ODY-C

CYCLE ONE

FOR JAMES COCKRELL, MARY WALSTON, BILL KING, LEROY
PERCY, CLYDE FOWLER, MARTHA DUNNIGAN:
TEACHERS ALL, LEADING ME TO ITHACA.
—MATT

FOR CATHERINE, FOR JOINING ME ON THIS JOURNEY.
—CHRISTIAN

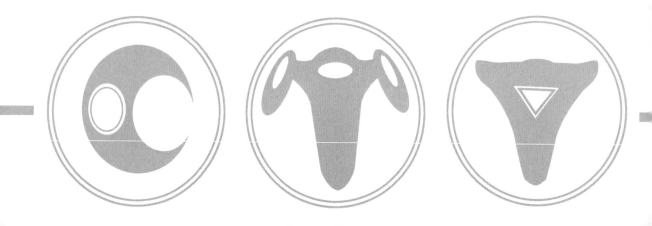

TABLE OF CONTENTS

IMAGE COMICS, INC.

Robert Kirkman – Chief Operating Officer
Erik Larsen – Chief Financial Officer
Todd McFarlane – President
Marc Silvestri – Chief Executive Officer
Jim Valentino – Vice-President

Eric Stephenson – Publisher
Corey Murphy – Director of Sales
Jeff Boison – Director of Publishing Planning & Book Trade Sales
Jeremy Sullivan – Director of Digital Sales
Kat Salazar – Director of PR & Marketing
Branwyn Bigglestone – Controller
Drew Gill – Art Director
Jonathan Chan – Production Manager
Meredith Wallace – Print Manager
Briah Skelly – Publicist
Sasha Head – Sales & Marketing Production Designer
Randy Okamura – Digital Production Designer
David Brothers – Branding Manager
Olivia Ngai – Content Manager
Addison Duke – Production Artist
Vincent Kukua – Production Artist
Tricia Ramos – Production Artist
Jeff Stang – Direct Market Sales Representative
Emilio Bautista – Digital Sales Associate
Leanna Caunter – Accounting Assistant
Chloe Ramos-Peterson – Library Market Sales Representative
IMAGECOMICS.COM

CYCLE ONE

STORY - MATT FRACTION
ART & COLORS - CHRISTIAN WARD

LETTERING - CHRIS ELIOPOULOS
FLATS - DEE CUNNIFFE
ESSAYS - DANI COLMAN

BOOK DESIGN - LAURENN MCCUBBIN

EDITOR - LAUREN SANKOVITCH

DESIGN - CHRISTIAN WARD & DREW GILL

ODY-C CREATED BY MATT FRACTION AND CHRISTIAN WARD

SPECIAL THANKS TO CATHERINE ROONEY-WARD,
PROF. BEN SAUNDERS, AND KATE MEYERS

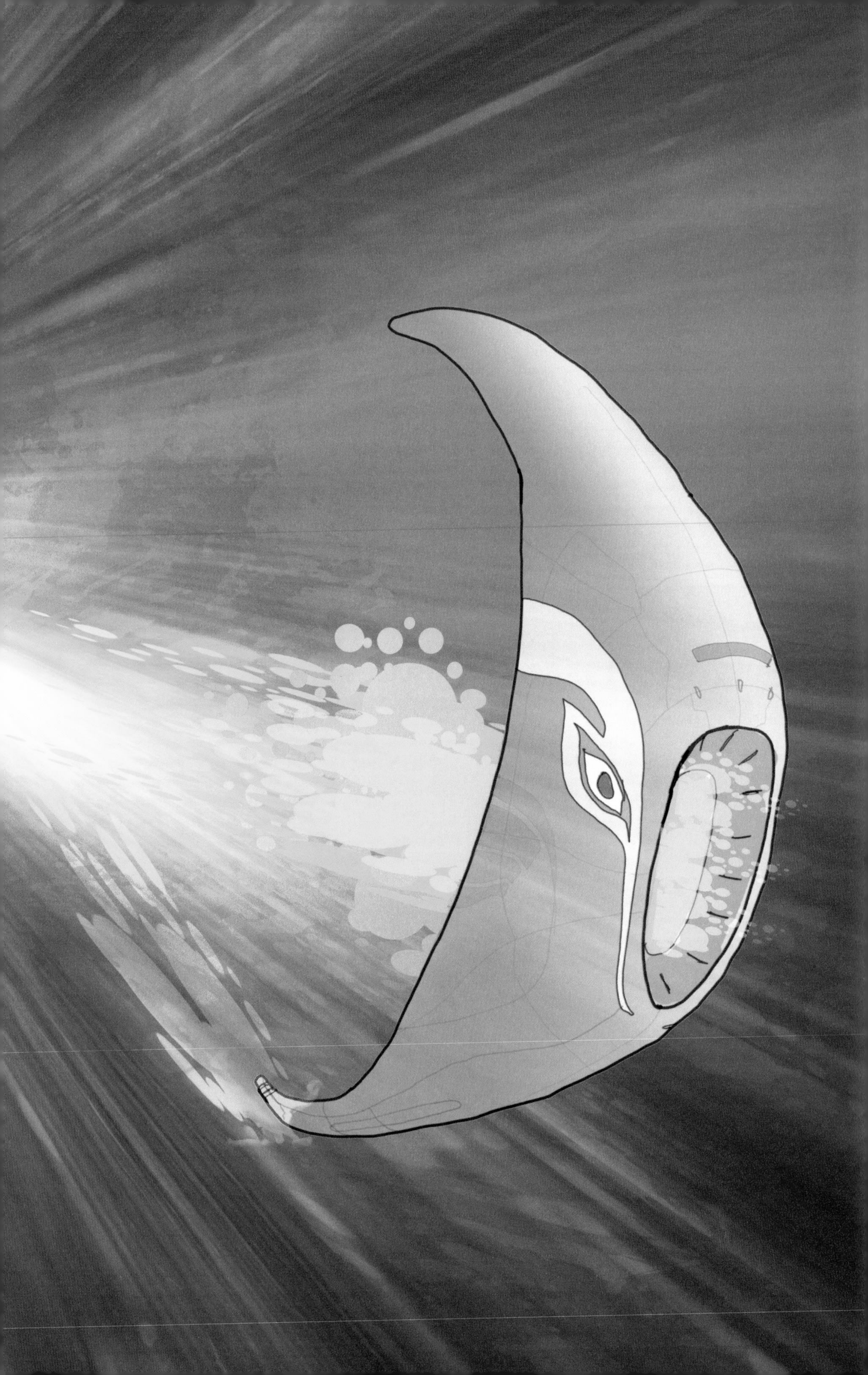

"AND I KNOW THERE IS SOMETHING ALL WRONG
ABOUT ME ––
BELIEVE ME. SOMETIMES I SHOCK MYSELF."

– SOPHOKLES,
FROM *AN ORESTEIA: ELEKTRA*
(TRANS. ANNE CARSON)

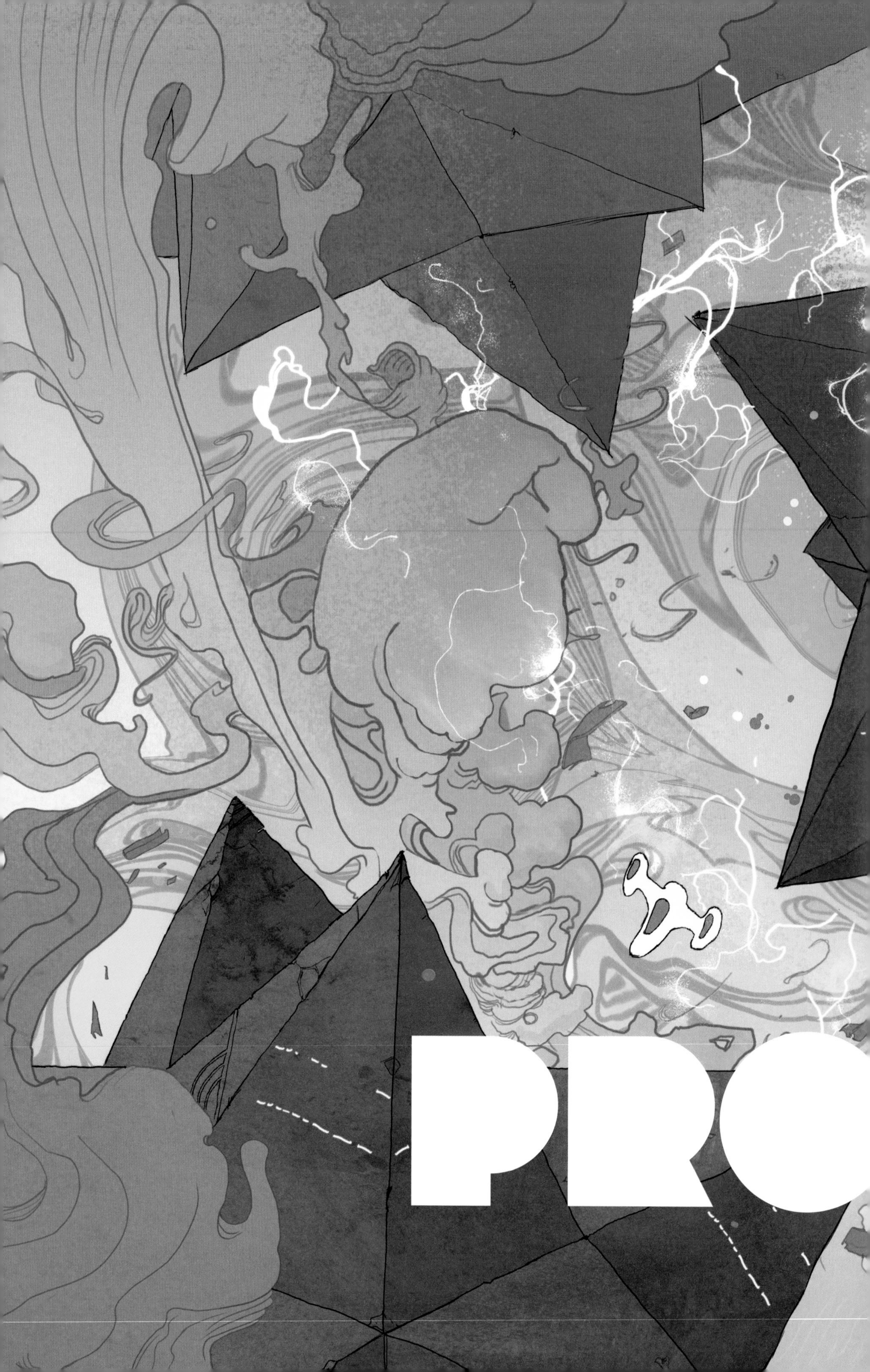
PRO

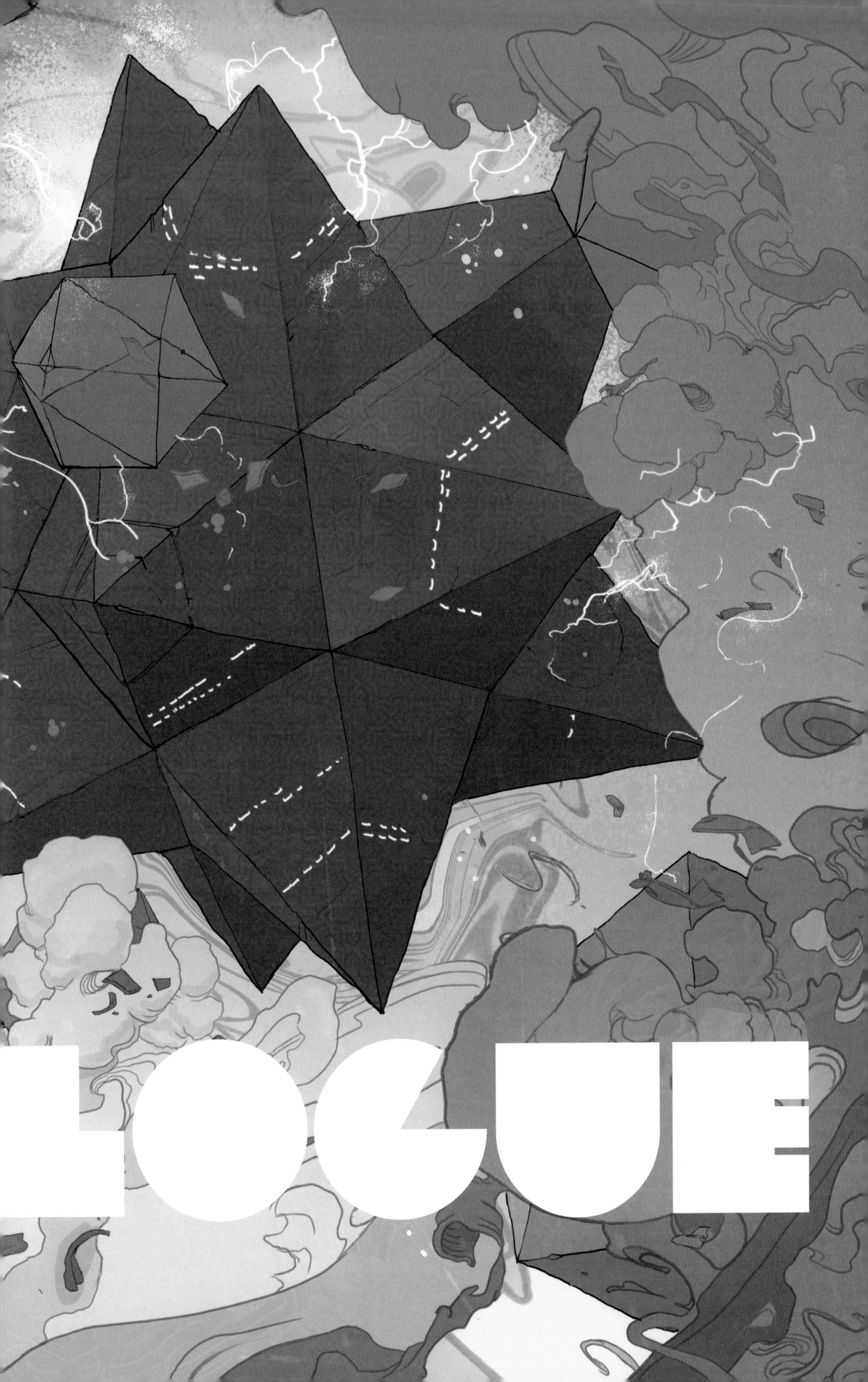
LOGUE

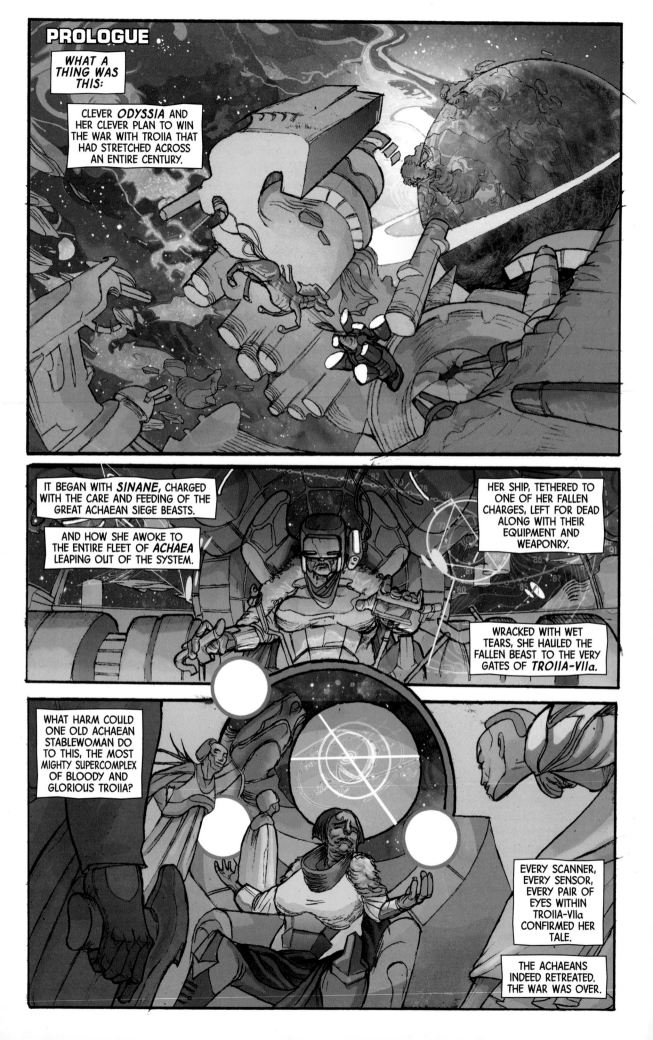

PROLOGUE

WHAT A THING WAS THIS:

CLEVER *ODYSSIA* AND HER CLEVER PLAN TO WIN THE WAR WITH TROIIA THAT HAD STRETCHED ACROSS AN ENTIRE CENTURY.

IT BEGAN WITH *SINANE*, CHARGED WITH THE CARE AND FEEDING OF THE GREAT ACHAEAN SIEGE BEASTS.

AND HOW SHE AWOKE TO THE ENTIRE FLEET OF *ACHAEA* LEAPING OUT OF THE SYSTEM.

HER SHIP, TETHERED TO ONE OF HER FALLEN CHARGES, LEFT FOR DEAD ALONG WITH THEIR EQUIPMENT AND WEAPONRY.

WRACKED WITH WET TEARS, SHE HAULED THE FALLEN BEAST TO THE VERY GATES OF *TROIIA-VIIa*.

WHAT HARM COULD ONE OLD ACHAEAN STABLEWOMAN DO TO THIS, THE MOST MIGHTY SUPERCOMPLEX OF BLOODY AND GLORIOUS TROIIA?

EVERY SCANNER, EVERY SENSOR, EVERY PAIR OF EYES WITHIN TROIIA-VIIa CONFIRMED HER TALE.

THE ACHAEANS INDEED RETREATED. THE WAR WAS OVER.

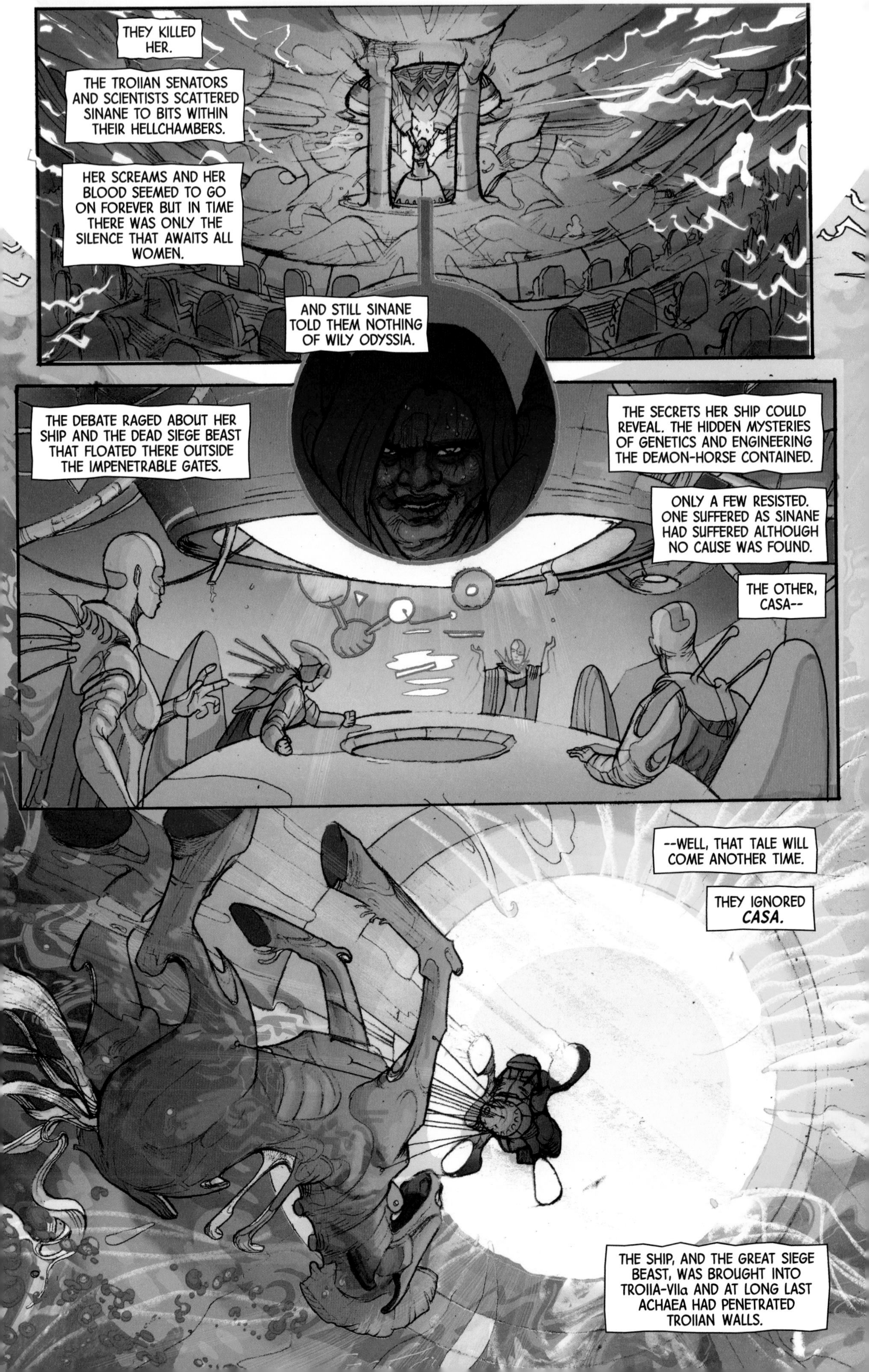
THEY KILLED HER.
THE TROIIAN SENATORS AND SCIENTISTS SCATTERED SINANE TO BITS WITHIN THEIR HELLCHAMBERS.
HER SCREAMS AND HER BLOOD SEEMED TO GO ON FOREVER BUT IN TIME THERE WAS ONLY THE SILENCE THAT AWAITS ALL WOMEN.
AND STILL SINANE TOLD THEM NOTHING OF WILY ODYSSIA.
THE DEBATE RAGED ABOUT HER SHIP AND THE DEAD SIEGE BEAST THAT FLOATED THERE OUTSIDE THE IMPENETRABLE GATES.
THE SECRETS HER SHIP COULD REVEAL. THE HIDDEN MYSTERIES OF GENETICS AND ENGINEERING THE DEMON-HORSE CONTAINED.
ONLY A FEW RESISTED. ONE SUFFERED AS SINANE HAD SUFFERED ALTHOUGH NO CAUSE WAS FOUND.
THE OTHER, CASA--
--WELL, THAT TALE WILL COME ANOTHER TIME.
THEY IGNORED *CASA.*
THE SHIP, AND THE GREAT SIEGE BEAST, WAS BROUGHT INTO TROIIA-VIIa AND AT LONG LAST ACHAEA HAD PENETRATED TROIIAN WALLS.

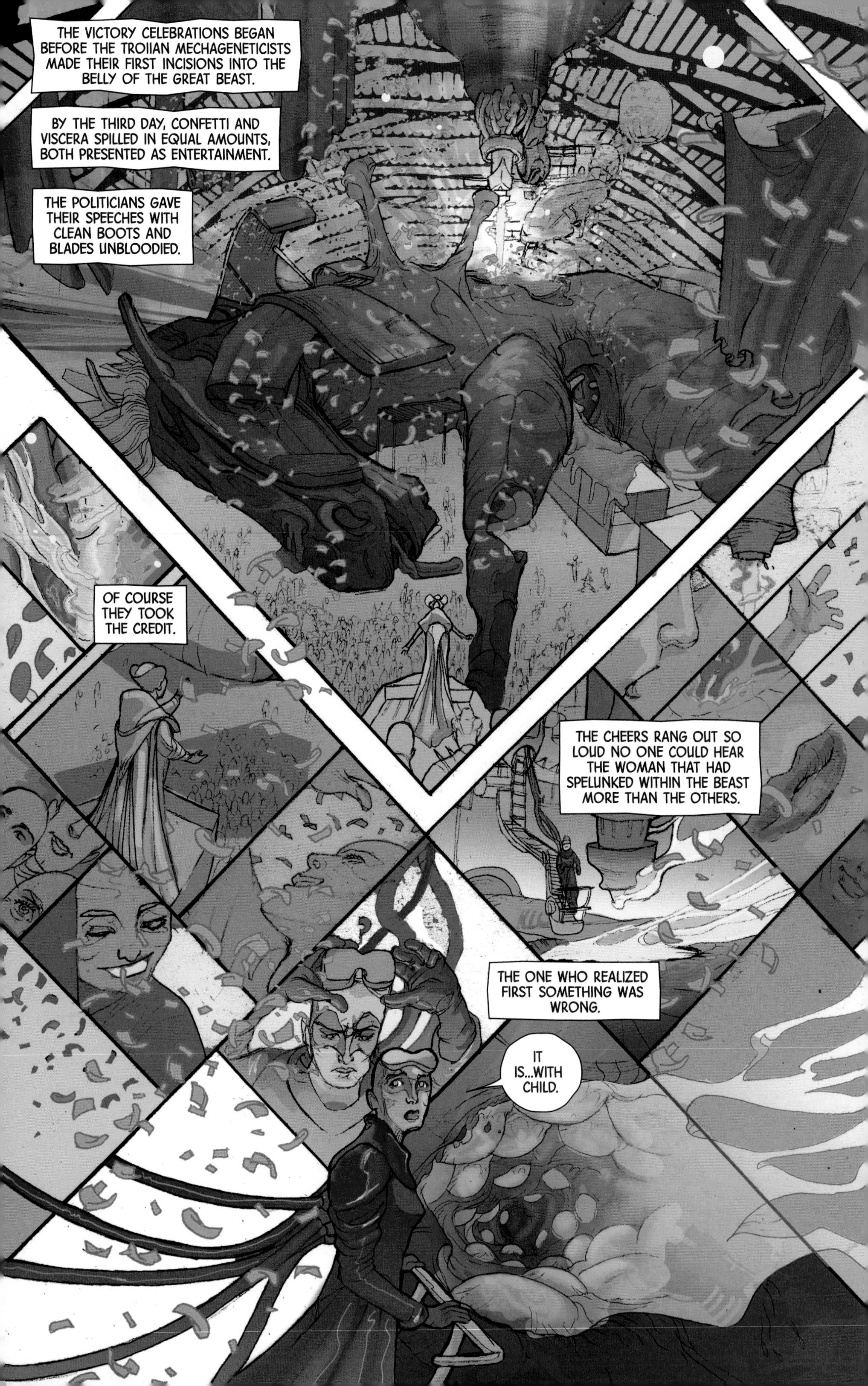
THE VICTORY CELEBRATIONS BEGAN BEFORE THE TROIIAN MECHAGENETICISTS MADE THEIR FIRST INCISIONS INTO THE BELLY OF THE GREAT BEAST.
BY THE THIRD DAY, CONFETTI AND VISCERA SPILLED IN EQUAL AMOUNTS, BOTH PRESENTED AS ENTERTAINMENT.
THE POLITICIANS GAVE THEIR SPEECHES WITH CLEAN BOOTS AND BLADES UNBLOODIED.
OF COURSE THEY TOOK THE CREDIT.
THE CHEERS RANG OUT SO LOUD NO ONE COULD HEAR THE WOMAN THAT HAD SPELUNKED WITHIN THE BEAST MORE THAN THE OTHERS.
THE ONE WHO REALIZED FIRST SOMETHING WAS WRONG.
IT IS...WITH CHILD.

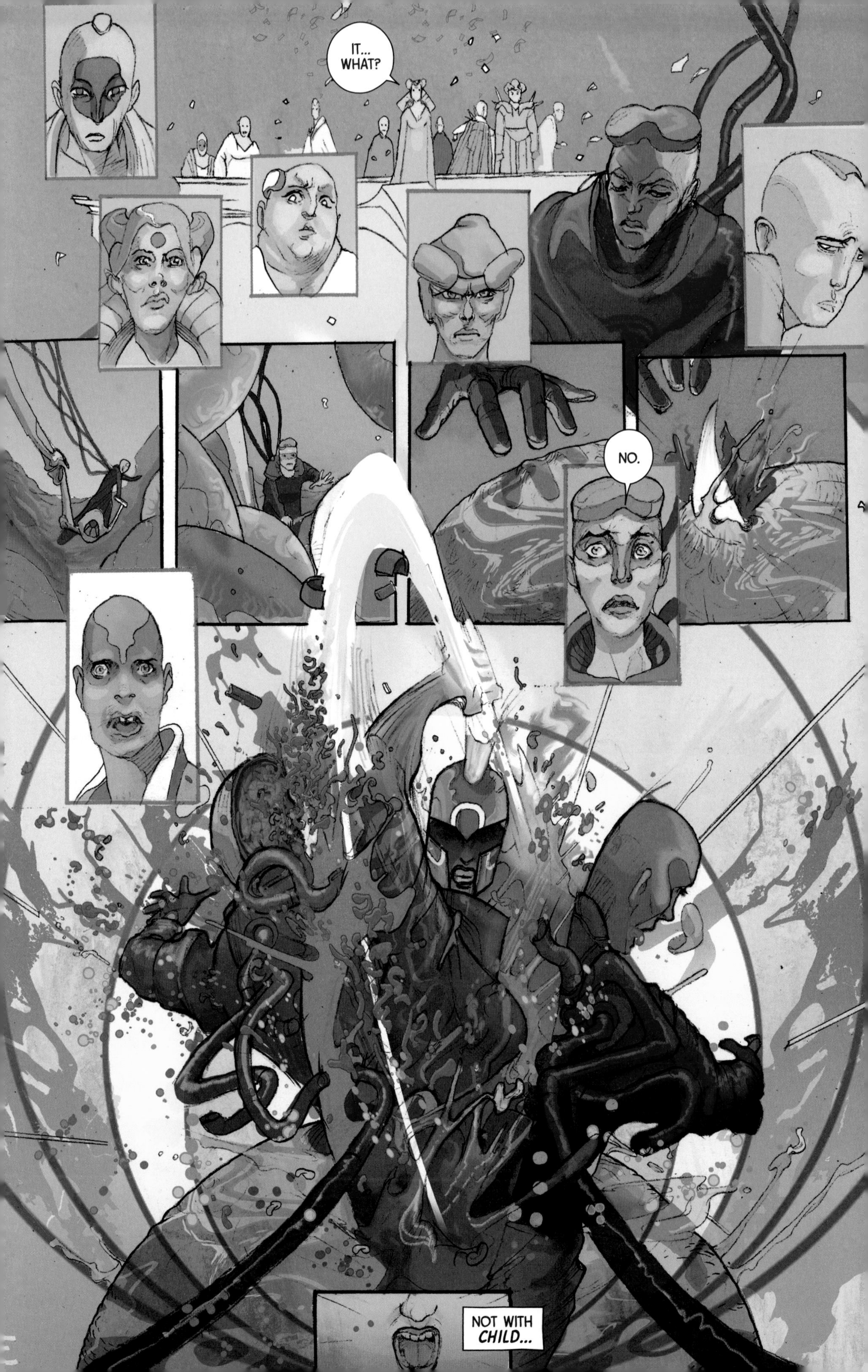

IT... WHAT?
NO.
NOT WITH CHILD...

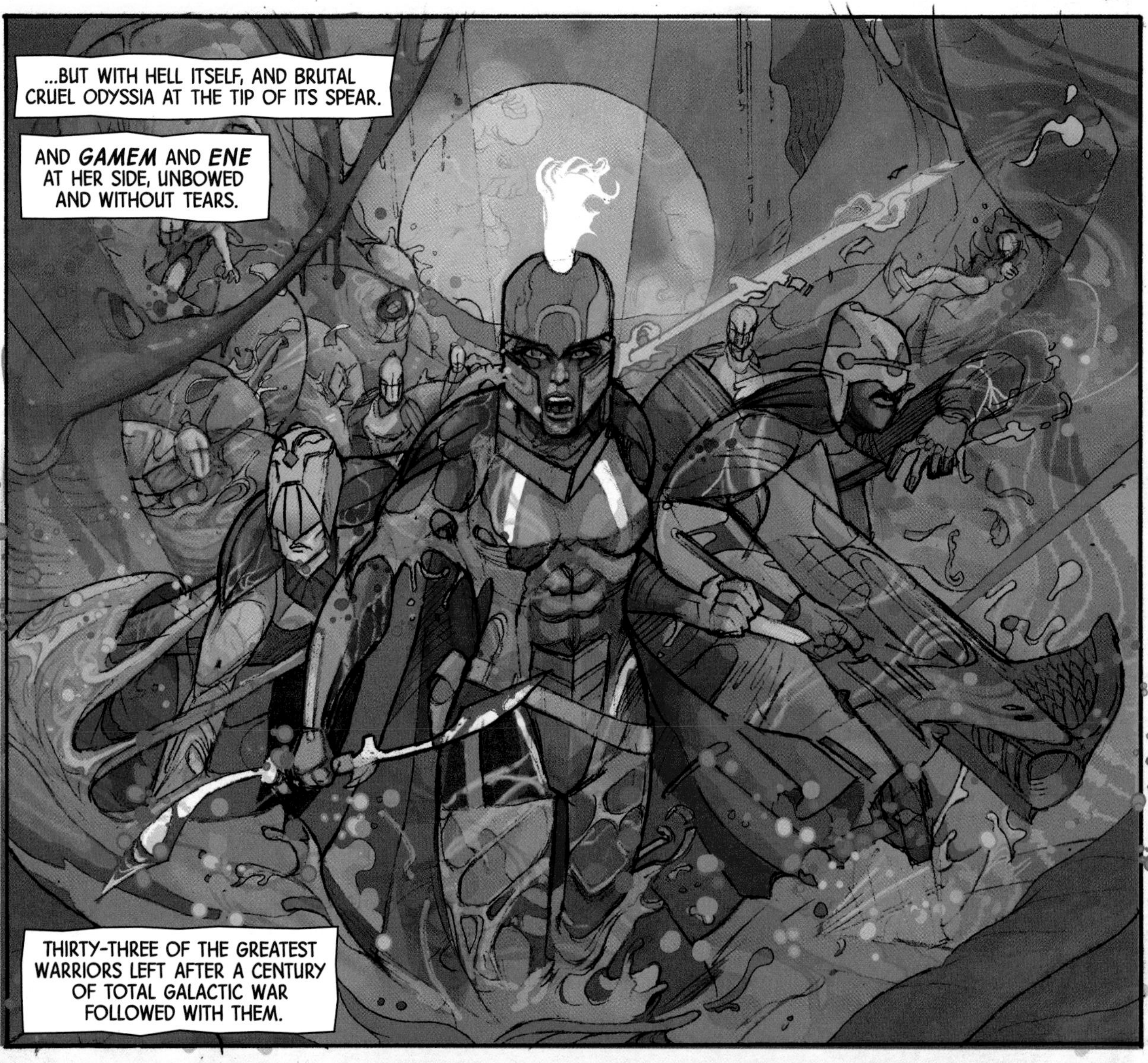
...BUT WITH HELL ITSELF, AND BRUTAL CRUEL ODYSSIA AT THE TIP OF ITS SPEAR.
AND GAMEM AND ENE AT HER SIDE, UNBOWED AND WITHOUT TEARS.
THIRTY-THREE OF THE GREATEST WARRIORS LEFT AFTER A CENTURY OF TOTAL GALACTIC WAR FOLLOWED WITH THEM.

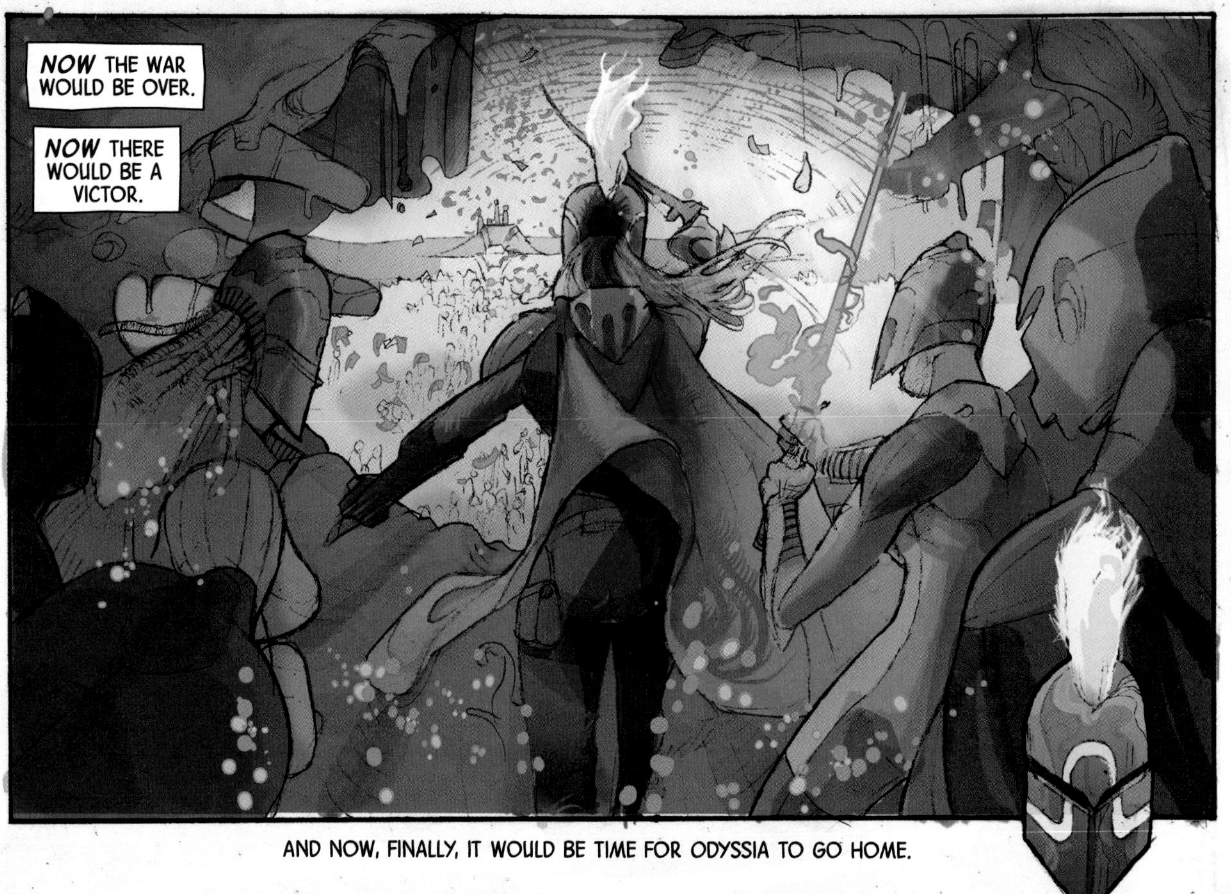
NOW THE WAR WOULD BE OVER.
NOW THERE WOULD BE A VICTOR.

AND NOW, FINALLY, IT WOULD BE TIME FOR ODYSSIA TO GO HOME.

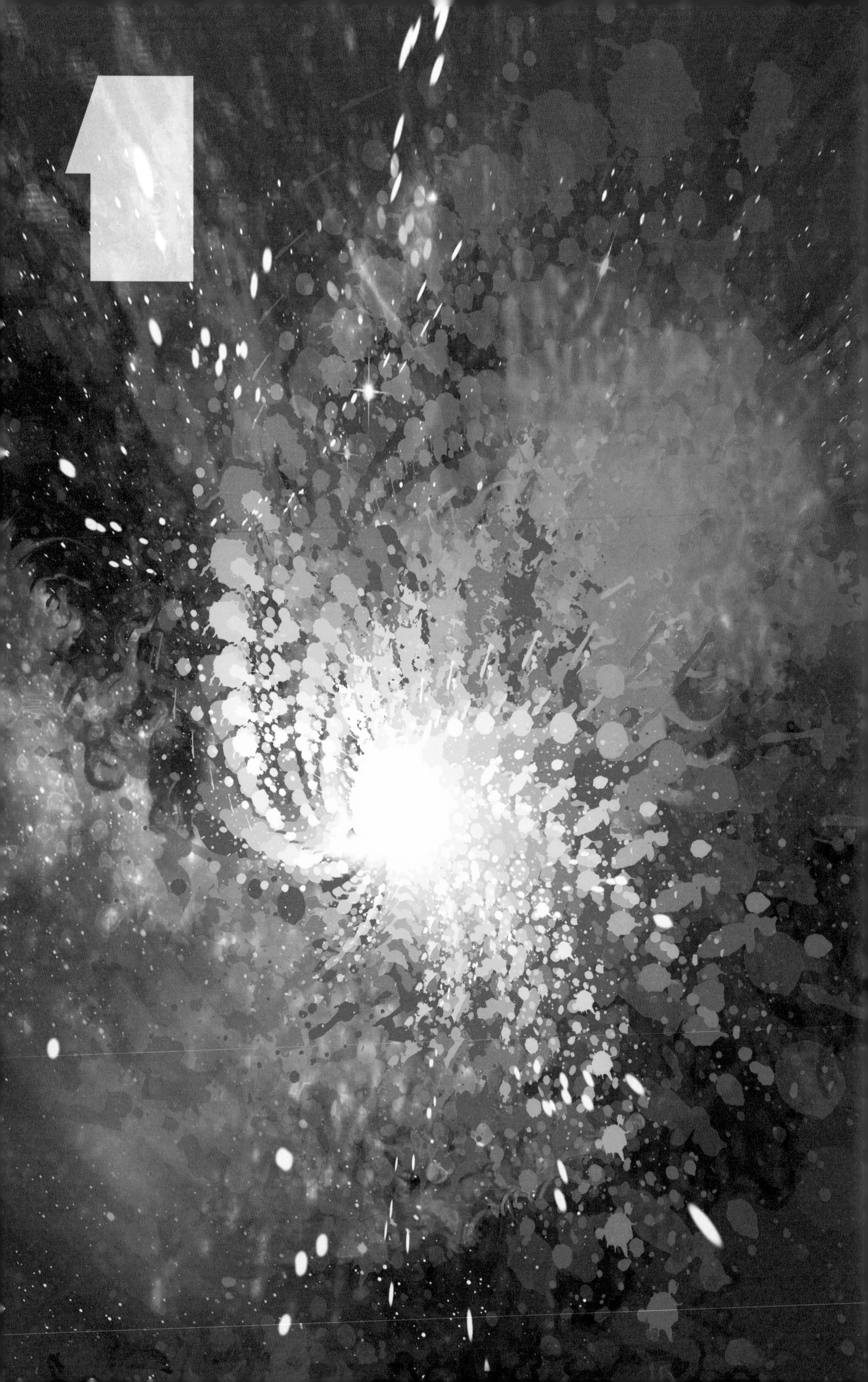
1

THE BIRTH OF ALL KNOWN THINGS

- THE GODS
- TITAN PROMETHENE
- COURTSHIP AND MARRIAGE OF THETIA AND PELENUS
- SERI, GODDESS OF STRIFE
- PARIS OF TROIIA-VII
- THE ACHAEAN HEROES
- PARIS AND HE
- ODYSSIA AND PENELOPE
- THE ILIAD

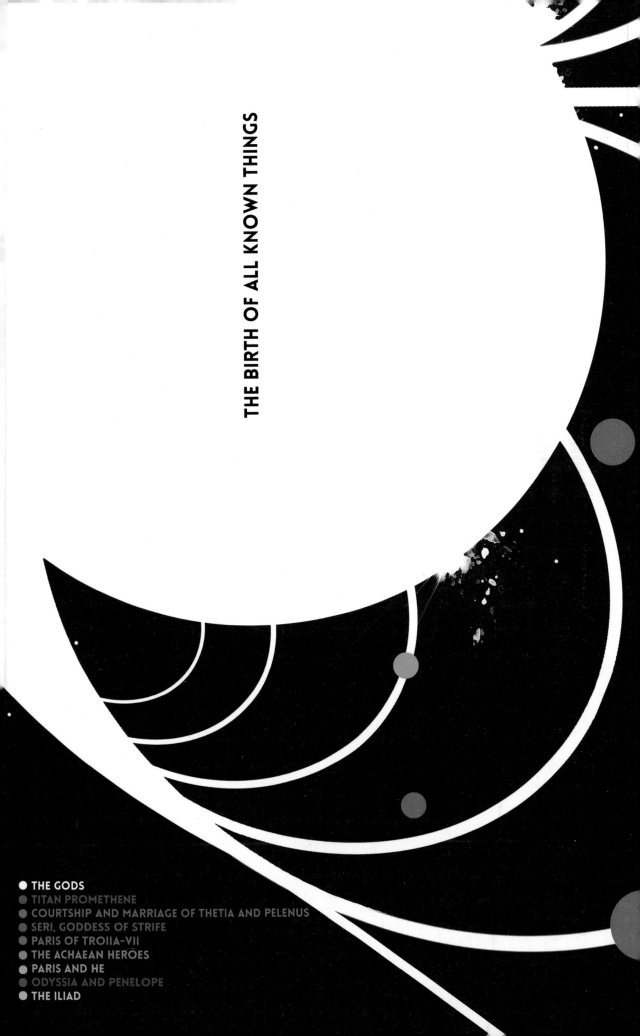

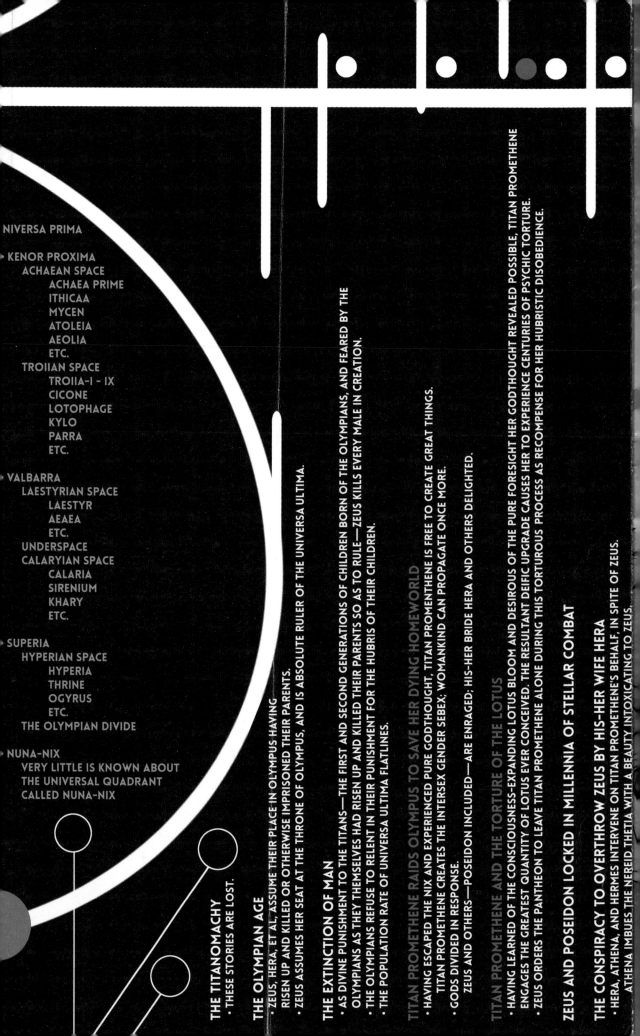

NIVERSA PRIMA

▶ KENOR PROXIMA
   ACHAEAN SPACE
      ACHAEA PRIME
      ITHICAA
      MYCEN
      ATOLEIA
      AEOLIA
      ETC.
   TROIIAN SPACE
      TROIIA-I - IX
      CICONE
      LOTOPHAGE
      KYLO
      PARRA
      ETC.

▶ VALBARRA
   LAESTYRIAN SPACE
      LAESTYR
      AEAEA
      ETC.
   UNDERSPACE
   CALARYIAN SPACE
      CALARIA
      SIRENIUM
      KHARY
      ETC.

▶ SUPERIA
   HYPERIAN SPACE
      HYPERIA
      THRINE
      OGYRUS
      ETC.
   THE OLYMPIAN DIVIDE

▶ NUNA-NIX
   VERY LITTLE IS KNOWN ABOUT
   THE UNIVERSAL QUADRANT
   CALLED NUNA-NIX

THE TITANOMACHY
· THESE STORIES ARE LOST.

THE OLYMPIAN AGE
· ZEUS, HERA, ET AL, ASSUME THEIR PLACE IN OLYMPUS HAVING RISEN UP AND KILLED OR OTHERWISE IMPRISONED THEIR PARENTS.
· ZEUS ASSUMES HER SEAT AT THE THRONE OF OLYMPUS, AND IS ABSOLUTE RULER OF THE UNIVERSA ULTIMA.

THE EXTINCTION OF MAN
· AS DIVINE PUNISHMENT TO THE TITANS—THE FIRST AND SECOND GENERATIONS OF CHILDREN BORN OF THE OLYMPIANS, AND FEARED BY THE OLYMPIANS AS THEY THEMSELVES HAD RISEN UP AND KILLED THEIR PARENTS SO AS TO RULE—ZEUS KILLS EVERY MALE IN CREATION.
· THE OLYMPIANS REFUSE TO RELENT IN THEIR PUNISHMENT FOR THE HUBRIS OF THEIR CHILDREN.
· THE POPULATION RATE OF UNIVERSA ULTIMA FLATLINES.

TITAN PROMETHENE RAIDS OLYMPUS TO SAVE HER DYING HOMEWORLD
· HAVING ESCAPED THE NIX AND EXPERIENCED PURE GODTHOUGHT, TITAN PROMETHENE IS FREE TO CREATE GREAT THINGS. TITAN PROMETHENE CREATES THE INTERSEX GENDER SEBEX; WOMANKIND CAN PROPAGATE ONCE MORE.
· GODS DIVIDED IN RESPONSE.
  ZEUS AND OTHERS—POSEIDON INCLUDED—ARE ENRAGED; HIS-HER BRIDE HERA AND OTHERS DELIGHTED.

TITAN PROMETHENE AND THE TORTURE OF THE LOTUS
· HAVING LEARNED OF THE CONSCIOUSNESS-EXPANDING LOTUS BLOOM AND DESIROUS OF THE PURE FORESIGHT HER GODTHOUGHT REVEALED POSSIBLE, TITAN PROMETHENE ENGAGES THE GREATEST QUANTITY OF LOTUS EVER CONCEIVED. THE RESULTANT DEIFIC UPGRADE CAUSES HER TO EXPERIENCE CENTURIES OF PSYCHIC TORTURE.
· ZEUS ORDERS THE PANTHEON TO LEAVE TITAN PROMETHENE ALONE DURING THIS TORTUROUS PROCESS AS RECOMPENSE FOR HER HUBRISTIC DISOBEDIENCE.

ZEUS AND POSEIDON LOCKED IN MILLENNIA OF STELLAR COMBAT

THE CONSPIRACY TO OVERTHROW ZEUS BY HIS-HER WIFE HERA
· HERA, ATHENA, AND HERMES INTERVENE ON TITAN PROMETHENE'S BEHALF, IN SPITE OF ZEUS.
  ATHENA MBUES THE NEREID THETIA WITH A BEAUTY INTOXICATING TO ZEUS.

THE OLYMPIAN DIVIDE

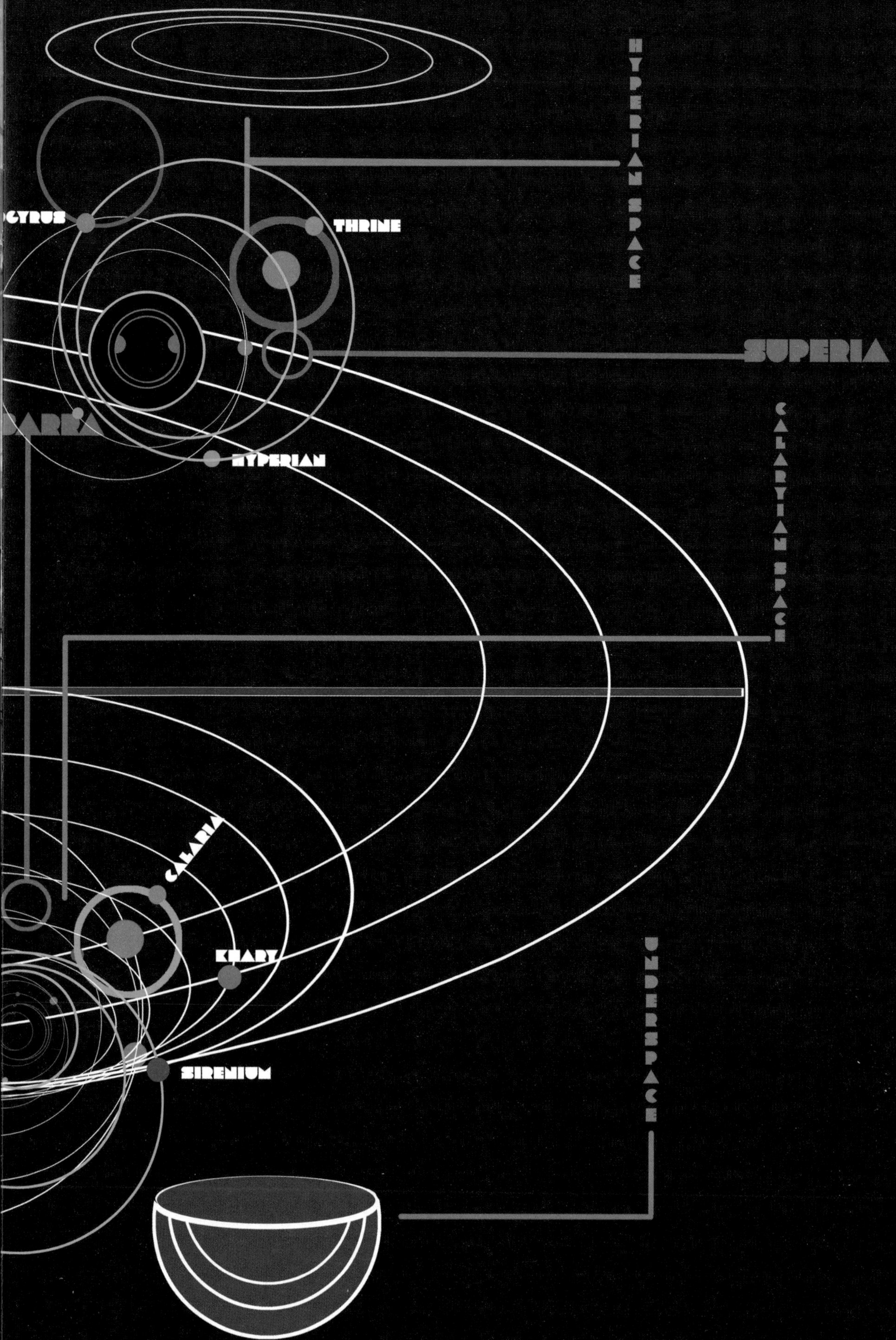
HYPERIAN SPACE
THRINE
SUPERIA
HYPERIAN
CALARYIAN SPACE
CALARIA
KHARY
SIRENIUM
UNDERSPACE

NUMA-NIX

SING IN US, MUSE
OF ODYSSIA
WITCHJACK AND WANDERER
HOMEWARD BOUND
WARLESS AT LAST

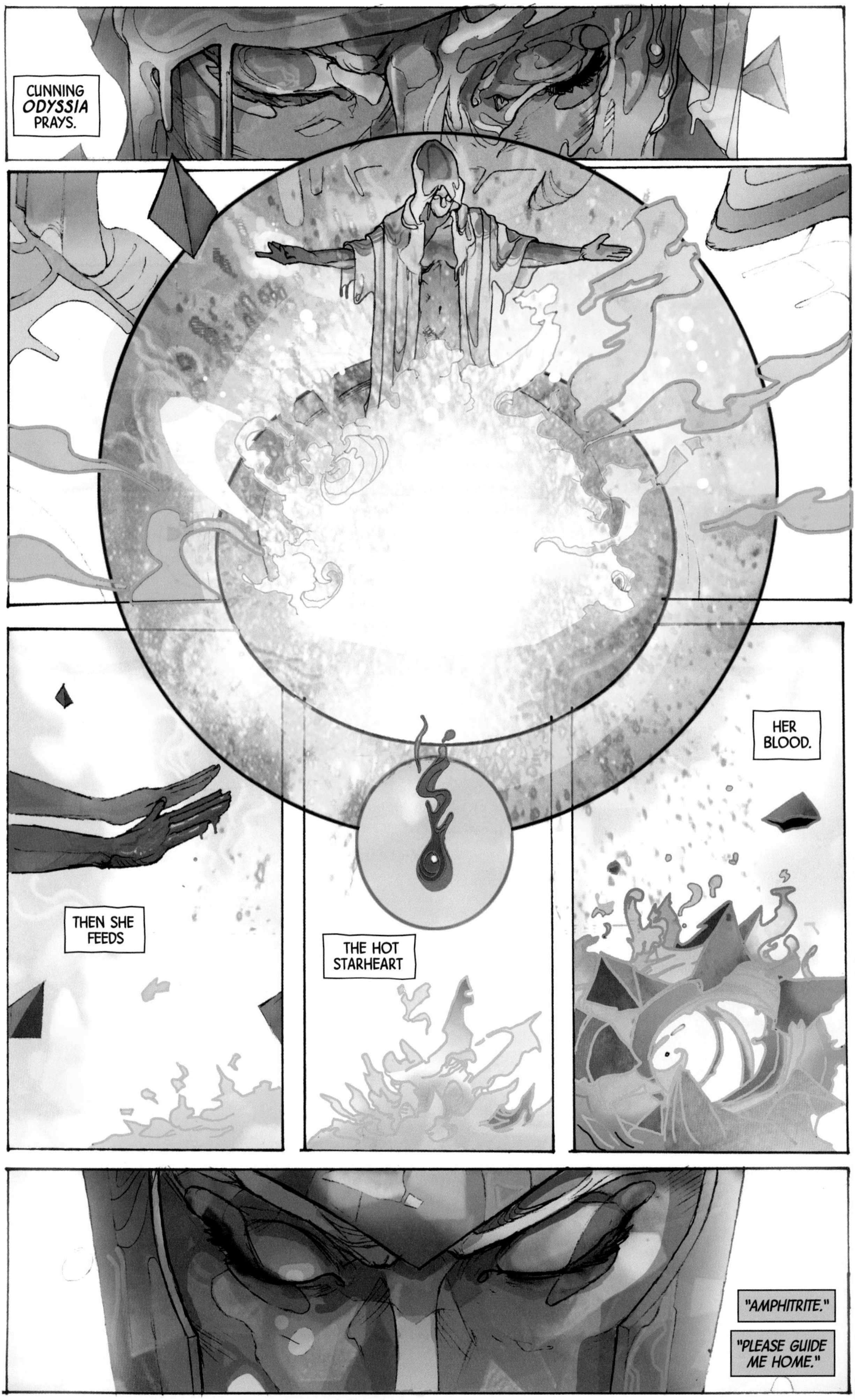
CUNNING *ODYSSIA* PRAYS.
THEN SHE FEEDS
THE HOT STARHEART
HER BLOOD.
"AMPHITRITE."
"PLEASE GUIDE ME HOME."

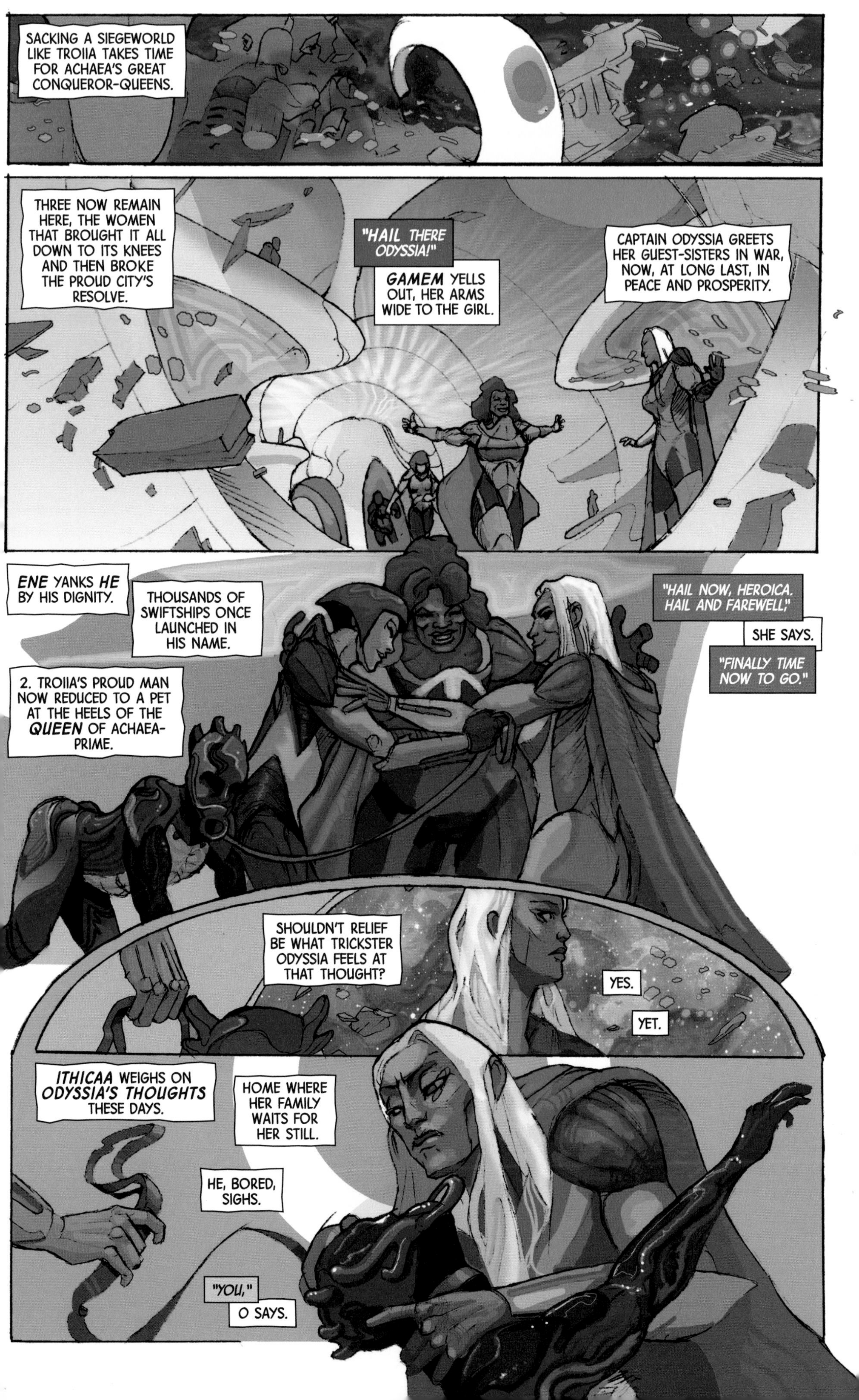
SACKING A SIEGEWORLD LIKE TROIIA TAKES TIME FOR ACHAEA'S GREAT CONQUEROR-QUEENS.
THREE NOW REMAIN HERE, THE WOMEN THAT BROUGHT IT ALL DOWN TO ITS KNEES AND THEN BROKE THE PROUD CITY'S RESOLVE.
"HAIL THERE ODYSSIA!"
GAMEM YELLS OUT, HER ARMS WIDE TO THE GIRL.
CAPTAIN ODYSSIA GREETS HER GUEST-SISTERS IN WAR, NOW, AT LONG LAST, IN PEACE AND PROSPERITY.
ENE YANKS HE BY HIS DIGNITY.
THOUSANDS OF SWIFTSHIPS ONCE LAUNCHED IN HIS NAME.
2. TROIIA'S PROUD MAN NOW REDUCED TO A PET AT THE HEELS OF THE QUEEN OF ACHAEA-PRIME.
"HAIL NOW, HEROICA. HAIL AND FAREWELL,"
SHE SAYS.
"FINALLY TIME NOW TO GO."
SHOULDN'T RELIEF BE WHAT TRICKSTER ODYSSIA FEELS AT THAT THOUGHT?
YES.
YET.
ITHICAA WEIGHS ON ODYSSIA'S THOUGHTS THESE DAYS.
HOME WHERE HER FAMILY WAITS FOR HER STILL.
HE, BORED, SIGHS.
"YOU,"
O SAYS.

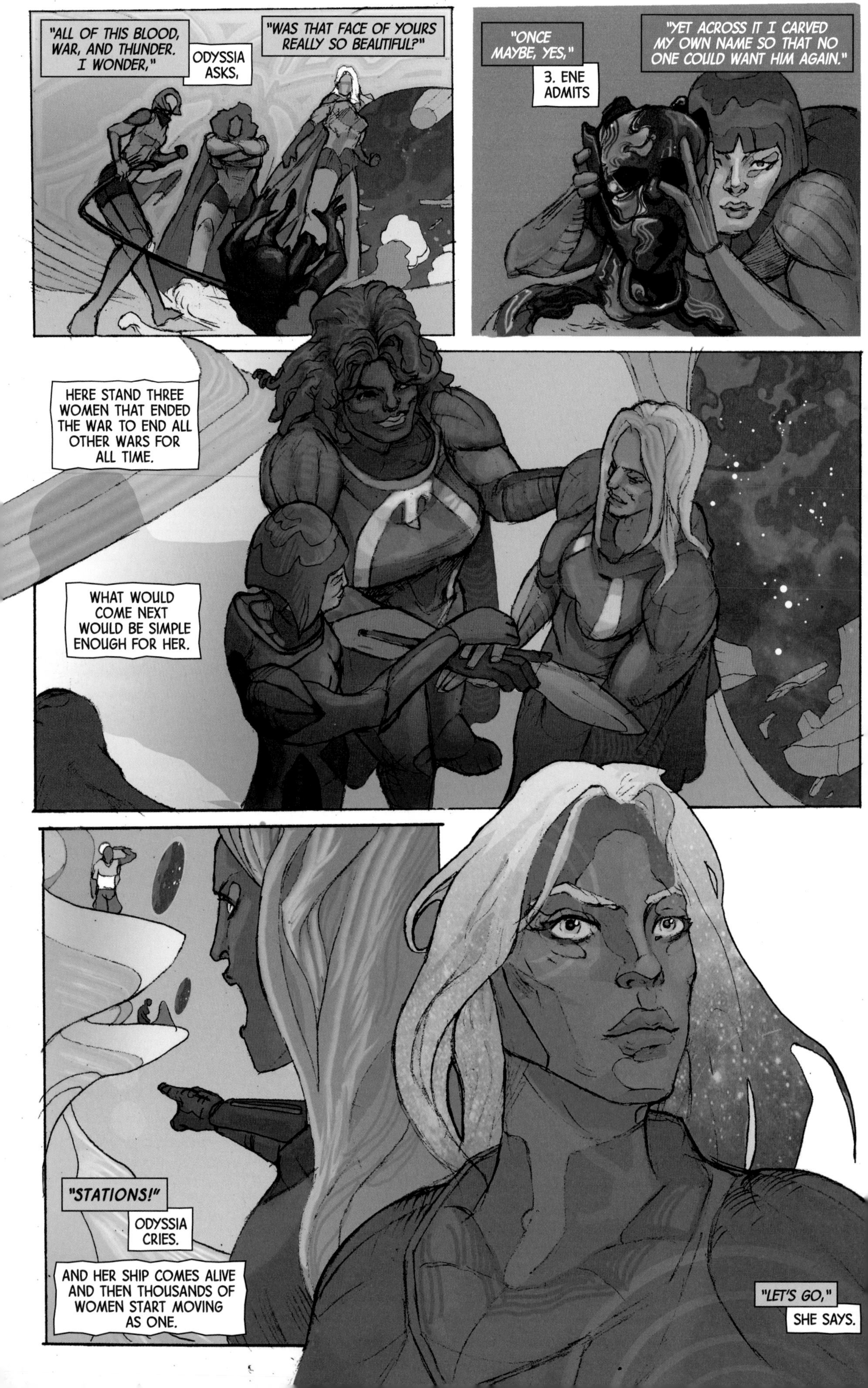
"ALL OF THIS BLOOD, WAR, AND THUNDER. I WONDER,"
ODYSSIA ASKS,
"WAS THAT FACE OF YOURS REALLY SO BEAUTIFUL?"
"ONCE MAYBE, YES,"
3. ENE ADMITS
"YET ACROSS IT I CARVED MY OWN NAME SO THAT NO ONE COULD WANT HIM AGAIN."
HERE STAND THREE WOMEN THAT ENDED THE WAR TO END ALL OTHER WARS FOR ALL TIME.
WHAT WOULD COME NEXT WOULD BE SIMPLE ENOUGH FOR HER.
"STATIONS!"
ODYSSIA CRIES.
AND HER SHIP COMES ALIVE AND THEN THOUSANDS OF WOMEN START MOVING AS ONE.
"LET'S GO,"
SHE SAYS.

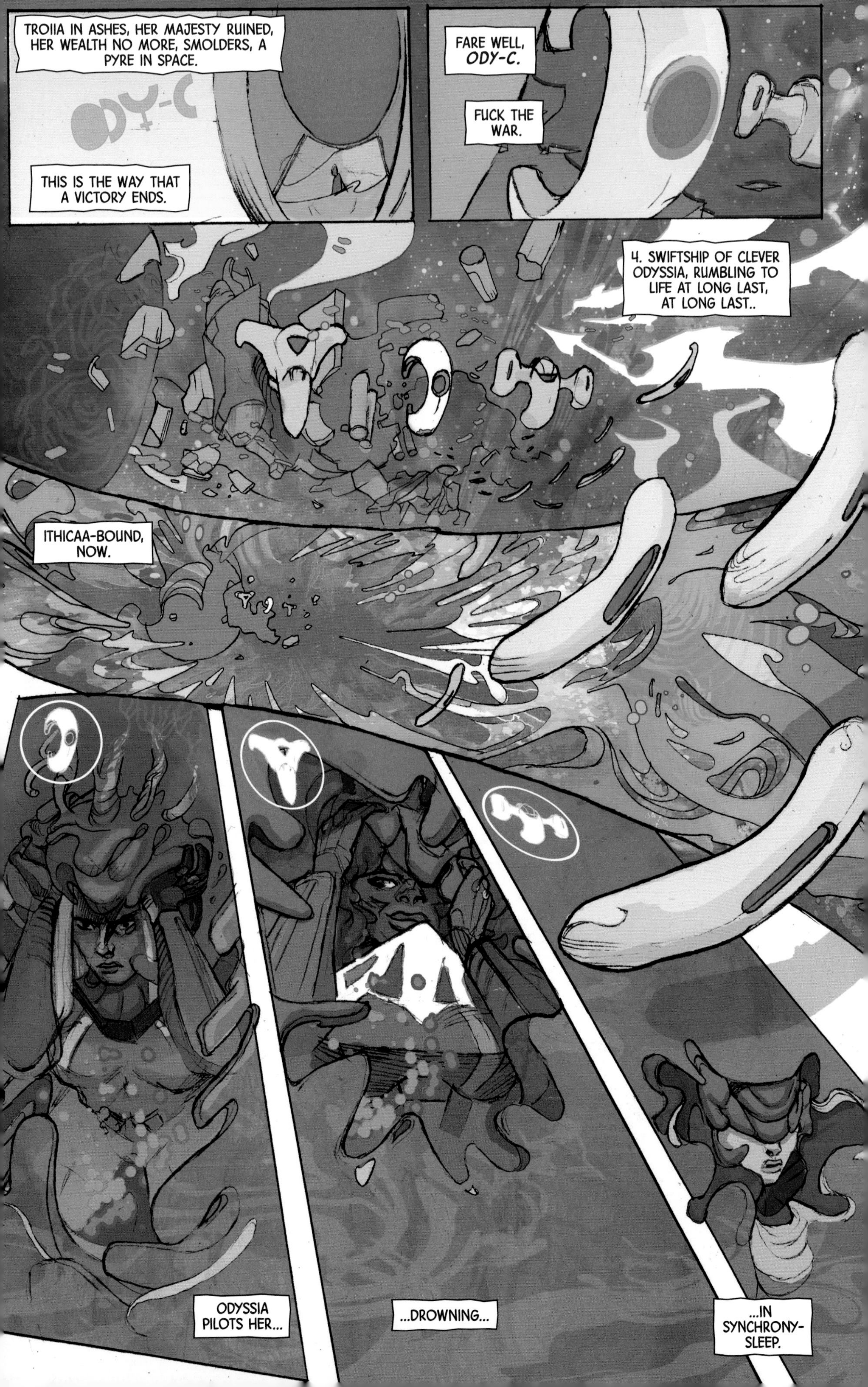
TROIIA IN ASHES, HER MAJESTY RUINED, HER WEALTH NO MORE, SMOLDERS, A PYRE IN SPACE.
ODY-C
THIS IS THE WAY THAT A VICTORY ENDS.
FARE WELL, ODY-C.
FUCK THE WAR.
4. SWIFTSHIP OF CLEVER ODYSSIA, RUMBLING TO LIFE AT LONG LAST, AT LONG LAST..
ITHICAA-BOUND, NOW.
ODYSSIA PILOTS HER...
...DROWNING...
...IN SYNCHRONY-SLEEP.

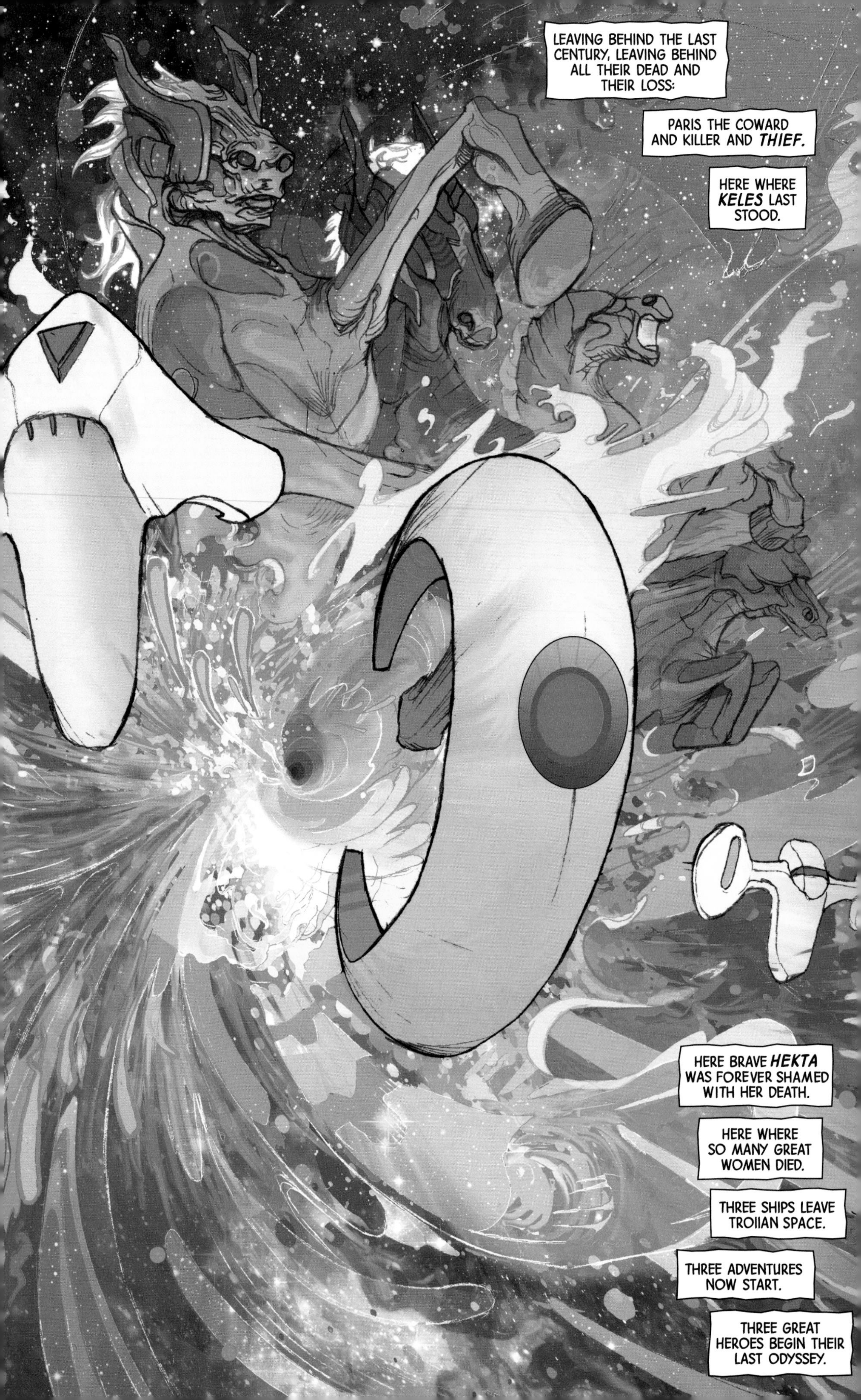
LEAVING BEHIND THE LAST CENTURY, LEAVING BEHIND ALL THEIR DEAD AND THEIR LOSS:
PARIS THE COWARD AND KILLER AND *THIEF.*
HERE WHERE ***KELES*** LAST STOOD.
HERE BRAVE ***HEKTA*** WAS FOREVER SHAMED WITH HER DEATH.
HERE WHERE SO MANY GREAT WOMEN DIED.
THREE SHIPS LEAVE TROIIAN SPACE.
THREE ADVENTURES NOW START.
THREE GREAT HEROES BEGIN THEIR LAST ODYSSEY.

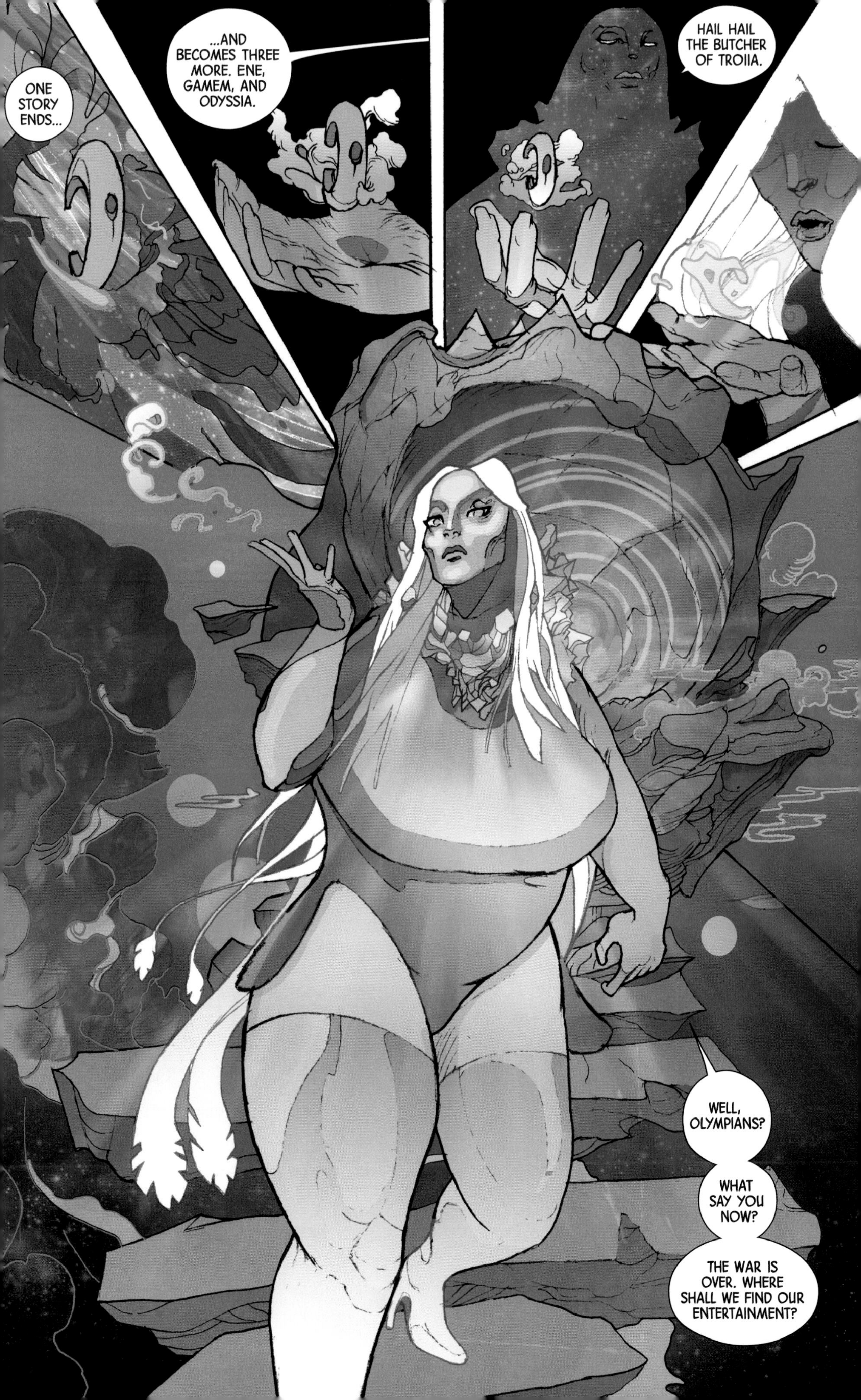
ONE STORY ENDS...
...AND BECOMES THREE MORE. ENE, GAMEM, AND ODYSSIA.
HAIL HAIL THE BUTCHER OF TROIIA.
WELL, OLYMPIANS?
WHAT SAY YOU NOW?
THE WAR IS OVER. WHERE SHALL WE FIND OUR ENTERTAINMENT?

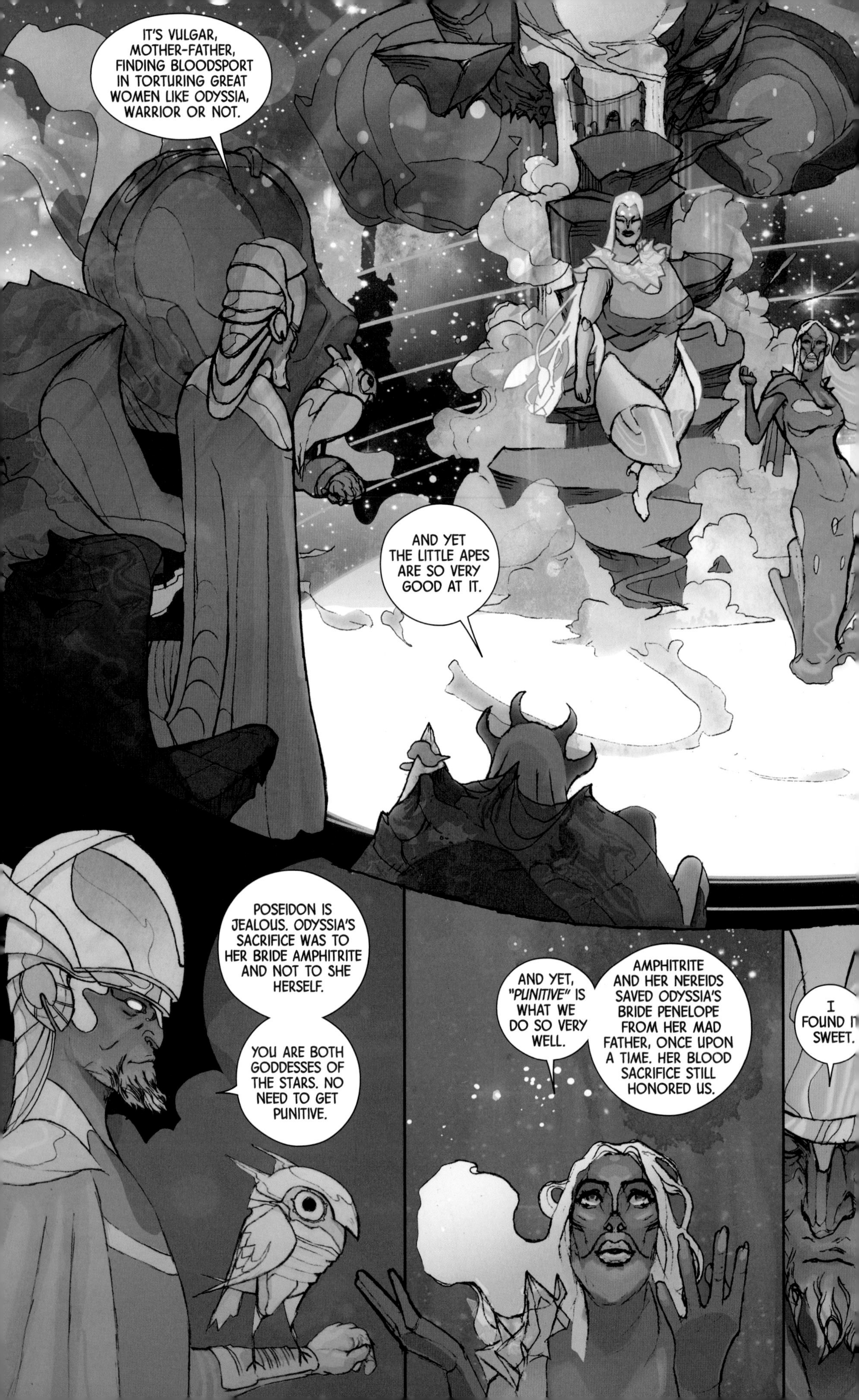
IT'S VULGAR, MOTHER-FATHER, FINDING BLOODSPORT IN TORTURING GREAT WOMEN LIKE ODYSSIA, WARRIOR OR NOT.
AND YET THE LITTLE APES ARE SO VERY GOOD AT IT.
POSEIDON IS JEALOUS. ODYSSIA'S SACRIFICE WAS TO HER BRIDE AMPHITRITE AND NOT TO SHE HERSELF.
YOU ARE BOTH GODDESSES OF THE STARS. NO NEED TO GET PUNITIVE.
AND YET, "PUNITIVE" IS WHAT WE DO SO VERY WELL.
AMPHITRITE AND HER NEREIDS SAVED ODYSSIA'S BRIDE PENELOPE FROM HER MAD FATHER, ONCE UPON A TIME. HER BLOOD SACRIFICE STILL HONORED US.
I FOUND I
SWEET.

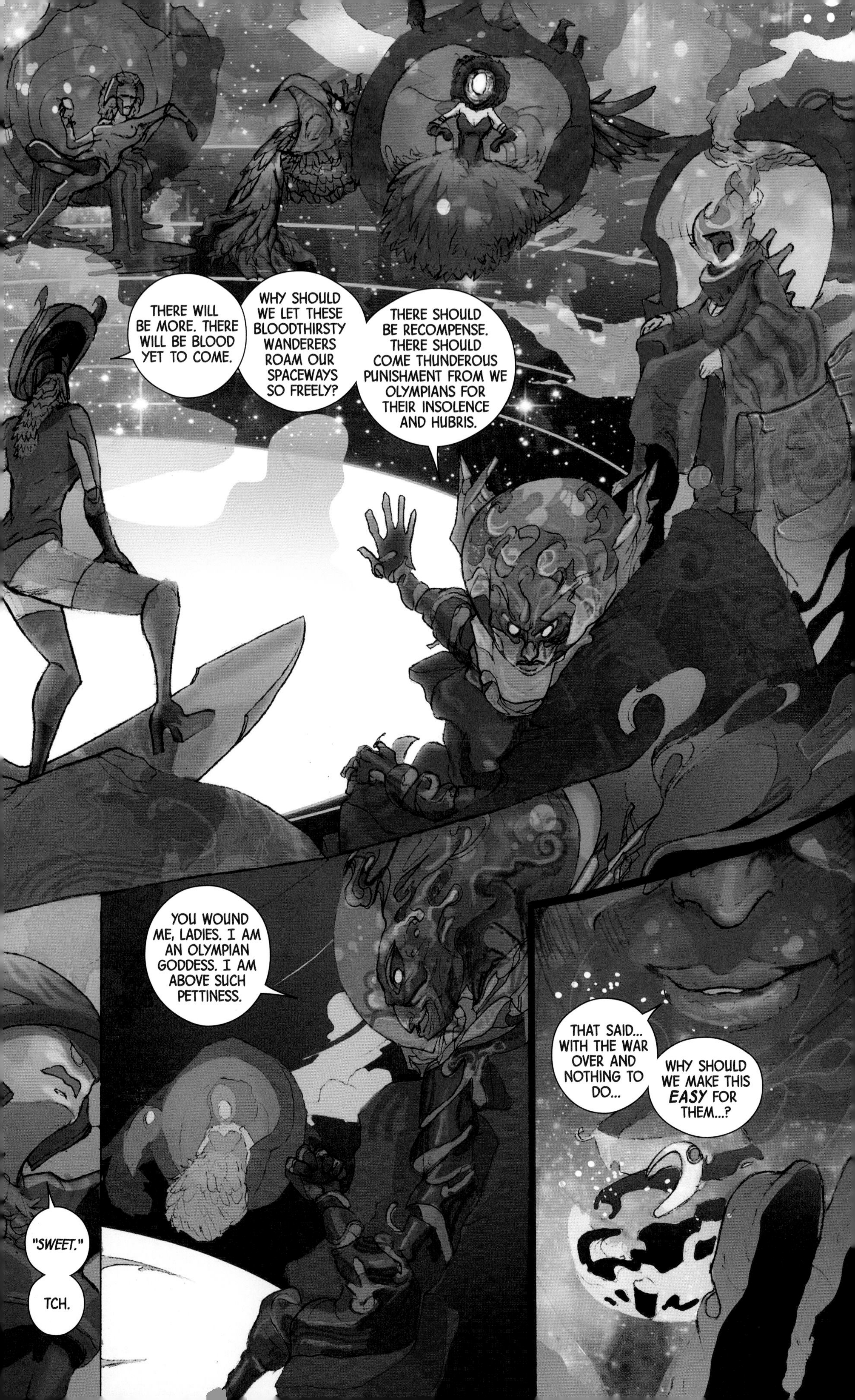

THERE WILL BE MORE. THERE WILL BE BLOOD YET TO COME.
WHY SHOULD WE LET THESE BLOODTHIRSTY WANDERERS ROAM OUR SPACEWAYS SO FREELY?
THERE SHOULD BE RECOMPENSE. THERE SHOULD COME THUNDEROUS PUNISHMENT FROM WE OLYMPIANS FOR THEIR INSOLENCE AND HUBRIS.
"SWEET."
TCH.
YOU WOUND ME, LADIES. I AM AN OLYMPIAN GODDESS. I AM ABOVE SUCH PETTINESS.
THAT SAID... WITH THE WAR OVER AND NOTHING TO DO...
WHY SHOULD WE MAKE THIS *EASY* FOR THEM...?

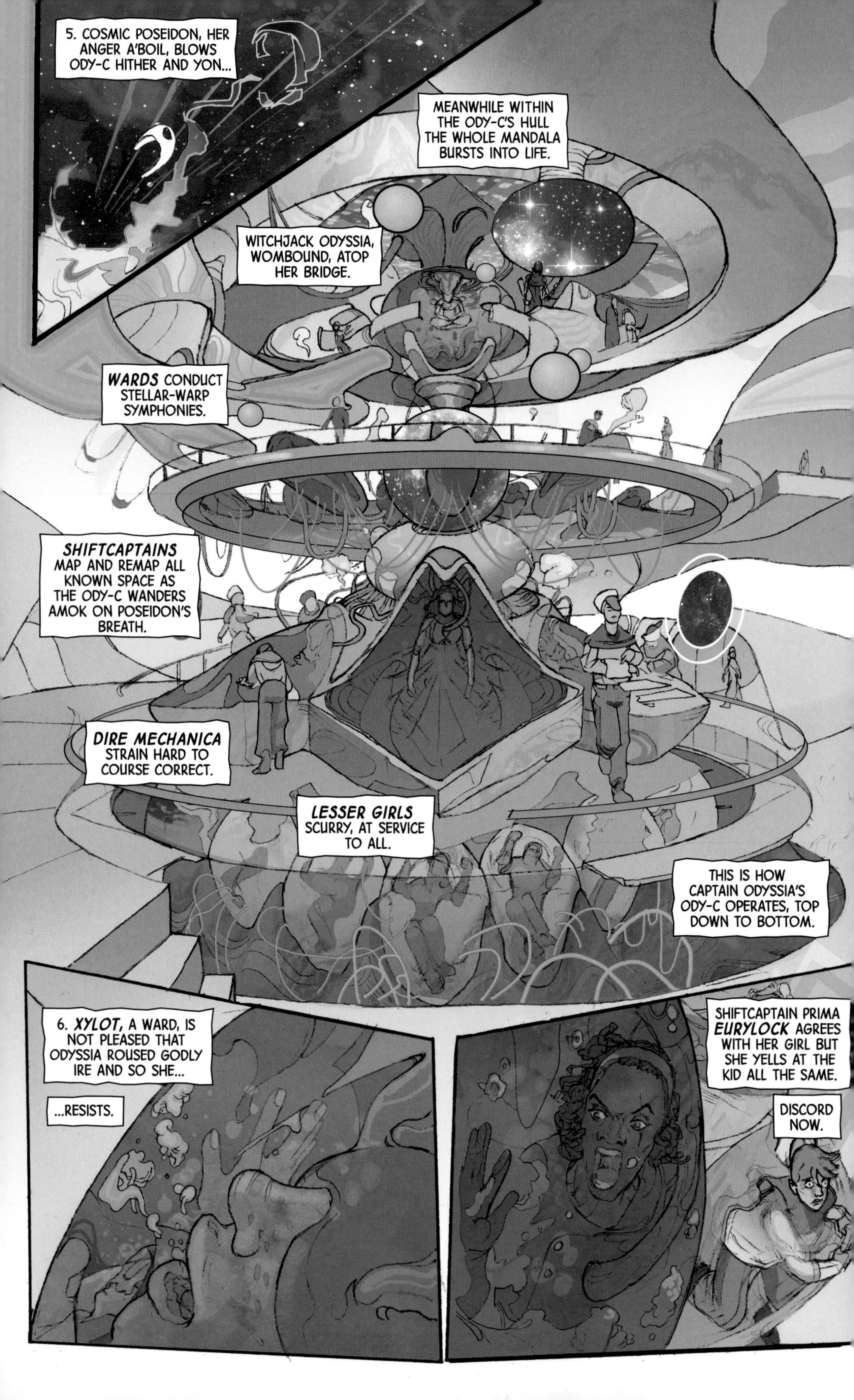
5. COSMIC POSEIDON, HER ANGER A'BOIL, BLOWS ODY-C HITHER AND YON...
MEANWHILE WITHIN THE ODY-C'S HULL THE WHOLE MANDALA BURSTS INTO LIFE.
WITCHJACK ODYSSIA, WOMBOUND, ATOP HER BRIDGE.
WARDS CONDUCT STELLAR-WARP SYMPHONIES.
SHIFTCAPTAINS MAP AND REMAP ALL KNOWN SPACE AS THE ODY-C WANDERS AMOK ON POSEIDON'S BREATH.
DIRE MECHANICA STRAIN HARD TO COURSE CORRECT.
LESSER GIRLS SCURRY, AT SERVICE TO ALL.
THIS IS HOW CAPTAIN ODYSSIA'S ODY-C OPERATES, TOP DOWN TO BOTTOM.
6. XYLOT, A WARD, IS NOT PLEASED THAT ODYSSIA ROUSED GODLY IRE AND SO SHE...
...RESISTS.
SHIFTCAPTAIN PRIMA EURYLOCK AGREES WITH HER GIRL BUT SHE YELLS AT THE KID ALL THE SAME.
DISCORD NOW.

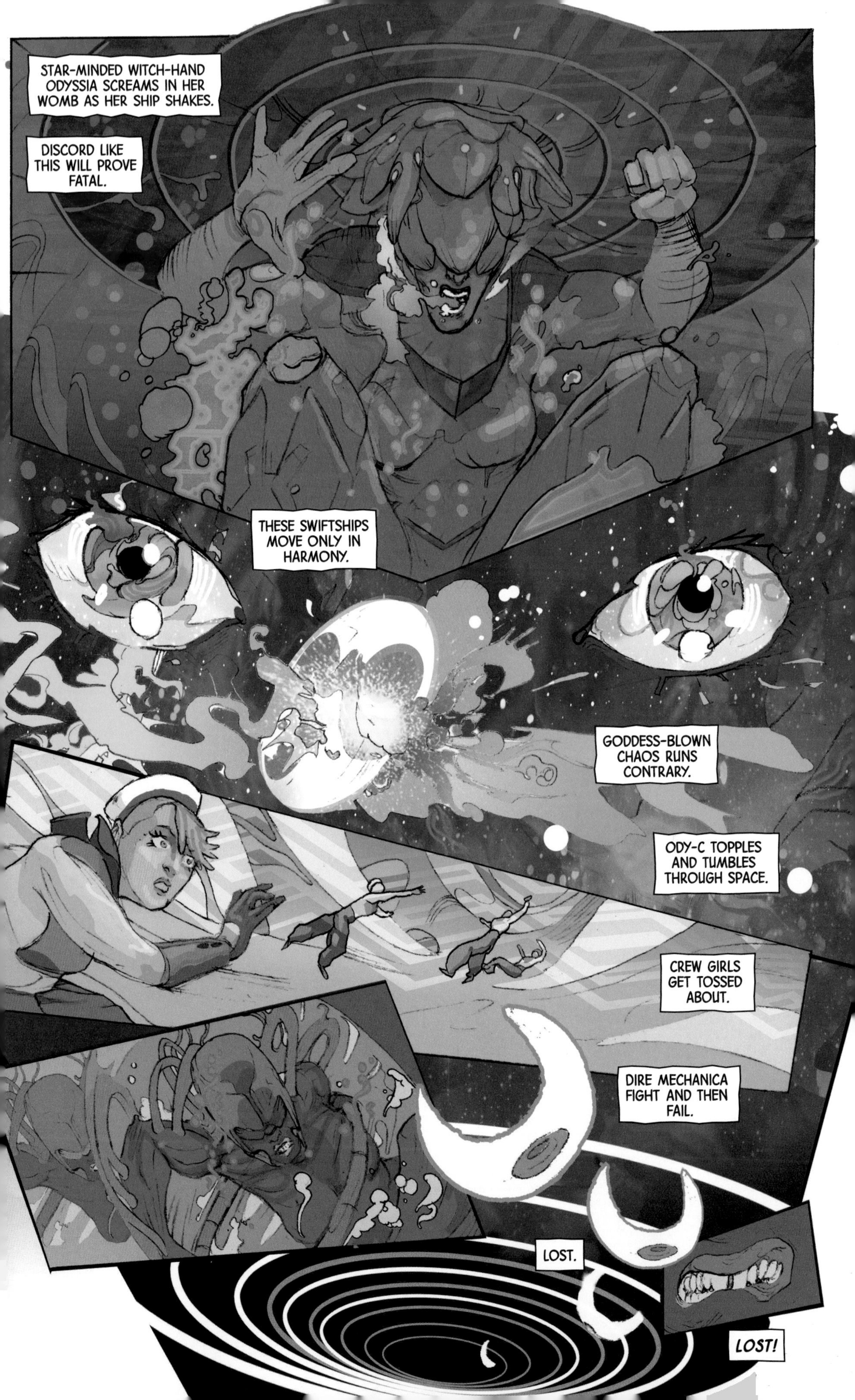

STAR-MINDED WITCH-HAND ODYSSIA SCREAMS IN HER WOMB AS HER SHIP SHAKES.
DISCORD LIKE THIS WILL PROVE FATAL.
THESE SWIFTSHIPS MOVE ONLY IN HARMONY.
GODDESS-BLOWN CHAOS RUNS CONTRARY.
ODY-C TOPPLES AND TUMBLES THROUGH SPACE.
CREW GIRLS GET TOSSED ABOUT.
DIRE MECHANICA FIGHT AND THEN FAIL.
LOST.
LOST!

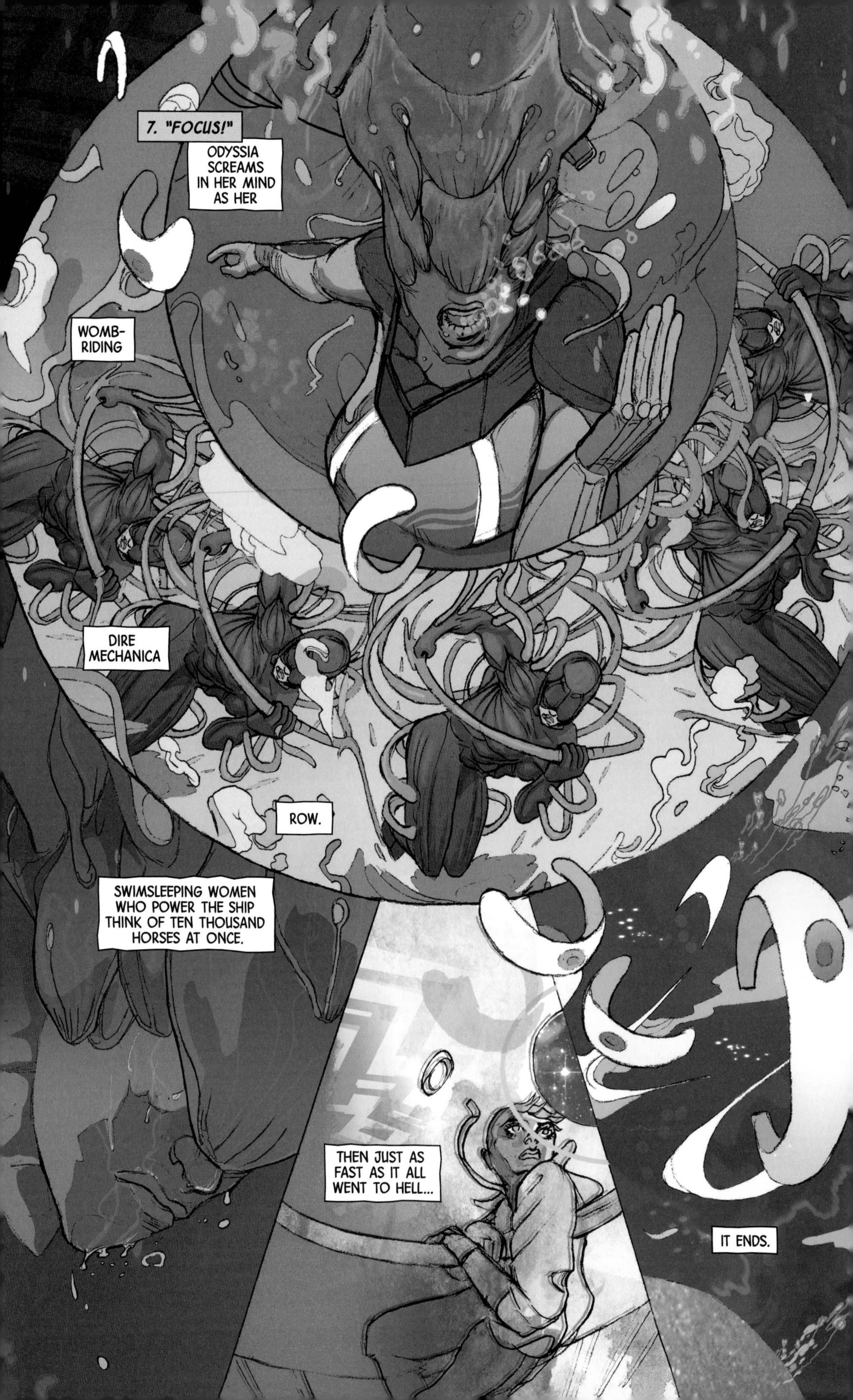
7. "FOCUS!"
ODYSSIA SCREAMS IN HER MIND AS HER
WOMB-RIDING
DIRE MECHANICA
ROW.
SWIMSLEEPING WOMEN WHO POWER THE SHIP THINK OF TEN THOUSAND HORSES AT ONCE.
THEN JUST AS FAST AS IT ALL WENT TO HELL...
IT ENDS.

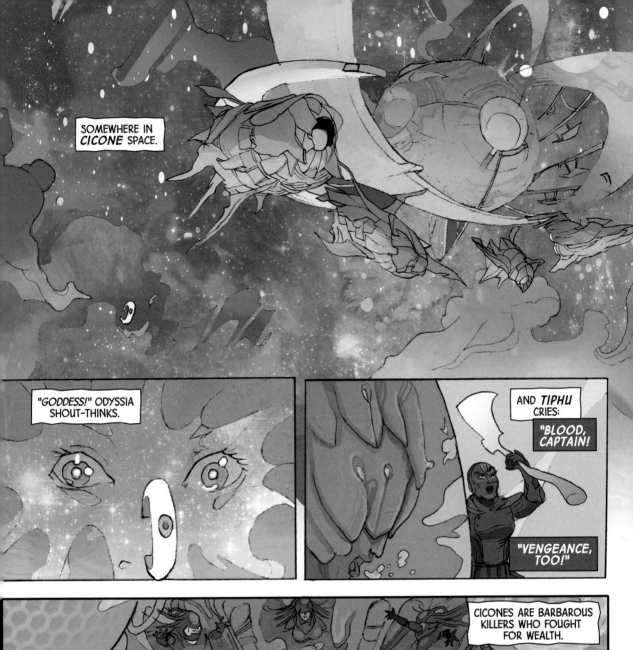

SOMEWHERE IN *CICONE* SPACE.

"*GODDESS!*" ODYSSIA SHOUT-THINKS.

AND *TIPHU* CRIES:

"*BLOOD, CAPTAIN!*"

"*VENGEANCE, TOO!*"

CICONES ARE BARBAROUS KILLERS WHO FOUGHT FOR WEALTH.

PAID BY THE TROIIAN REGIME.

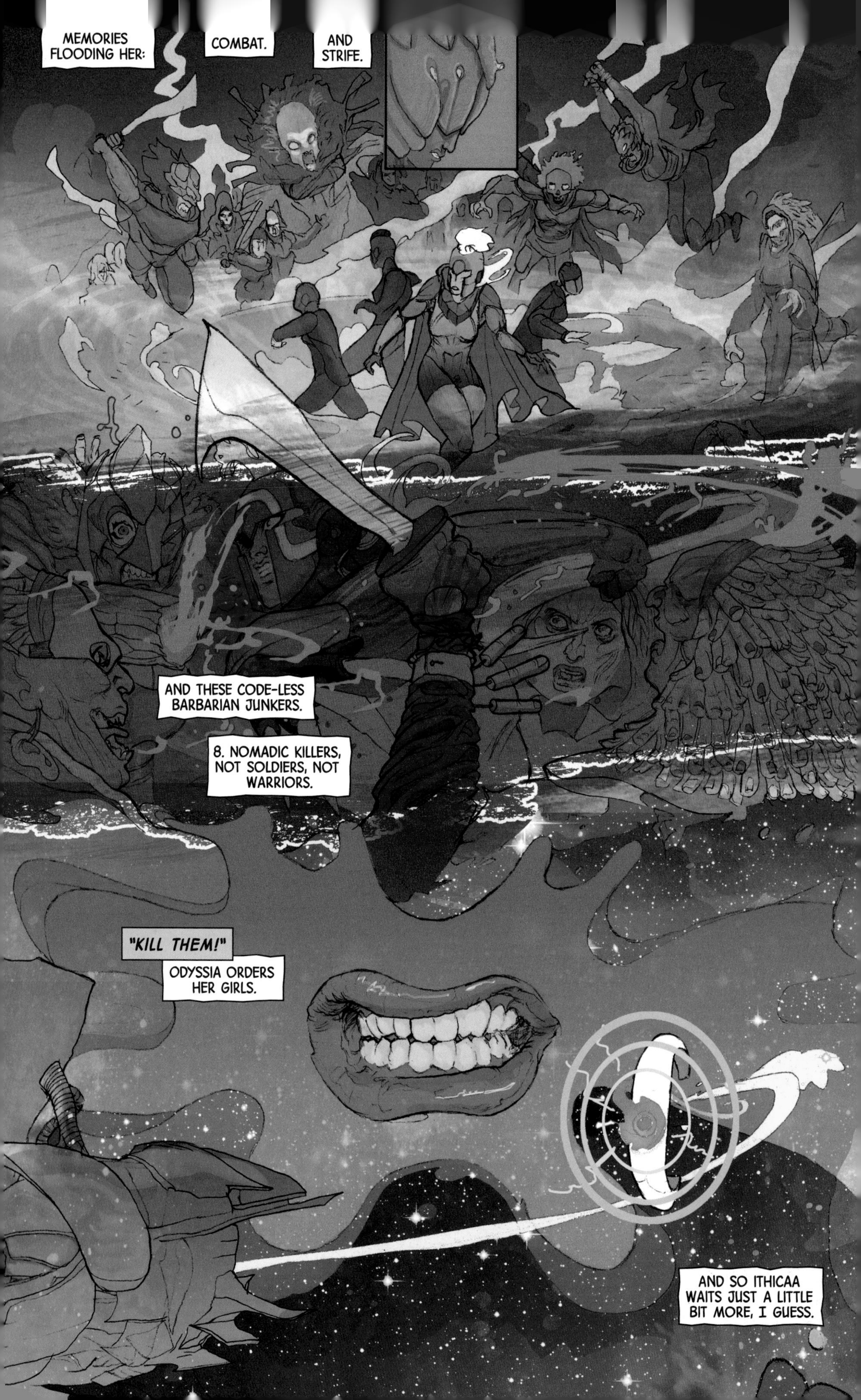
MEMORIES FLOODING HER:
COMBAT.
AND STRIFE.
AND THESE CODE-LESS BARBARIAN JUNKERS.
8. NOMADIC KILLERS, NOT SOLDIERS, NOT WARRIORS.
"KILL THEM!"
ODYSSIA ORDERS HER GIRLS.
AND SO ITHICAA WAITS JUST A LITTLE BIT MORE, I GUESS.

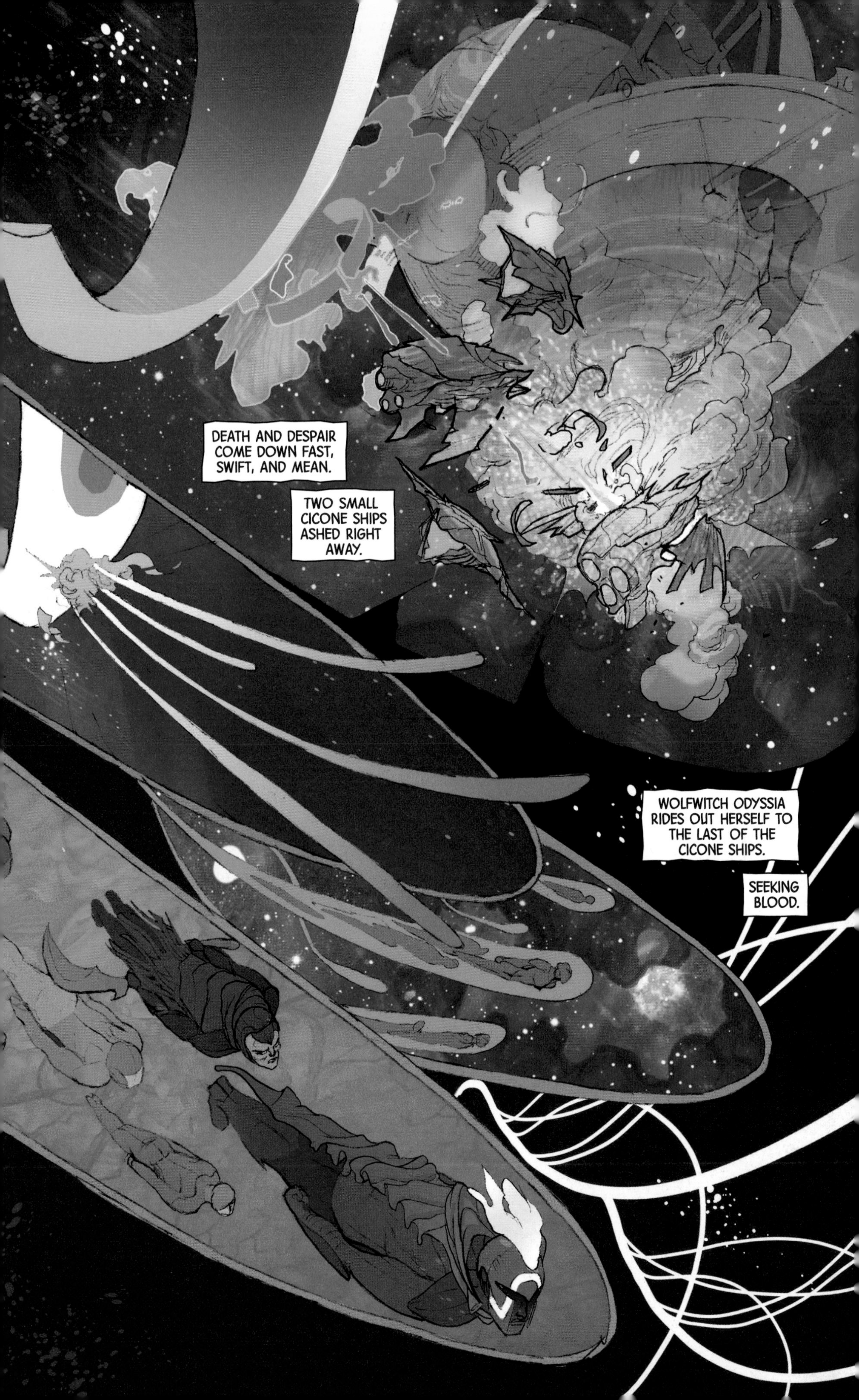
DEATH AND DESPAIR COME DOWN FAST, SWIFT, AND MEAN.
TWO SMALL CICONE SHIPS ASHED RIGHT AWAY.
WOLFWITCH ODYSSIA RIDES OUT HERSELF TO THE LAST OF THE CICONE SHIPS.
SEEKING BLOOD.

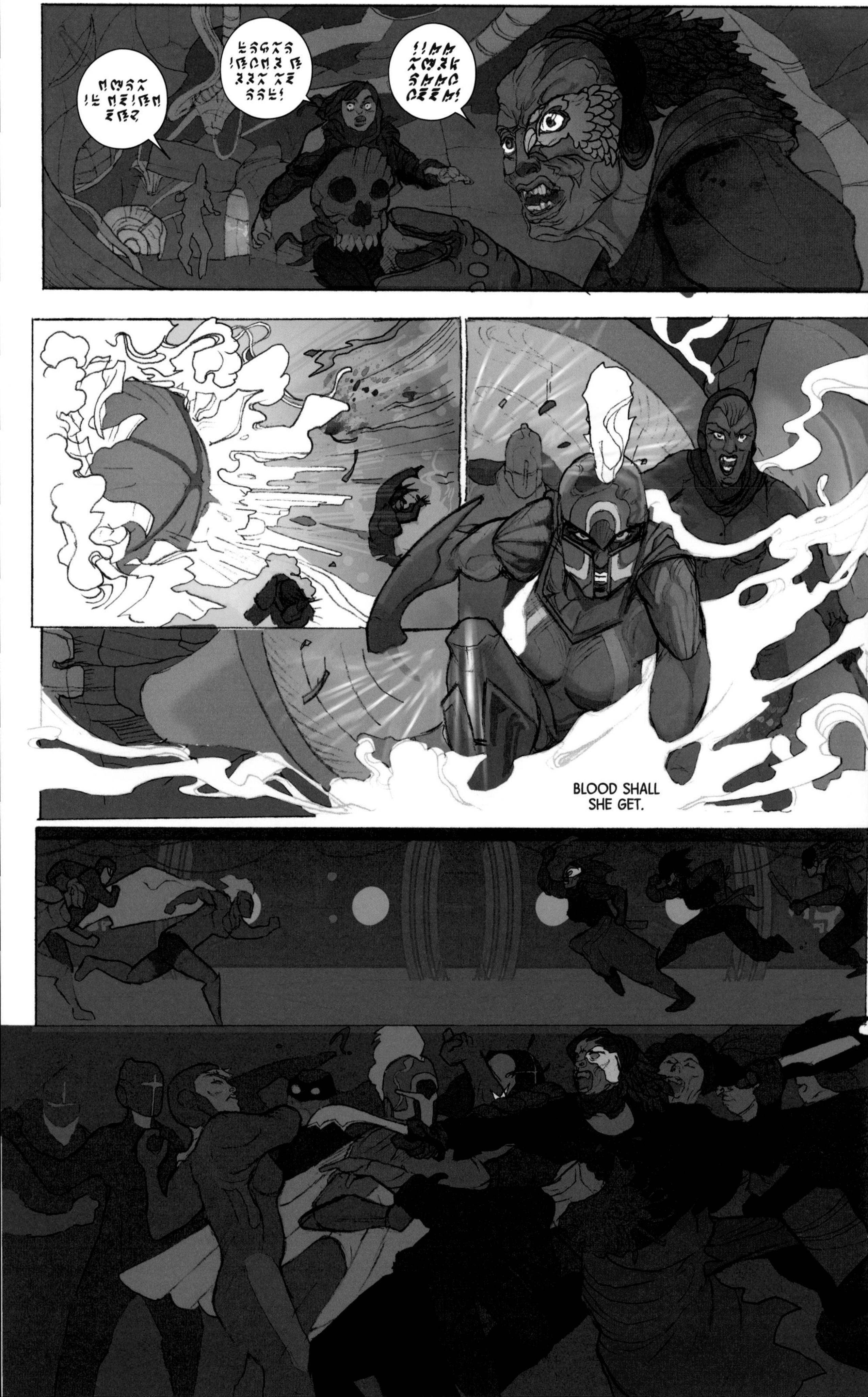
BLOOD SHALL SHE GET.

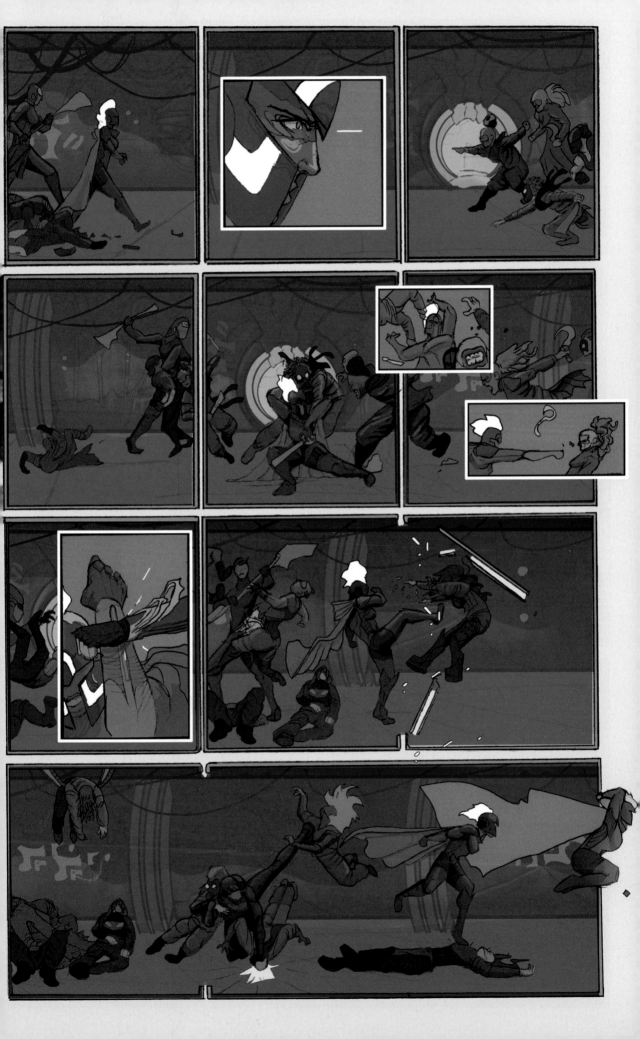

AND THUS MURDEROUS WOLFHEART ODYSSIA SETTLES UP.

AND THEN:

"WARRIOR QUEENS!"

THEIR ODYSSIA BELLOWS OUT.

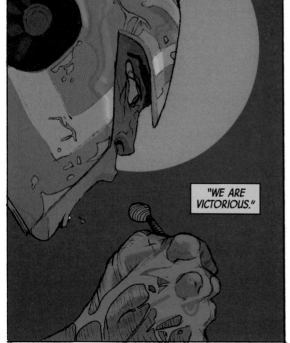

"WE ARE VICTORIOUS."

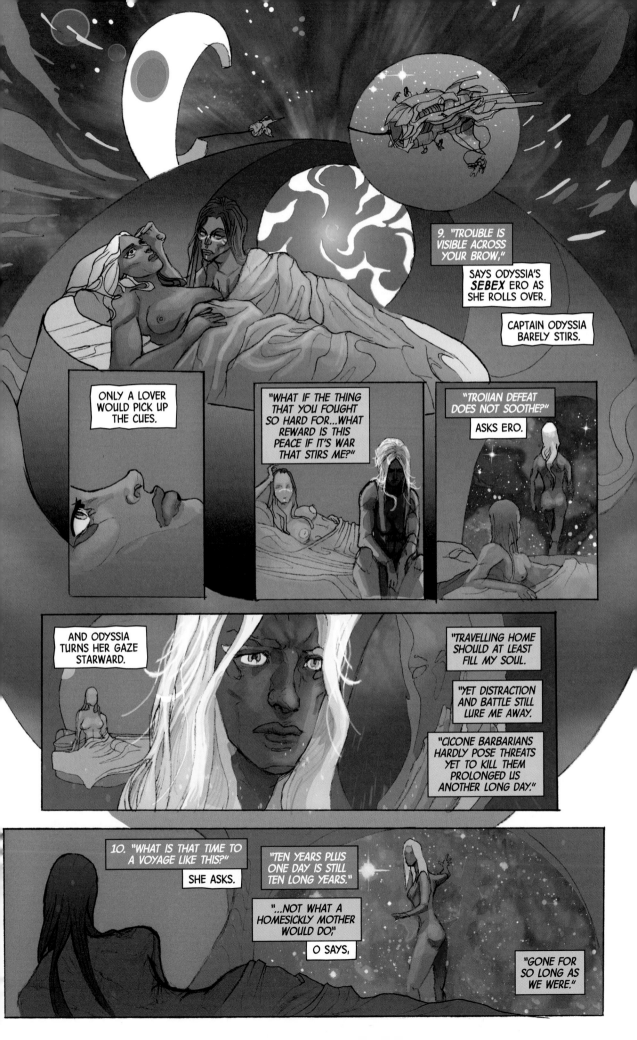

9. "TROUBLE IS VISIBLE ACROSS YOUR BROW,"

SAYS ODYSSIA'S *SEBEX* ERO AS SHE ROLLS OVER.

CAPTAIN ODYSSIA BARELY STIRS.

ONLY A LOVER WOULD PICK UP THE CUES.

"WHAT IF THE THING THAT YOU FOUGHT SO HARD FOR...WHAT REWARD IS THIS PEACE IF IT'S WAR THAT STIRS ME?"

"TROIIAN DEFEAT DOES NOT SOOTHE?"

ASKS ERO.

AND ODYSSIA TURNS HER GAZE STARWARD.

"TRAVELLING HOME SHOULD AT LEAST FILL MY SOUL.

"YET DISTRACTION AND BATTLE STILL LURE ME AWAY.

"CICONE BARBARIANS HARDLY POSE THREATS YET TO KILL THEM PROLONGED US ANOTHER LONG DAY."

10. "WHAT IS THAT TIME TO A VOYAGE LIKE THIS?"

SHE ASKS.

"TEN YEARS PLUS ONE DAY IS STILL TEN LONG YEARS."

"...NOT WHAT A HOMESICKLY MOTHER WOULD DO,"

O SAYS,

"GONE FOR SO LONG AS WE WERE."

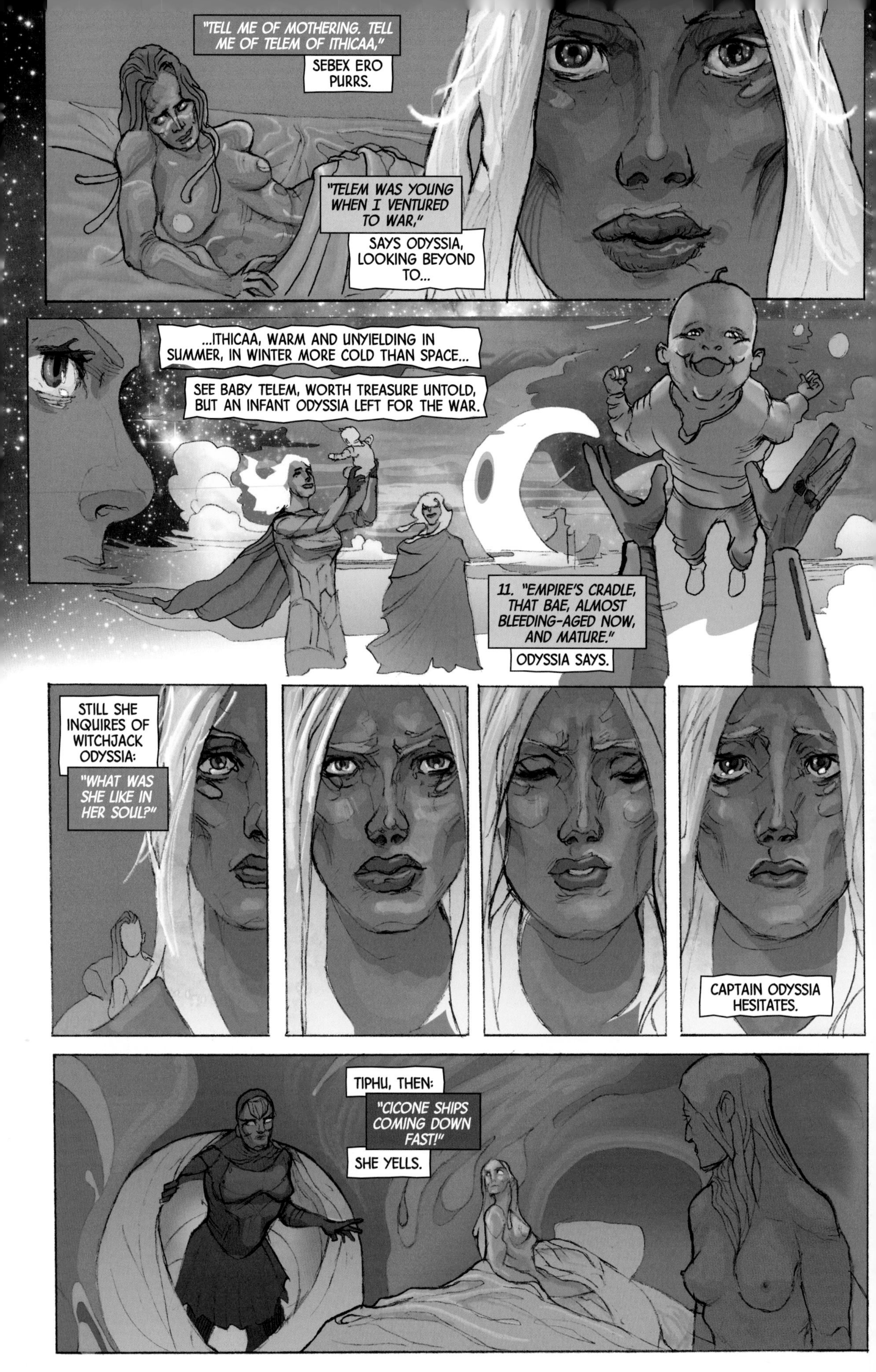
"TELL ME OF MOTHERING. TELL ME OF TELEM OF ITHICAA,"
SEBEX ERO PURRS.
"TELEM WAS YOUNG WHEN I VENTURED TO WAR,"
SAYS ODYSSIA, LOOKING BEYOND TO...
...ITHICAA, WARM AND UNYIELDING IN SUMMER, IN WINTER MORE COLD THAN SPACE...
SEE BABY TELEM, WORTH TREASURE UNTOLD, BUT AN INFANT ODYSSIA LEFT FOR THE WAR.
11. "EMPIRE'S CRADLE, THAT BAE, ALMOST BLEEDING-AGED NOW, AND MATURE."
ODYSSIA SAYS.
STILL SHE INQUIRES OF WITCHJACK ODYSSIA:
"WHAT WAS SHE LIKE IN HER SOUL?"
CAPTAIN ODYSSIA HESITATES.
TIPHU, THEN:
"CICONE SHIPS COMING DOWN FAST!"
SHE YELLS.

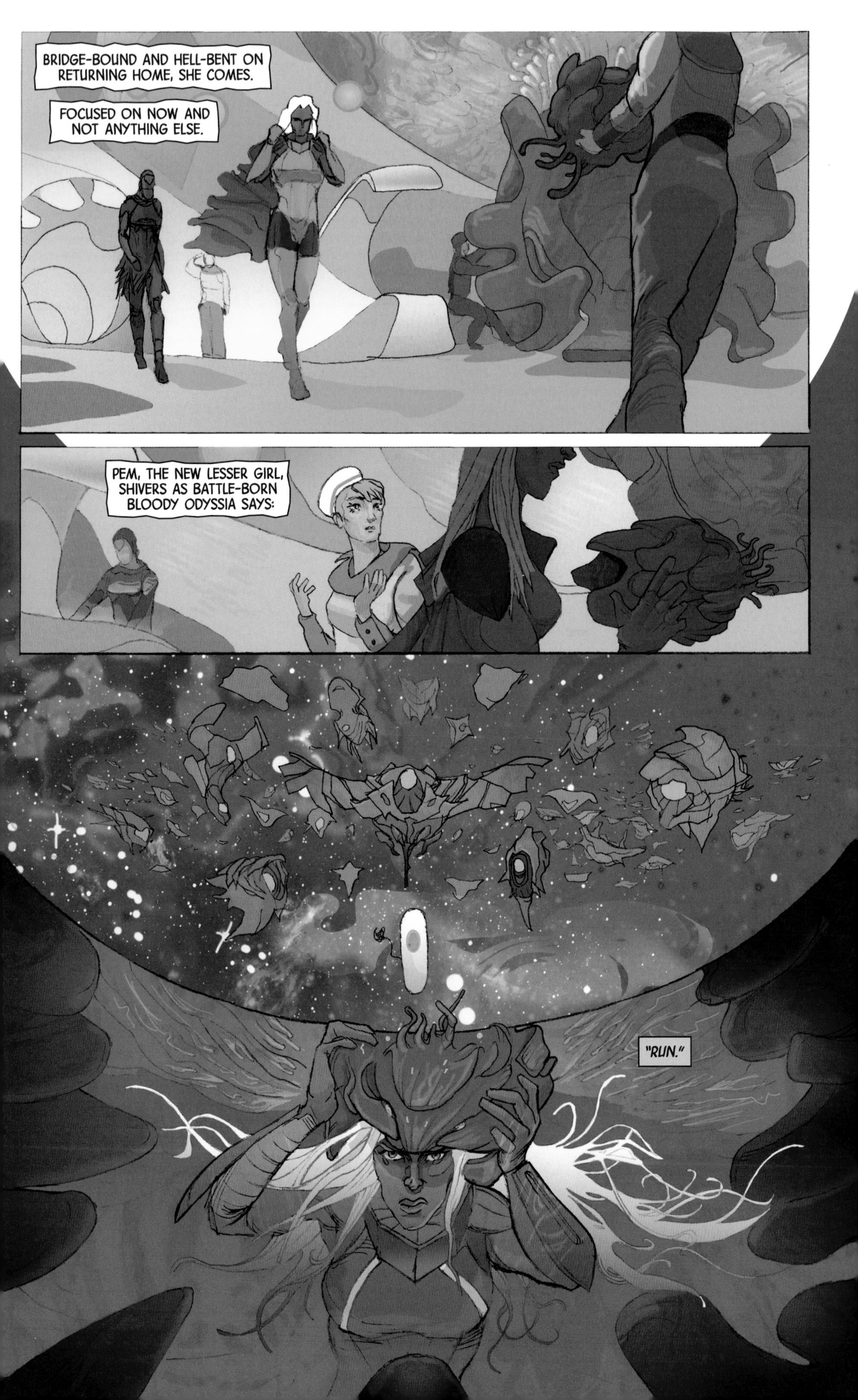
BRIDGE-BOUND AND HELL-BENT ON RETURNING HOME, SHE COMES.
FOCUSED ON NOW AND NOT ANYTHING ELSE.
PEM, THE NEW LESSER GIRL, SHIVERS AS BATTLE-BORN BLOODY ODYSSIA SAYS:
"RUN."

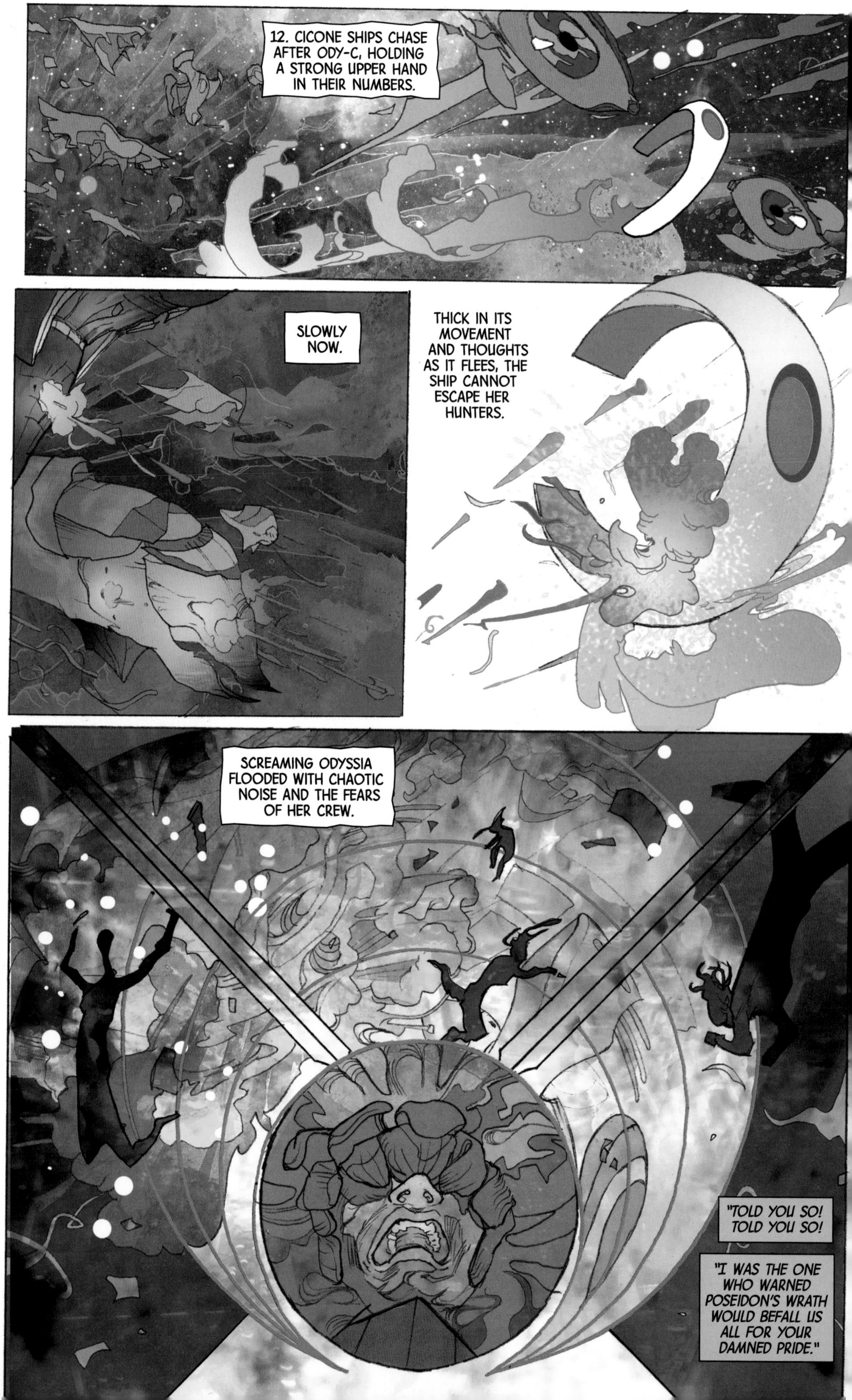
12. CICONE SHIPS CHASE AFTER ODY-C, HOLDING A STRONG UPPER HAND IN THEIR NUMBERS.
SLOWLY NOW.
THICK IN ITS MOVEMENT AND THOUGHTS AS IT FLEES, THE SHIP CANNOT ESCAPE HER HUNTERS.
SCREAMING ODYSSIA FLOODED WITH CHAOTIC NOISE AND THE FEARS OF HER CREW.
"TOLD YOU SO! TOLD YOU SO!
"I WAS THE ONE WHO WARNED POSEIDON'S WRATH WOULD BEFALL US ALL FOR YOUR DAMNED PRIDE."

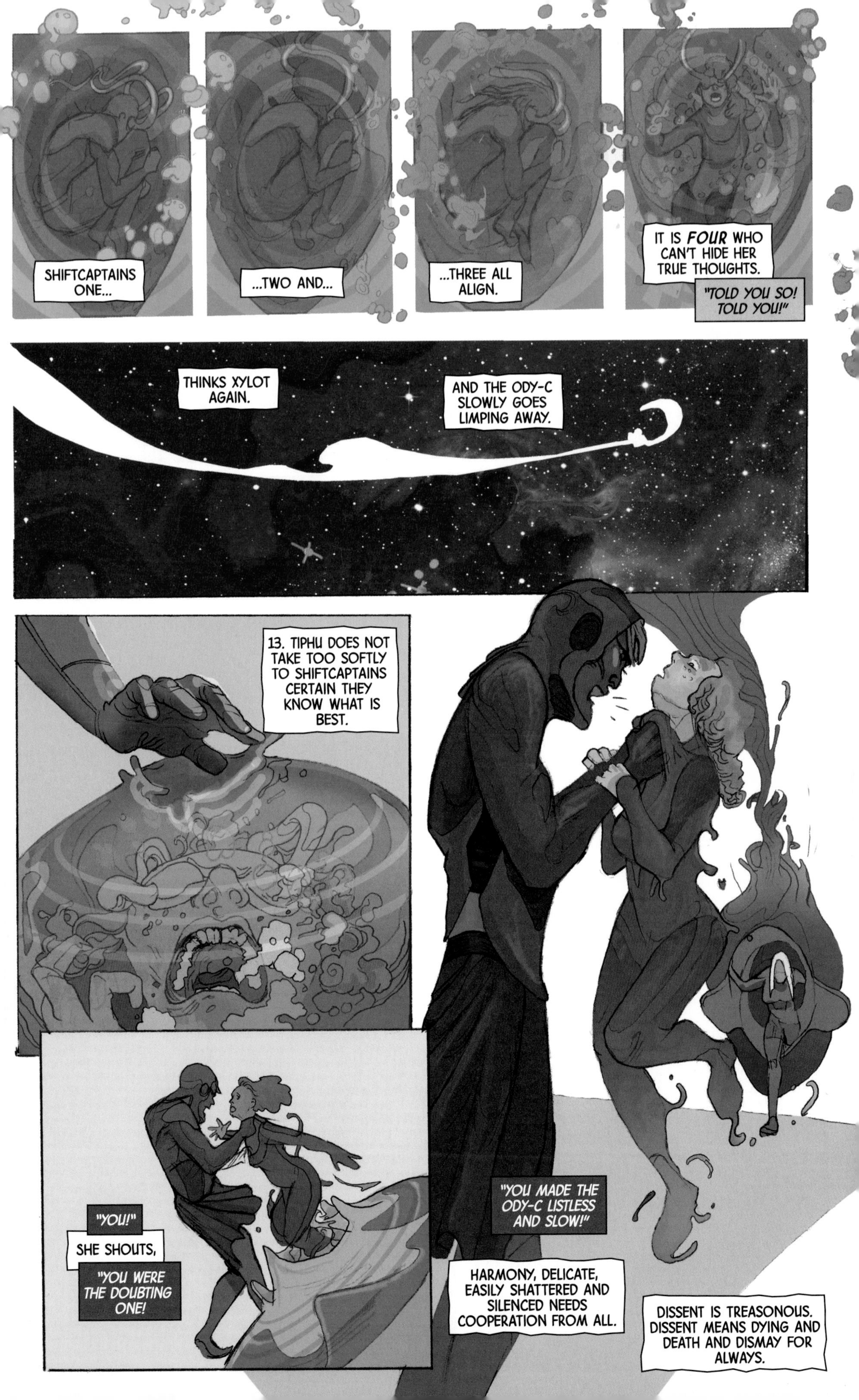
SHIFTCAPTAINS ONE...
...TWO AND...
...THREE ALL ALIGN.
IT IS FOUR WHO CAN'T HIDE HER TRUE THOUGHTS.
"TOLD YOU SO! TOLD YOU!"
THINKS XYLOT AGAIN.
AND THE ODY-C SLOWLY GOES LIMPING AWAY.
13. TIPHU DOES NOT TAKE TOO SOFTLY TO SHIFTCAPTAINS CERTAIN THEY KNOW WHAT IS BEST.
"YOU!"
SHE SHOUTS,
"YOU WERE THE DOUBTING ONE!
"YOU MADE THE ODY-C LISTLESS AND SLOW!"
HARMONY, DELICATE, EASILY SHATTERED AND SILENCED NEEDS COOPERATION FROM ALL.
DISSENT IS TREASONOUS. DISSENT MEANS DYING AND DEATH AND DISMAY FOR ALWAYS.

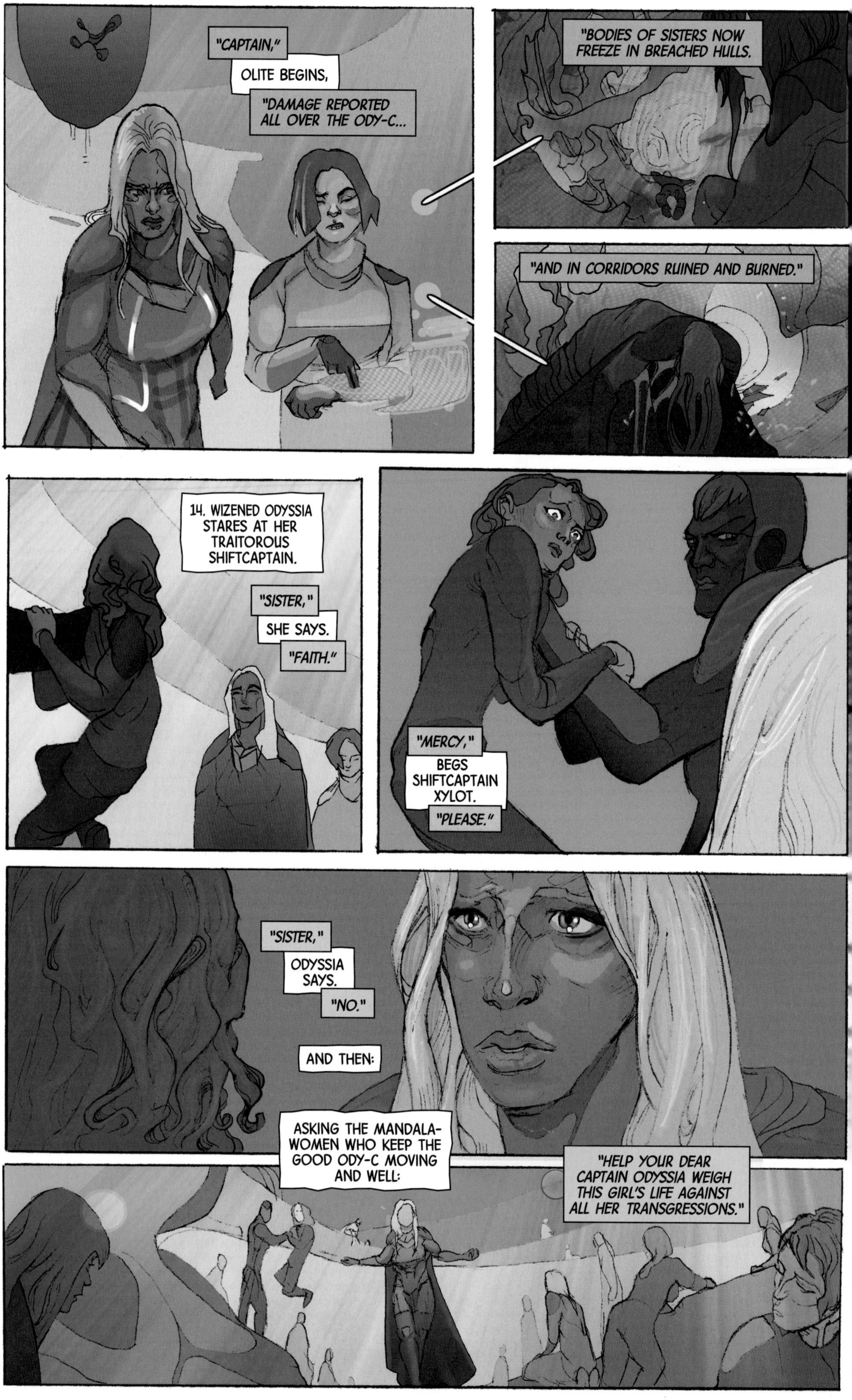
"CAPTAIN,"
OLITE BEGINS,
"DAMAGE REPORTED ALL OVER THE ODY-C...
"BODIES OF SISTERS NOW FREEZE IN BREACHED HULLS.
"AND IN CORRIDORS RUINED AND BURNED."
14. WIZENED ODYSSIA STARES AT HER TRAITOROUS SHIFTCAPTAIN.
"SISTER,"
SHE SAYS.
"FAITH."
"MERCY,"
BEGS SHIFTCAPTAIN XYLOT.
"PLEASE."
"SISTER,"
ODYSSIA SAYS.
"NO."
AND THEN:
ASKING THE MANDALA-WOMEN WHO KEEP THE GOOD ODY-C MOVING AND WELL:
"HELP YOUR DEAR CAPTAIN ODYSSIA WEIGH THIS GIRL'S LIFE AGAINST ALL HER TRANSGRESSIONS."

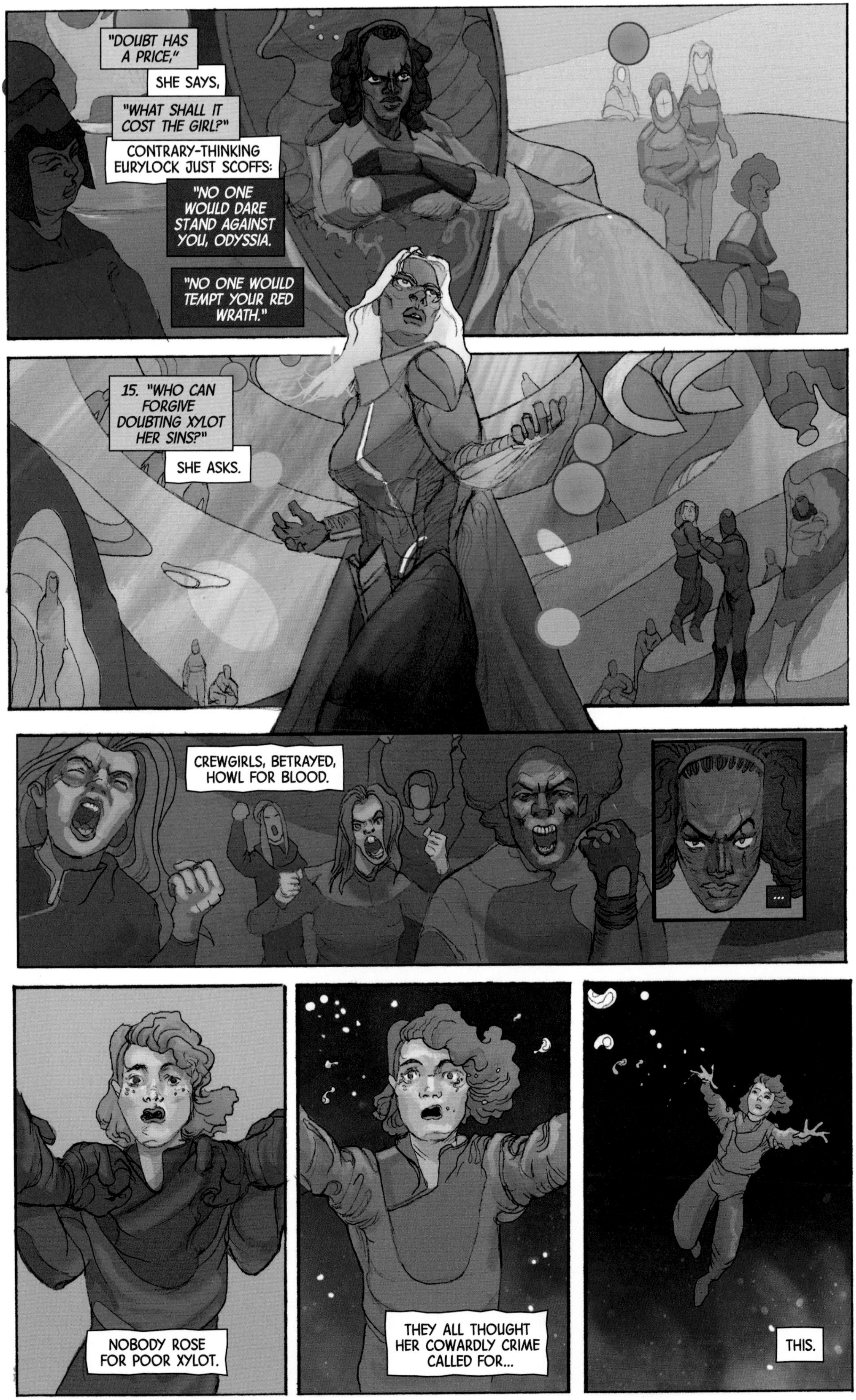
"DOUBT HAS A PRICE,"
SHE SAYS,
"WHAT SHALL IT COST THE GIRL?"
CONTRARY-THINKING EURYLOCK JUST SCOFFS:
"NO ONE WOULD DARE STAND AGAINST YOU, ODYSSIA.
"NO ONE WOULD TEMPT YOUR RED WRATH."
15. "WHO CAN FORGIVE DOUBTING XYLOT HER SINS?"
SHE ASKS.
CREWGIRLS, BETRAYED, HOWL FOR BLOOD.
...
NOBODY ROSE FOR POOR XYLOT.
THEY ALL THOUGHT HER COWARDLY CRIME CALLED FOR...
THIS.

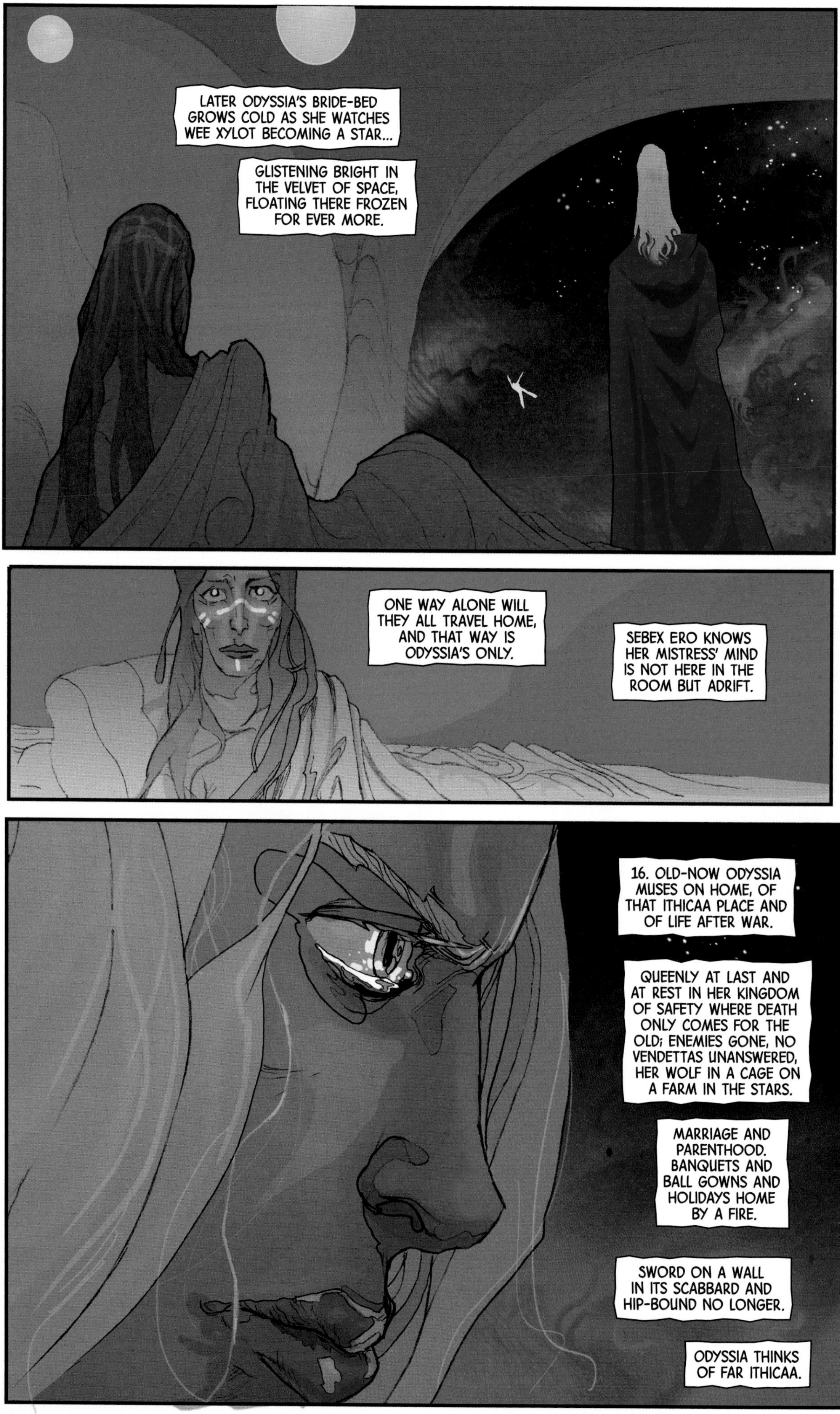
LATER ODYSSIA'S BRIDE-BED GROWS COLD AS SHE WATCHES WEE XYLOT BECOMING A STAR...
GLISTENING BRIGHT IN THE VELVET OF SPACE, FLOATING THERE FROZEN FOR EVER MORE.
ONE WAY ALONE WILL THEY ALL TRAVEL HOME, AND THAT WAY IS ODYSSIA'S ONLY.
SEBEX ERO KNOWS HER MISTRESS' MIND IS NOT HERE IN THE ROOM BUT ADRIFT.
16. OLD-NOW ODYSSIA MUSES ON HOME, OF THAT ITHICAA PLACE AND OF LIFE AFTER WAR.
QUEENLY AT LAST AND AT REST IN HER KINGDOM OF SAFETY WHERE DEATH ONLY COMES FOR THE OLD; ENEMIES GONE, NO VENDETTAS UNANSWERED, HER WOLF IN A CAGE ON A FARM IN THE STARS.
MARRIAGE AND PARENTHOOD. BANQUETS AND BALL GOWNS AND HOLIDAYS HOME BY A FIRE.
SWORD ON A WALL IN ITS SCABBARD AND HIP-BOUND NO LONGER.
ODYSSIA THINKS OF FAR ITHICAA.

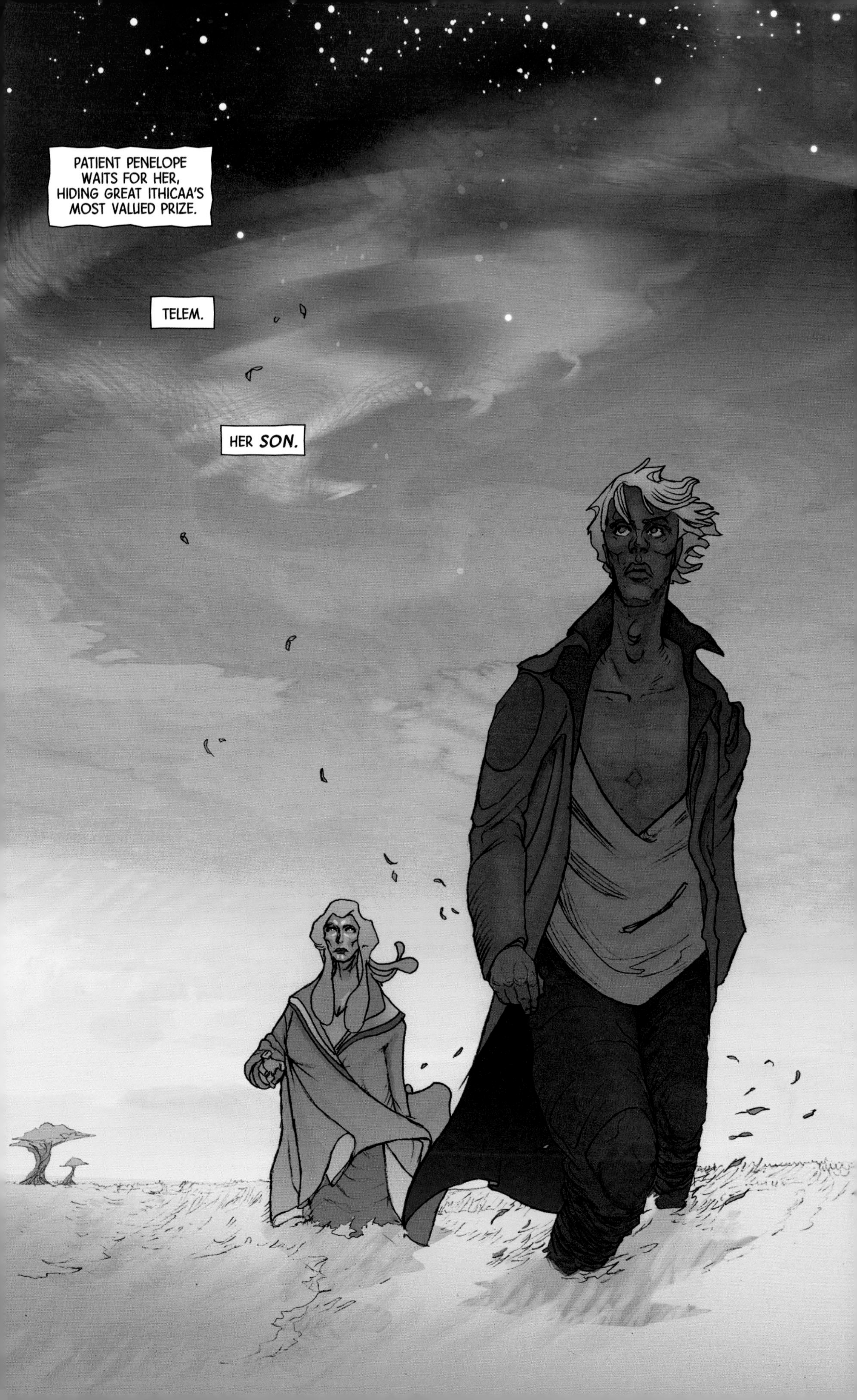
PATIENT PENELOPE WAITS FOR HER, HIDING GREAT ITHICAA'S MOST VALUED PRIZE.
TELEM.
HER SON.

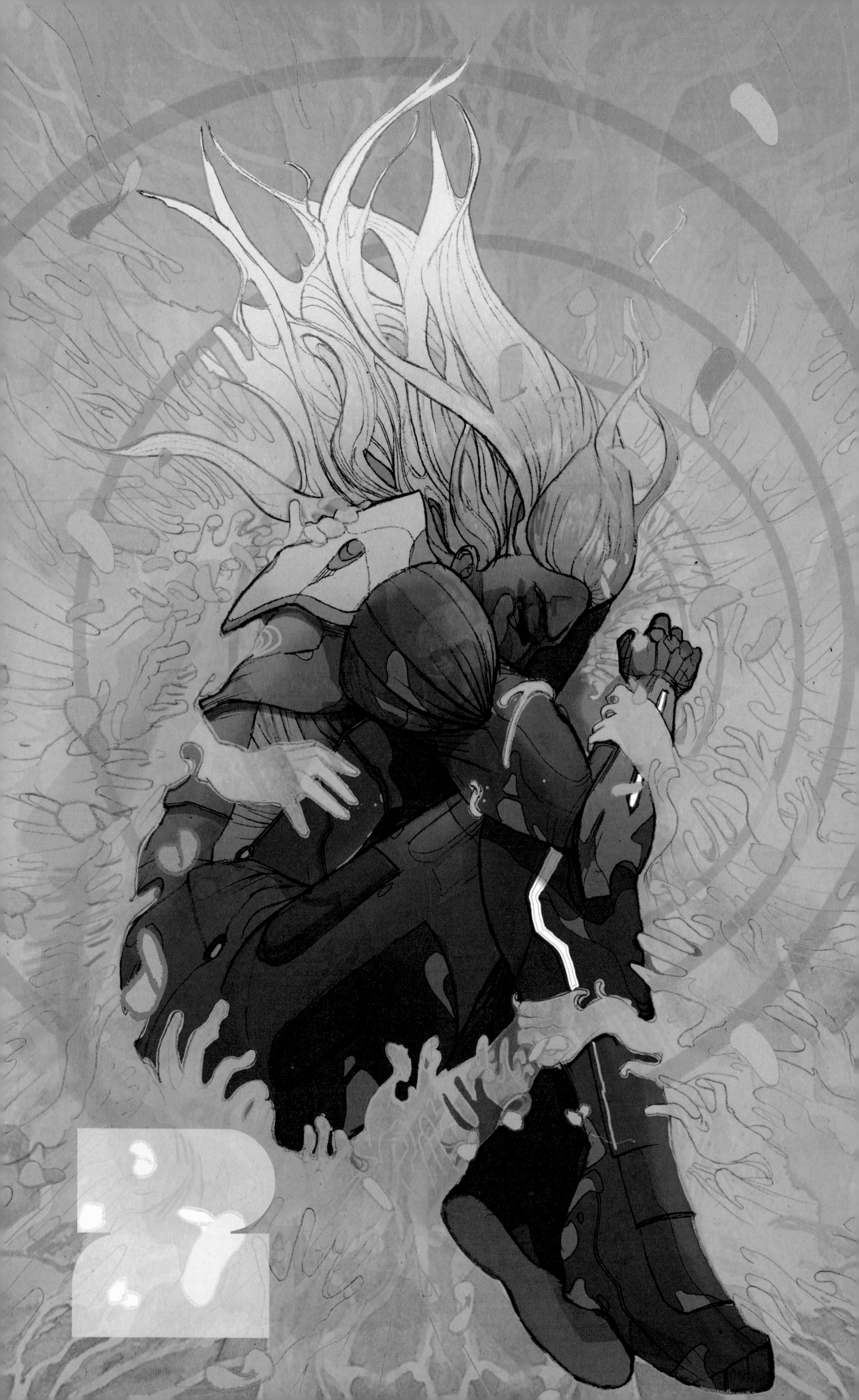
2

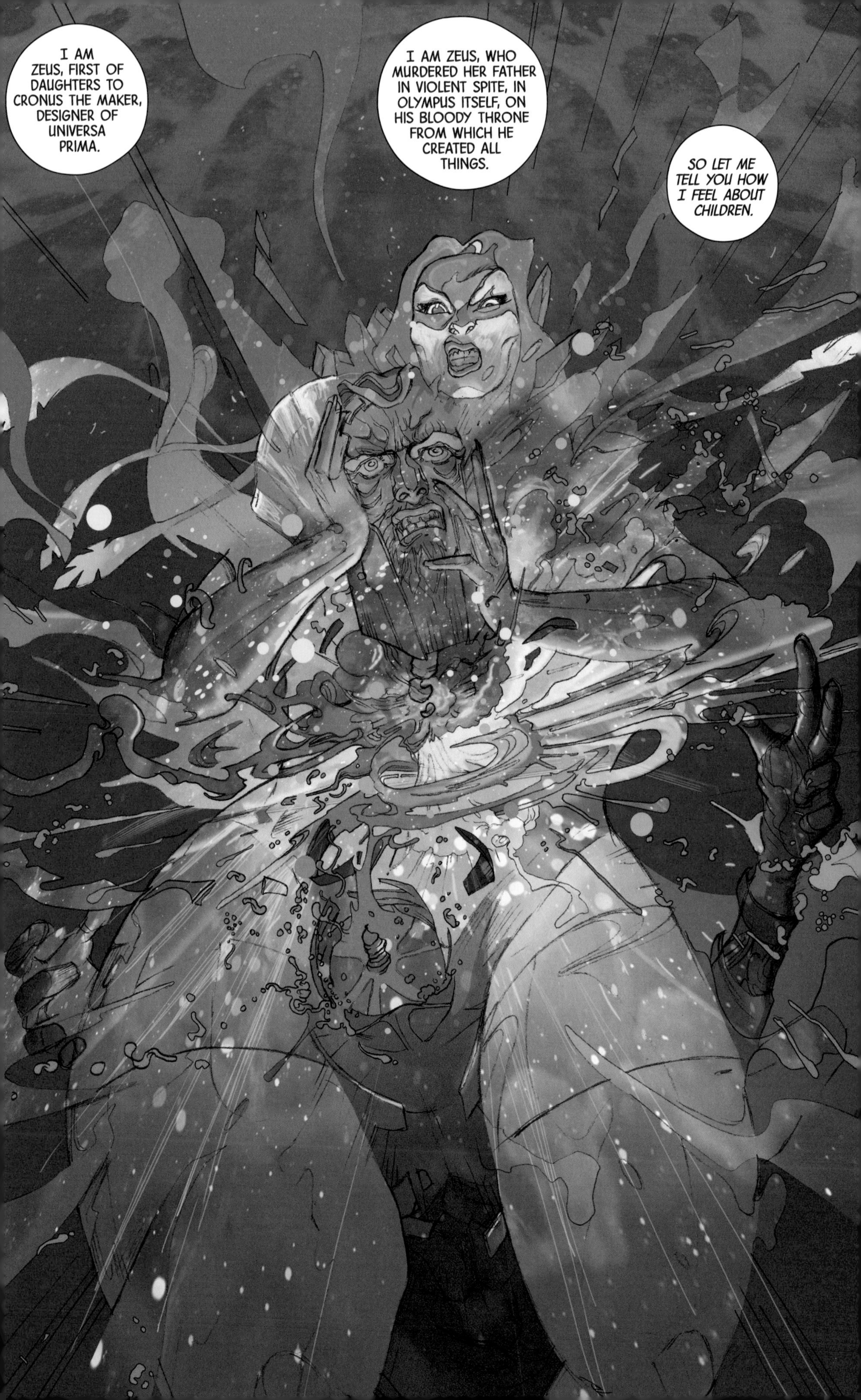
I AM ZEUS, FIRST OF DAUGHTERS TO CRONUS THE MAKER, DESIGNER OF UNIVERSA PRIMA.
I AM ZEUS, WHO MURDERED HER FATHER IN VIOLENT SPITE, IN OLYMPUS ITSELF, ON HIS BLOODY THRONE FROM WHICH HE CREATED ALL THINGS.
SO LET ME TELL YOU HOW I FEEL ABOUT CHILDREN.

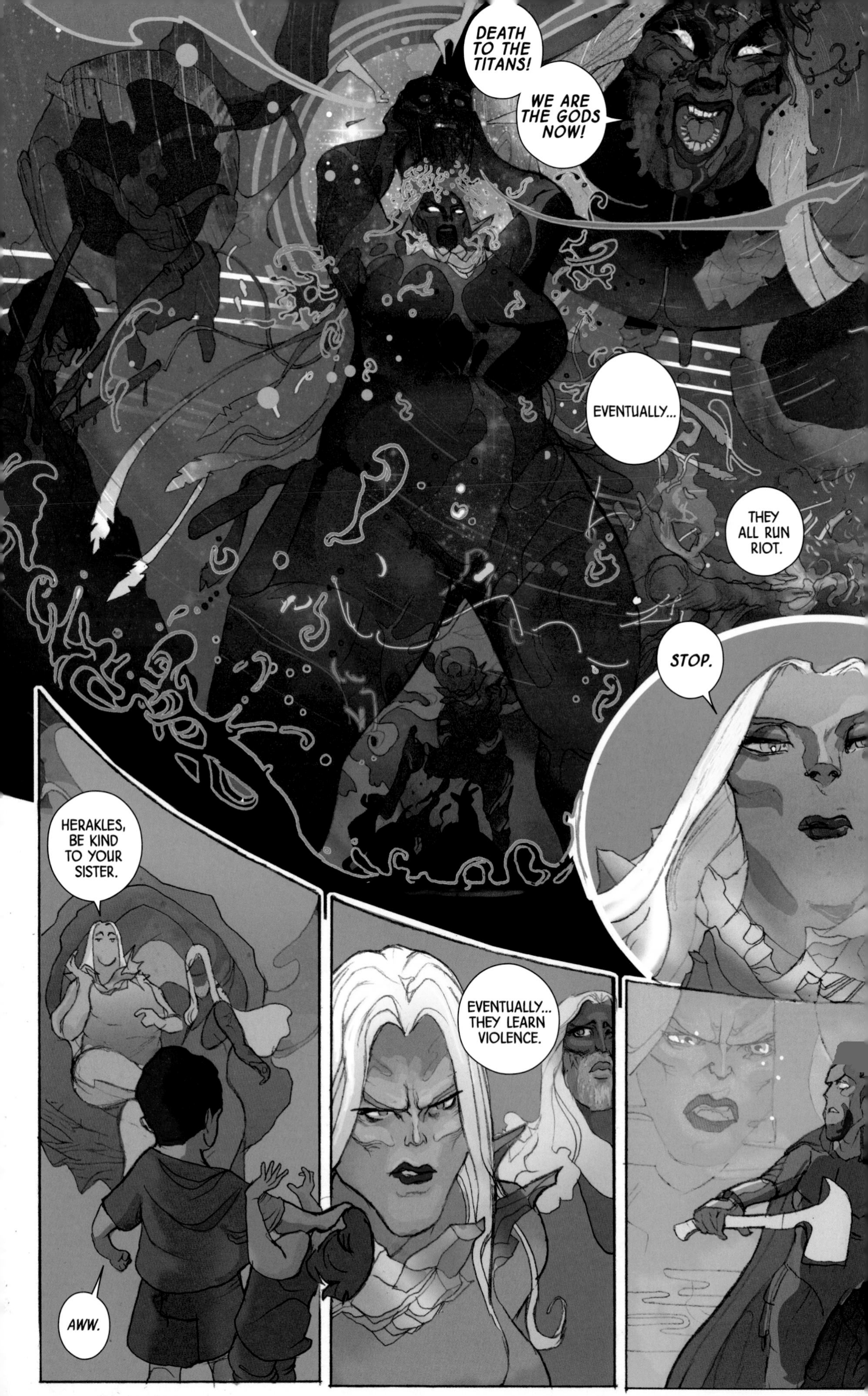
DEATH TO THE TITANS!
WE ARE THE GODS NOW!
EVENTUALLY...
THEY ALL RUN RIOT.
STOP.
HERAKLES, BE KIND TO YOUR SISTER.
AWW.
EVENTUALLY... THEY LEARN VIOLENCE.

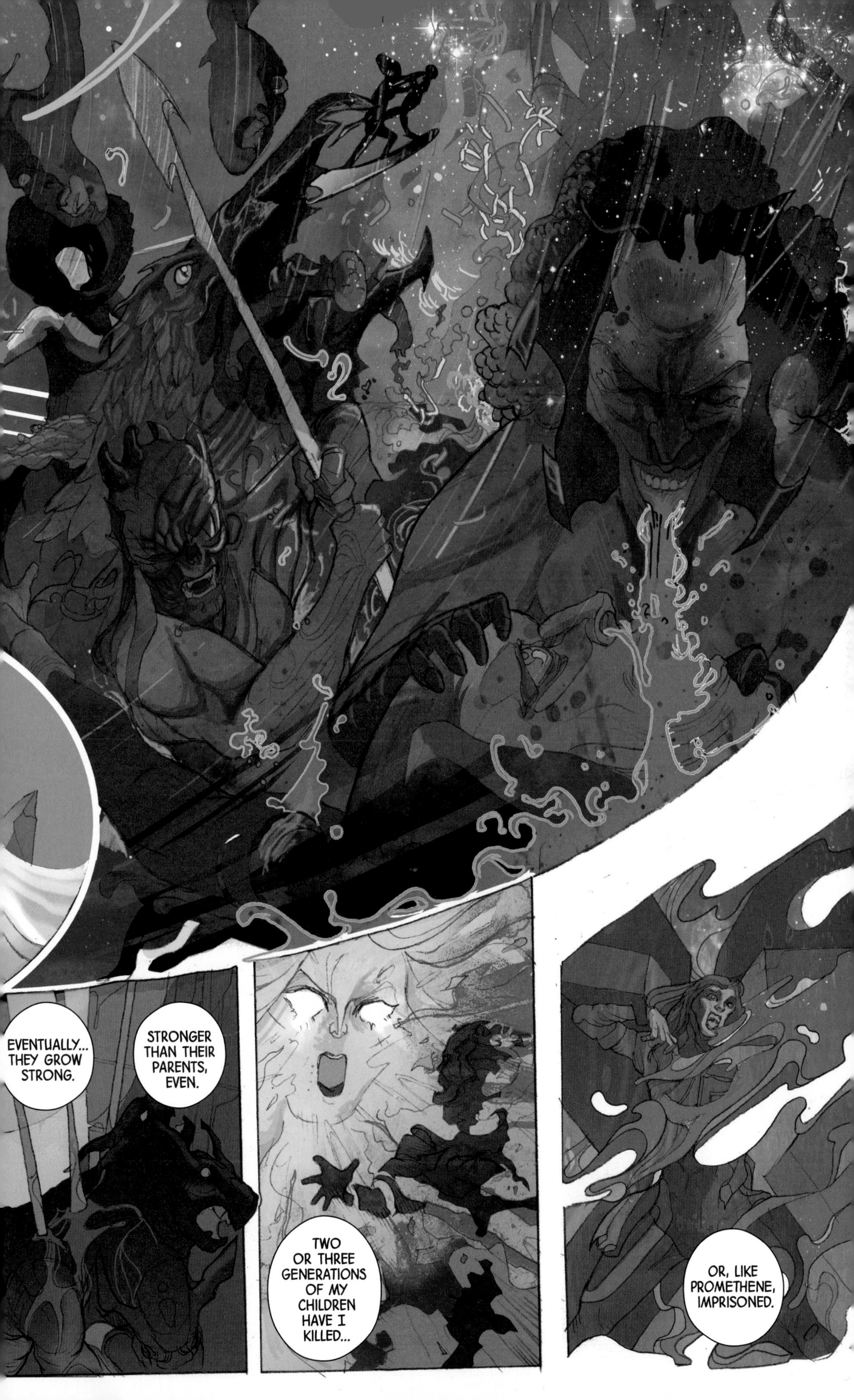
EVENTUALLY... THEY GROW STRONG.
STRONGER THAN THEIR PARENTS, EVEN.
TWO OR THREE GENERATIONS OF MY CHILDREN HAVE I KILLED...
OR, LIKE PROMETHENE, IMPRISONED.

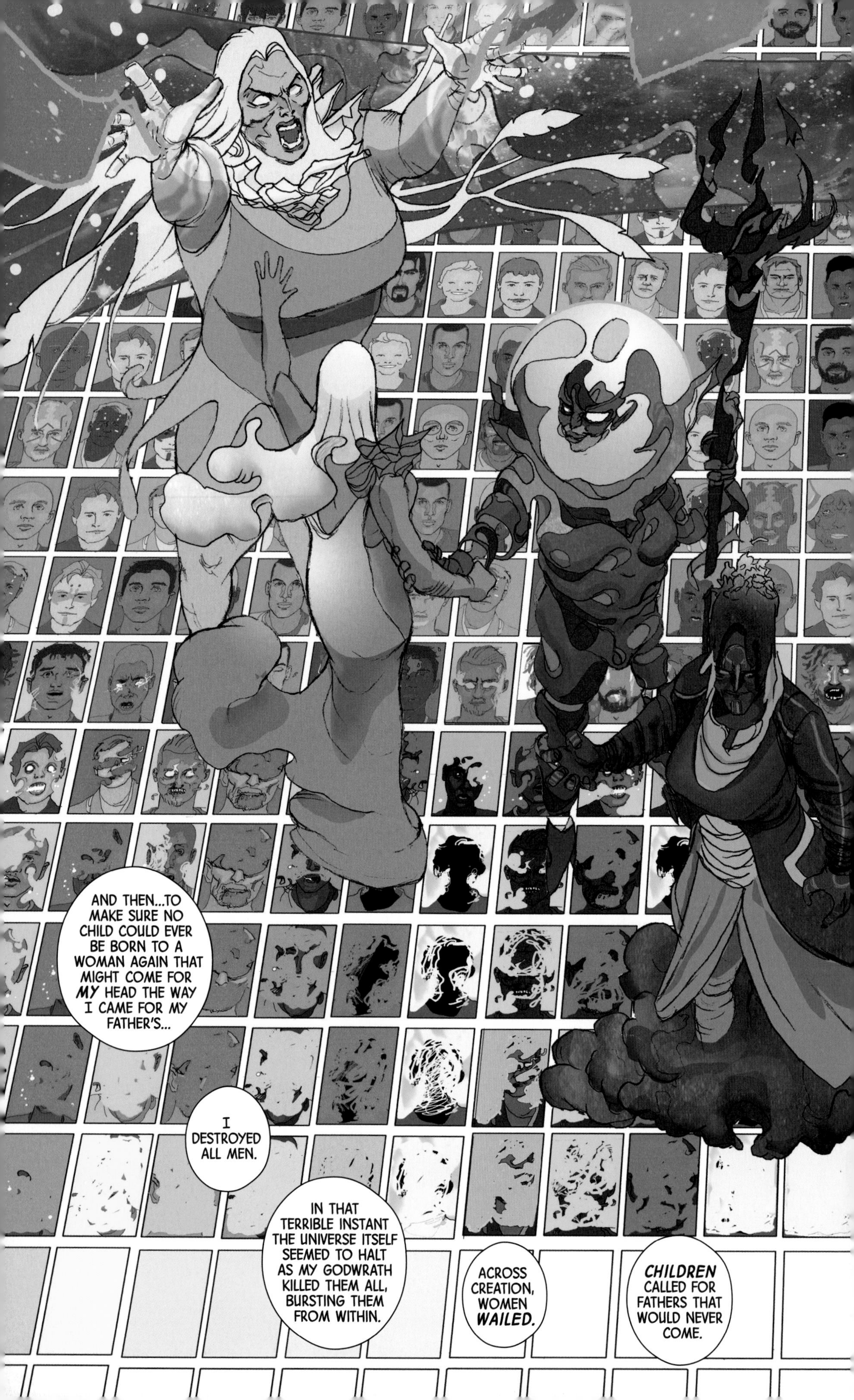
AND THEN...TO MAKE SURE NO CHILD COULD EVER BE BORN TO A WOMAN AGAIN THAT MIGHT COME FOR *MY* HEAD THE WAY I CAME FOR MY FATHER'S...
I DESTROYED ALL MEN.
IN THAT TERRIBLE INSTANT THE UNIVERSE ITSELF SEEMED TO HALT AS MY GODWRATH KILLED THEM ALL, BURSTING THEM FROM WITHIN.
ACROSS CREATION, WOMEN *WAILED.*
CHILDREN CALLED FOR FATHERS THAT WOULD NEVER COME.

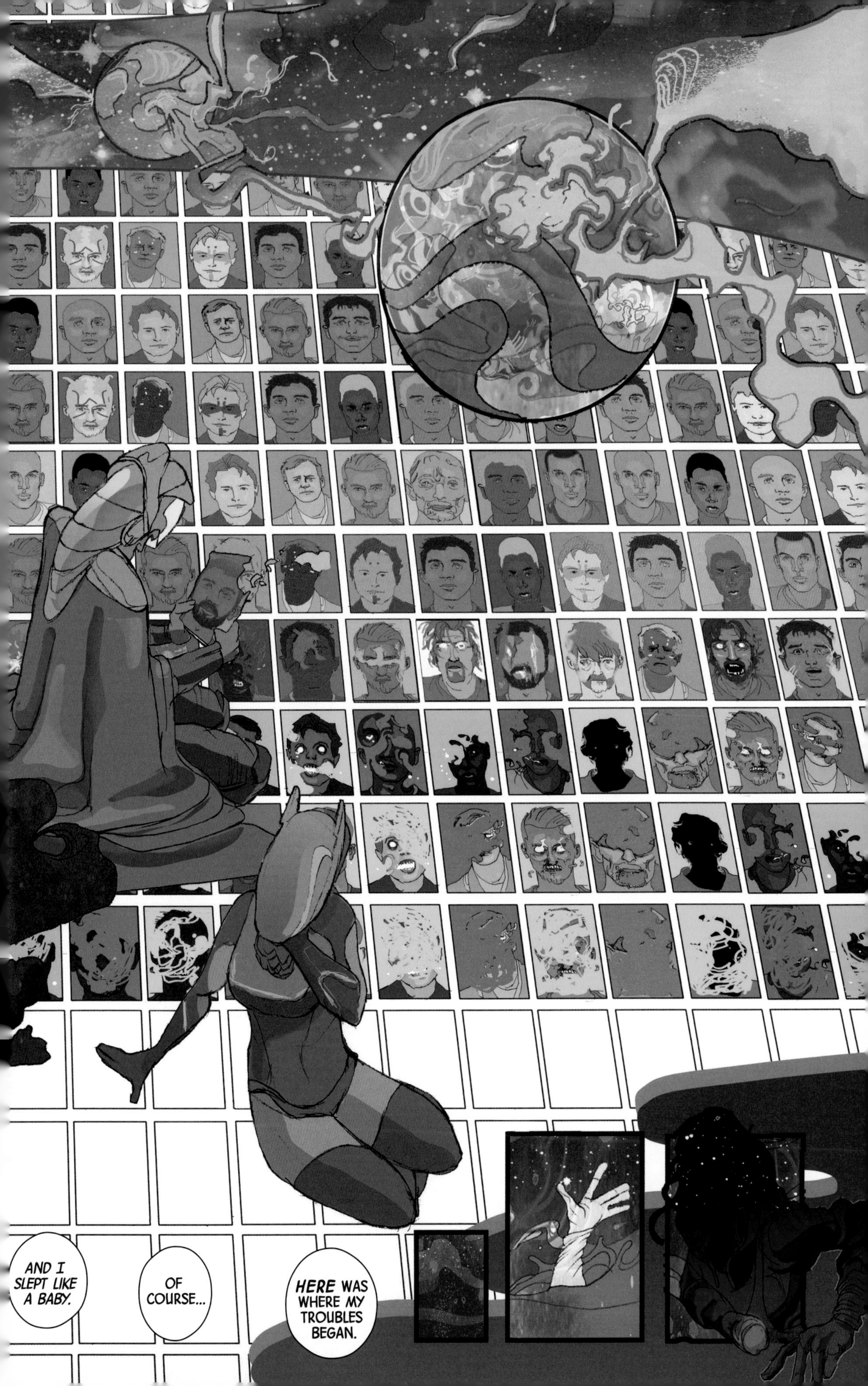
AND I SLEPT LIKE A BABY.
OF COURSE...
HERE WAS WHERE MY TROUBLES BEGAN.

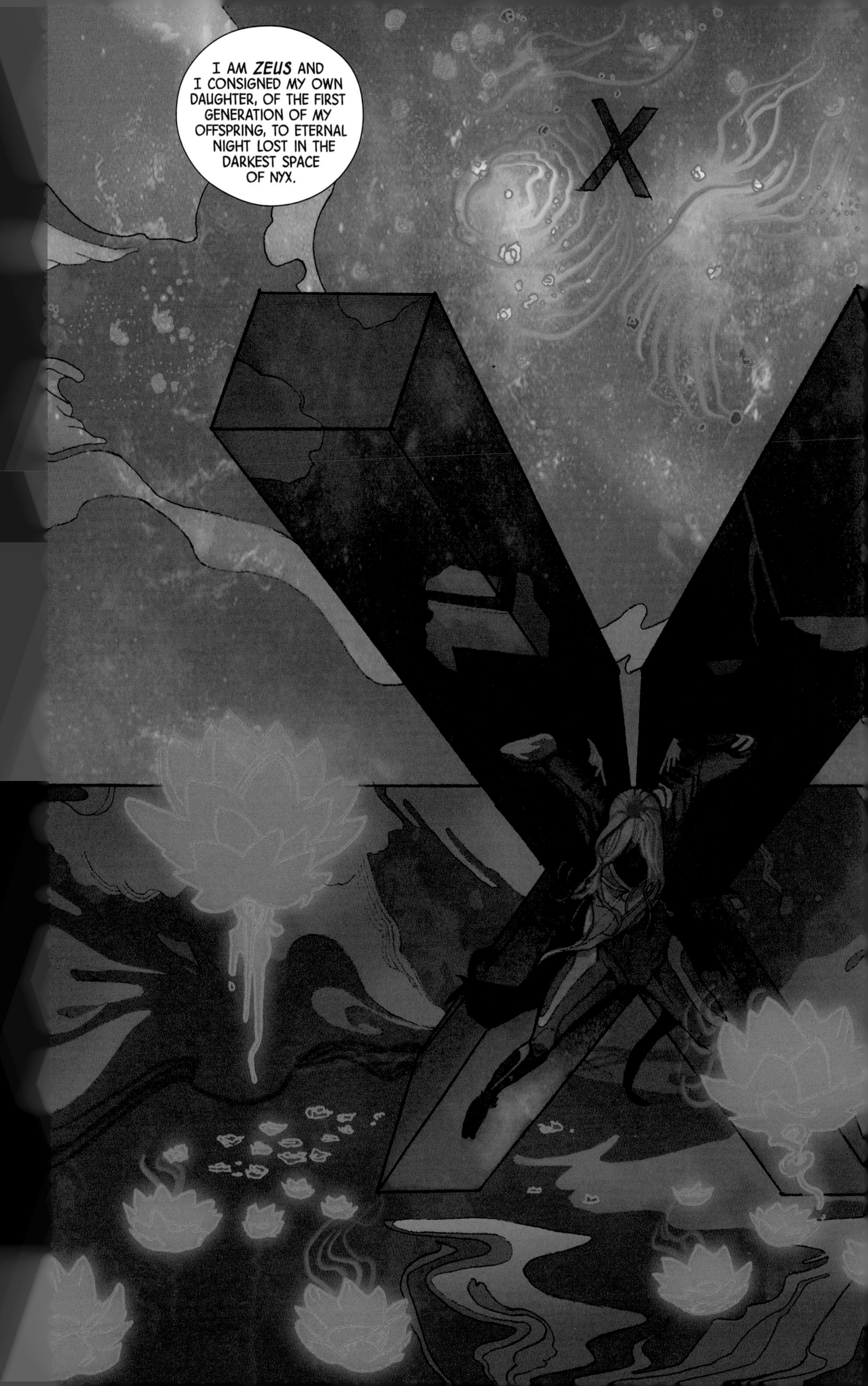
I AM ZEUS AND I CONSIGNED MY OWN DAUGHTER, OF THE FIRST GENERATION OF MY OFFSPRING, TO ETERNAL NIGHT LOST IN THE DARKEST SPACE OF NYX.
X

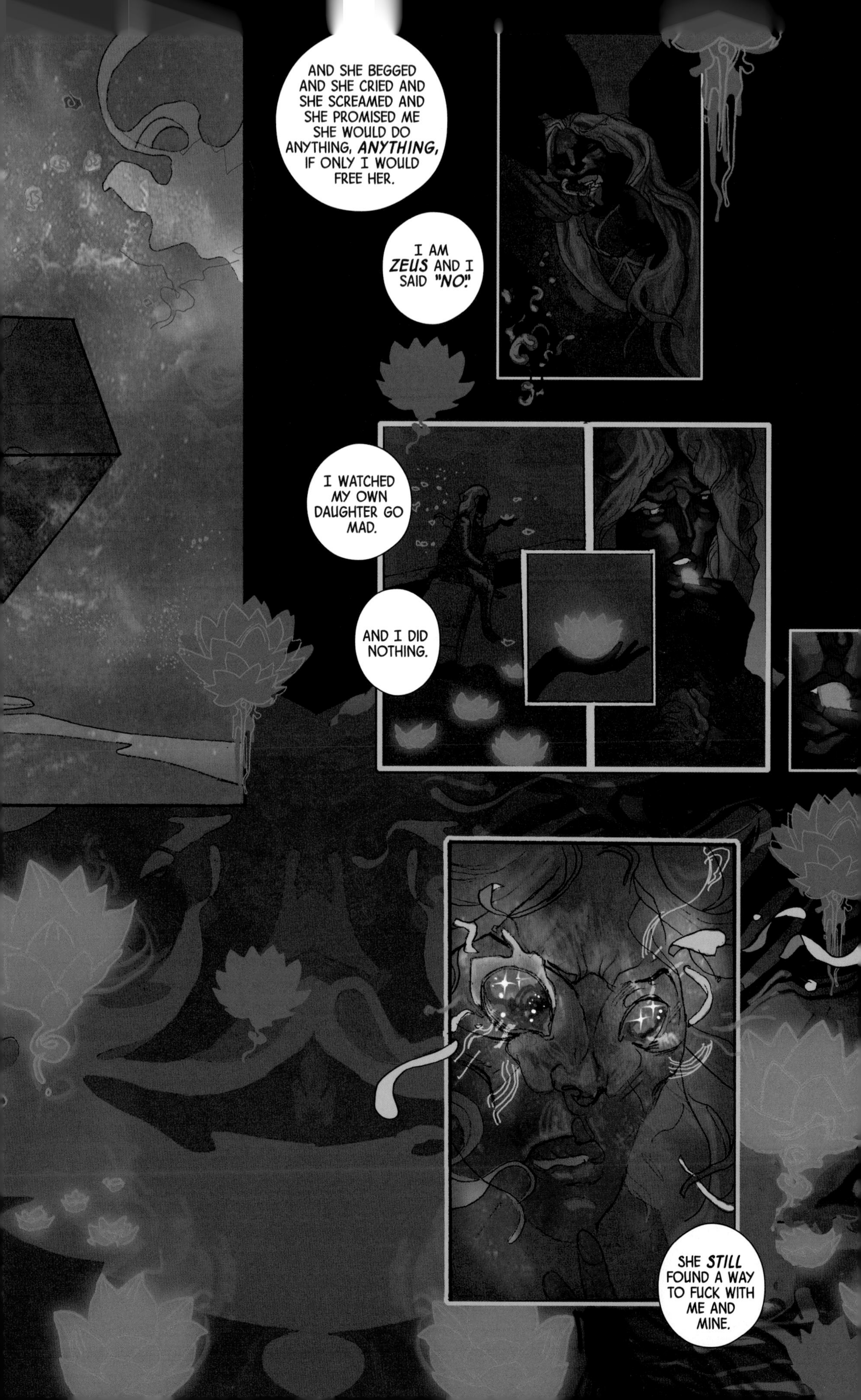
AND SHE BEGGED AND SHE CRIED AND SHE SCREAMED AND SHE PROMISED ME SHE WOULD DO ANYTHING, ANYTHING, IF ONLY I WOULD FREE HER.
I AM ZEUS AND I SAID "NO."
I WATCHED MY OWN DAUGHTER GO MAD.
AND I DID NOTHING.
SHE STILL FOUND A WAY TO FUCK WITH ME AND MINE.

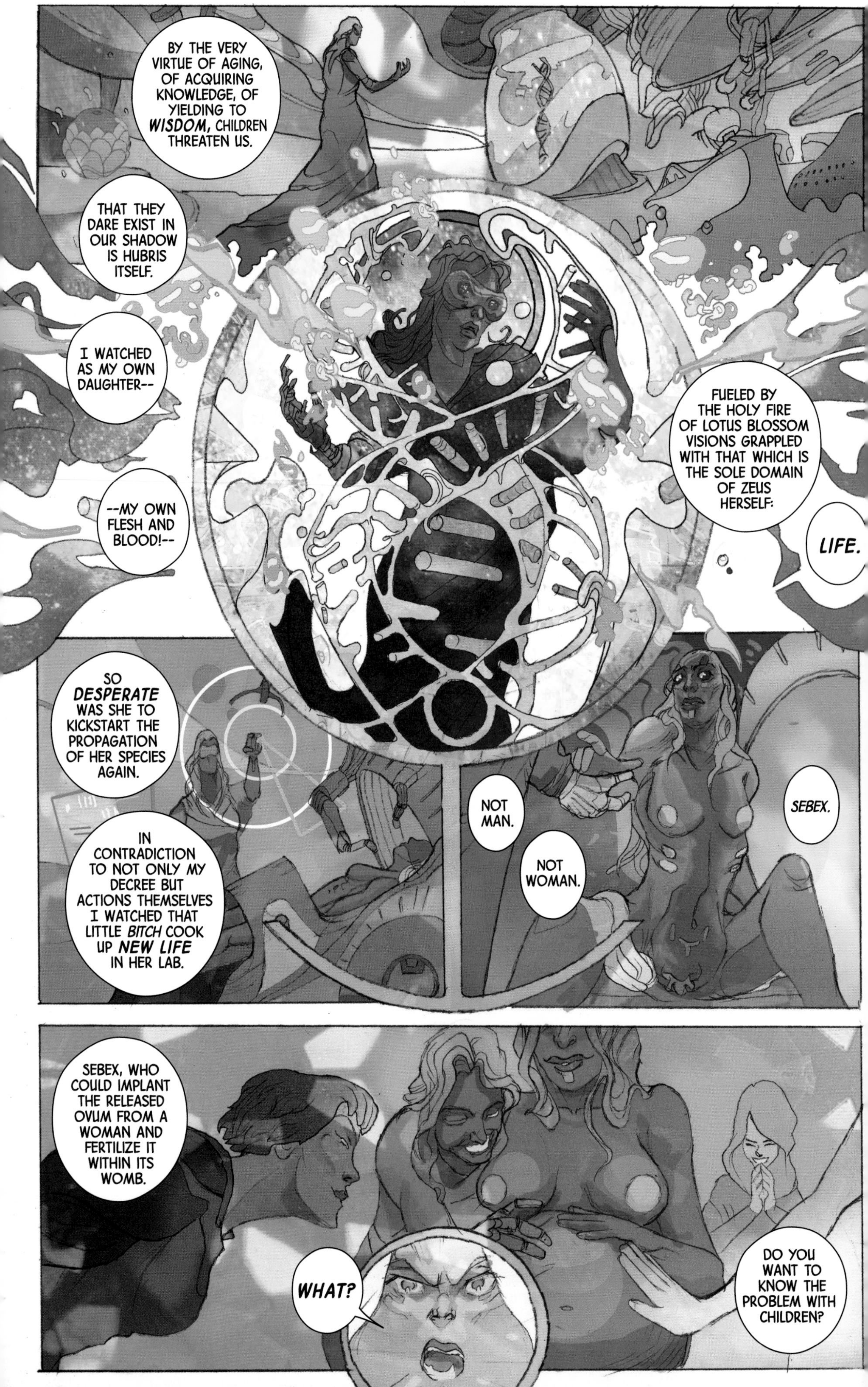
BY THE VERY VIRTUE OF AGING, OF ACQUIRING KNOWLEDGE, OF YIELDING TO WISDOM, CHILDREN THREATEN US.
THAT THEY DARE EXIST IN OUR SHADOW IS HUBRIS ITSELF.
I WATCHED AS MY OWN DAUGHTER--
--MY OWN FLESH AND BLOOD!--
FUELED BY THE HOLY FIRE OF LOTUS BLOSSOM VISIONS GRAPPLED WITH THAT WHICH IS THE SOLE DOMAIN OF ZEUS HERSELF:
LIFE.
SO DESPERATE WAS SHE TO KICKSTART THE PROPAGATION OF HER SPECIES AGAIN.
IN CONTRADICTION TO NOT ONLY MY DECREE BUT ACTIONS THEMSELVES I WATCHED THAT LITTLE BITCH COOK UP NEW LIFE IN HER LAB.
NOT MAN.
NOT WOMAN.
SEBEX.
SEBEX, WHO COULD IMPLANT THE RELEASED OVUM FROM A WOMAN AND FERTILIZE IT WITHIN ITS WOMB.
WHAT?
DO YOU WANT TO KNOW THE PROBLEM WITH CHILDREN?

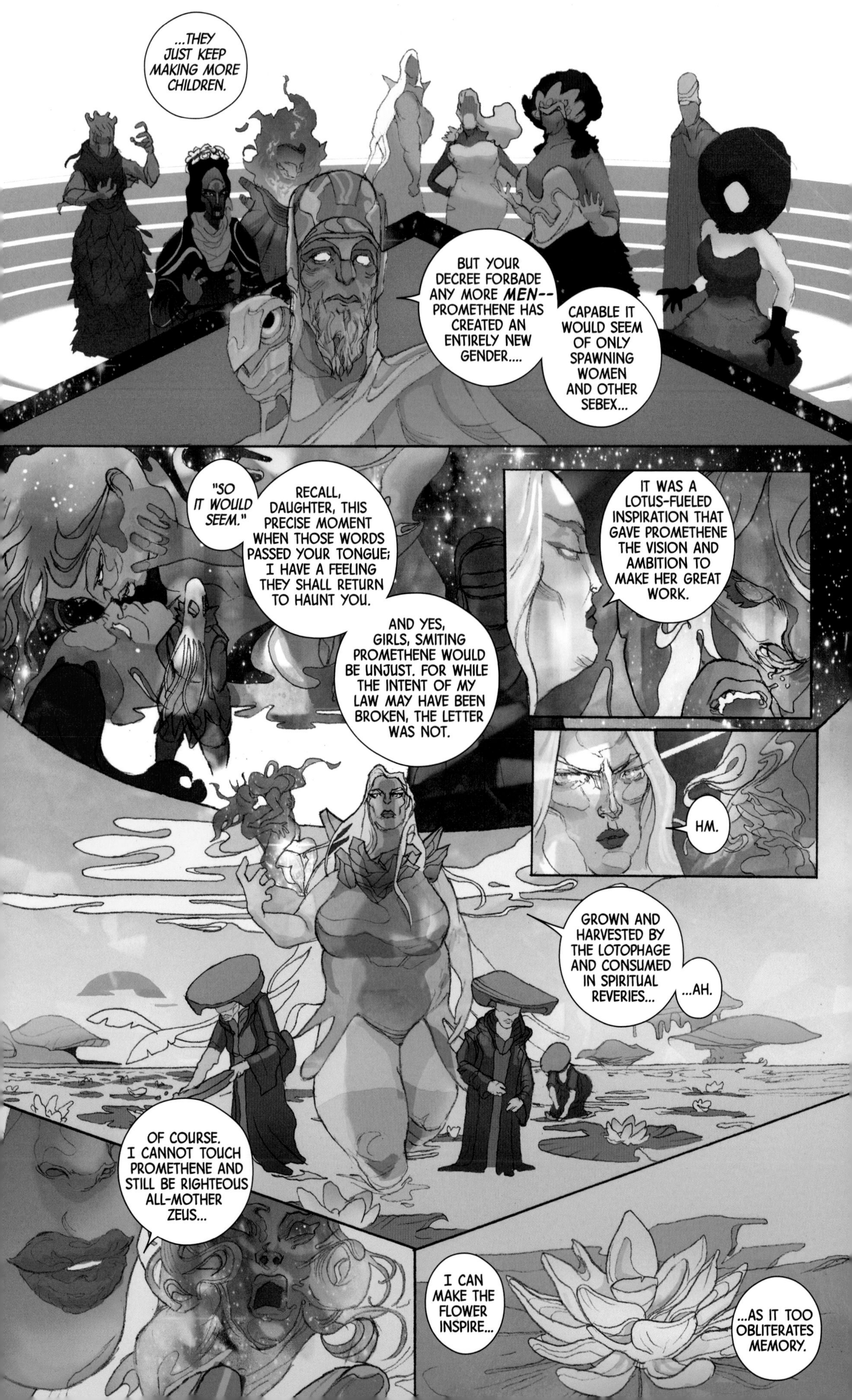
...THEY JUST KEEP MAKING MORE CHILDREN.
BUT YOUR DECREE FORBADE ANY MORE *MEN*-- PROMETHENE HAS CREATED AN ENTIRELY NEW GENDER....
CAPABLE IT WOULD SEEM OF ONLY SPAWNING WOMEN AND OTHER SEBEX...
"SO IT WOULD SEEM."
RECALL, DAUGHTER, THIS PRECISE MOMENT WHEN THOSE WORDS PASSED YOUR TONGUE; I HAVE A FEELING THEY SHALL RETURN TO HAUNT YOU.
AND YES, GIRLS, SMITING PROMETHENE WOULD BE UNJUST. FOR WHILE THE INTENT OF MY LAW MAY HAVE BEEN BROKEN, THE LETTER WAS NOT.
IT WAS A LOTUS-FUELED INSPIRATION THAT GAVE PROMETHENE THE VISION AND AMBITION TO MAKE HER GREAT WORK.
HM.
GROWN AND HARVESTED BY THE LOTOPHAGE AND CONSUMED IN SPIRITUAL REVERIES...
...AH.
OF COURSE. I CANNOT TOUCH PROMETHENE AND STILL BE RIGHTEOUS ALL-MOTHER ZEUS...
I CAN MAKE THE FLOWER INSPIRE...
...AS IT TOO OBLITERATES MEMORY.

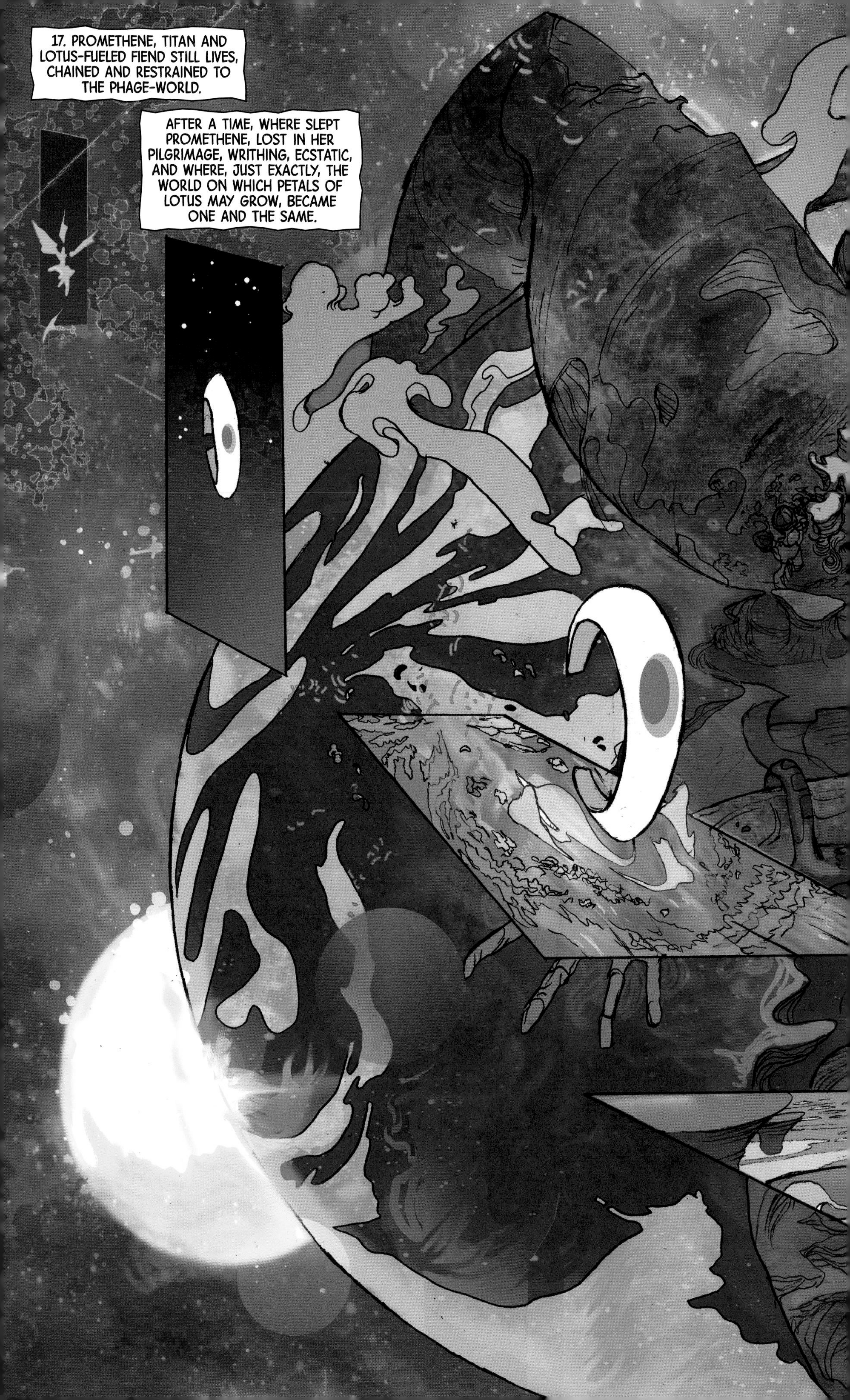
17. PROMETHENE, TITAN AND LOTUS-FUELED FIEND STILL LIVES, CHAINED AND RESTRAINED TO THE PHAGE-WORLD.
AFTER A TIME, WHERE SLEPT PROMETHENE, LOST IN HER PILGRIMAGE, WRITHING, ECSTATIC, AND WHERE, JUST EXACTLY, THE WORLD ON WHICH PETALS OF LOTUS MAY GROW, BECAME ONE AND THE SAME.

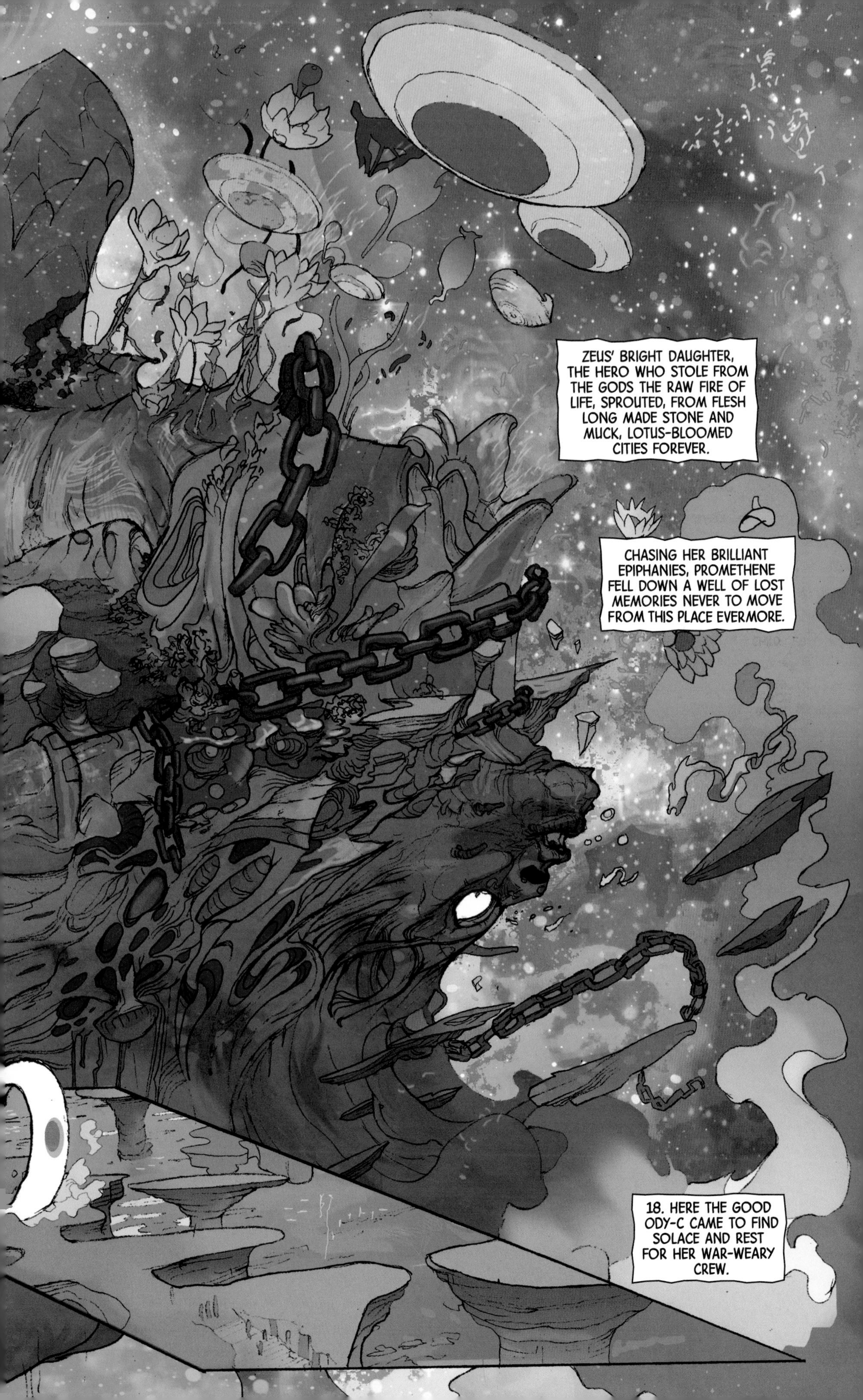
ZEUS' BRIGHT DAUGHTER, THE HERO WHO STOLE FROM THE GODS THE RAW FIRE OF LIFE, SPROUTED, FROM FLESH LONG MADE STONE AND MUCK, LOTUS-BLOOMED CITIES FOREVER.
CHASING HER BRILLIANT EPIPHANIES, PROMETHENE FELL DOWN A WELL OF LOST MEMORIES NEVER TO MOVE FROM THIS PLACE EVERMORE.
18. HERE THE GOOD ODY-C CAME TO FIND SOLACE AND REST FOR HER WAR-WEARY CREW.

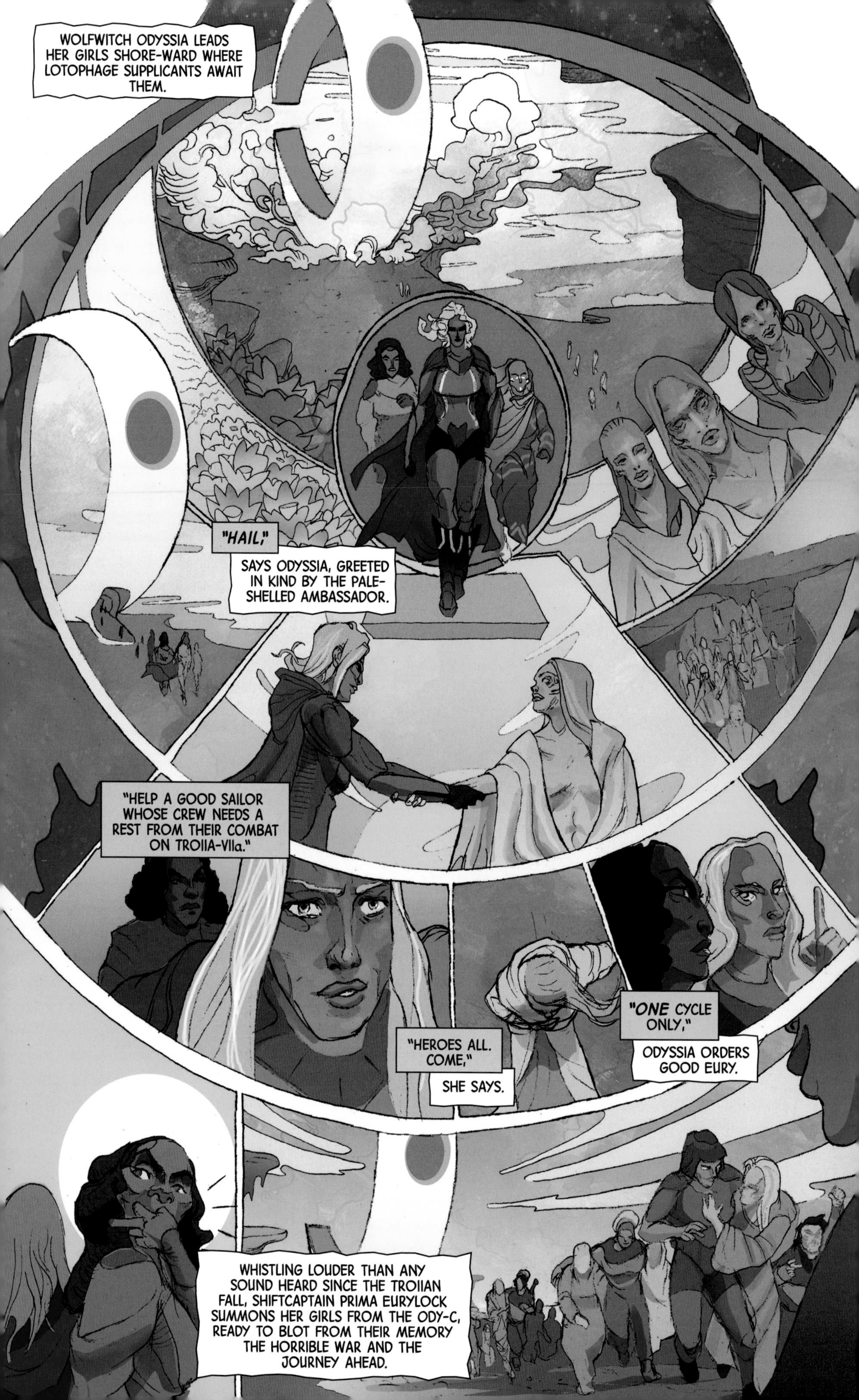
WOLFWITCH ODYSSIA LEADS HER GIRLS SHORE-WARD WHERE LOTOPHAGE SUPPLICANTS AWAIT THEM.
"HAIL,"
SAYS ODYSSIA, GREETED IN KIND BY THE PALE-SHELLED AMBASSADOR.
"HELP A GOOD SAILOR WHOSE CREW NEEDS A REST FROM THEIR COMBAT ON TROIIA-VIIa."
"HEROES ALL. COME,"
SHE SAYS.
"ONE CYCLE ONLY,"
ODYSSIA ORDERS GOOD EURY.
WHISTLING LOUDER THAN ANY SOUND HEARD SINCE THE TROIIAN FALL, SHIFTCAPTAIN PRIMA EURYLOCK SUMMONS HER GIRLS FROM THE ODY-C, READY TO BLOT FROM THEIR MEMORY THE HORRIBLE WAR AND THE JOURNEY AHEAD.

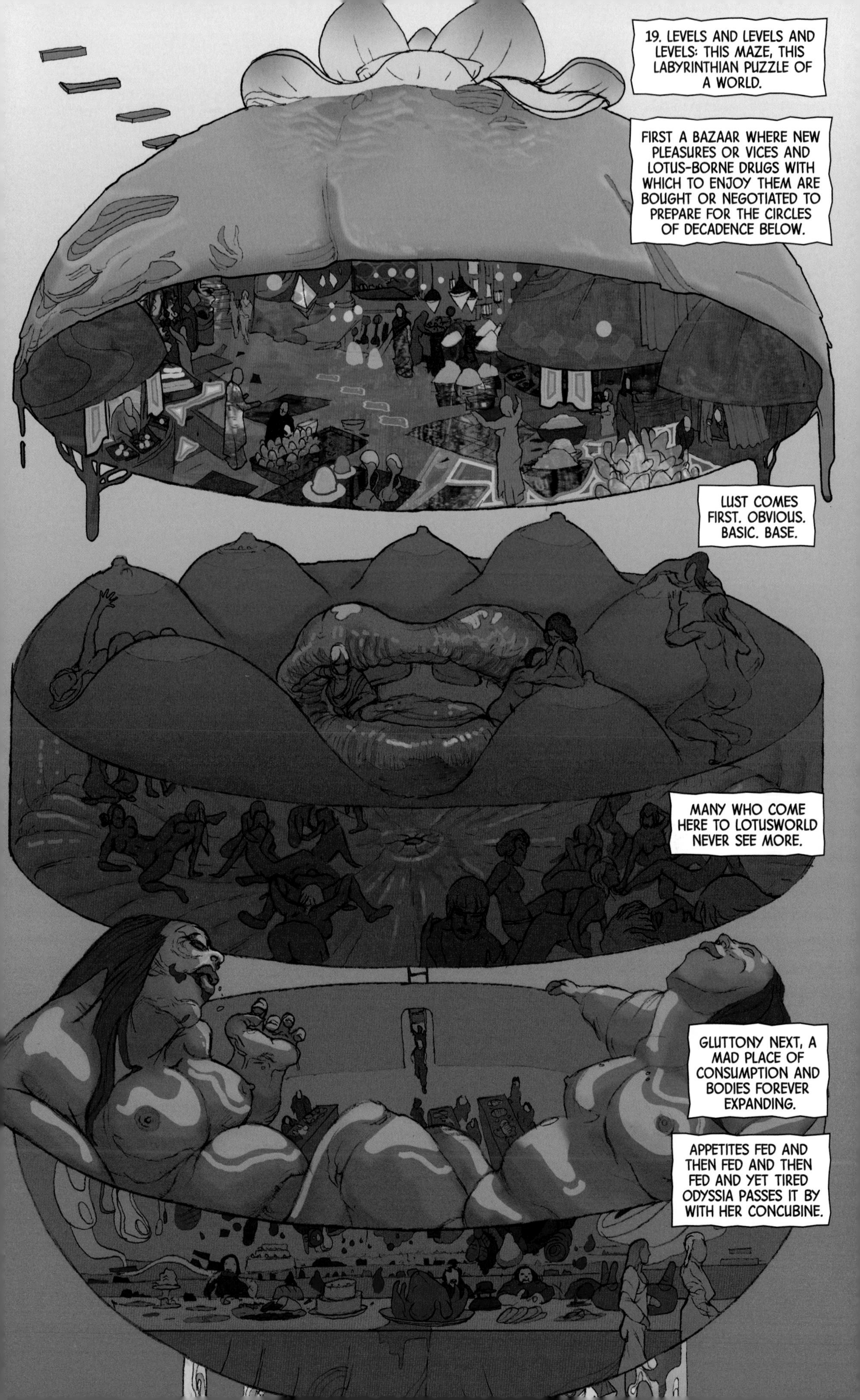
19. LEVELS AND LEVELS AND LEVELS: THIS MAZE, THIS LABYRINTHIAN PUZZLE OF A WORLD.
FIRST A BAZAAR WHERE NEW PLEASURES OR VICES AND LOTUS-BORNE DRUGS WITH WHICH TO ENJOY THEM ARE BOUGHT OR NEGOTIATED TO PREPARE FOR THE CIRCLES OF DECADENCE BELOW.
LUST COMES FIRST. OBVIOUS. BASIC. BASE.
MANY WHO COME HERE TO LOTUSWORLD NEVER SEE MORE.
GLUTTONY NEXT, A MAD PLACE OF CONSUMPTION AND BODIES FOREVER EXPANDING.
APPETITES FED AND THEN FED AND THEN FED AND YET TIRED ODYSSIA PASSES IT BY WITH HER CONCUBINE.

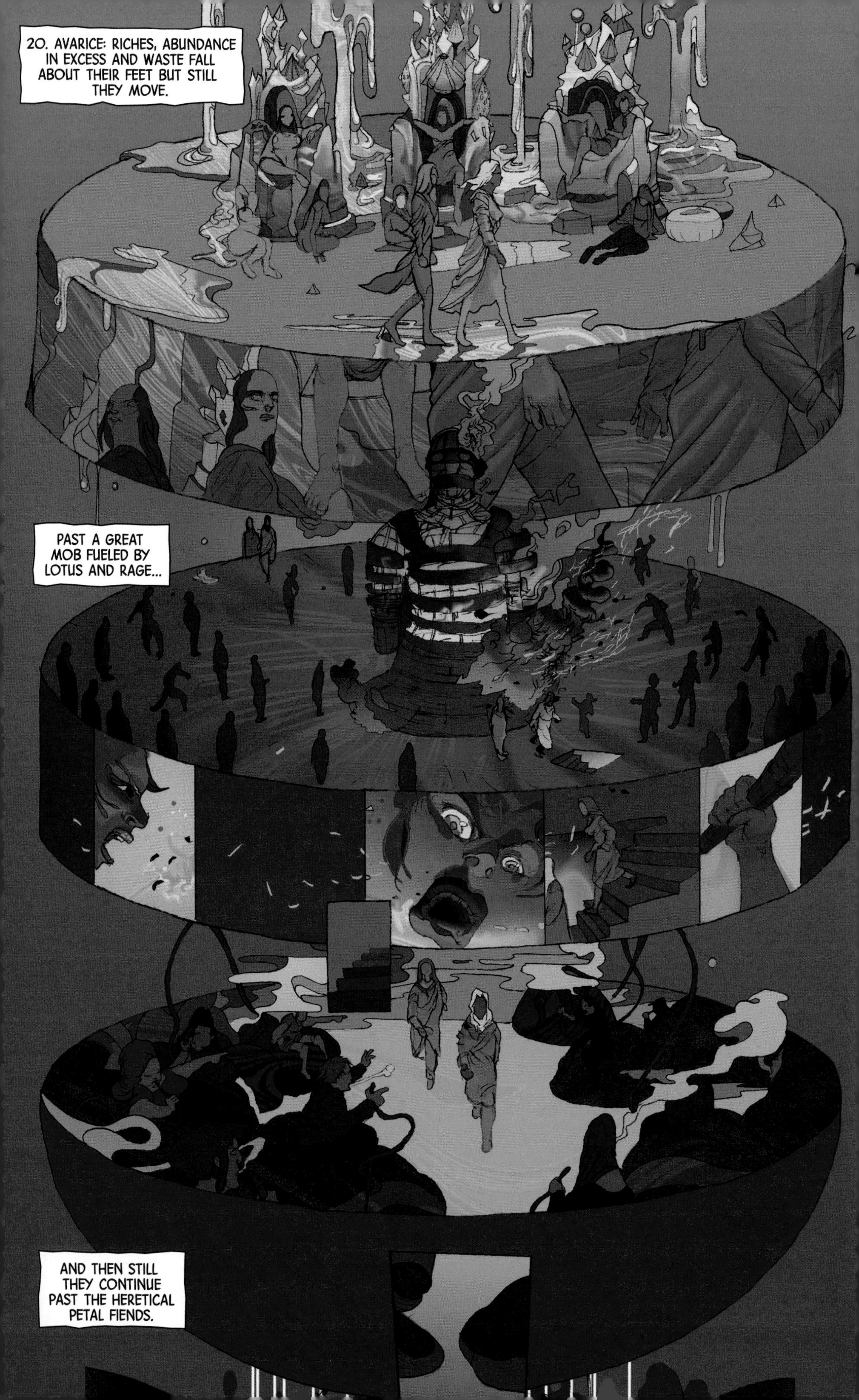
20. AVARICE: RICHES, ABUNDANCE IN EXCESS AND WASTE FALL ABOUT THEIR FEET BUT STILL THEY MOVE.
PAST A GREAT MOB FUELED BY LOTUS AND RAGE...
AND THEN STILL THEY CONTINUE PAST THE HERETICAL PETAL FIENDS.

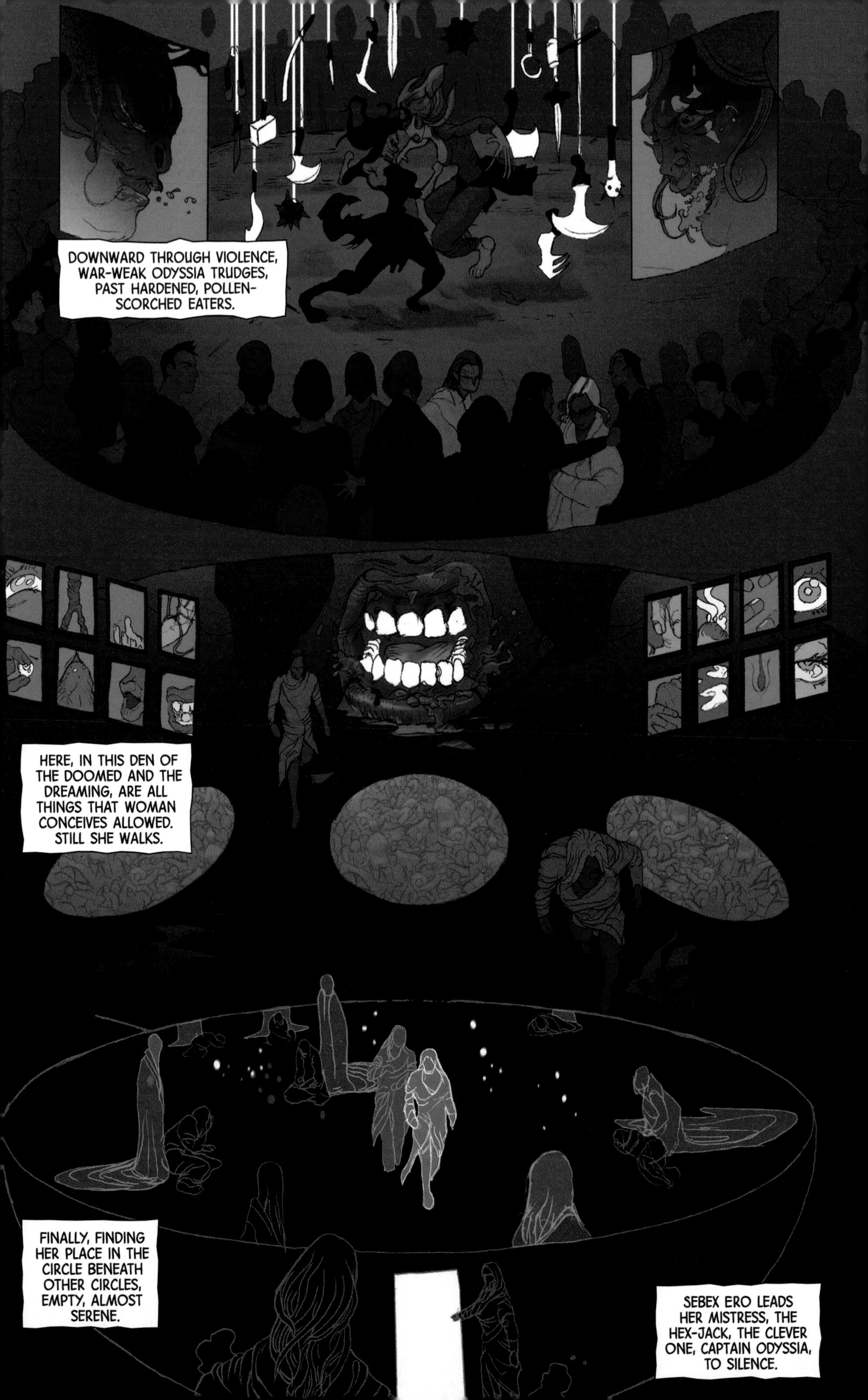
DOWNWARD THROUGH VIOLENCE, WAR-WEAK ODYSSIA TRUDGES, PAST HARDENED, POLLEN-SCORCHED EATERS.
HERE, IN THIS DEN OF THE DOOMED AND THE DREAMING, ARE ALL THINGS THAT WOMAN CONCEIVES ALLOWED. STILL SHE WALKS.
FINALLY, FINDING HER PLACE IN THE CIRCLE BENEATH OTHER CIRCLES, EMPTY, ALMOST SERENE.
SEBEX ERO LEADS HER MISTRESS, THE HEX-JACK, THE CLEVER ONE, CAPTAIN ODYSSIA, TO SILENCE.

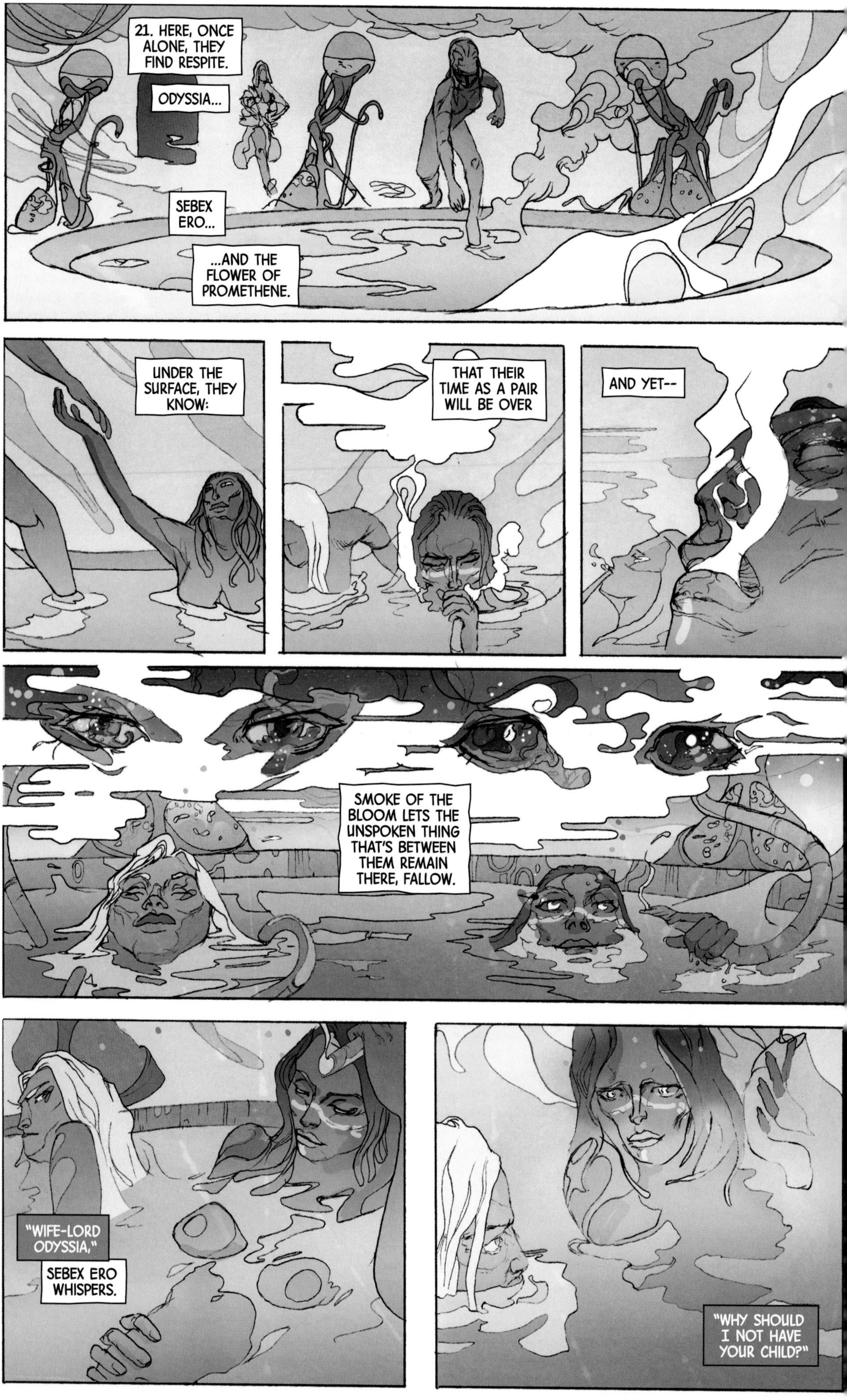
21. HERE, ONCE ALONE, THEY FIND RESPITE.
ODYSSIA...
SEBEX ERO...
...AND THE FLOWER OF PROMETHENE.
UNDER THE SURFACE, THEY KNOW:
THAT THEIR TIME AS A PAIR WILL BE OVER
AND YET--
SMOKE OF THE BLOOM LETS THE UNSPOKEN THING THAT'S BETWEEN THEM REMAIN THERE, FALLOW.
"WIFE-LORD ODYSSIA,"
SEBEX ERO WHISPERS.
"WHY SHOULD I NOT HAVE YOUR CHILD?"

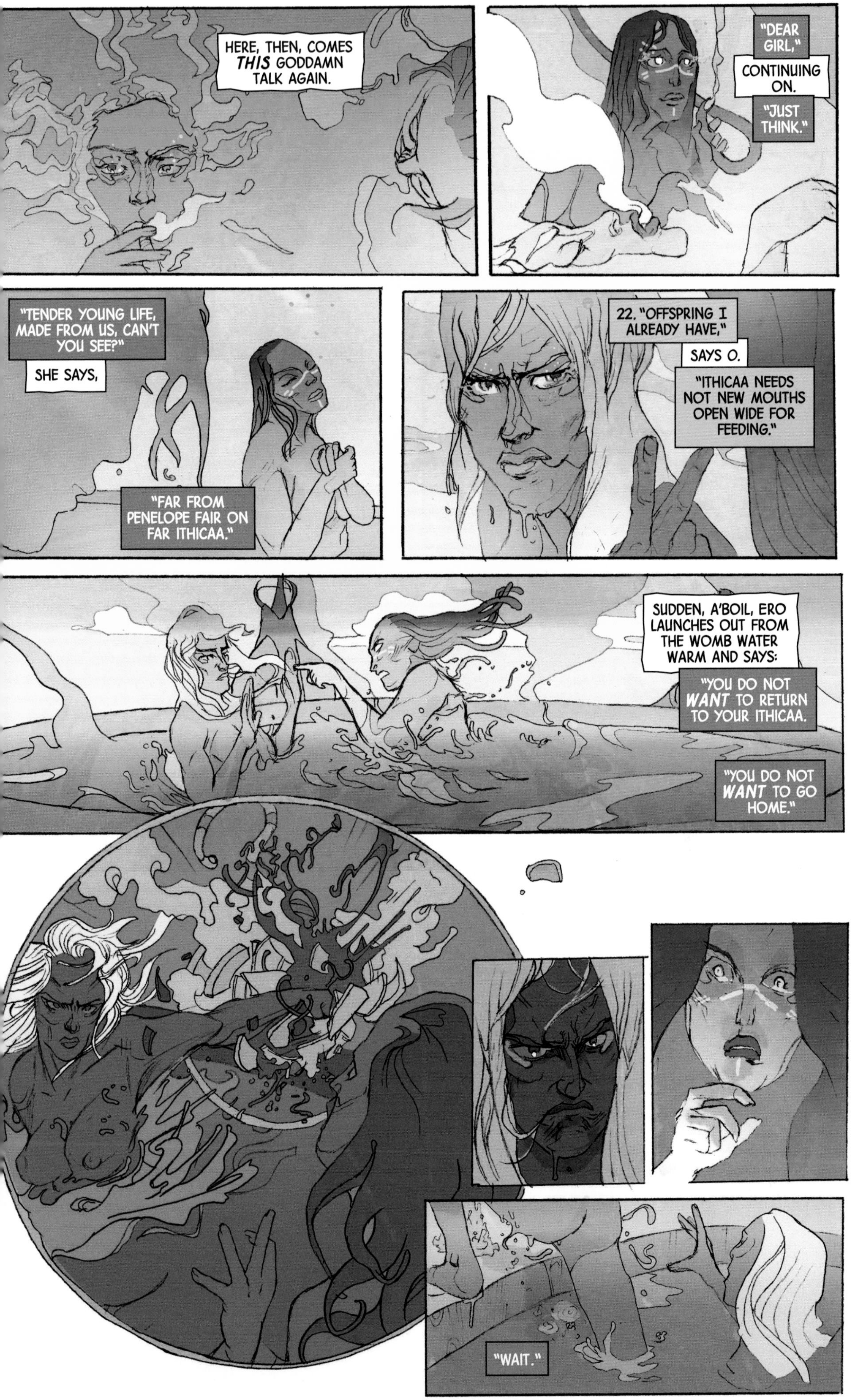
HERE, THEN, COMES *THIS* GODDAMN TALK AGAIN.
"DEAR GIRL,"
CONTINUING ON.
"JUST THINK."
"TENDER YOUNG LIFE, MADE FROM US, CAN'T YOU SEE?"
SHE SAYS,
"FAR FROM PENELOPE FAIR ON FAR ITHICAA."
22. "OFFSPRING I ALREADY HAVE,"
SAYS O.
"ITHICAA NEEDS NOT NEW MOUTHS OPEN WIDE FOR FEEDING."
SUDDEN, A'BOIL, ERO LAUNCHES OUT FROM THE WOMB WATER WARM AND SAYS:
"YOU DO NOT *WANT* TO RETURN TO YOUR ITHICAA.
"YOU DO NOT *WANT* TO GO HOME."
"WAIT."

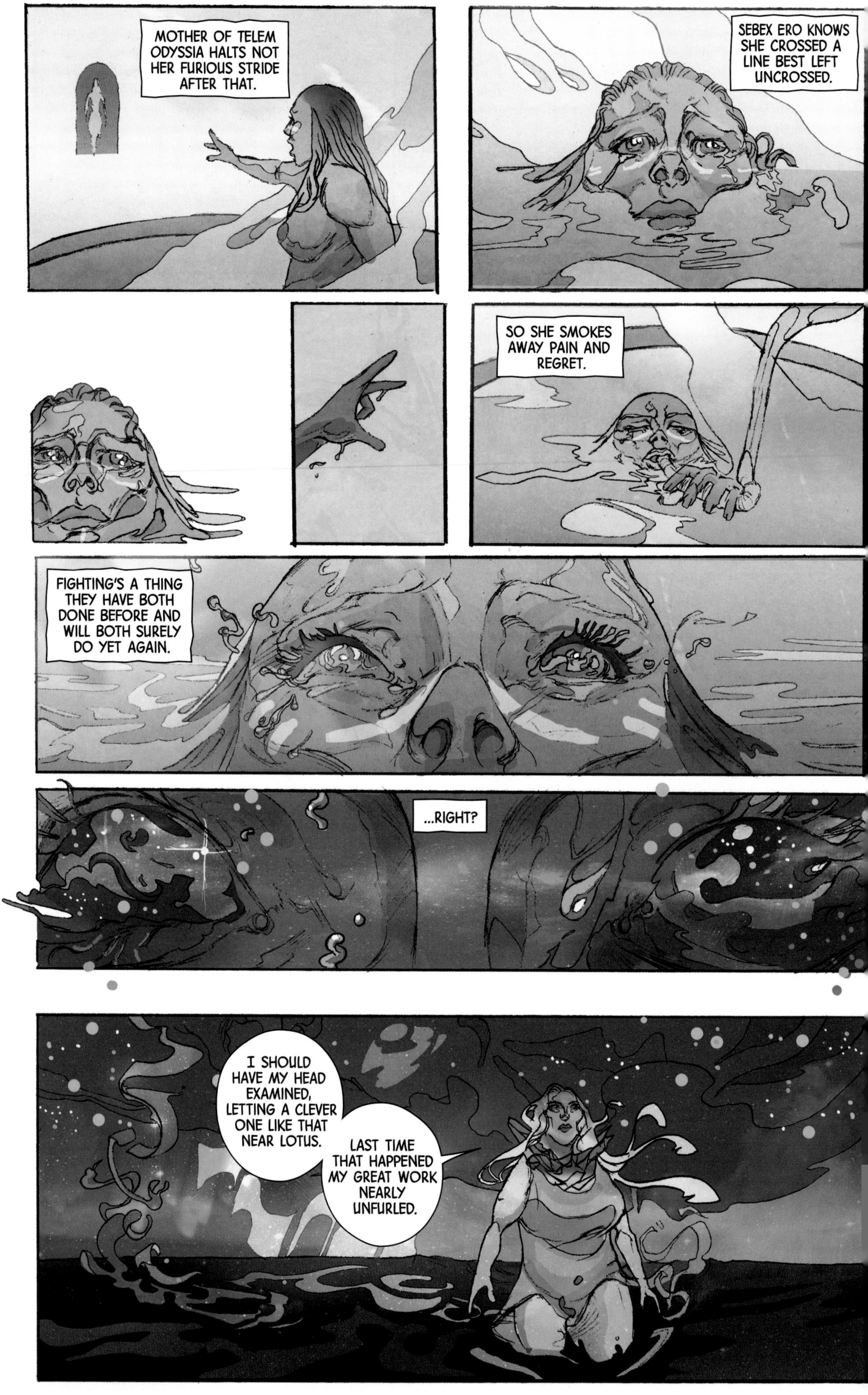

MOTHER OF TELEM ODYSSIA HALTS NOT HER FURIOUS STRIDE AFTER THAT.
SEBEX ERO KNOWS SHE CROSSED A LINE BEST LEFT UNCROSSED.
SO SHE SMOKES AWAY PAIN AND REGRET.
FIGHTING'S A THING THEY HAVE BOTH DONE BEFORE AND WILL BOTH SURELY DO YET AGAIN.
...RIGHT?
I SHOULD HAVE MY HEAD EXAMINED, LETTING A CLEVER ONE LIKE THAT NEAR LOTUS.
LAST TIME THAT HAPPENED MY GREAT WORK NEARLY UNFURLED.

YESTERDAY SHE WAS ENTERTAINMENT. TODAY SHE VEXES YOU. WHY? YOU'RE ZEUS. YOU SIT ON HIGH ABOVE ALL.

BECAUSE ONCE UPON A TIME I WAS A CLEVER GIRL TOO. AND NOW...

...I AM ZEUS AND I SIT ON HIGH ABOVE ALL.

I REMEMBER HOW I GOT HERE. I REMEMBER HOW **WE** GOT HERE.

NOTHING GOLD CAN STAY.

ODYSSIA'S CLEVER BUT SHE'S NOT THAT CLEVER. AND SHE HARDLY SEEMS THE TYPE TO COME FOR THE THRONE OF THRONES.

THERE IS A LINE OF BLOOD FROM ODYSSIA TO CRONUS HIMSELF THAT GOES RIGHT THROUGH ME.

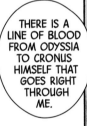

AND EVERY CHILD COMES LOOKING FOR ITS INHERITANCE EVENTUALLY.

SHE DIDN'T EVEN WANT TO FIGHT! REMEMBER HER, FEIGNING MADNESS TO ESCAPE HER CONSCRIPTION, AT WAR'S DAWN. SHE DOESN'T--

WHY ARE YOU OF ALL GODS DEFENDING HER? DID SHE NOT SPITE YOU? DID NOT PAY YOU YOUR TRIBUTE?

AHH, SHE DID, SHE DID.

I'M BEGINNING TO FEEL LIKE I'M BEING SET UP.

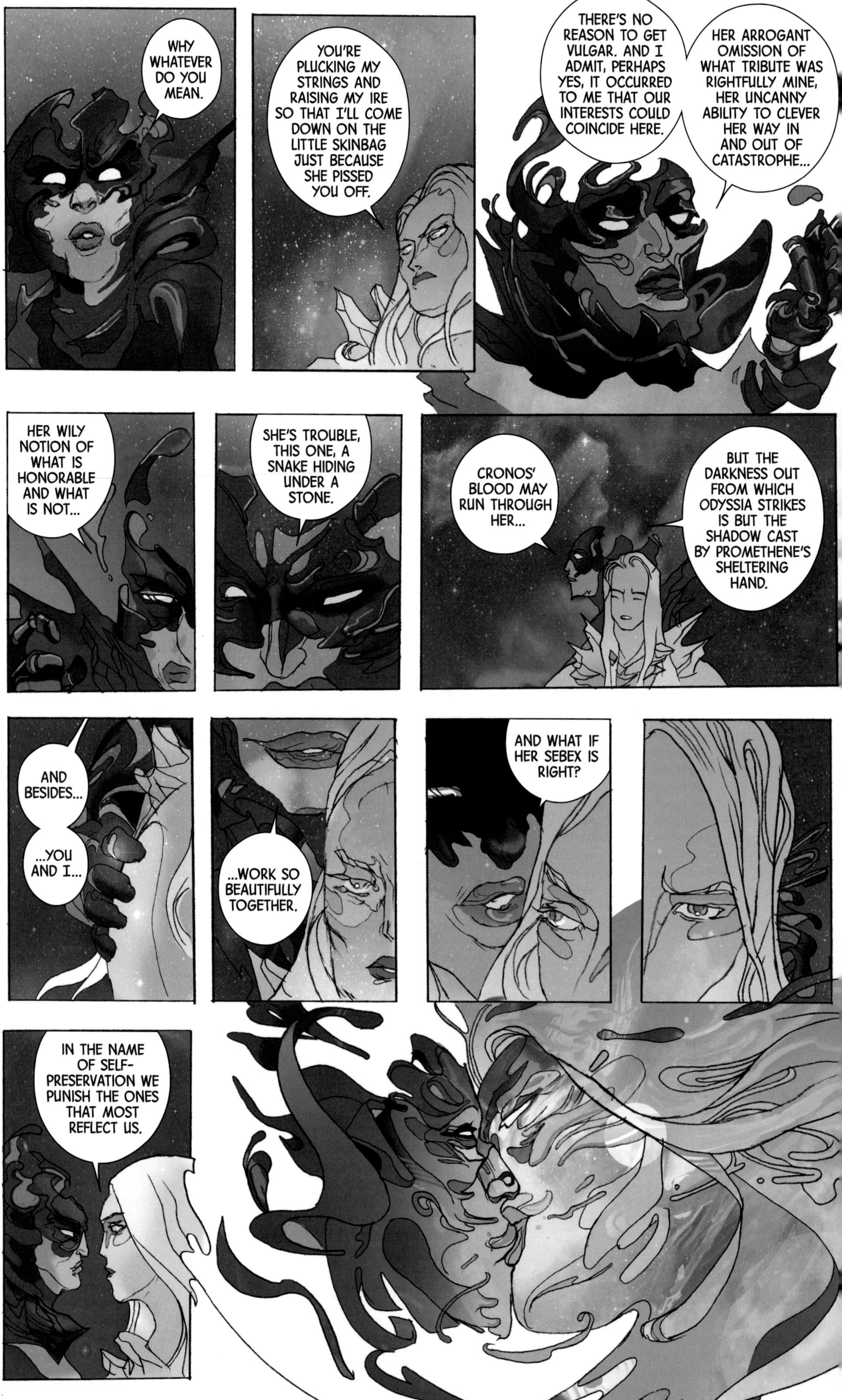
WHY WHATEVER DO YOU MEAN.
YOU'RE PLUCKING MY STRINGS AND RAISING MY IRE SO THAT I'LL COME DOWN ON THE LITTLE SKINBAG JUST BECAUSE SHE PISSED YOU OFF.
THERE'S NO REASON TO GET VULGAR. AND I ADMIT, PERHAPS YES, IT OCCURRED TO ME THAT OUR INTERESTS COULD COINCIDE HERE.
HER ARROGANT OMISSION OF WHAT TRIBUTE WAS RIGHTFULLY MINE, HER UNCANNY ABILITY TO CLEVER HER WAY IN AND OUT OF CATASTROPHE...
HER WILY NOTION OF WHAT IS HONORABLE AND WHAT IS NOT...
SHE'S TROUBLE, THIS ONE, A SNAKE HIDING UNDER A STONE.
CRONOS' BLOOD MAY RUN THROUGH HER...
BUT THE DARKNESS OUT FROM WHICH ODYSSIA STRIKES IS BUT THE SHADOW CAST BY PROMETHENE'S SHELTERING HAND.
AND BESIDES...
...YOU AND I...
...WORK SO BEAUTIFULLY TOGETHER.
AND WHAT IF HER SEBEX IS RIGHT?
IN THE NAME OF SELF-PRESERVATION WE PUNISH THE ONES THAT MOST REFLECT US.

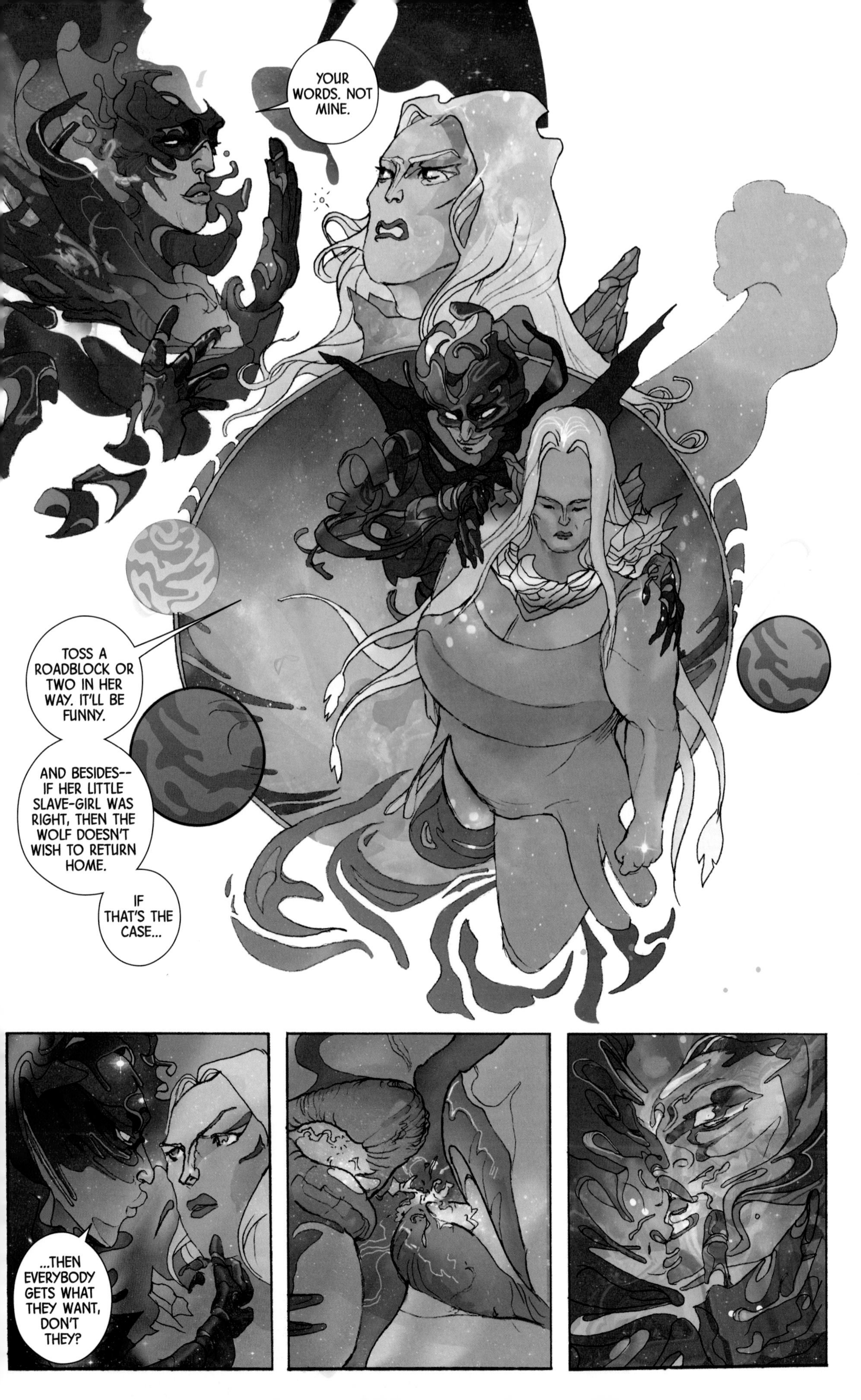
YOUR WORDS. NOT MINE.
TOSS A ROADBLOCK OR TWO IN HER WAY. IT'LL BE FUNNY.
AND BESIDES-- IF HER LITTLE SLAVE-GIRL WAS RIGHT, THEN THE WOLF DOESN'T WISH TO RETURN HOME.
IF THAT'S THE CASE...
...THEN EVERYBODY GETS WHAT THEY WANT, DON'T THEY?

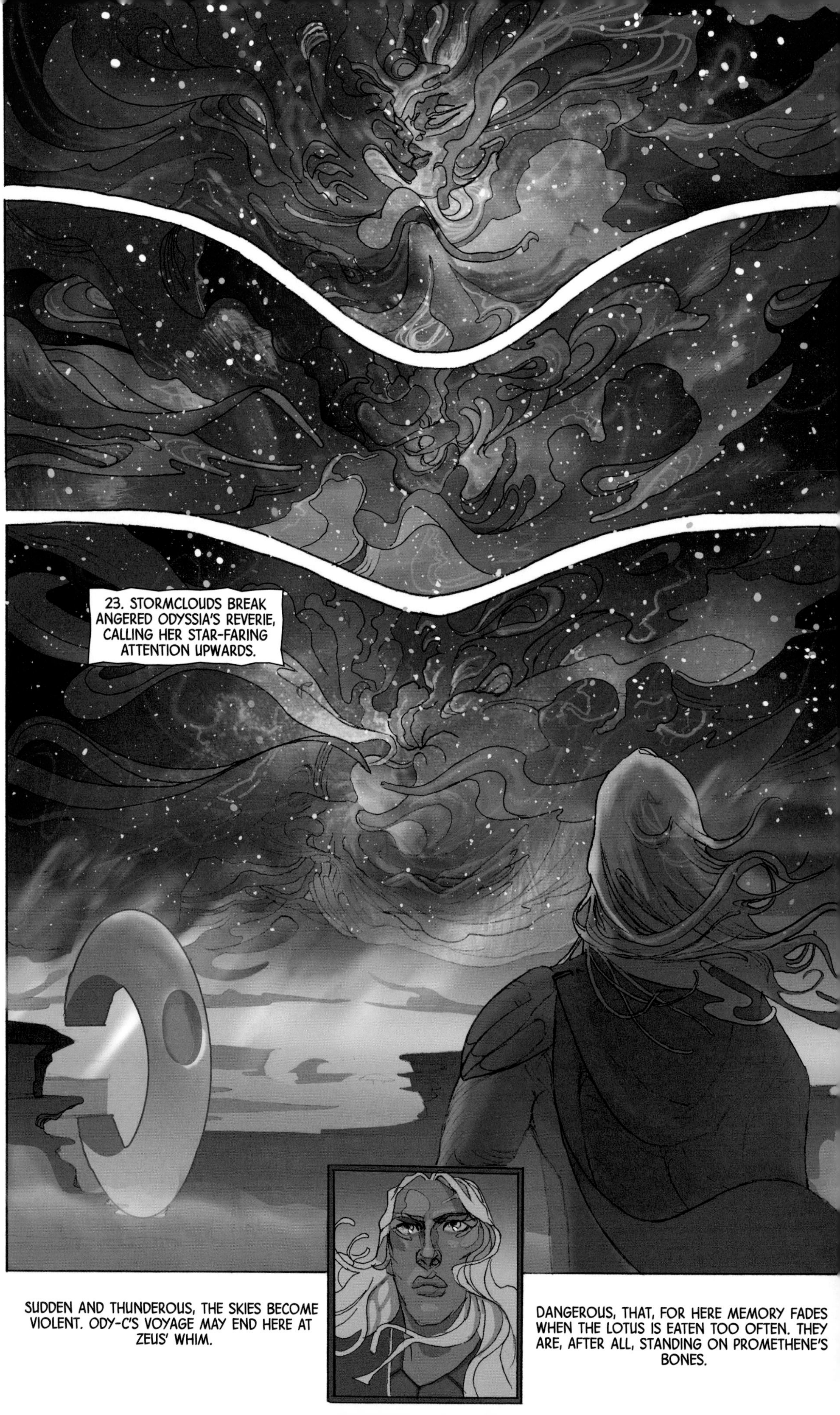
23. STORMCLOUDS BREAK ANGERED ODYSSIA'S REVERIE, CALLING HER STAR-FARING ATTENTION UPWARDS.
SUDDEN AND THUNDEROUS, THE SKIES BECOME VIOLENT. ODY-C'S VOYAGE MAY END HERE AT ZEUS' WHIM.
DANGEROUS, THAT, FOR HERE MEMORY FADES WHEN THE LOTUS IS EATEN TOO OFTEN. THEY ARE, AFTER ALL, STANDING ON PROMETHENE'S BONES.

THEN COMES EURYLOCK WHO GLANCED SKYWARD TOO. SHE SAYS:

"ZEUS ABOVE HEARD NOT OUR PRAYERS."

"SHE ANSWERS EVERYONE'S PRAYERS,"

O SAYS,

"SOMETIMES HER ANSWER IS NO, JUST THE SAME."

SHIPGIRLS ASSEMBLE THEMSELVES. AND EURYLOCK ASKS:

"EVERY LAST SOUL IS ABOARD?"

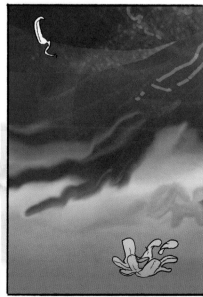

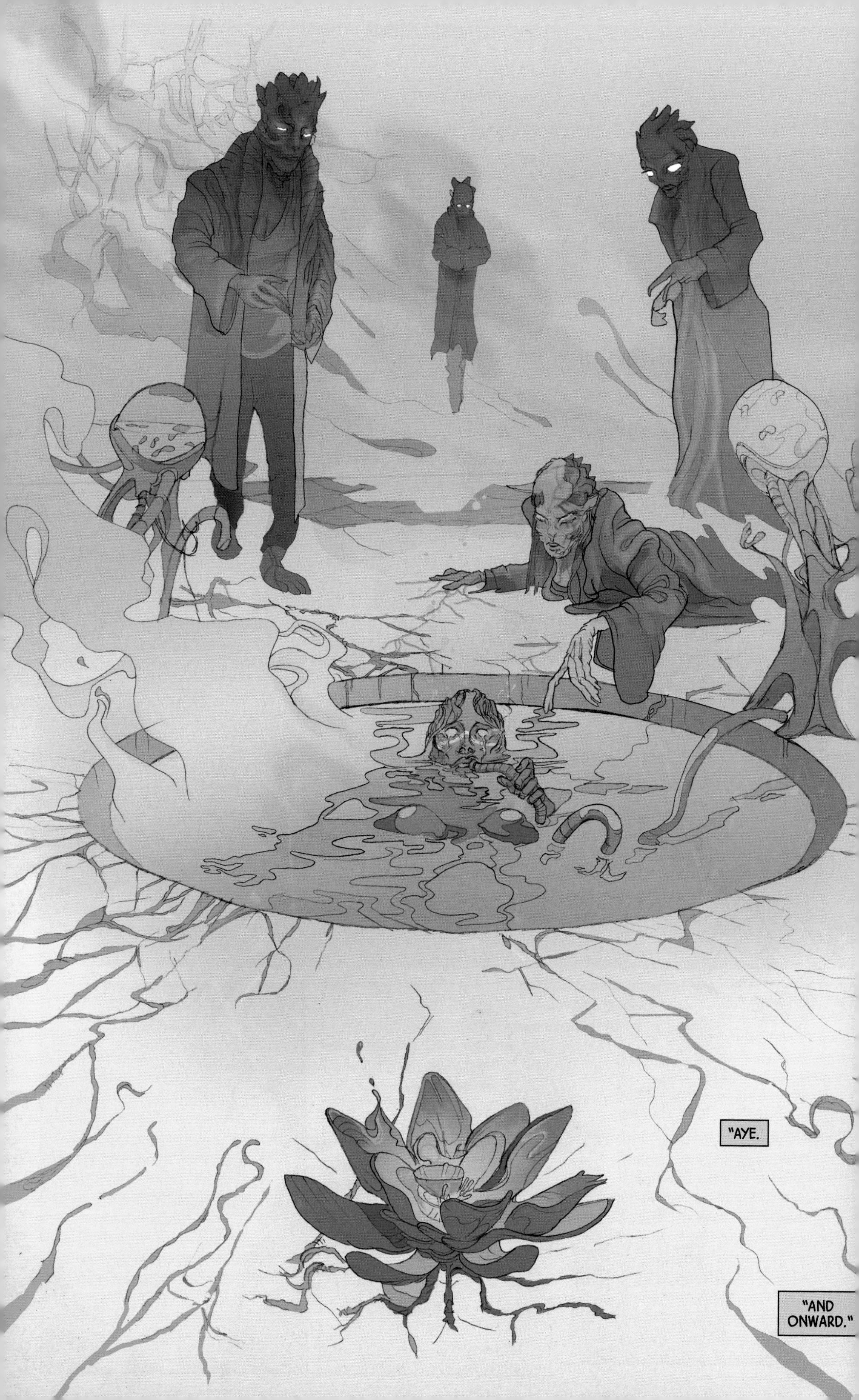
"AYE.
"AND ONWARD."

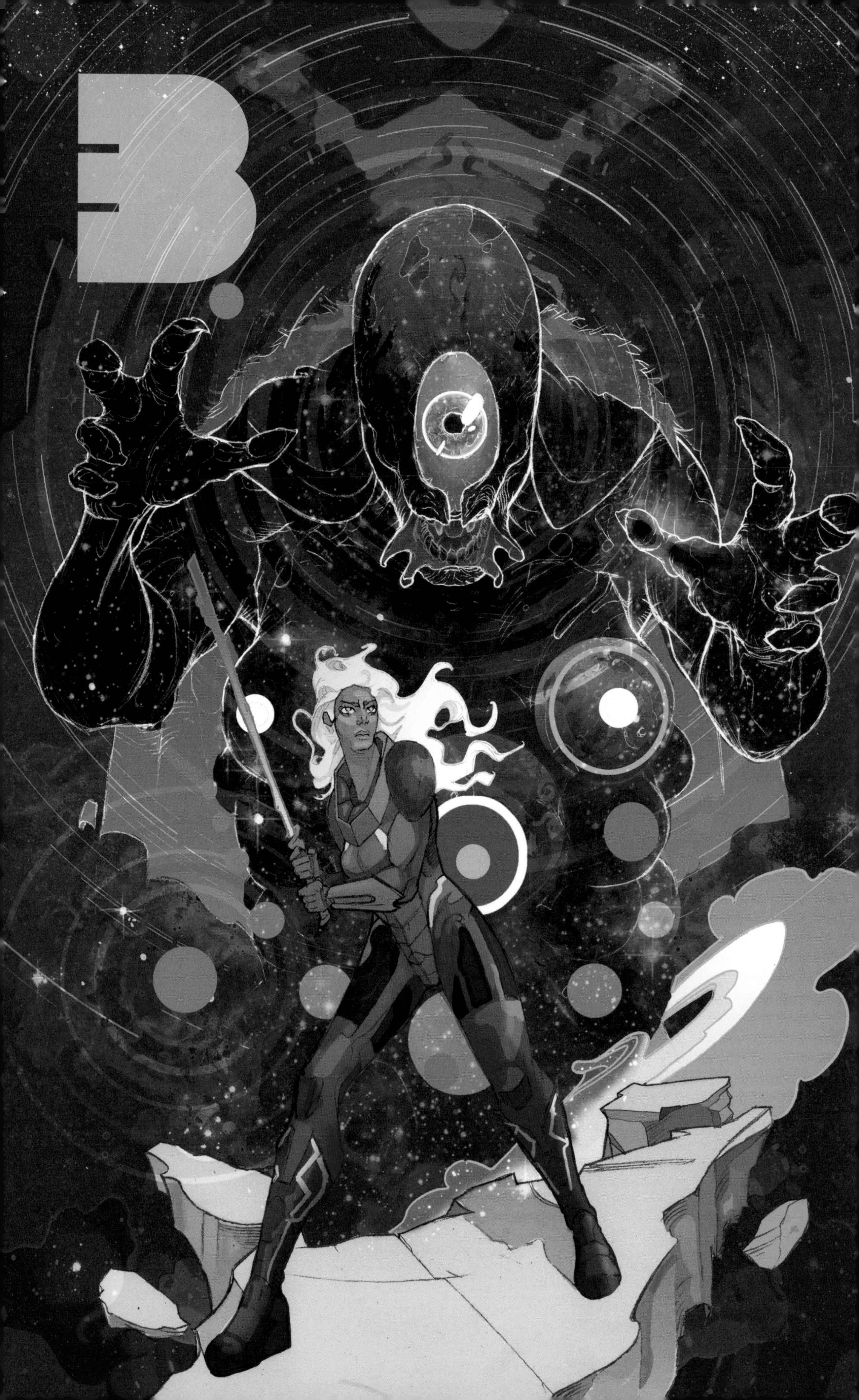

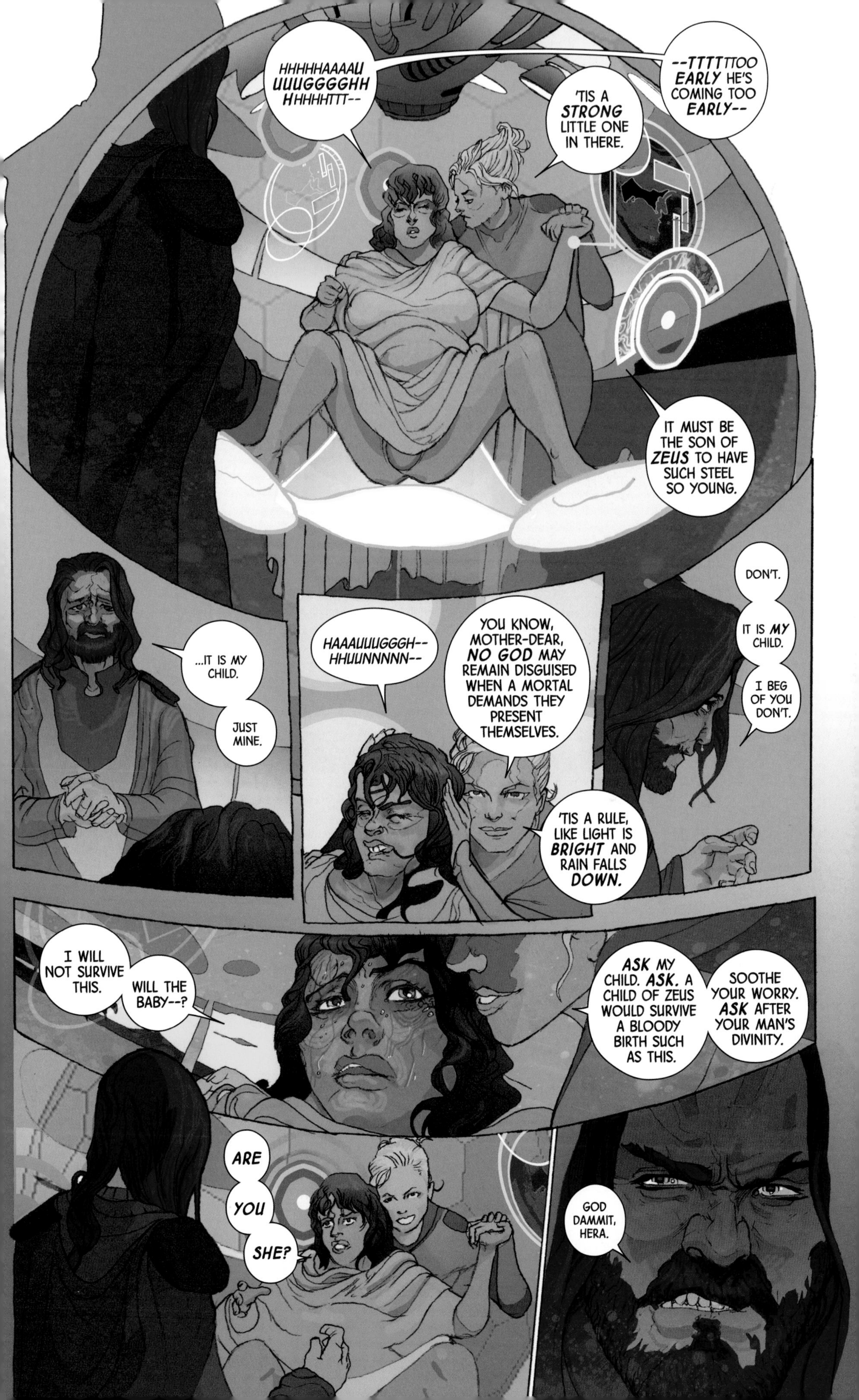

HHHHHAAAAU UUUGGGGHH HHHHHTTT--
--TTTTTTOO EARLY HE'S COMING TOO EARLY--
'TIS A STRONG LITTLE ONE IN THERE.
IT MUST BE THE SON OF ZEUS TO HAVE SUCH STEEL SO YOUNG.
...IT IS MY CHILD.
JUST MINE.
HAAAUUUGGGH-- HHUUNNNNN--
YOU KNOW, MOTHER-DEAR, NO GOD MAY REMAIN DISGUISED WHEN A MORTAL DEMANDS THEY PRESENT THEMSELVES.
'TIS A RULE, LIKE LIGHT IS BRIGHT AND RAIN FALLS DOWN.
DON'T.
IT IS MY CHILD.
I BEG OF YOU DON'T.
I WILL NOT SURVIVE THIS.
WILL THE BABY--?
ASK MY CHILD. ASK. A CHILD OF ZEUS WOULD SURVIVE A BLOODY BIRTH SUCH AS THIS.
SOOTHE YOUR WORRY. ASK AFTER YOUR MAN'S DIVINITY.
ARE
YOU
SHE?
GOD DAMMIT, HERA.

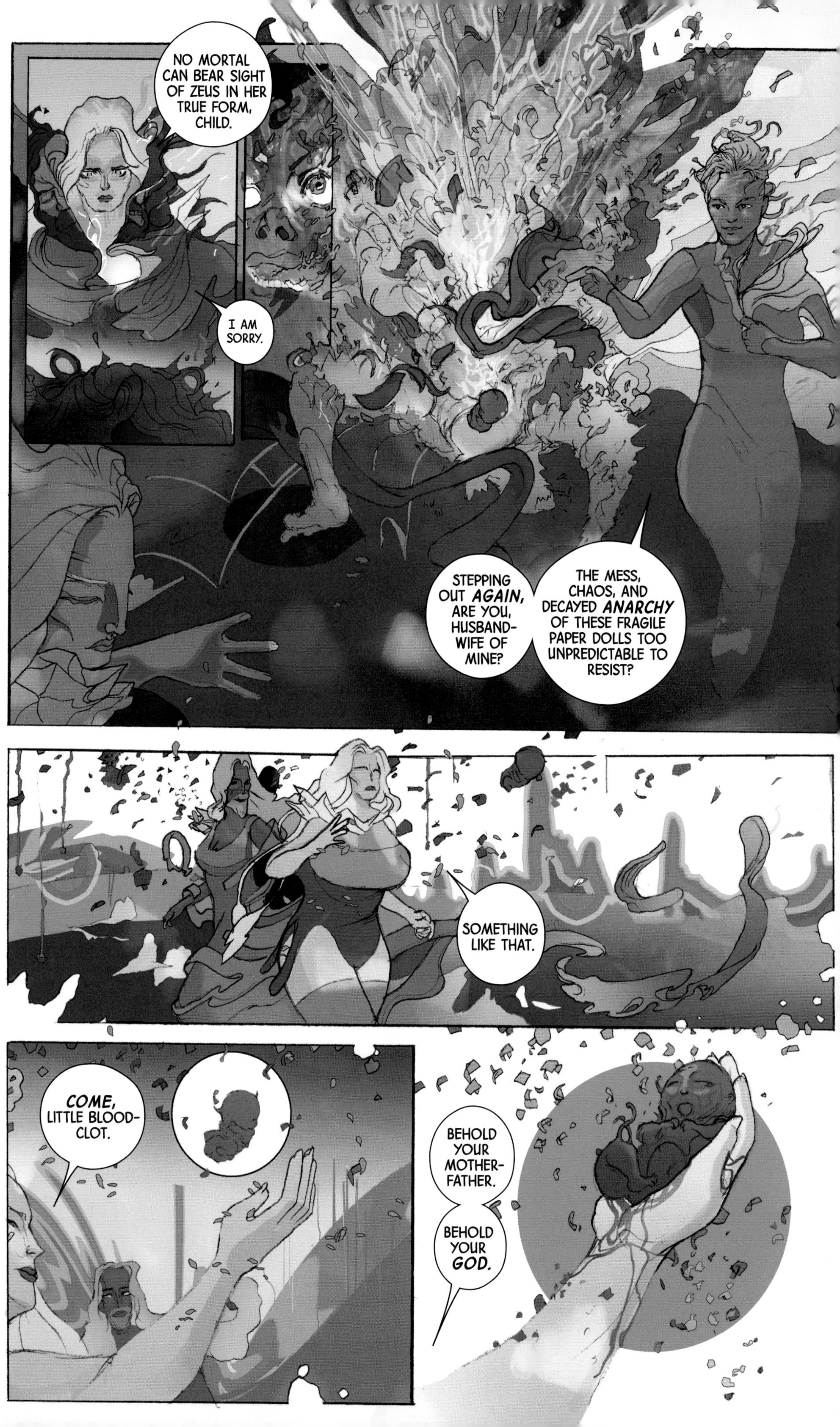
NO MORTAL CAN BEAR SIGHT OF ZEUS IN HER TRUE FORM, CHILD.
I AM SORRY.
STEPPING OUT AGAIN, ARE YOU, HUSBAND-WIFE OF MINE?
THE MESS, CHAOS, AND DECAYED ANARCHY OF THESE FRAGILE PAPER DOLLS TOO UNPREDICTABLE TO RESIST?
SOMETHING LIKE THAT.
COME, LITTLE BLOOD-CLOT.
BEHOLD YOUR MOTHER-FATHER.
BEHOLD YOUR GOD.

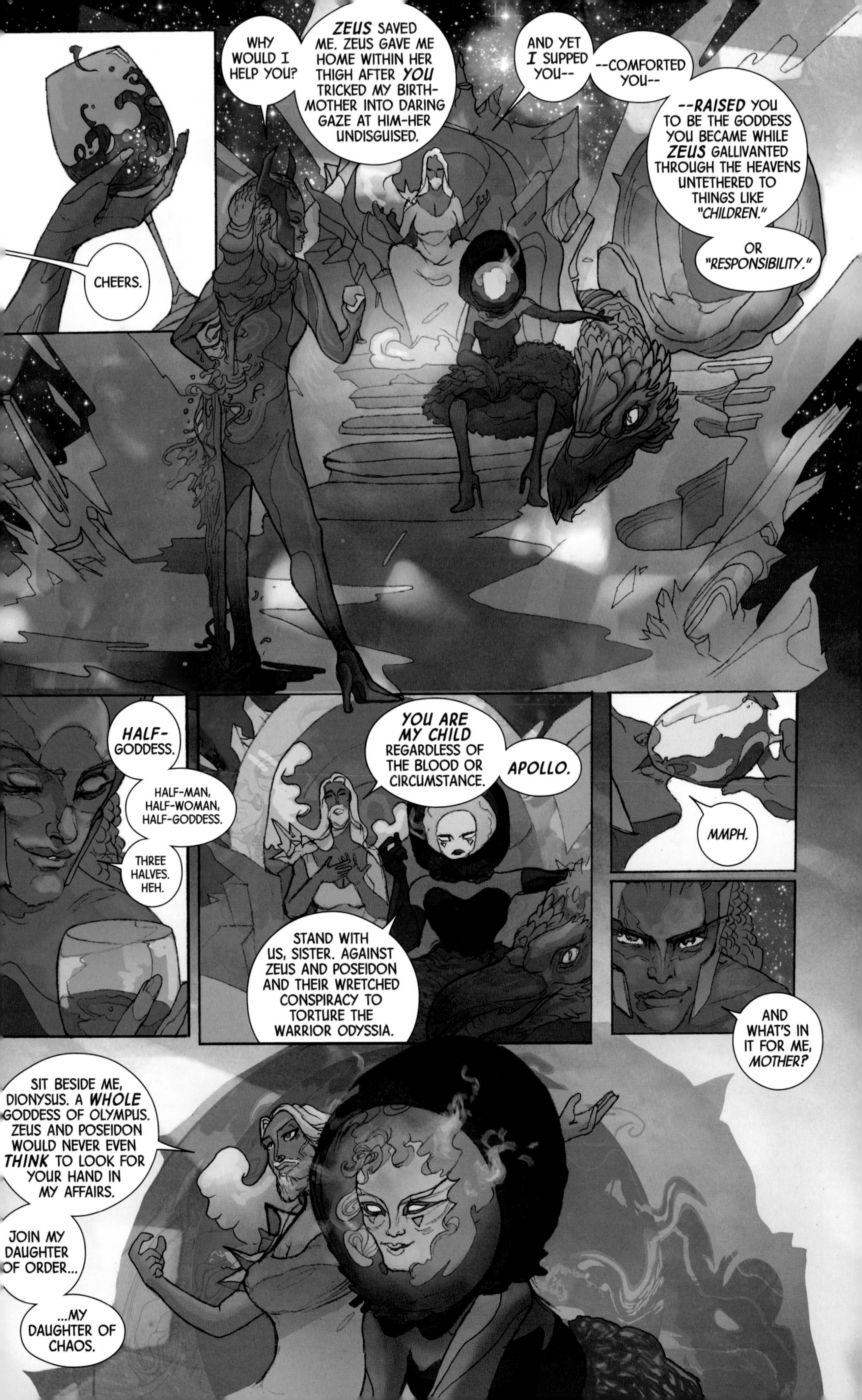
CHEERS.
WHY WOULD I HELP YOU?
ZEUS SAVED ME. ZEUS GAVE ME HOME WITHIN HER THIGH AFTER YOU TRICKED MY BIRTH-MOTHER INTO DARING GAZE AT HIM-HER UNDISGUISED.
AND YET I SUPPED YOU--
--COMFORTED YOU--
--RAISED YOU TO BE THE GODDESS YOU BECAME WHILE ZEUS GALLIVANTED THROUGH THE HEAVENS UNTETHERED TO THINGS LIKE "CHILDREN."
OR "RESPONSIBILITY."
HALF-GODDESS.
HALF-MAN, HALF-WOMAN, HALF-GODDESS.
THREE HALVES. HEH.
YOU ARE MY CHILD REGARDLESS OF THE BLOOD OR CIRCUMSTANCE.
APOLLO.
STAND WITH US, SISTER. AGAINST ZEUS AND POSEIDON AND THEIR WRETCHED CONSPIRACY TO TORTURE THE WARRIOR ODYSSIA.
MMPH.
AND WHAT'S IN IT FOR ME, MOTHER?
SIT BESIDE ME, DIONYSUS. A WHOLE GODDESS OF OLYMPUS. ZEUS AND POSEIDON WOULD NEVER EVEN THINK TO LOOK FOR YOUR HAND IN MY AFFAIRS.
JOIN MY DAUGHTER OF ORDER...
...MY DAUGHTER OF CHAOS.

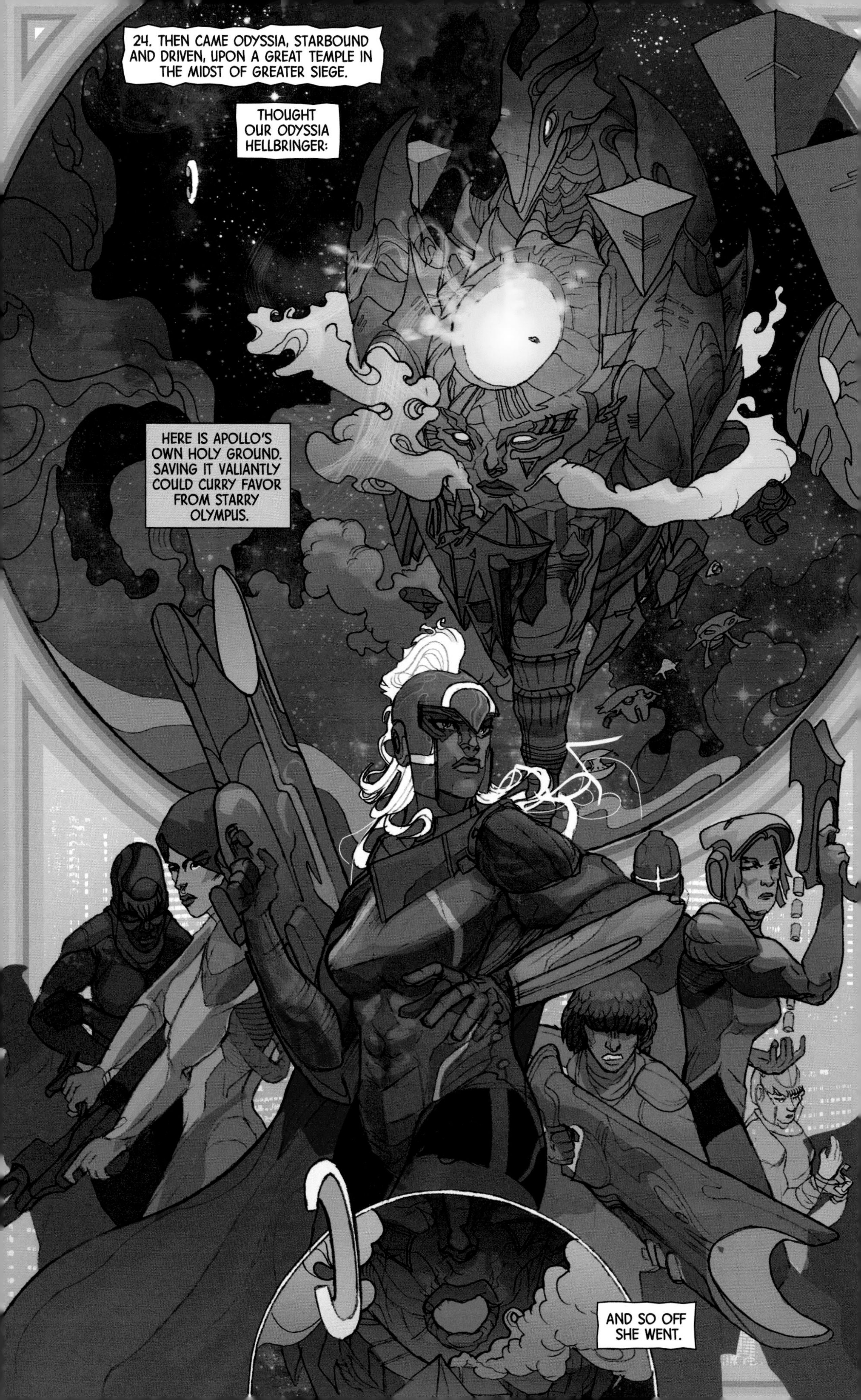
24. THEN CAME ODYSSIA, STARBOUND AND DRIVEN, UPON A GREAT TEMPLE IN THE MIDST OF GREATER SIEGE.
THOUGHT OUR ODYSSIA HELLBRINGER:
HERE IS APOLLO'S OWN HOLY GROUND. SAVING IT VALIANTLY COULD CURRY FAVOR FROM STARRY OLYMPUS.
AND SO OFF SHE WENT.

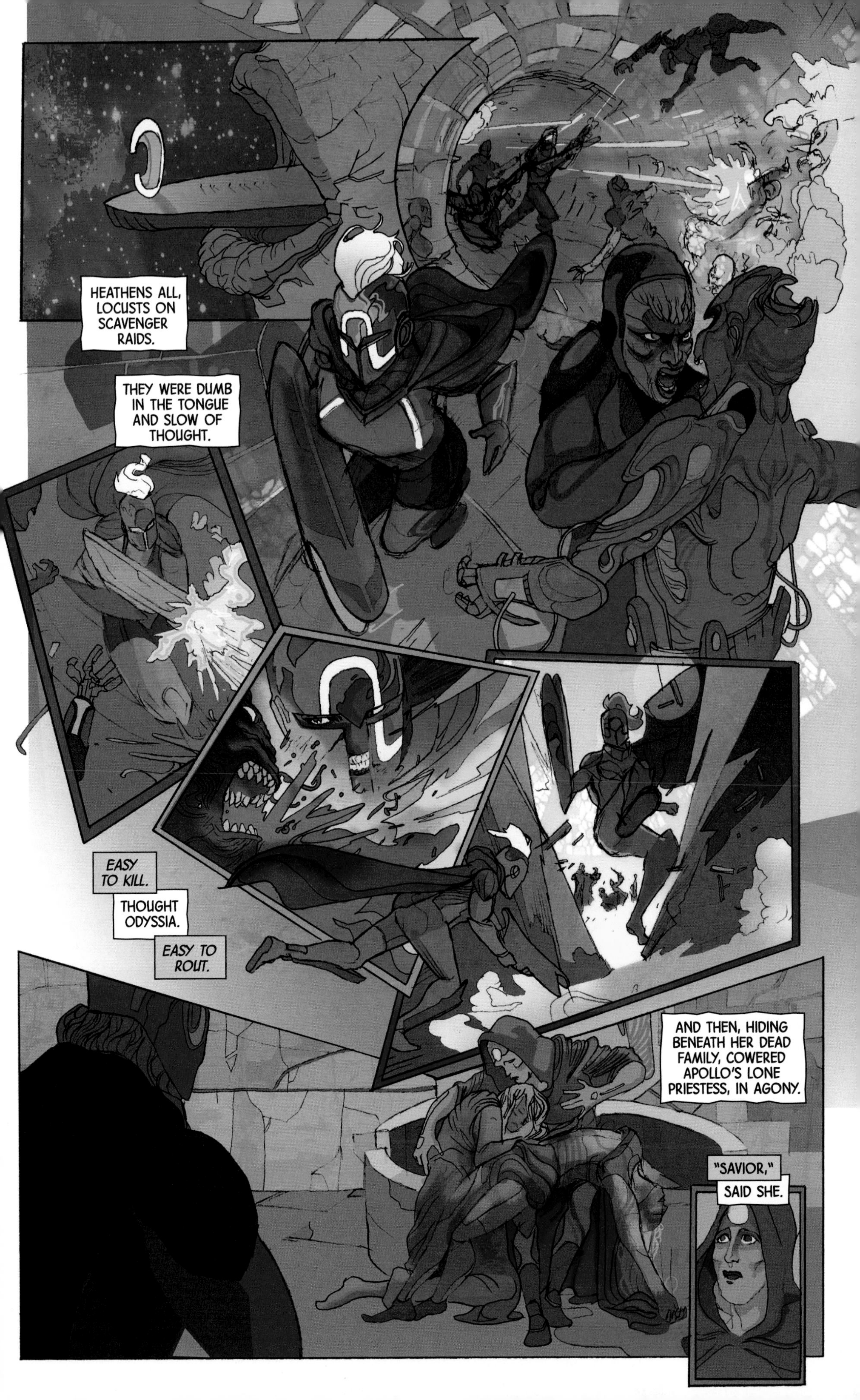
HEATHENS ALL, LOCUSTS ON SCAVENGER RAIDS.
THEY WERE DUMB IN THE TONGUE AND SLOW OF THOUGHT.
EASY TO KILL.
THOUGHT ODYSSIA.
EASY TO ROUT.
AND THEN, HIDING BENEATH HER DEAD FAMILY, COWERED APOLLO'S LONE PRIESTESS, IN AGONY.
"SAVIOR,"
SAID SHE.

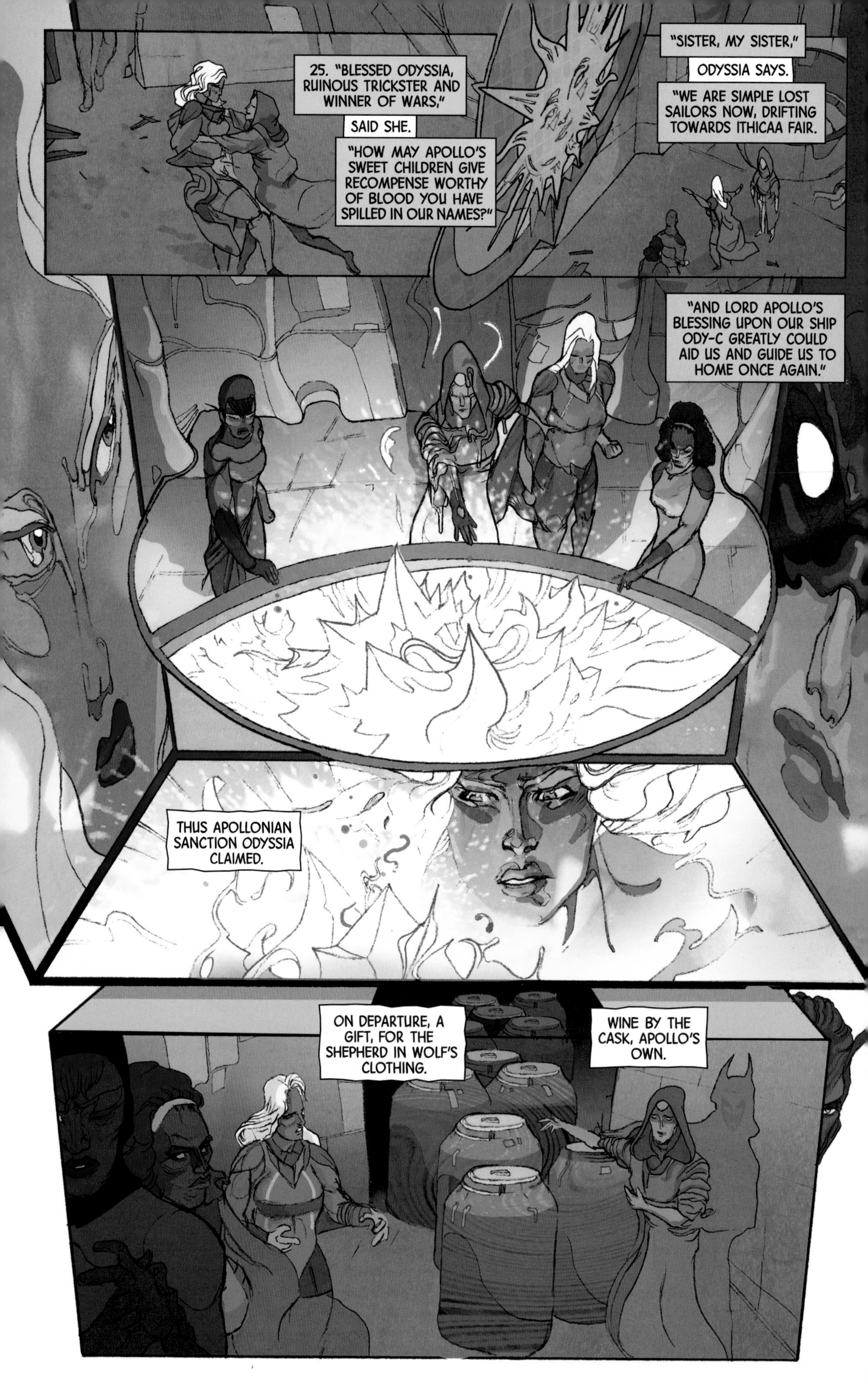
25. "BLESSED ODYSSIA, RUINOUS TRICKSTER AND WINNER OF WARS,"
SAID SHE.
"HOW MAY APOLLO'S SWEET CHILDREN GIVE RECOMPENSE WORTHY OF BLOOD YOU HAVE SPILLED IN OUR NAMES?"
"SISTER, MY SISTER,"
ODYSSIA SAYS.
"WE ARE SIMPLE LOST SAILORS NOW, DRIFTING TOWARDS ITHICAA FAIR.
"AND LORD APOLLO'S BLESSING UPON OUR SHIP ODY-C GREATLY COULD AID US AND GUIDE US TO HOME ONCE AGAIN."
THUS APOLLONIAN SANCTION ODYSSIA CLAIMED.
ON DEPARTURE, A GIFT, FOR THE SHEPHERD IN WOLF'S CLOTHING.
WINE BY THE CASK, APOLLO'S OWN.

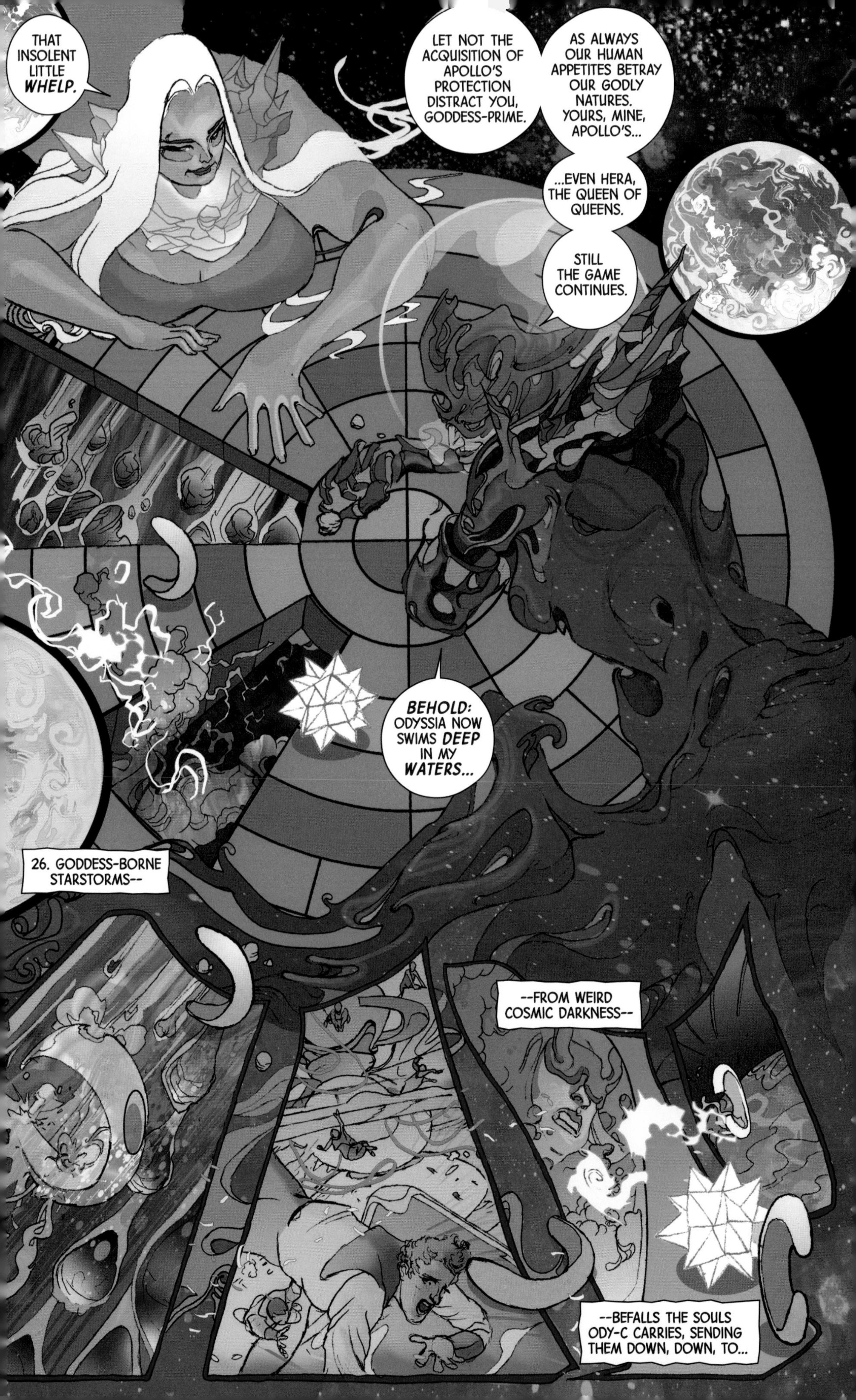
THAT INSOLENT LITTLE WHELP.
LET NOT THE ACQUISITION OF APOLLO'S PROTECTION DISTRACT YOU, GODDESS-PRIME.
AS ALWAYS OUR HUMAN APPETITES BETRAY OUR GODLY NATURES. YOURS, MINE, APOLLO'S...
...EVEN HERA, THE QUEEN OF QUEENS.
STILL THE GAME CONTINUES.
BEHOLD: ODYSSIA NOW SWIMS DEEP IN MY WATERS...
26. GODDESS-BORNE STARSTORMS--
--FROM WEIRD COSMIC DARKNESS--
--BEFALLS THE SOULS ODY-C CARRIES, SENDING THEM DOWN, DOWN, TO...

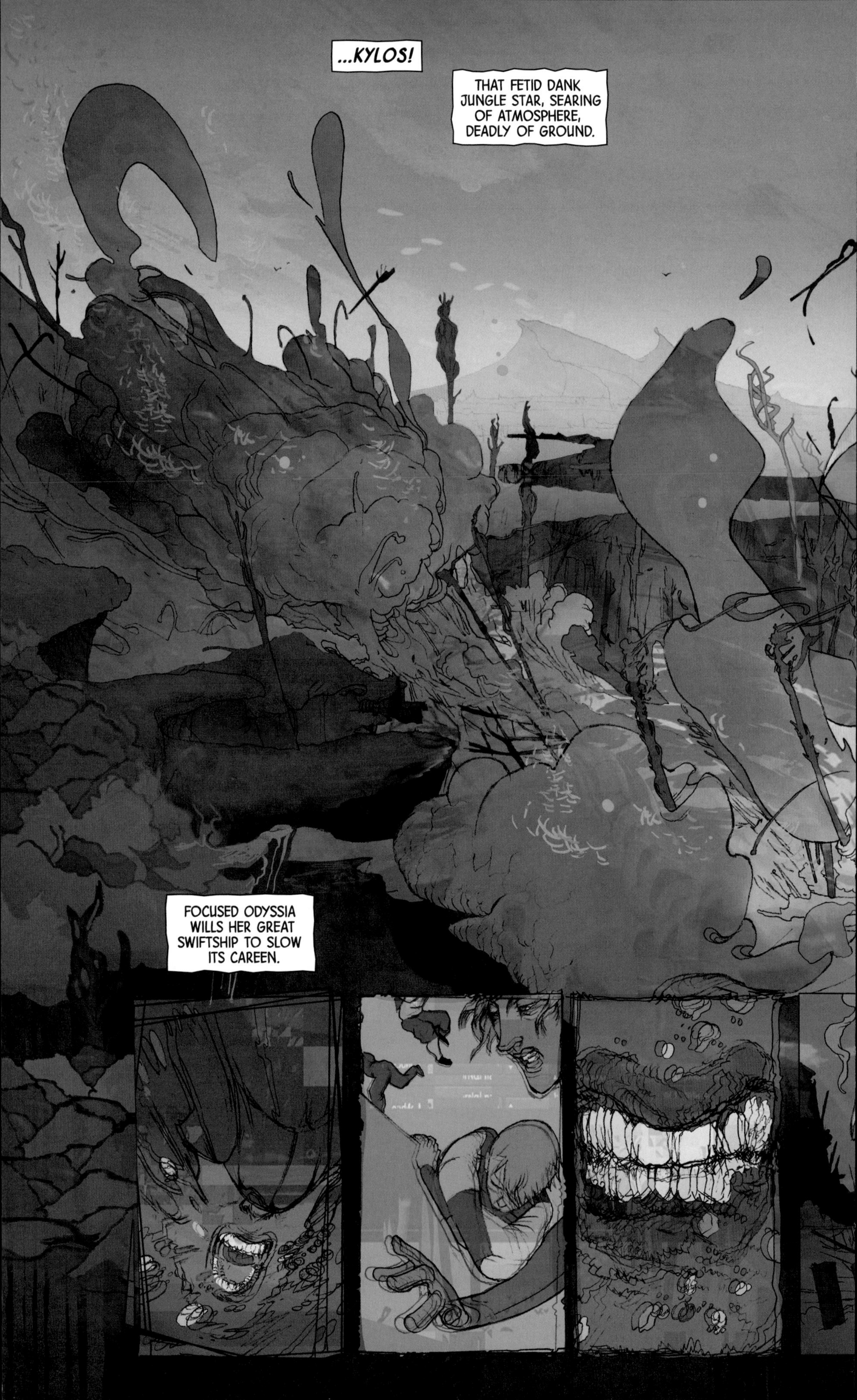
...KYLOS!
THAT FETID DANK JUNGLE STAR, SEARING OF ATMOSPHERE, DEADLY OF GROUND.
FOCUSED ODYSSIA WILLS HER GREAT SWIFTSHIP TO SLOW ITS CAREEN.

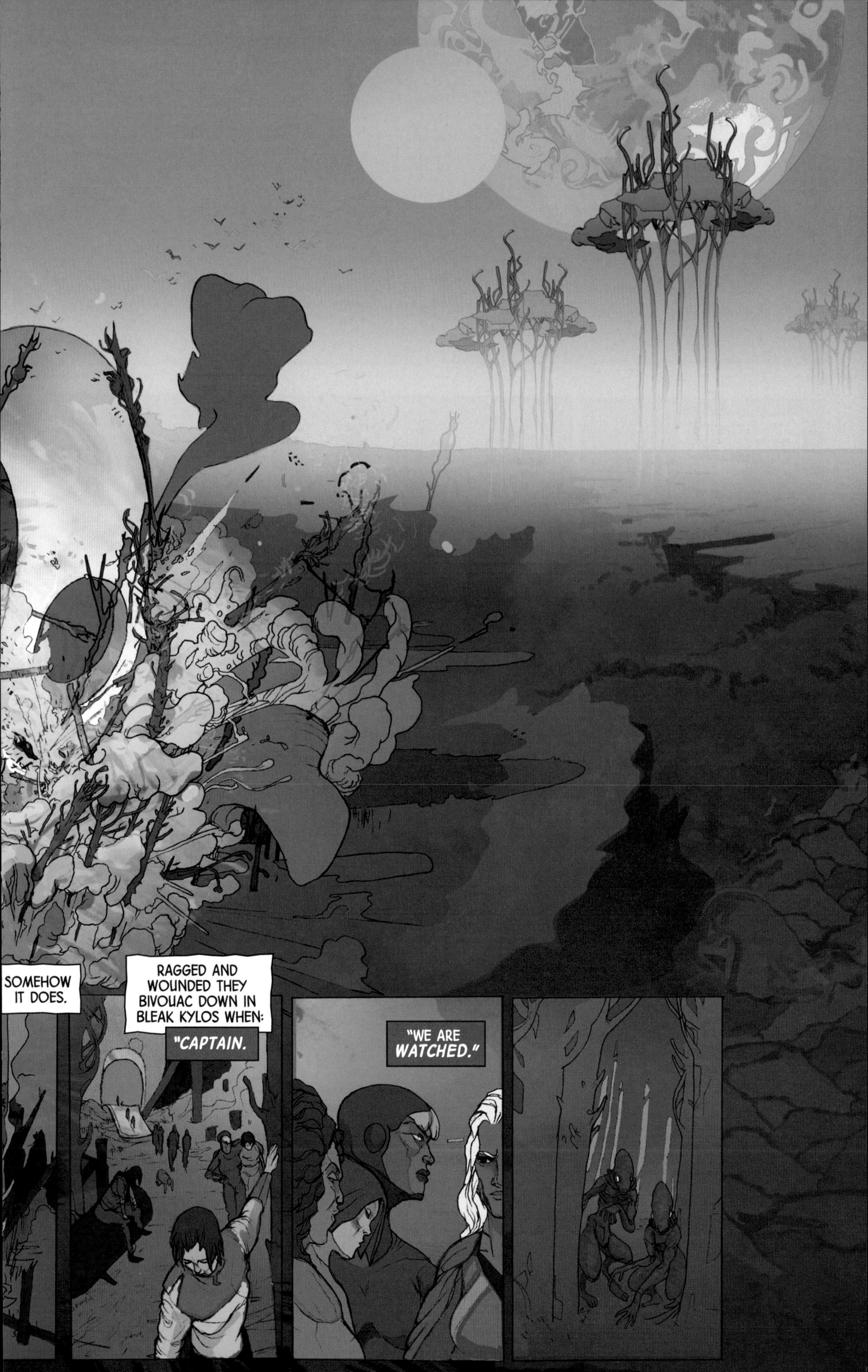
SOMEHOW IT DOES.
RAGGED AND WOUNDED THEY BIVOUAC DOWN IN BLEAK KYLOS WHEN:
"CAPTAIN.
"WE ARE WATCHED."

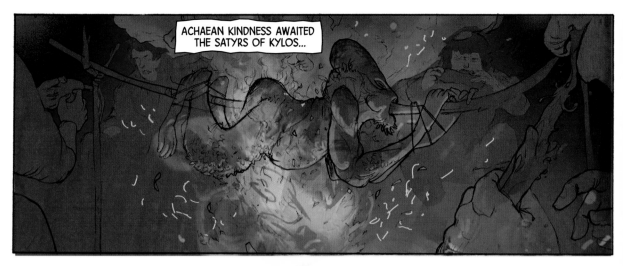

ACHAEAN KINDNESS AWAITED
THE SATYRS OF KYLOS...

...OF WHOM IT IS
SAID WERE QUITE
"NOURISHING."

"CAPTAIN
ODYSSIA!"

LESSER GIRL PEM
CRIES FROM WITHIN
GREAT BRANCHES.

"LOOK."

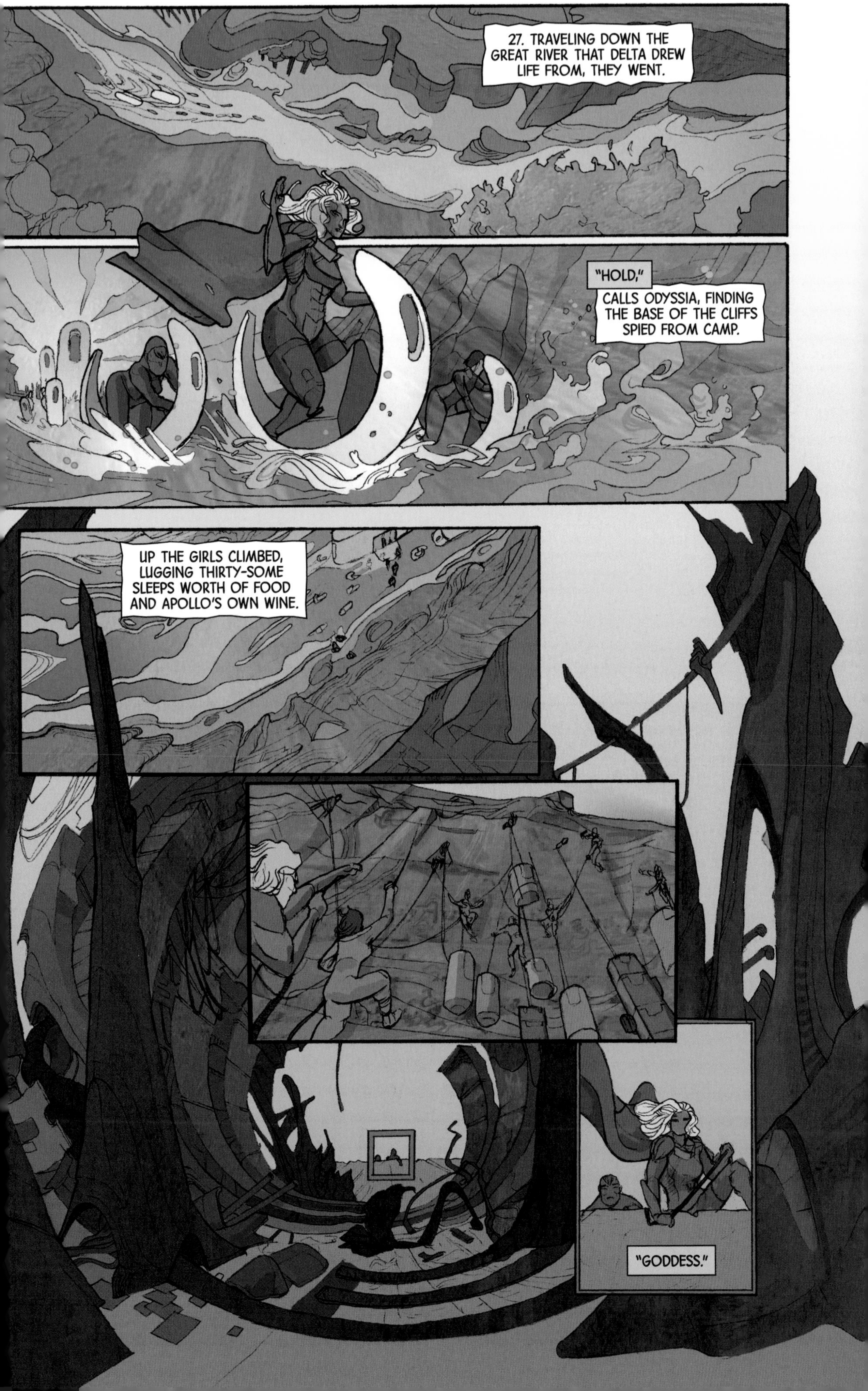
27. TRAVELING DOWN THE GREAT RIVER THAT DELTA DREW LIFE FROM, THEY WENT.
"HOLD,"
CALLS ODYSSIA, FINDING THE BASE OF THE CLIFFS SPIED FROM CAMP.
UP THE GIRLS CLIMBED, LUGGING THIRTY-SOME SLEEPS WORTH OF FOOD AND APOLLO'S OWN WINE.
"GODDESS."

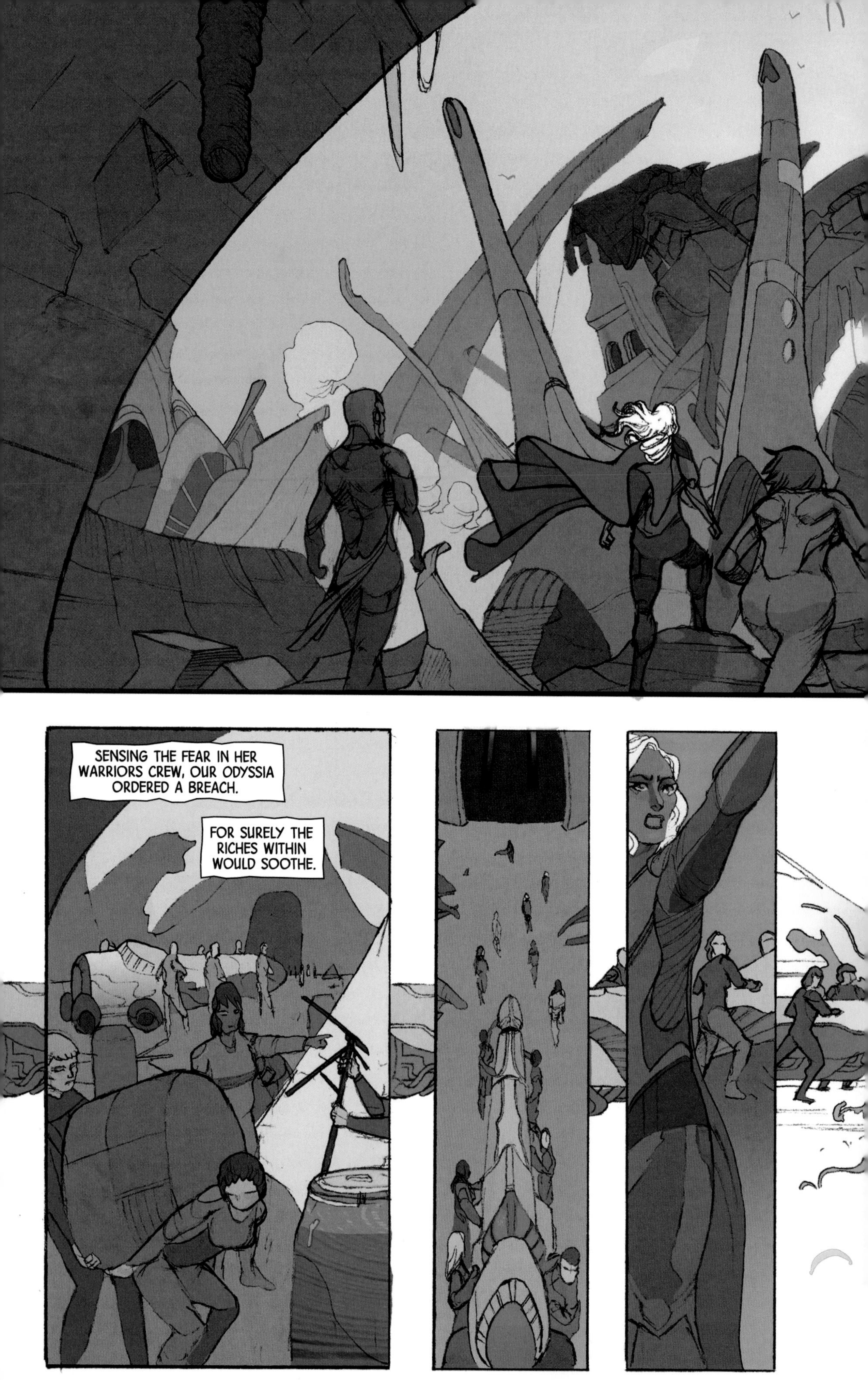
SENSING THE FEAR IN HER WARRIORS CREW, OUR ODYSSIA ORDERED A BREACH.
FOR SURELY THE RICHES WITHIN WOULD SOOTHE.

VERYTHING FOUND
TOP DWARFED THE
ACHAEANS.

THE *WOLF*
SMELLED PLUNDER
FOR TAKING.

"CAPTAIN!"

THE GIRLS OF
THE ODY-C
BEGGED.

"WHAT *THING*
NEEDS A FRONT
DOOR SO
LARGE?"

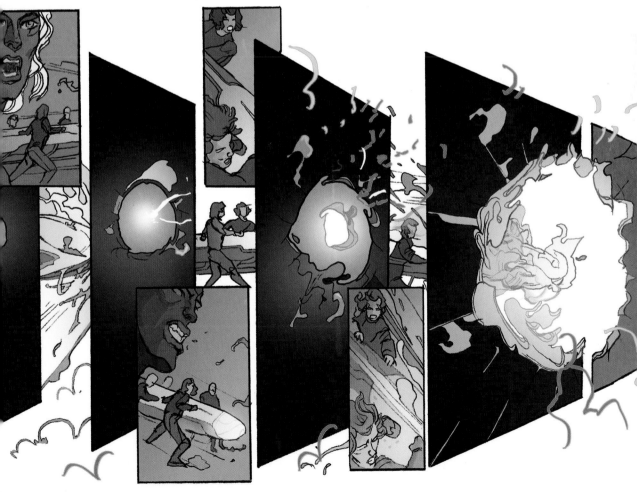

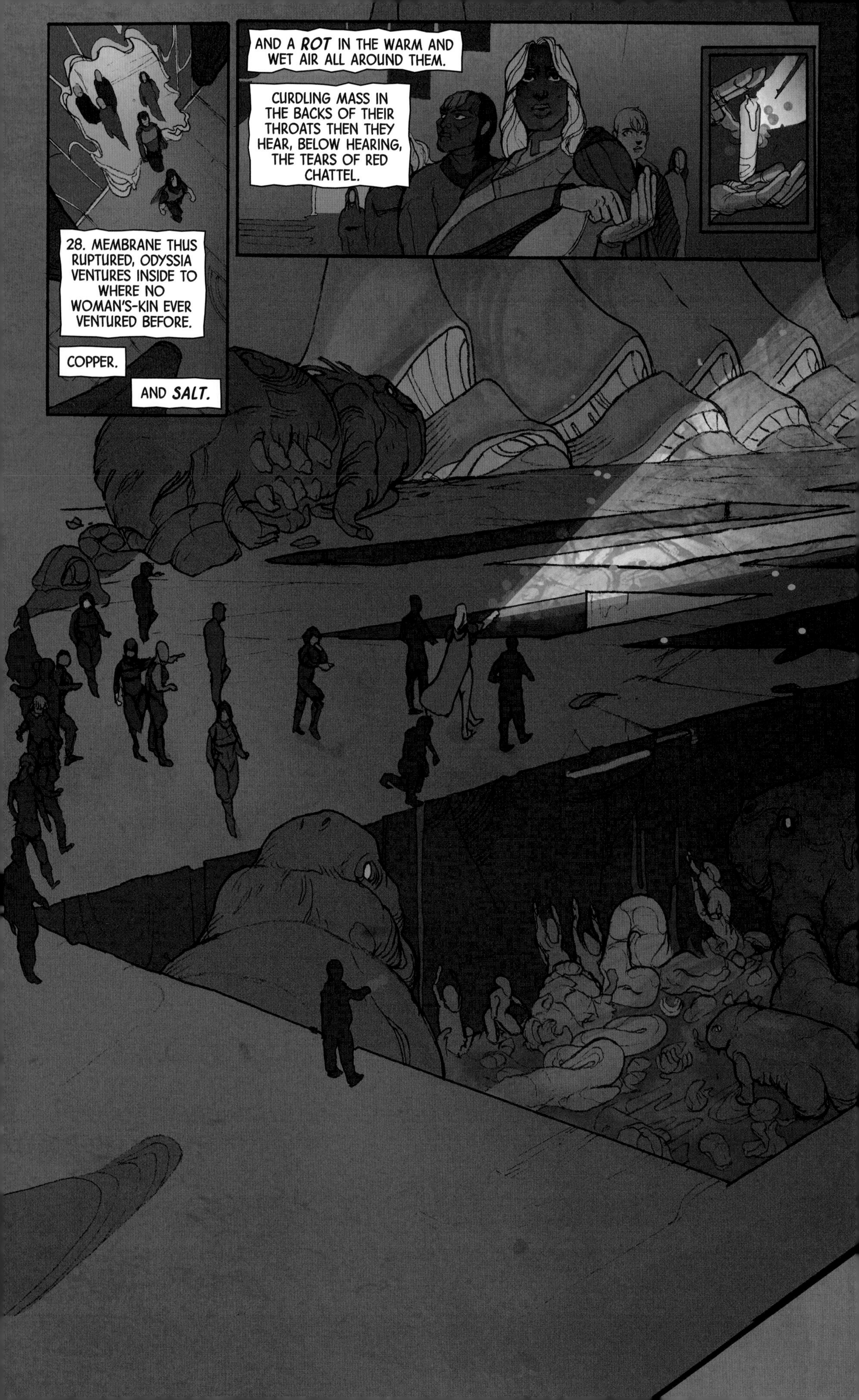

28. MEMBRANE THUS RUPTURED, ODYSSIA VENTURES INSIDE TO WHERE NO WOMAN'S-KIN EVER VENTURED BEFORE.
COPPER.
AND *SALT.*
AND A *ROT* IN THE WARM AND WET AIR ALL AROUND THEM.
CURDLING MASS IN THE BACKS OF THEIR THROATS THEN THEY HEAR, BELOW HEARING, THE TEARS OF RED CHATTEL.

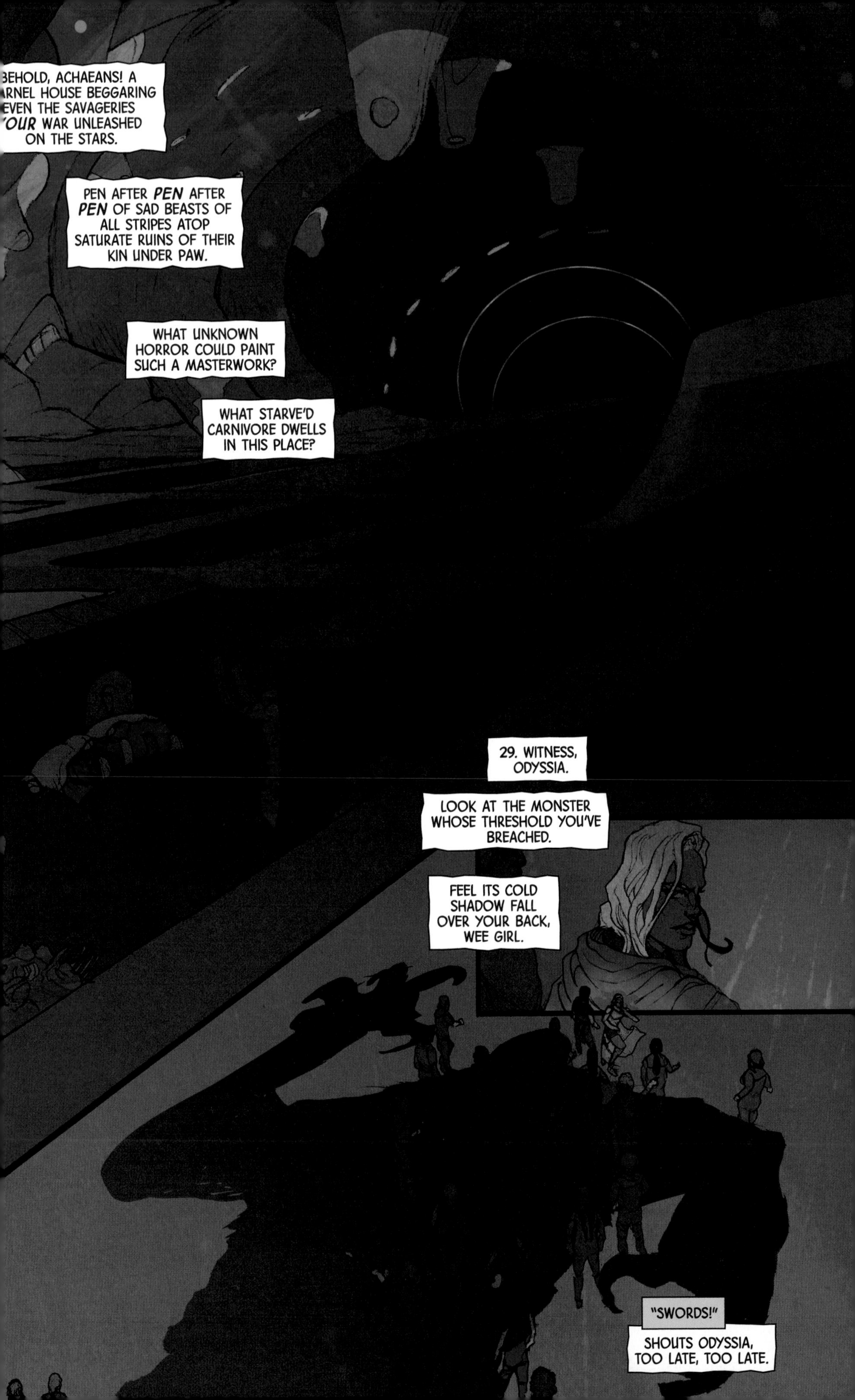
EHOLD, ACHAEANS! A RNEL HOUSE BEGGARING EVEN THE SAVAGERIES OUR WAR UNLEASHED ON THE STARS.
PEN AFTER PEN AFTER PEN OF SAD BEASTS OF ALL STRIPES ATOP SATURATE RUINS OF THEIR KIN UNDER PAW.
WHAT UNKNOWN HORROR COULD PAINT SUCH A MASTERWORK?
WHAT STARVE'D CARNIVORE DWELLS IN THIS PLACE?
29. WITNESS, ODYSSIA.
LOOK AT THE MONSTER WHOSE THRESHOLD YOU'VE BREACHED.
FEEL ITS COLD SHADOW FALL OVER YOUR BACK, WEE GIRL.
"SWORDS!"
SHOUTS ODYSSIA, TOO LATE, TOO LATE.

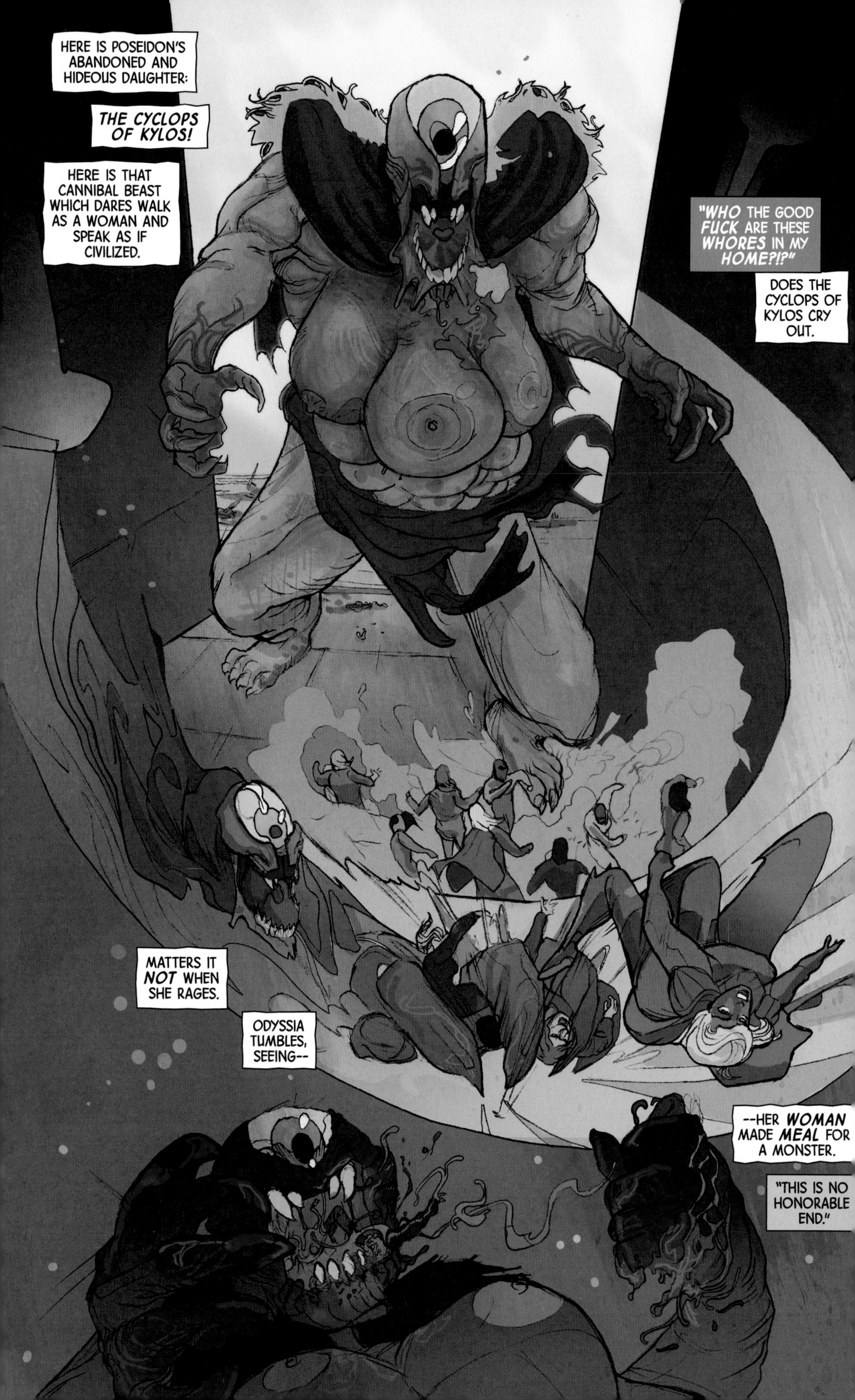
HERE IS POSEIDON'S ABANDONED AND HIDEOUS DAUGHTER:
THE CYCLOPS OF KYLOS!
HERE IS THAT CANNIBAL BEAST WHICH DARES WALK AS A WOMAN AND SPEAK AS IF CIVILIZED.
"WHO THE GOOD FUCK ARE THESE WHORES IN MY HOME?!?"
DOES THE CYCLOPS OF KYLOS CRY OUT.
MATTERS IT NOT WHEN SHE RAGES.
ODYSSIA TUMBLES, SEEING--
--HER WOMAN MADE MEAL FOR A MONSTER.
"THIS IS NO HONORABLE END."

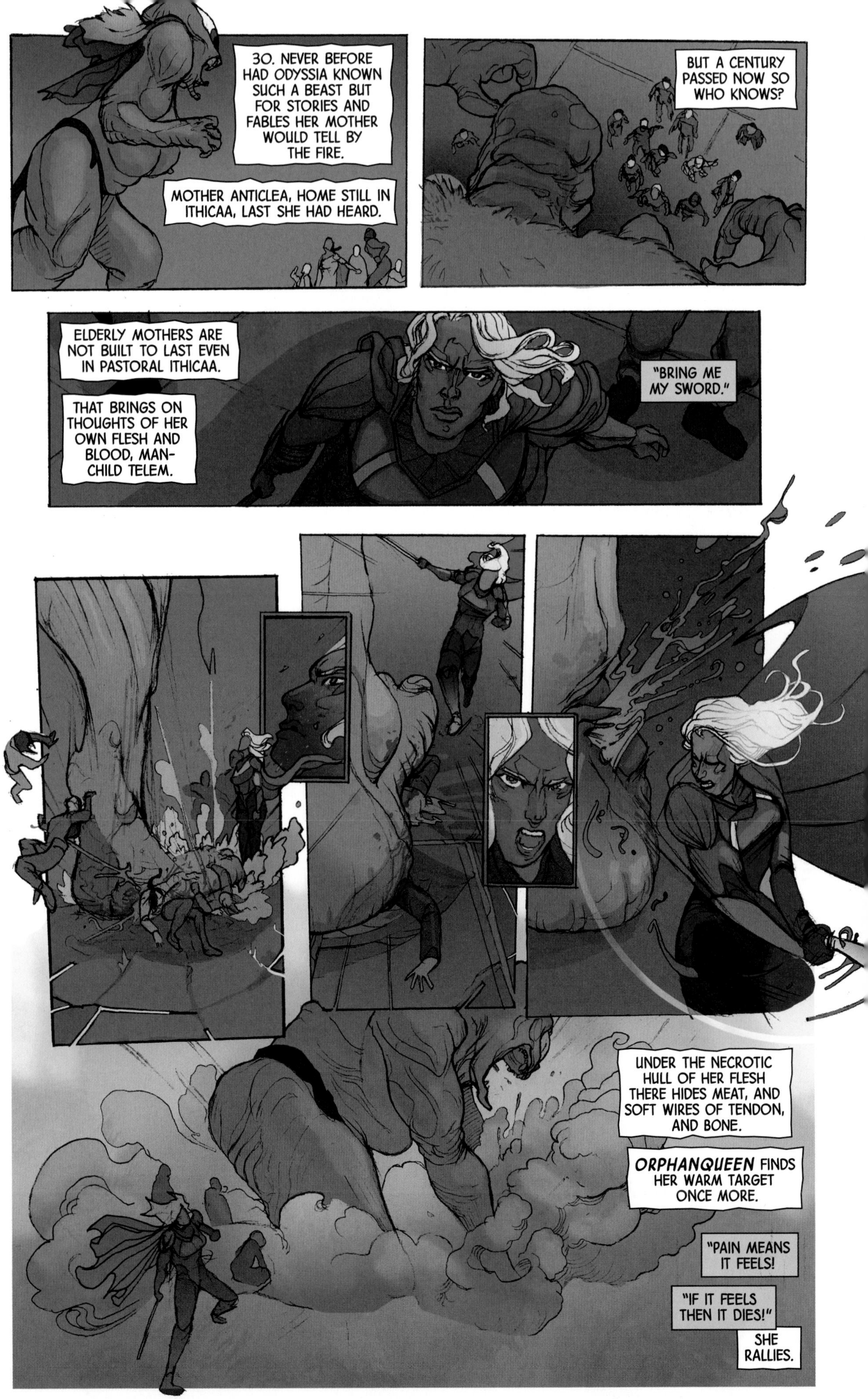
30. NEVER BEFORE HAD ODYSSIA KNOWN SUCH A BEAST BUT FOR STORIES AND FABLES HER MOTHER WOULD TELL BY THE FIRE.
MOTHER ANTICLEA, HOME STILL IN ITHICAA, LAST SHE HAD HEARD.
BUT A CENTURY PASSED NOW SO WHO KNOWS?
ELDERLY MOTHERS ARE NOT BUILT TO LAST EVEN IN PASTORAL ITHICAA.
THAT BRINGS ON THOUGHTS OF HER OWN FLESH AND BLOOD, MAN-CHILD TELEM.
"BRING ME MY SWORD."
UNDER THE NECROTIC HULL OF HER FLESH THERE HIDES MEAT, AND SOFT WIRES OF TENDON, AND BONE.
ORPHANQUEEN FINDS HER WARM TARGET ONCE MORE.
"PAIN MEANS IT FEELS!
"IF IT FEELS THEN IT DIES!"
SHE RALLIES.

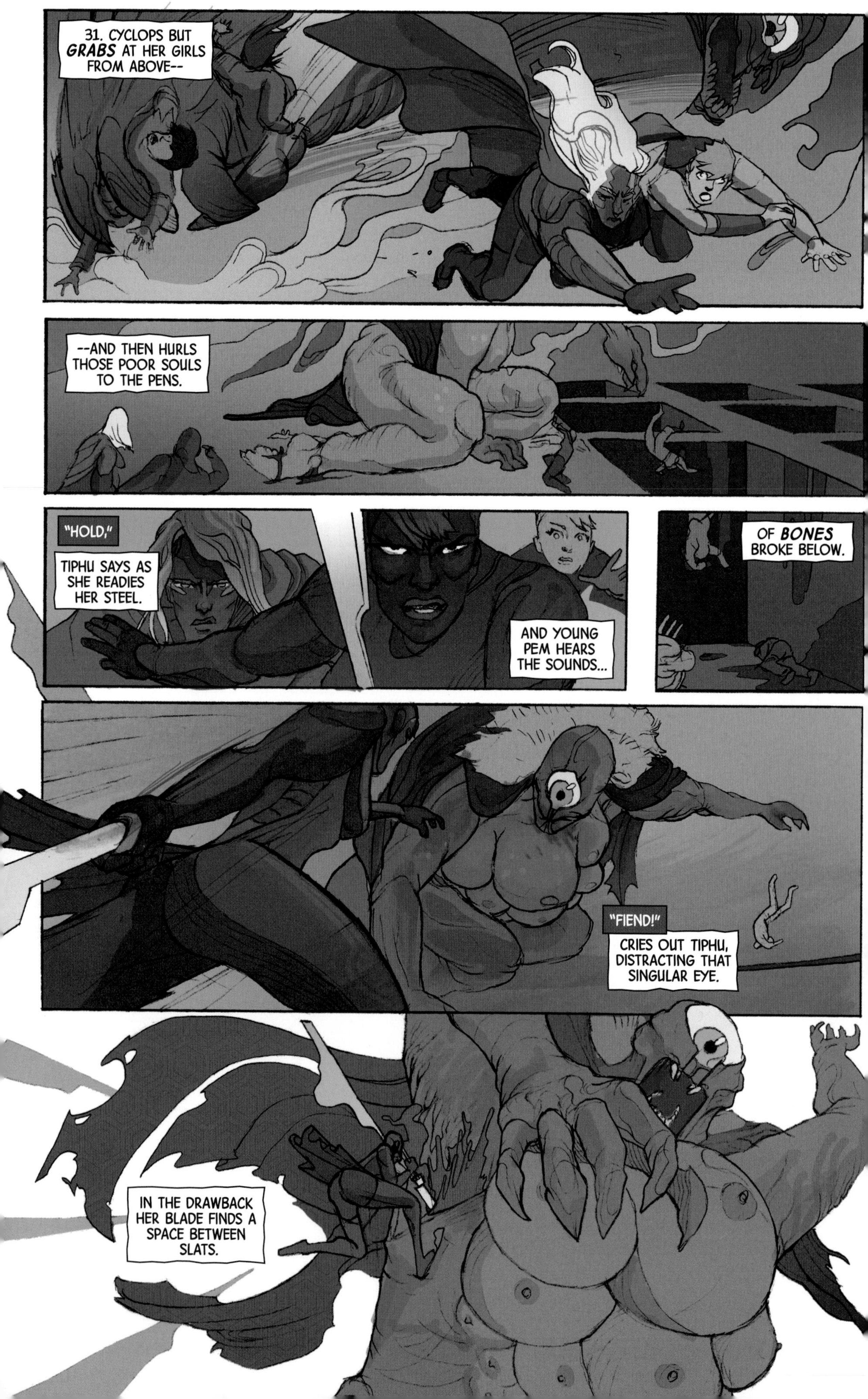
31. CYCLOPS BUT GRABS AT HER GIRLS FROM ABOVE--
--AND THEN HURLS THOSE POOR SOULS TO THE PENS.
"HOLD,"
TIPHU SAYS AS SHE READIES HER STEEL.
AND YOUNG PEM HEARS THE SOUNDS...
OF BONES BROKE BELOW.
"FIEND!"
CRIES OUT TIPHU, DISTRACTING THAT SINGULAR EYE.
IN THE DRAWBACK HER BLADE FINDS A SPACE BETWEEN SLATS.

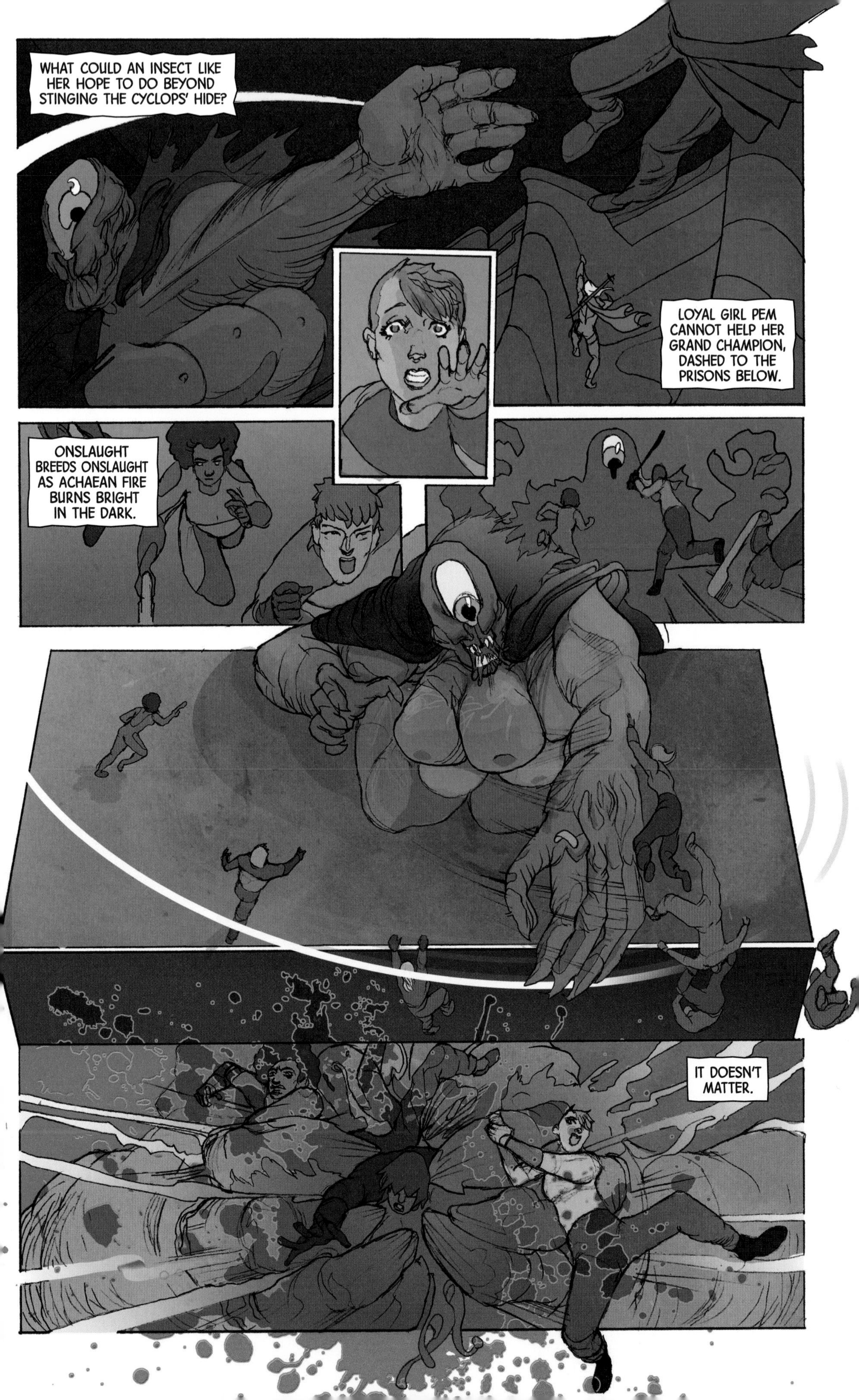
WHAT COULD AN INSECT LIKE HER HOPE TO DO BEYOND STINGING THE CYCLOPS' HIDE?
LOYAL GIRL PEM CANNOT HELP HER GRAND CHAMPION, DASHED TO THE PRISONS BELOW.
ONSLAUGHT BREEDS ONSLAUGHT AS ACHAEAN FIRE BURNS BRIGHT IN THE DARK.
IT DOESN'T MATTER.

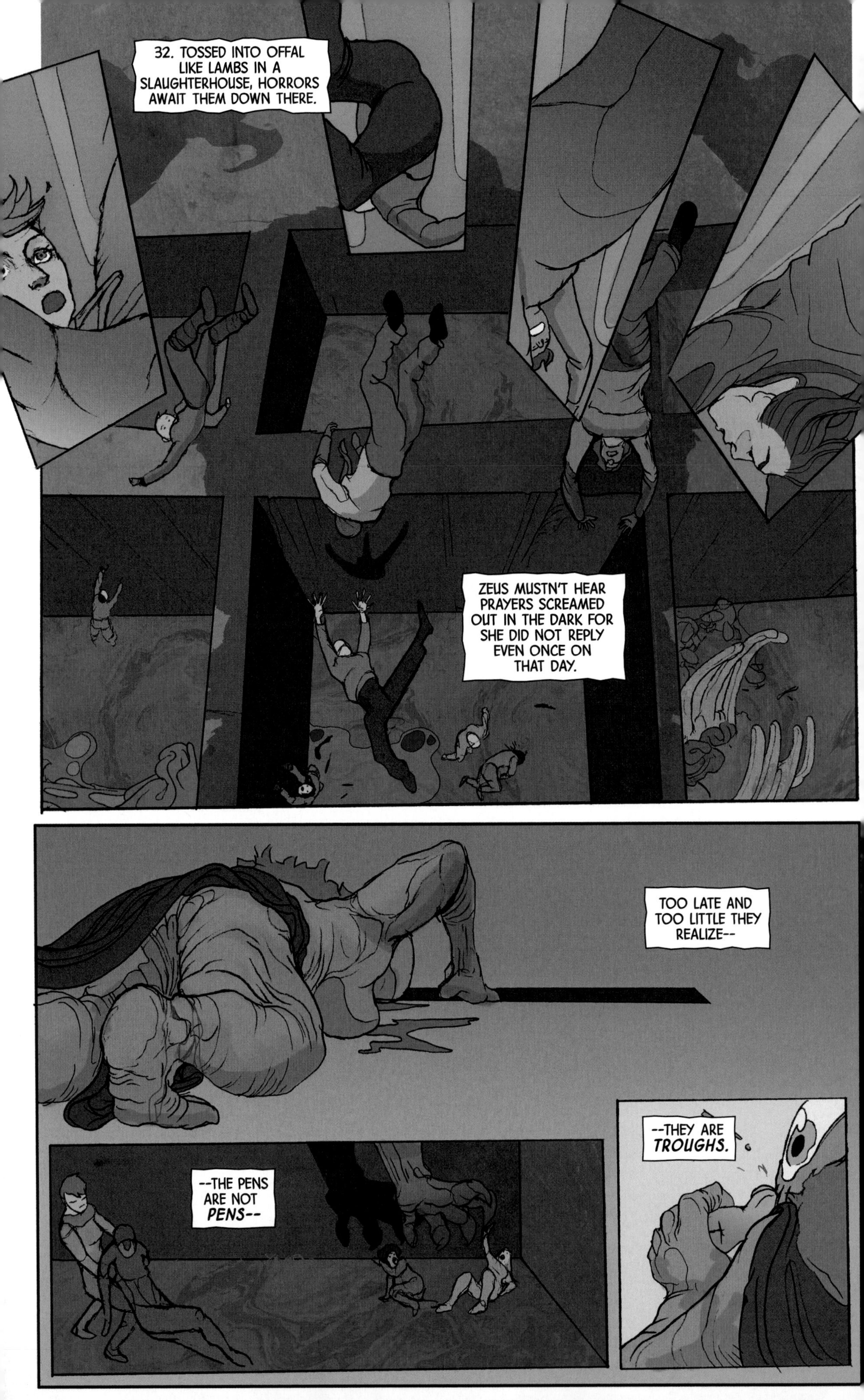
32. TOSSED INTO OFFAL LIKE LAMBS IN A SLAUGHTERHOUSE, HORRORS AWAIT THEM DOWN THERE.
ZEUS MUSTN'T HEAR PRAYERS SCREAMED OUT IN THE DARK FOR SHE DID NOT REPLY EVEN ONCE ON THAT DAY.
TOO LATE AND TOO LITTLE THEY REALIZE--
--THE PENS ARE NOT *PENS*--
--THEY ARE *TROUGHS.*

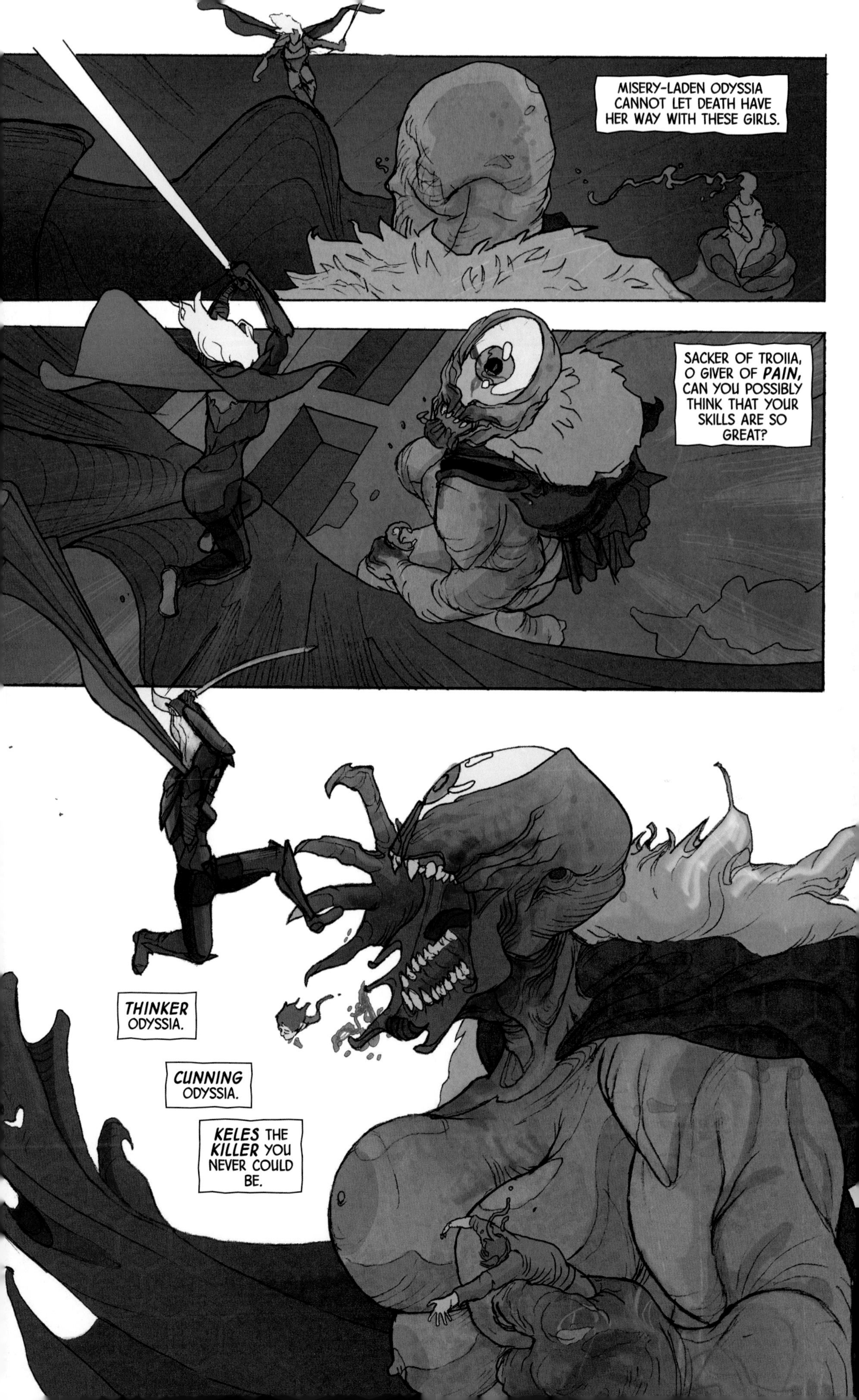
MISERY-LADEN ODYSSIA CANNOT LET DEATH HAVE HER WAY WITH THESE GIRLS.
SACKER OF TROIIA, O GIVER OF PAIN, CAN YOU POSSIBLY THINK THAT YOUR SKILLS ARE SO GREAT?
THINKER ODYSSIA.
CUNNING ODYSSIA.
KELES THE KILLER YOU NEVER COULD BE.

SEE?

33. DOWN IN THE RUINOUS PILES OF VISCERA ONCE HER COMMAND AND HER CREW...

...ODYSSIA RECALIBRATES.

WATCHING THE CYCLOPS OF KYLOS MAKE FEAST OF THE ODY-C'S GIRLS THEY KNOW--

--FOR THE FIRST TIME SINCE TROIIA DID FALL--

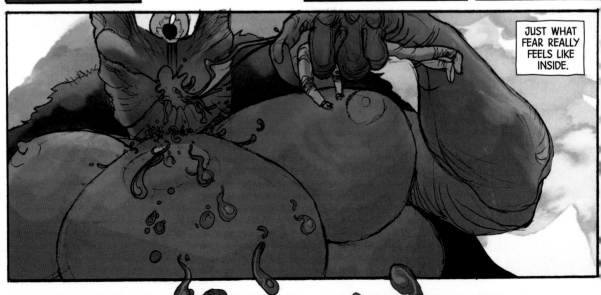

JUST WHAT FEAR REALLY FEELS LIKE INSIDE.

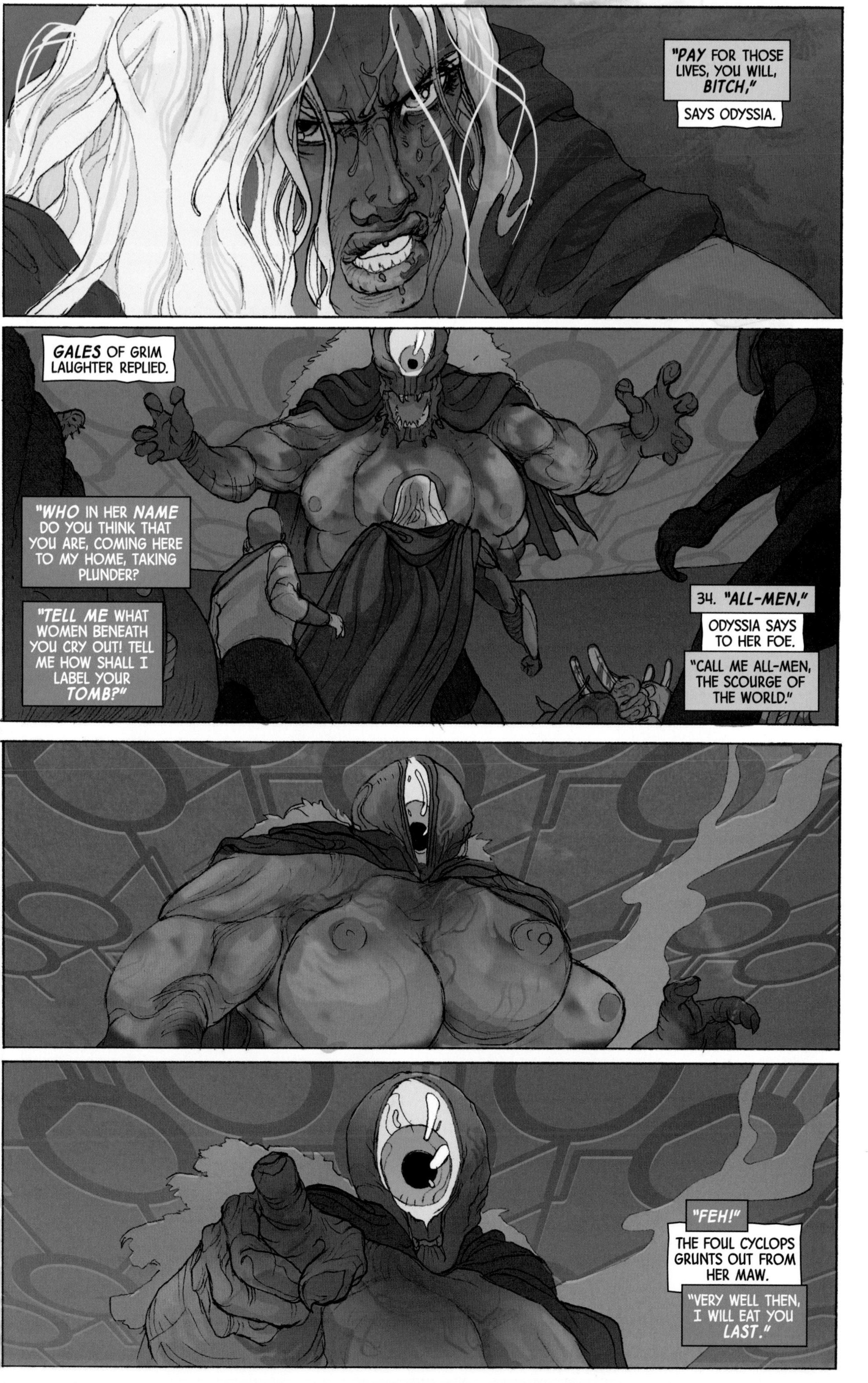
"PAY FOR THOSE LIVES, YOU WILL, BITCH,"
SAYS ODYSSIA.
GALES OF GRIM LAUGHTER REPLIED.
"WHO IN HER NAME DO YOU THINK THAT YOU ARE, COMING HERE TO MY HOME, TAKING PLUNDER?
"TELL ME WHAT WOMEN BENEATH YOU CRY OUT! TELL ME HOW SHALL I LABEL YOUR TOMB?"
34. "ALL-MEN,"
ODYSSIA SAYS TO HER FOE.
"CALL ME ALL-MEN, THE SCOURGE OF THE WORLD."
"FEH!"
THE FOUL CYCLOPS GRUNTS OUT FROM HER MAW.
"VERY WELL THEN, I WILL EAT YOU LAST."

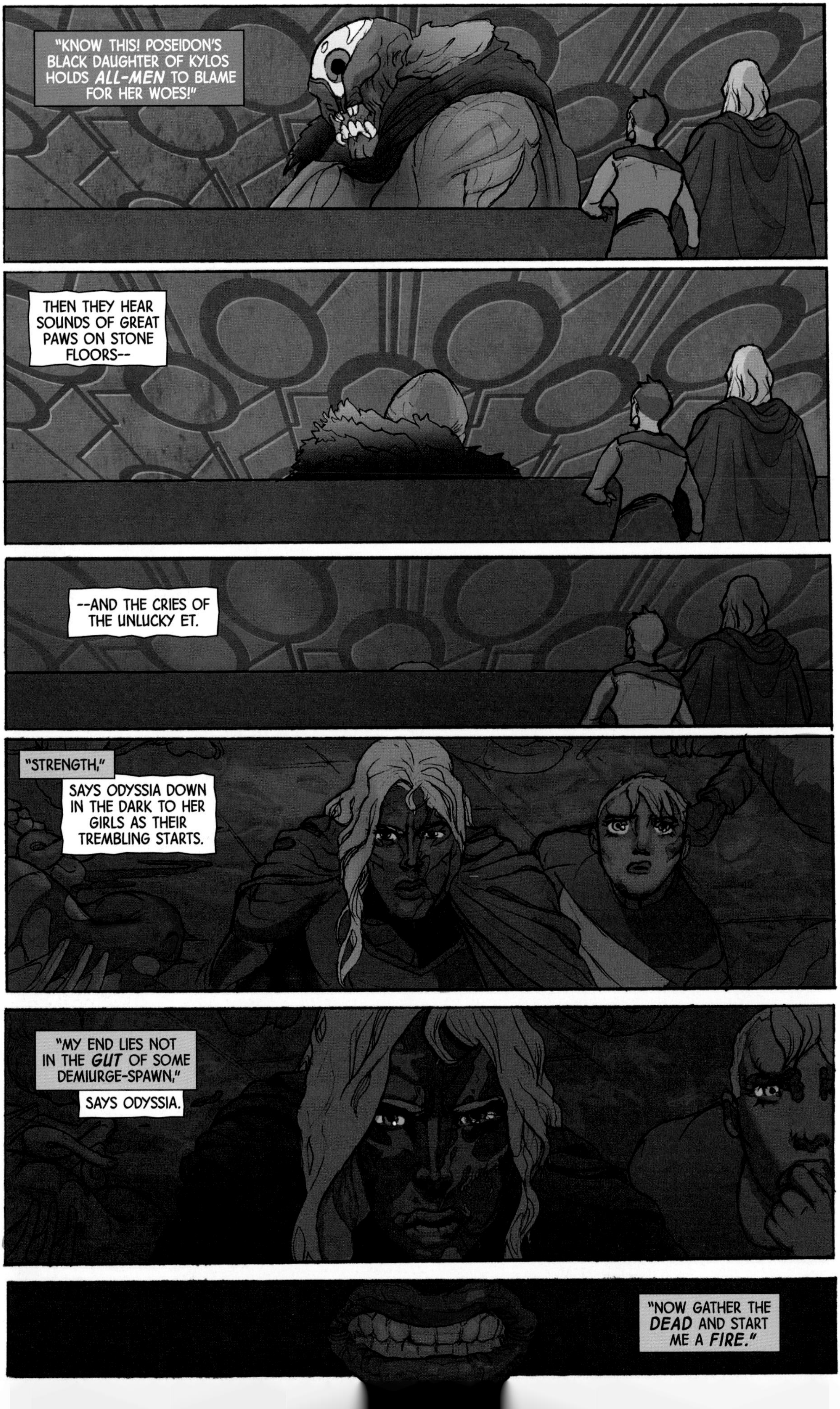
"KNOW THIS! POSEIDON'S BLACK DAUGHTER OF KYLOS HOLDS ALL-MEN TO BLAME FOR HER WOES!"
THEN THEY HEAR SOUNDS OF GREAT PAWS ON STONE FLOORS--
--AND THE CRIES OF THE UNLUCKY ET.
"STRENGTH,"
SAYS ODYSSIA DOWN IN THE DARK TO HER GIRLS AS THEIR TREMBLING STARTS.
"MY END LIES NOT IN THE GUT OF SOME DEMIURGE-SPAWN,"
SAYS ODYSSIA.
"NOW GATHER THE DEAD AND START ME A FIRE."

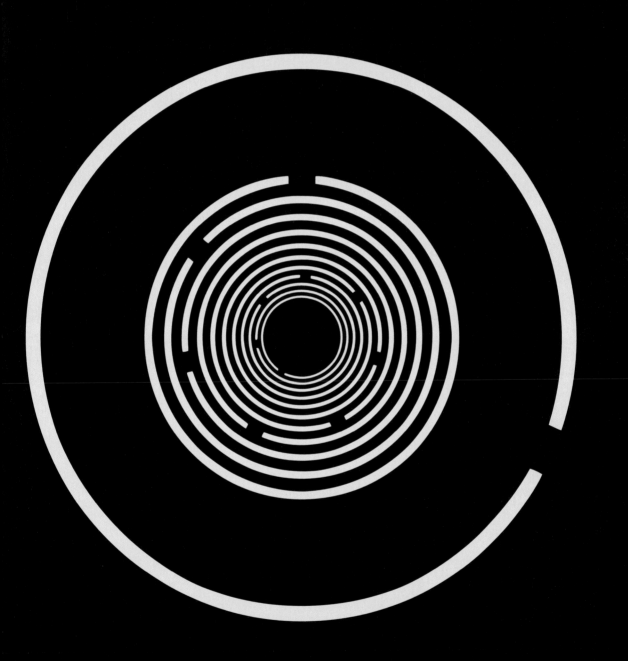

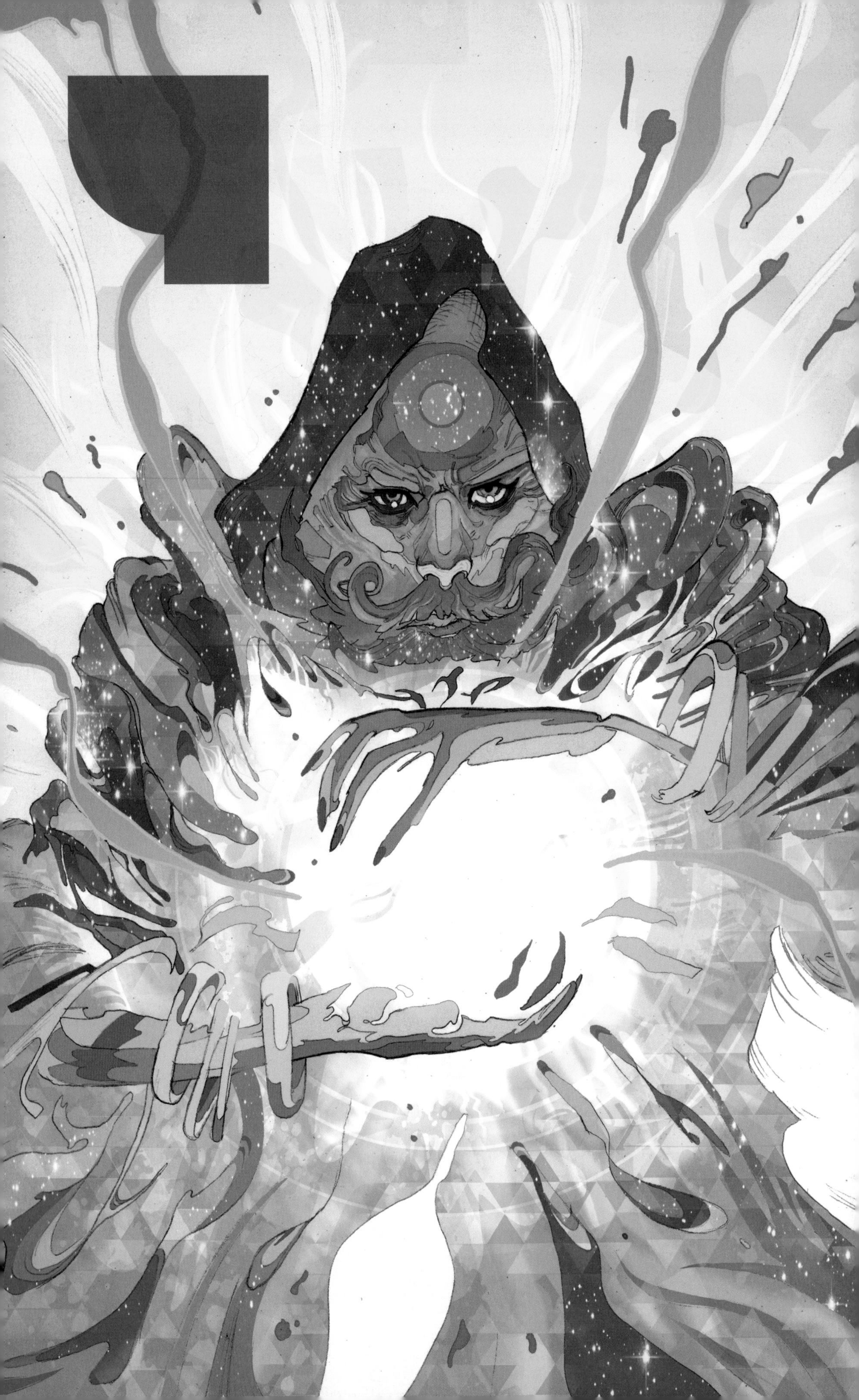

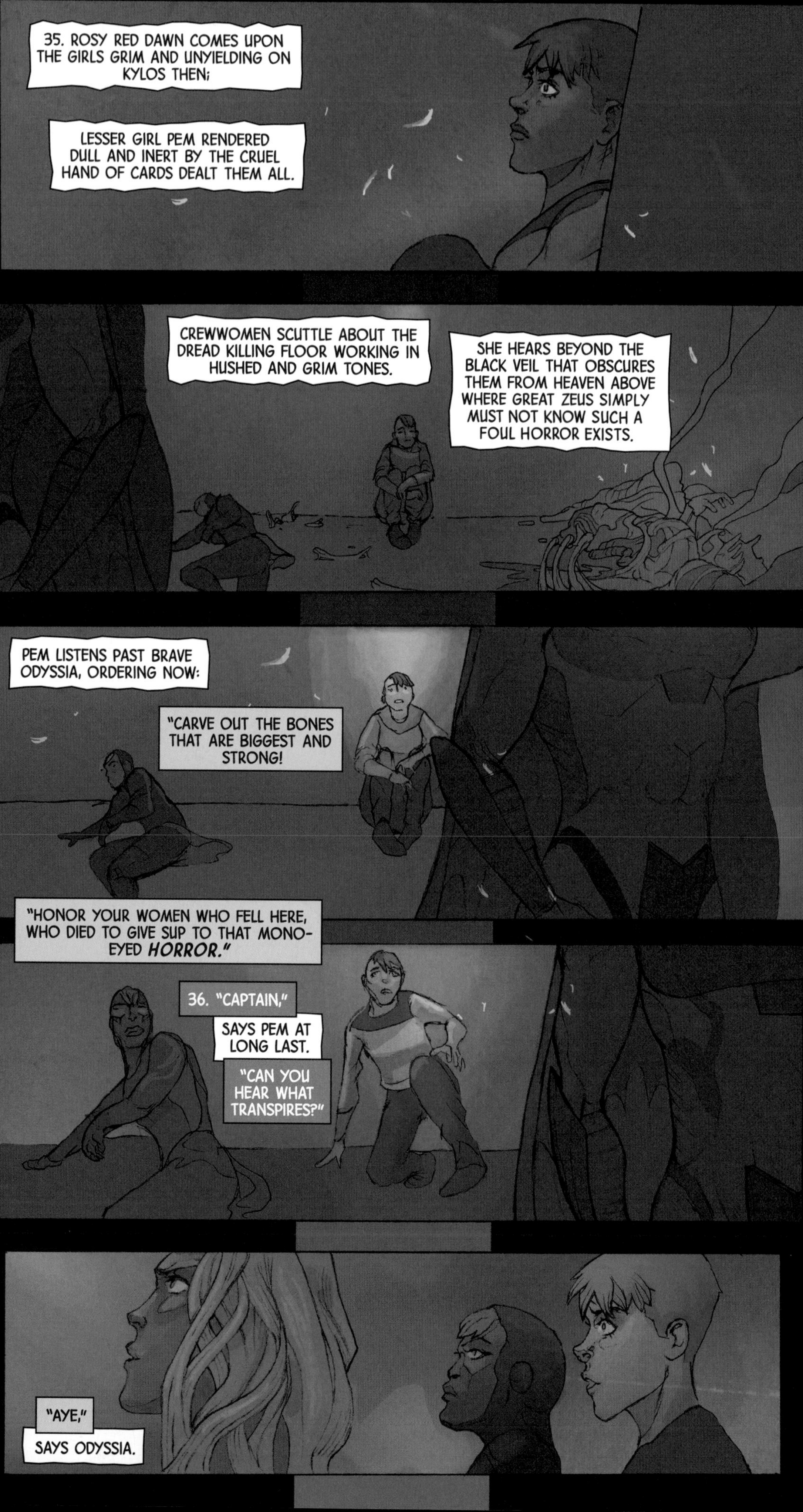
35. ROSY RED DAWN COMES UPON THE GIRLS GRIM AND UNYIELDING ON KYLOS THEN;
LESSER GIRL PEM RENDERED DULL AND INERT BY THE CRUEL HAND OF CARDS DEALT THEM ALL.
CREWWOMEN SCUTTLE ABOUT THE DREAD KILLING FLOOR WORKING IN HUSHED AND GRIM TONES.
SHE HEARS BEYOND THE BLACK VEIL THAT OBSCURES THEM FROM HEAVEN ABOVE WHERE GREAT ZEUS SIMPLY MUST NOT KNOW SUCH A FOUL HORROR EXISTS.
PEM LISTENS PAST BRAVE ODYSSIA, ORDERING NOW:
"CARVE OUT THE BONES THAT ARE BIGGEST AND STRONG!
"HONOR YOUR WOMEN WHO FELL HERE, WHO DIED TO GIVE SUP TO THAT MONO-EYED HORROR."
36. "CAPTAIN,"
SAYS PEM AT LONG LAST.
"CAN YOU HEAR WHAT TRANSPIRES?"
"AYE,"
SAYS ODYSSIA.

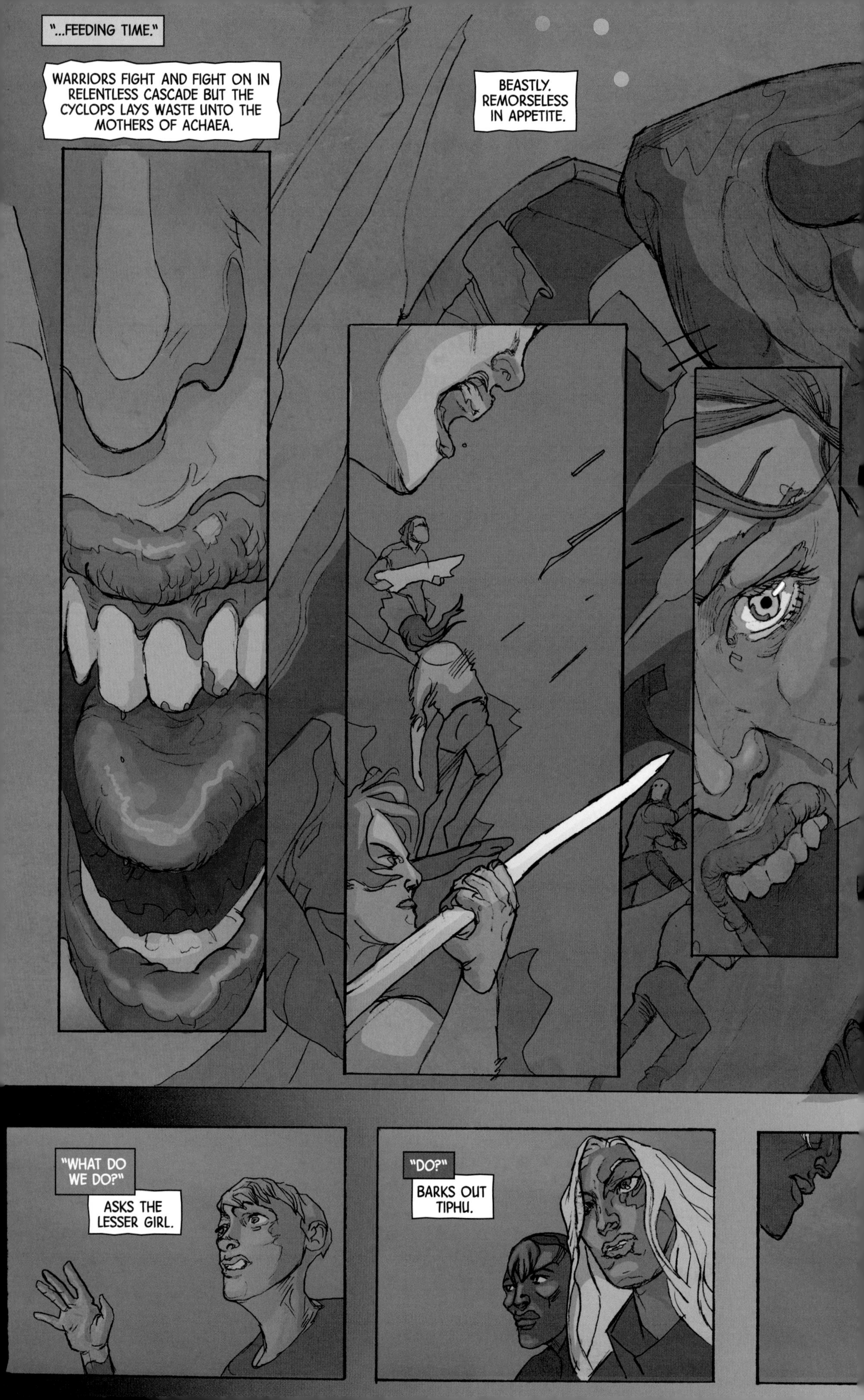
"...FEEDING TIME."
WARRIORS FIGHT AND FIGHT ON IN RELENTLESS CASCADE BUT THE CYCLOPS LAYS WASTE UNTO THE MOTHERS OF ACHAEA.
BEASTLY. REMORSELESS IN APPETITE.
"WHAT DO WE DO?"
ASKS THE LESSER GIRL.
"DO?"
BARKS OUT TIPHU.

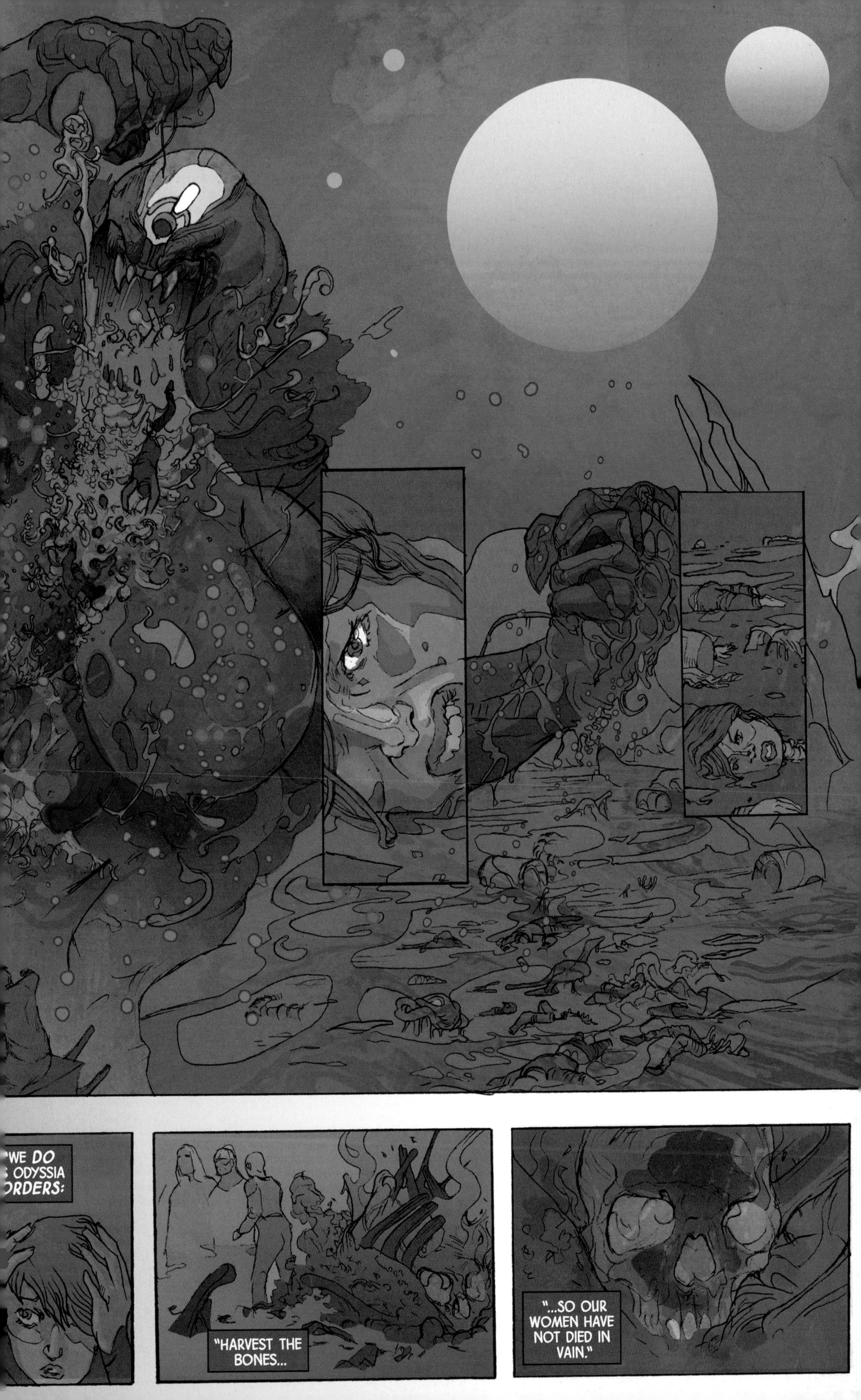

WE DO
ODYSSIA
ORDERS:
"HARVEST THE BONES...
"...SO OUR WOMEN HAVE NOT DIED IN VAIN."

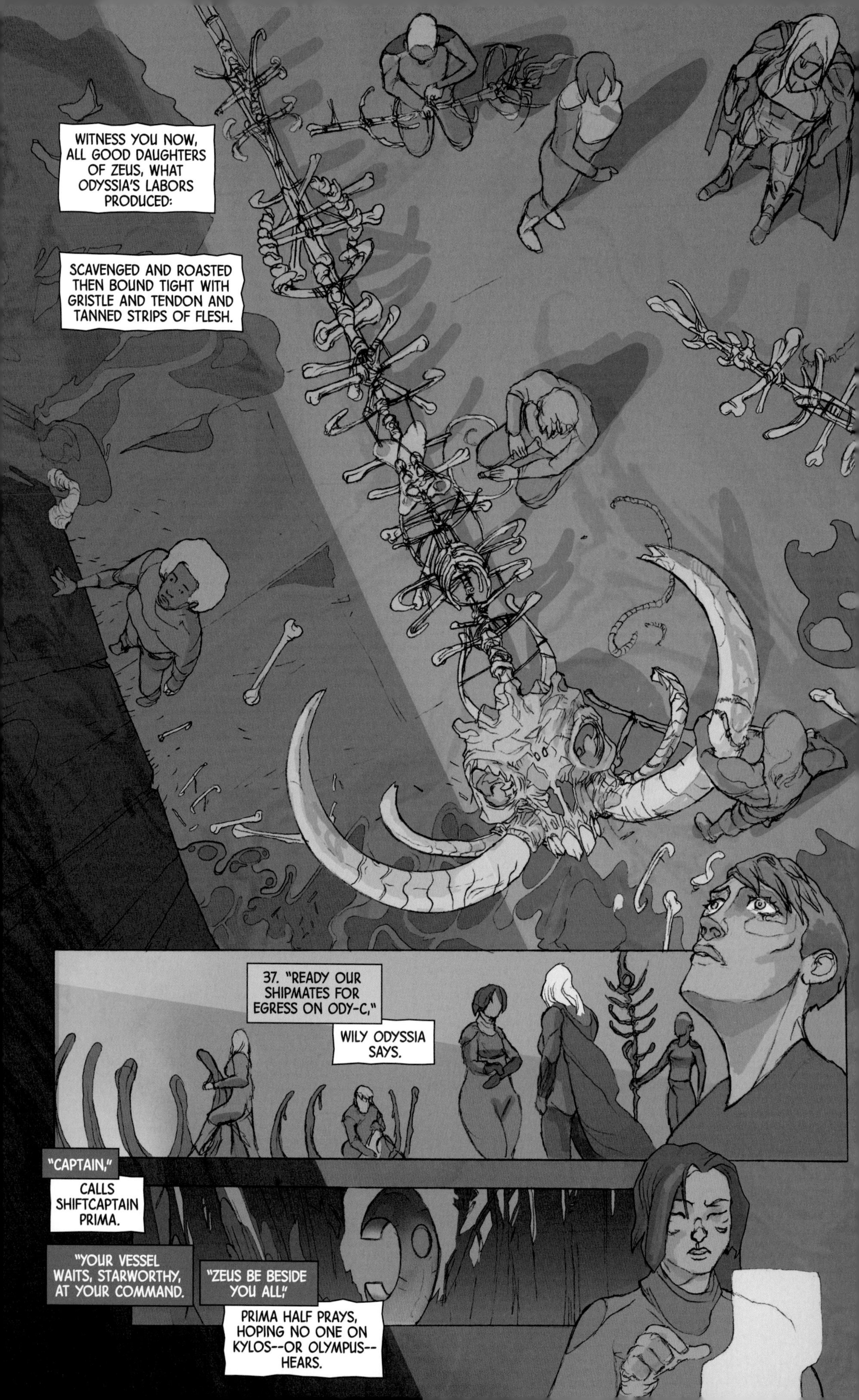
WITNESS YOU NOW, ALL GOOD DAUGHTERS OF ZEUS, WHAT ODYSSIA'S LABORS PRODUCED:
SCAVENGED AND ROASTED THEN BOUND TIGHT WITH GRISTLE AND TENDON AND TANNED STRIPS OF FLESH.
37. "READY OUR SHIPMATES FOR EGRESS ON ODY-C,"
WILY ODYSSIA SAYS.
"CAPTAIN,"
CALLS SHIFTCAPTAIN PRIMA.
"YOUR VESSEL WAITS, STARWORTHY, AT YOUR COMMAND.
"ZEUS BE BESIDE YOU ALL,"
PRIMA HALF PRAYS, HOPING NO ONE ON KYLOS--OR OLYMPUS--HEARS.

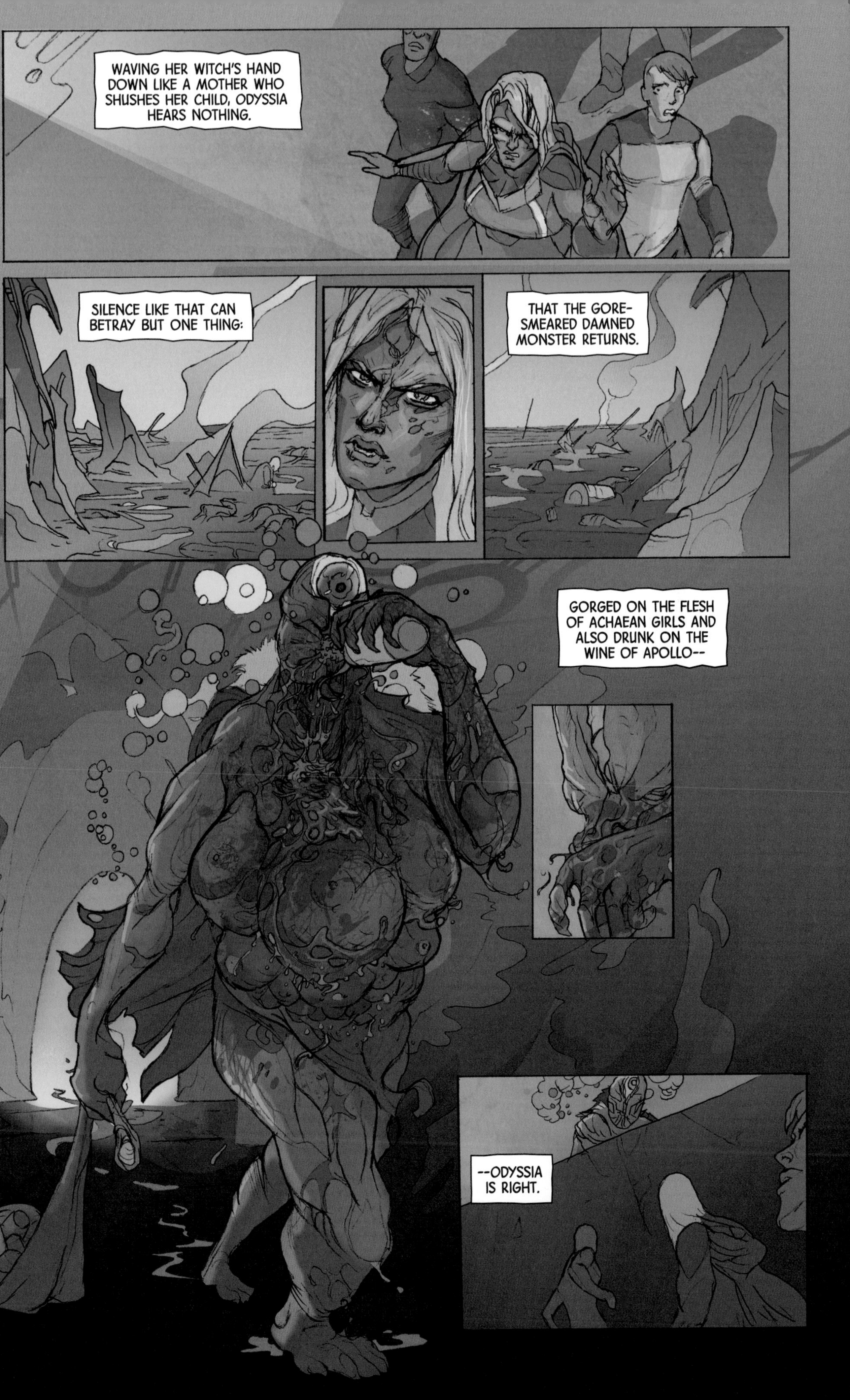
WAVING HER WITCH'S HAND DOWN LIKE A MOTHER WHO SHUSHES HER CHILD, ODYSSIA HEARS NOTHING.
SILENCE LIKE THAT CAN BETRAY BUT ONE THING:
THAT THE GORE-SMEARED DAMNED MONSTER RETURNS.
GORGED ON THE FLESH OF ACHAEAN GIRLS AND ALSO DRUNK ON THE WINE OF APOLLO--
--ODYSSIA IS RIGHT.

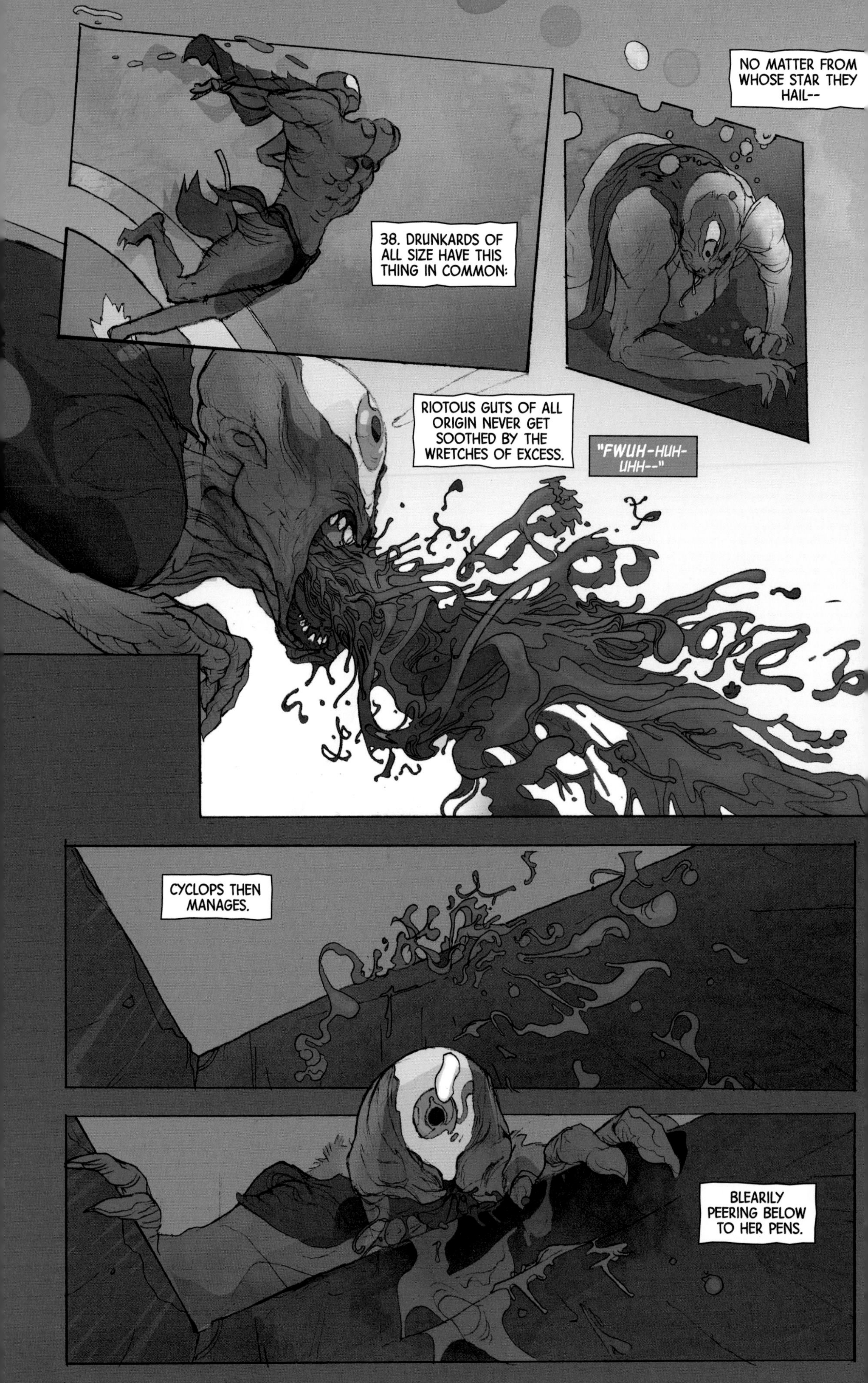
38. DRUNKARDS OF ALL SIZE HAVE THIS THING IN COMMON:
NO MATTER FROM WHOSE STAR THEY HAIL--
RIOTOUS GUTS OF ALL ORIGIN NEVER GET SOOTHED BY THE WRETCHES OF EXCESS.
"FWUH-HUH-UHH--"
CYCLOPS THEN MANAGES.
BLEARILY PEERING BELOW TO HER PENS.

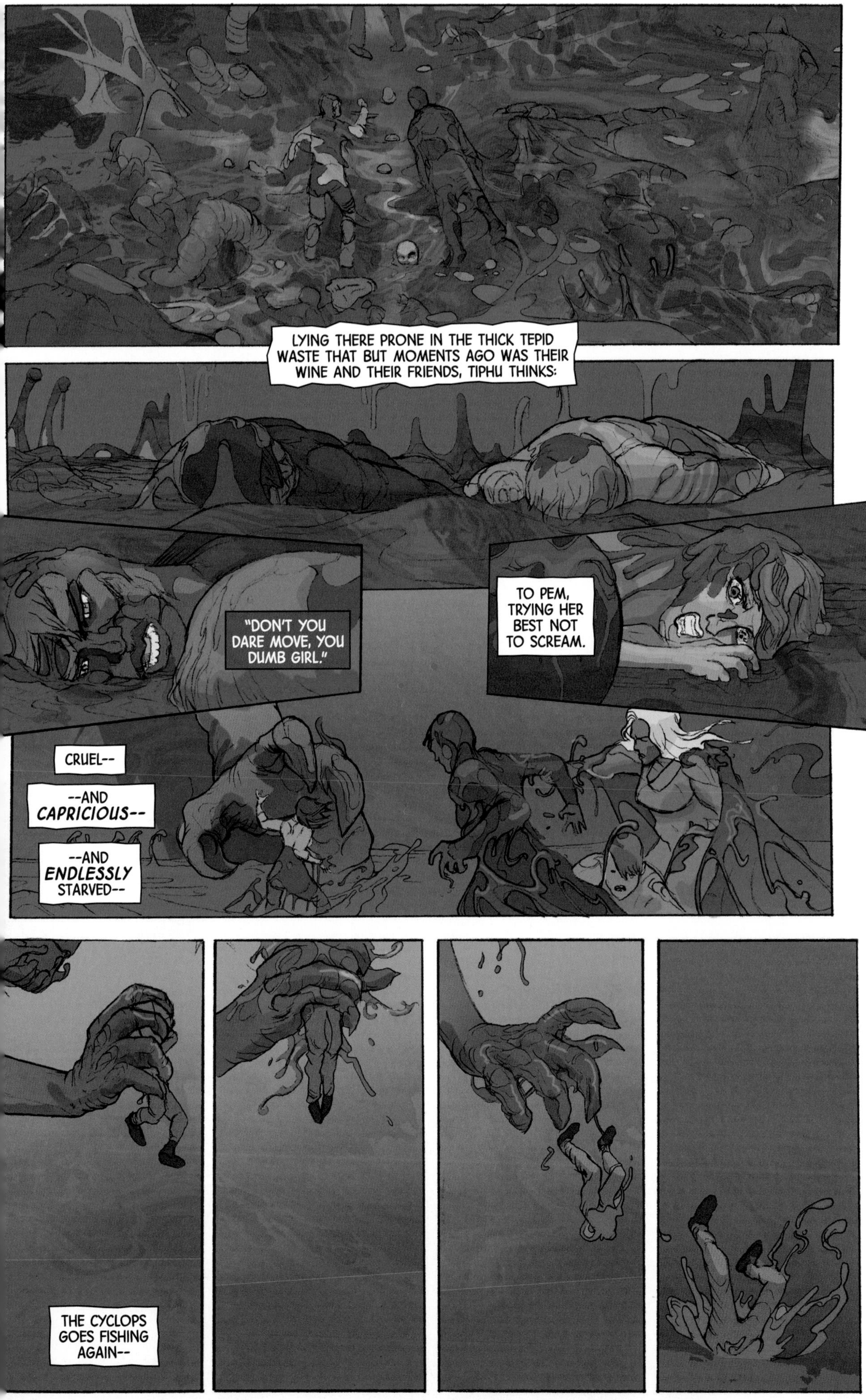
LYING THERE PRONE IN THE THICK TEPID WASTE THAT BUT MOMENTS AGO WAS THEIR WINE AND THEIR FRIENDS, TIPHU THINKS:
"DON'T YOU DARE MOVE, YOU DUMB GIRL."
TO PEM, TRYING HER BEST NOT TO SCREAM.
CRUEL--
--AND CAPRICIOUS--
--AND ENDLESSLY STARVED--
THE CYCLOPS GOES FISHING AGAIN--

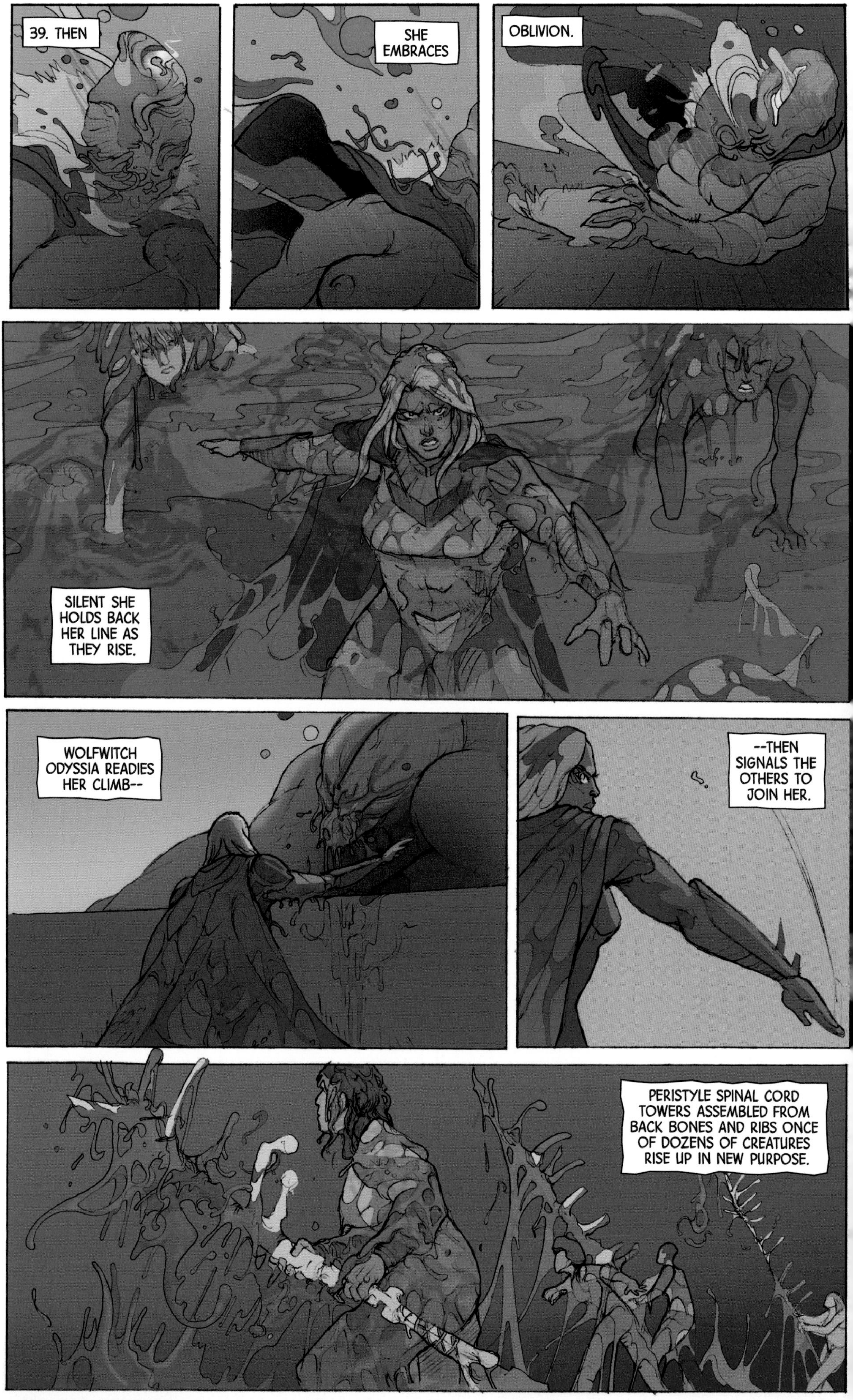

39. THEN
SHE EMBRACES
OBLIVION.
SILENT SHE HOLDS BACK HER LINE AS THEY RISE.
WOLFWITCH ODYSSIA READIES HER CLIMB--
--THEN SIGNALS THE OTHERS TO JOIN HER.
PERISTYLE SPINAL CORD TOWERS ASSEMBLED FROM BACK BONES AND RIBS ONCE OF DOZENS OF CREATURES RISE UP IN NEW PURPOSE.

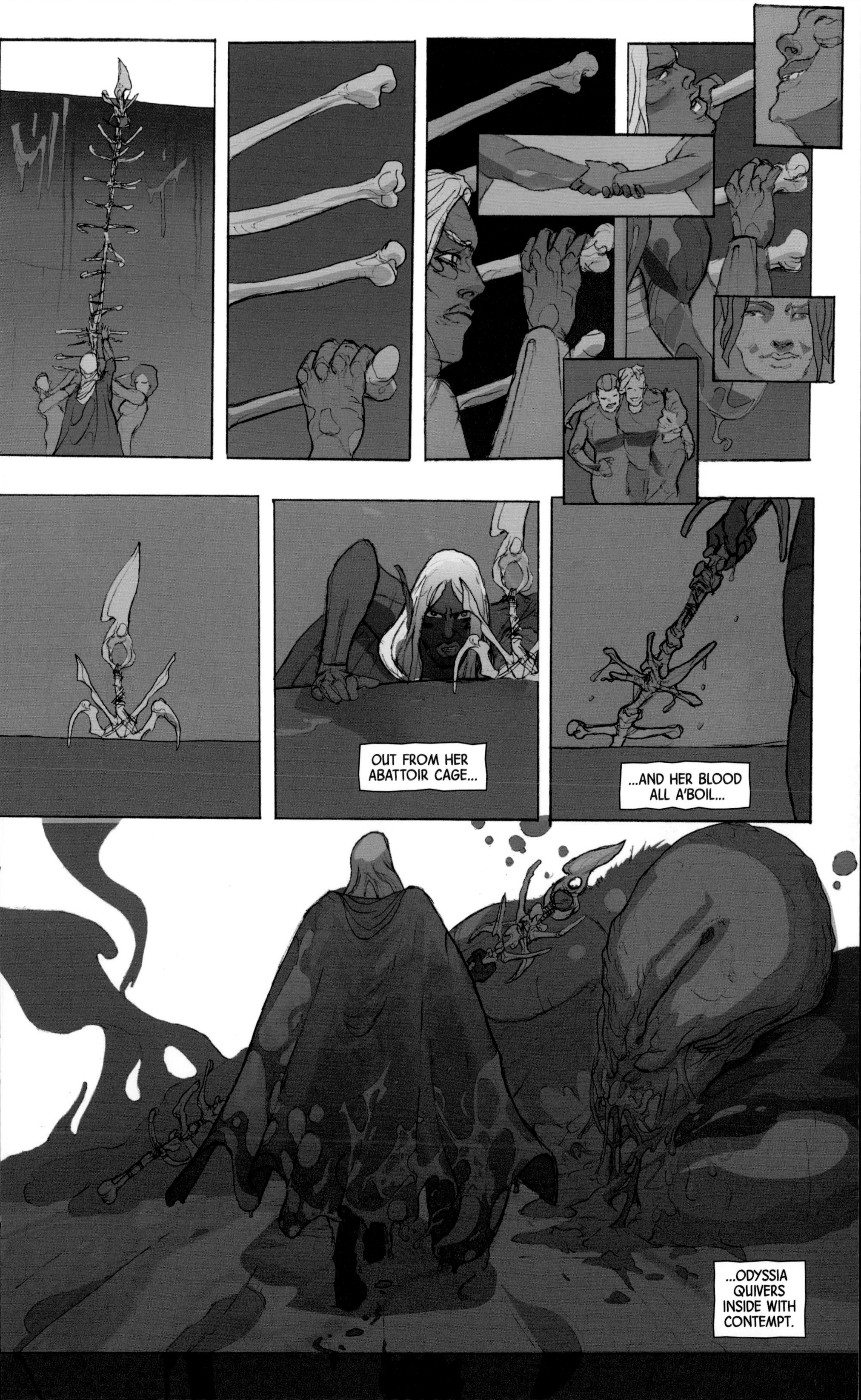
OUT FROM HER ABATTOIR CAGE...
...AND HER BLOOD ALL A'BOIL...
...ODYSSIA QUIVERS INSIDE WITH CONTEMPT.

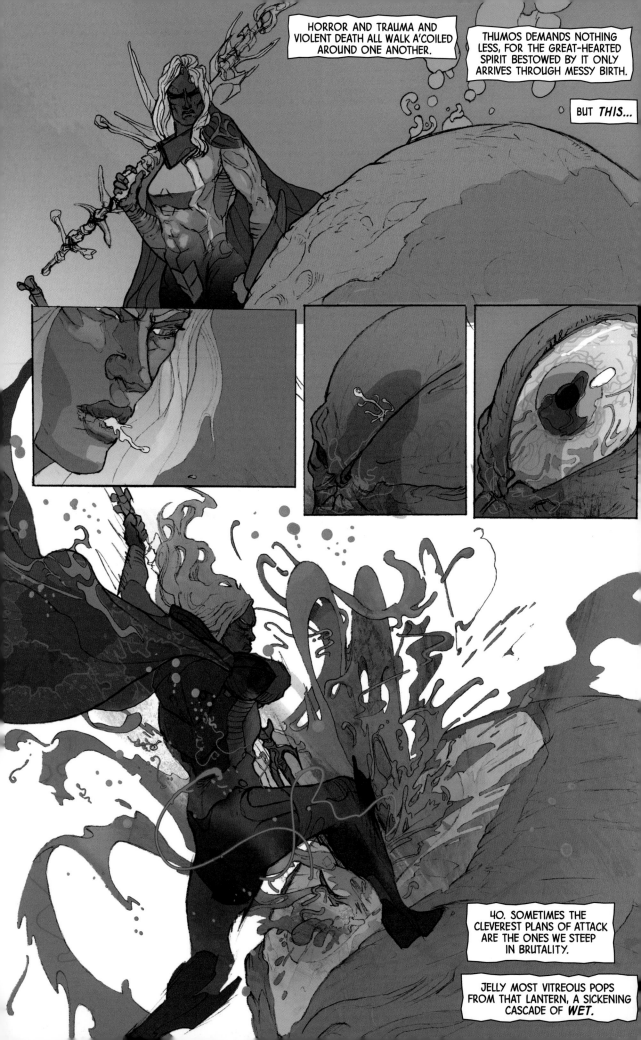

HORROR AND TRAUMA AND VIOLENT DEATH ALL WALK A'COILED AROUND ONE ANOTHER.

THUMOS DEMANDS NOTHING LESS, FOR THE GREAT-HEARTED SPIRIT BESTOWED BY IT ONLY ARRIVES THROUGH MESSY BIRTH.

BUT *THIS*...

40. SOMETIMES THE CLEVEREST PLANS OF ATTACK ARE THE ONES WE STEEP IN BRUTALITY.

JELLY MOST VITREOUS POPS FROM THAT LANTERN, A SICKENING CASCADE OF *WET*.

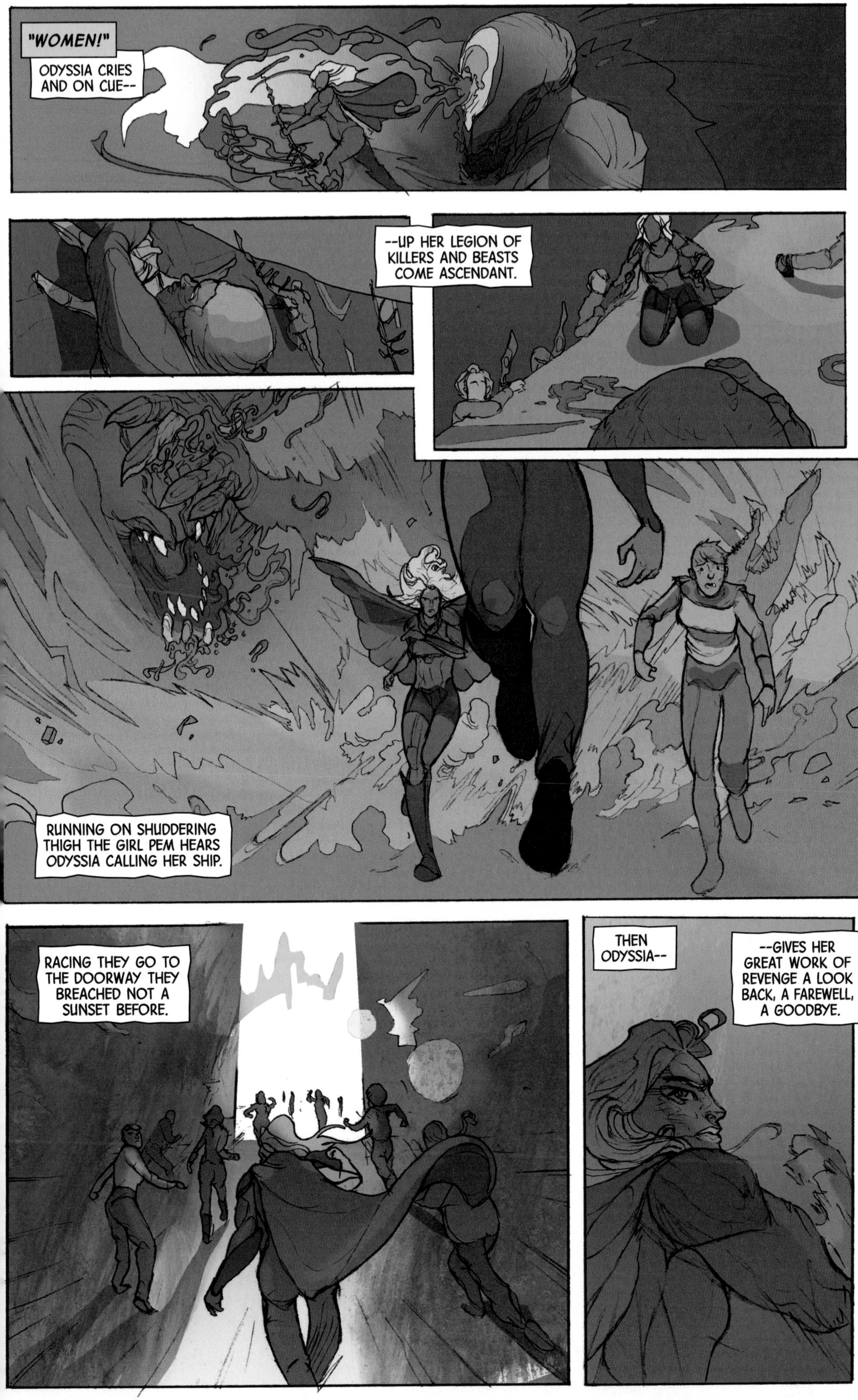
"WOMEN!"
ODYSSIA CRIES AND ON CUE--
--UP HER LEGION OF KILLERS AND BEASTS COME ASCENDANT.
RUNNING ON SHUDDERING THIGH THE GIRL PEM HEARS ODYSSIA CALLING HER SHIP.
RACING THEY GO TO THE DOORWAY THEY BREACHED NOT A SUNSET BEFORE.
THEN ODYSSIA--
--GIVES HER GREAT WORK OF REVENGE A LOOK BACK, A FAREWELL, A GOODBYE.

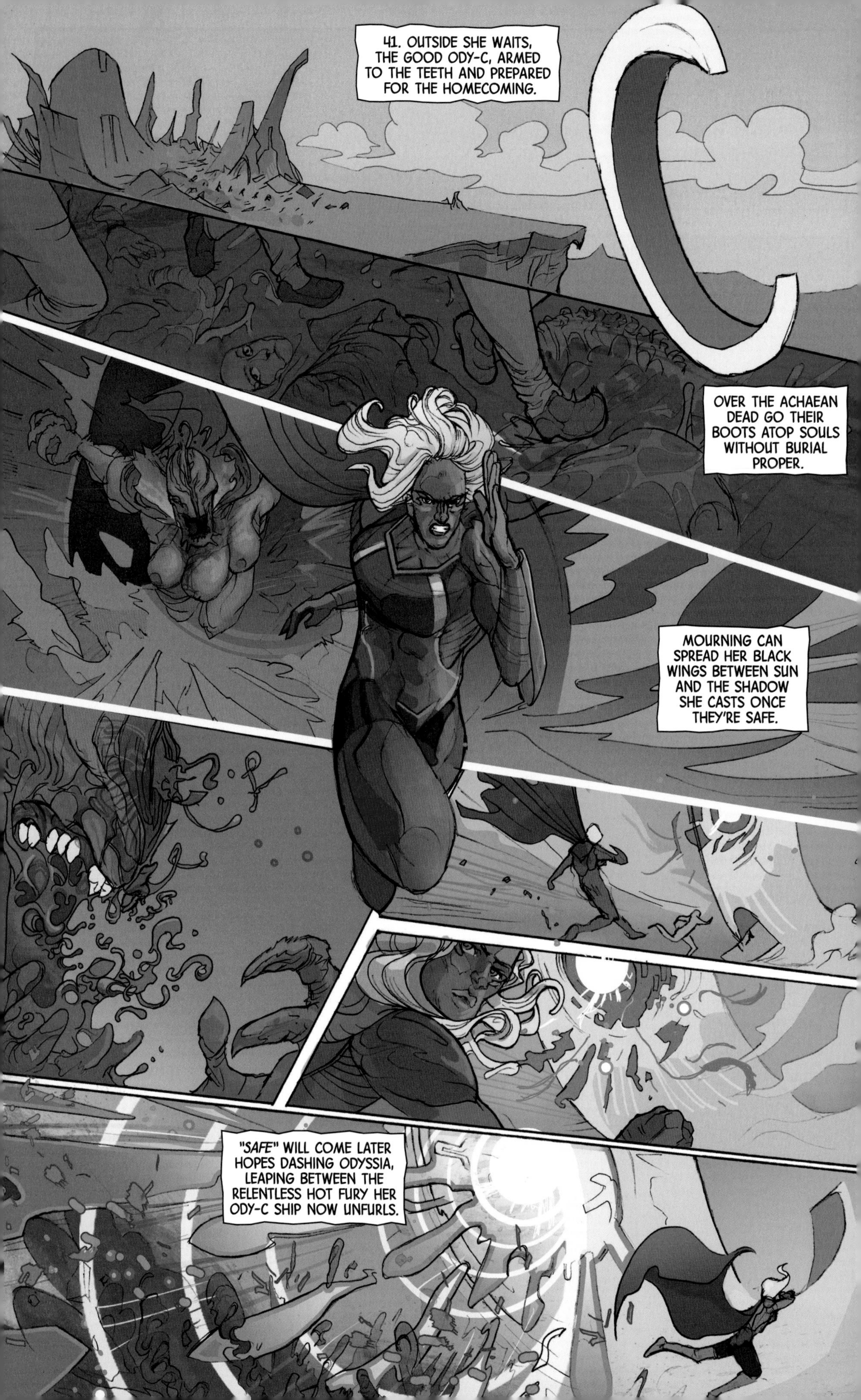
41. OUTSIDE SHE WAITS, THE GOOD ODY-C, ARMED TO THE TEETH AND PREPARED FOR THE HOMECOMING.
OVER THE ACHAEAN DEAD GO THEIR BOOTS ATOP SOULS WITHOUT BURIAL PROPER.
MOURNING CAN SPREAD HER BLACK WINGS BETWEEN SUN AND THE SHADOW SHE CASTS ONCE THEY'RE SAFE.
"*SAFE*" WILL COME LATER HOPES DASHING ODYSSIA, LEAPING BETWEEN THE RELENTLESS HOT FURY HER ODY-C SHIP NOW UNFURLS.

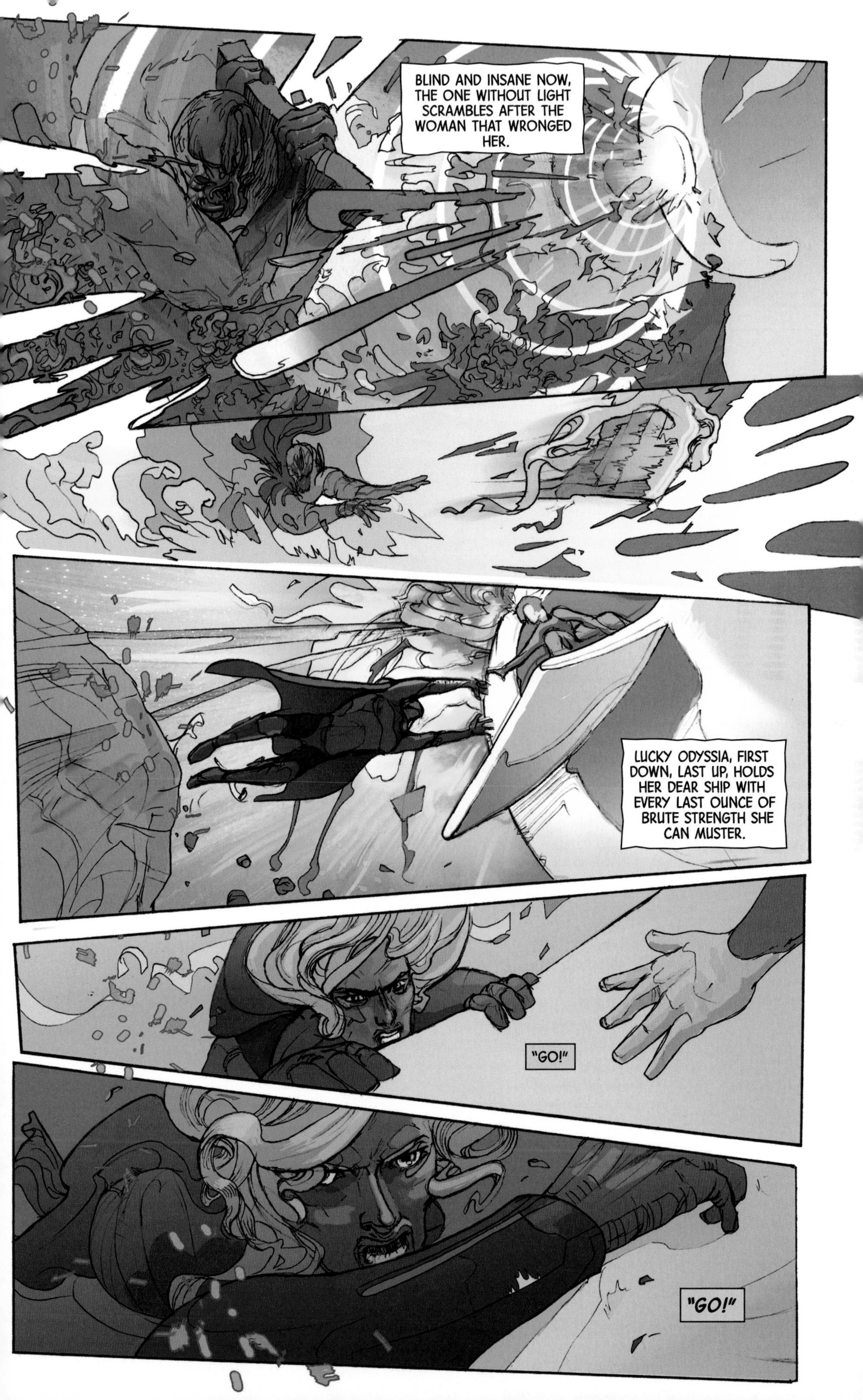
BLIND AND INSANE NOW, THE ONE WITHOUT LIGHT SCRAMBLES AFTER THE WOMAN THAT WRONGED HER.
LUCKY ODYSSIA, FIRST DOWN, LAST UP, HOLDS HER DEAR SHIP WITH EVERY LAST OUNCE OF BRUTE STRENGTH SHE CAN MUSTER.
"GO!"
"GO!"

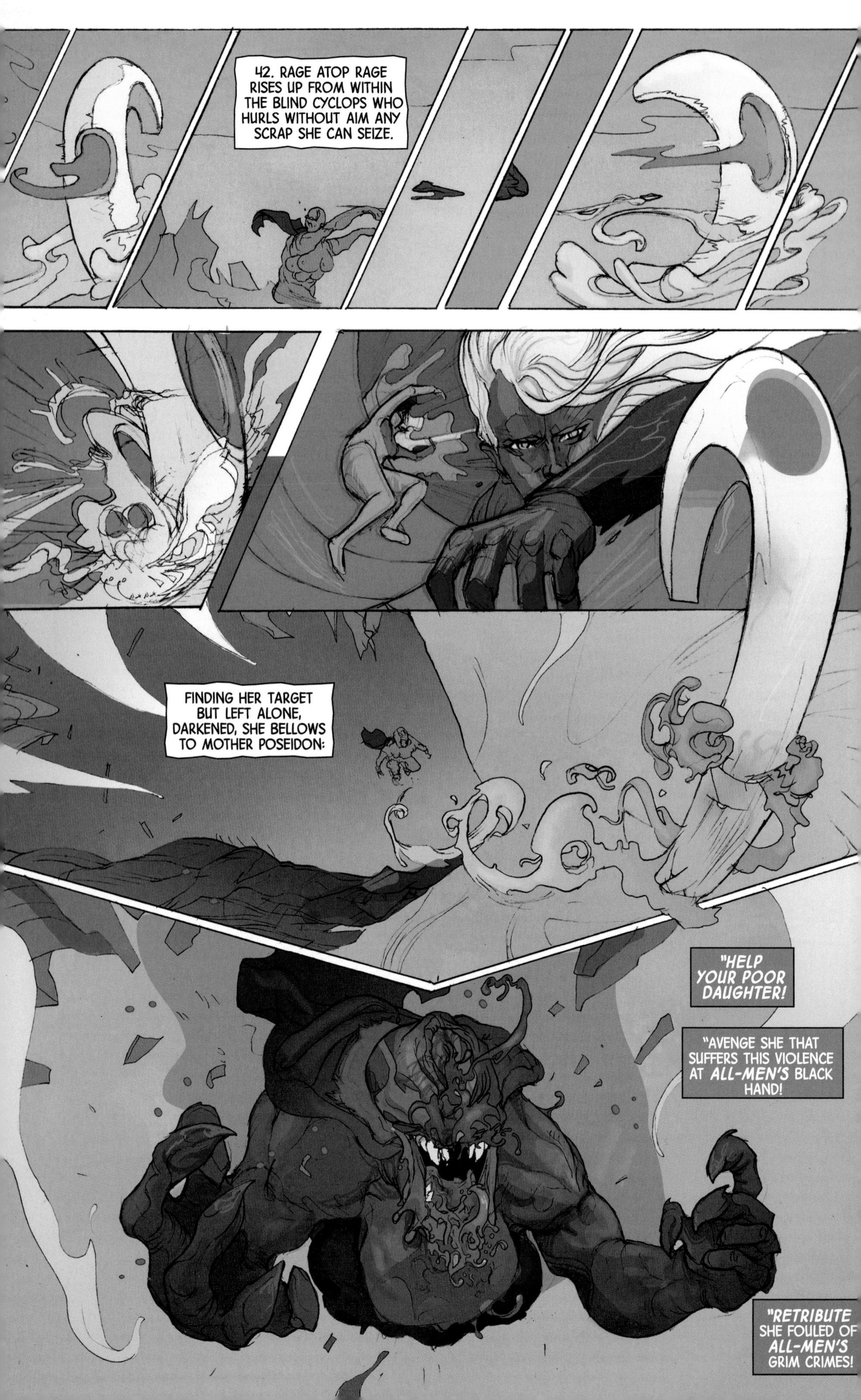
42. RAGE ATOP RAGE RISES UP FROM WITHIN THE BLIND CYCLOPS WHO HURLS WITHOUT AIM ANY SCRAP SHE CAN SEIZE.
FINDING HER TARGET BUT LEFT ALONE, DARKENED, SHE BELLOWS TO MOTHER POSEIDON:
"HELP YOUR POOR DAUGHTER!
"AVENGE SHE THAT SUFFERS THIS VIOLENCE AT ALL-MEN'S BLACK HAND!
"RETRIBUTE SHE FOULED OF ALL-MEN'S GRIM CRIMES!

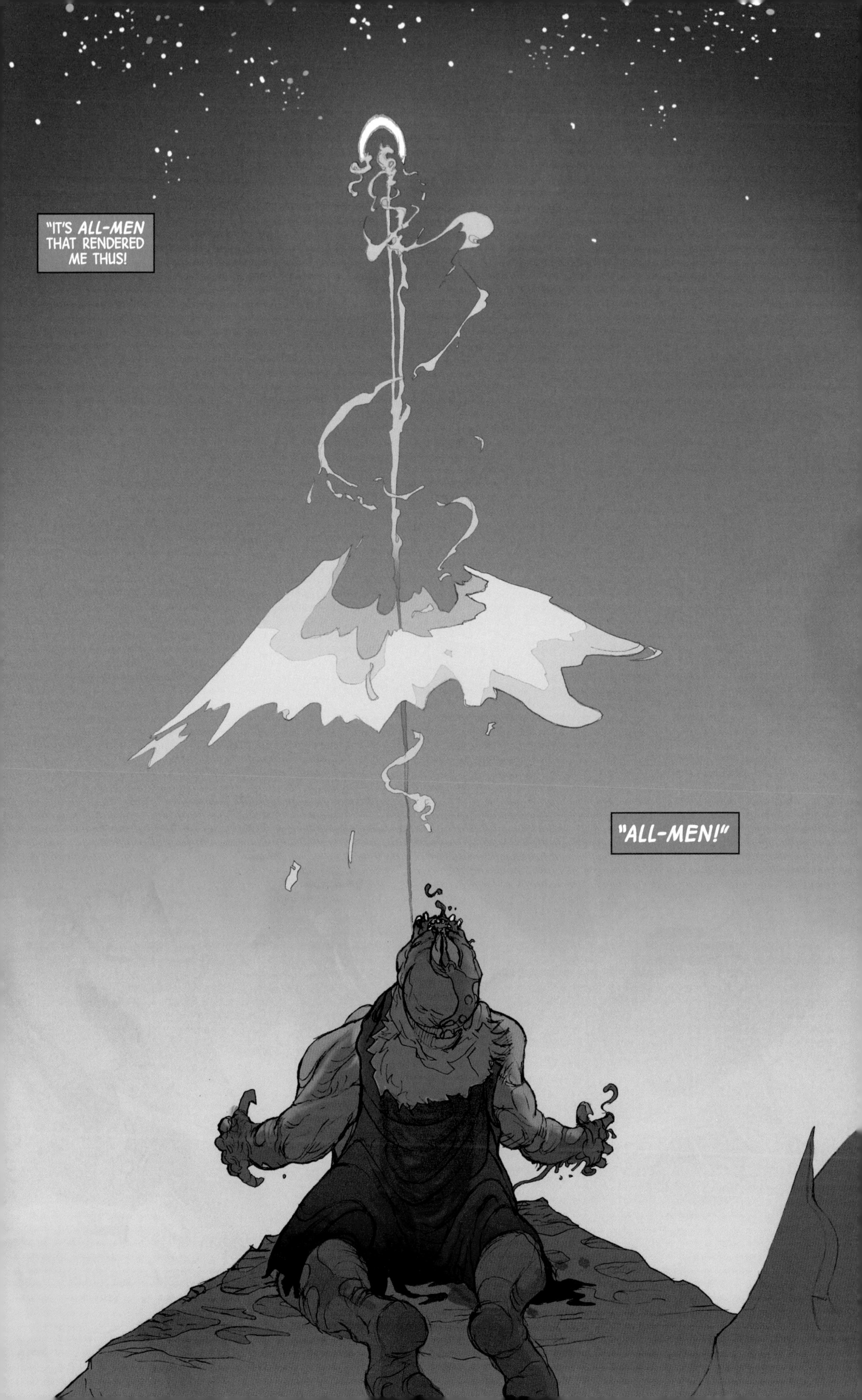
"IT'S ALL-MEN THAT RENDERED ME THUS!
"ALL-MEN!"

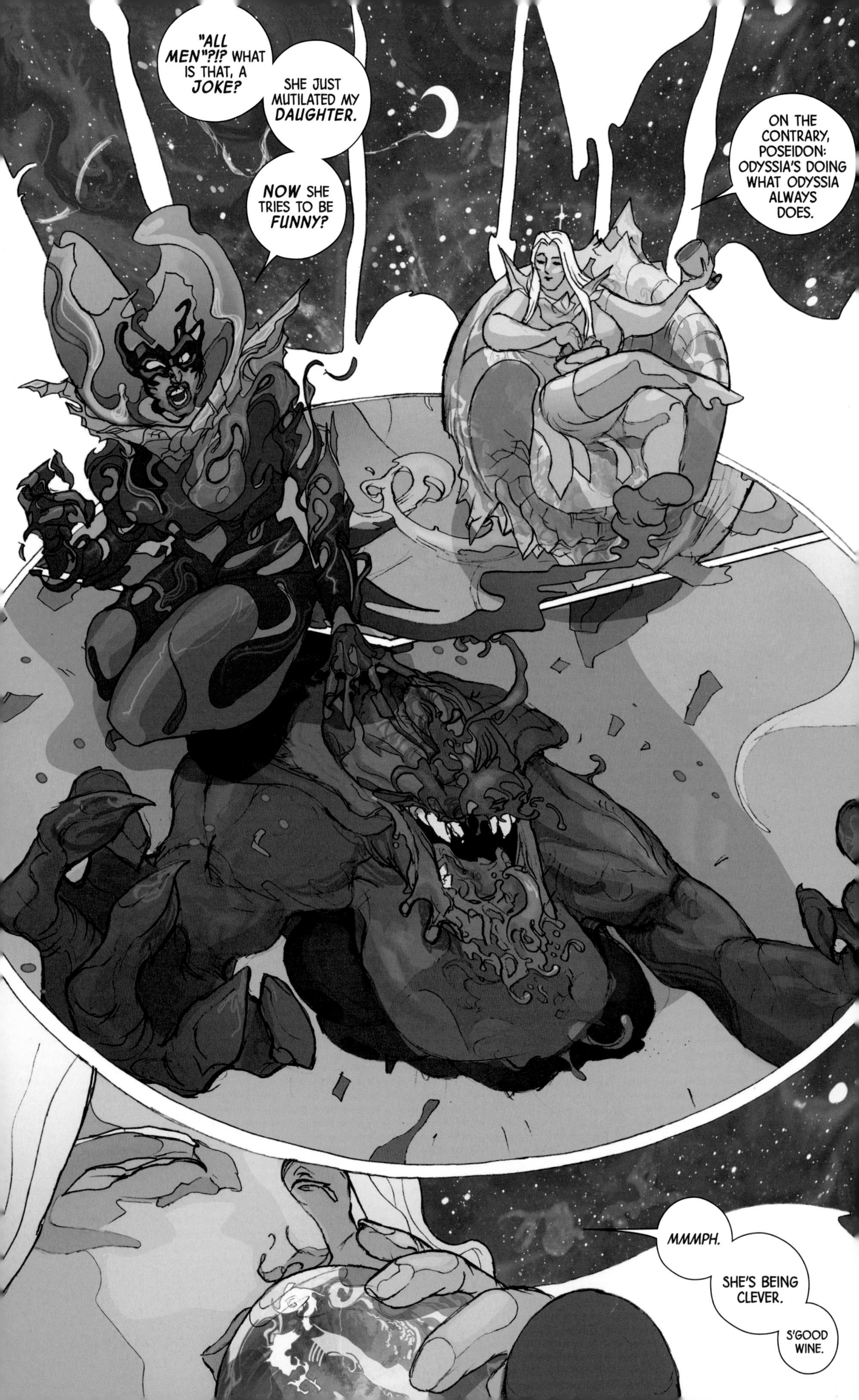
"ALL MEN"?!? WHAT IS THAT, A JOKE?
SHE JUST MUTILATED MY DAUGHTER.
NOW SHE TRIES TO BE FUNNY?
ON THE CONTRARY, POSEIDON: ODYSSIA'S DOING WHAT ODYSSIA ALWAYS DOES.
MMMPH.
SHE'S BEING CLEVER.
S'GOOD WINE.

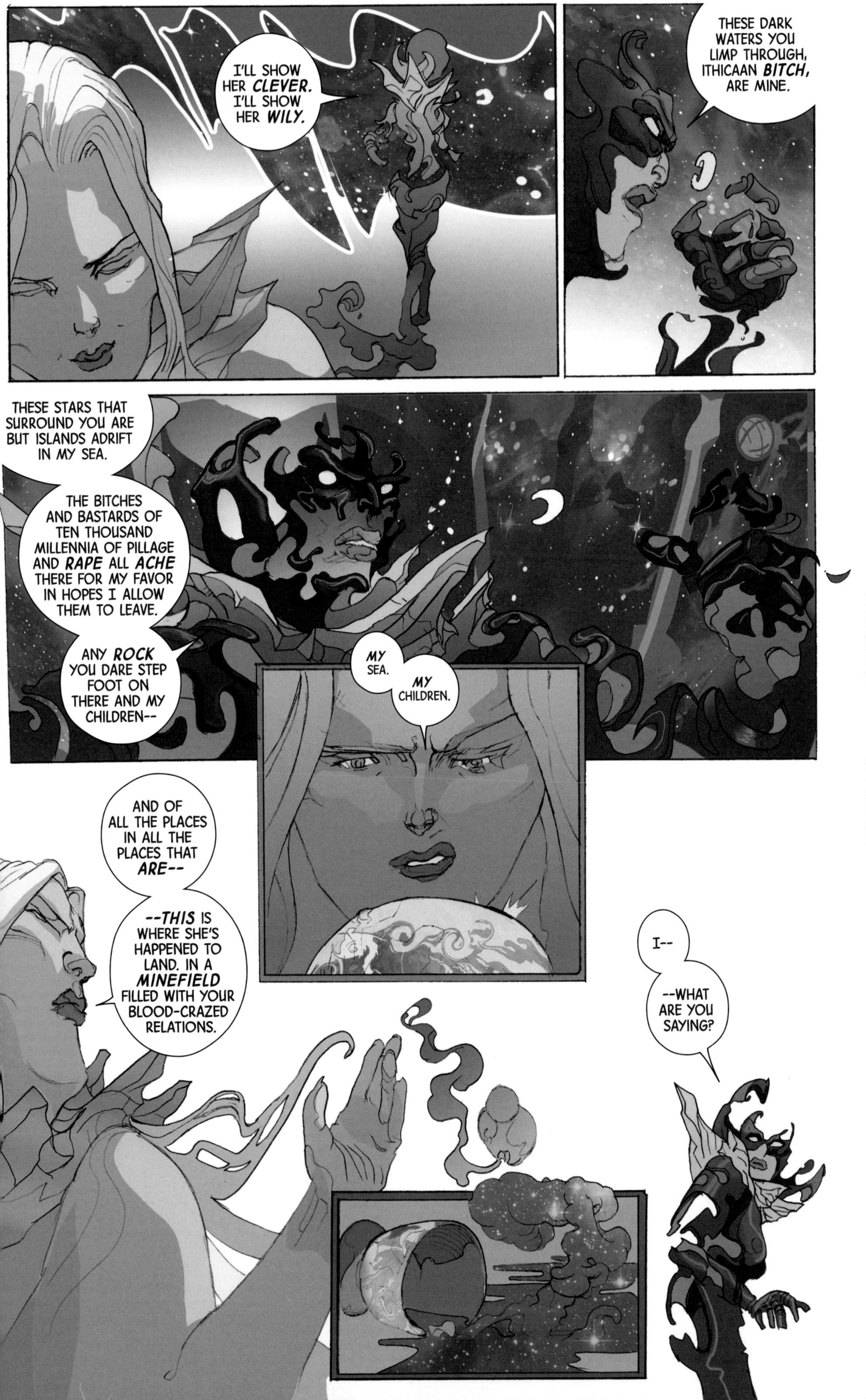
I'LL SHOW HER CLEVER. I'LL SHOW HER WILY.
THESE DARK WATERS YOU LIMP THROUGH, ITHICAAN BITCH, ARE MINE.
THESE STARS THAT SURROUND YOU ARE BUT ISLANDS ADRIFT IN MY SEA.
THE BITCHES AND BASTARDS OF TEN THOUSAND MILLENNIA OF PILLAGE AND RAPE ALL ACHE THERE FOR MY FAVOR IN HOPES I ALLOW THEM TO LEAVE.
ANY ROCK YOU DARE STEP FOOT ON THERE AND MY CHILDREN--
MY SEA.
MY CHILDREN.
AND OF ALL THE PLACES IN ALL THE PLACES THAT ARE--
--THIS IS WHERE SHE'S HAPPENED TO LAND. IN A MINEFIELD FILLED WITH YOUR BLOOD-CRAZED RELATIONS.
I--
--WHAT ARE YOU SAYING?

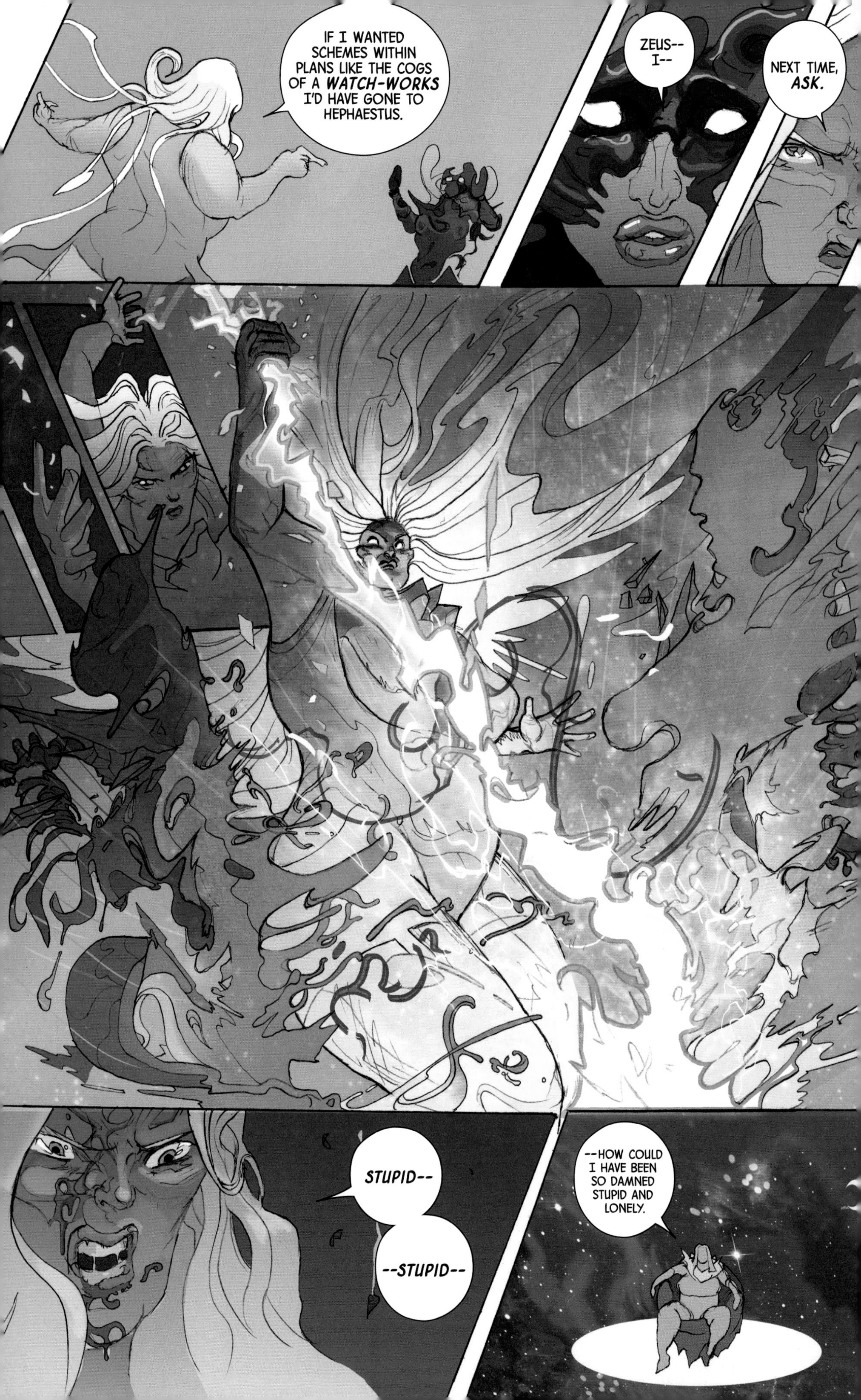
IF I WANTED SCHEMES WITHIN PLANS LIKE THE COGS OF A WATCH-WORKS I'D HAVE GONE TO HEPHAESTUS.
ZEUS-- I--
NEXT TIME, ASK.
STUPID--
--STUPID--
--HOW COULD I HAVE BEEN SO DAMNED STUPID AND LONELY.

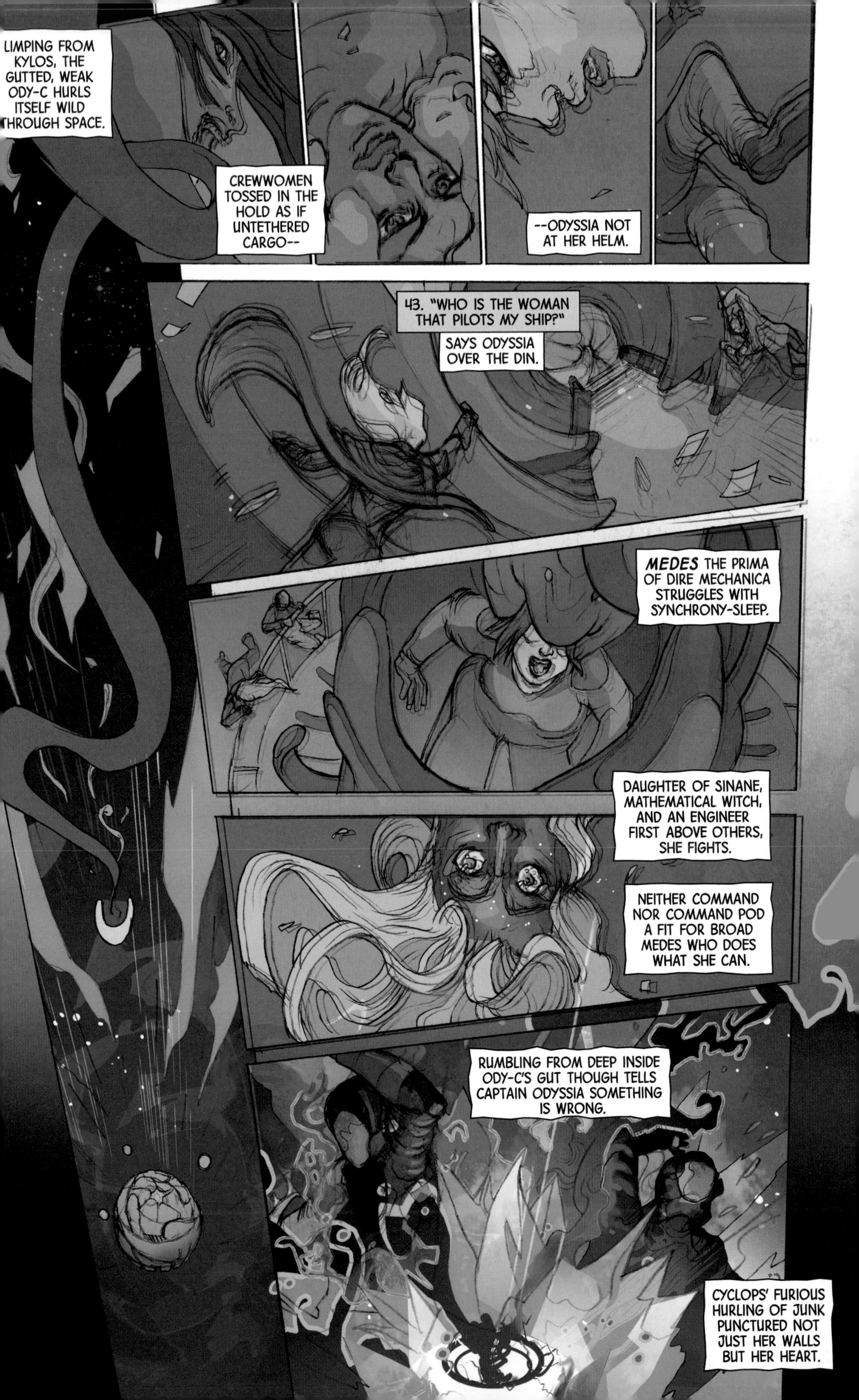
LIMPING FROM KYLOS, THE GUTTED, WEAK ODY-C HURLS ITSELF WILD THROUGH SPACE.
CREWWOMEN TOSSED IN THE HOLD AS IF UNTETHERED CARGO--
--ODYSSIA NOT AT HER HELM.
43. "WHO IS THE WOMAN THAT PILOTS MY SHIP?"
SAYS ODYSSIA OVER THE DIN.
MEDES THE PRIMA OF DIRE MECHANICA STRUGGLES WITH SYNCHRONY-SLEEP.
DAUGHTER OF SINANE, MATHEMATICAL WITCH, AND AN ENGINEER FIRST ABOVE OTHERS, SHE FIGHTS.
NEITHER COMMAND NOR COMMAND POD A FIT FOR BROAD MEDES WHO DOES WHAT SHE CAN.
RUMBLING FROM DEEP INSIDE ODY-C'S GUT THOUGH TELLS CAPTAIN ODYSSIA SOMETHING IS WRONG.
CYCLOPS' FURIOUS HURLING OF JUNK PUNCTURED NOT JUST HER WALLS BUT HER HEART.

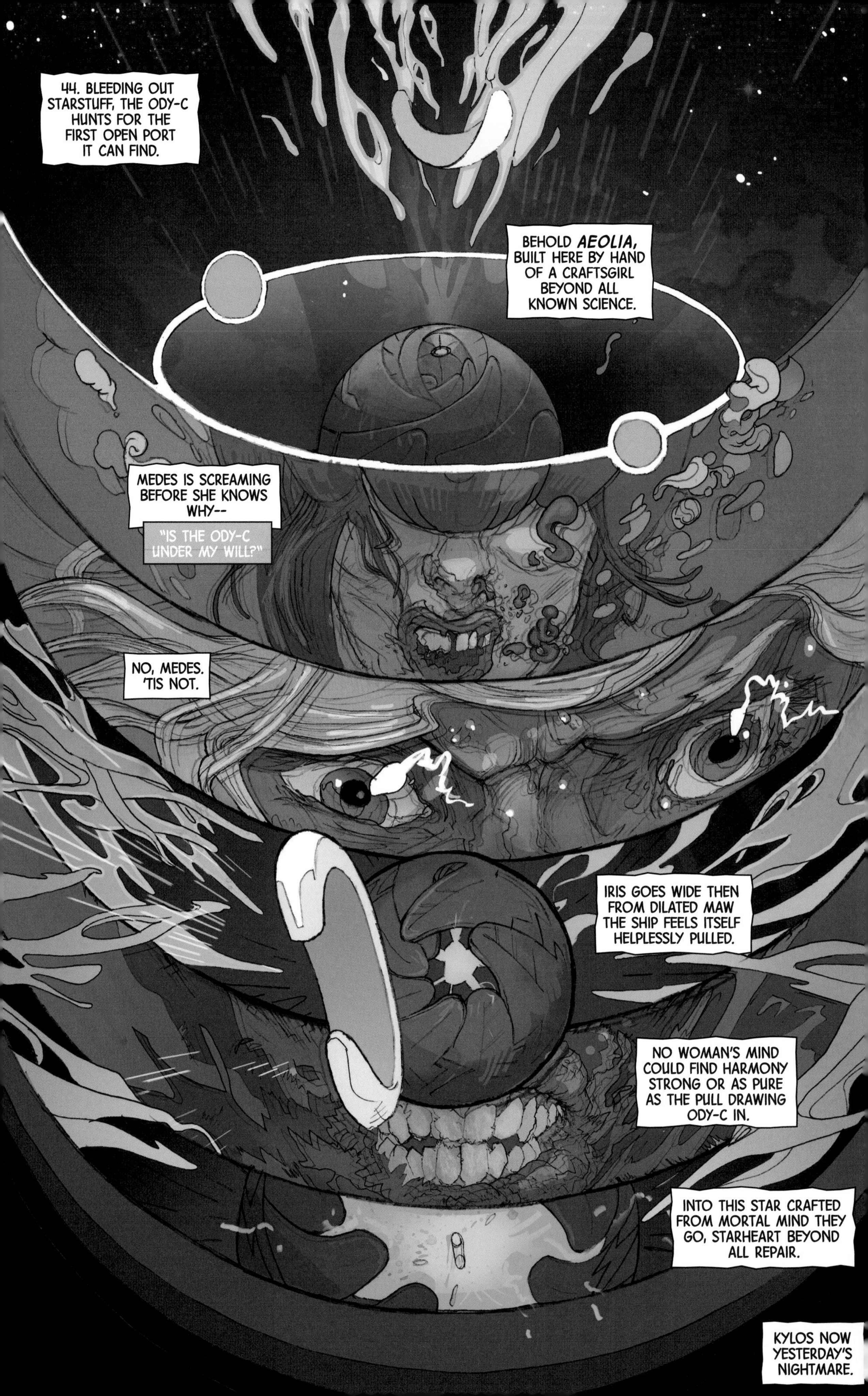
44. BLEEDING OUT STARSTUFF, THE ODY-C HUNTS FOR THE FIRST OPEN PORT IT CAN FIND.
BEHOLD AEOLIA, BUILT HERE BY HAND OF A CRAFTSGIRL BEYOND ALL KNOWN SCIENCE.
MEDES IS SCREAMING BEFORE SHE KNOWS WHY--
"IS THE ODY-C UNDER MY WILL?"
NO, MEDES. 'TIS NOT.
IRIS GOES WIDE THEN FROM DILATED MAW THE SHIP FEELS ITSELF HELPLESSLY PULLED.
NO WOMAN'S MIND COULD FIND HARMONY STRONG OR AS PURE AS THE PULL DRAWING ODY-C IN.
INTO THIS STAR CRAFTED FROM MORTAL MIND THEY GO, STARHEART BEYOND ALL REPAIR.
KYLOS NOW YESTERDAY'S NIGHTMARE.

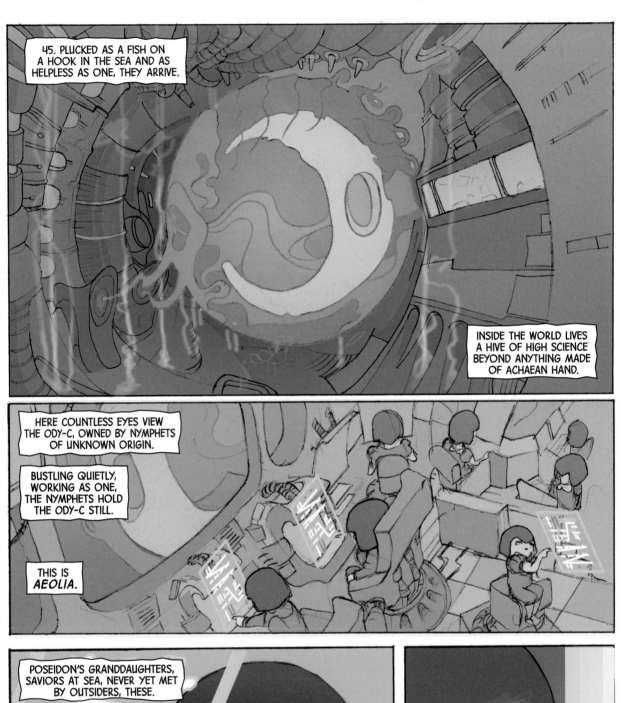

45. PLUCKED AS A FISH ON A HOOK IN THE SEA AND AS HELPLESS AS ONE, THEY ARRIVE.

INSIDE THE WORLD LIVES A HIVE OF HIGH SCIENCE BEYOND ANYTHING MADE OF ACHAEAN HAND.

HERE COUNTLESS EYES VIEW THE ODY-C, OWNED BY NYMPHETS OF UNKNOWN ORIGIN.

BUSTLING QUIETLY, WORKING AS ONE, THE NYMPHETS HOLD THE ODY-C STILL.

THIS IS AEOLIA.

POSEIDON'S GRANDDAUGHTERS, SAVIORS AT SEA, NEVER YET MET BY OUTSIDERS, THESE.

"AEOLUS..."

SAYS THE NYMPHET THAT SEEMS MOST IN CHARGE.

"TELL US, WHAT DO YOU COMMAND?"

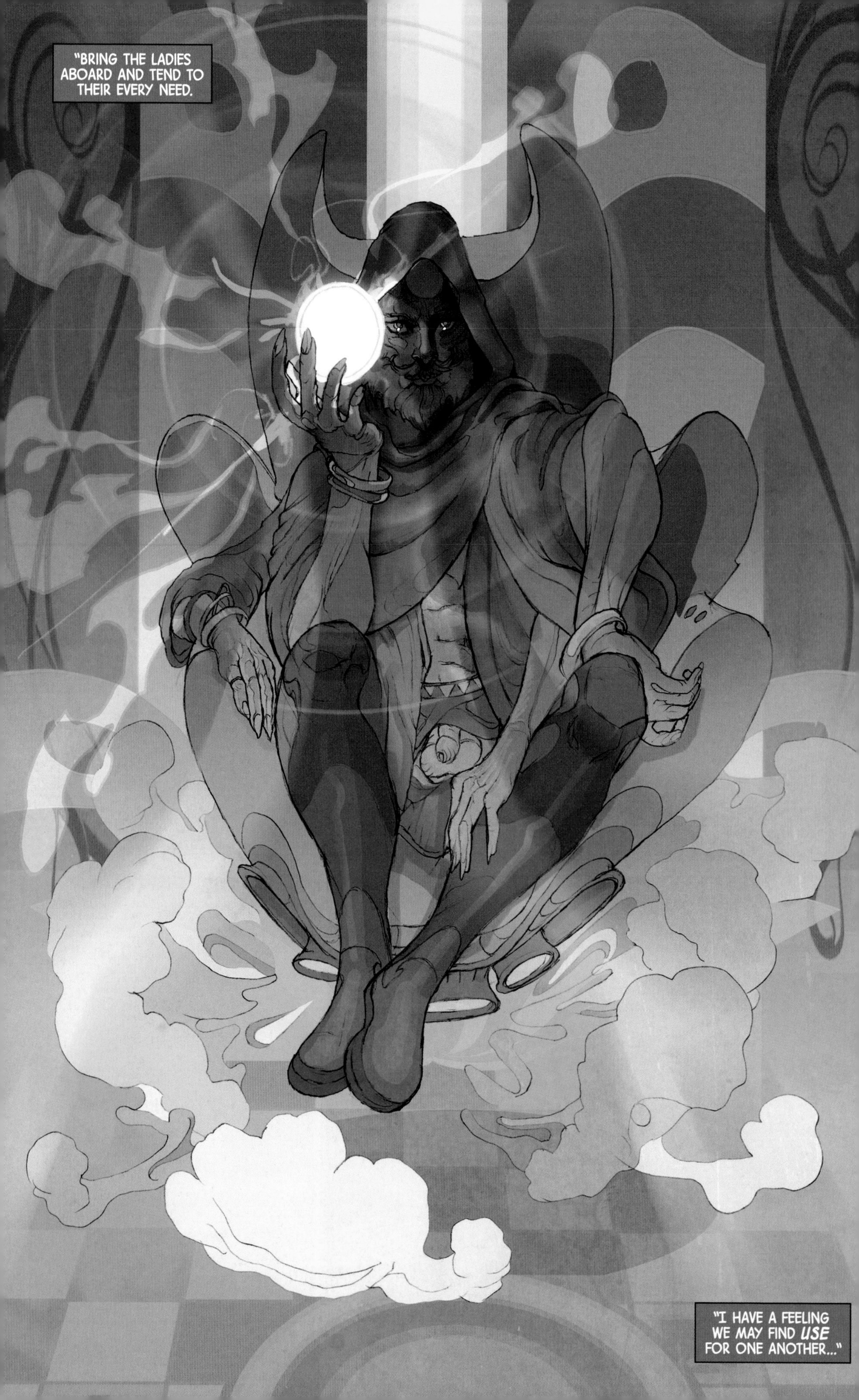
"BRING THE LADIES ABOARD AND TEND TO THEIR EVERY NEED.
"I HAVE A FEELING WE MAY FIND USE FOR ONE ANOTHER..."

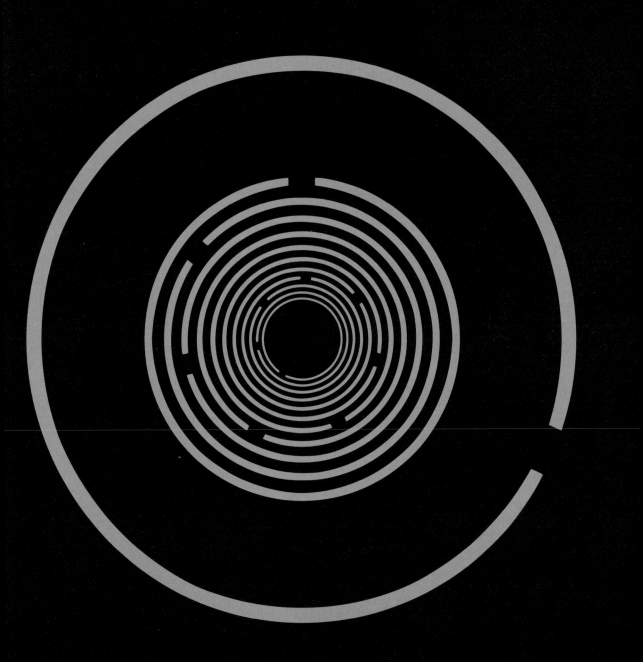

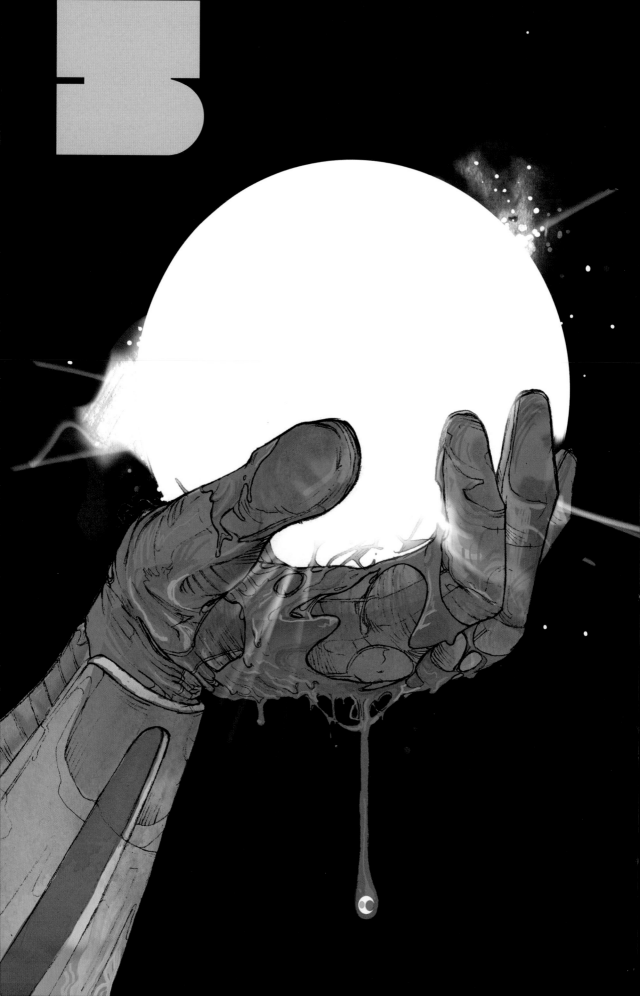

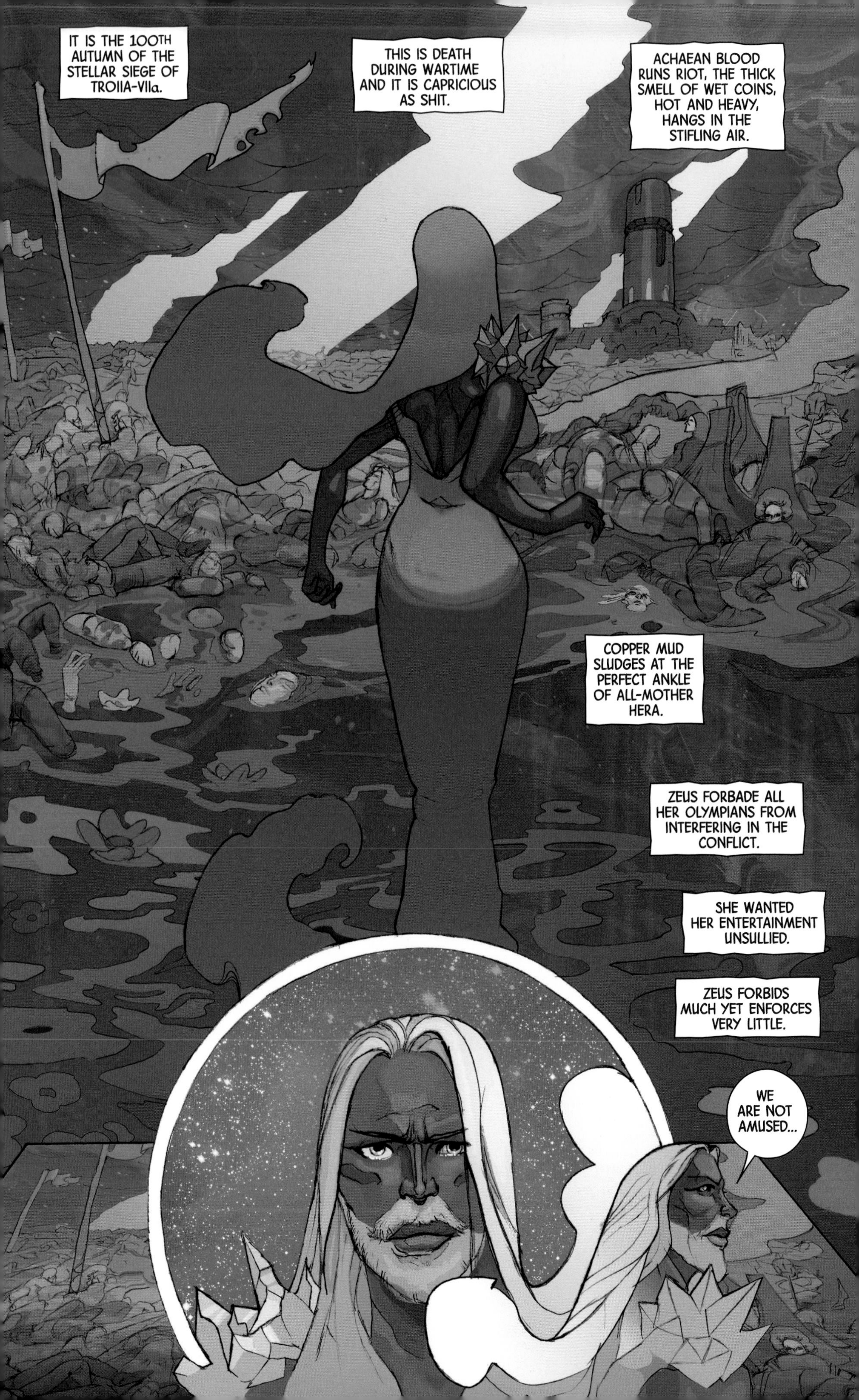

IT IS THE 100TH AUTUMN OF THE STELLAR SIEGE OF TROIIA-VIIa.
THIS IS DEATH DURING WARTIME AND IT IS CAPRICIOUS AS SHIT.
ACHAEAN BLOOD RUNS RIOT, THE THICK SMELL OF WET COINS, HOT AND HEAVY, HANGS IN THE STIFLING AIR.
COPPER MUD SLUDGES AT THE PERFECT ANKLE OF ALL-MOTHER HERA.
ZEUS FORBADE ALL HER OLYMPIANS FROM INTERFERING IN THE CONFLICT.
SHE WANTED HER ENTERTAINMENT UNSULLIED.
ZEUS FORBIDS MUCH YET ENFORCES VERY LITTLE.
WE ARE NOT AMUSED...

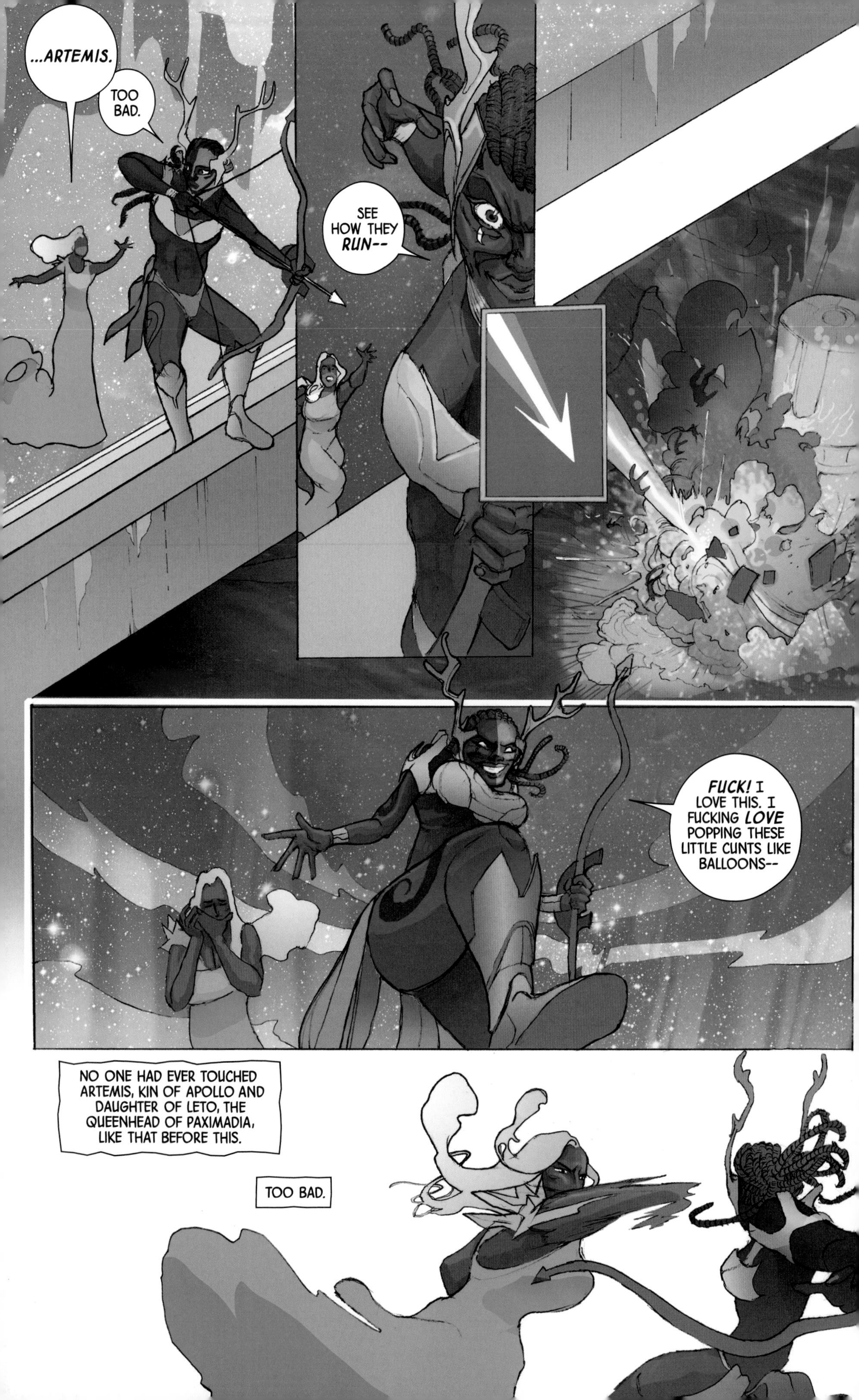
...ARTEMIS.
TOO BAD.
SEE HOW THEY RUN--
FUCK! I LOVE THIS. I FUCKING LOVE POPPING THESE LITTLE CUNTS LIKE BALLOONS--
NO ONE HAD EVER TOUCHED ARTEMIS, KIN OF APOLLO AND DAUGHTER OF LETO, THE QUEENHEAD OF PAXIMADIA, LIKE THAT BEFORE THIS.
TOO BAD.

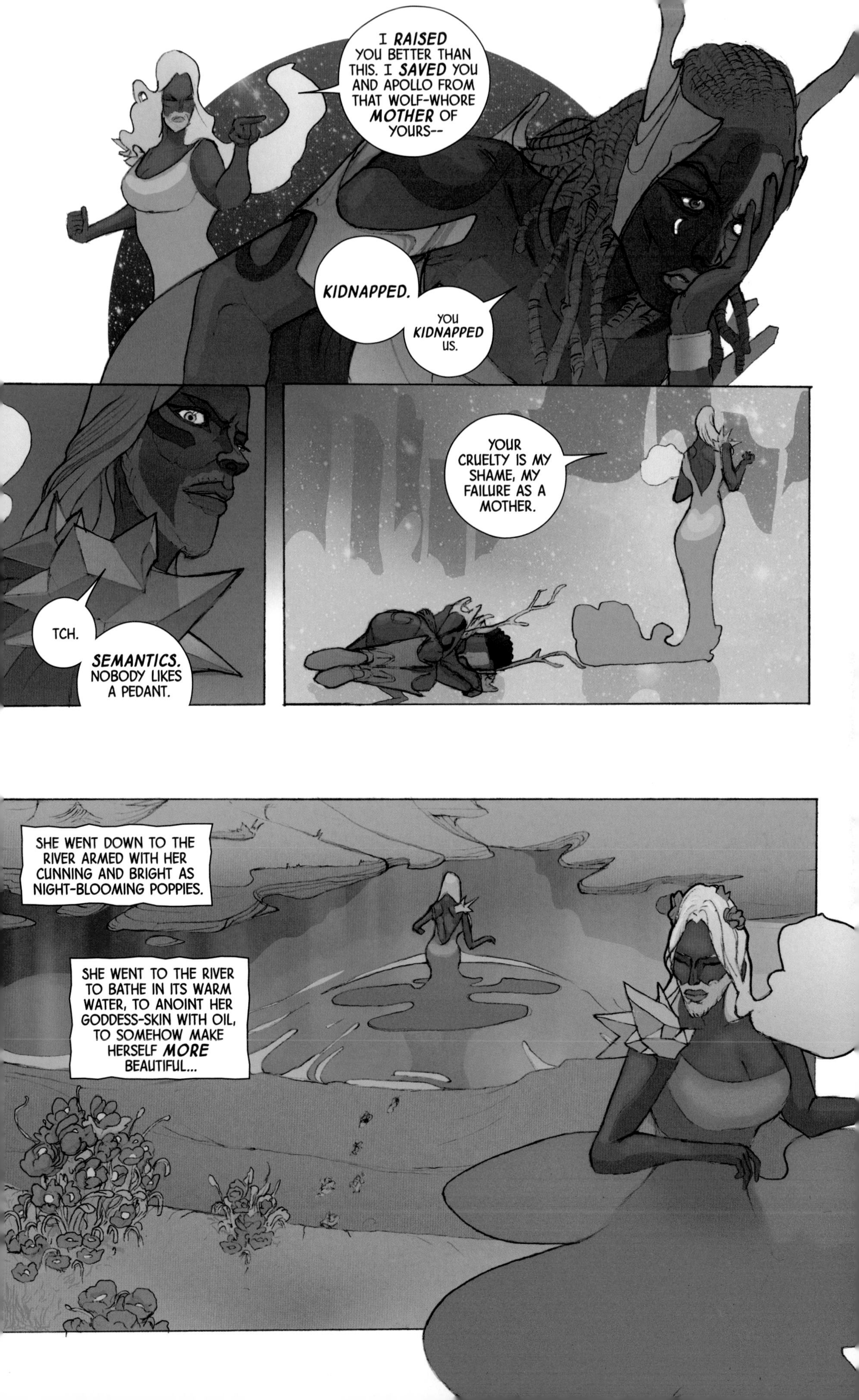
I RAISED YOU BETTER THAN THIS. I SAVED YOU AND APOLLO FROM THAT WOLF-WHORE MOTHER OF YOURS--
KIDNAPPED.
YOU KIDNAPPED US.
TCH.
SEMANTICS. NOBODY LIKES A PEDANT.
YOUR CRUELTY IS MY SHAME, MY FAILURE AS A MOTHER.
SHE WENT DOWN TO THE RIVER ARMED WITH HER CUNNING AND BRIGHT AS NIGHT-BLOOMING POPPIES.
SHE WENT TO THE RIVER TO BATHE IN ITS WARM WATER, TO ANOINT HER GODDESS-SKIN WITH OIL, TO SOMEHOW MAKE HERSELF MORE BEAUTIFUL...

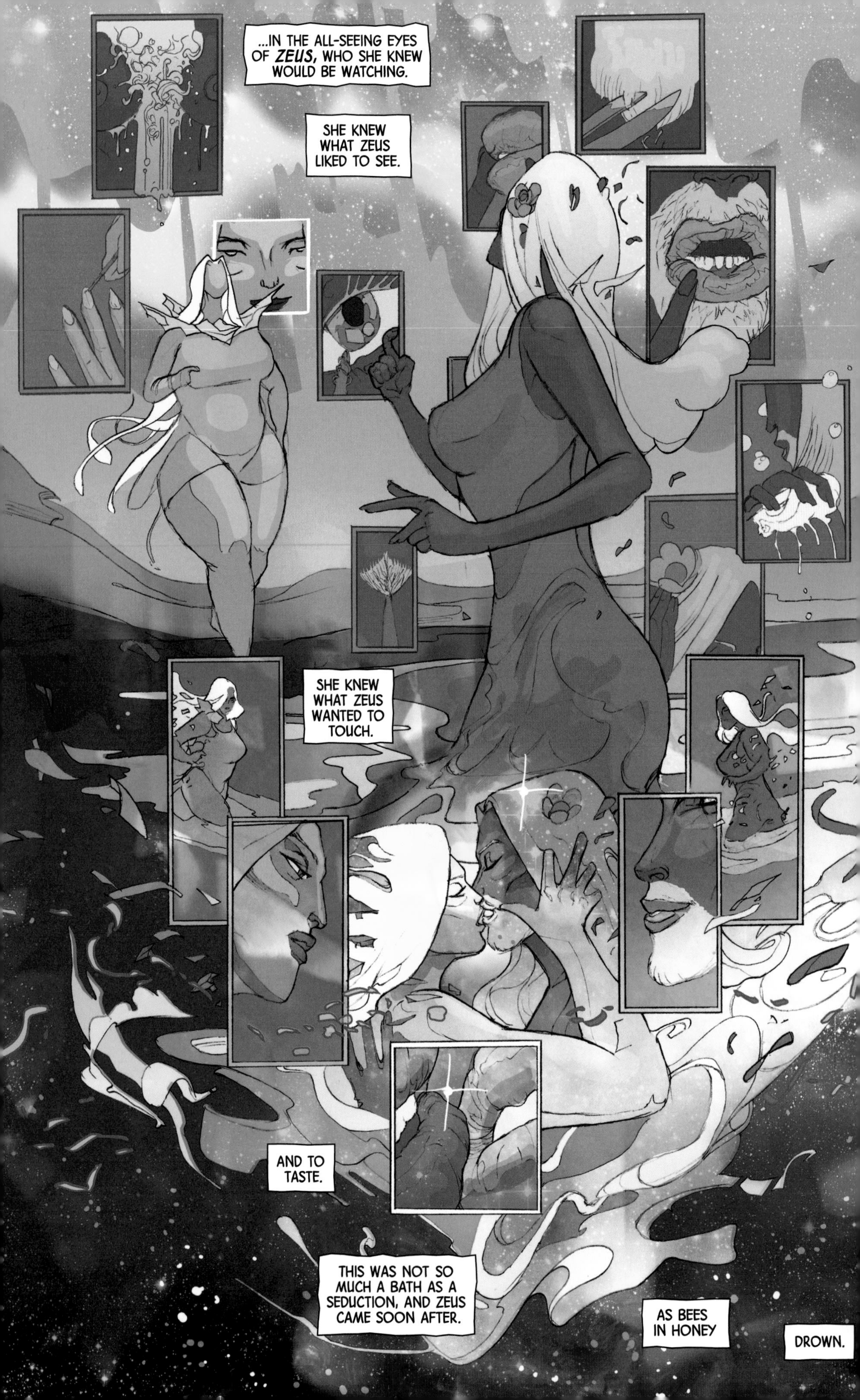
...IN THE ALL-SEEING EYES OF ZEUS, WHO SHE KNEW WOULD BE WATCHING.
SHE KNEW WHAT ZEUS LIKED TO SEE.
SHE KNEW WHAT ZEUS WANTED TO TOUCH.
AND TO TASTE.
THIS WAS NOT SO MUCH A BATH AS A SEDUCTION, AND ZEUS CAME SOON AFTER.
AS BEES IN HONEY
DROWN.

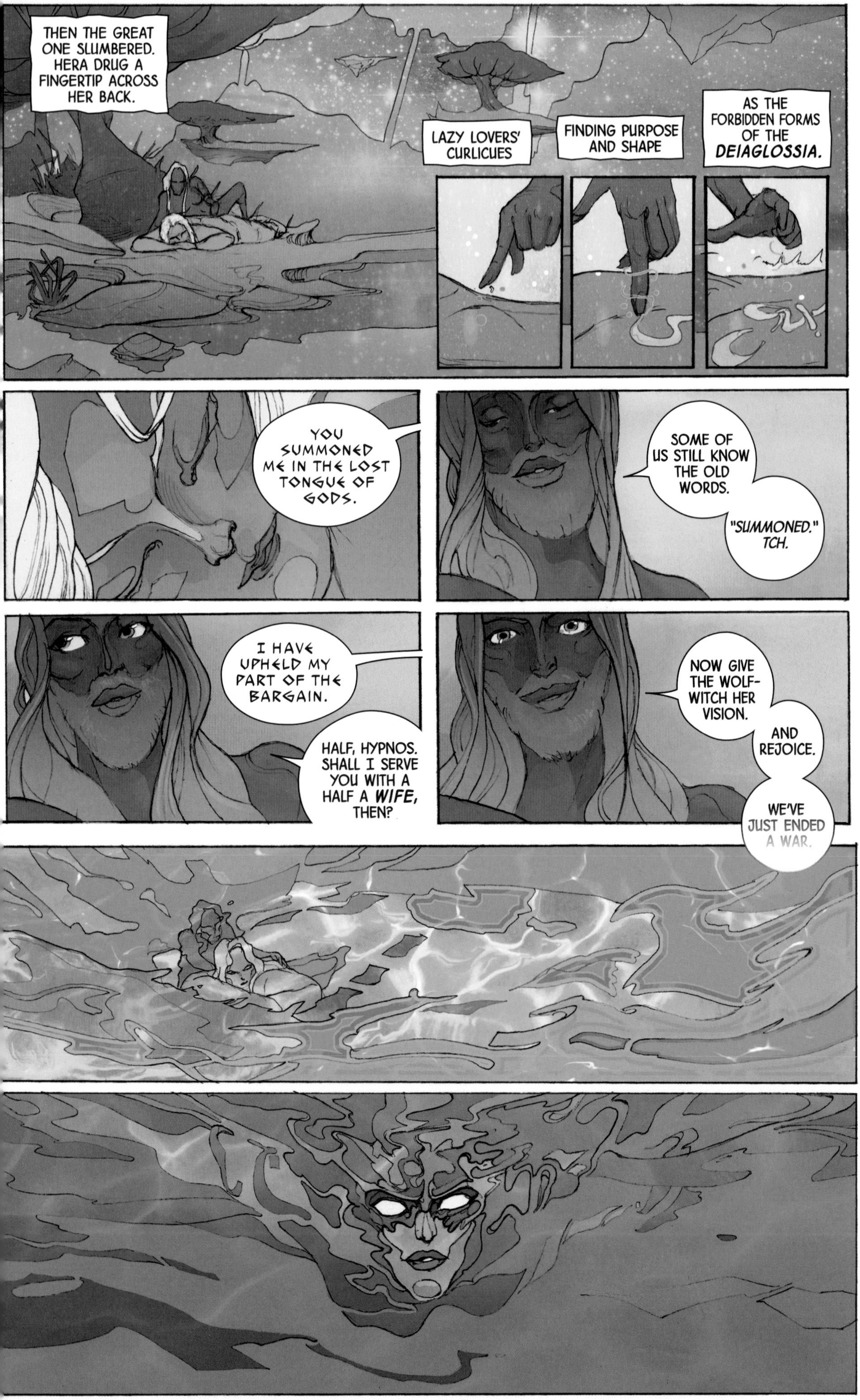
THEN THE GREAT ONE SLUMBERED. HERA DRUG A FINGERTIP ACROSS HER BACK.
LAZY LOVERS' CURLICUES
FINDING PURPOSE AND SHAPE
AS THE FORBIDDEN FORMS OF THE DEIAGLOSSIA.
YOU SUMMONED ME IN THE LOST TONGUE OF GODS.
SOME OF US STILL KNOW THE OLD WORDS.
"SUMMONED." TCH.
I HAVE UPHELD MY PART OF THE BARGAIN.
HALF, HYPNOS. SHALL I SERVE YOU WITH A HALF A WIFE, THEN?
NOW GIVE THE WOLF-WITCH HER VISION.
AND REJOICE.
WE'VE JUST ENDED A WAR.

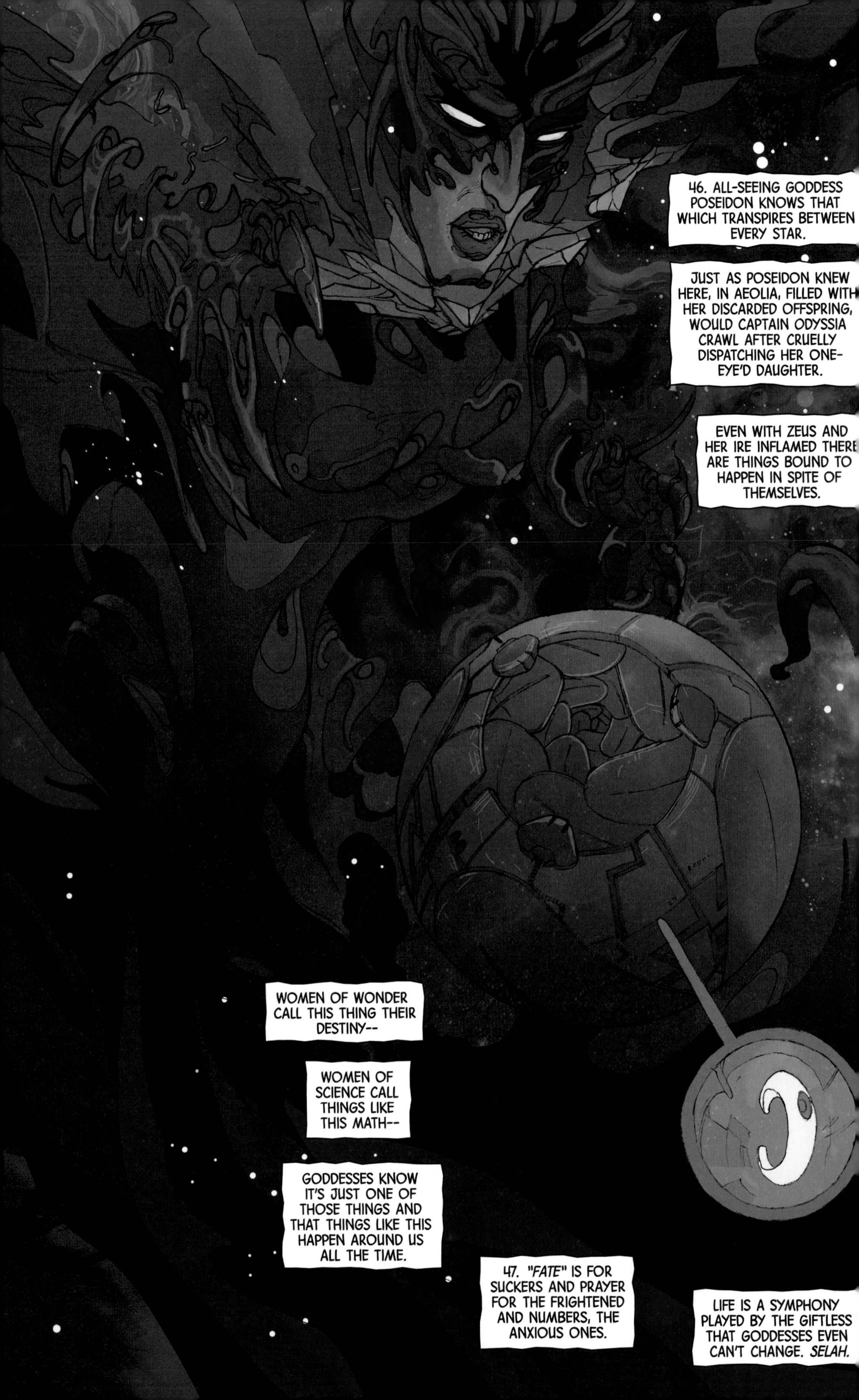
46. ALL-SEEING GODDESS POSEIDON KNOWS THAT WHICH TRANSPIRES BETWEEN EVERY STAR.
JUST AS POSEIDON KNEW HERE, IN AEOLIA, FILLED WITH HER DISCARDED OFFSPRING, WOULD CAPTAIN ODYSSIA CRAWL AFTER CRUELLY DISPATCHING HER ONE-EYE'D DAUGHTER.
EVEN WITH ZEUS AND HER IRE INFLAMED THERE ARE THINGS BOUND TO HAPPEN IN SPITE OF THEMSELVES.
WOMEN OF WONDER CALL THIS THING THEIR DESTINY--
WOMEN OF SCIENCE CALL THINGS LIKE THIS MATH--
GODDESSES KNOW IT'S JUST ONE OF THOSE THINGS AND THAT THINGS LIKE THIS HAPPEN AROUND US ALL THE TIME.
47. *"FATE"* IS FOR SUCKERS AND PRAYER FOR THE FRIGHTENED AND NUMBERS, THE ANXIOUS ONES.
LIFE IS A SYMPHONY PLAYED BY THE GIFTLESS THAT GODDESSES EVEN CAN'T CHANGE. *SELAH.*

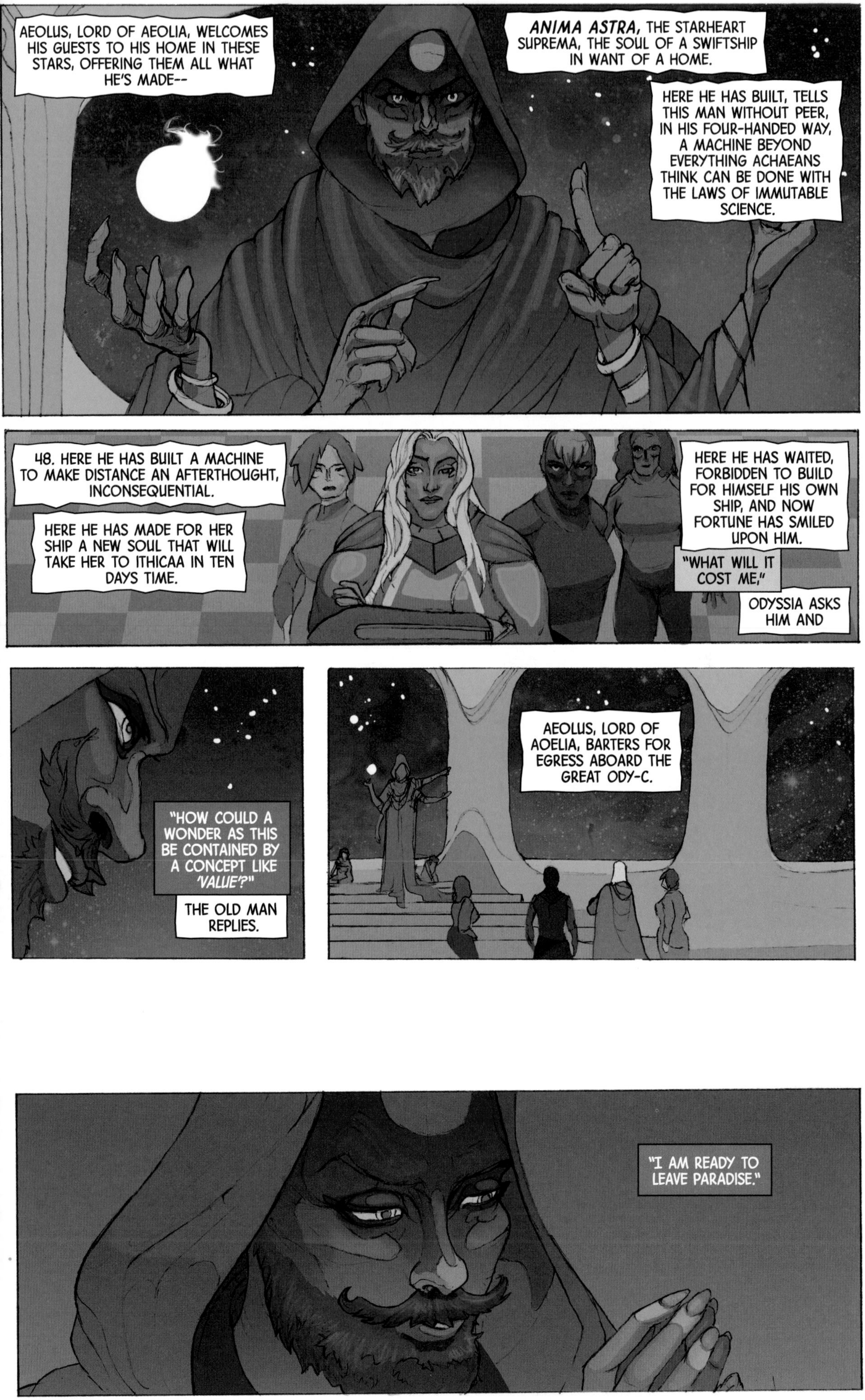
AEOLUS, LORD OF AEOLIA, WELCOMES HIS GUESTS TO HIS HOME IN THESE STARS, OFFERING THEM ALL WHAT HE'S MADE--
ANIMA ASTRA, THE STARHEART SUPREMA, THE SOUL OF A SWIFTSHIP IN WANT OF A HOME.
HERE HE HAS BUILT, TELLS THIS MAN WITHOUT PEER, IN HIS FOUR-HANDED WAY, A MACHINE BEYOND EVERYTHING ACHAEANS THINK CAN BE DONE WITH THE LAWS OF IMMUTABLE SCIENCE.
48. HERE HE HAS BUILT A MACHINE TO MAKE DISTANCE AN AFTERTHOUGHT, INCONSEQUENTIAL.
HERE HE HAS MADE FOR HER SHIP A NEW SOUL THAT WILL TAKE HER TO ITHICAA IN TEN DAYS TIME.
HERE HE HAS WAITED, FORBIDDEN TO BUILD FOR HIMSELF HIS OWN SHIP, AND NOW FORTUNE HAS SMILED UPON HIM.
"WHAT WILL IT COST ME,"
ODYSSIA ASKS HIM AND
"HOW COULD A WONDER AS THIS BE CONTAINED BY A CONCEPT LIKE *'VALUE'?*"
THE OLD MAN REPLIES.
AEOLUS, LORD OF AOELIA, BARTERS FOR EGRESS ABOARD THE GREAT ODY-C.
"I AM READY TO LEAVE PARADISE."

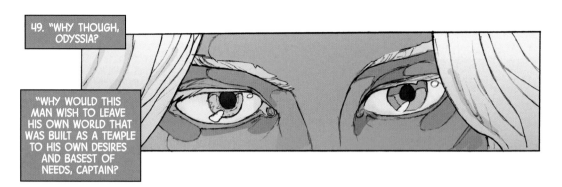

49. "WHY THOUGH, ODYSSIA?

"WHY WOULD THIS MAN WISH TO LEAVE HIS OWN WORLD THAT WAS BUILT AS A TEMPLE TO HIS OWN DESIRES AND BASEST OF NEEDS, CAPTAIN?

"SCADS OF NYMPHETS WAITING ONLY FOR AEOLUS, BENT OF THE KNEE AND BOWED OF THE HEAD,"

SAYS EURY.

MEDES SAYS:

"THINK OF IT: AEOLUS, HERE AND ALONE, THE SOLE MAN AMONG THOUSANDS AND THOUSANDS OF STARS.

AND CONTINUES:

"MY CAPTAIN, THESE STARLOST YOUNG WOMEN NOW BOW AT HIS FEET AS THOUGH HE WERE SOME SORT OF GOD."

"AND WHY NOT?"

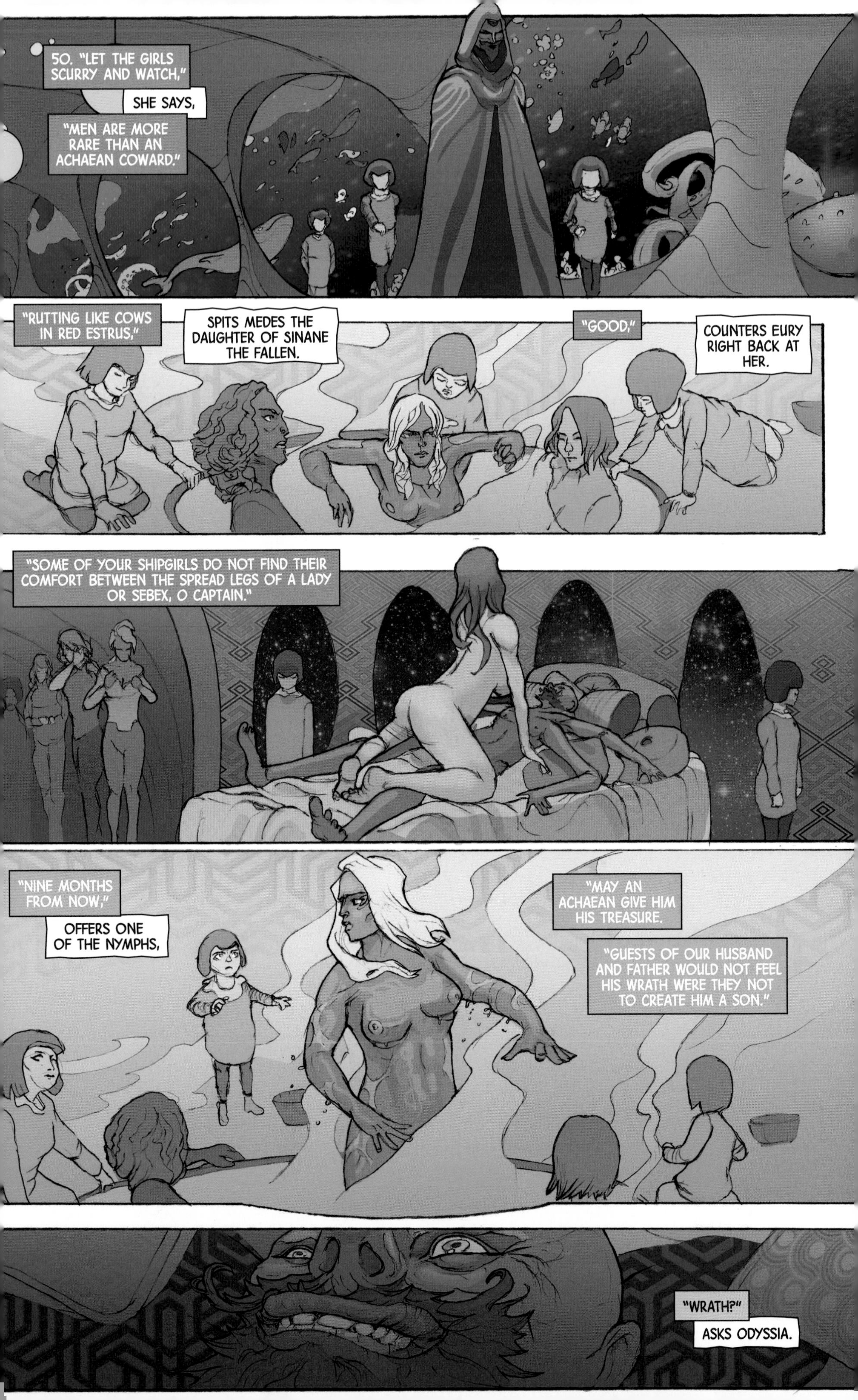
50. "LET THE GIRLS SCURRY AND WATCH,"
SHE SAYS,
"MEN ARE MORE RARE THAN AN ACHAEAN COWARD."
"RUTTING LIKE COWS IN RED ESTRUS,"
SPITS MEDES THE DAUGHTER OF SINANE THE FALLEN.
"GOOD,"
COUNTERS EURY RIGHT BACK AT HER.
"SOME OF YOUR SHIPGIRLS DO NOT FIND THEIR COMFORT BETWEEN THE SPREAD LEGS OF A LADY OR SEBEX, O CAPTAIN."
"NINE MONTHS FROM NOW,"
OFFERS ONE OF THE NYMPHS,
"MAY AN ACHAEAN GIVE HIM HIS TREASURE.
"GUESTS OF OUR HUSBAND AND FATHER WOULD NOT FEEL HIS WRATH WERE THEY NOT TO CREATE HIM A SON."
"WRATH?"
ASKS ODYSSIA.

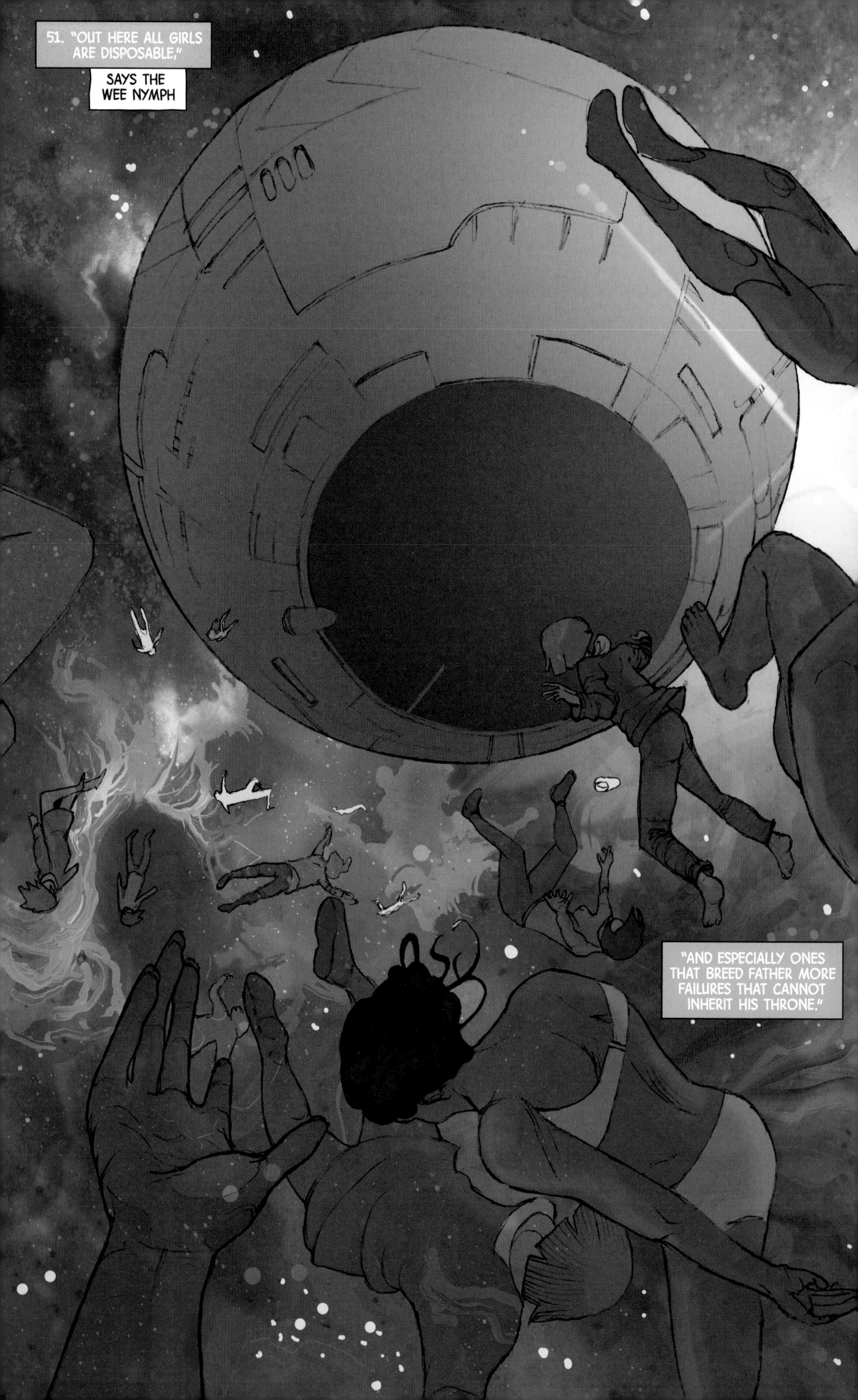
51. "OUT HERE ALL GIRLS ARE DISPOSABLE,"
SAYS THE WEE NYMPH
"AND ESPECIALLY ONES THAT BREED FATHER MORE FAILURES THAT CANNOT INHERIT HIS THRONE."

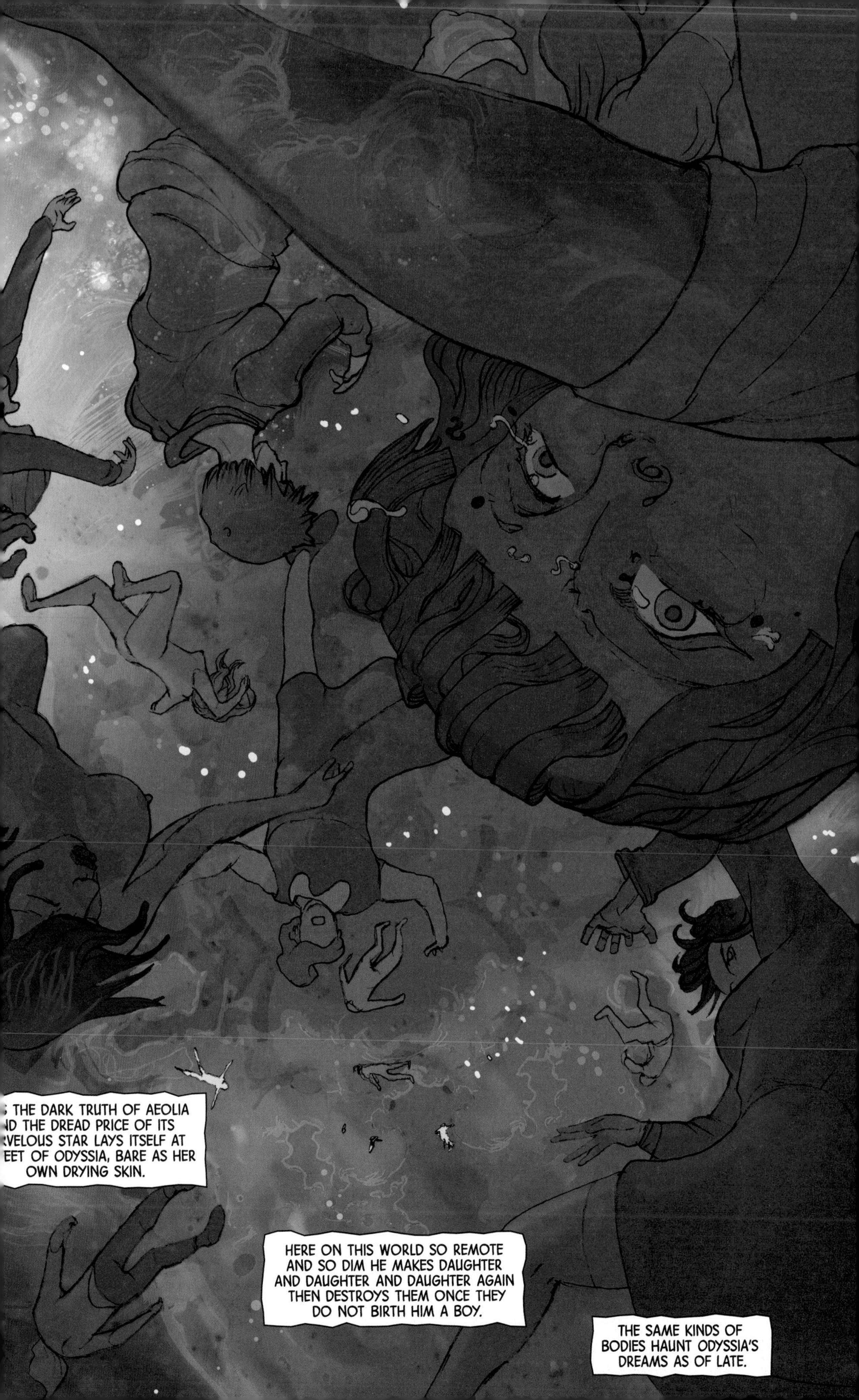
S THE DARK TRUTH OF AEOLIA
ND THE DREAD PRICE OF ITS
RVELOUS STAR LAYS ITSELF AT
EET OF ODYSSIA, BARE AS HER
OWN DRYING SKIN.
HERE ON THIS WORLD SO REMOTE AND SO DIM HE MAKES DAUGHTER AND DAUGHTER AND DAUGHTER AGAIN THEN DESTROYS THEM ONCE THEY DO NOT BIRTH HIM A BOY.
THE SAME KINDS OF BODIES HAUNT ODYSSIA'S DREAMS AS OF LATE.

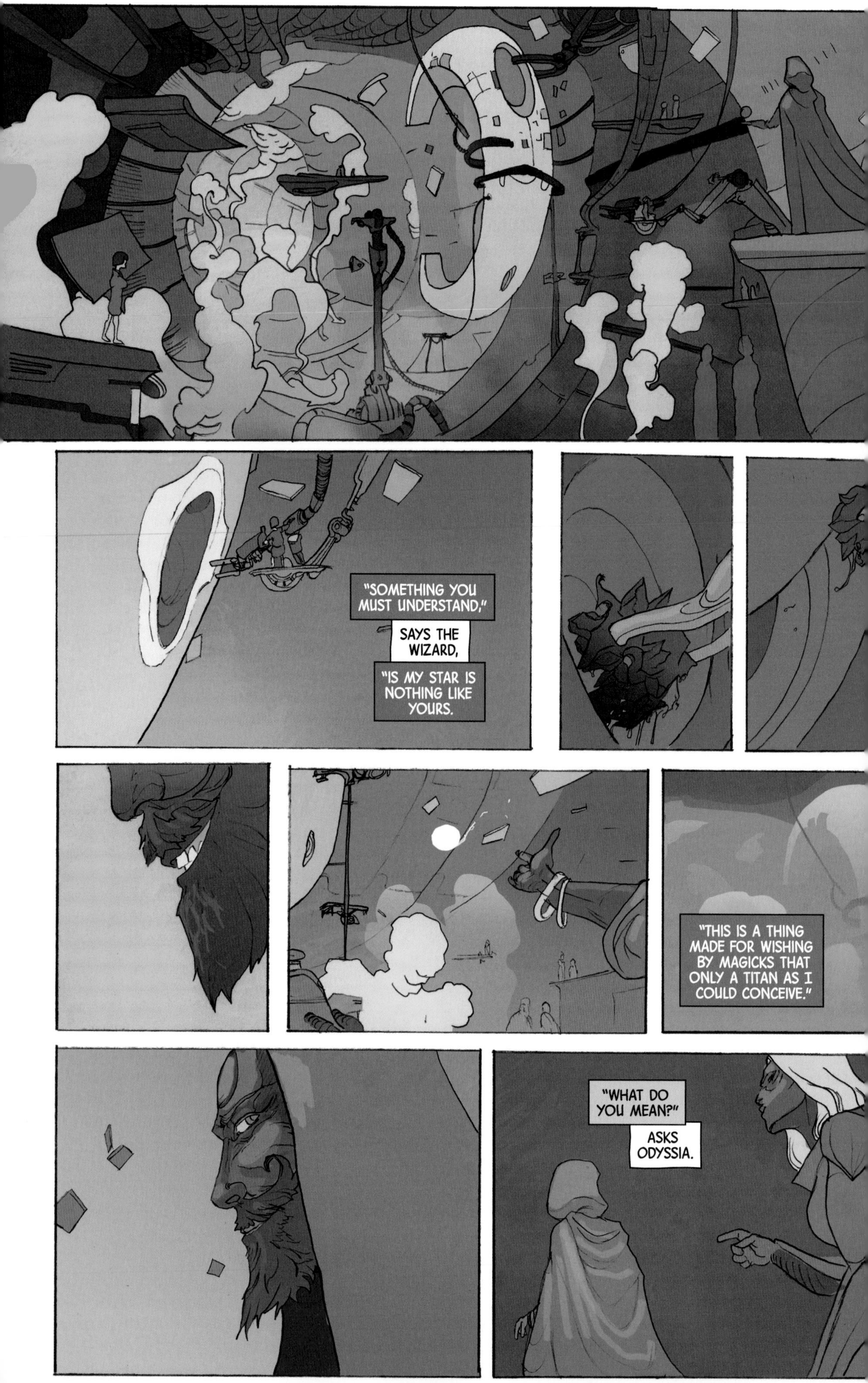
"SOMETHING YOU MUST UNDERSTAND,"
SAYS THE WIZARD,
"IS MY STAR IS NOTHING LIKE YOURS.
"THIS IS A THING MADE FOR WISHING BY MAGICKS THAT ONLY A TITAN AS I COULD CONCEIVE."
"WHAT DO YOU MEAN?"
ASKS ODYSSIA.

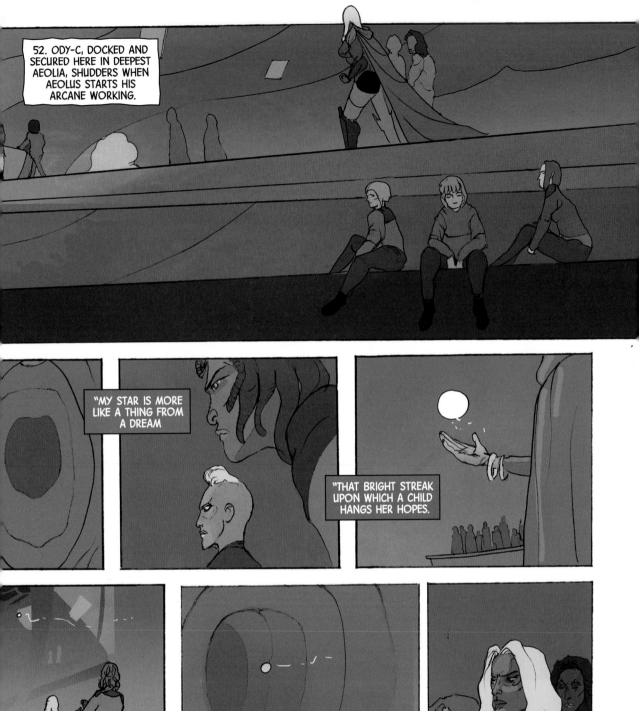

52. ODY-C, DOCKED AND SECURED HERE IN DEEPEST AEOLIA, SHUDDERS WHEN AEOLUS STARTS HIS ARCANE WORKING.

"MY STAR IS MORE LIKE A THING FROM A DREAM

"THAT BRIGHT STREAK UPON WHICH A CHILD HANGS HER HOPES.

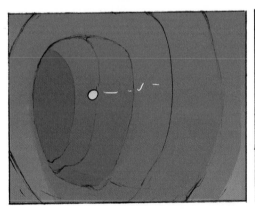

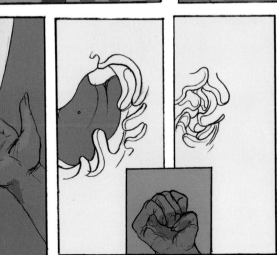

"WISHES ARE LIMITED ONLY BY WISHING,"

SAYS HE.

"SO, NOW, CAPTAIN-- WISH BIG."

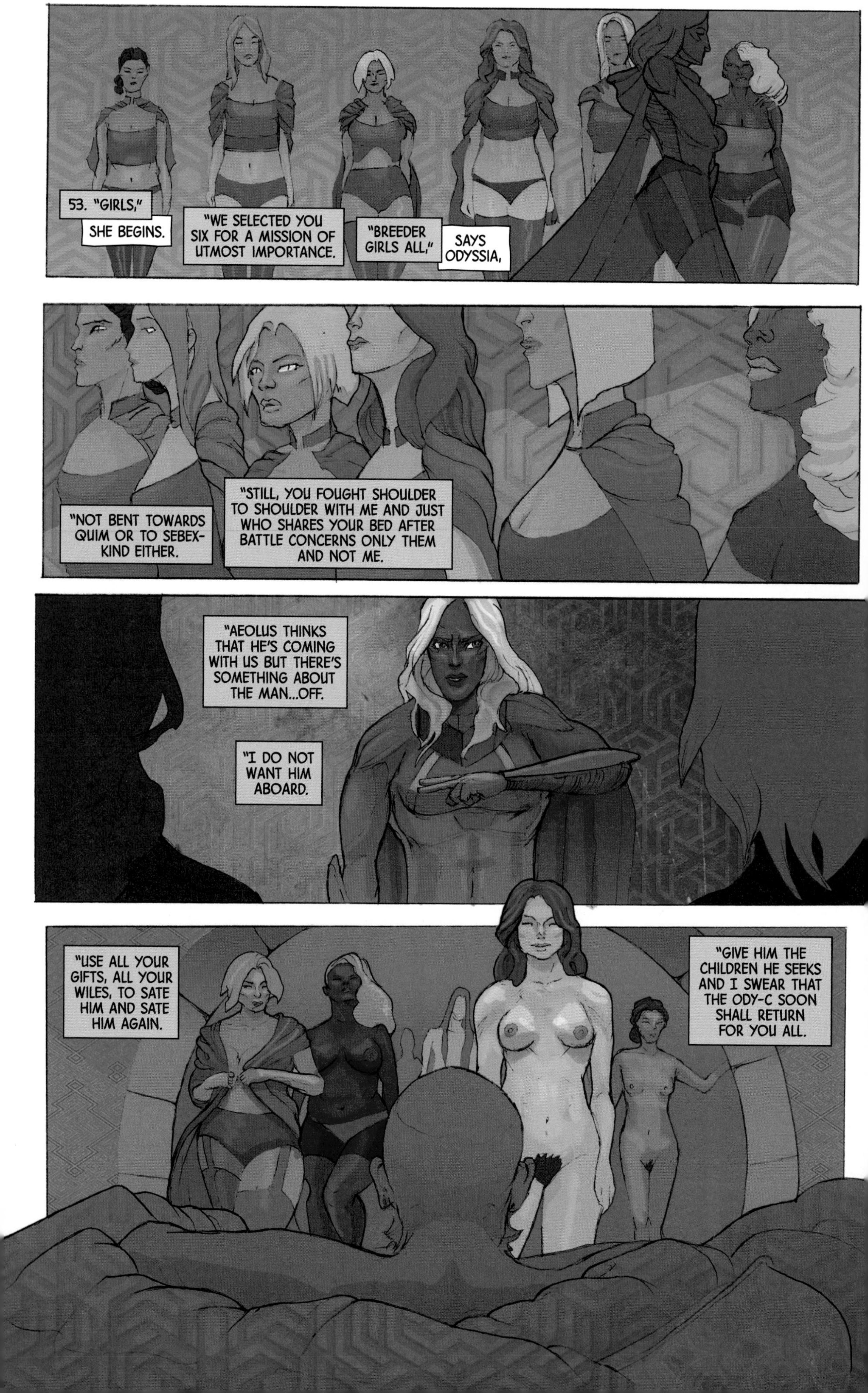
53. "GIRLS,"
SHE BEGINS.
"WE SELECTED YOU SIX FOR A MISSION OF UTMOST IMPORTANCE.
"BREEDER GIRLS ALL,"
SAYS ODYSSIA,
"NOT BENT TOWARDS QUIM OR TO SEBEX-KIND EITHER.
"STILL, YOU FOUGHT SHOULDER TO SHOULDER WITH ME AND JUST WHO SHARES YOUR BED AFTER BATTLE CONCERNS ONLY THEM AND NOT ME.
"AEOLUS THINKS THAT HE'S COMING WITH US BUT THERE'S SOMETHING ABOUT THE MAN...OFF.
"I DO NOT WANT HIM ABOARD.
"USE ALL YOUR GIFTS, ALL YOUR WILES, TO SATE HIM AND SATE HIM AGAIN.
"GIVE HIM THE CHILDREN HE SEEKS AND I SWEAR THAT THE ODY-C SOON SHALL RETURN FOR YOU ALL.

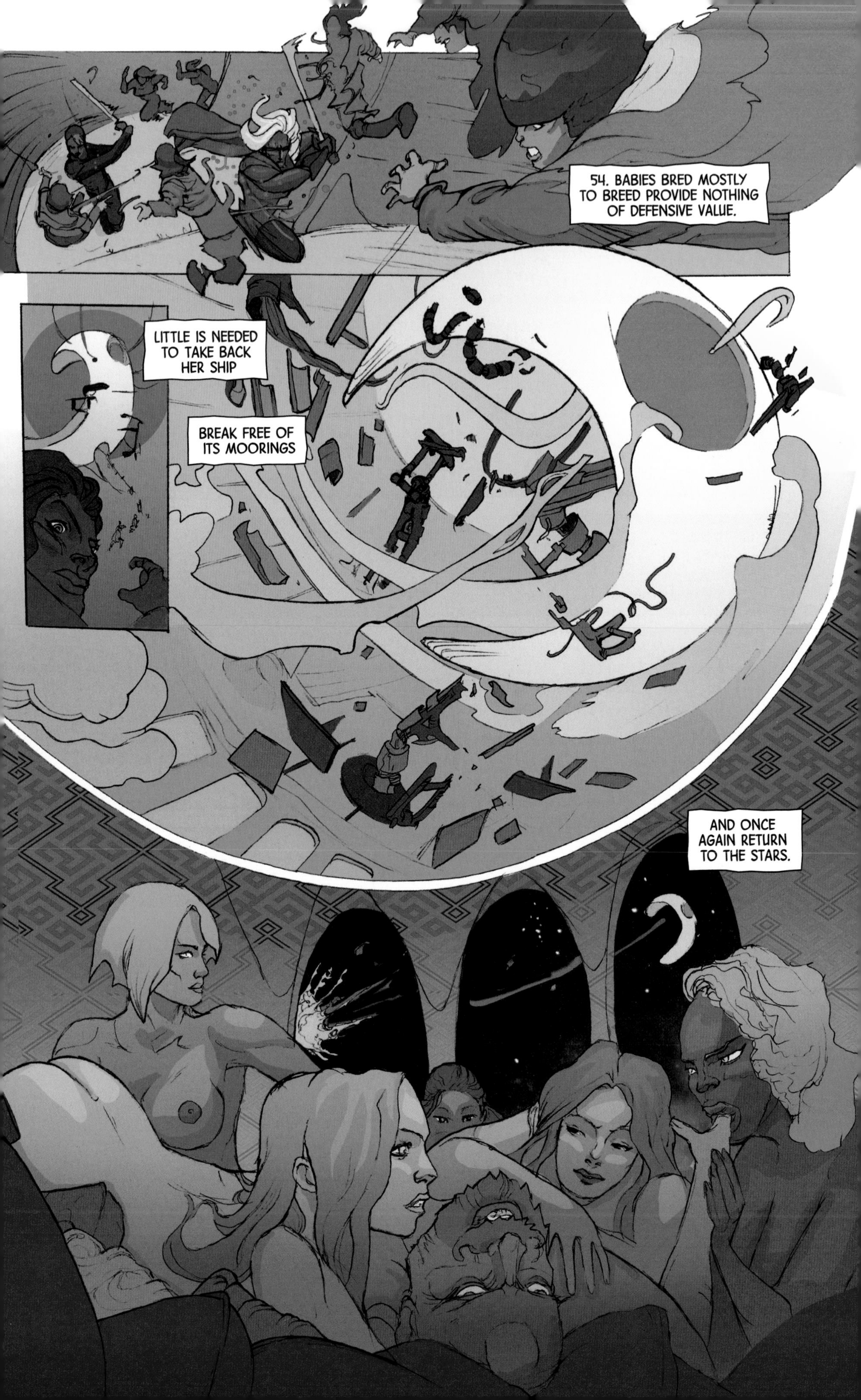
54. BABIES BRED MOSTLY TO BREED PROVIDE NOTHING OF DEFENSIVE VALUE.
LITTLE IS NEEDED TO TAKE BACK HER SHIP
BREAK FREE OF ITS MOORINGS
AND ONCE AGAIN RETURN TO THE STARS.

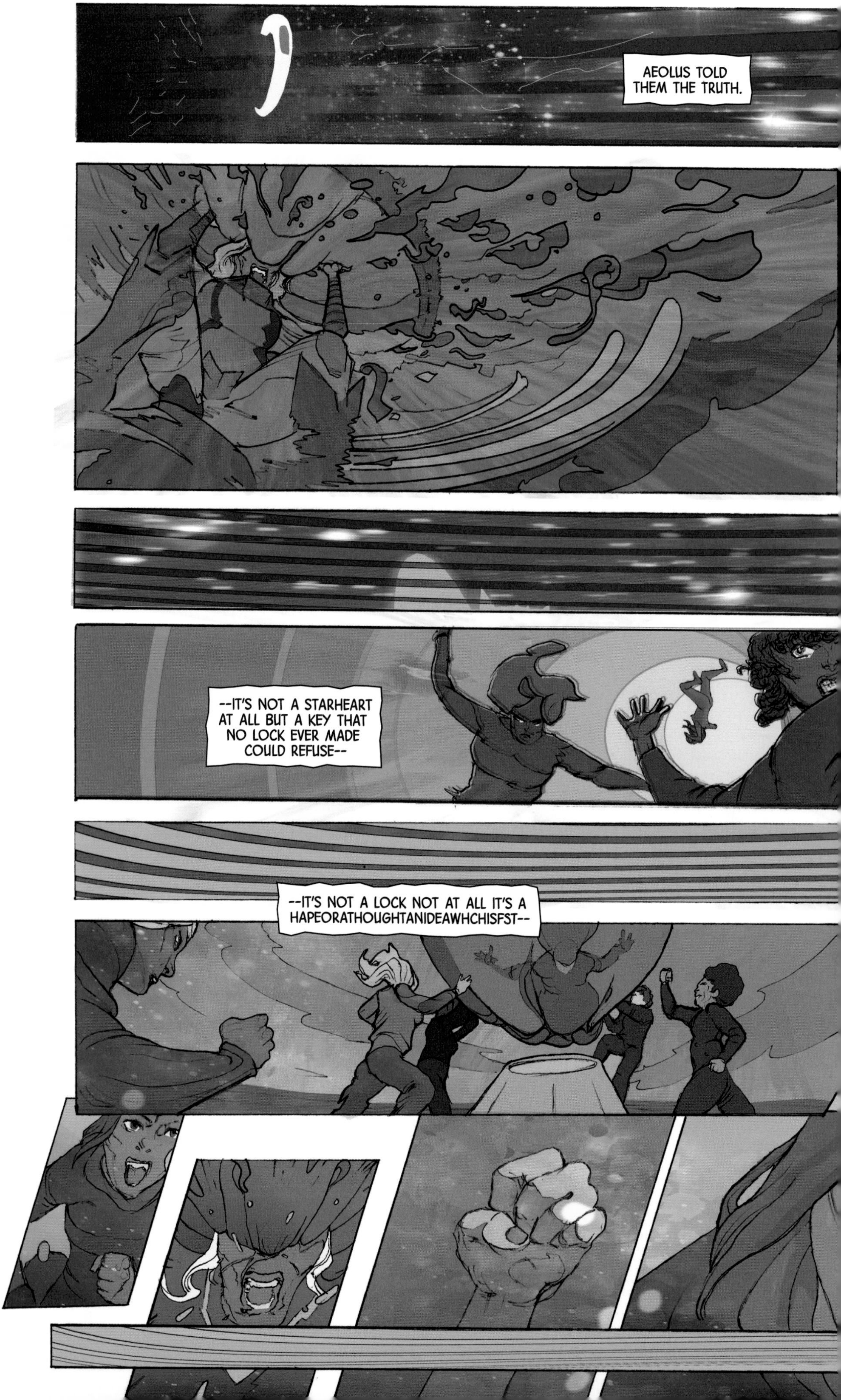
AEOLUS TOLD THEM THE TRUTH.
--IT'S NOT A STARHEART AT ALL BUT A KEY THAT NO LOCK EVER MADE COULD REFUSE--
--IT'S NOT A LOCK NOT AT ALL IT'S A HAPEORATHOUGHTANIDEAWHCHISFST--

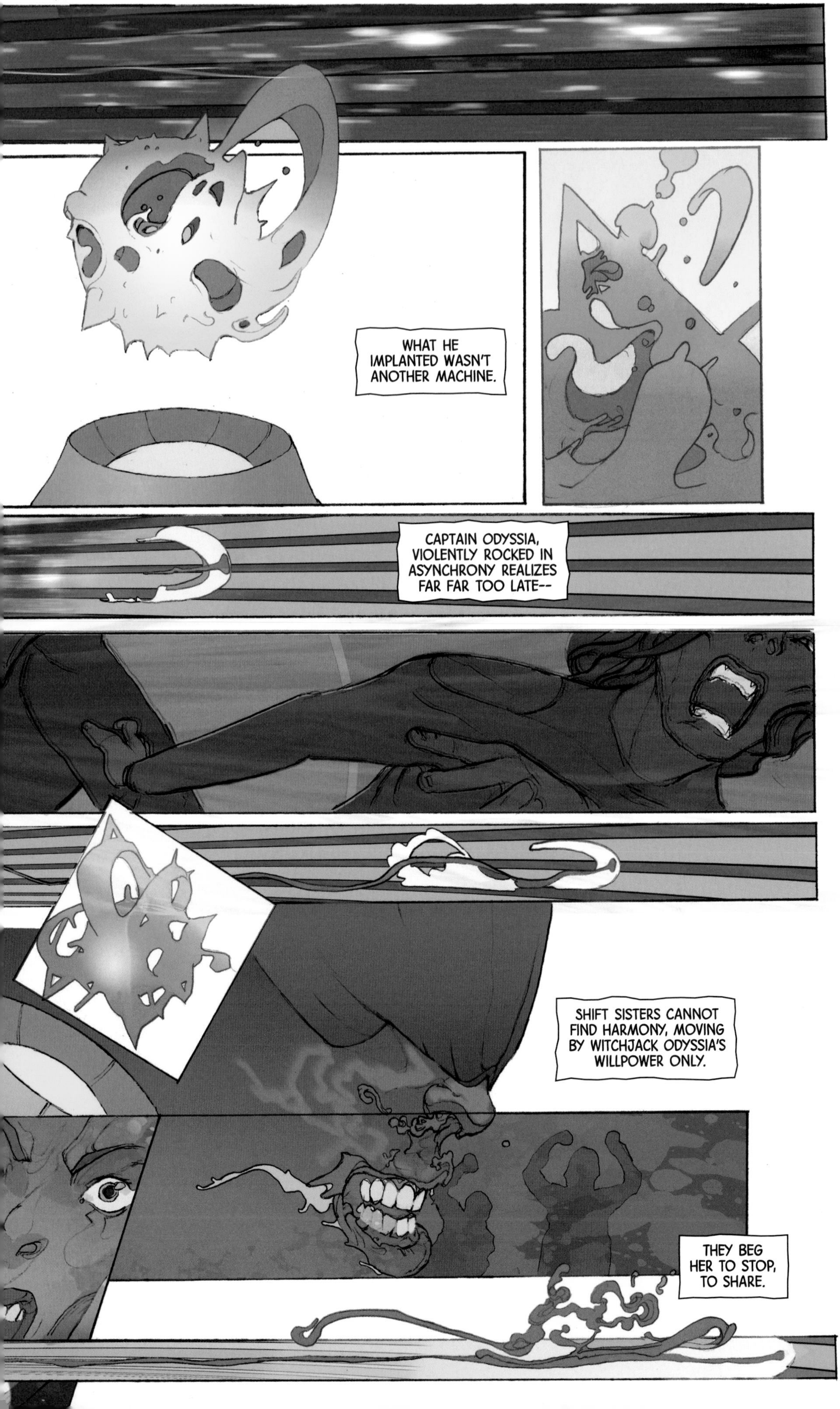
WHAT HE
IMPLANTED WASN'T
ANOTHER MACHINE.
CAPTAIN ODYSSIA,
VIOLENTLY ROCKED IN
ASYNCHRONY REALIZES
FAR FAR TOO LATE--
SHIFT SISTERS CANNOT
FIND HARMONY, MOVING
BY WITCHJACK ODYSSIA'S
WILLPOWER ONLY.
THEY BEG
HER TO STOP,
TO SHARE.

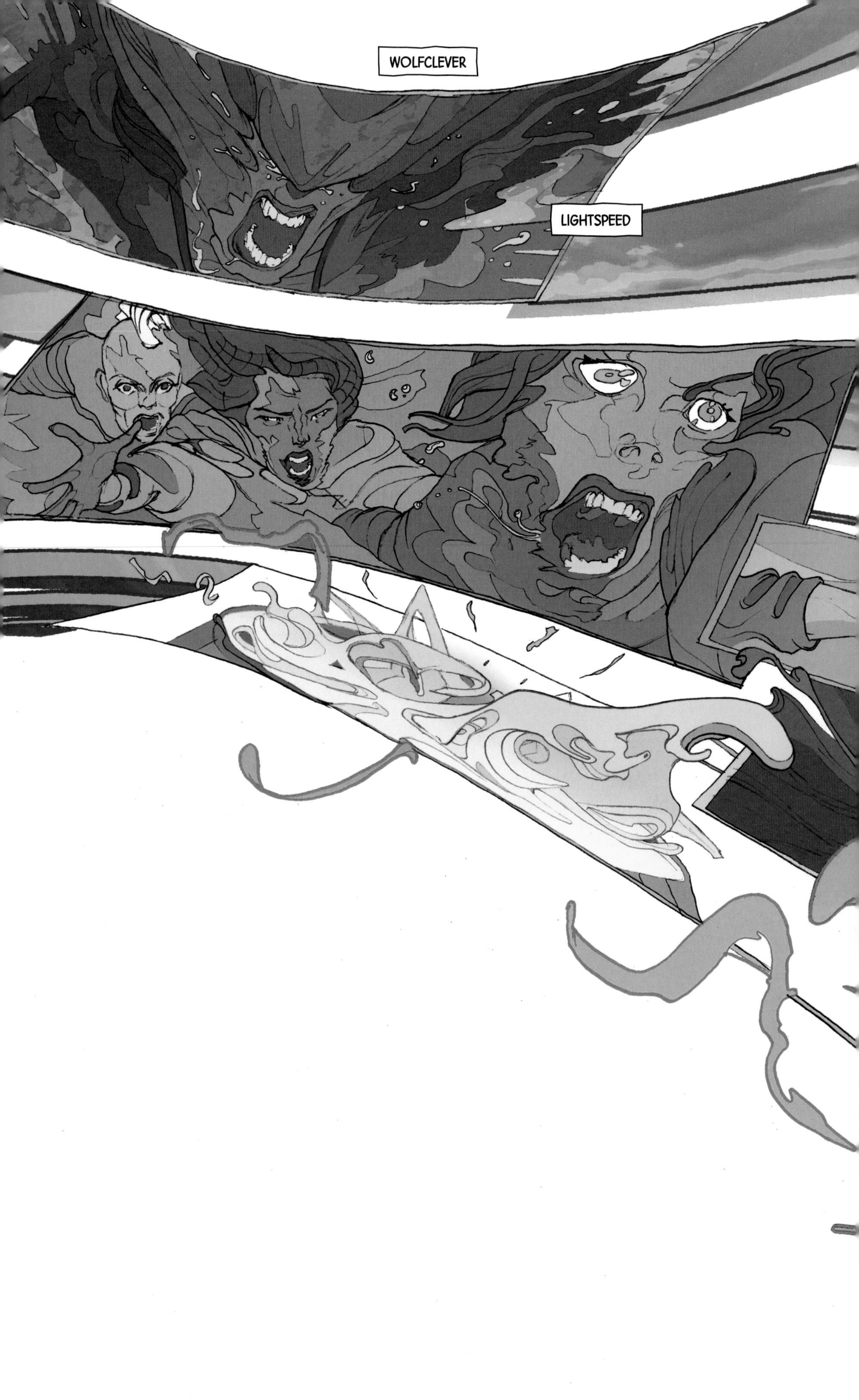
WOLFCLEVER
LIGHTSPEED

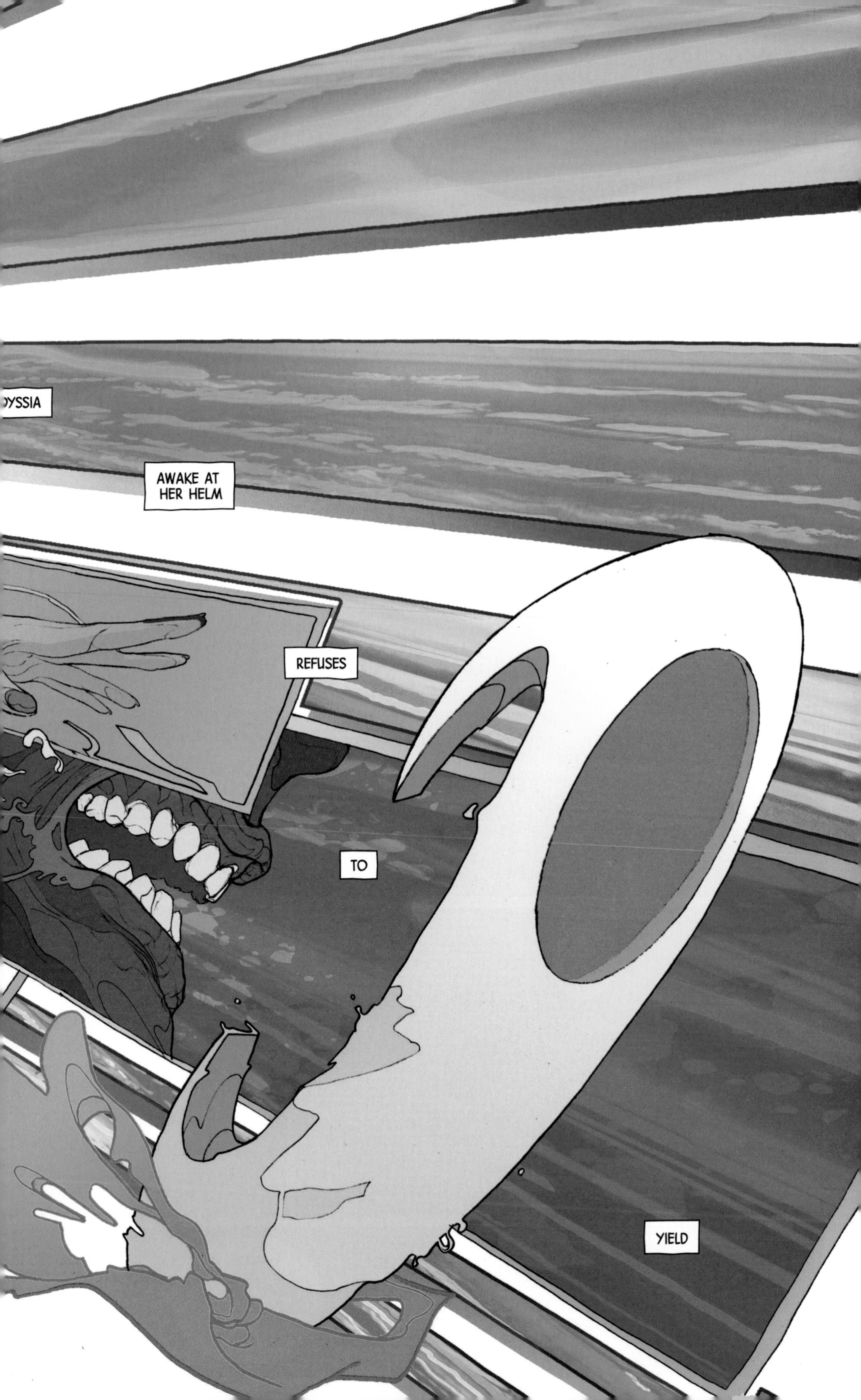

YSSIA
AWAKE AT HER HELM
REFUSES
TO
YIELD

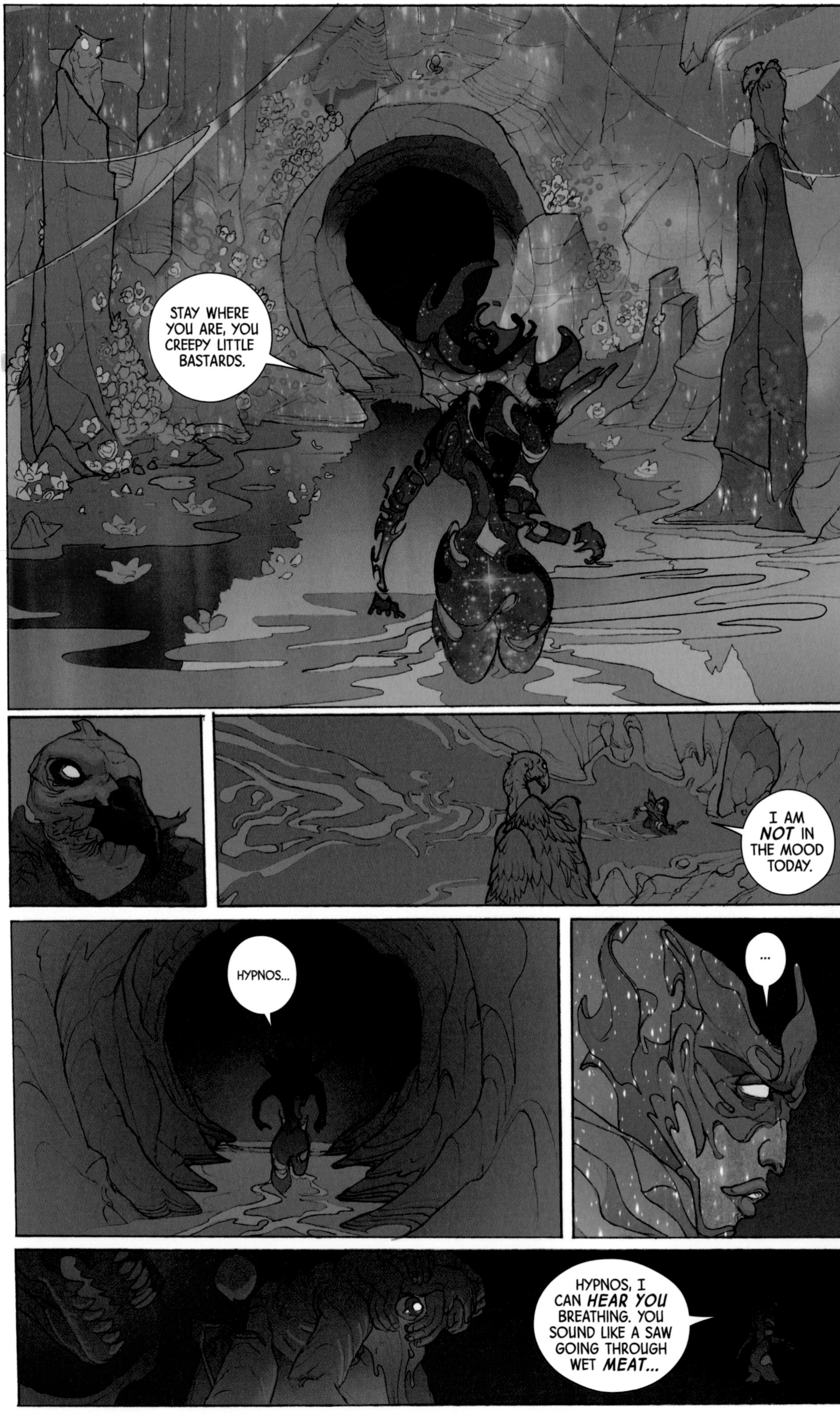
STAY WHERE YOU ARE, YOU CREEPY LITTLE BASTARDS.
I AM *NOT* IN THE MOOD TODAY.
HYPNOS...
...
HYPNOS, I CAN *HEAR YOU* BREATHING. YOU SOUND LIKE A SAW GOING THROUGH WET *MEAT*...

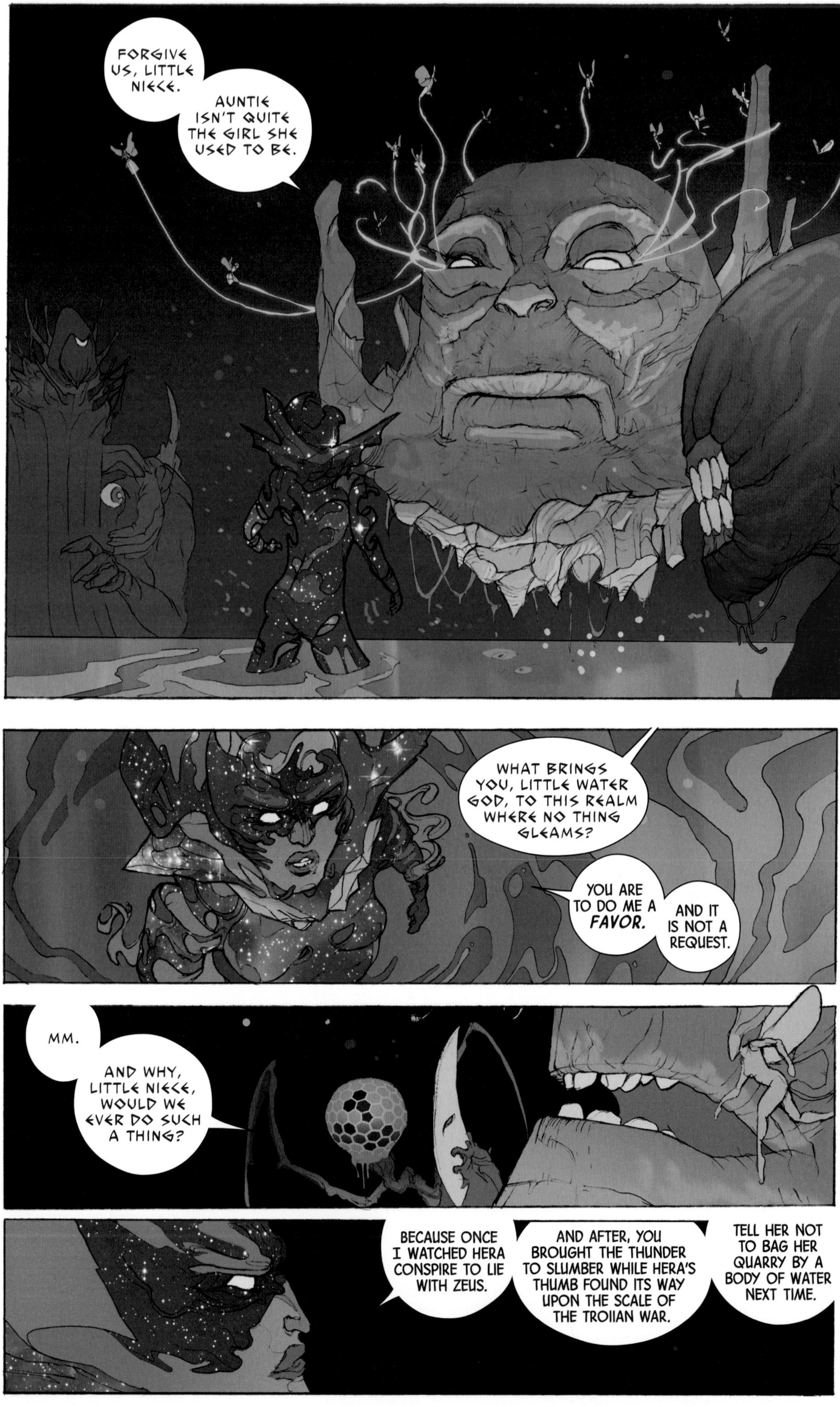
FORGIVE US, LITTLE NIECE.
AUNTIE ISN'T QUITE THE GIRL SHE USED TO BE.
WHAT BRINGS YOU, LITTLE WATER GOD, TO THIS REALM WHERE NO THING GLEAMS?
YOU ARE TO DO ME A *FAVOR.*
AND IT IS NOT A REQUEST.
MM.
AND WHY, LITTLE NIECE, WOULD WE EVER DO SUCH A THING?
BECAUSE ONCE I WATCHED HERA CONSPIRE TO LIE WITH ZEUS.
AND AFTER, YOU BROUGHT THE THUNDER TO SLUMBER WHILE HERA'S THUMB FOUND ITS WAY UPON THE SCALE OF THE TROJIAN WAR.
TELL HER NOT TO BAG HER QUARRY BY A BODY OF WATER NEXT TIME.

"AND THE WOLFWITCH ODYSSIA TASTED YOUR POPPY AND WAS GIVEN A DREAM...

"A VISION THAT WOULD WIN HER THE WAR.

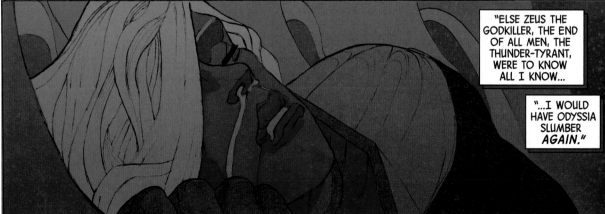

"ELSE ZEUS THE GODKILLER, THE END OF ALL MEN, THE THUNDER-TYRANT, WERE TO KNOW ALL I KNOW...

"...I WOULD HAVE ODYSSIA SLUMBER *AGAIN.*"

"IT SHOULDN'T BE *HARD* FOR YOU, HYPNOS.

"ODYSSIA'S STAYED AWAKE AND AT HER HELM FOR *NINE DAYS.*

"WITHOUT HER GUILT-BORN IRON-CLAD WILL AT THE HELM OF HER SHIP, THE STELLAR WINDS OF AEOLUS, SON OF POSEIDON, HAVE NO MASTER.

"MAD WITH THE POTENTIAL OF THE VERY THING THAT BRINGS THEM HOME, HER OWN WOMEN WILL DISOBEY HER.

"AND IN THE NEAR-MUTINY THEY WILL HOPE TO FORCE THIS WISHING MACHINE TO YIELD UNTO THEM TREASURES UNTOLD."

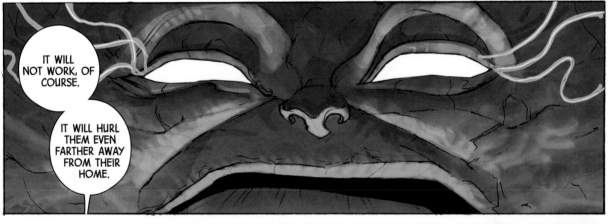

IT WILL NOT WORK, OF COURSE.

IT WILL HURL THEM EVEN FARTHER AWAY FROM THEIR HOME.

"*LUST* AND *GREED* MAY DRIVE THE SPIRIT BUT THEY ARE NOT *WILL--*"

BUT THEN AGAIN, THE GREAT AND GOOD ZEUS KNOWS ALL ABOUT THAT, DOESN'T SHE?

WHY...

...ARE YOU *TELLING* ME ALL THIS?

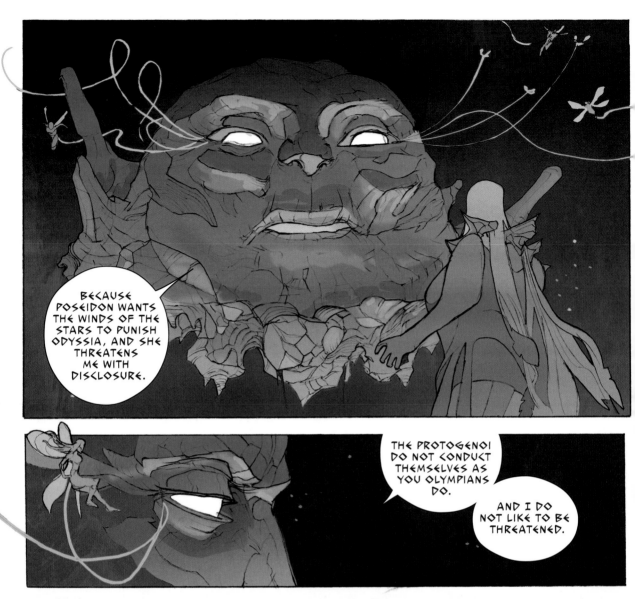

BECAUSE POSEIDON WANTS THE WINDS OF THE STARS TO PUNISH ODYSSIA, AND SHE THREATENS ME WITH DISCLOSURE.

THE PROTOGENOI DO NOT CONDUCT THEMSELVES AS YOU OLYMPIANS DO.

AND I DO NOT LIKE TO BE THREATENED.

AND SO YOU THREATEN ME?

NO, NO COUSIN-THUNDER.

I MERELY SUGGEST THAT BEFORE MOTHER NIGHT DOES IT FOR YOU...

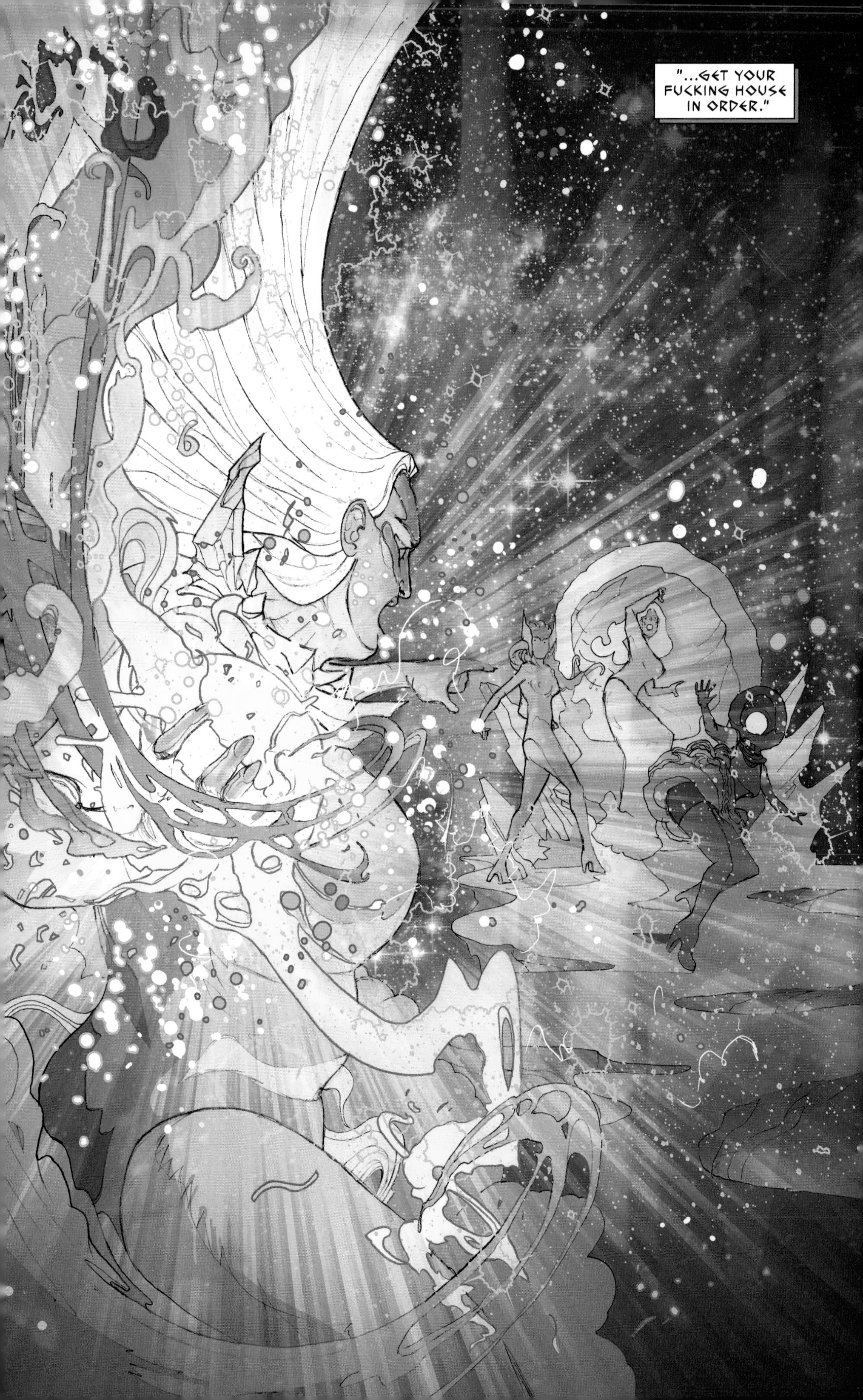
"...GET YOUR FUCKING HOUSE IN ORDER."

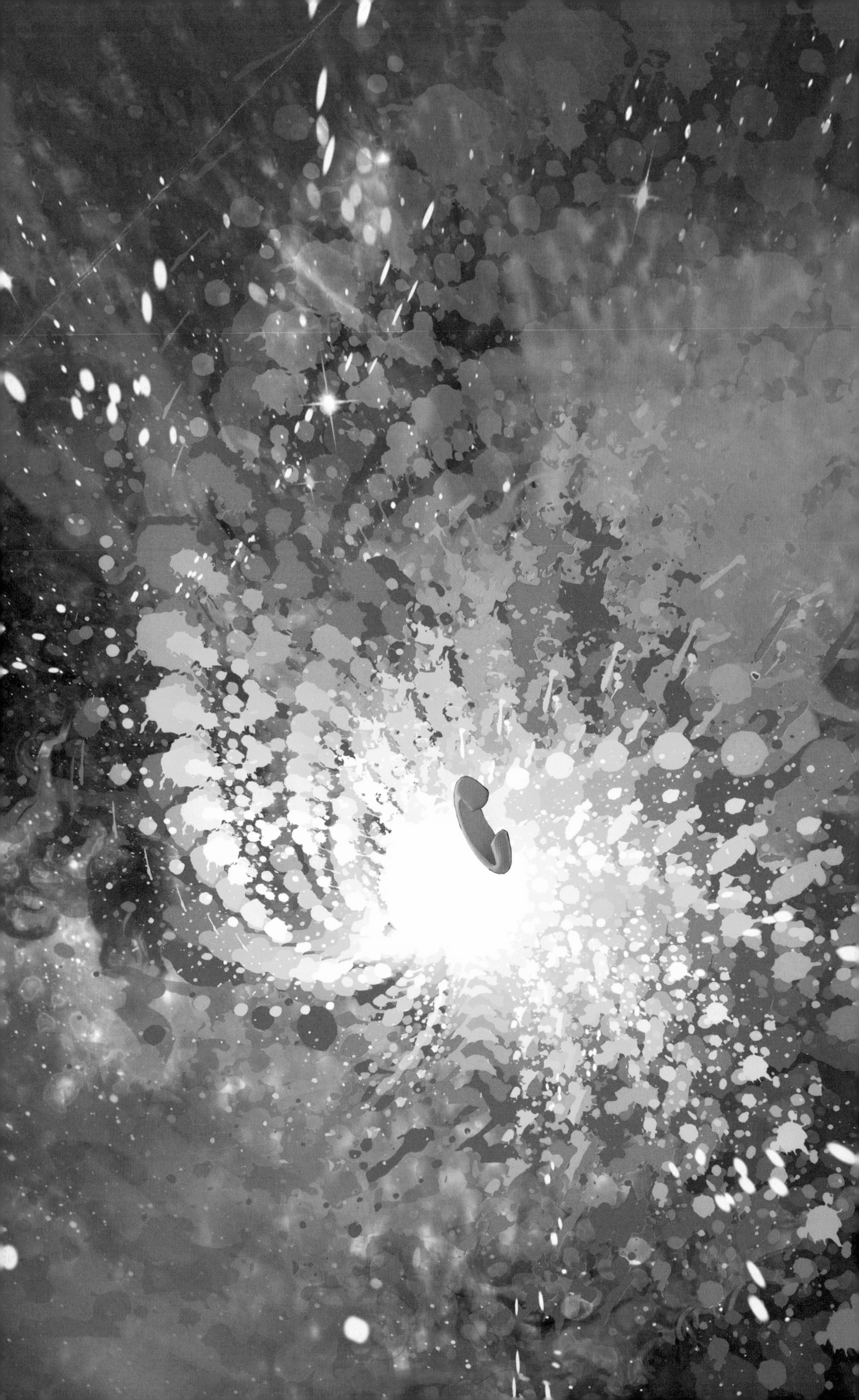

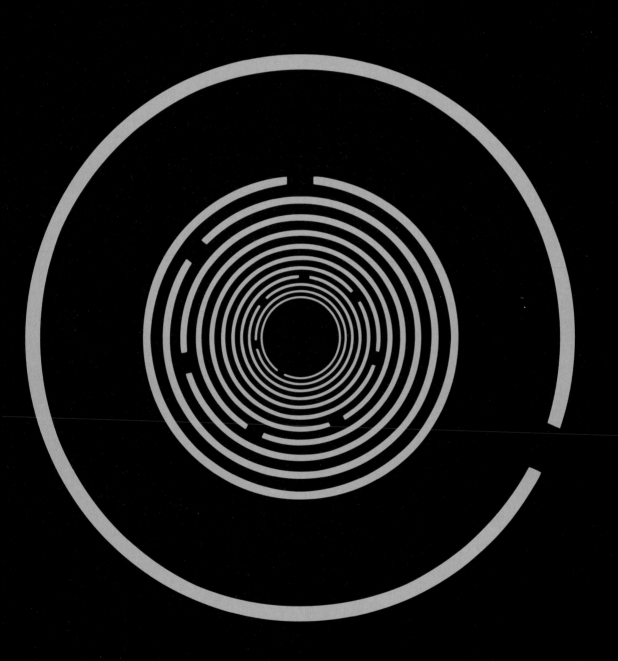

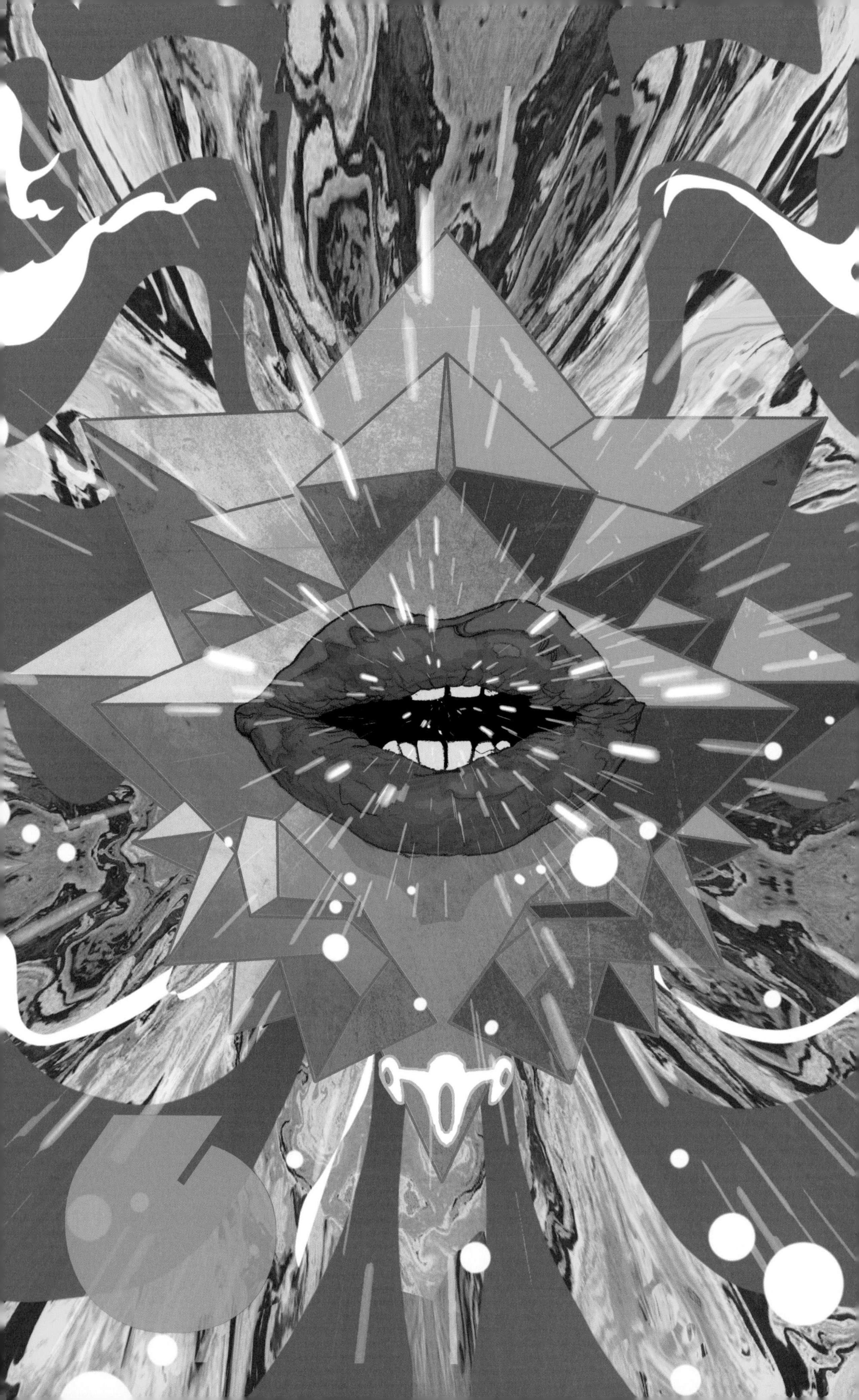

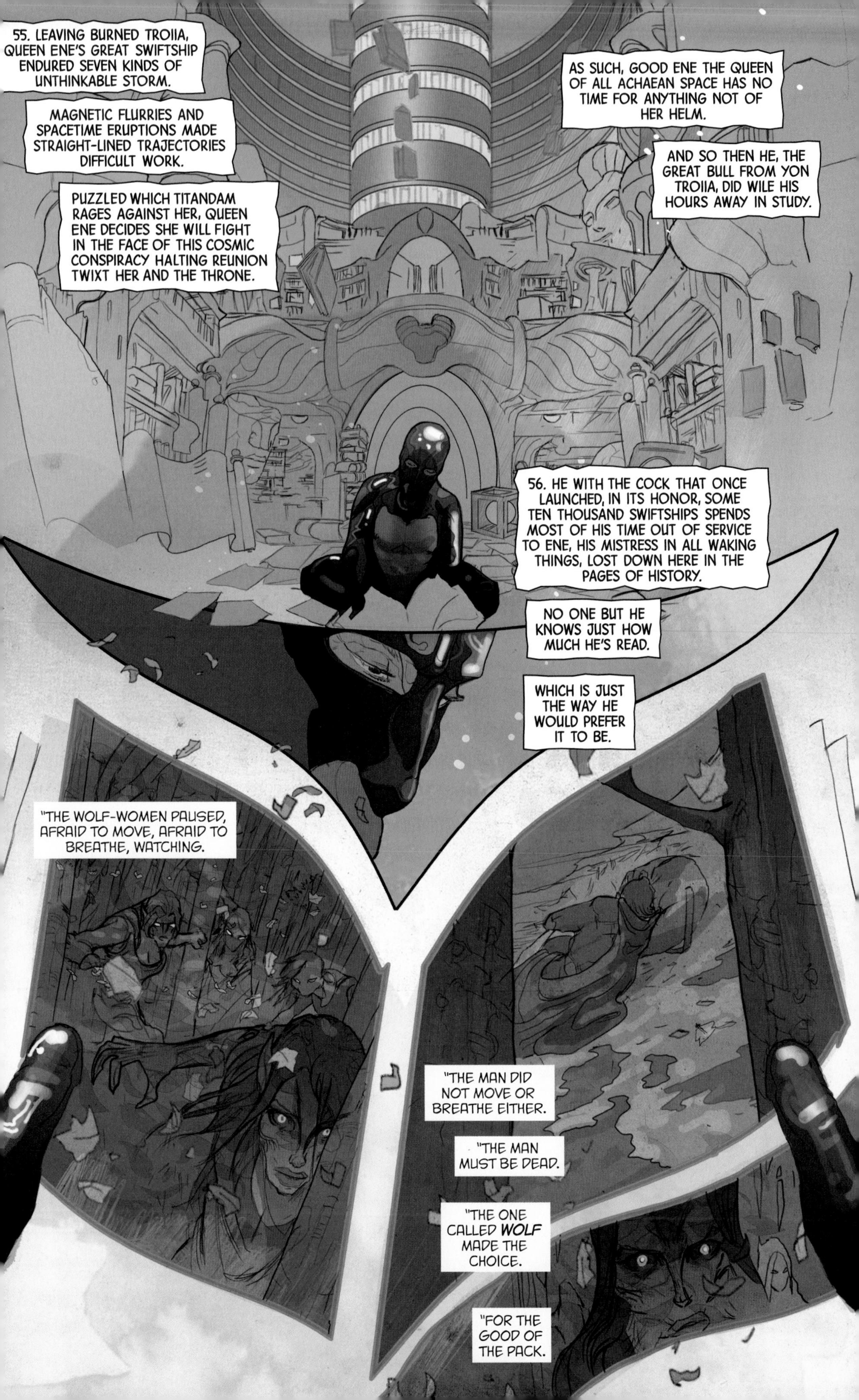
55. LEAVING BURNED TROIIA, QUEEN ENE'S GREAT SWIFTSHIP ENDURED SEVEN KINDS OF UNTHINKABLE STORM.
MAGNETIC FLURRIES AND SPACETIME ERUPTIONS MADE STRAIGHT-LINED TRAJECTORIES DIFFICULT WORK.
PUZZLED WHICH TITANDAM RAGES AGAINST HER, QUEEN ENE DECIDES SHE WILL FIGHT IN THE FACE OF THIS COSMIC CONSPIRACY HALTING REUNION TWIXT HER AND THE THRONE.
AS SUCH, GOOD ENE THE QUEEN OF ALL ACHAEAN SPACE HAS NO TIME FOR ANYTHING NOT OF HER HELM.
AND SO THEN HE, THE GREAT BULL FROM YON TROIIA, DID WILE HIS HOURS AWAY IN STUDY.
56. HE WITH THE COCK THAT ONCE LAUNCHED, IN ITS HONOR, SOME TEN THOUSAND SWIFTSHIPS SPENDS MOST OF HIS TIME OUT OF SERVICE TO ENE, HIS MISTRESS IN ALL WAKING THINGS, LOST DOWN HERE IN THE PAGES OF HISTORY.
NO ONE BUT HE KNOWS JUST HOW MUCH HE'S READ.
WHICH IS JUST THE WAY HE WOULD PREFER IT TO BE.
"THE WOLF-WOMEN PAUSED, AFRAID TO MOVE, AFRAID TO BREATHE, WATCHING.
"THE MAN DID NOT MOVE OR BREATHE EITHER.
"THE MAN MUST BE DEAD.
"THE ONE CALLED ***WOLF*** MADE THE CHOICE.
"FOR THE GOOD OF THE PACK.

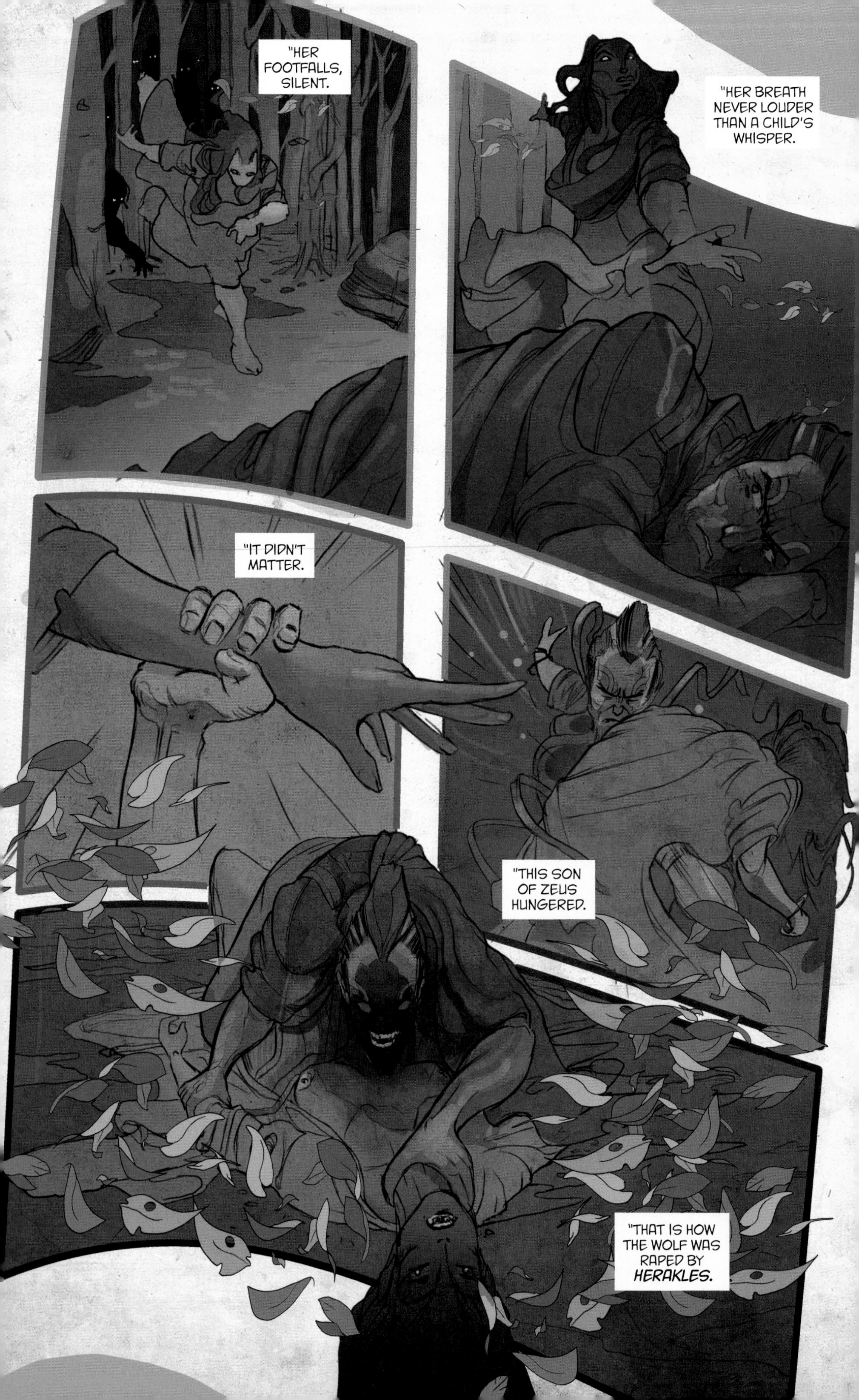
"HER FOOTFALLS, SILENT.
"HER BREATH NEVER LOUDER THAN A CHILD'S WHISPER.
"IT DIDN'T MATTER.
"THIS SON OF ZEUS HUNGERED.
"THAT IS HOW THE WOLF WAS RAPED BY *HERAKLES.*

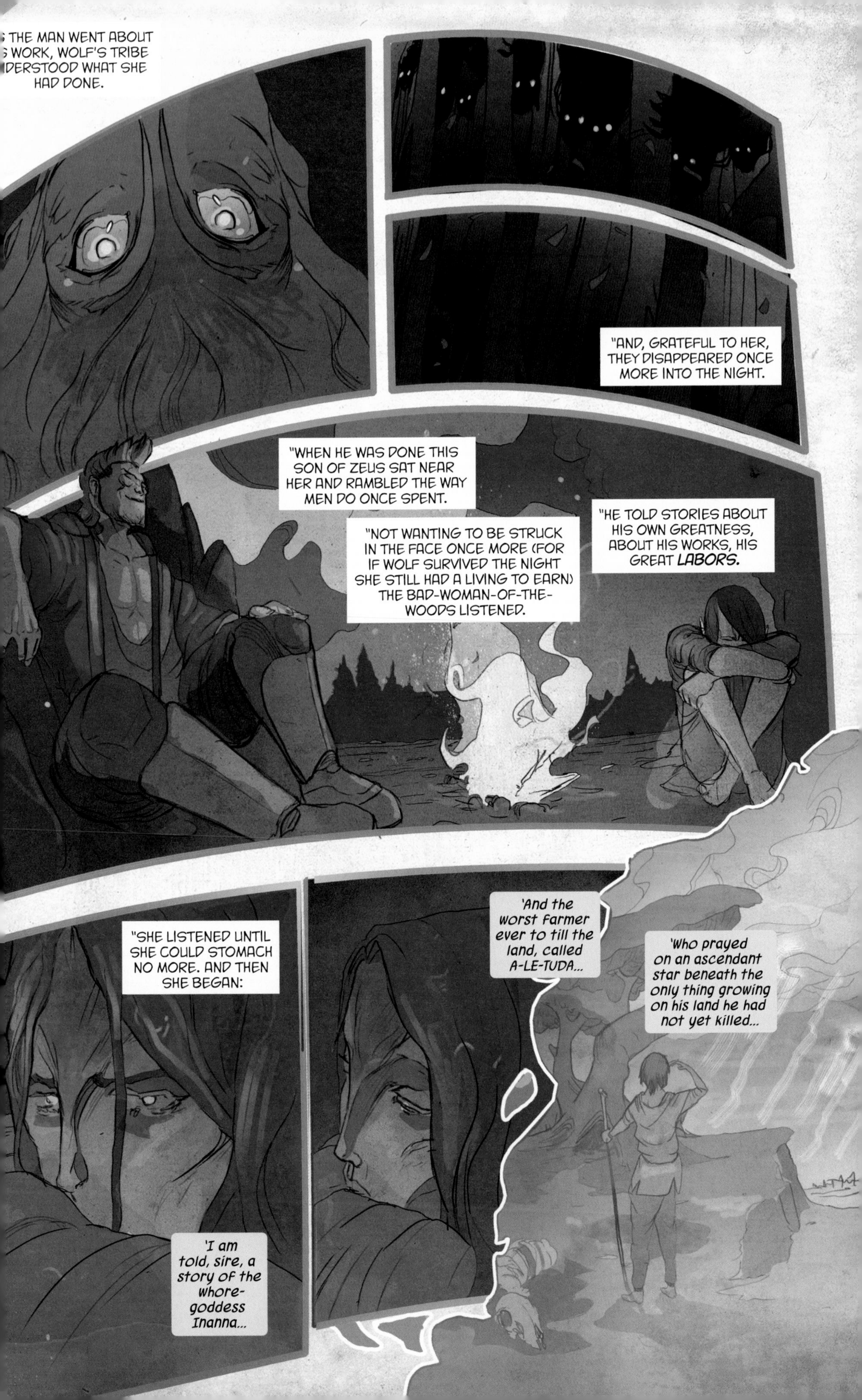
S THE MAN WENT ABOUT S WORK, WOLF'S TRIBE DERSTOOD WHAT SHE HAD DONE.
"AND, GRATEFUL TO HER, THEY DISAPPEARED ONCE MORE INTO THE NIGHT.
"WHEN HE WAS DONE THIS SON OF ZEUS SAT NEAR HER AND RAMBLED THE WAY MEN DO ONCE SPENT.
"NOT WANTING TO BE STRUCK IN THE FACE ONCE MORE (FOR IF WOLF SURVIVED THE NIGHT SHE STILL HAD A LIVING TO EARN) THE BAD-WOMAN-OF-THE-WOODS LISTENED.
"HE TOLD STORIES ABOUT HIS OWN GREATNESS, ABOUT HIS WORKS, HIS GREAT LABORS.
"SHE LISTENED UNTIL SHE COULD STOMACH NO MORE. AND THEN SHE BEGAN:
'I am told, sire, a story of the whore-goddess Inanna...
'And the worst farmer ever to till the land, called A-LE-TUDA...
'Who prayed on an ascendant star beneath the only thing growing on his land he had not yet killed...

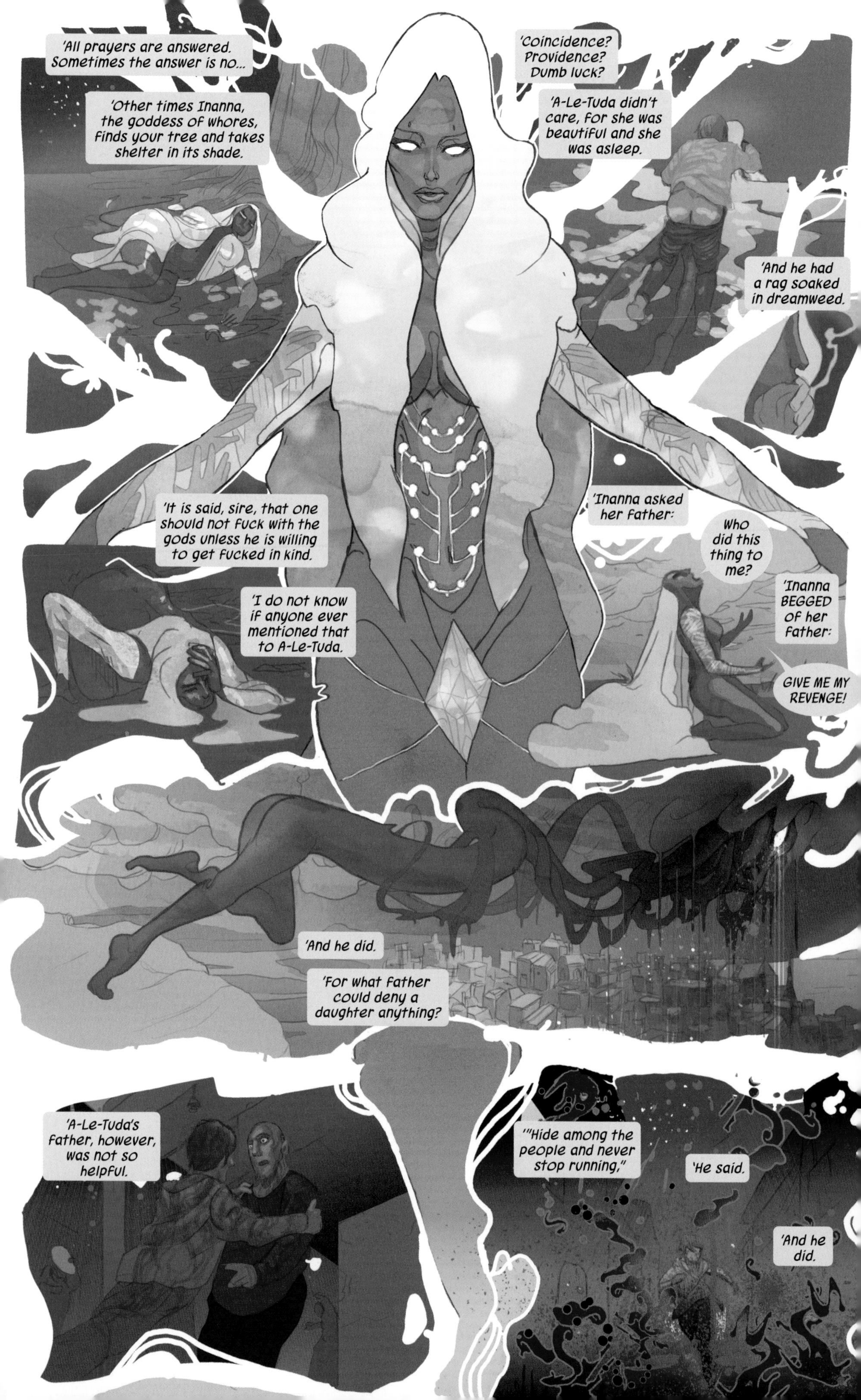
'All prayers are answered. Sometimes the answer is no...
'Other times Inanna, the goddess of whores, finds your tree and takes shelter in its shade.
'Coincidence? Providence? Dumb luck?
'A-Le-Tuda didn't care, for she was beautiful and she was asleep.
'And he had a rag soaked in dreamweed.
'It is said, sire, that one should not fuck with the gods unless he is willing to get fucked in kind.
'I do not know if anyone ever mentioned that to A-Le-Tuda.
'Inanna asked her father:
Who did this thing to me?
'Inanna BEGGED of her father:
GIVE ME MY REVENGE!
'And he did.
'For what father could deny a daughter anything?
'A-Le-Tuda's father, however, was not so helpful.
'"Hide among the people and never stop running,"
'He said.
'And he did.

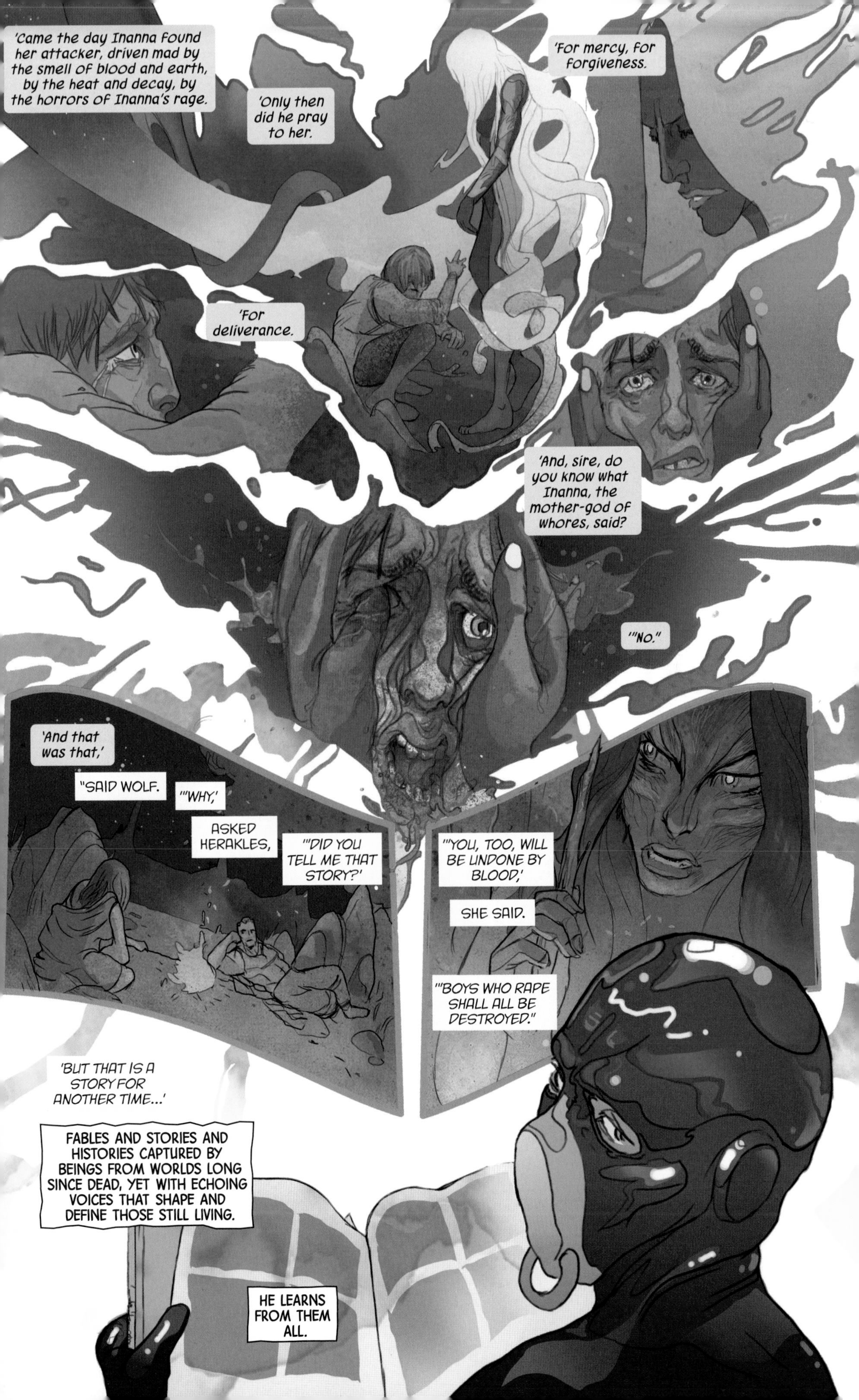

'Came the day Inanna found her attacker, driven mad by the smell of blood and earth, by the heat and decay, by the horrors of Inanna's rage.
'Only then did he pray to her.
'For mercy, for forgiveness.
'For deliverance.
'And, sire, do you know what Inanna, the mother-god of whores, said?
'"No."
'And that was that,'
"SAID WOLF.
'"WHY,'
ASKED HERAKLES,
'"DID YOU TELL ME THAT STORY?'
'"YOU, TOO, WILL BE UNDONE BY BLOOD,'
SHE SAID.
'"BOYS WHO RAPE SHALL ALL BE DESTROYED."
'BUT THAT IS A STORY FOR ANOTHER TIME...'
FABLES AND STORIES AND HISTORIES CAPTURED BY BEINGS FROM WORLDS LONG SINCE DEAD, YET WITH ECHOING VOICES THAT SHAPE AND DEFINE THOSE STILL LIVING.
HE LEARNS FROM THEM ALL.

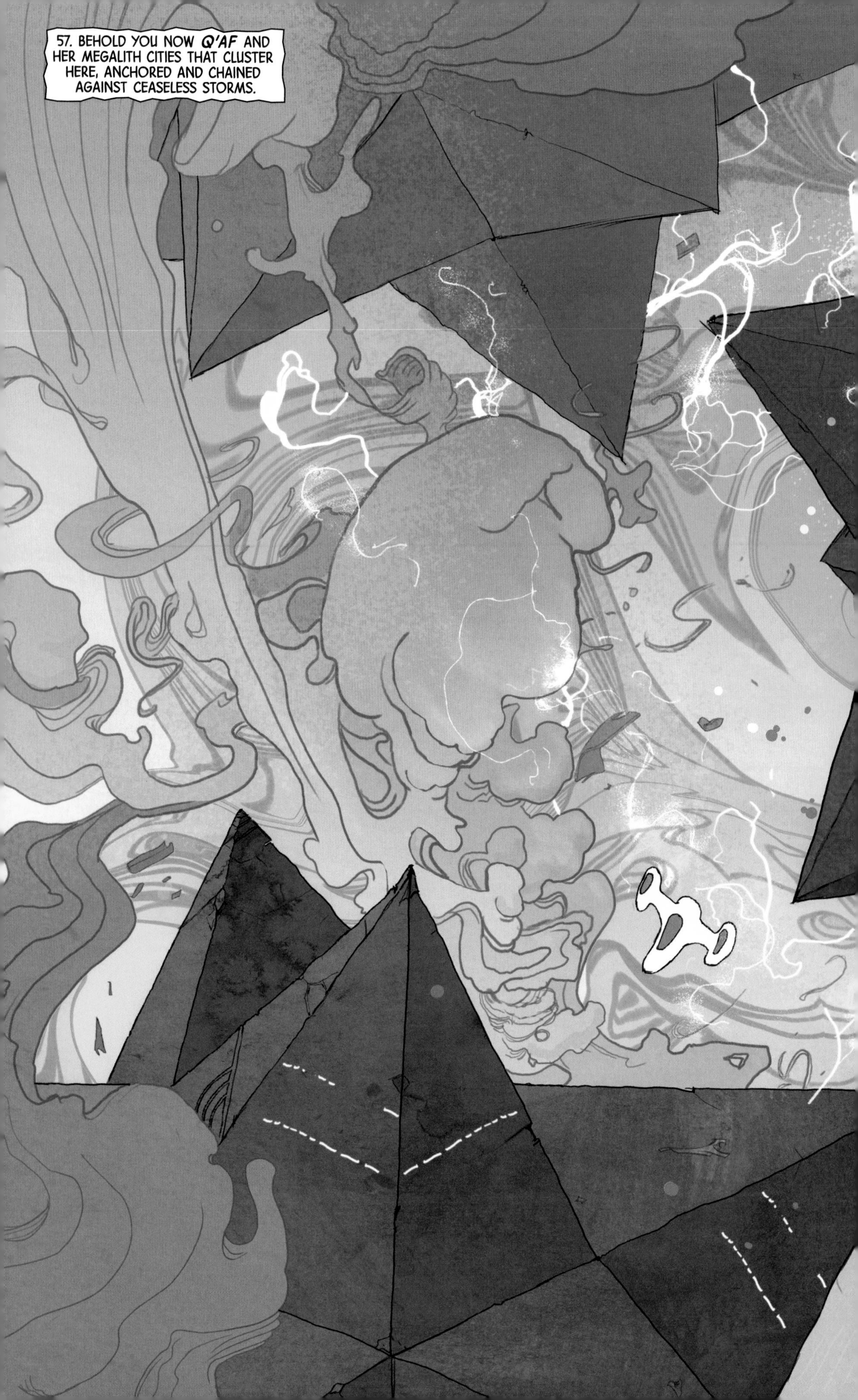
57. BEHOLD YOU NOW Q'AF AND HER MEGALITH CITIES THAT CLUSTER HERE, ANCHORED AND CHAINED AGAINST CEASELESS STORMS.

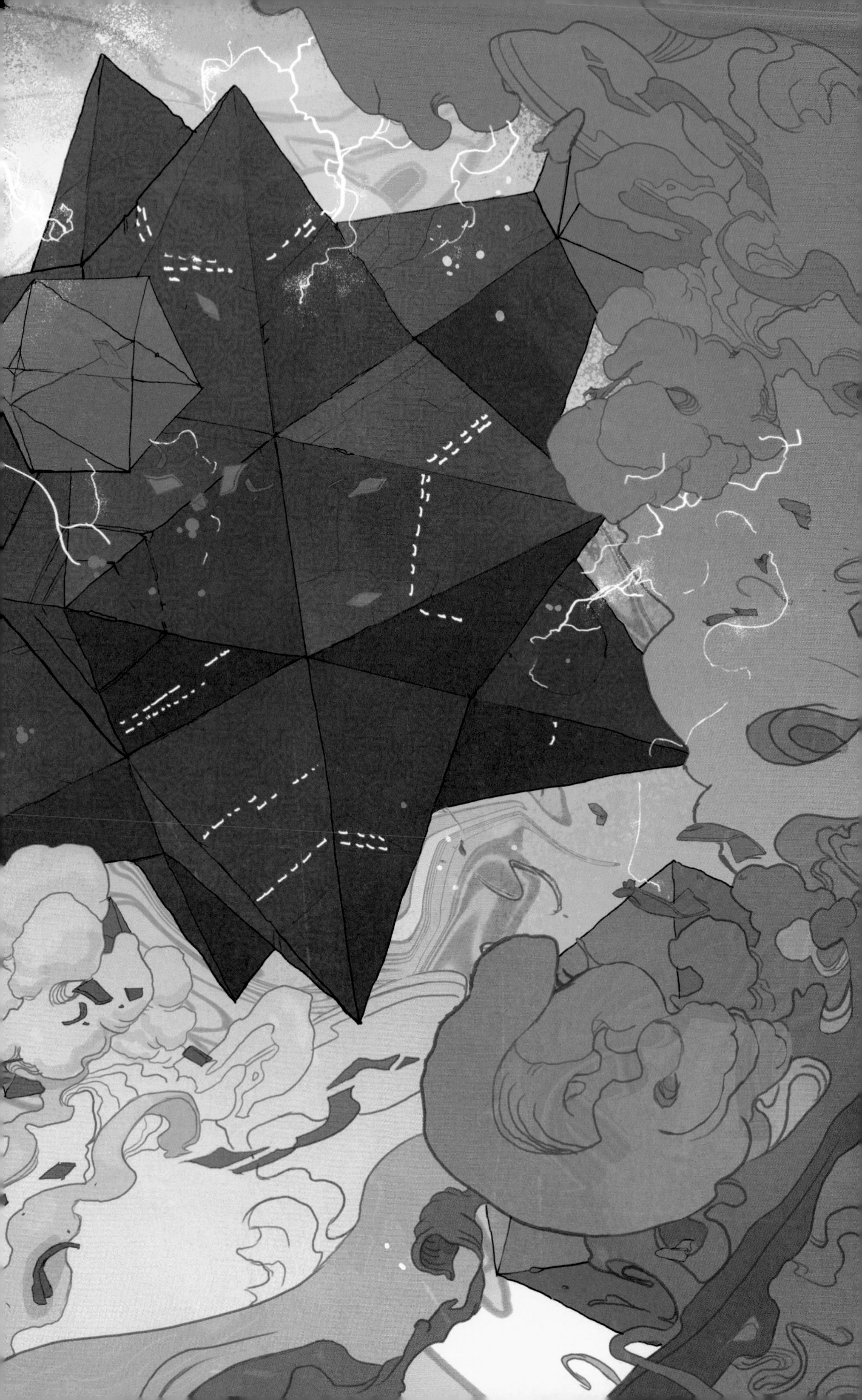

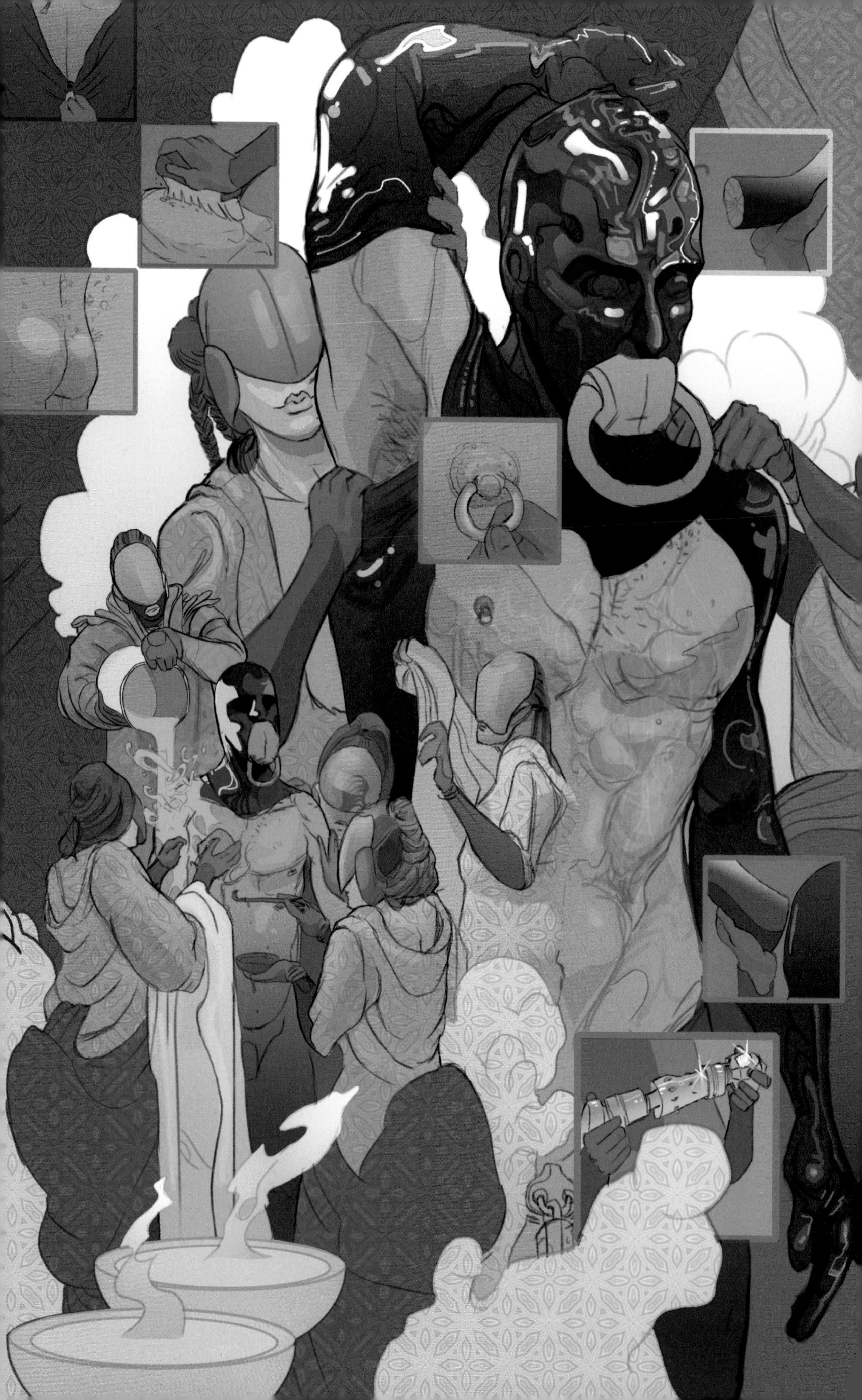

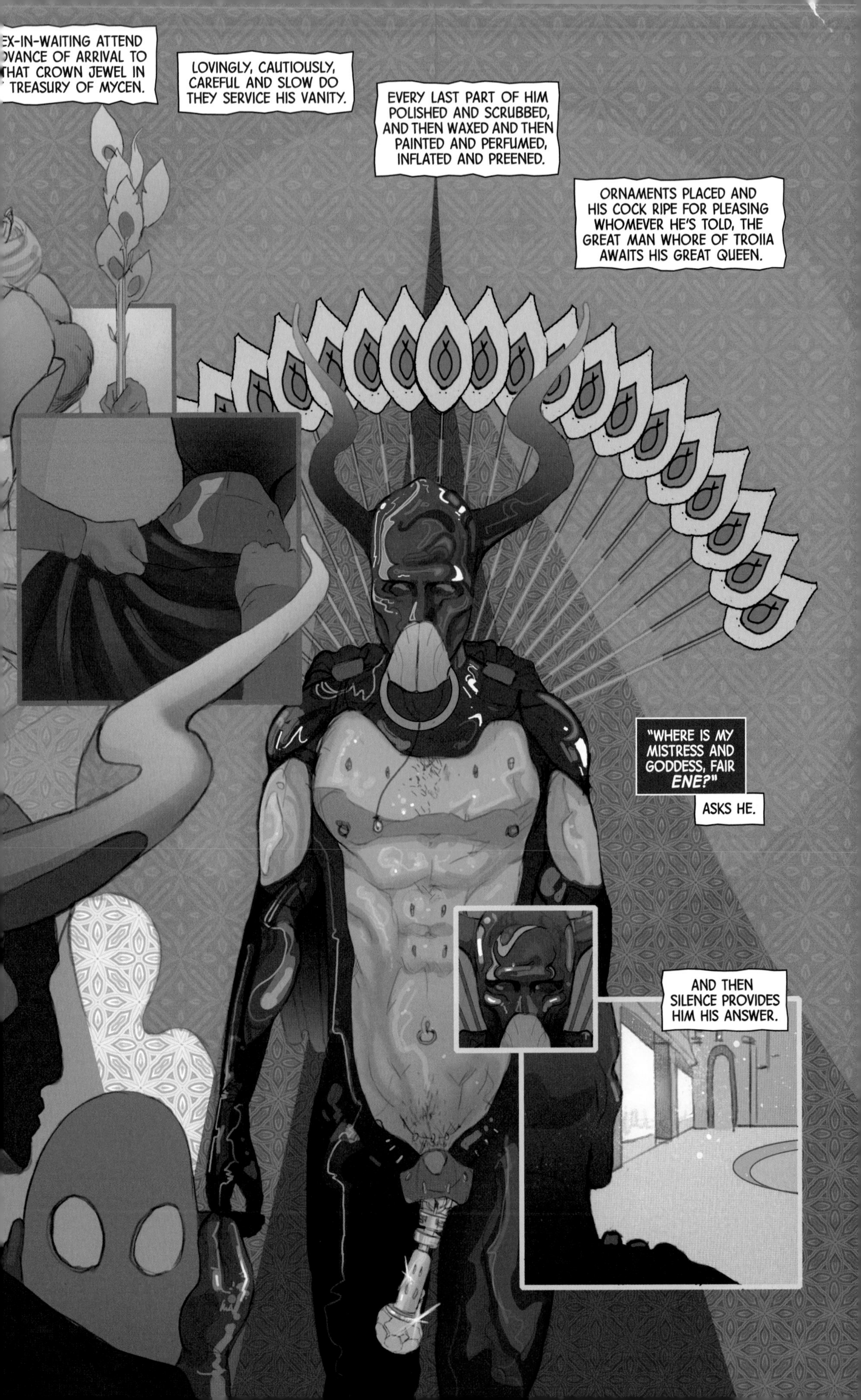

EX-IN-WAITING ATTEND DVANCE OF ARRIVAL TO THAT CROWN JEWEL IN TREASURY OF MYCEN.
LOVINGLY, CAUTIOUSLY, CAREFUL AND SLOW DO THEY SERVICE HIS VANITY.
EVERY LAST PART OF HIM POLISHED AND SCRUBBED, AND THEN WAXED AND THEN PAINTED AND PERFUMED, INFLATED AND PREENED.
ORNAMENTS PLACED AND HIS COCK RIPE FOR PLEASING WHOMEVER HE'S TOLD, THE GREAT MAN WHORE OF TROIIA AWAITS HIS GREAT QUEEN.
"WHERE IS MY MISTRESS AND GODDESS, FAIR *ENE?*"
ASKS HE.
AND THEN SILENCE PROVIDES HIM HIS ANSWER.

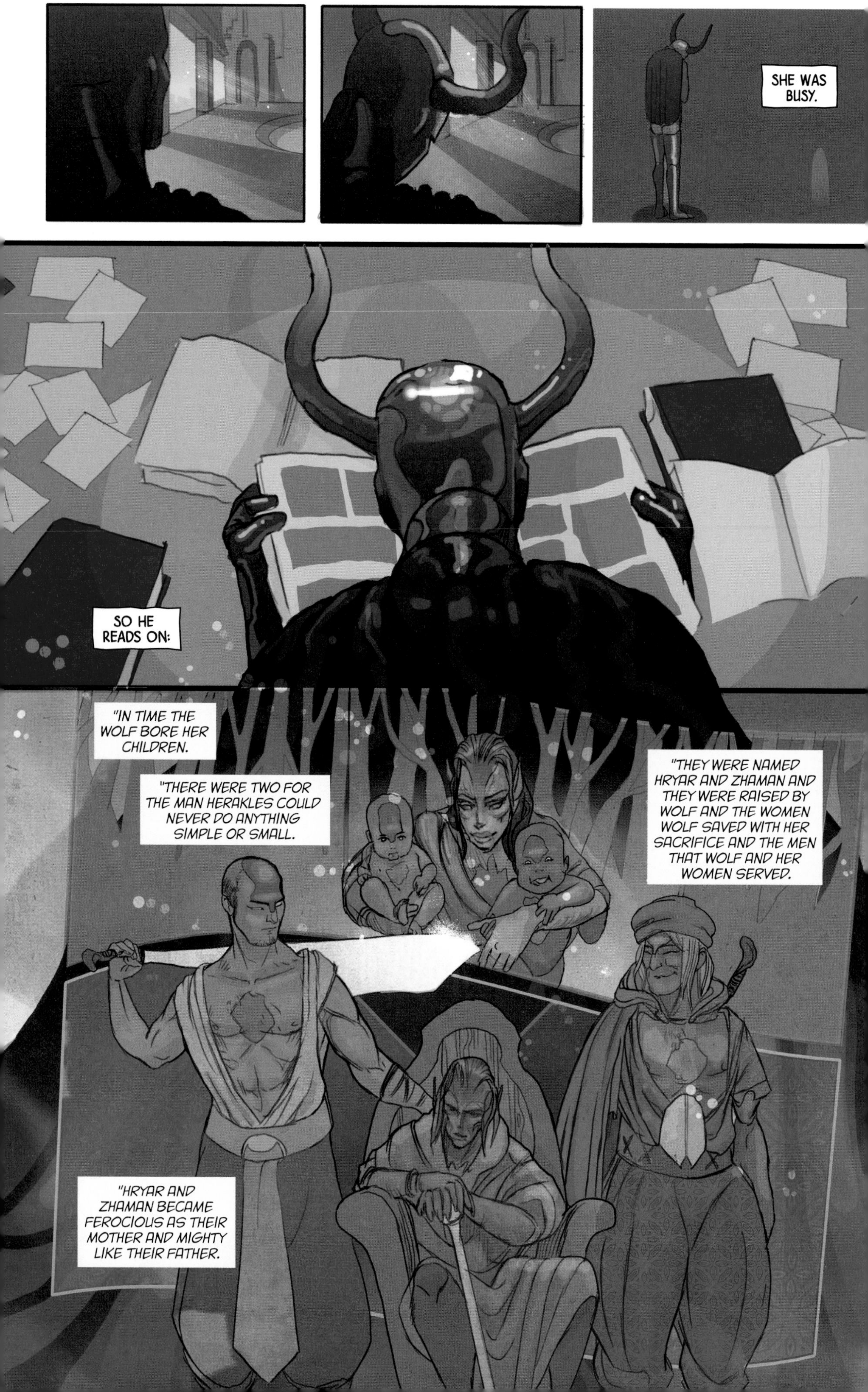
SHE WAS BUSY.
SO HE READS ON:
"IN TIME THE WOLF BORE HER CHILDREN.
"THERE WERE TWO FOR THE MAN HERAKLES COULD NEVER DO ANYTHING SIMPLE OR SMALL.
"THEY WERE NAMED HRYAR AND ZHAMAN AND THEY WERE RAISED BY WOLF AND THE WOMEN WOLF SAVED WITH HER SACRIFICE AND THE MEN THAT WOLF AND HER WOMEN SERVED.
"HRYAR AND ZHAMAN BECAME FEROCIOUS AS THEIR MOTHER AND MIGHTY LIKE THEIR FATHER.

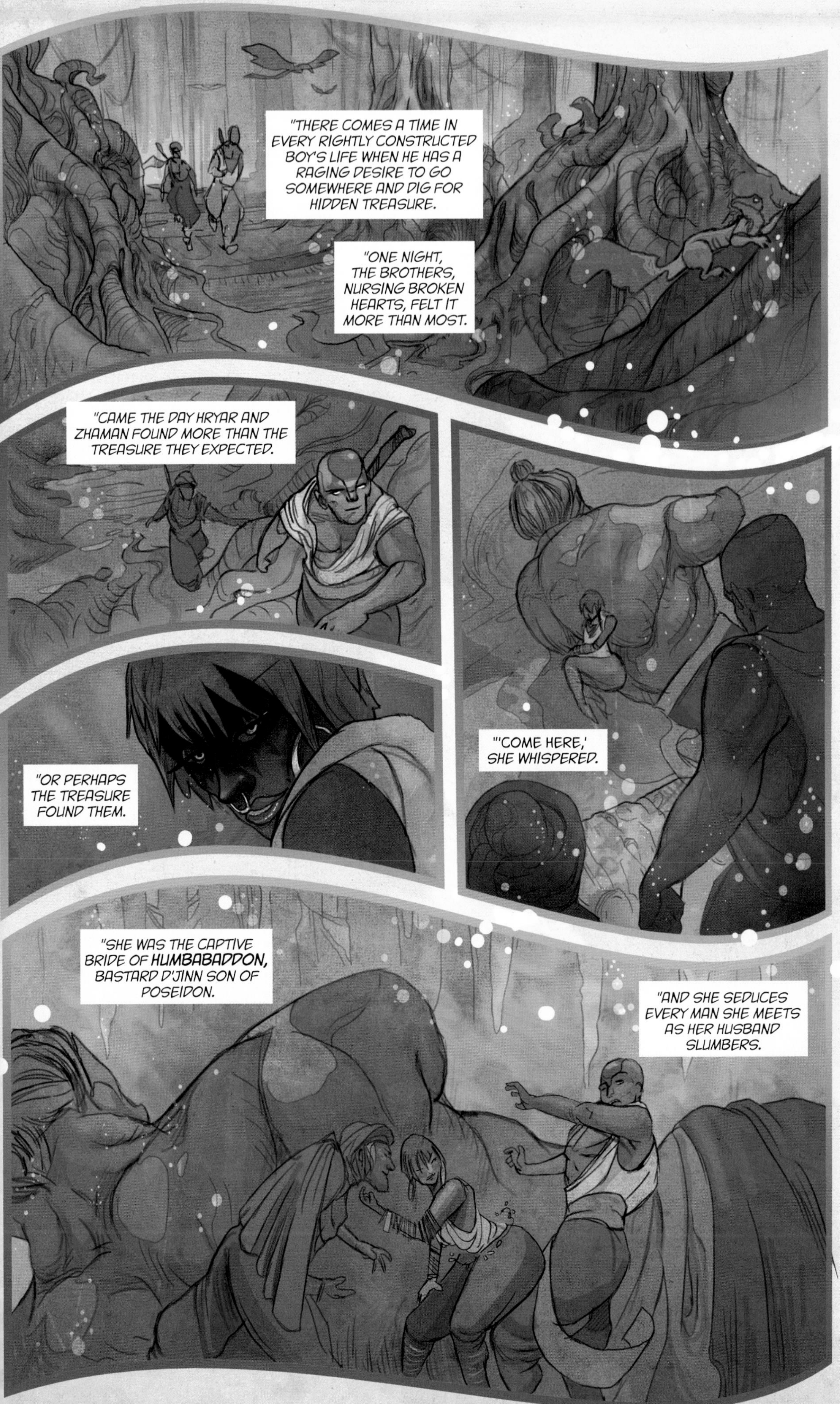
"THERE COMES A TIME IN EVERY RIGHTLY CONSTRUCTED BOY'S LIFE WHEN HE HAS A RAGING DESIRE TO GO SOMEWHERE AND DIG FOR HIDDEN TREASURE.
"ONE NIGHT, THE BROTHERS, NURSING BROKEN HEARTS, FELT IT MORE THAN MOST.
"CAME THE DAY HRYAR AND ZHAMAN FOUND MORE THAN THE TREASURE THEY EXPECTED.
"OR PERHAPS THE TREASURE FOUND THEM.
"'COME HERE,' SHE WHISPERED.
"SHE WAS THE CAPTIVE BRIDE OF **HUMBABADDON,** BASTARD D'JINN SON OF POSEIDON.
"AND SHE SEDUCES EVERY MAN SHE MEETS AS HER HUSBAND SLUMBERS.

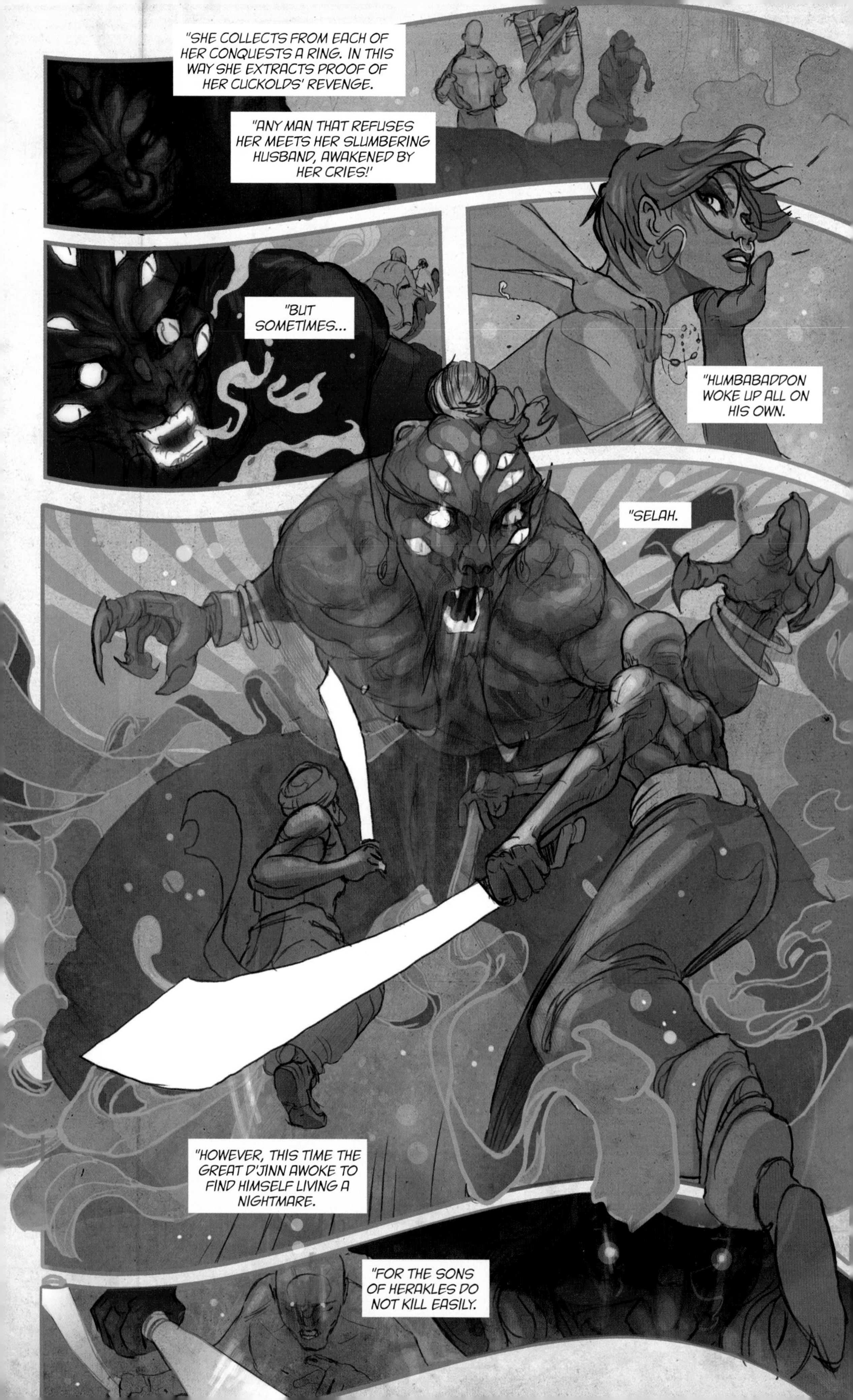
"SHE COLLECTS FROM EACH OF HER CONQUESTS A RING. IN THIS WAY SHE EXTRACTS PROOF OF HER CUCKOLDS' REVENGE.
"ANY MAN THAT REFUSES HER MEETS HER SLUMBERING HUSBAND, AWAKENED BY HER CRIES!'
"BUT SOMETIMES...
"HUMBABADDON WOKE UP ALL ON HIS OWN.
"SELAH.
"HOWEVER, THIS TIME THE GREAT D'JINN AWOKE TO FIND HIMSELF LIVING A NIGHTMARE.
"FOR THE SONS OF HERAKLES DO NOT KILL EASILY.

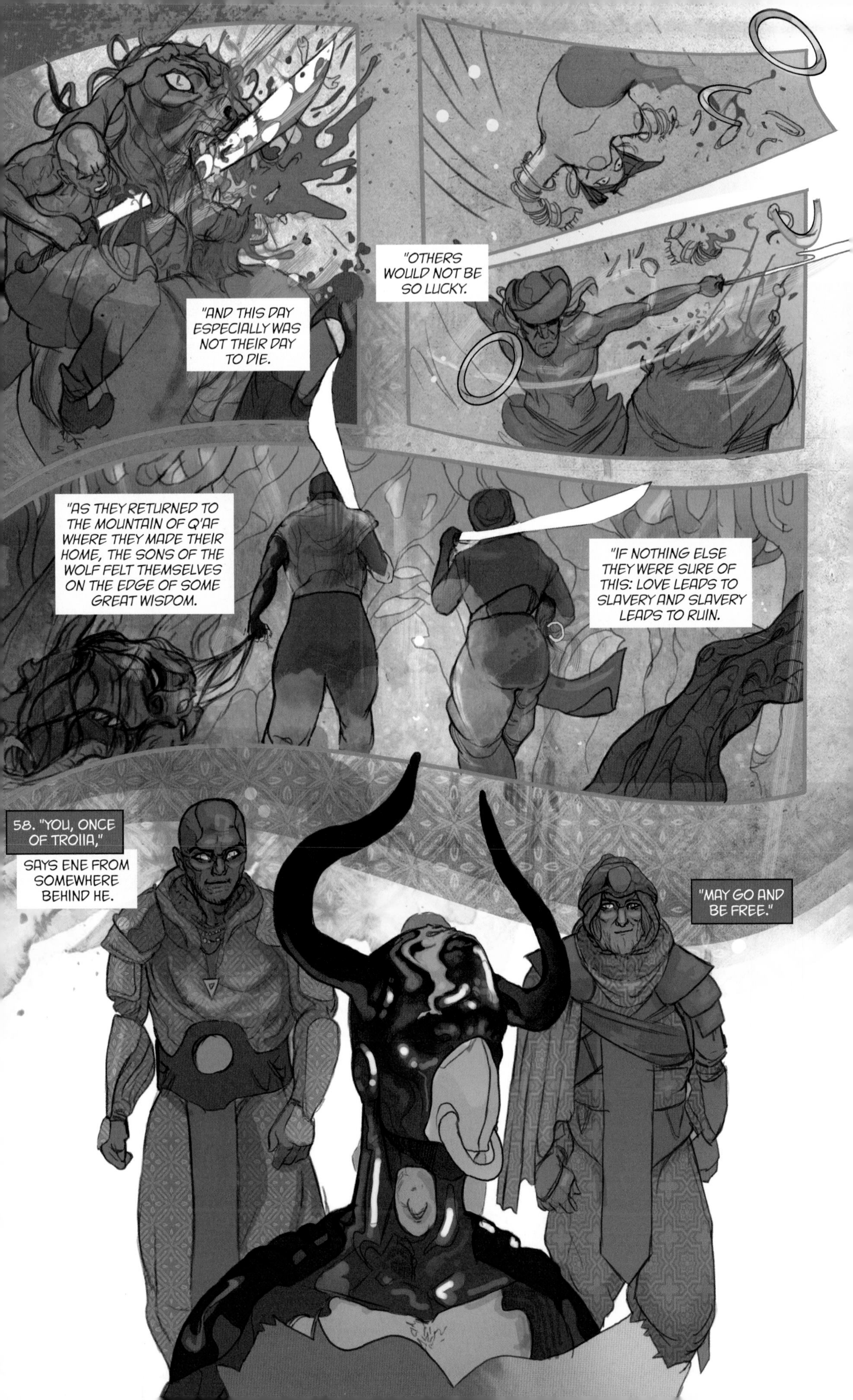
"AND THIS DAY ESPECIALLY WAS NOT THEIR DAY TO DIE.
"OTHERS WOULD NOT BE SO LUCKY.
"AS THEY RETURNED TO THE MOUNTAIN OF Q'AF WHERE THEY MADE THEIR HOME, THE SONS OF THE WOLF FELT THEMSELVES ON THE EDGE OF SOME GREAT WISDOM.
"IF NOTHING ELSE THEY WERE SURE OF THIS: LOVE LEADS TO SLAVERY AND SLAVERY LEADS TO RUIN.
58. "YOU, ONCE OF TROIIA,"
SAYS ENE FROM SOMEWHERE BEHIND HE.
"MAY GO AND BE FREE."

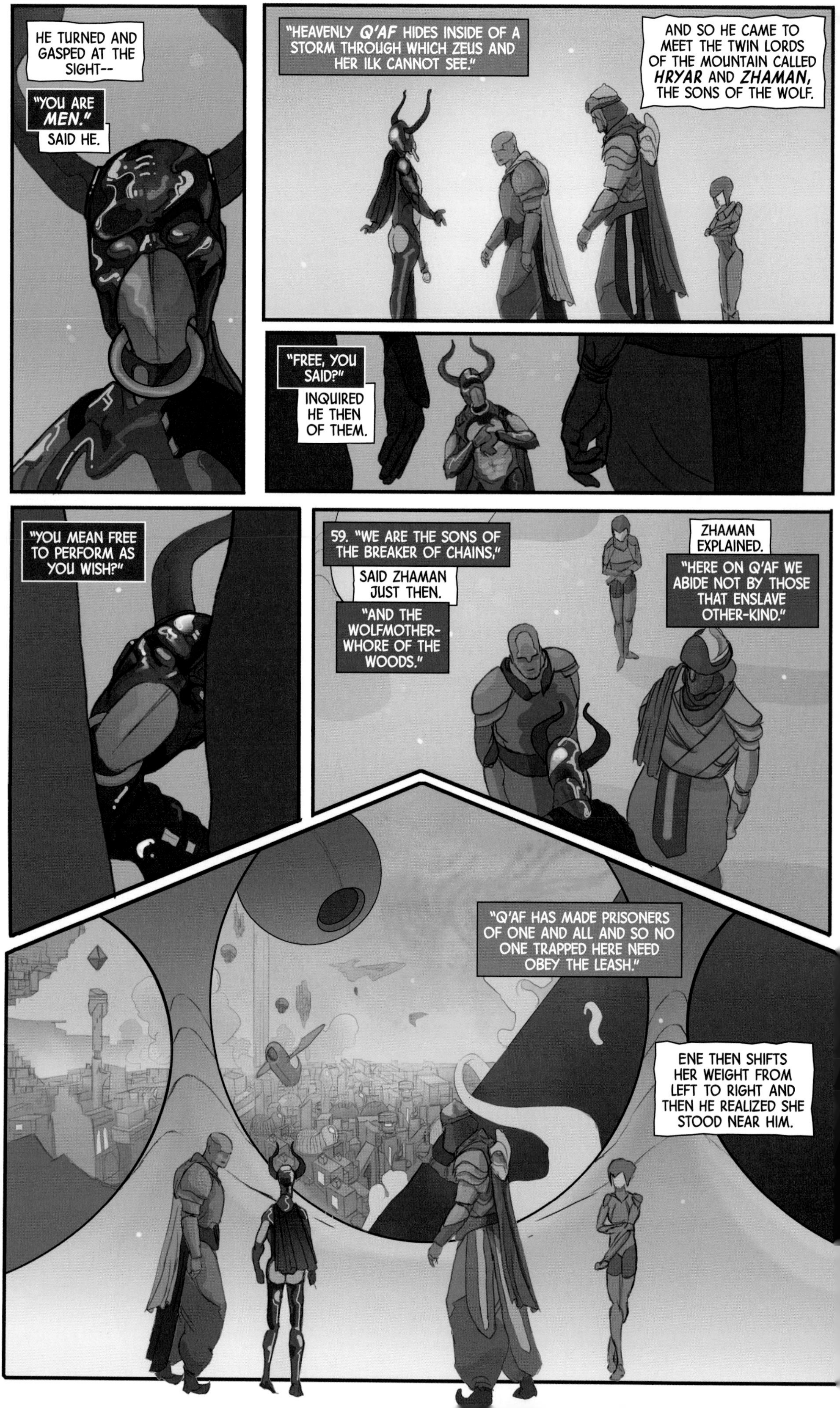
HE TURNED AND GASPED AT THE SIGHT--
"YOU ARE MEN."
SAID HE.
"HEAVENLY Q'AF HIDES INSIDE OF A STORM THROUGH WHICH ZEUS AND HER ILK CANNOT SEE."
AND SO HE CAME TO MEET THE TWIN LORDS OF THE MOUNTAIN CALLED HRYAR AND ZHAMAN, THE SONS OF THE WOLF.
"FREE, YOU SAID?"
INQUIRED HE THEN OF THEM.
"YOU MEAN FREE TO PERFORM AS YOU WISH?"
59. "WE ARE THE SONS OF THE BREAKER OF CHAINS,"
SAID ZHAMAN JUST THEN.
"AND THE WOLFMOTHER-WHORE OF THE WOODS."
ZHAMAN EXPLAINED.
"HERE ON Q'AF WE ABIDE NOT BY THOSE THAT ENSLAVE OTHER-KIND."
"Q'AF HAS MADE PRISONERS OF ONE AND ALL AND SO NO ONE TRAPPED HERE NEED OBEY THE LEASH."
ENE THEN SHIFTS HER WEIGHT FROM LEFT TO RIGHT AND THEN HE REALIZED SHE STOOD NEAR HIM.

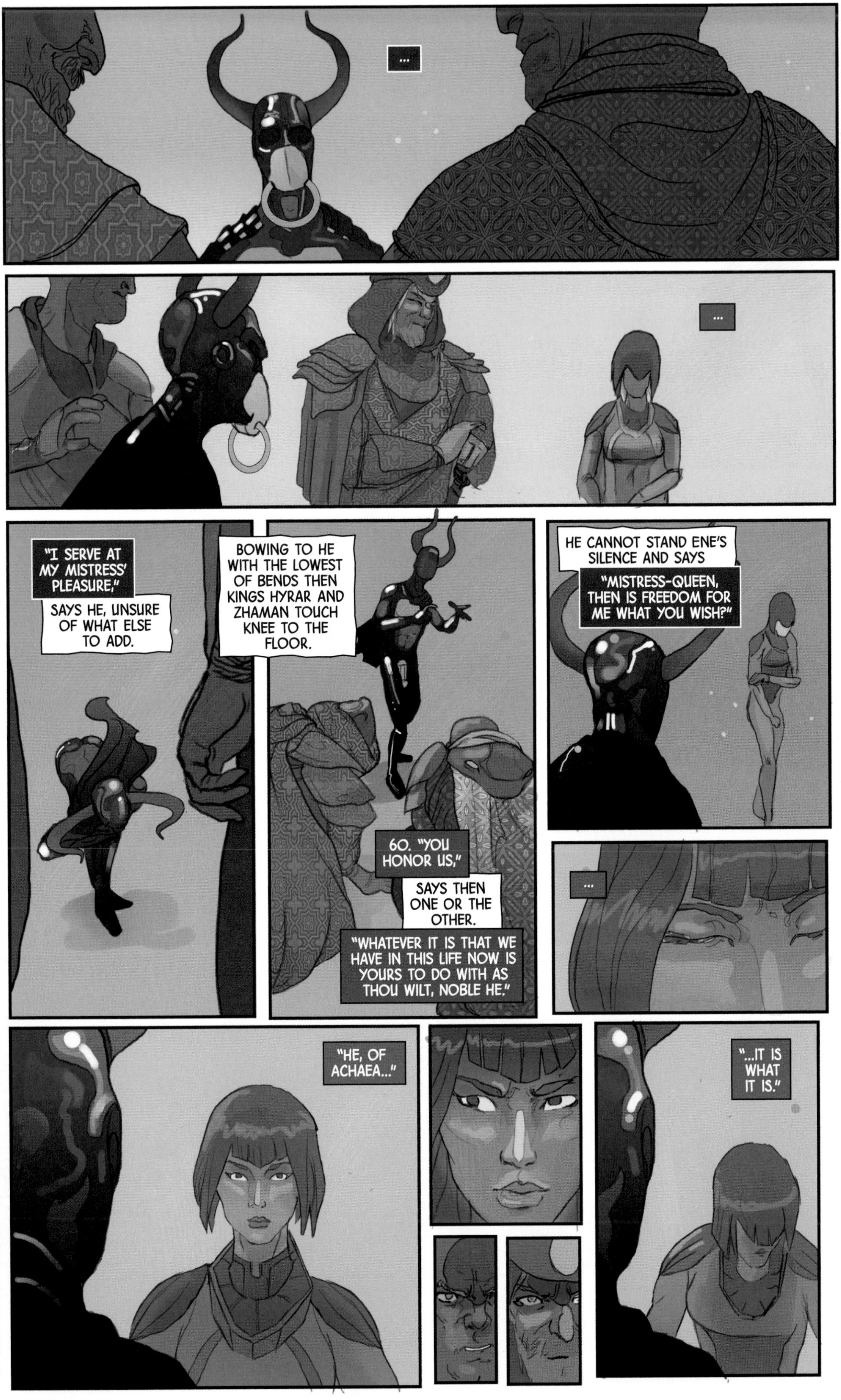
...
...
"I SERVE AT MY MISTRESS' PLEASURE,"
SAYS HE, UNSURE OF WHAT ELSE TO ADD.
BOWING TO HE WITH THE LOWEST OF BENDS THEN KINGS HYRAR AND ZHAMAN TOUCH KNEE TO THE FLOOR.
60. "YOU HONOR US,"
SAYS THEN ONE OR THE OTHER.
"WHATEVER IT IS THAT WE HAVE IN THIS LIFE NOW IS YOURS TO DO WITH AS THOU WILT, NOBLE HE."
HE CANNOT STAND ENE'S SILENCE AND SAYS
"MISTRESS-QUEEN, THEN IS FREEDOM FOR ME WHAT YOU WISH?"
...
"HE, OF ACHAEA..."
"...IT IS WHAT IT IS."

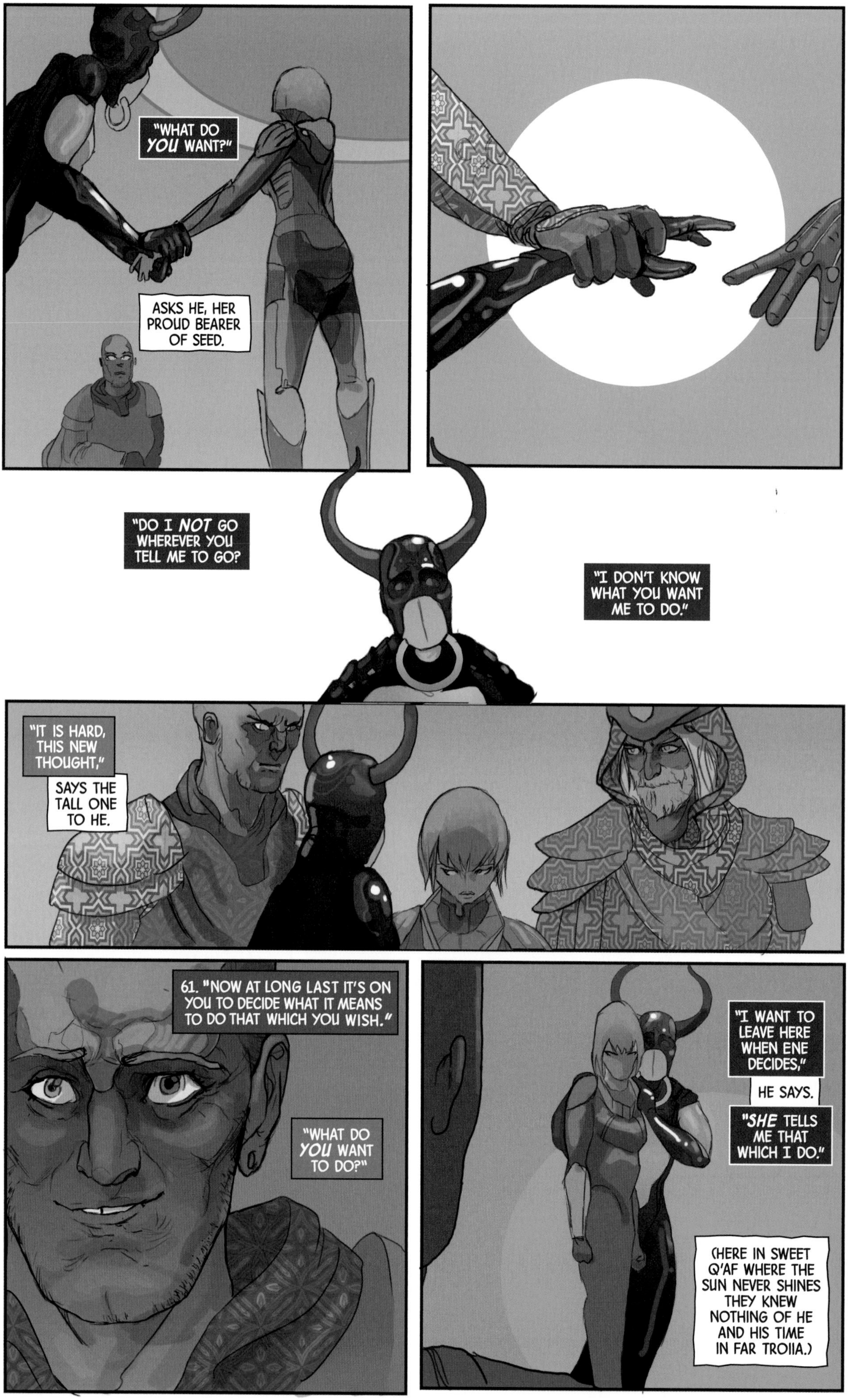
"WHAT DO YOU WANT?"
ASKS HE, HER PROUD BEARER OF SEED.
"DO I NOT GO WHEREVER YOU TELL ME TO GO?
"I DON'T KNOW WHAT YOU WANT ME TO DO."
"IT IS HARD, THIS NEW THOUGHT,"
SAYS THE TALL ONE TO HE.
61. "NOW AT LONG LAST IT'S ON YOU TO DECIDE WHAT IT MEANS TO DO THAT WHICH YOU WISH."
"WHAT DO YOU WANT TO DO?"
"I WANT TO LEAVE HERE WHEN ENE DECIDES,"
HE SAYS.
"SHE TELLS ME THAT WHICH I DO."
(HERE IN SWEET Q'AF WHERE THE SUN NEVER SHINES THEY KNEW NOTHING OF HE AND HIS TIME IN FAR TROIIA.)

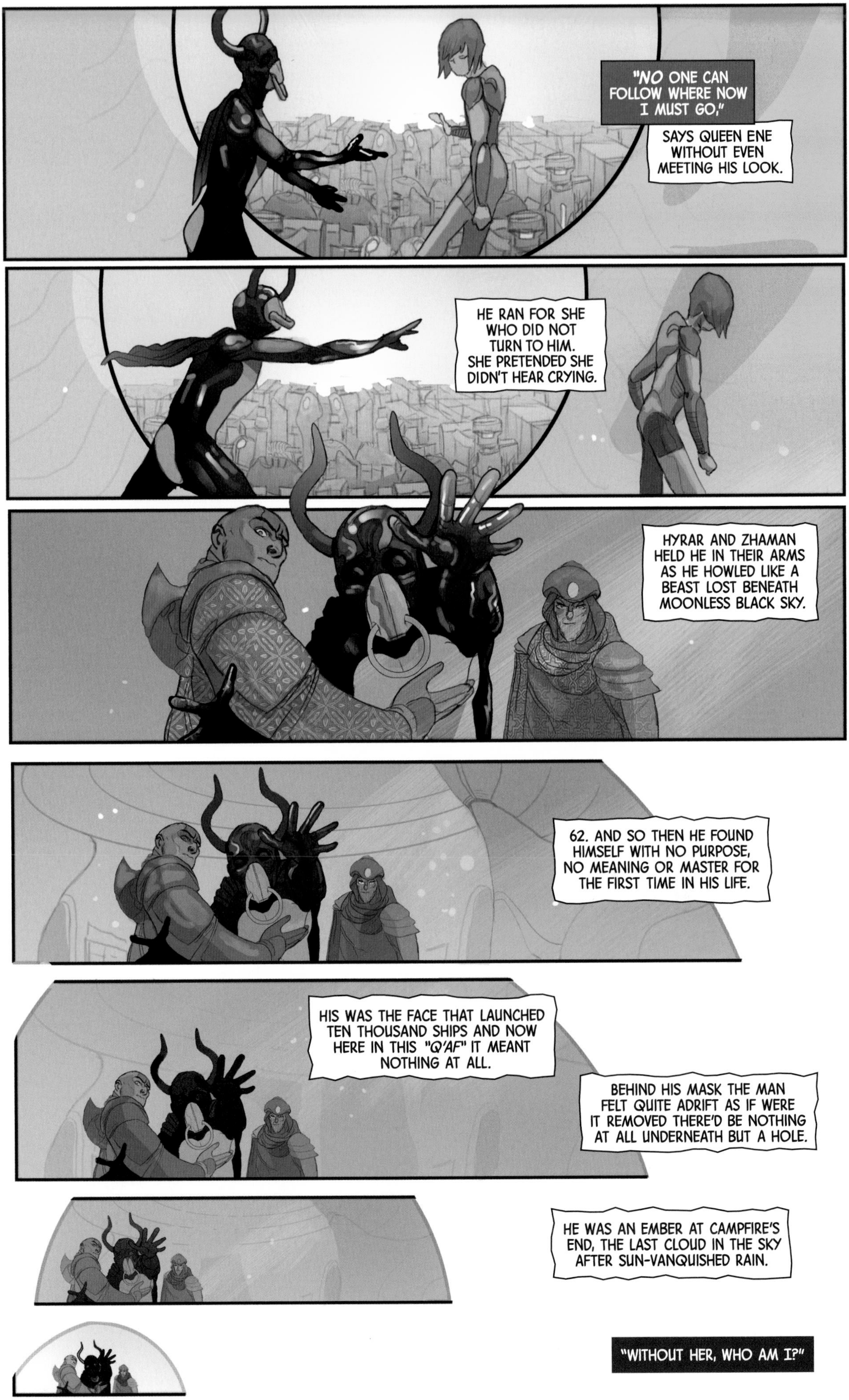
"NO ONE CAN FOLLOW WHERE NOW I MUST GO,"
SAYS QUEEN ENE WITHOUT EVEN MEETING HIS LOOK.
HE RAN FOR SHE WHO DID NOT TURN TO HIM. SHE PRETENDED SHE DIDN'T HEAR CRYING.
HYRAR AND ZHAMAN HELD HE IN THEIR ARMS AS HE HOWLED LIKE A BEAST LOST BENEATH MOONLESS BLACK SKY.
62. AND SO THEN HE FOUND HIMSELF WITH NO PURPOSE, NO MEANING OR MASTER FOR THE FIRST TIME IN HIS LIFE.
HIS WAS THE FACE THAT LAUNCHED TEN THOUSAND SHIPS AND NOW HERE IN THIS "Q'AF" IT MEANT NOTHING AT ALL.
BEHIND HIS MASK THE MAN FELT QUITE ADRIFT AS IF WERE IT REMOVED THERE'D BE NOTHING AT ALL UNDERNEATH BUT A HOLE.
HE WAS AN EMBER AT CAMPFIRE'S END, THE LAST CLOUD IN THE SKY AFTER SUN-VANQUISHED RAIN.
"WITHOUT HER, WHO AM I?"

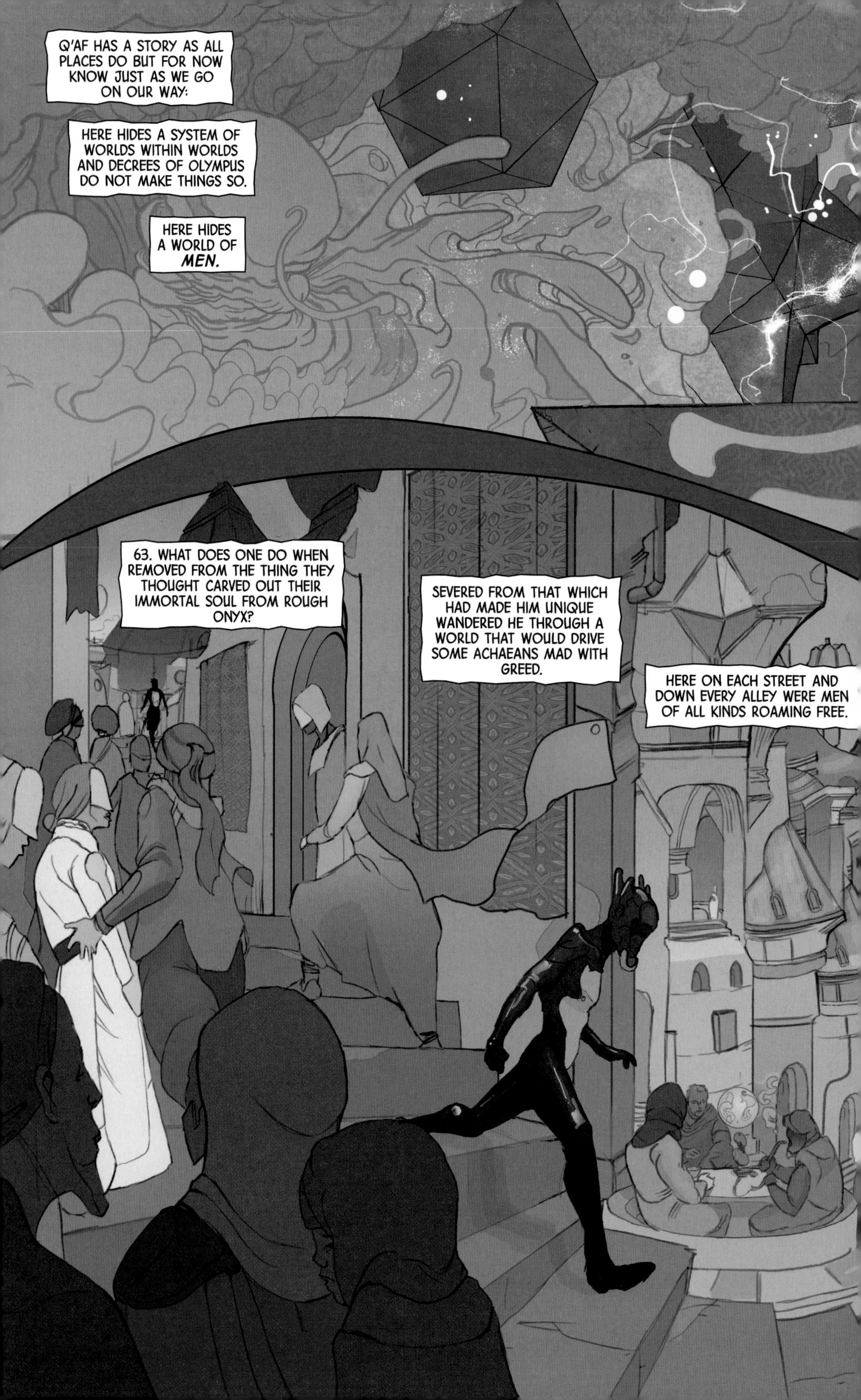
Q'AF HAS A STORY AS ALL PLACES DO BUT FOR NOW KNOW JUST AS WE GO ON OUR WAY:
HERE HIDES A SYSTEM OF WORLDS WITHIN WORLDS AND DECREES OF OLYMPUS DO NOT MAKE THINGS SO.
HERE HIDES A WORLD OF MEN.
63. WHAT DOES ONE DO WHEN REMOVED FROM THE THING THEY THOUGHT CARVED OUT THEIR IMMORTAL SOUL FROM ROUGH ONYX?
SEVERED FROM THAT WHICH HAD MADE HIM UNIQUE WANDERED HE THROUGH A WORLD THAT WOULD DRIVE SOME ACHAEANS MAD WITH GREED.
HERE ON EACH STREET AND DOWN EVERY ALLEY WERE MEN OF ALL KINDS ROAMING FREE.

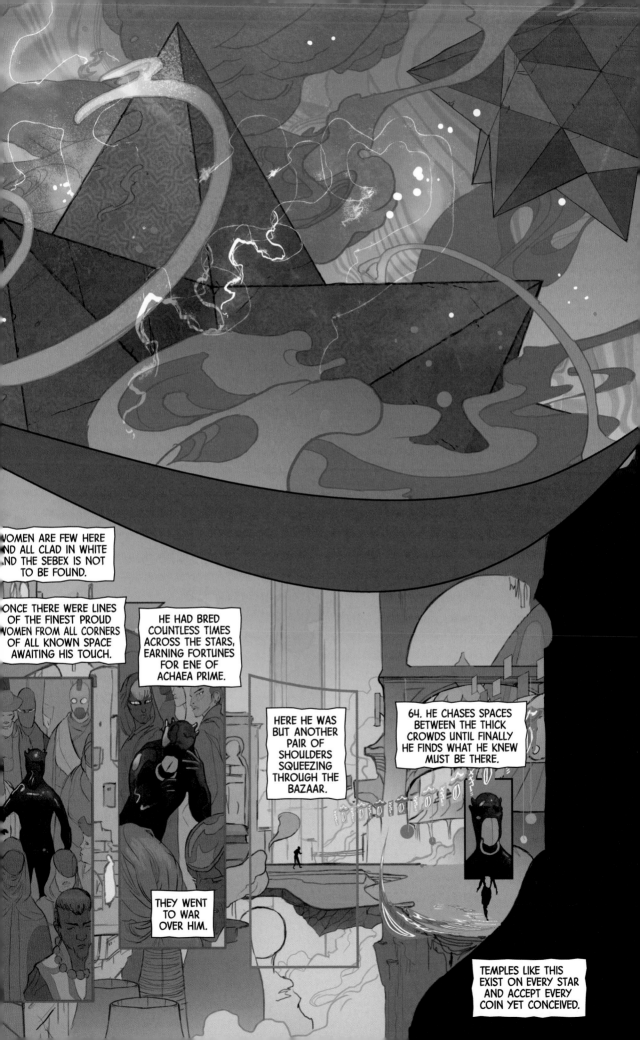

WOMEN ARE FEW HERE AND ALL CLAD IN WHITE AND THE SEBEX IS NOT TO BE FOUND.

ONCE THERE WERE LINES OF THE FINEST PROUD WOMEN FROM ALL CORNERS OF ALL KNOWN SPACE AWAITING HIS TOUCH.

HE HAD BRED COUNTLESS TIMES ACROSS THE STARS, EARNING FORTUNES FOR ENE OF ACHAEA PRIME.

HERE HE WAS BUT ANOTHER PAIR OF SHOULDERS SQUEEZING THROUGH THE BAZAAR.

64. HE CHASES SPACES BETWEEN THE THICK CROWDS UNTIL FINALLY HE FINDS WHAT HE KNEW MUST BE THERE.

THEY WENT TO WAR OVER HIM.

TEMPLES LIKE THIS EXIST ON EVERY STAR AND ACCEPT EVERY COIN YET CONCEIVED.

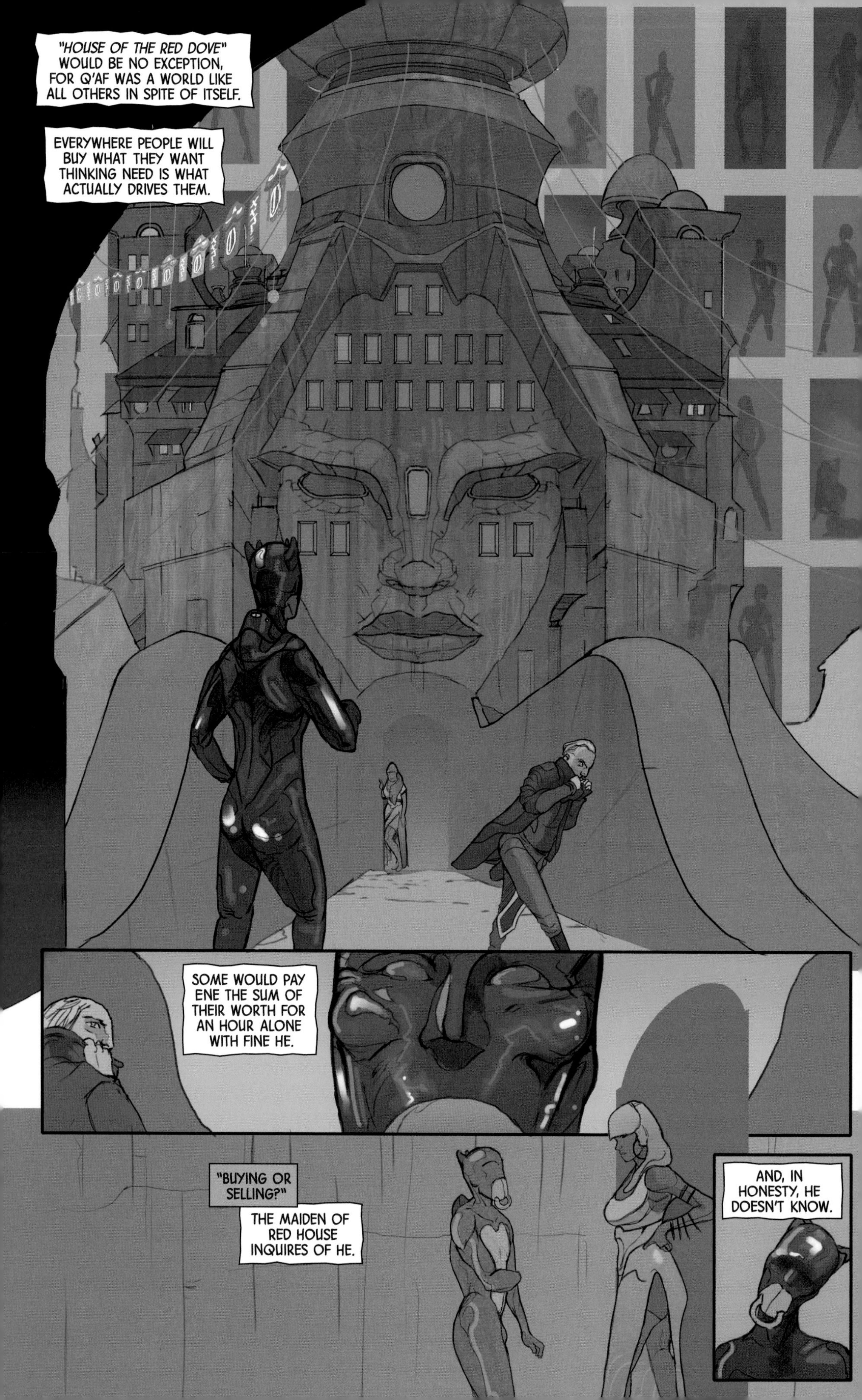
"HOUSE OF THE RED DOVE" WOULD BE NO EXCEPTION, FOR Q'AF WAS A WORLD LIKE ALL OTHERS IN SPITE OF ITSELF.
EVERYWHERE PEOPLE WILL BUY WHAT THEY WANT THINKING NEED IS WHAT ACTUALLY DRIVES THEM.
SOME WOULD PAY ENE THE SUM OF THEIR WORTH FOR AN HOUR ALONE WITH FINE HE.
"BUYING OR SELLING?"
THE MAIDEN OF RED HOUSE INQUIRES OF HE.
AND, IN HONESTY, HE DOESN'T KNOW.

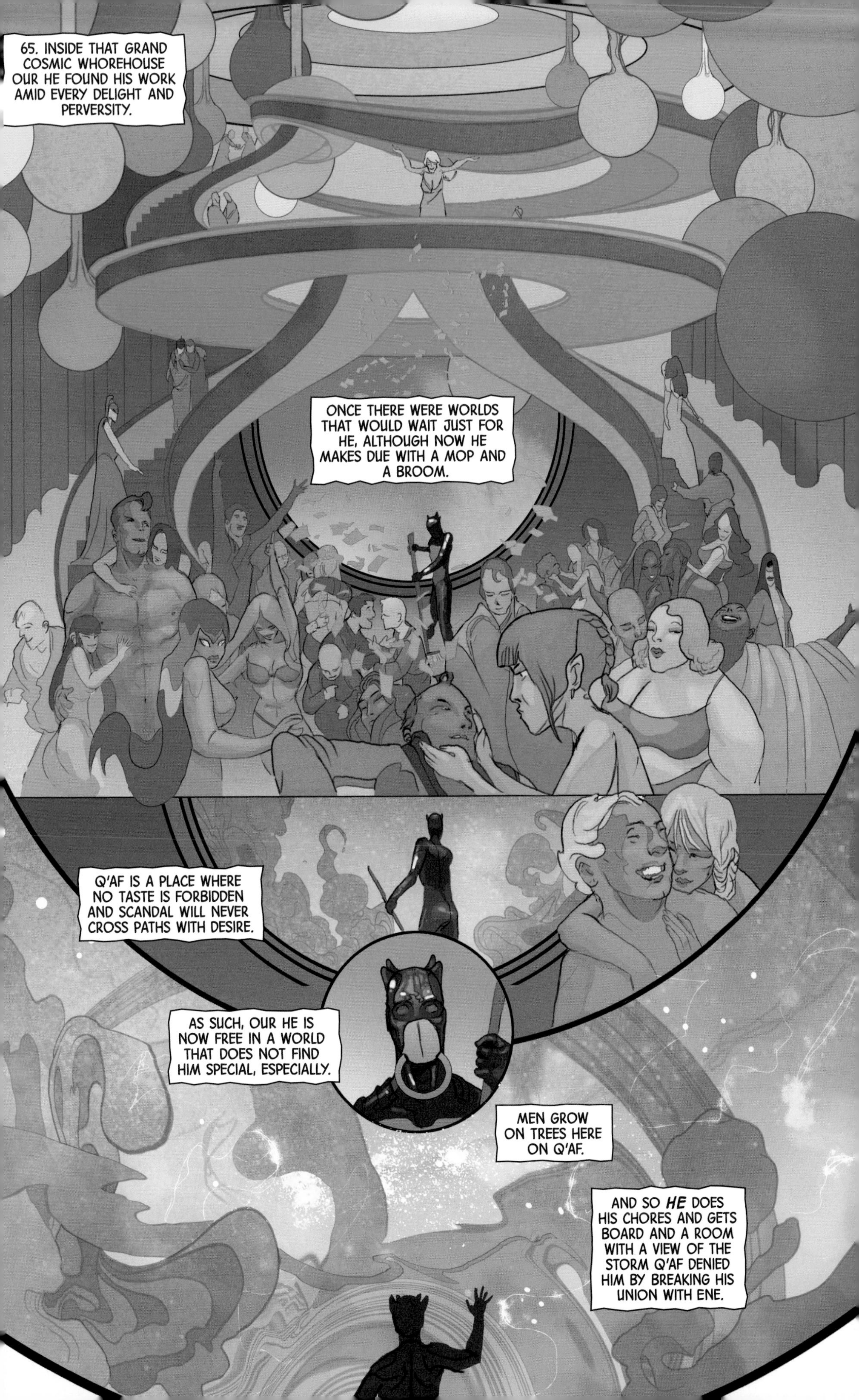
65. INSIDE THAT GRAND COSMIC WHOREHOUSE OUR HE FOUND HIS WORK AMID EVERY DELIGHT AND PERVERSITY.
ONCE THERE WERE WORLDS THAT WOULD WAIT JUST FOR HE, ALTHOUGH NOW HE MAKES DUE WITH A MOP AND A BROOM.
Q'AF IS A PLACE WHERE NO TASTE IS FORBIDDEN AND SCANDAL WILL NEVER CROSS PATHS WITH DESIRE.
AS SUCH, OUR HE IS NOW FREE IN A WORLD THAT DOES NOT FIND HIM SPECIAL, ESPECIALLY.
MEN GROW ON TREES HERE ON Q'AF.
AND SO ***HE*** DOES HIS CHORES AND GETS BOARD AND A ROOM WITH A VIEW OF THE STORM Q'AF DENIED HIM BY BREAKING HIS UNION WITH ENE.

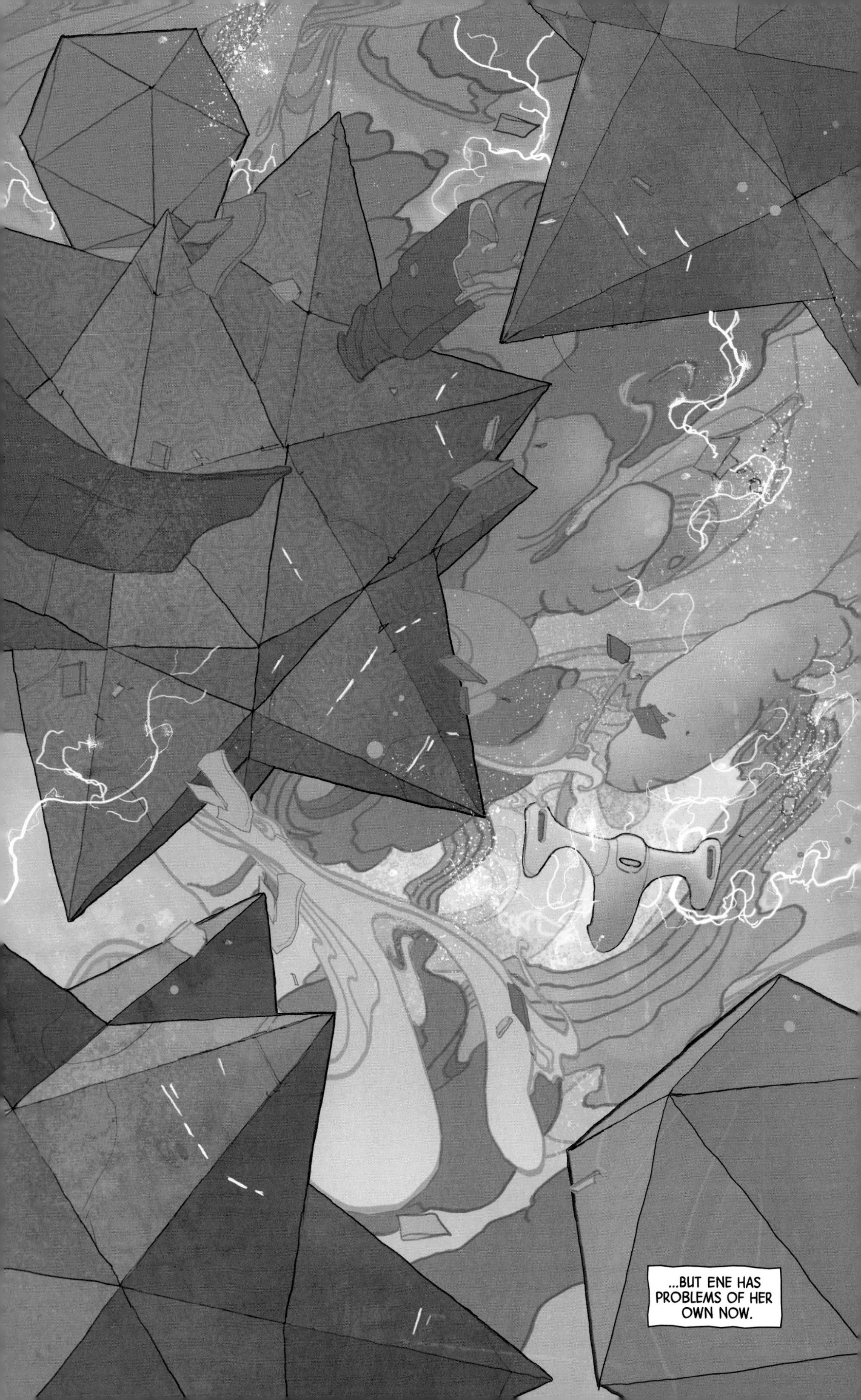
...BUT ENE HAS PROBLEMS OF HER OWN NOW.

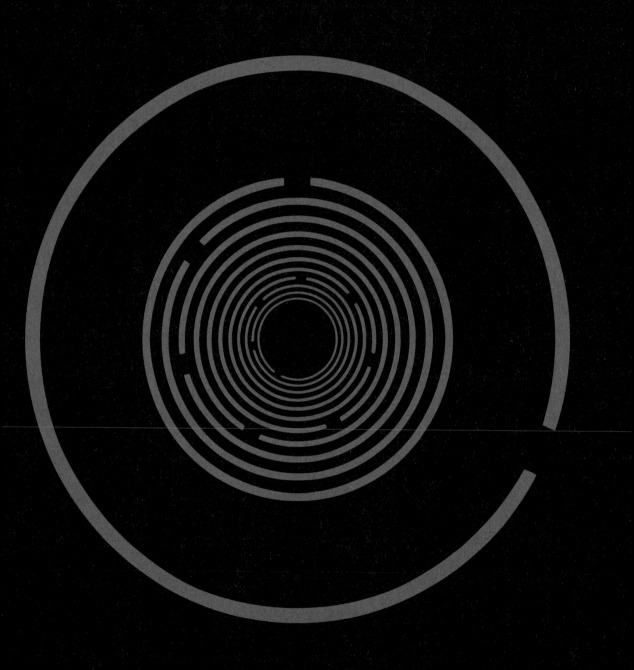

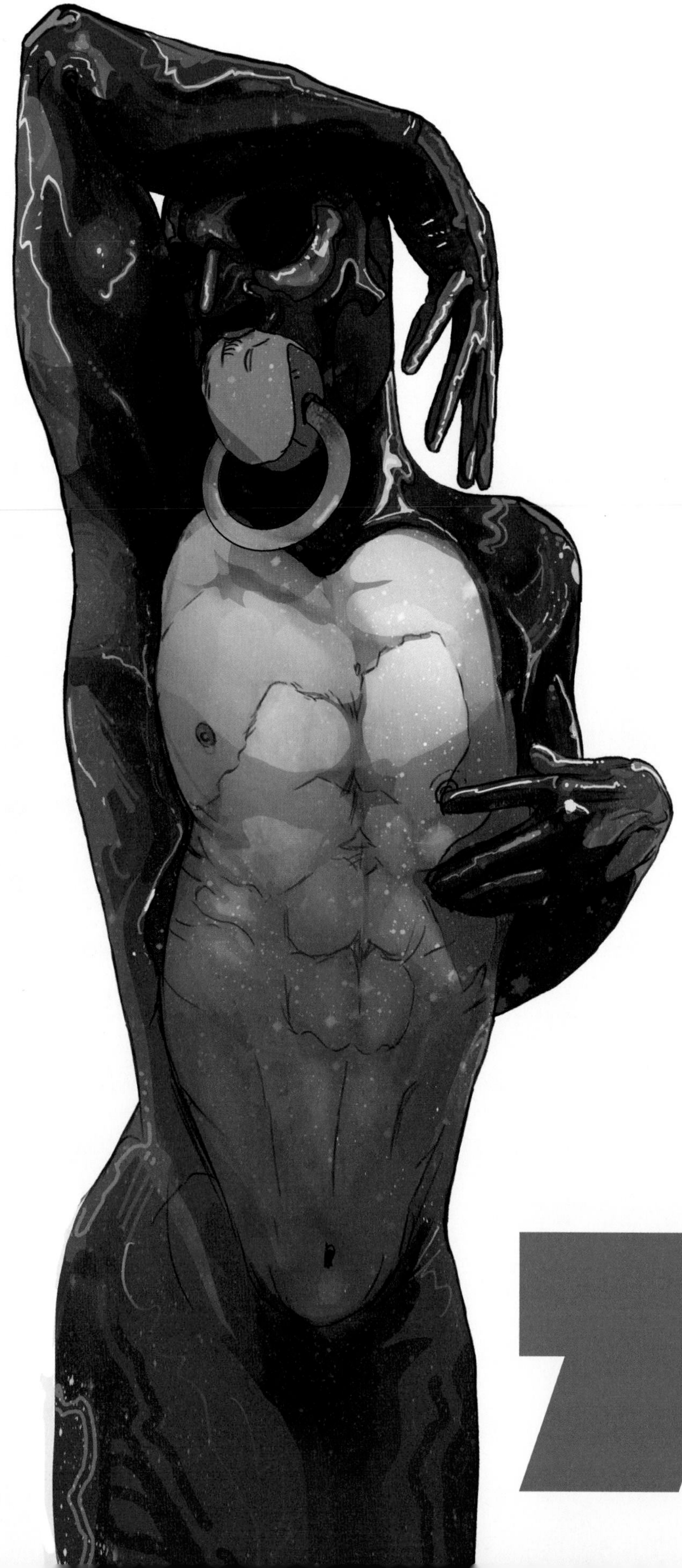

7

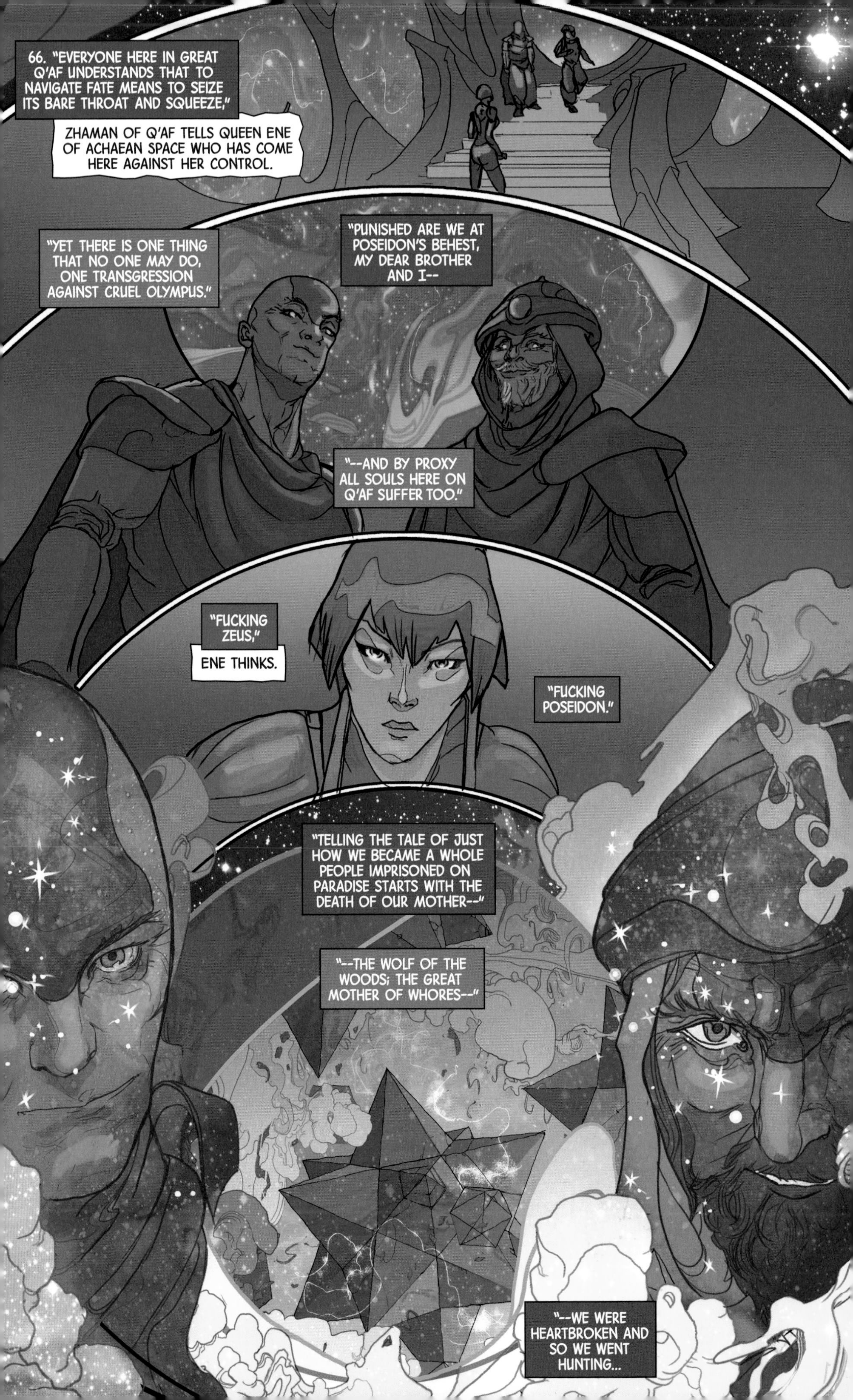
66. "EVERYONE HERE IN GREAT Q'AF UNDERSTANDS THAT TO NAVIGATE FATE MEANS TO SEIZE ITS BARE THROAT AND SQUEEZE,"
ZHAMAN OF Q'AF TELLS QUEEN ENE OF ACHAEAN SPACE WHO HAS COME HERE AGAINST HER CONTROL.
"YET THERE IS ONE THING THAT NO ONE MAY DO, ONE TRANSGRESSION AGAINST CRUEL OLYMPUS."
"PUNISHED ARE WE AT POSEIDON'S BEHEST, MY DEAR BROTHER AND I--
"--AND BY PROXY ALL SOULS HERE ON Q'AF SUFFER TOO."
"FUCKING ZEUS,"
ENE THINKS.
"FUCKING POSEIDON."
"TELLING THE TALE OF JUST HOW WE BECAME A WHOLE PEOPLE IMPRISONED ON PARADISE STARTS WITH THE DEATH OF OUR MOTHER--"
"--THE WOLF OF THE WOODS; THE GREAT MOTHER OF WHORES--"
"--WE WERE HEARTBROKEN AND SO WE WENT HUNTING...

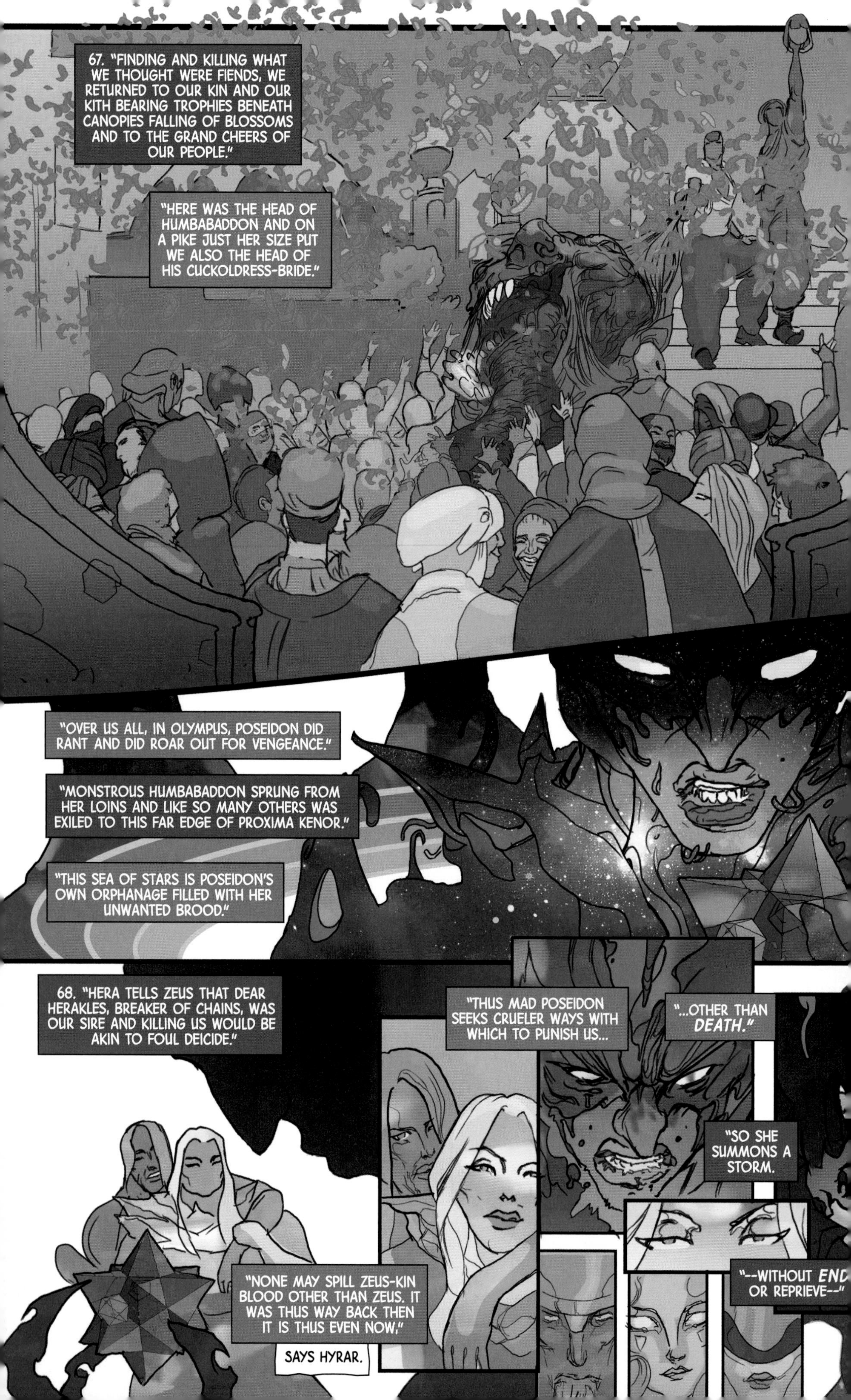
67. "FINDING AND KILLING WHAT WE THOUGHT WERE FIENDS, WE RETURNED TO OUR KIN AND OUR KITH BEARING TROPHIES BENEATH CANOPIES FALLING OF BLOSSOMS AND TO THE GRAND CHEERS OF OUR PEOPLE."
"HERE WAS THE HEAD OF HUMBABADDON AND ON A PIKE JUST HER SIZE PUT WE ALSO THE HEAD OF HIS CUCKOLDRESS-BRIDE."
"OVER US ALL, IN OLYMPUS, POSEIDON DID RANT AND DID ROAR OUT FOR VENGEANCE."
"MONSTROUS HUMBABADDON SPRUNG FROM HER LOINS AND LIKE SO MANY OTHERS WAS EXILED TO THIS FAR EDGE OF PROXIMA KENOR."
"THIS SEA OF STARS IS POSEIDON'S OWN ORPHANAGE FILLED WITH HER UNWANTED BROOD."
68. "HERA TELLS ZEUS THAT DEAR HERAKLES, BREAKER OF CHAINS, WAS OUR SIRE AND KILLING US WOULD BE AKIN TO FOUL DEICIDE."
"NONE MAY SPILL ZEUS-KIN BLOOD OTHER THAN ZEUS. IT WAS THUS WAY BACK THEN IT IS THUS EVEN NOW,"
SAYS HYRAR.
"THUS MAD POSEIDON SEEKS CRUELER WAYS WITH WHICH TO PUNISH US...
"...OTHER THAN DEATH."
"SO SHE SUMMONS A STORM.
"--WITHOUT END OR REPRIEVE--"

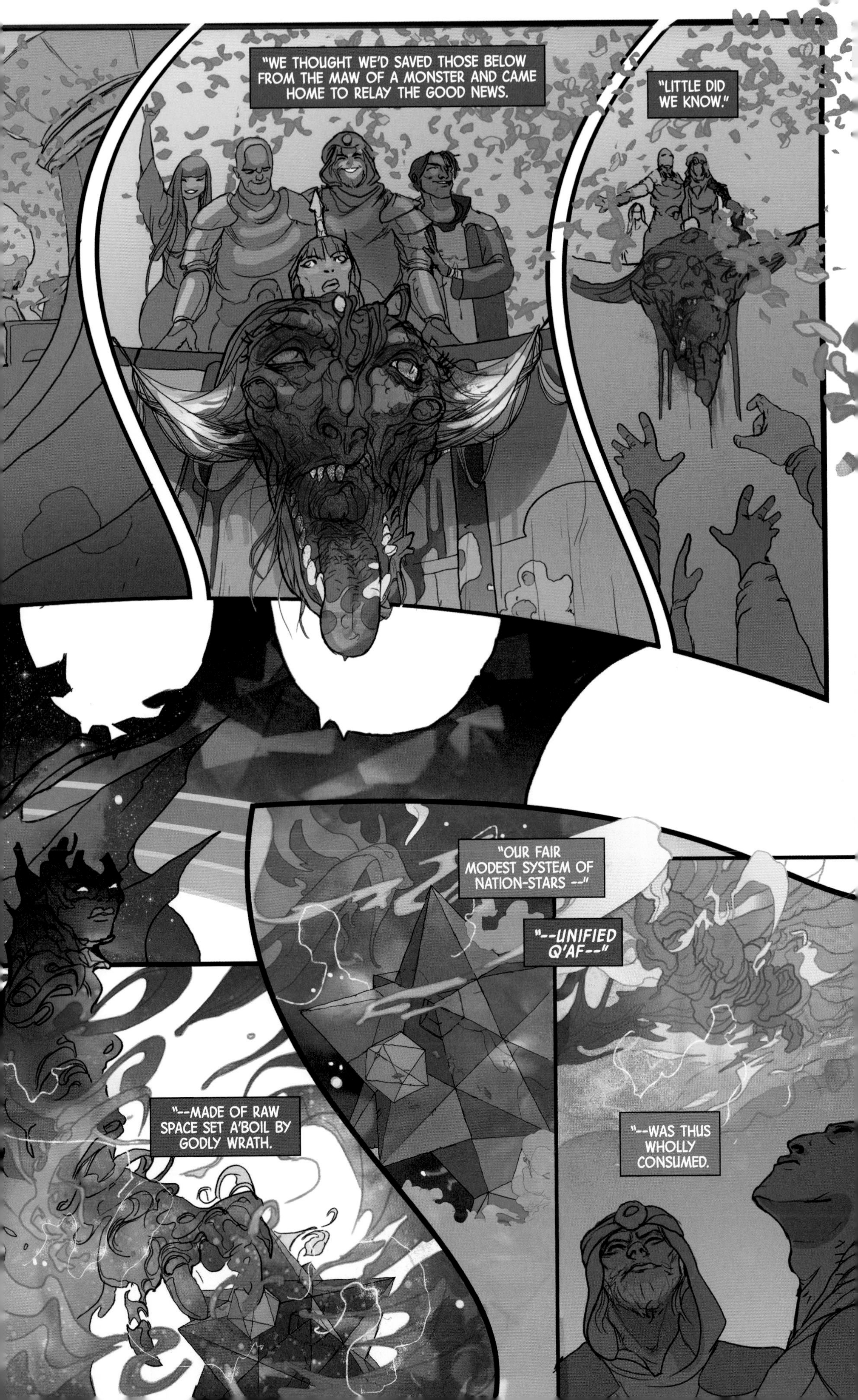
"WE THOUGHT WE'D SAVED THOSE BELOW FROM THE MAW OF A MONSTER AND CAME HOME TO RELAY THE GOOD NEWS.
"LITTLE DID WE KNOW."
"OUR FAIR MODEST SYSTEM OF NATION-STARS --"
"--UNIFIED Q'AF--"
"--MADE OF RAW SPACE SET A'BOIL BY GODLY WRATH.
"--WAS THUS WHOLLY CONSUMED.

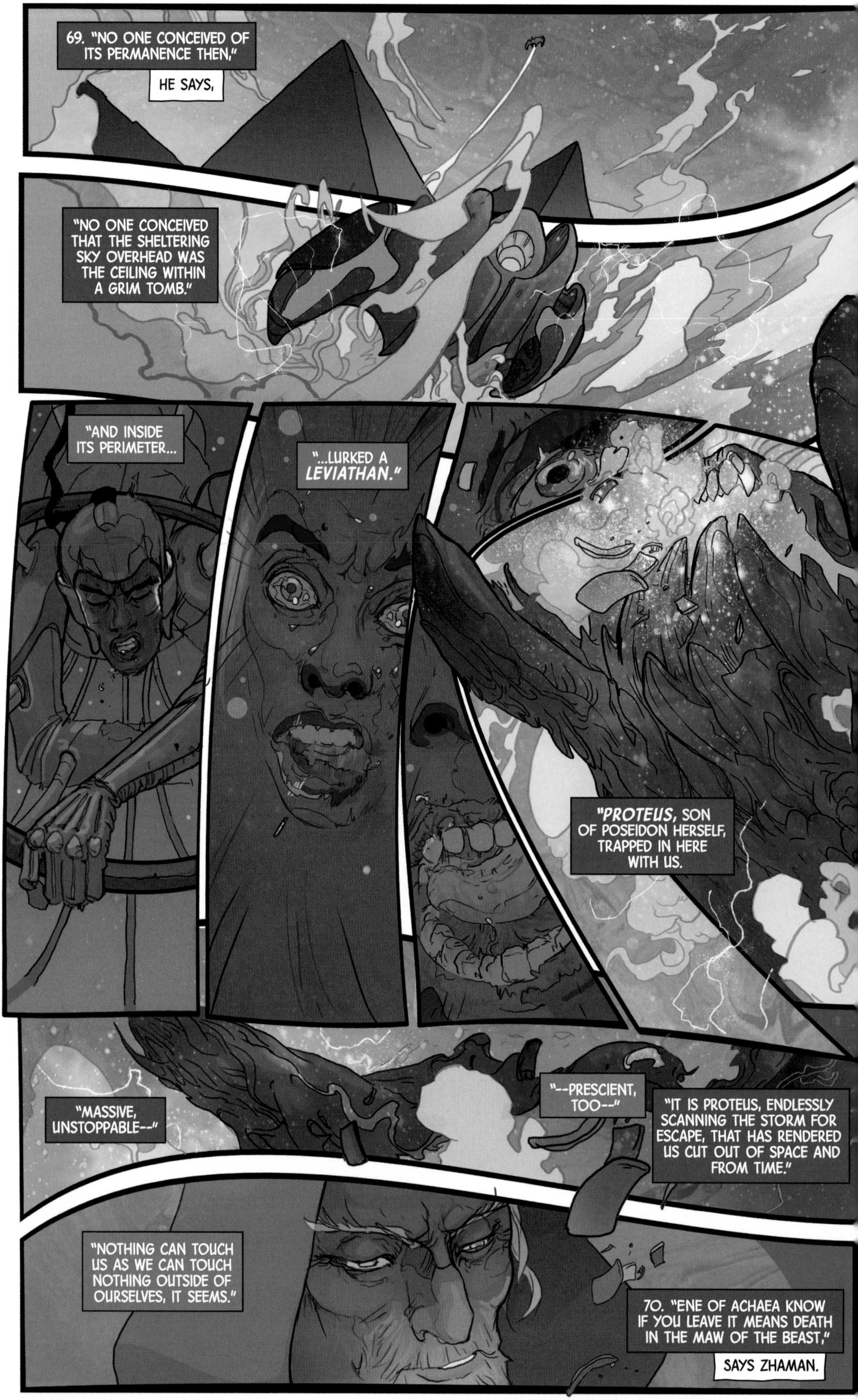
69. "NO ONE CONCEIVED OF ITS PERMANENCE THEN,"
HE SAYS,
"NO ONE CONCEIVED THAT THE SHELTERING SKY OVERHEAD WAS THE CEILING WITHIN A GRIM TOMB."
"AND INSIDE ITS PERIMETER...
"...LURKED A *LEVIATHAN.*"
"*PROTEUS,* SON OF POSEIDON HERSELF, TRAPPED IN HERE WITH US.
"MASSIVE, UNSTOPPABLE--"
"--PRESCIENT, TOO--"
"IT IS PROTEUS, ENDLESSLY SCANNING THE STORM FOR ESCAPE, THAT HAS RENDERED US CUT OUT OF SPACE AND FROM TIME."
"NOTHING CAN TOUCH US AS WE CAN TOUCH NOTHING OUTSIDE OF OURSELVES, IT SEEMS."
70. "ENE OF ACHAEA KNOW IF YOU LEAVE IT MEANS DEATH IN THE MAW OF THE BEAST,"
SAYS ZHAMAN.

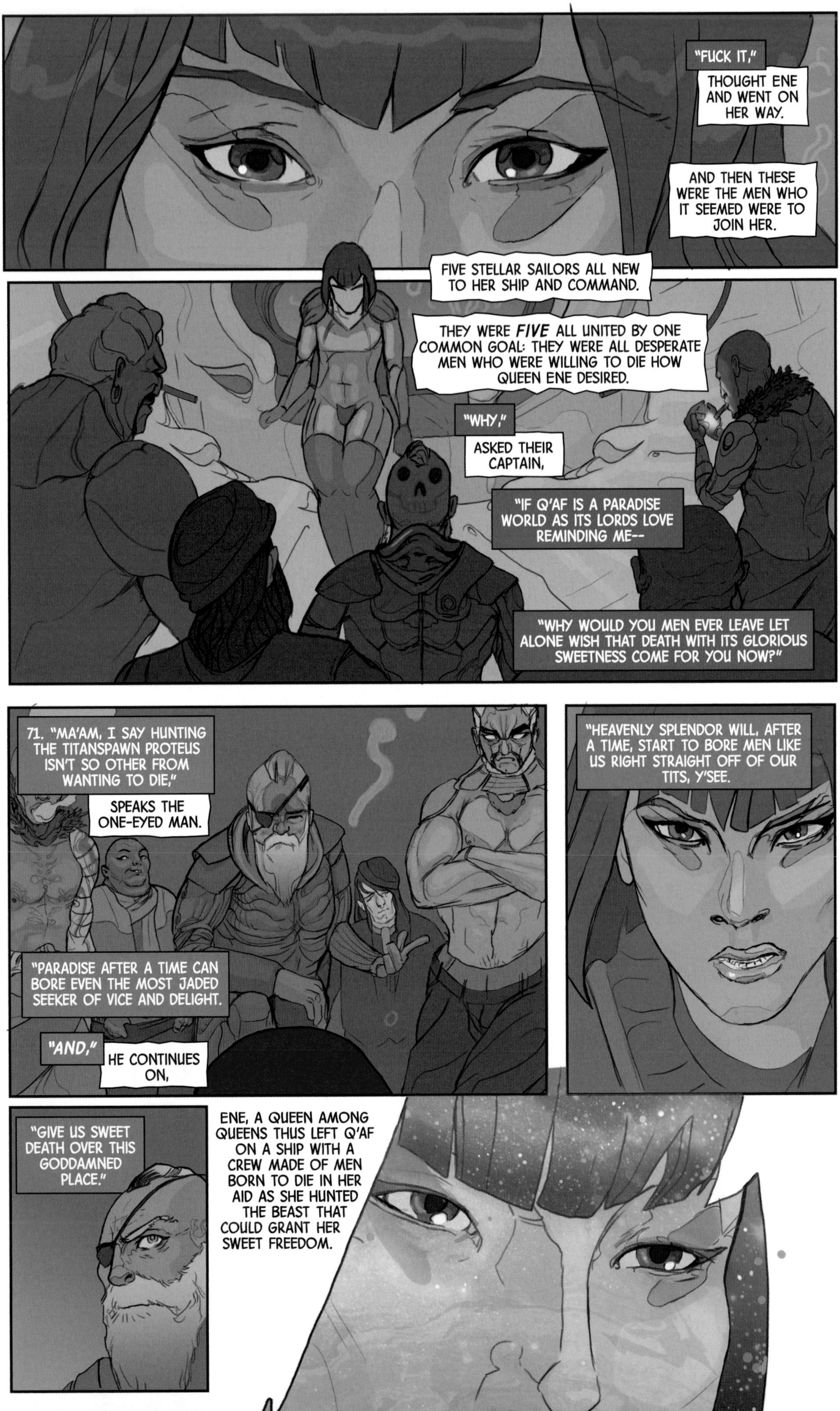
"FUCK IT,"
THOUGHT ENE AND WENT ON HER WAY.
AND THEN THESE WERE THE MEN WHO IT SEEMED WERE TO JOIN HER.
FIVE STELLAR SAILORS ALL NEW TO HER SHIP AND COMMAND.
THEY WERE *FIVE* ALL UNITED BY ONE COMMON GOAL: THEY WERE ALL DESPERATE MEN WHO WERE WILLING TO DIE HOW QUEEN ENE DESIRED.
"WHY,"
ASKED THEIR CAPTAIN,
"IF Q'AF IS A PARADISE WORLD AS ITS LORDS LOVE REMINDING ME--
"WHY WOULD YOU MEN EVER LEAVE LET ALONE WISH THAT DEATH WITH ITS GLORIOUS SWEETNESS COME FOR YOU NOW?"
71. "MA'AM, I SAY HUNTING THE TITANSPAWN PROTEUS ISN'T SO OTHER FROM WANTING TO DIE,"
SPEAKS THE ONE-EYED MAN.
"PARADISE AFTER A TIME CAN BORE EVEN THE MOST JADED SEEKER OF VICE AND DELIGHT.
"AND,"
HE CONTINUES ON,
"HEAVENLY SPLENDOR WILL, AFTER A TIME, START TO BORE MEN LIKE US RIGHT STRAIGHT OFF OF OUR TITS, Y'SEE.
"GIVE US SWEET DEATH OVER THIS GODDAMNED PLACE."
ENE, A QUEEN AMONG QUEENS THUS LEFT Q'AF ON A SHIP WITH A CREW MADE OF MEN BORN TO DIE IN HER AID AS SHE HUNTED THE BEAST THAT COULD GRANT HER SWEET FREEDOM.

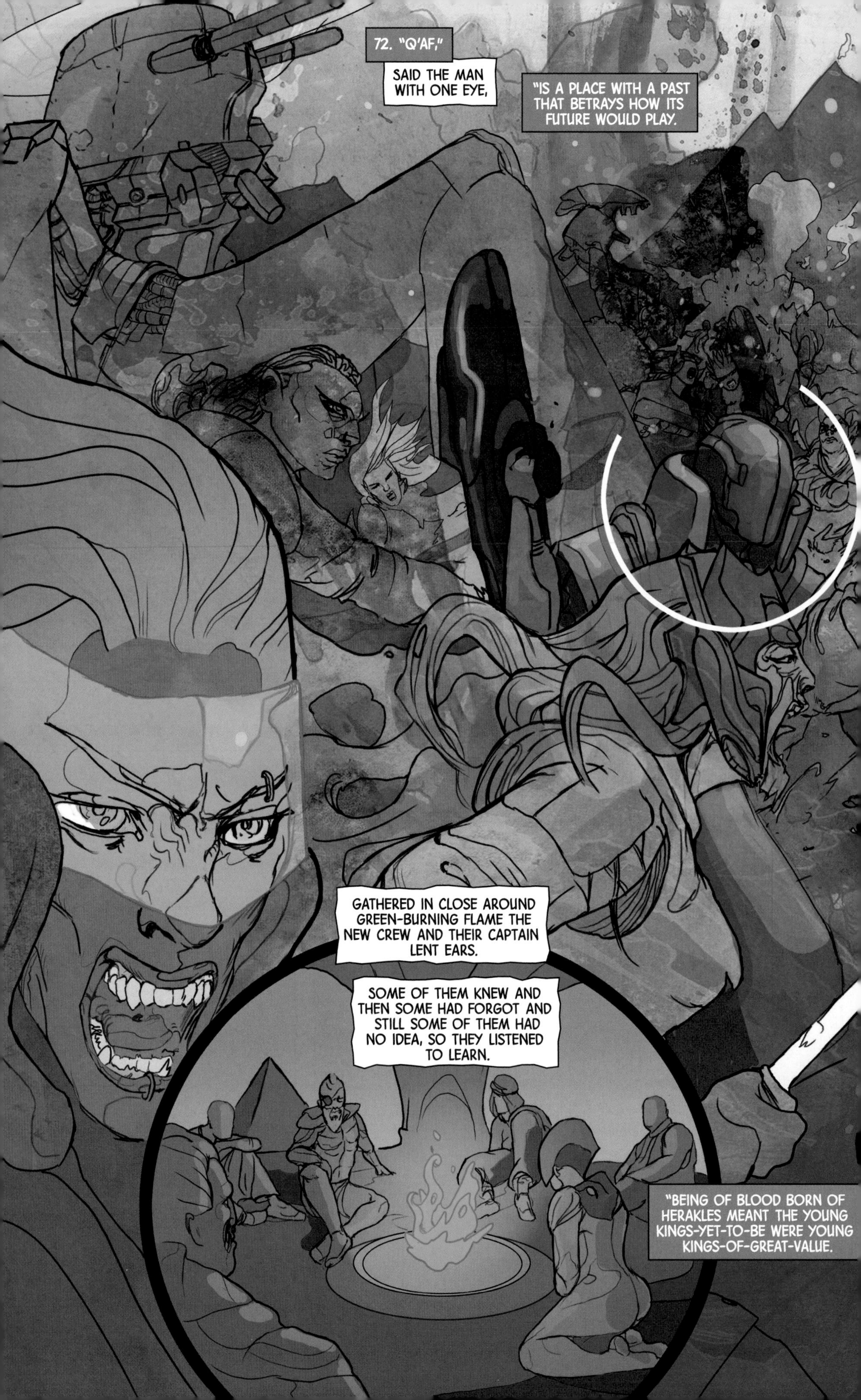
72. "Q'AF,"
SAID THE MAN WITH ONE EYE,
"IS A PLACE WITH A PAST THAT BETRAYS HOW ITS FUTURE WOULD PLAY.
GATHERED IN CLOSE AROUND GREEN-BURNING FLAME THE NEW CREW AND THEIR CAPTAIN LENT EARS.
SOME OF THEM KNEW AND THEN SOME HAD FORGOT AND STILL SOME OF THEM HAD NO IDEA, SO THEY LISTENED TO LEARN.
"BEING OF BLOOD BORN OF HERAKLES MEANT THE YOUNG KINGS-YET-TO-BE WERE YOUNG KINGS-OF-GREAT-VALUE.

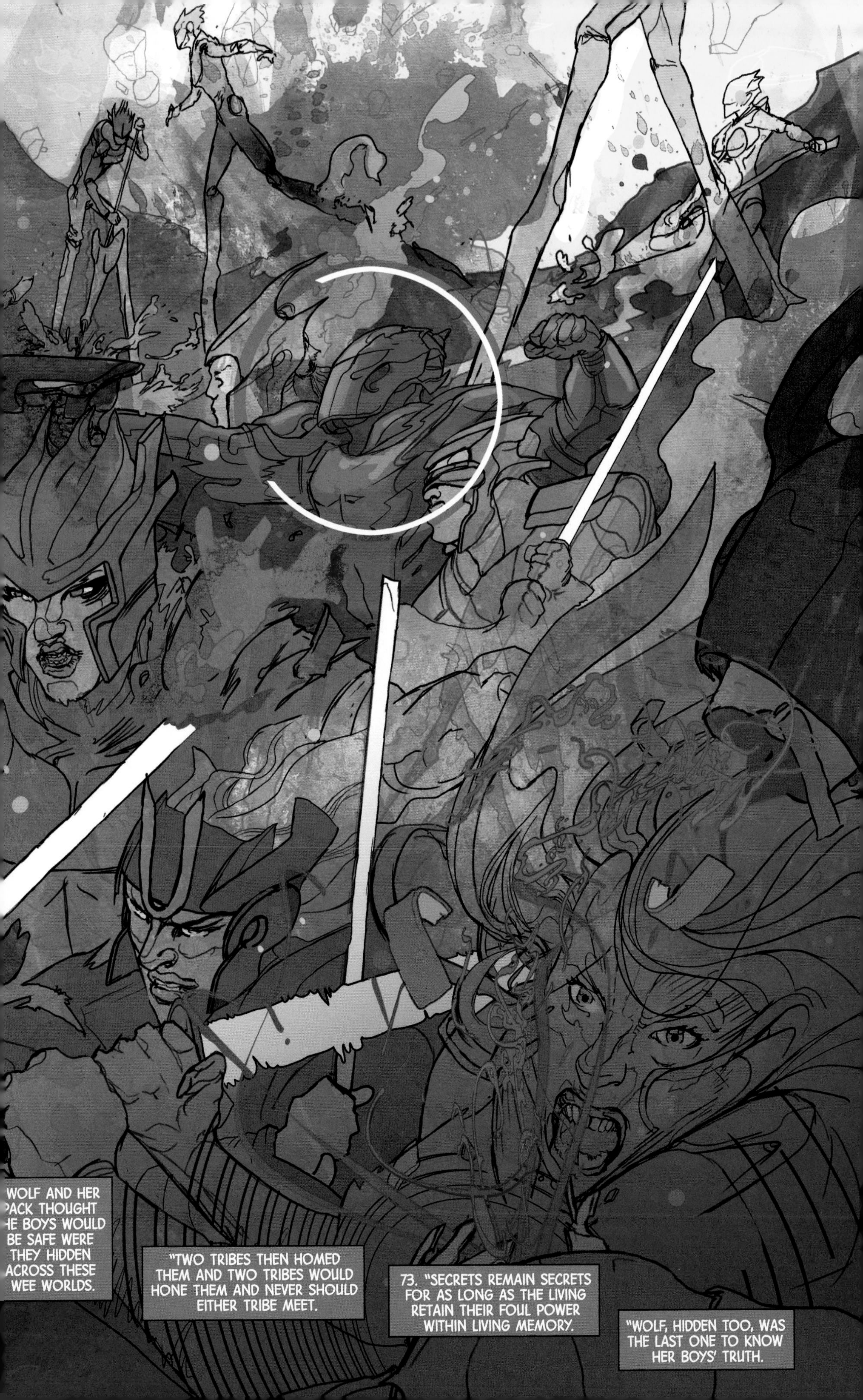
WOLF AND HER ACK THOUGHT HE BOYS WOULD BE SAFE WERE THEY HIDDEN ACROSS THESE WEE WORLDS.
"TWO TRIBES THEN HOMED THEM AND TWO TRIBES WOULD HONE THEM AND NEVER SHOULD EITHER TRIBE MEET.
73. "SECRETS REMAIN SECRETS FOR AS LONG AS THE LIVING RETAIN THEIR FOUL POWER WITHIN LIVING MEMORY.
"WOLF, HIDDEN TOO, WAS THE LAST ONE TO KNOW HER BOYS' TRUTH.

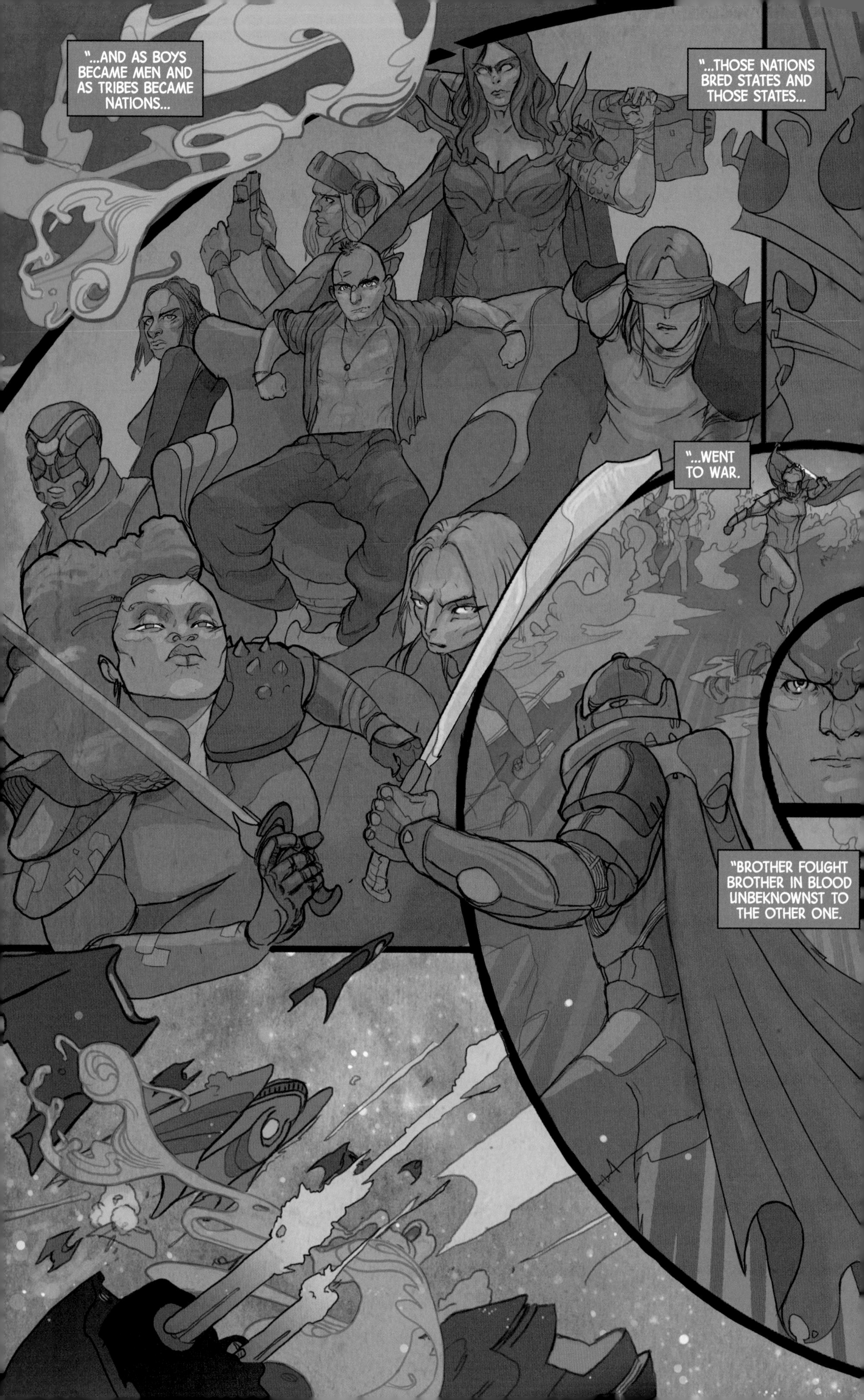
"...AND AS BOYS BECAME MEN AND AS TRIBES BECAME NATIONS...
"...THOSE NATIONS BRED STATES AND THOSE STATES...
"...WENT TO WAR.
"BROTHER FOUGHT BROTHER IN BLOOD UNBEKNOWNST TO THE OTHER ONE.

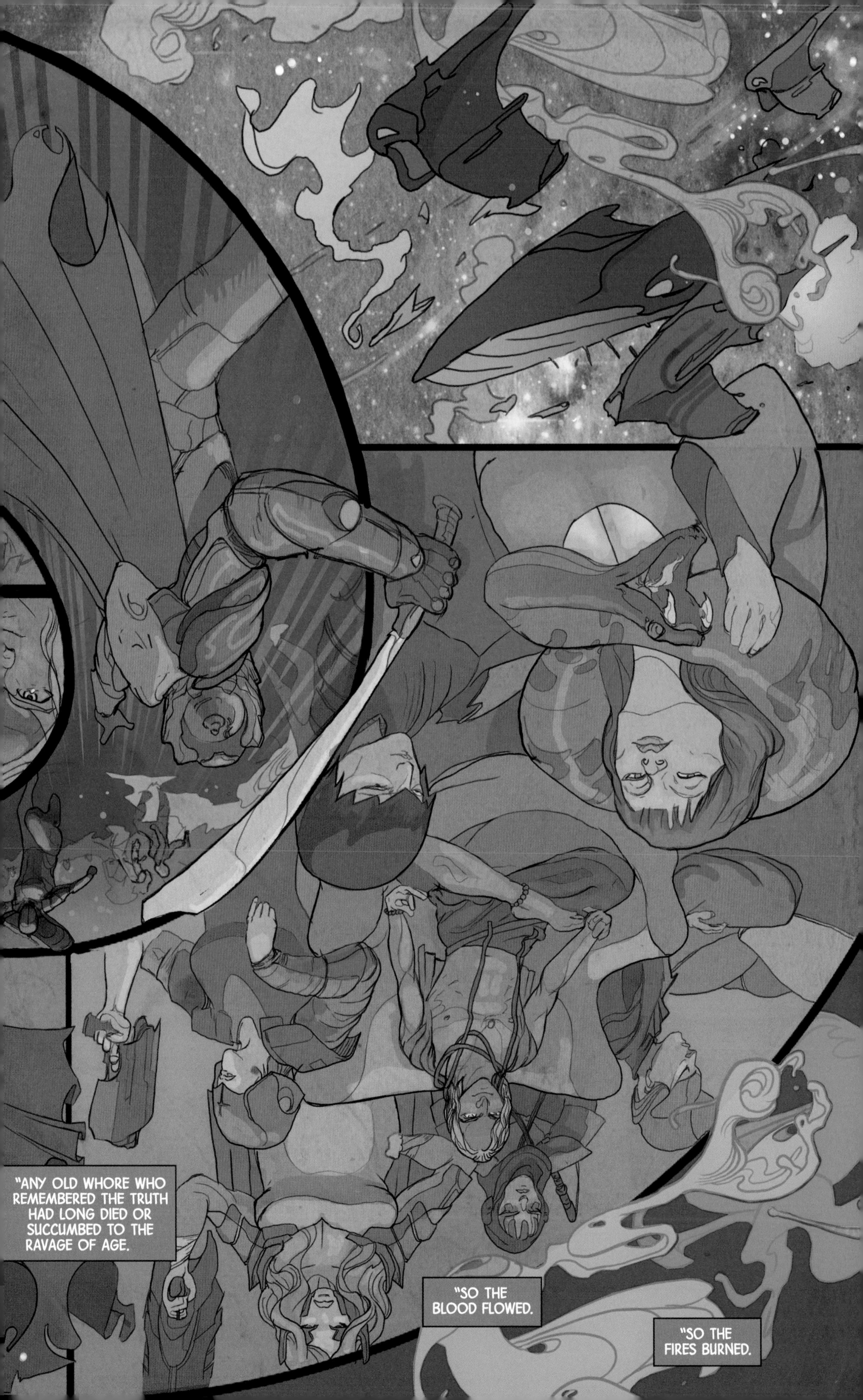
"ANY OLD WHORE WHO REMEMBERED THE TRUTH HAD LONG DIED OR SUCCUMBED TO THE RAVAGE OF AGE.
"SO THE BLOOD FLOWED.
"SO THE FIRES BURNED.

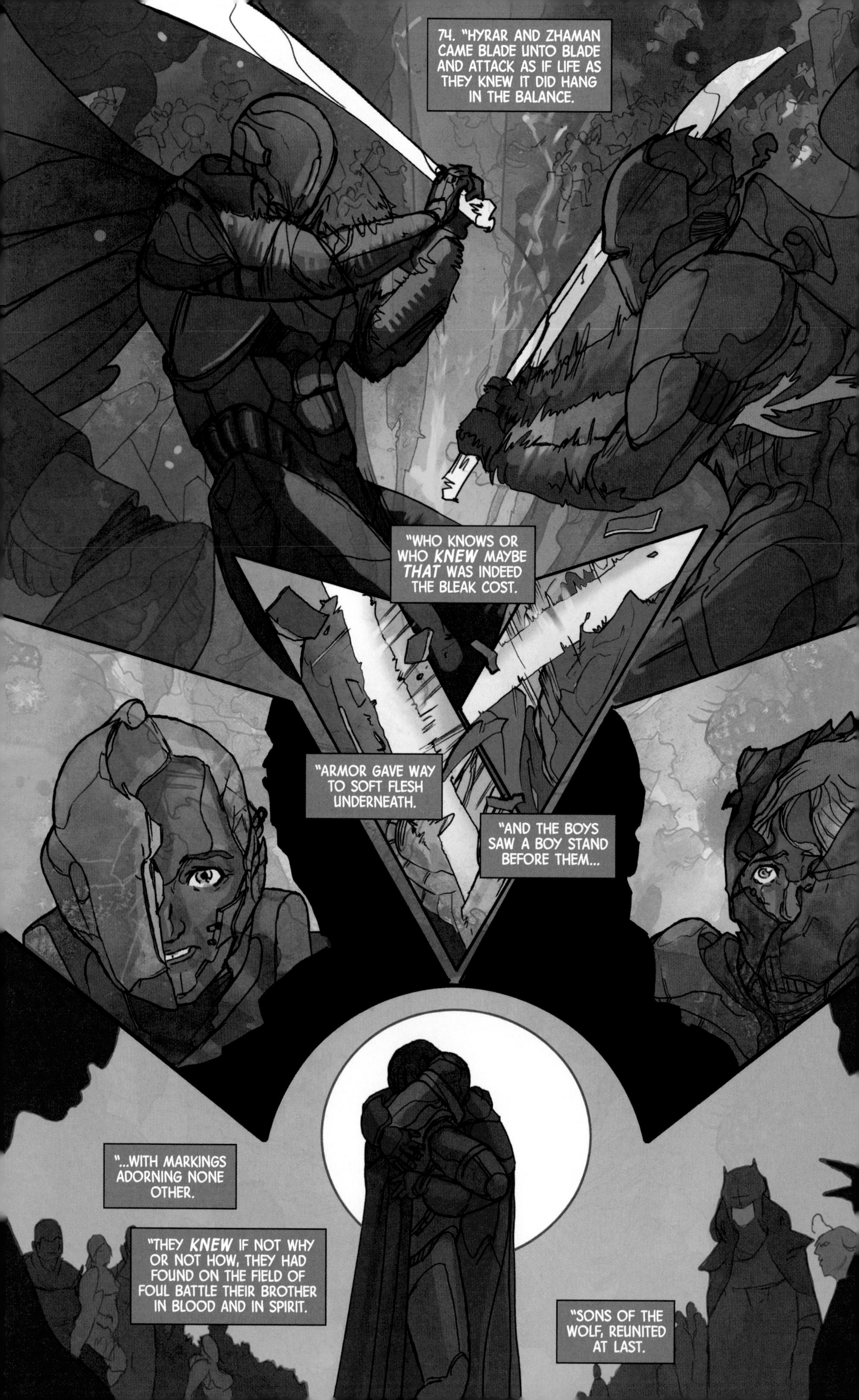
74. "HYRAR AND ZHAMAN CAME BLADE UNTO BLADE AND ATTACK AS IF LIFE AS THEY KNEW IT DID HANG IN THE BALANCE.
"WHO KNOWS OR WHO KNEW MAYBE THAT WAS INDEED THE BLEAK COST.
"ARMOR GAVE WAY TO SOFT FLESH UNDERNEATH.
"AND THE BOYS SAW A BOY STAND BEFORE THEM...
"...WITH MARKINGS ADORNING NONE OTHER.
"THEY KNEW IF NOT WHY OR NOT HOW, THEY HAD FOUND ON THE FIELD OF FOUL BATTLE THEIR BROTHER IN BLOOD AND IN SPIRIT.
"SONS OF THE WOLF, REUNITED AT LAST.

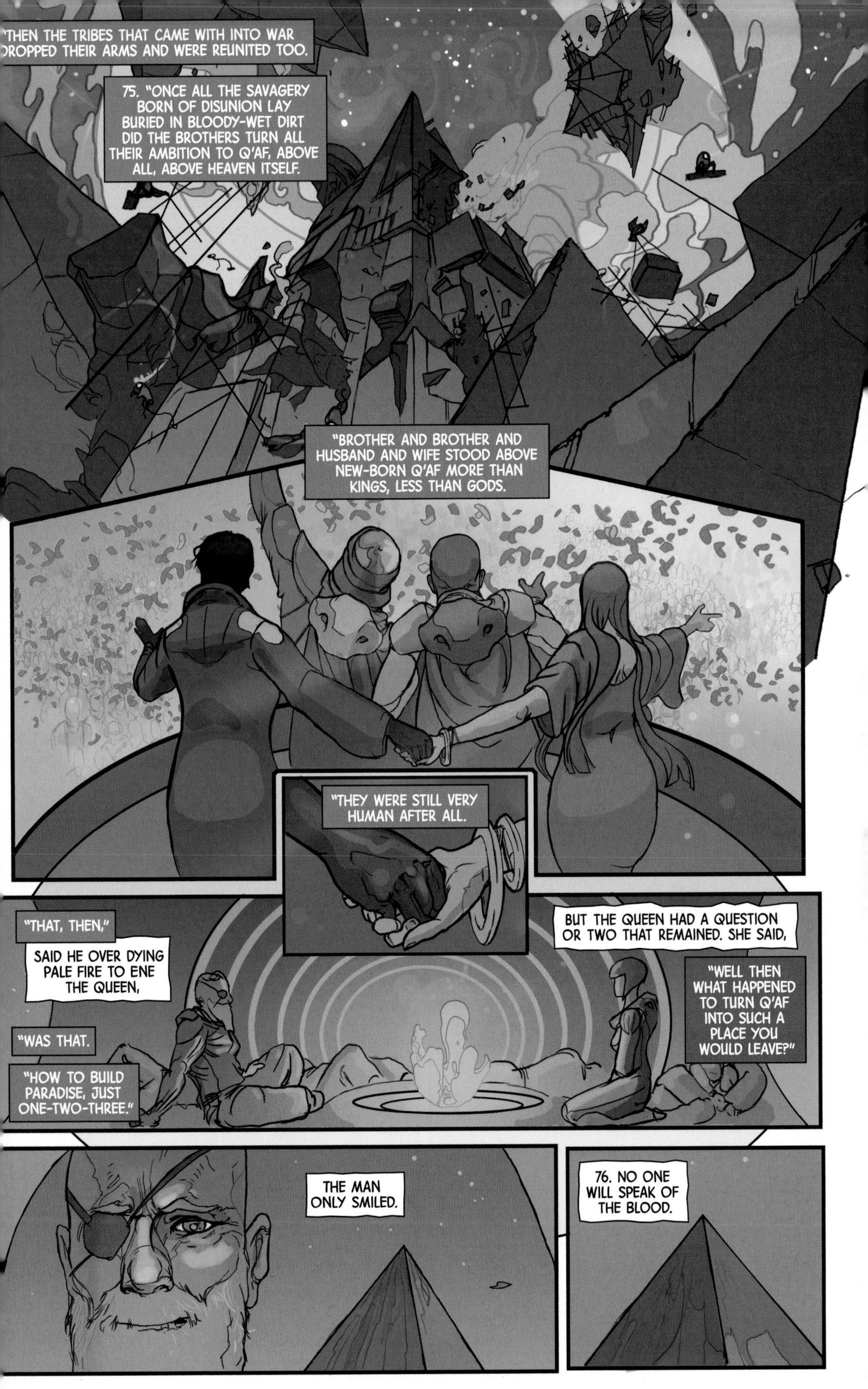
"THEN THE TRIBES THAT CAME WITH INTO WAR
DROPPED THEIR ARMS AND WERE REUNITED TOO.
75. "ONCE ALL THE SAVAGERY BORN OF DISUNION LAY BURIED IN BLOODY-WET DIRT DID THE BROTHERS TURN ALL THEIR AMBITION TO Q'AF, ABOVE ALL, ABOVE HEAVEN ITSELF.
"BROTHER AND BROTHER AND HUSBAND AND WIFE STOOD ABOVE NEW-BORN Q'AF MORE THAN KINGS, LESS THAN GODS.
"THEY WERE STILL VERY HUMAN AFTER ALL.
"THAT, THEN,"
SAID HE OVER DYING PALE FIRE TO ENE THE QUEEN,
"WAS THAT.
"HOW TO BUILD PARADISE, JUST ONE-TWO-THREE."
BUT THE QUEEN HAD A QUESTION OR TWO THAT REMAINED. SHE SAID,
"WELL THEN WHAT HAPPENED TO TURN Q'AF INTO SUCH A PLACE YOU WOULD LEAVE?"
THE MAN ONLY SMILED.
76. NO ONE WILL SPEAK OF THE BLOOD.

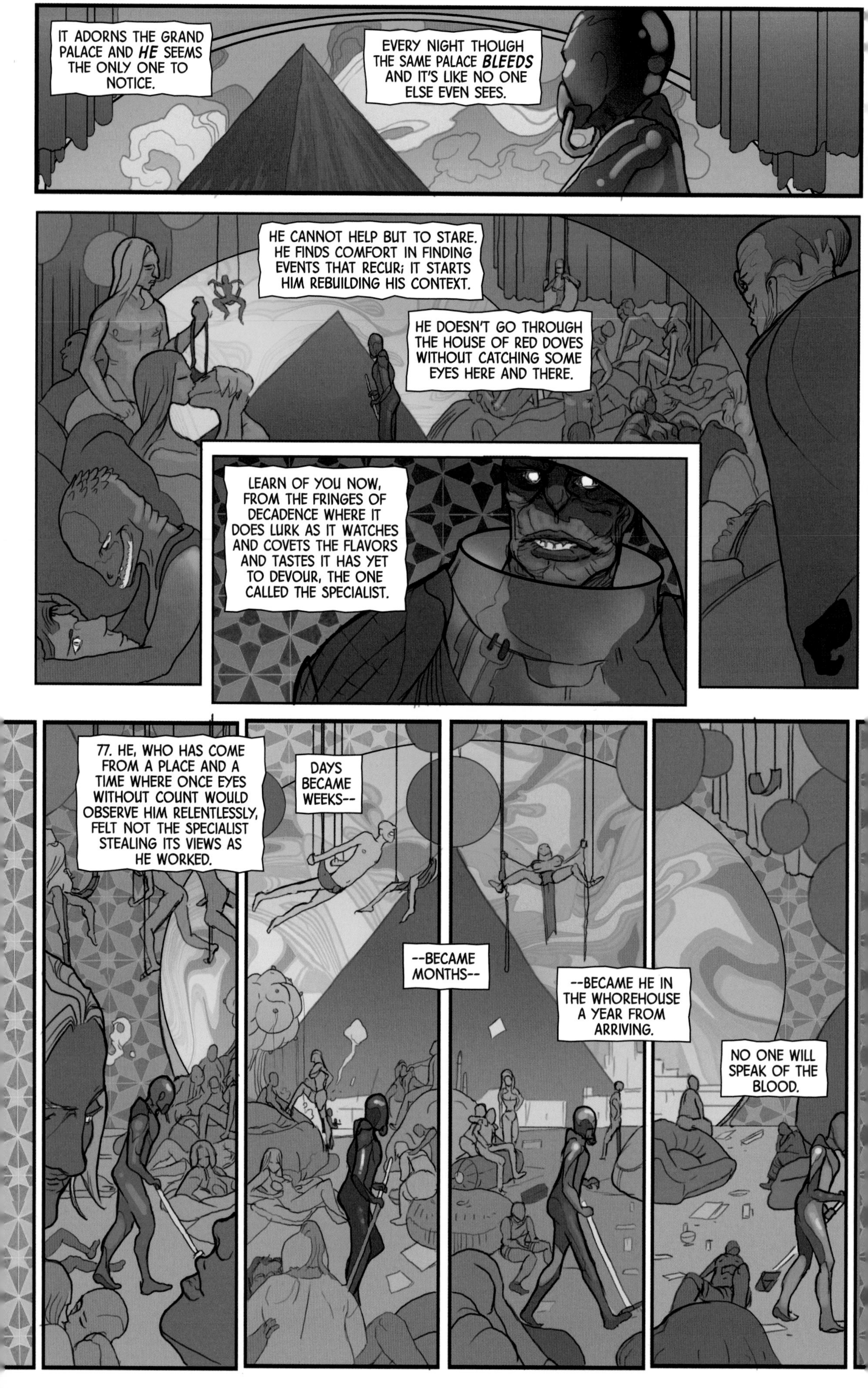
IT ADORNS THE GRAND PALACE AND HE SEEMS THE ONLY ONE TO NOTICE.
EVERY NIGHT THOUGH THE SAME PALACE BLEEDS AND IT'S LIKE NO ONE ELSE EVEN SEES.
HE CANNOT HELP BUT TO STARE. HE FINDS COMFORT IN FINDING EVENTS THAT RECUR; IT STARTS HIM REBUILDING HIS CONTEXT.
HE DOESN'T GO THROUGH THE HOUSE OF RED DOVES WITHOUT CATCHING SOME EYES HERE AND THERE.
LEARN OF YOU NOW, FROM THE FRINGES OF DECADENCE WHERE IT DOES LURK AS IT WATCHES AND COVETS THE FLAVORS AND TASTES IT HAS YET TO DEVOUR, THE ONE CALLED THE SPECIALIST.
77. HE, WHO HAS COME FROM A PLACE AND A TIME WHERE ONCE EYES WITHOUT COUNT WOULD OBSERVE HIM RELENTLESSLY, FELT NOT THE SPECIALIST STEALING ITS VIEWS AS HE WORKED.
DAYS BECAME WEEKS--
--BECAME MONTHS--
--BECAME HE IN THE WHOREHOUSE A YEAR FROM ARRIVING.
NO ONE WILL SPEAK OF THE BLOOD.

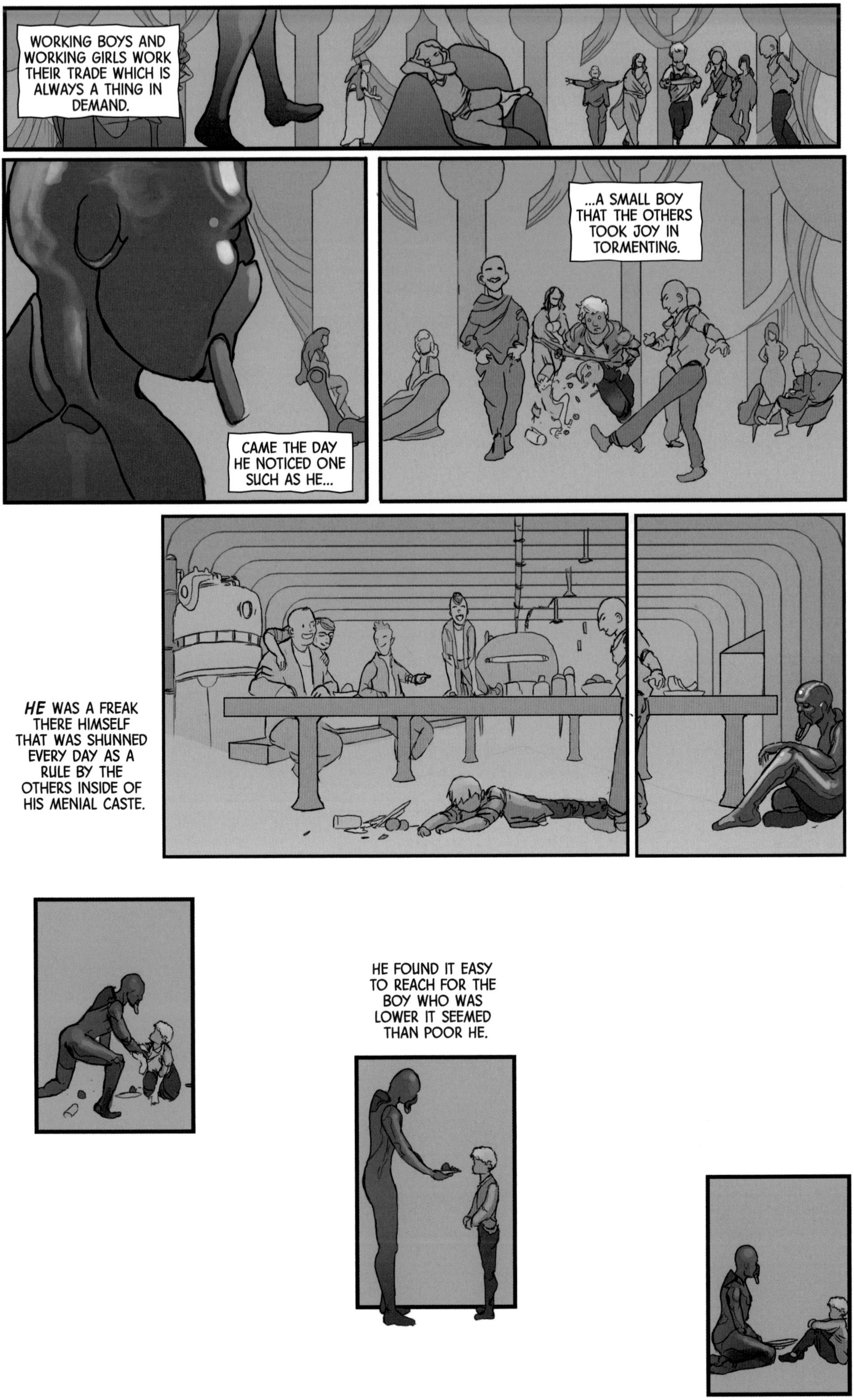
WORKING BOYS AND WORKING GIRLS WORK THEIR TRADE WHICH IS ALWAYS A THING IN DEMAND.
CAME THE DAY HE NOTICED ONE SUCH AS HE...
...A SMALL BOY THAT THE OTHERS TOOK JOY IN TORMENTING.
HE WAS A FREAK THERE HIMSELF THAT WAS SHUNNED EVERY DAY AS A RULE BY THE OTHERS INSIDE OF HIS MENIAL CASTE.
HE FOUND IT EASY TO REACH FOR THE BOY WHO WAS LOWER IT SEEMED THAN POOR HE.

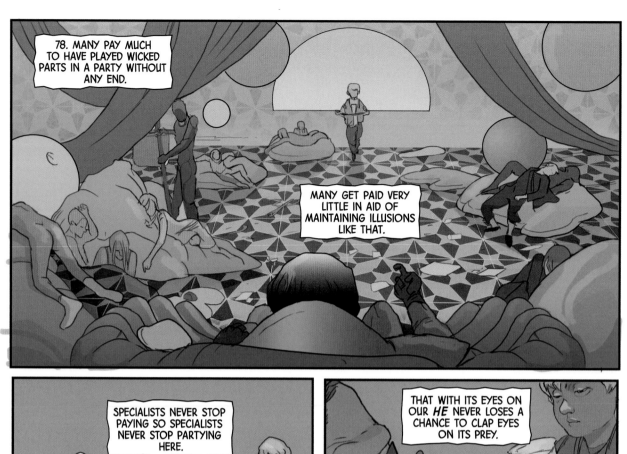

78. MANY PAY MUCH TO HAVE PLAYED WICKED PARTS IN A PARTY WITHOUT ANY END.

MANY GET PAID VERY LITTLE IN AID OF MAINTAINING ILLUSIONS LIKE THAT.

SPECIALISTS NEVER STOP PAYING SO SPECIALISTS NEVER STOP PARTYING HERE.

THAT WITH ITS EYES ON OUR *HE* NEVER LOSES A CHANCE TO CLAP EYES ON ITS PREY.

HE AND THE BOY ARE SO CHARMED BY EACH OTHER THEY DON'T EVEN SEE THEY ARE STALKED.

HE TAKES THE BOY BENEATH WING AND BEGINS TEACHING FACTS, MATHS, AND HISTORY TO HIM.

THEY ARE LEFT LARGELY ALONE.

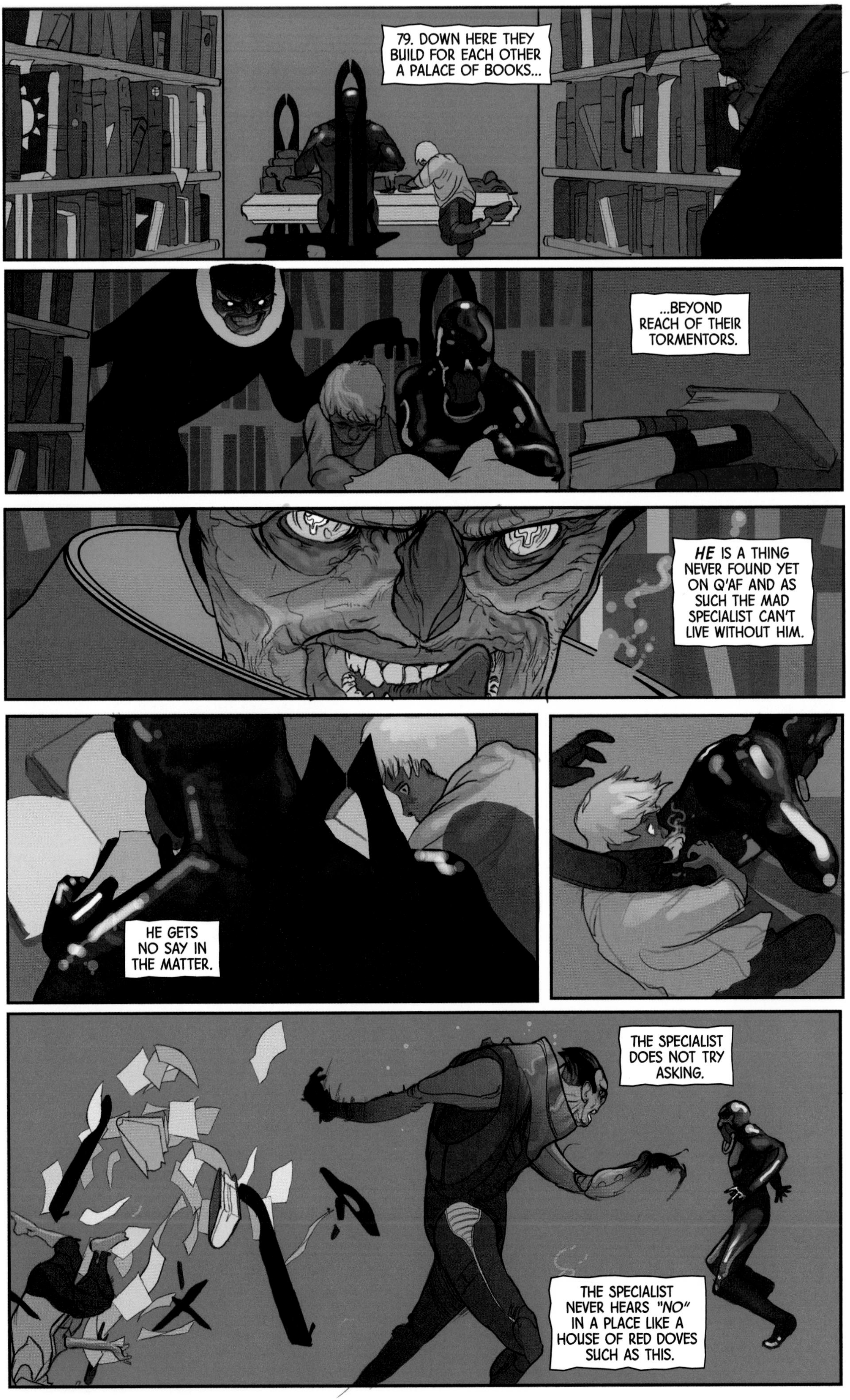
79. DOWN HERE THEY BUILD FOR EACH OTHER A PALACE OF BOOKS...
...BEYOND REACH OF THEIR TORMENTORS.
HE IS A THING NEVER FOUND YET ON Q'AF AND AS SUCH THE MAD SPECIALIST CAN'T LIVE WITHOUT HIM.
HE GETS NO SAY IN THE MATTER.
THE SPECIALIST DOES NOT TRY ASKING.
THE SPECIALIST NEVER HEARS "NO" IN A PLACE LIKE A HOUSE OF RED DOVES SUCH AS THIS.

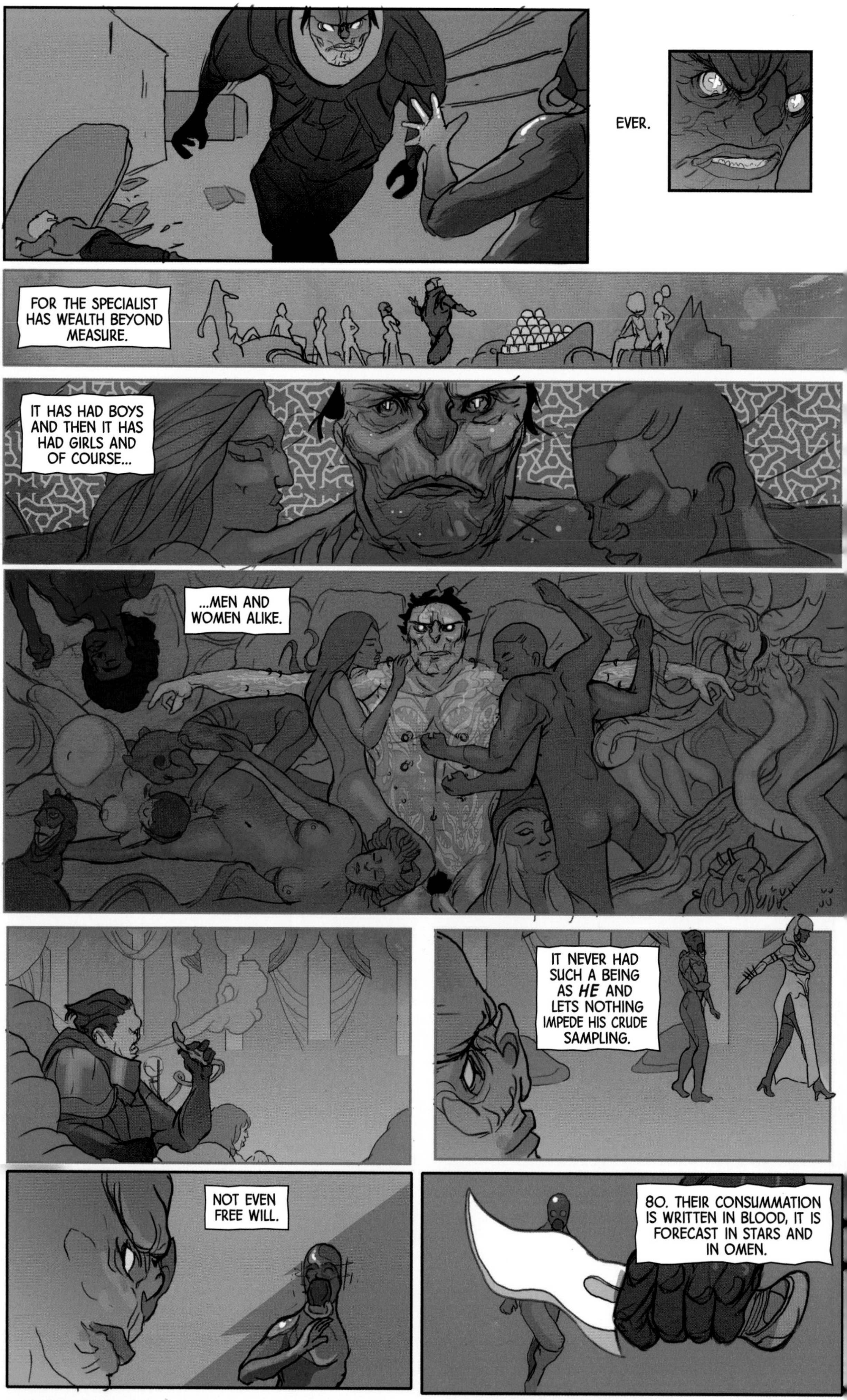
EVER.
FOR THE SPECIALIST HAS WEALTH BEYOND MEASURE.
IT HAS HAD BOYS AND THEN IT HAS HAD GIRLS AND OF COURSE...
...MEN AND WOMEN ALIKE.
IT NEVER HAD SUCH A BEING AS HE AND LETS NOTHING IMPEDE HIS CRUDE SAMPLING.
NOT EVEN FREE WILL.
80. THEIR CONSUMMATION IS WRITTEN IN BLOOD, IT IS FORECAST IN STARS AND IN OMEN.

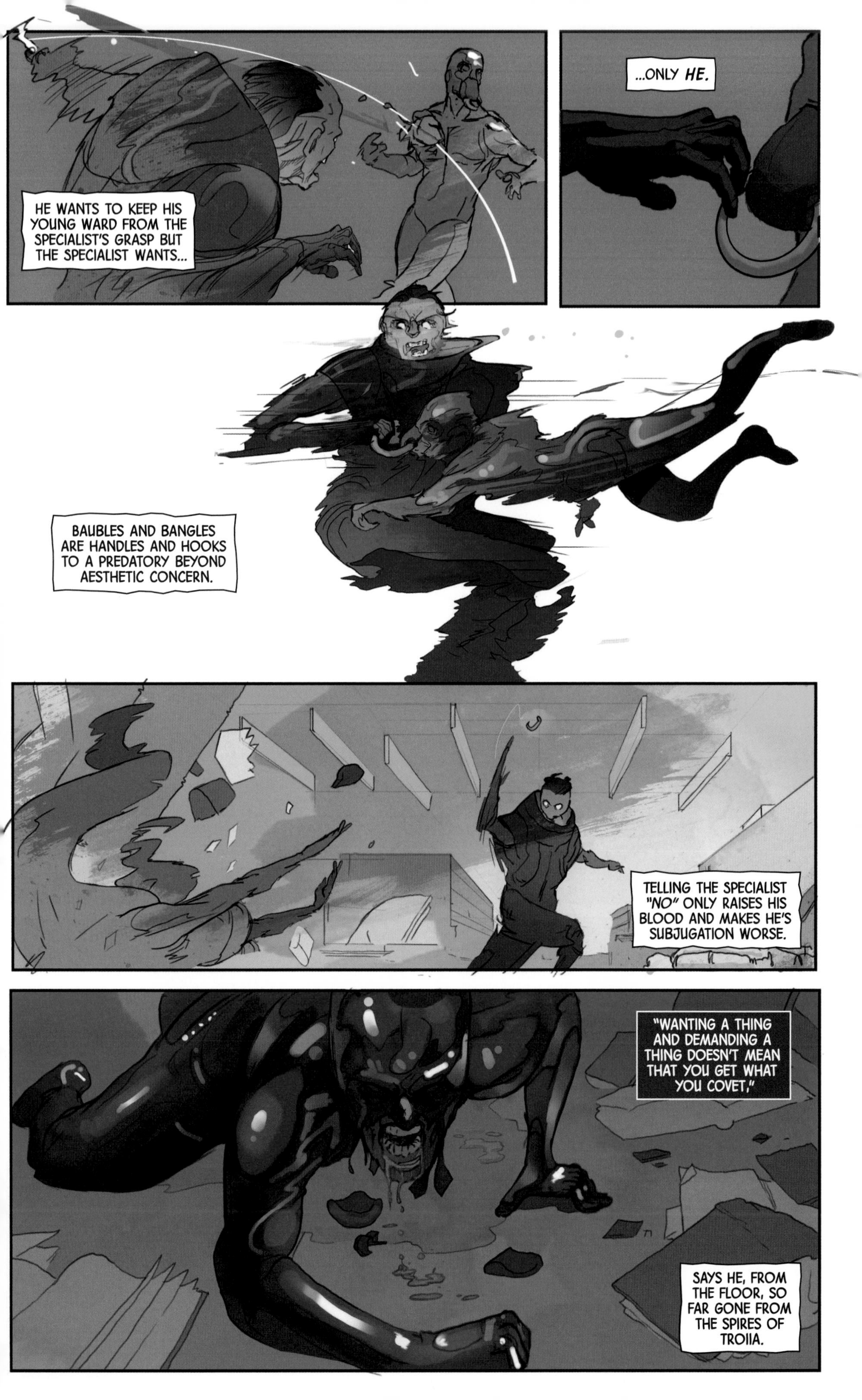
HE WANTS TO KEEP HIS YOUNG WARD FROM THE SPECIALIST'S GRASP BUT THE SPECIALIST WANTS...
...ONLY HE.
BAUBLES AND BANGLES ARE HANDLES AND HOOKS TO A PREDATORY BEYOND AESTHETIC CONCERN.
TELLING THE SPECIALIST "NO" ONLY RAISES HIS BLOOD AND MAKES HE'S SUBJUGATION WORSE.
"WANTING A THING AND DEMANDING A THING DOESN'T MEAN THAT YOU GET WHAT YOU COVET,"
SAYS HE, FROM THE FLOOR, SO FAR GONE FROM THE SPIRES OF TROIIA.

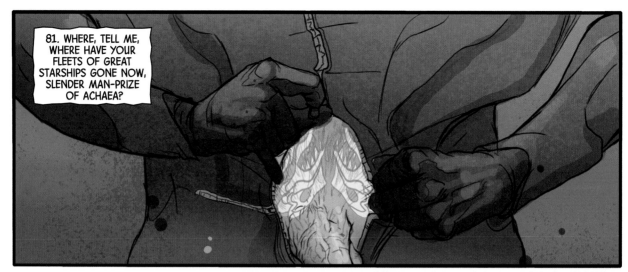

81. WHERE, TELL ME, WHERE HAVE YOUR FLEETS OF GREAT STARSHIPS GONE NOW, SLENDER MAN-PRIZE OF ACHAEA?

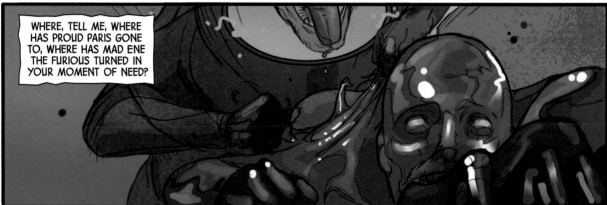

WHERE, TELL ME, WHERE HAS PROUD PARIS GONE TO, WHERE HAS MAD ENE THE FURIOUS TURNED IN YOUR MOMENT OF NEED?

HERE IN CRUEL Q'AF FAR BENEATH DAYLIGHTS' GLOW THEY HAVE LEFT YOU ALONE, LITTLE HE.

HERE IN THE DARK YOU MUST REAP WHAT YOU'VE SOWN AND DOWN HERE WHAT YOU'VE SOWN IS--

--BROTHERHOOD.

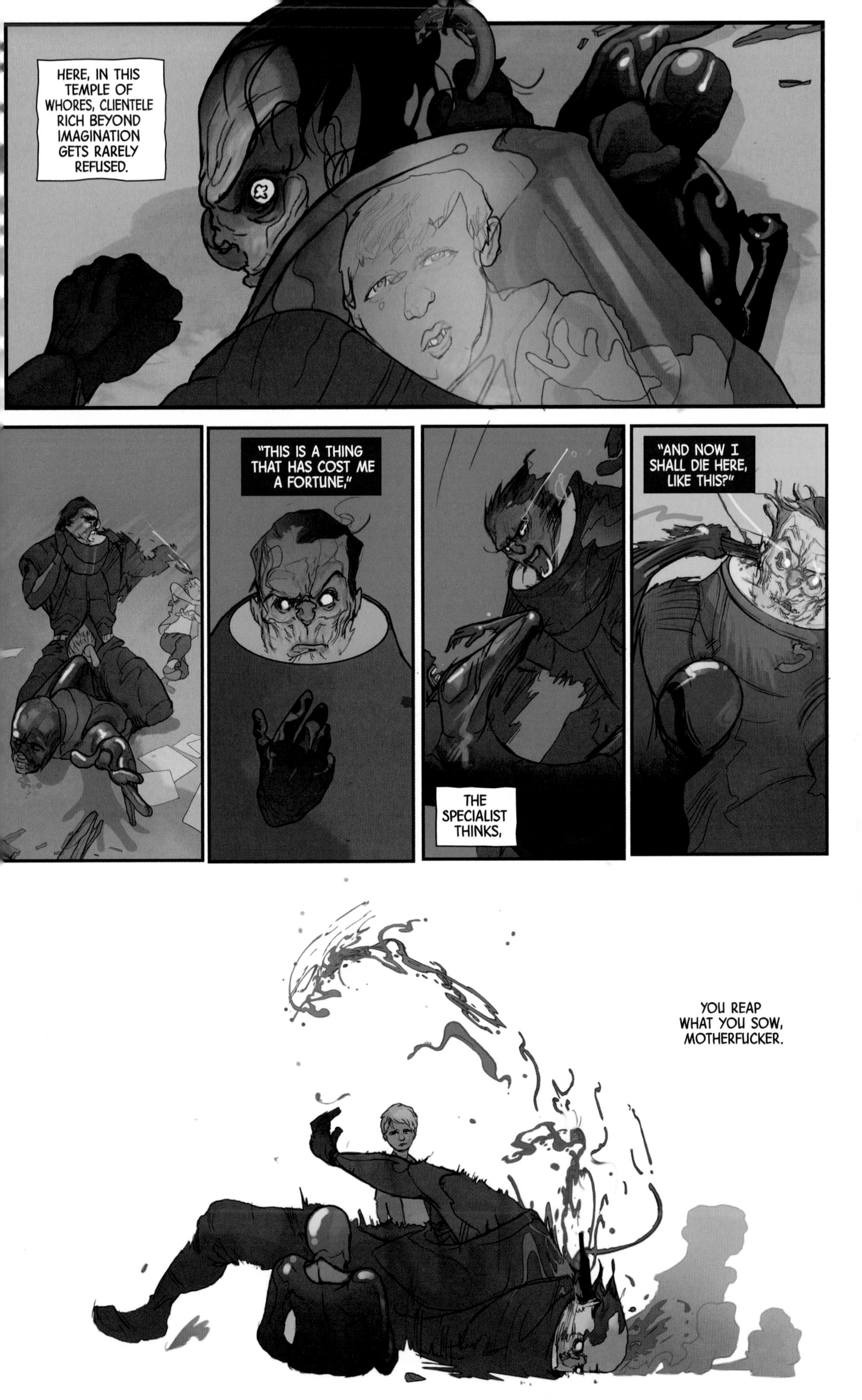
HERE, IN THIS TEMPLE OF WHORES, CLIENTELE RICH BEYOND IMAGINATION GETS RARELY REFUSED.
"THIS IS A THING THAT HAS COST ME A FORTUNE,"
THE SPECIALIST THINKS,
"AND NOW I SHALL DIE HERE, LIKE THIS?"
YOU REAP WHAT YOU SOW, MOTHERFUCKER.

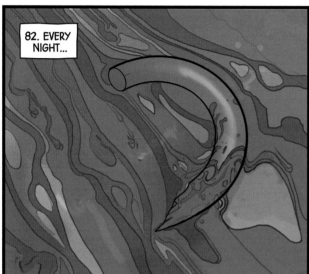

82. EVERY NIGHT...

...AS THE DAWN STARTS TO BREAK...

...FROM THE APEX OF Q'AF'S ROYAL PALACE A WEEPING OF BLOOD GREETS THE DAY WITHOUT FAIL.

AND, AS ALWAYS, PROUD HE BEARS MUTE WITNESS.

"I KNOW WHY,"

SAYS THE BOY.

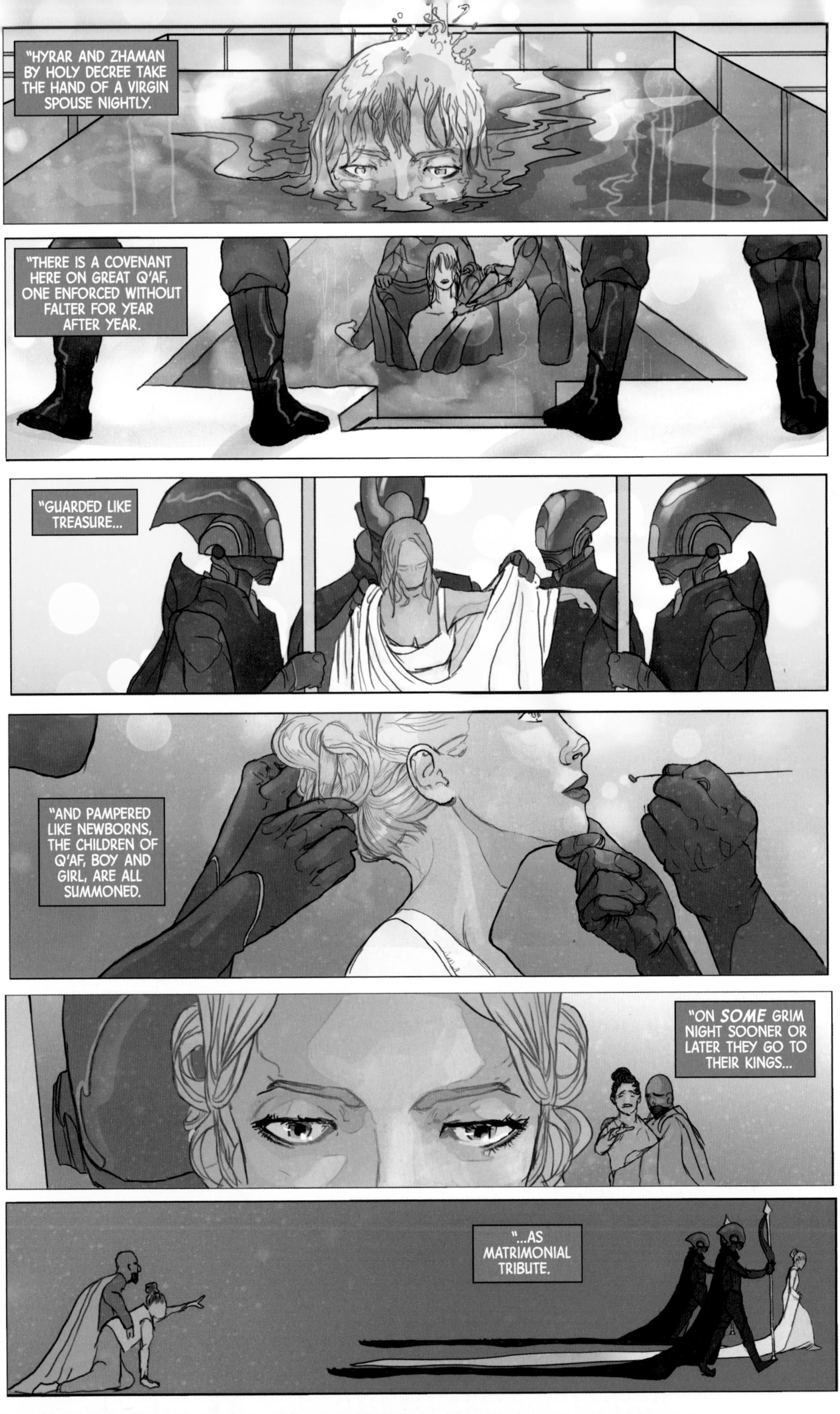
"HYRAR AND ZHAMAN BY HOLY DECREE TAKE THE HAND OF A VIRGIN SPOUSE NIGHTLY.
"THERE IS A COVENANT HERE ON GREAT Q'AF, ONE ENFORCED WITHOUT FALTER FOR YEAR AFTER YEAR.
"GUARDED LIKE TREASURE...
"AND PAMPERED LIKE NEWBORNS, THE CHILDREN OF Q'AF, BOY AND GIRL, ARE ALL SUMMONED.
"ON SOME GRIM NIGHT SOONER OR LATER THEY GO TO THEIR KINGS...
"...AS MATRIMONIAL TRIBUTE.

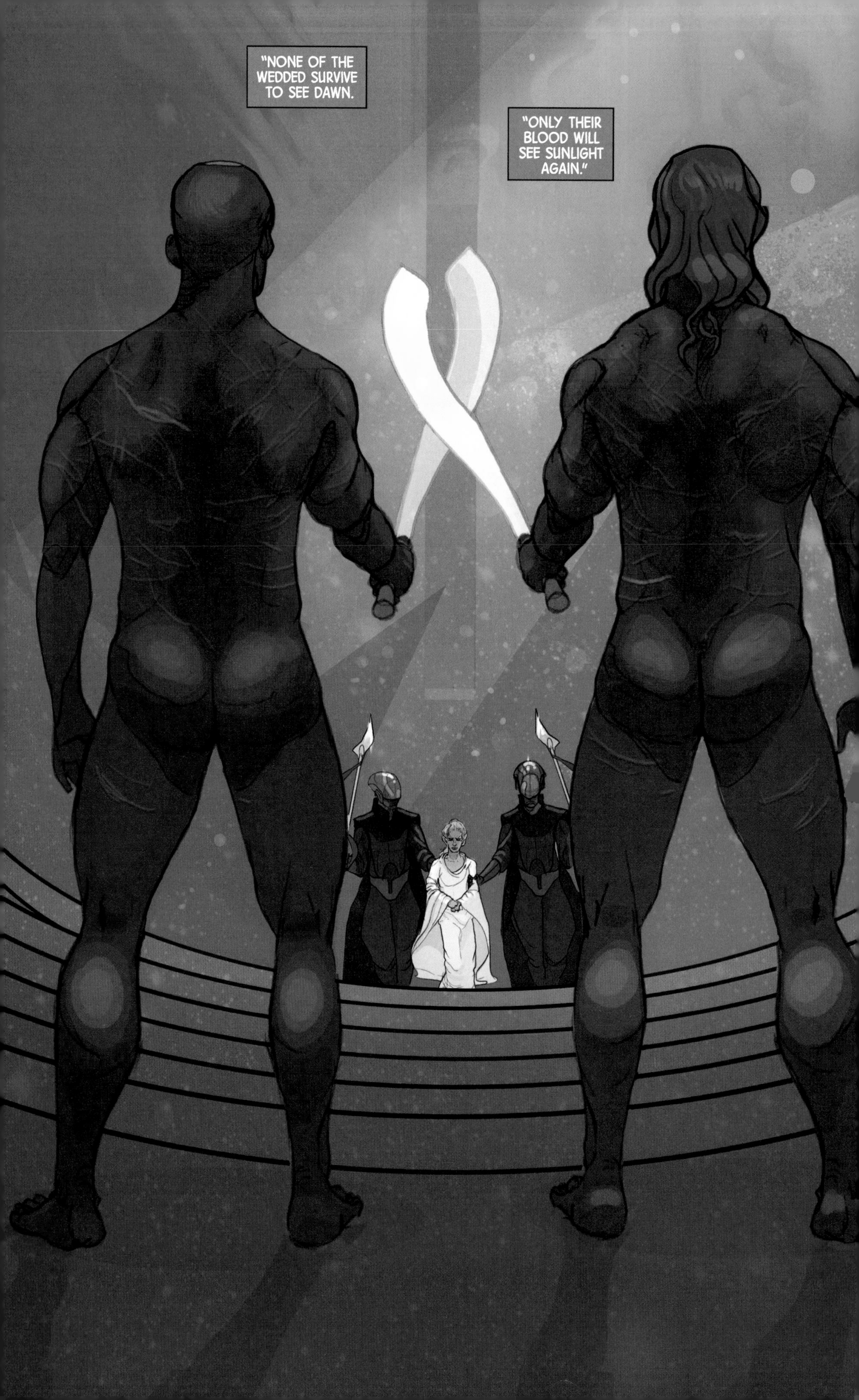
"NONE OF THE WEDDED SURVIVE TO SEE DAWN.
"ONLY THEIR BLOOD WILL SEE SUNLIGHT AGAIN."

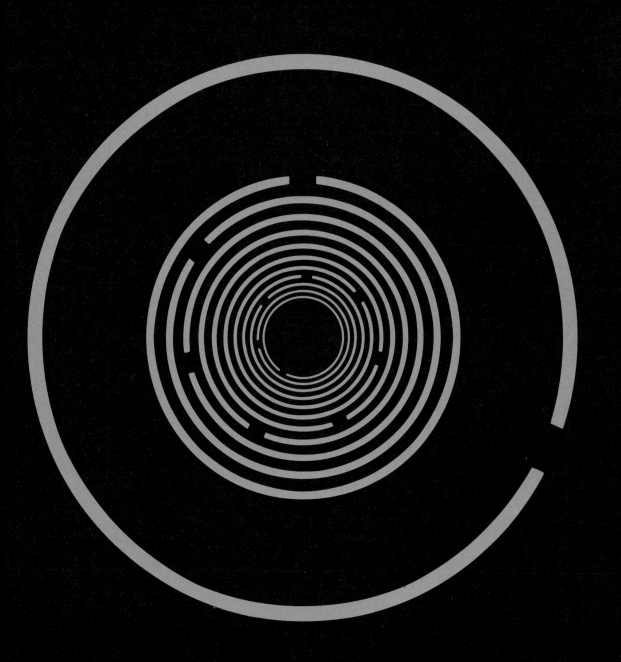

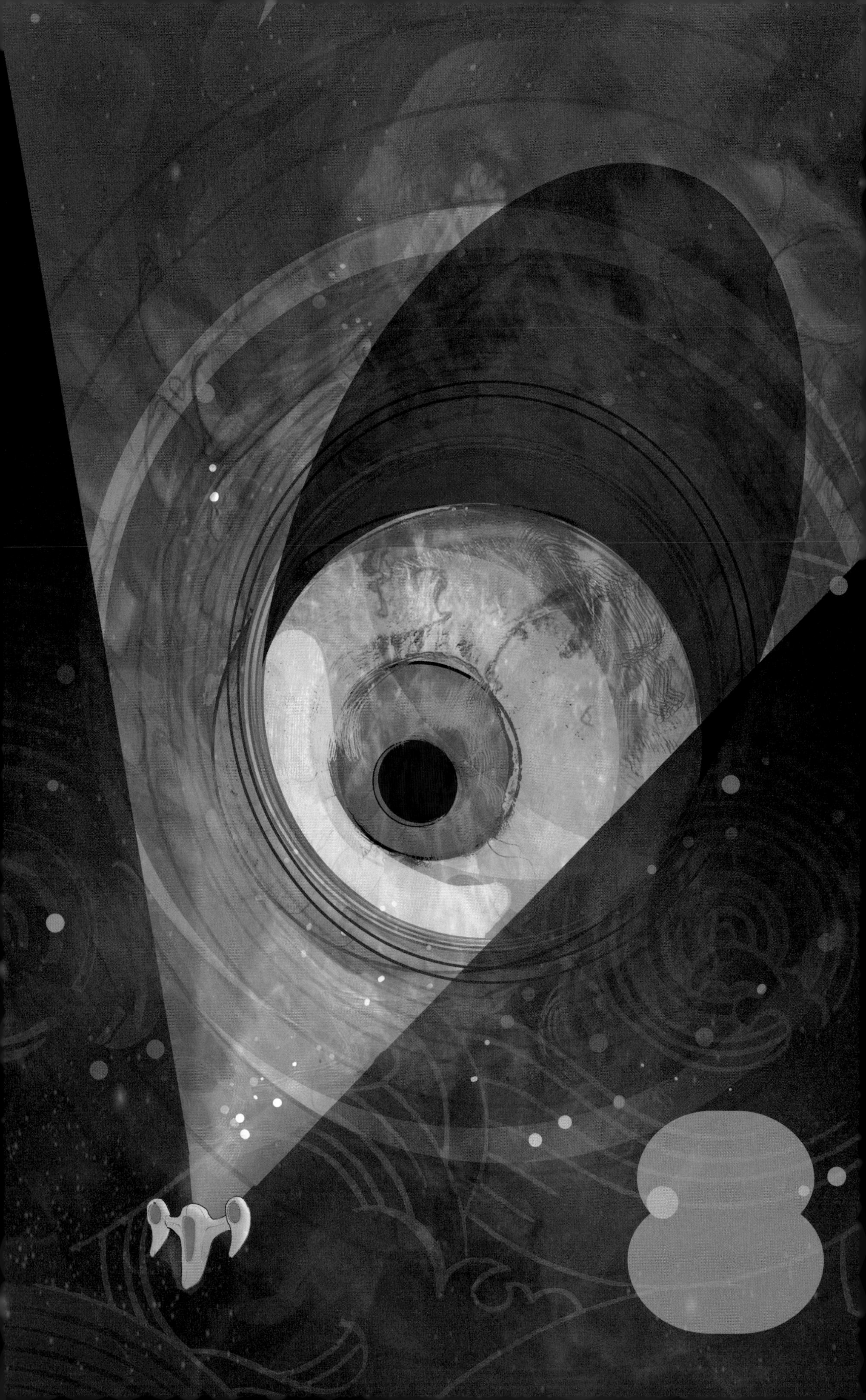

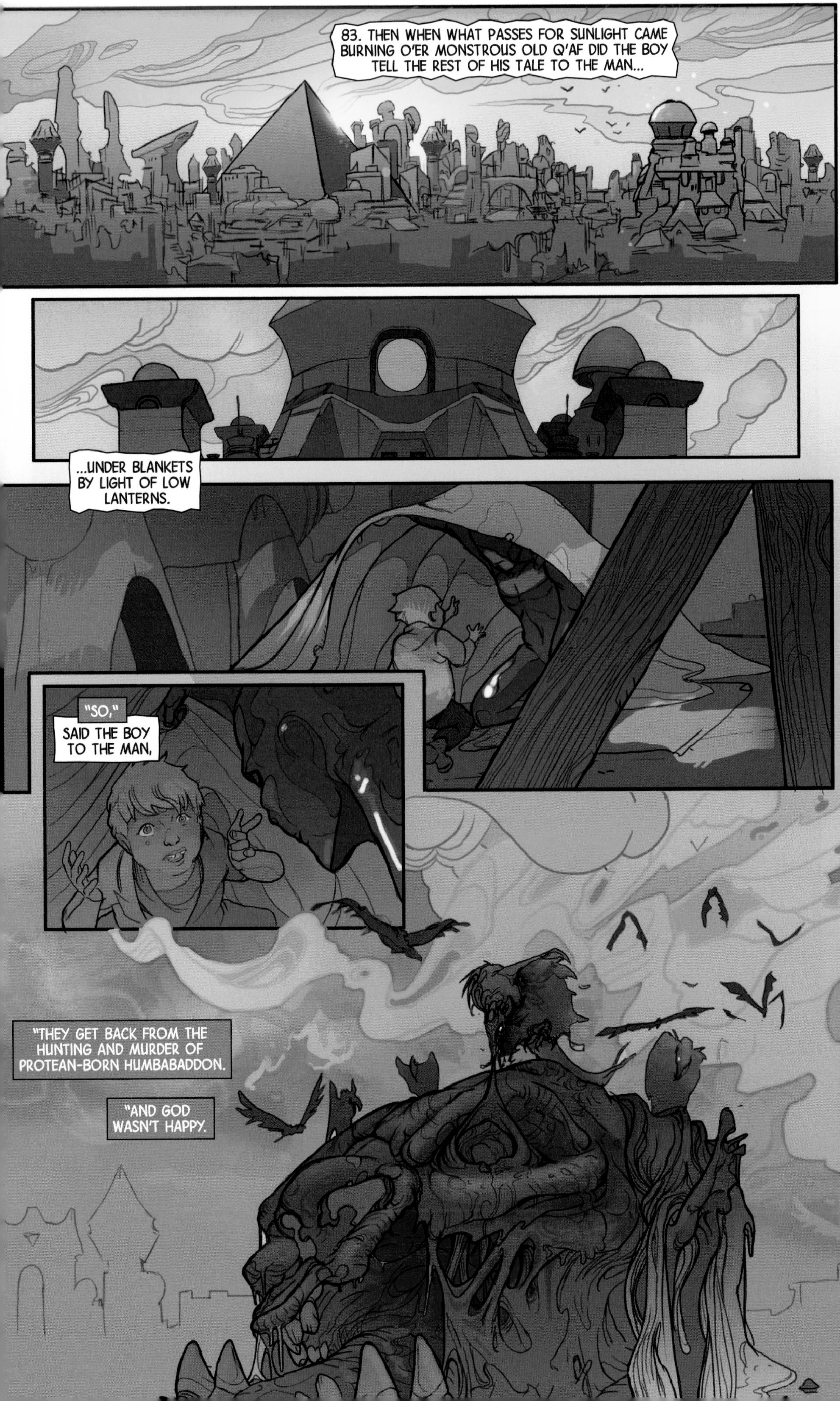
83. THEN WHEN WHAT PASSES FOR SUNLIGHT CAME BURNING O'ER MONSTROUS OLD Q'AF DID THE BOY TELL THE REST OF HIS TALE TO THE MAN...
...UNDER BLANKETS BY LIGHT OF LOW LANTERNS.
"SO,"
SAID THE BOY TO THE MAN,
"THEY GET BACK FROM THE HUNTING AND MURDER OF PROTEAN-BORN HUMBABADDON.
"AND GOD WASN'T HAPPY.

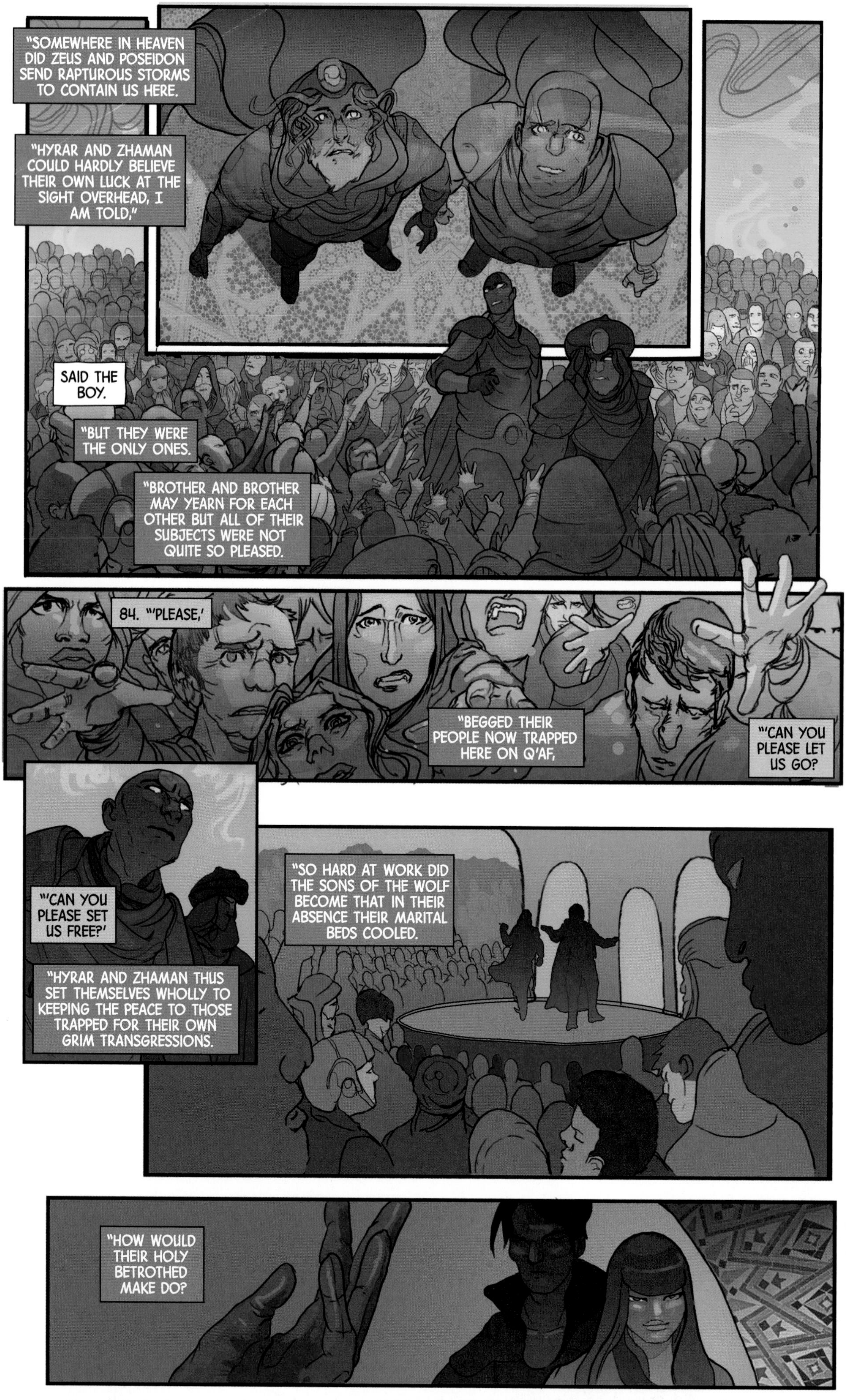
"SOMEWHERE IN HEAVEN DID ZEUS AND POSEIDON SEND RAPTUROUS STORMS TO CONTAIN US HERE.
"HYRAR AND ZHAMAN COULD HARDLY BELIEVE THEIR OWN LUCK AT THE SIGHT OVERHEAD, I AM TOLD,"
SAID THE BOY.
"BUT THEY WERE THE ONLY ONES.
"BROTHER AND BROTHER MAY YEARN FOR EACH OTHER BUT ALL OF THEIR SUBJECTS WERE NOT QUITE SO PLEASED.
84. "'PLEASE,'
"BEGGED THEIR PEOPLE NOW TRAPPED HERE ON Q'AF,
"'CAN YOU PLEASE LET US GO?
"'CAN YOU PLEASE SET US FREE?'
"HYRAR AND ZHAMAN THUS SET THEMSELVES WHOLLY TO KEEPING THE PEACE TO THOSE TRAPPED FOR THEIR OWN GRIM TRANSGRESSIONS.
"SO HARD AT WORK DID THE SONS OF THE WOLF BECOME THAT IN THEIR ABSENCE THEIR MARITAL BEDS COOLED.
"HOW WOULD THEIR HOLY BETROTHED MAKE DO?

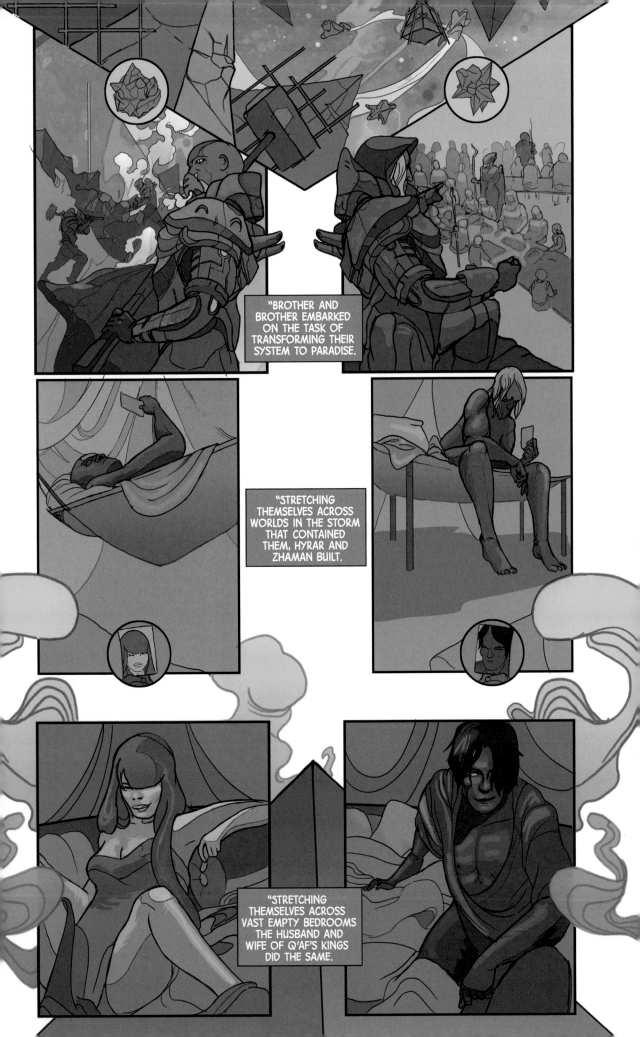

"BROTHER AND BROTHER EMBARKED ON THE TASK OF TRANSFORMING THEIR SYSTEM TO PARADISE.

"STRETCHING THEMSELVES ACROSS WORLDS IN THE STORM THAT CONTAINED THEM, HYRAR AND ZHAMAN BUILT.

"STRETCHING THEMSELVES ACROSS VAST EMPTY BEDROOMS THE HUSBAND AND WIFE OF Q'AF'S KINGS DID THE SAME.

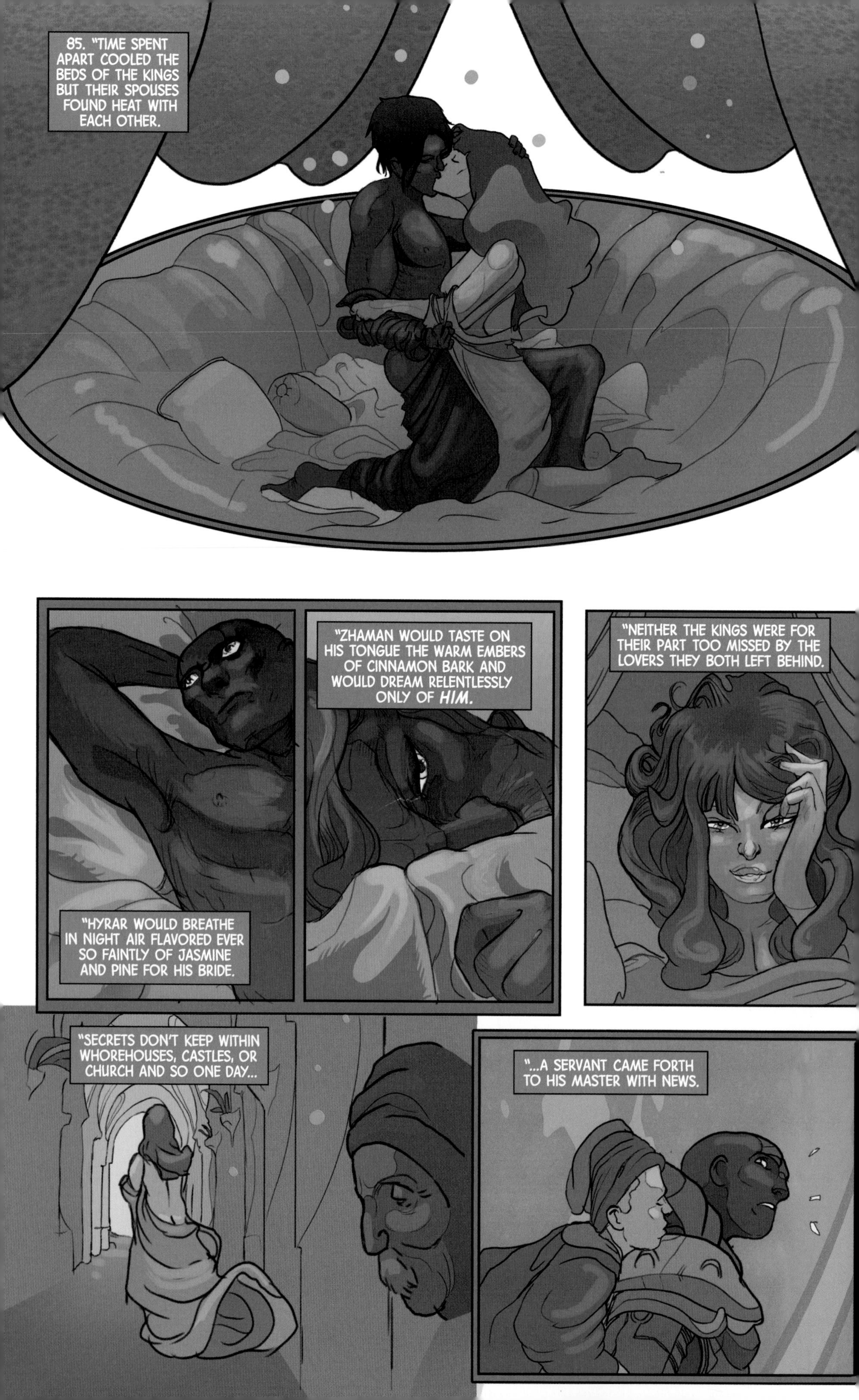
85. "TIME SPENT APART COOLED THE BEDS OF THE KINGS BUT THEIR SPOUSES FOUND HEAT WITH EACH OTHER.
"HYRAR WOULD BREATHE IN NIGHT AIR FLAVORED EVER SO FAINTLY OF JASMINE AND PINE FOR HIS BRIDE.
"ZHAMAN WOULD TASTE ON HIS TONGUE THE WARM EMBERS OF CINNAMON BARK AND WOULD DREAM RELENTLESSLY ONLY OF *HIM*.
"NEITHER THE KINGS WERE FOR THEIR PART TOO MISSED BY THE LOVERS THEY BOTH LEFT BEHIND.
"SECRETS DON'T KEEP WITHIN WHOREHOUSES, CASTLES, OR CHURCH AND SO ONE DAY...
"...A SERVANT CAME FORTH TO HIS MASTER WITH NEWS.

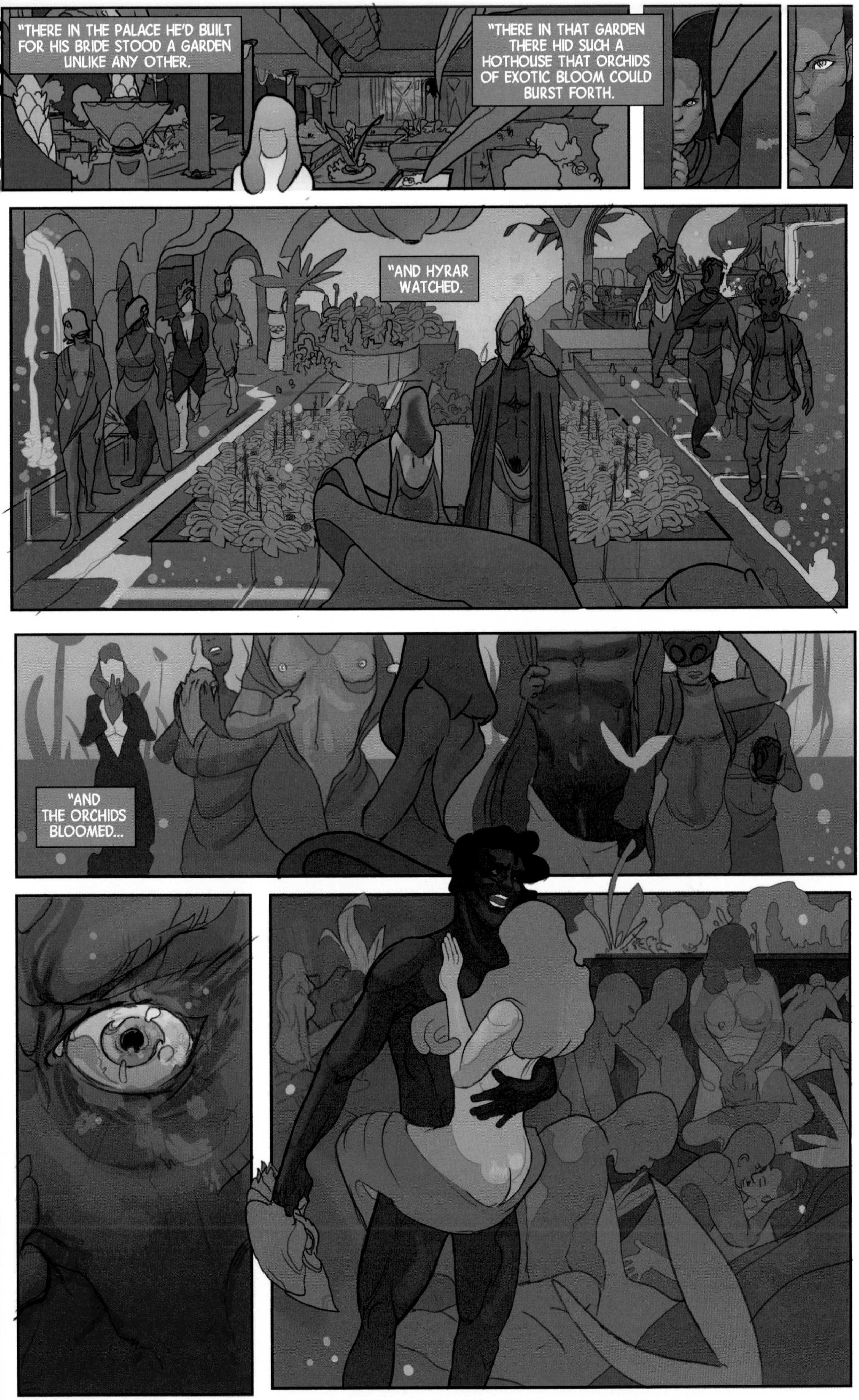
"THERE IN THE PALACE HE'D BUILT FOR HIS BRIDE STOOD A GARDEN UNLIKE ANY OTHER.
"THERE IN THAT GARDEN THERE HID SUCH A HOTHOUSE THAT ORCHIDS OF EXOTIC BLOOM COULD BURST FORTH.
"AND HYRAR WATCHED.
"AND THE ORCHIDS BLOOMED...

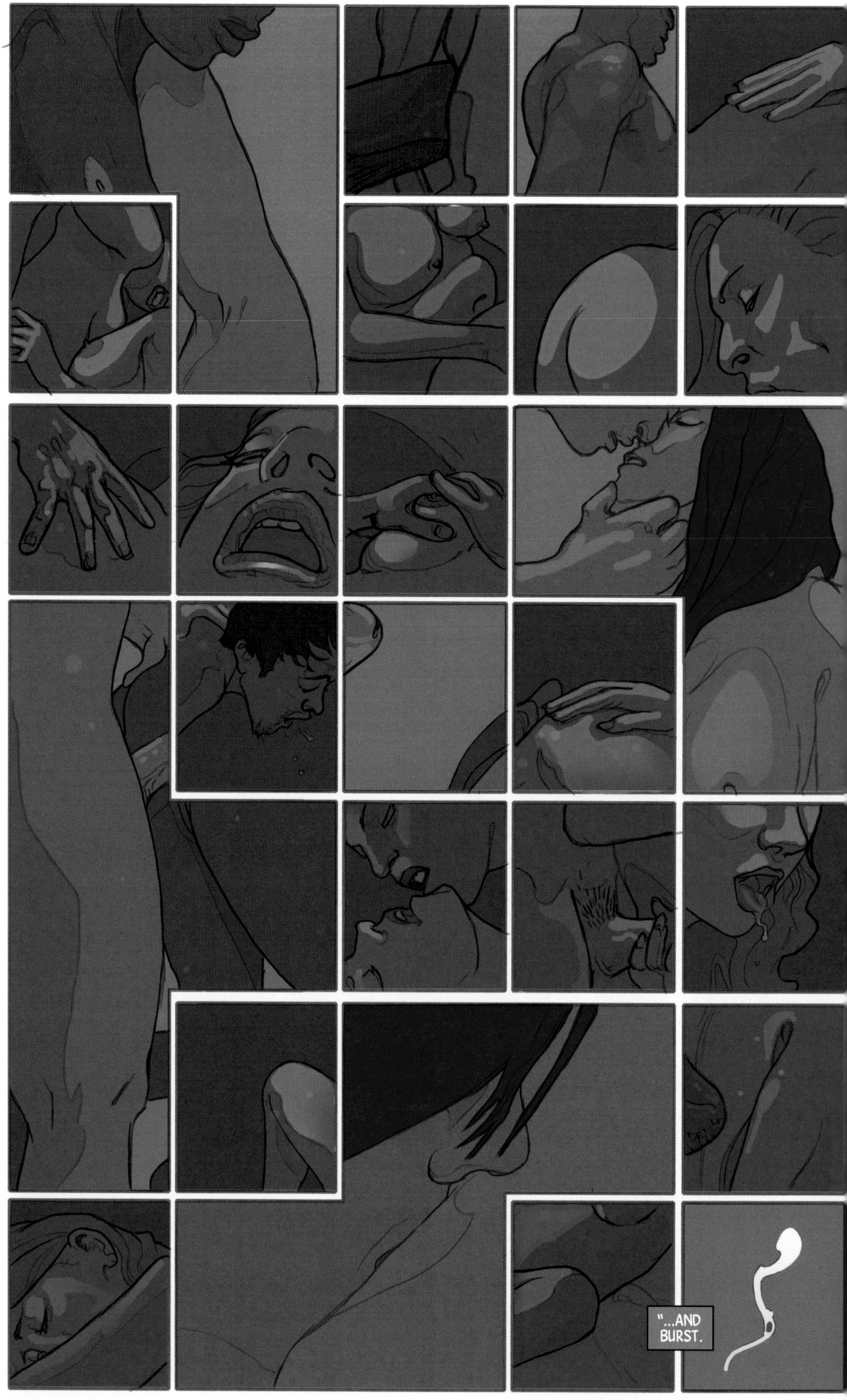
"...AND BURST.

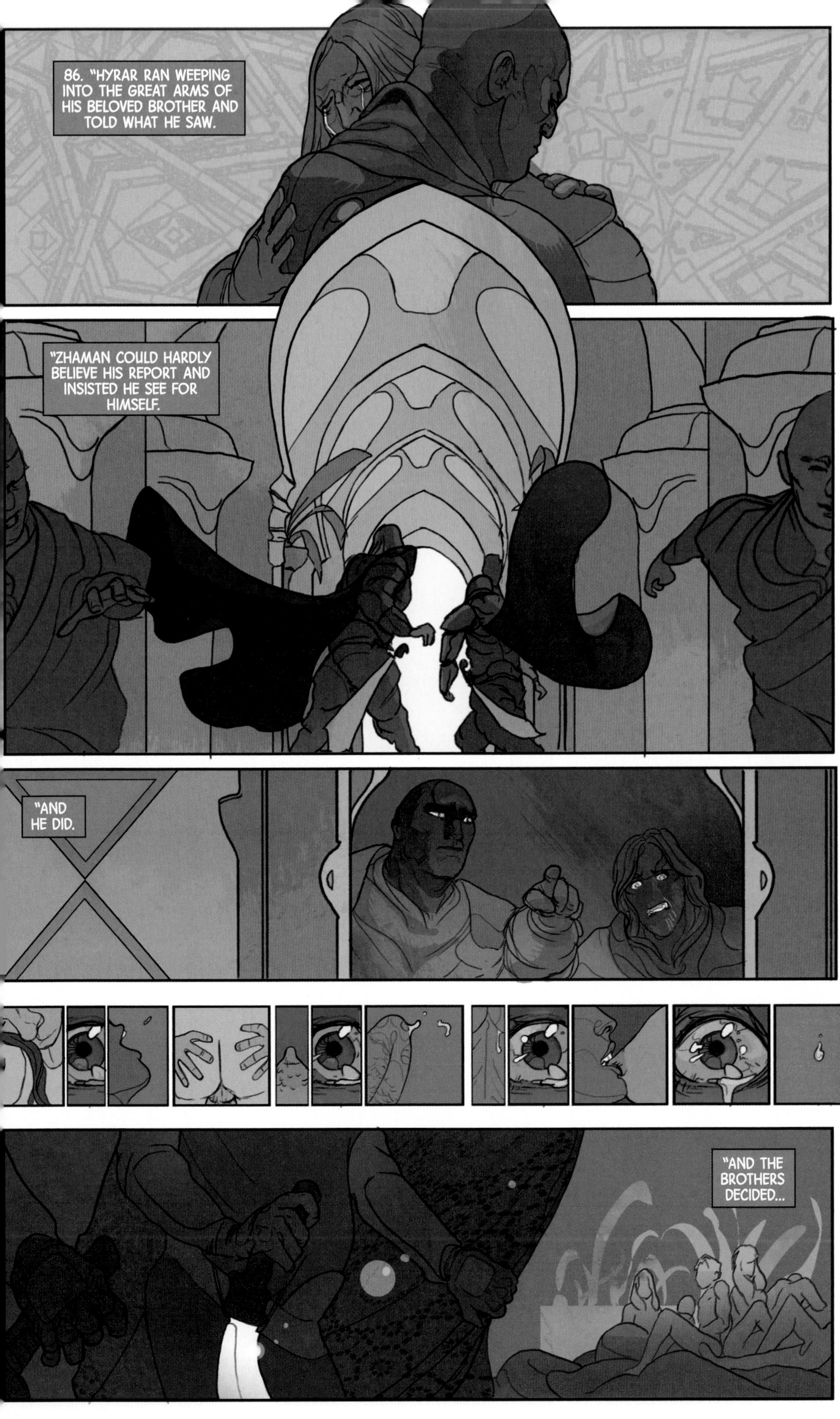
86. "HYRAR RAN WEEPING INTO THE GREAT ARMS OF HIS BELOVED BROTHER AND TOLD WHAT HE SAW.
"ZHAMAN COULD HARDLY BELIEVE HIS REPORT AND INSISTED HE SEE FOR HIMSELF.
"AND HE DID.
"AND THE BROTHERS DECIDED...

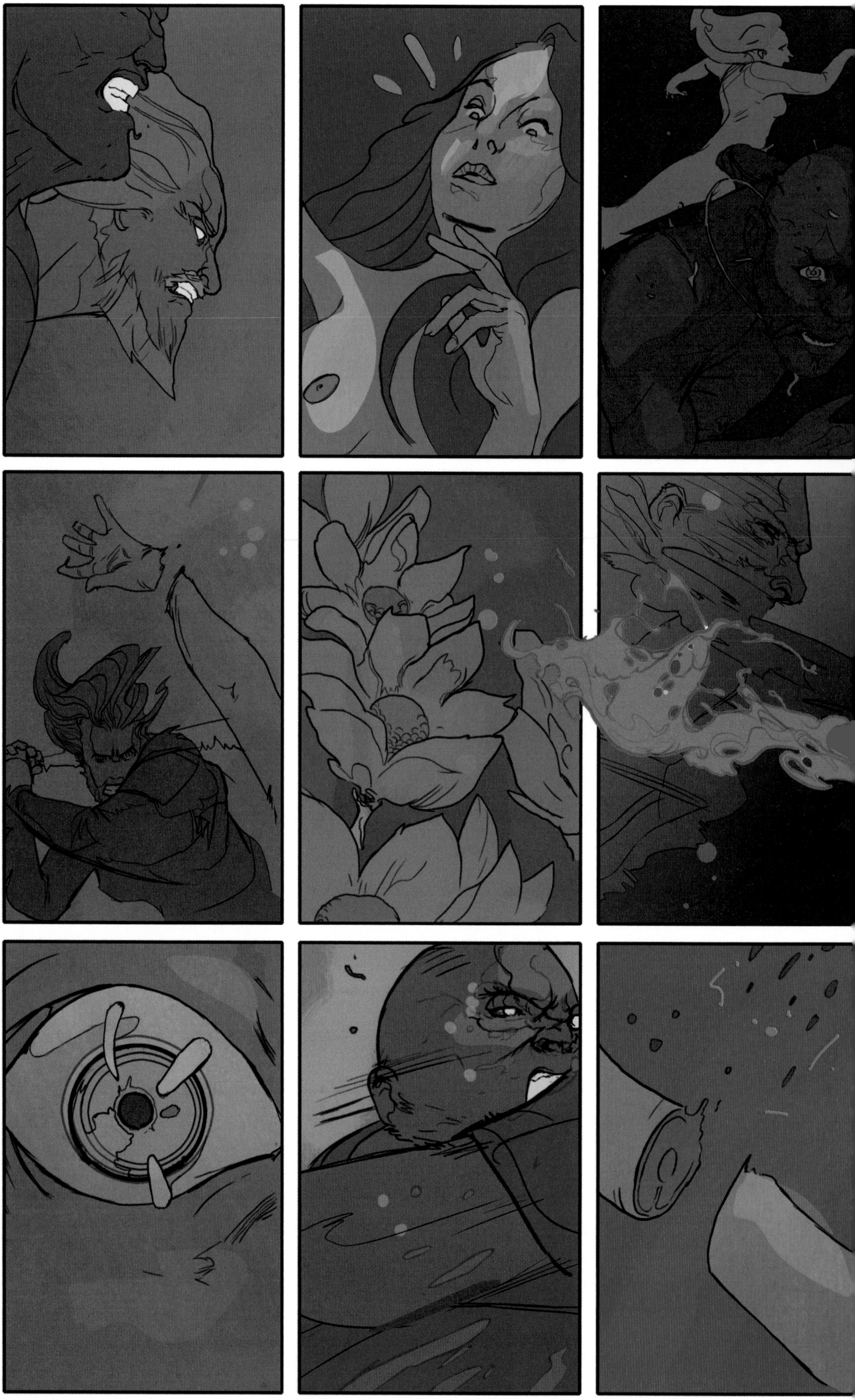

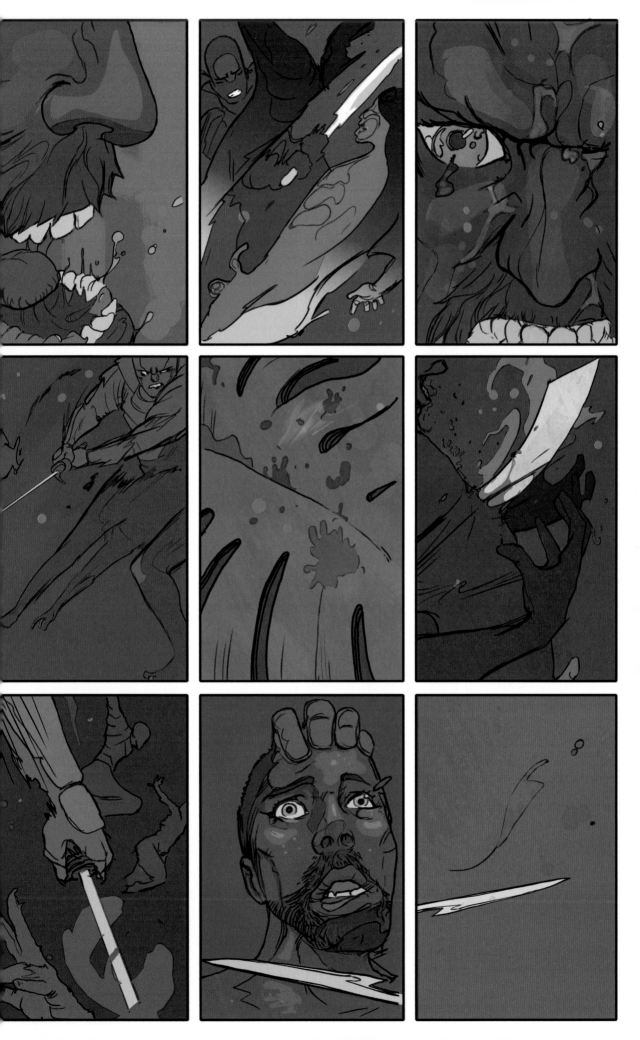

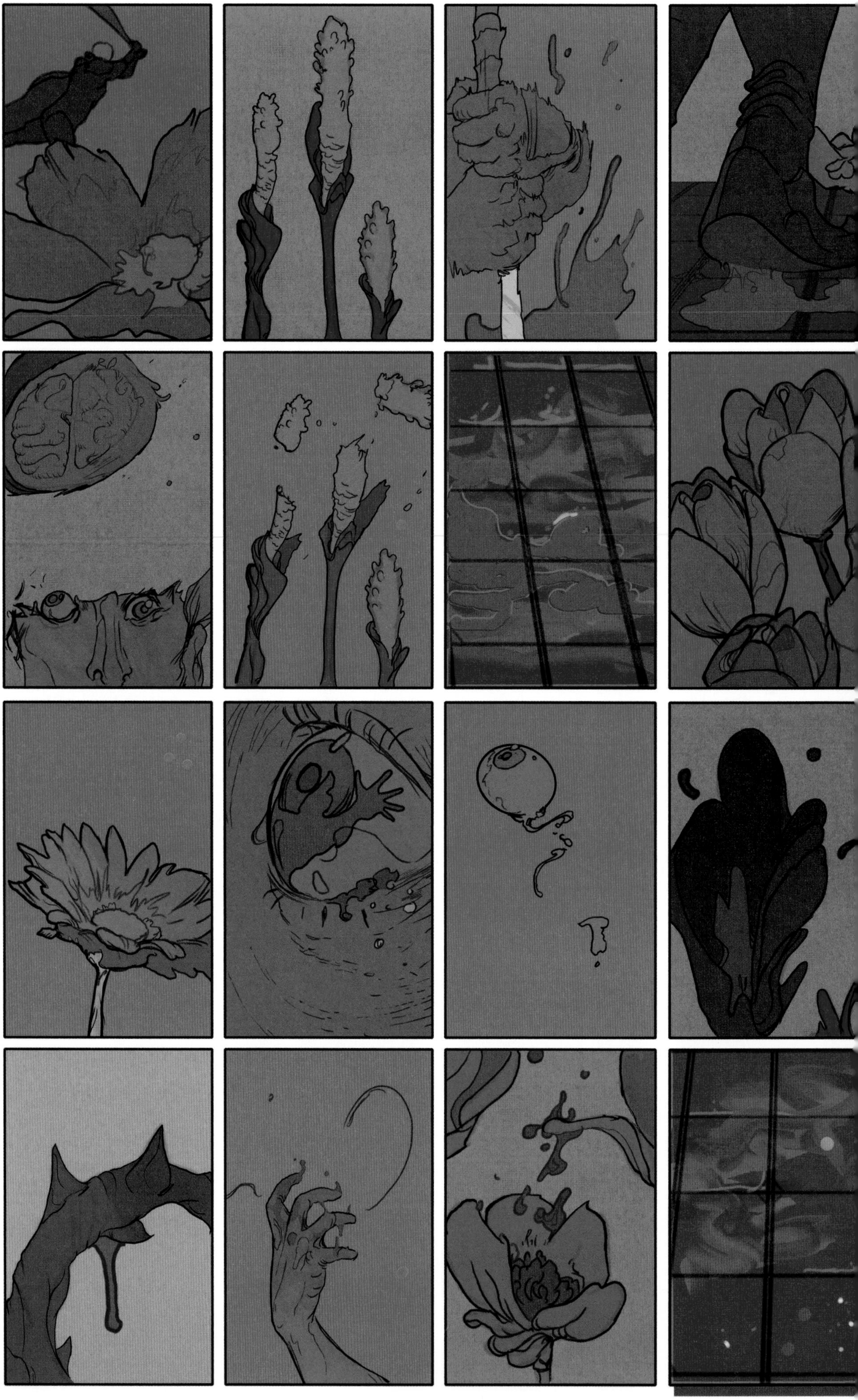

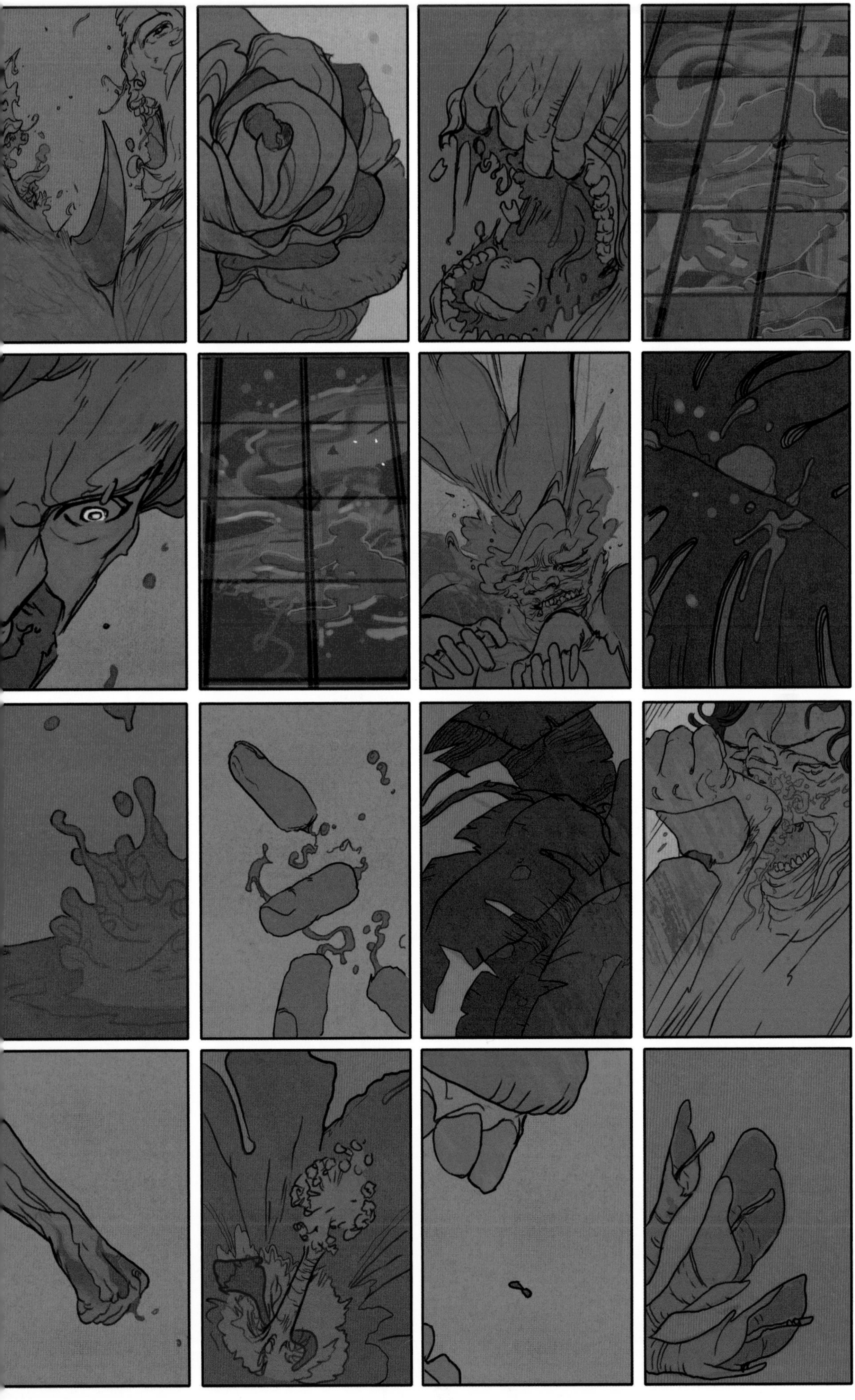

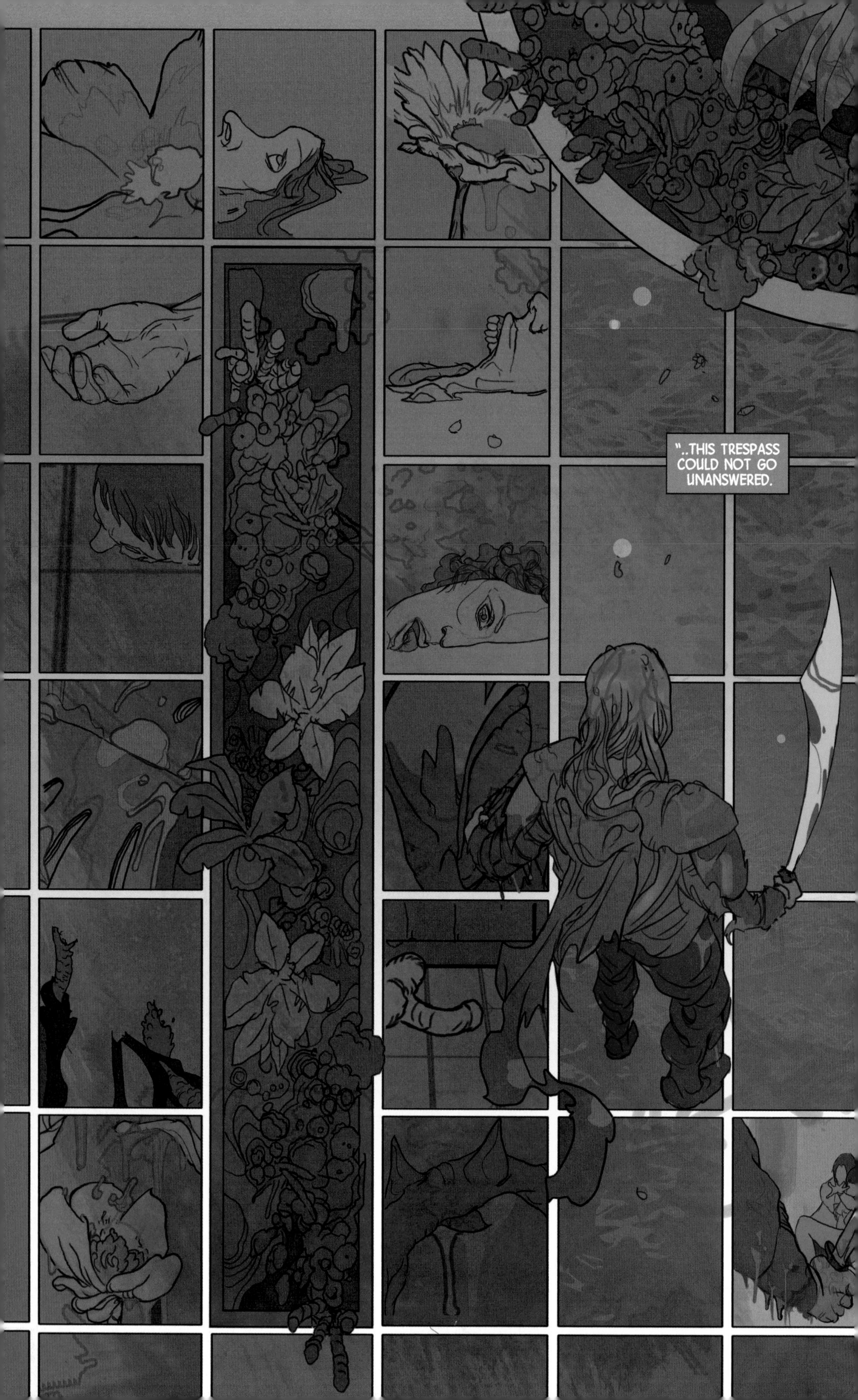
"..THIS TRESPASS COULD NOT GO UNANSWERED.

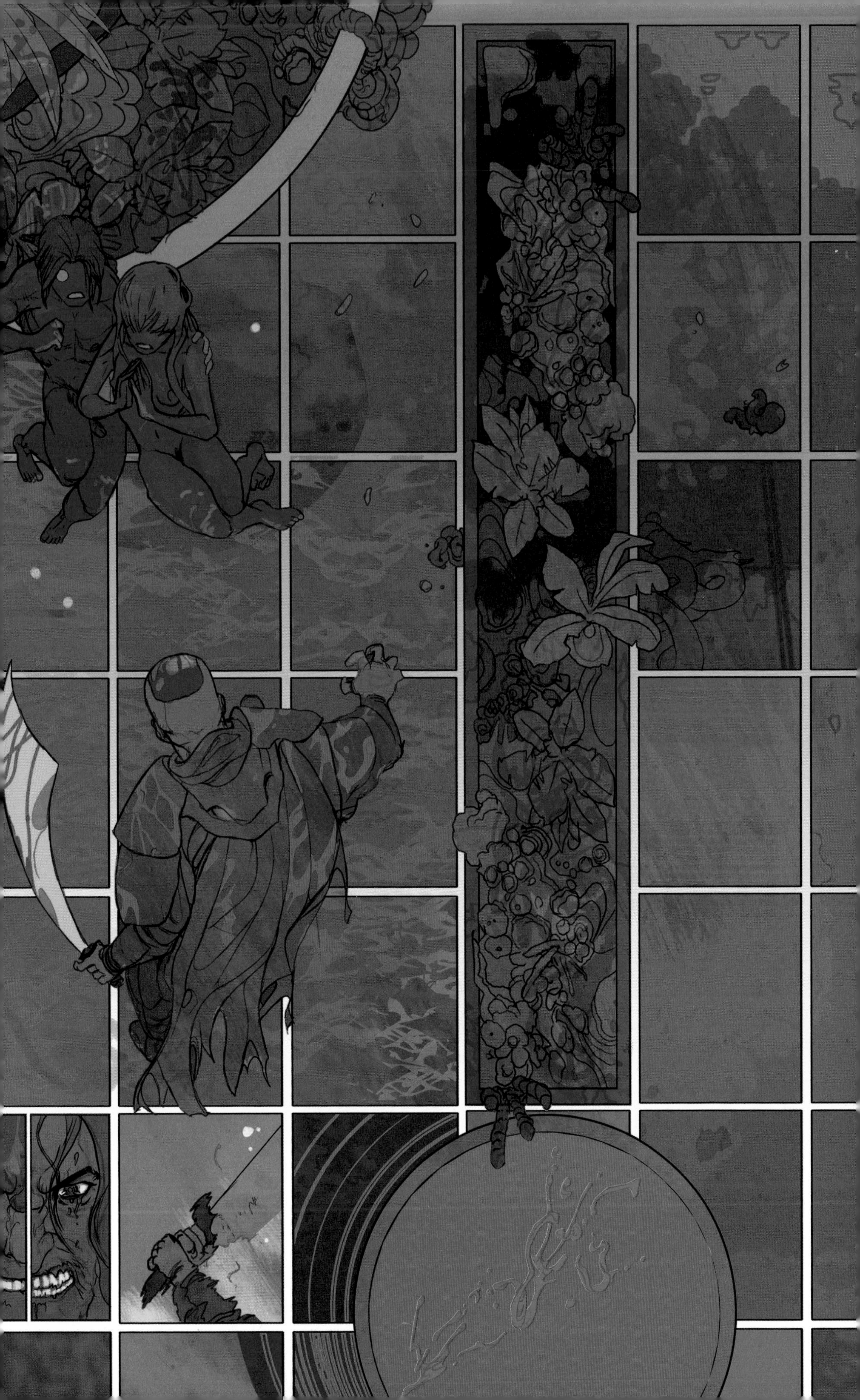

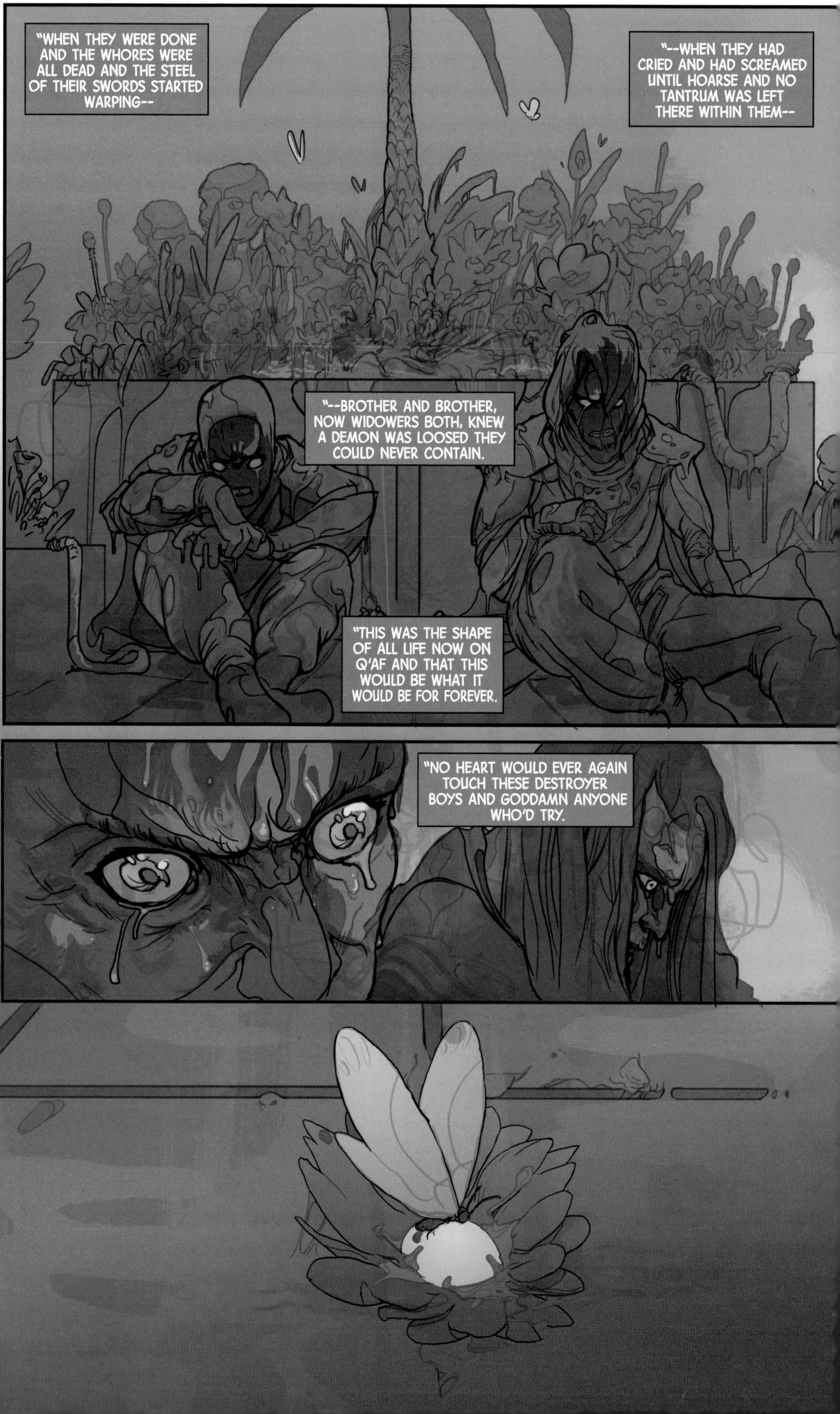
"WHEN THEY WERE DONE AND THE WHORES WERE ALL DEAD AND THE STEEL OF THEIR SWORDS STARTED WARPING--
"--WHEN THEY HAD CRIED AND HAD SCREAMED UNTIL HOARSE AND NO TANTRUM WAS LEFT THERE WITHIN THEM--
"--BROTHER AND BROTHER, NOW WIDOWERS BOTH, KNEW A DEMON WAS LOOSED THEY COULD NEVER CONTAIN.
"THIS WAS THE SHAPE OF ALL LIFE NOW ON Q'AF AND THAT THIS WOULD BE WHAT IT WOULD BE FOR FOREVER.
"NO HEART WOULD EVER AGAIN TOUCH THESE DESTROYER BOYS AND GODDAMN ANYONE WHO'D TRY.

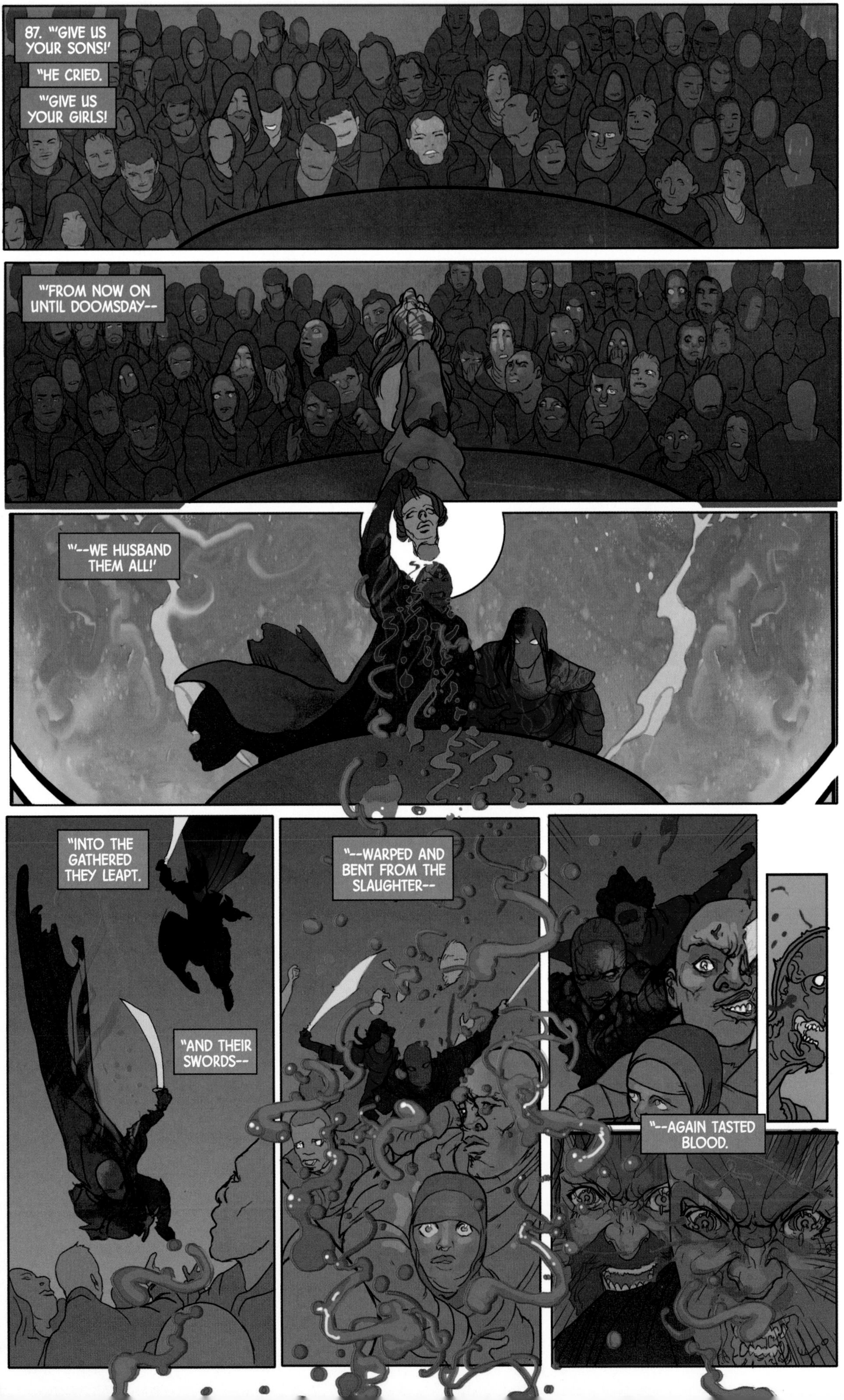
87. "'GIVE US YOUR SONS!'
"HE CRIED.
"'GIVE US YOUR GIRLS!
"FROM NOW ON UNTIL DOOMSDAY--
"--WE HUSBAND THEM ALL!'
"INTO THE GATHERED THEY LEAPT.
"AND THEIR SWORDS--
"--WARPED AND BENT FROM THE SLAUGHTER--
"--AGAIN TASTED BLOOD.

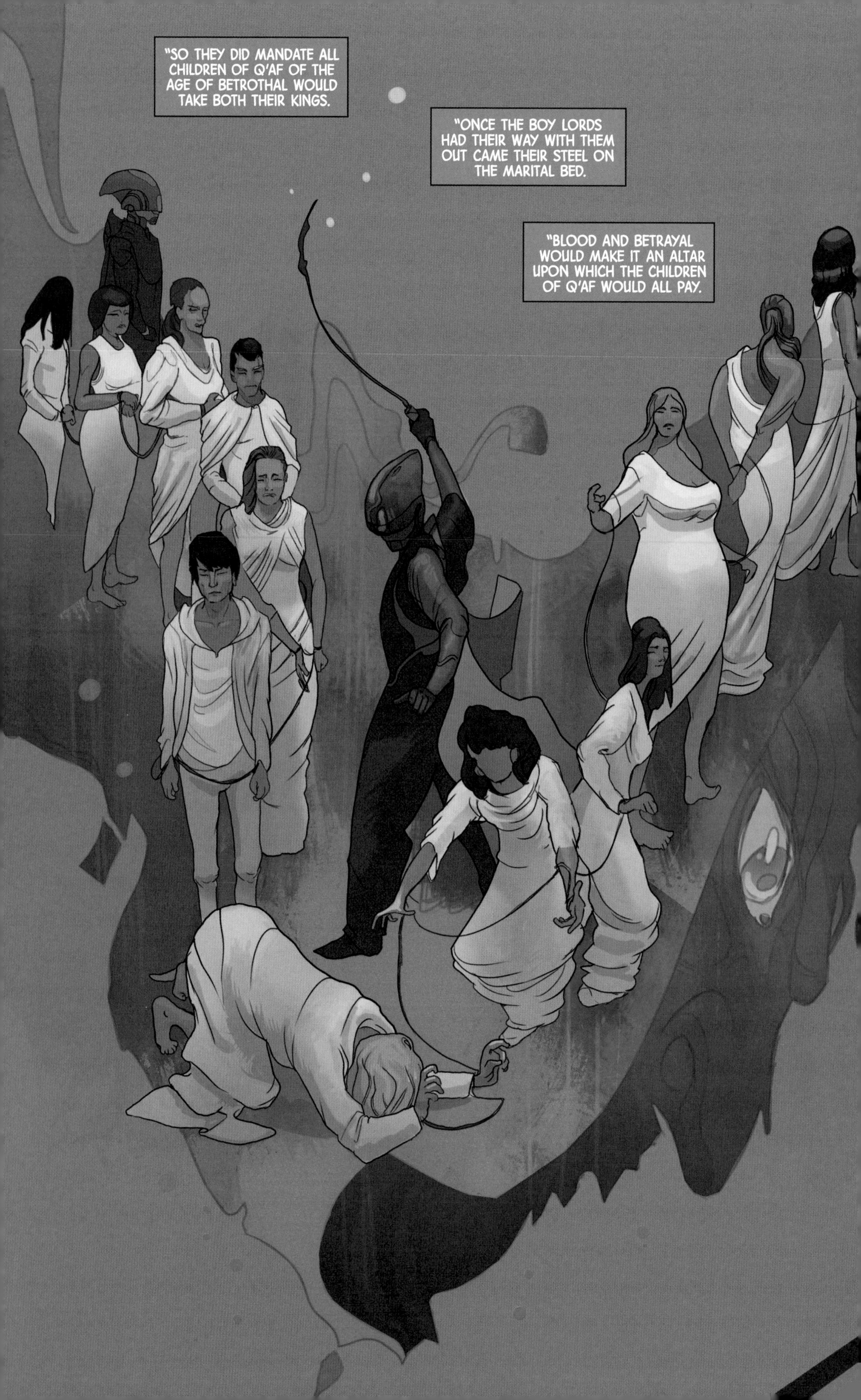
"SO THEY DID MANDATE ALL CHILDREN OF Q'AF OF THE AGE OF BETROTHAL WOULD TAKE BOTH THEIR KINGS.
"ONCE THE BOY LORDS HAD THEIR WAY WITH THEM OUT CAME THEIR STEEL ON THE MARITAL BED.
"BLOOD AND BETRAYAL WOULD MAKE IT AN ALTAR UPON WHICH THE CHILDREN OF Q'AF WOULD ALL PAY.

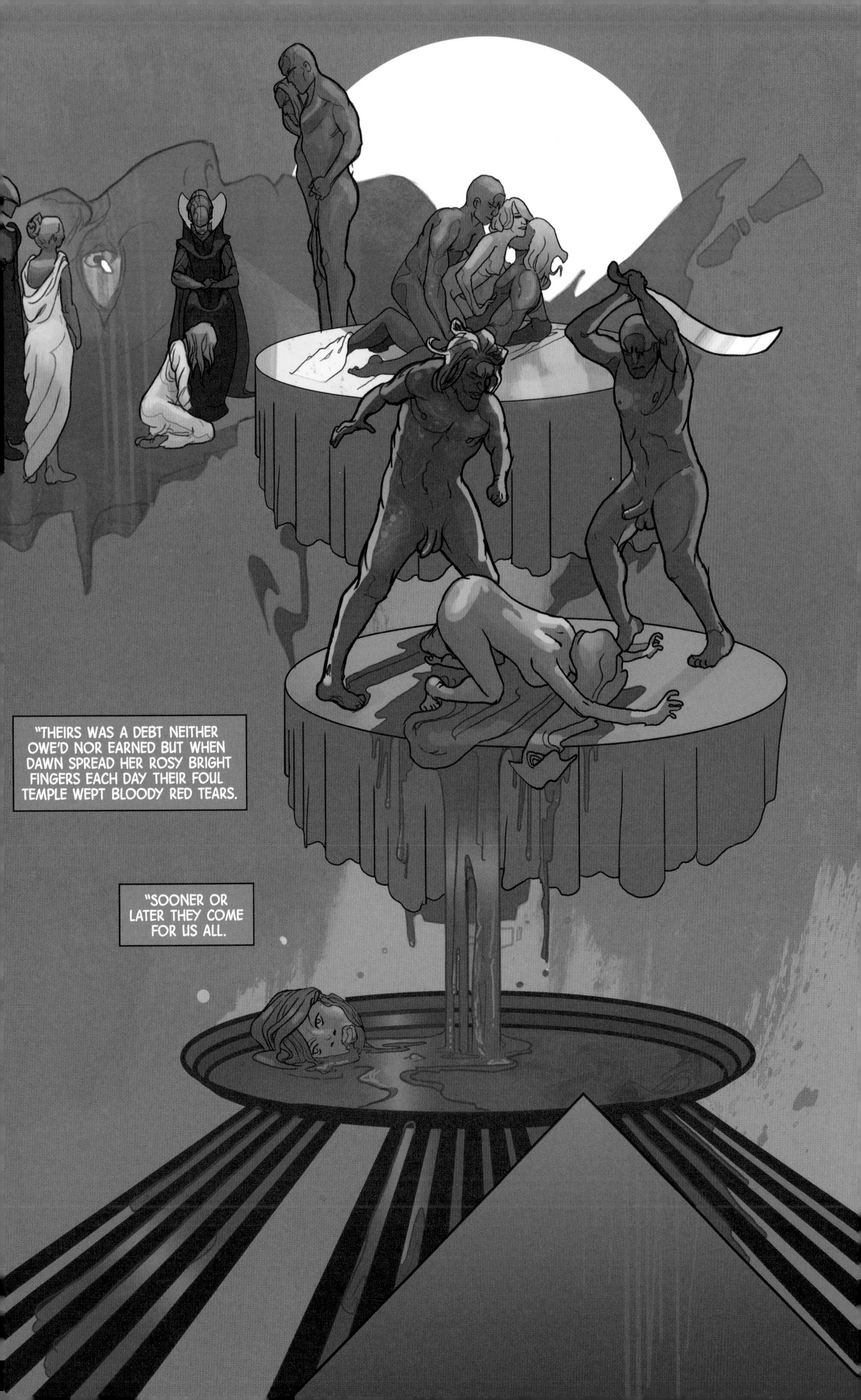
"THEIRS WAS A DEBT NEITHER OWE'D NOR EARNED BUT WHEN DAWN SPREAD HER ROSY BRIGHT FINGERS EACH DAY THEIR FOUL TEMPLE WEPT BLOODY RED TEARS.
"SOONER OR LATER THEY COME FOR US ALL.

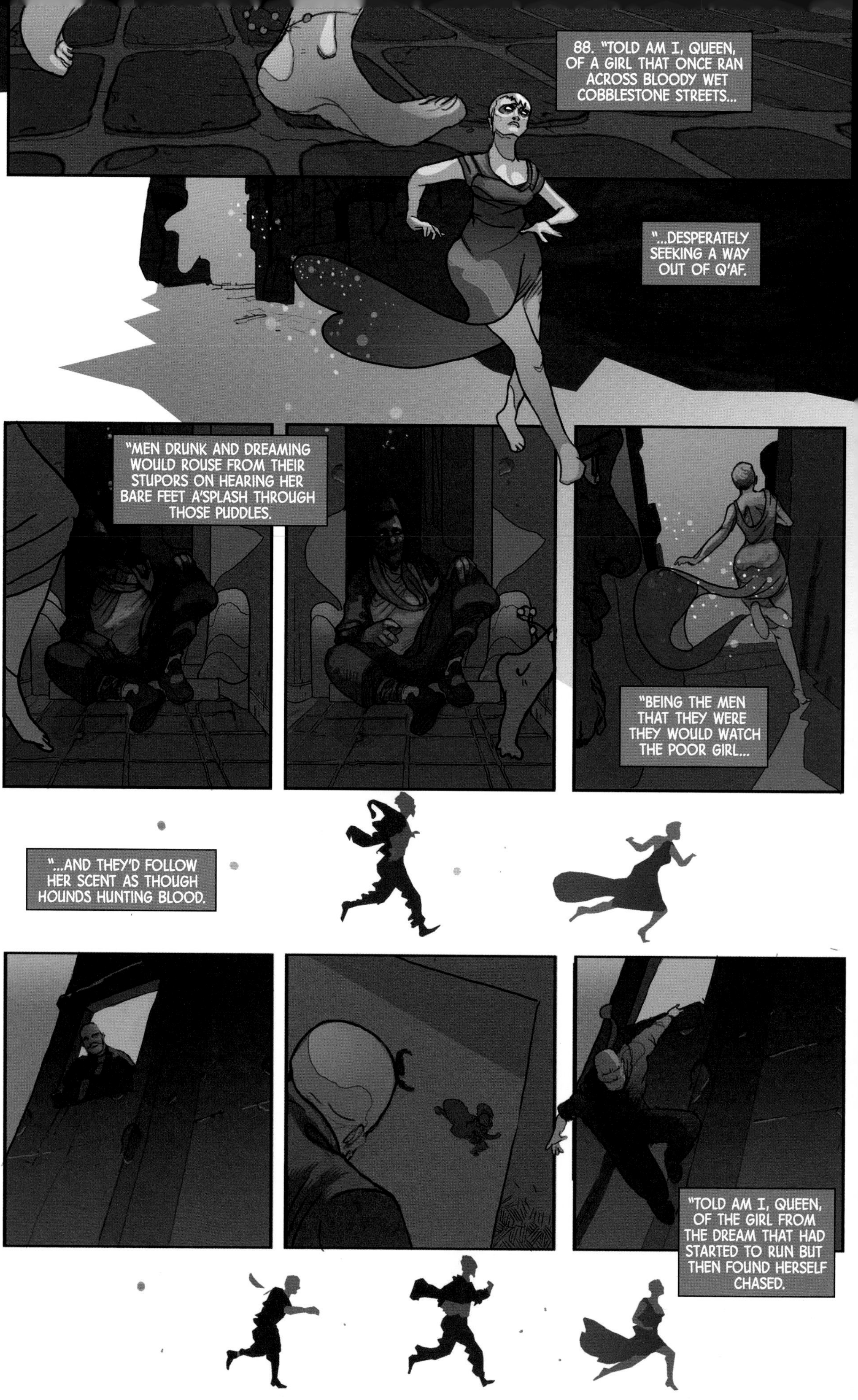

88. "TOLD AM I, QUEEN, OF A GIRL THAT ONCE RAN ACROSS BLOODY WET COBBLESTONE STREETS...
"...DESPERATELY SEEKING A WAY OUT OF Q'AF.
"MEN DRUNK AND DREAMING WOULD ROUSE FROM THEIR STUPORS ON HEARING HER BARE FEET A'SPLASH THROUGH THOSE PUDDLES.
"BEING THE MEN THAT THEY WERE THEY WOULD WATCH THE POOR GIRL...
"...AND THEY'D FOLLOW HER SCENT AS THOUGH HOUNDS HUNTING BLOOD.
"TOLD AM I, QUEEN, OF THE GIRL FROM THE DREAM THAT HAD STARTED TO RUN BUT THEN FOUND HERSELF CHASED.

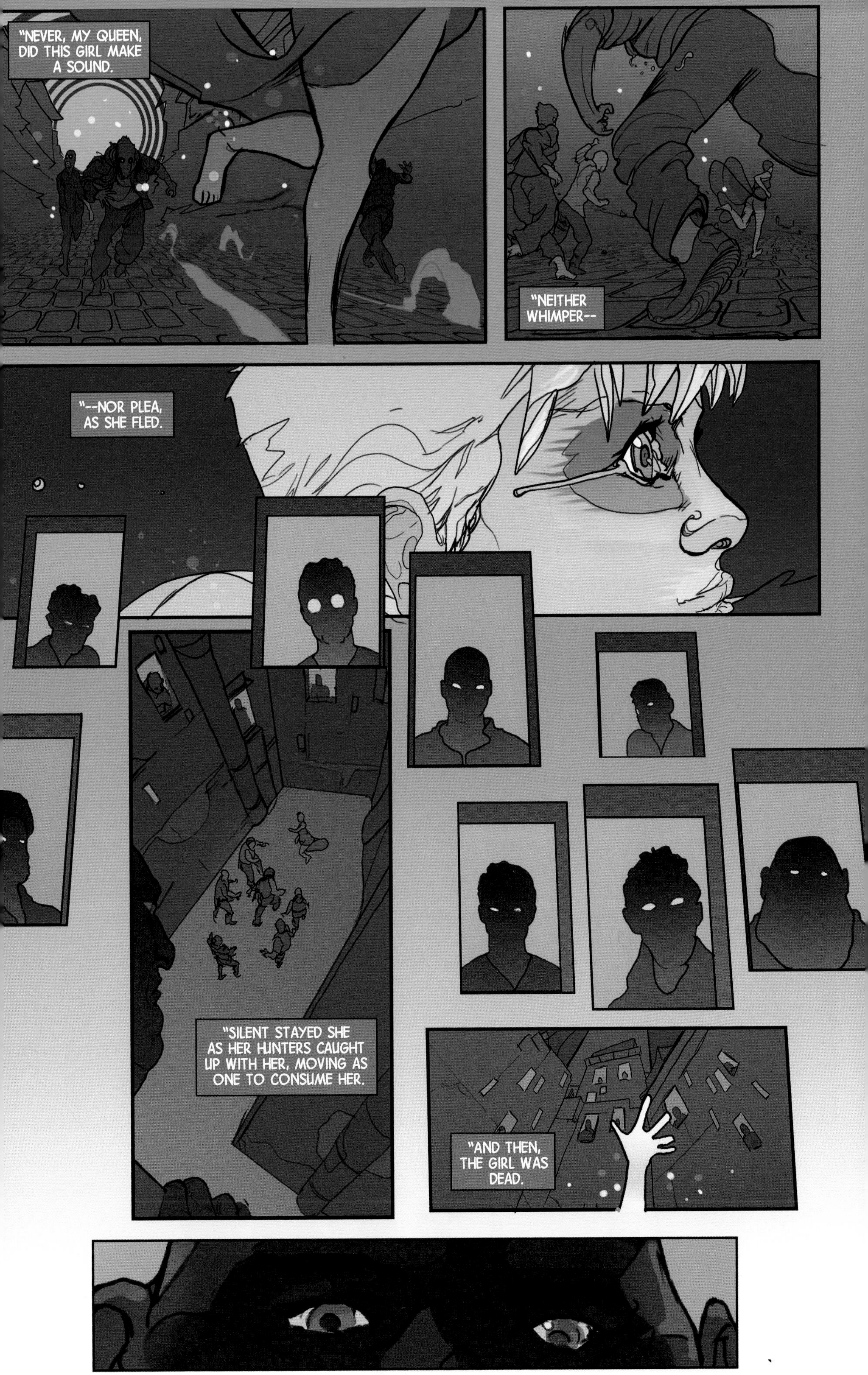
"NEVER, MY QUEEN, DID THIS GIRL MAKE A SOUND.
"NEITHER WHIMPER--
"--NOR PLEA, AS SHE FLED.
"SILENT STAYED SHE AS HER HUNTERS CAUGHT UP WITH HER, MOVING AS ONE TO CONSUME HER.
"AND THEN, THE GIRL WAS DEAD.

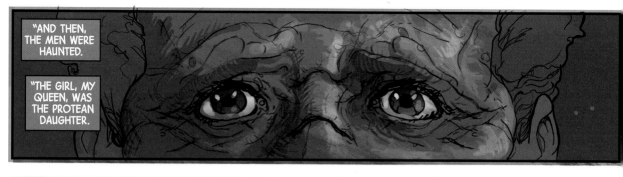

"AND THEN, THE MEN WERE HAUNTED.

"THE GIRL, MY QUEEN, WAS THE PROTEAN DAUGHTER.

"SHE WAS DEAD.

"*THEY* WERE VERY MUCH ALIVE.

"THE HAUNTED MAN STARTED TO DIG AT THE SITE OF HIS SIN.

"THE HAUNTED *MEN*.

89. "TOLD AM I, QUEEN, THAT THE MEN FOUND THEMSELVES OUTSIDE SLEEP'S TENDER WALLS, SO ASHAMED OF THEIR DEEDS, SO EMPTY, UNFED.

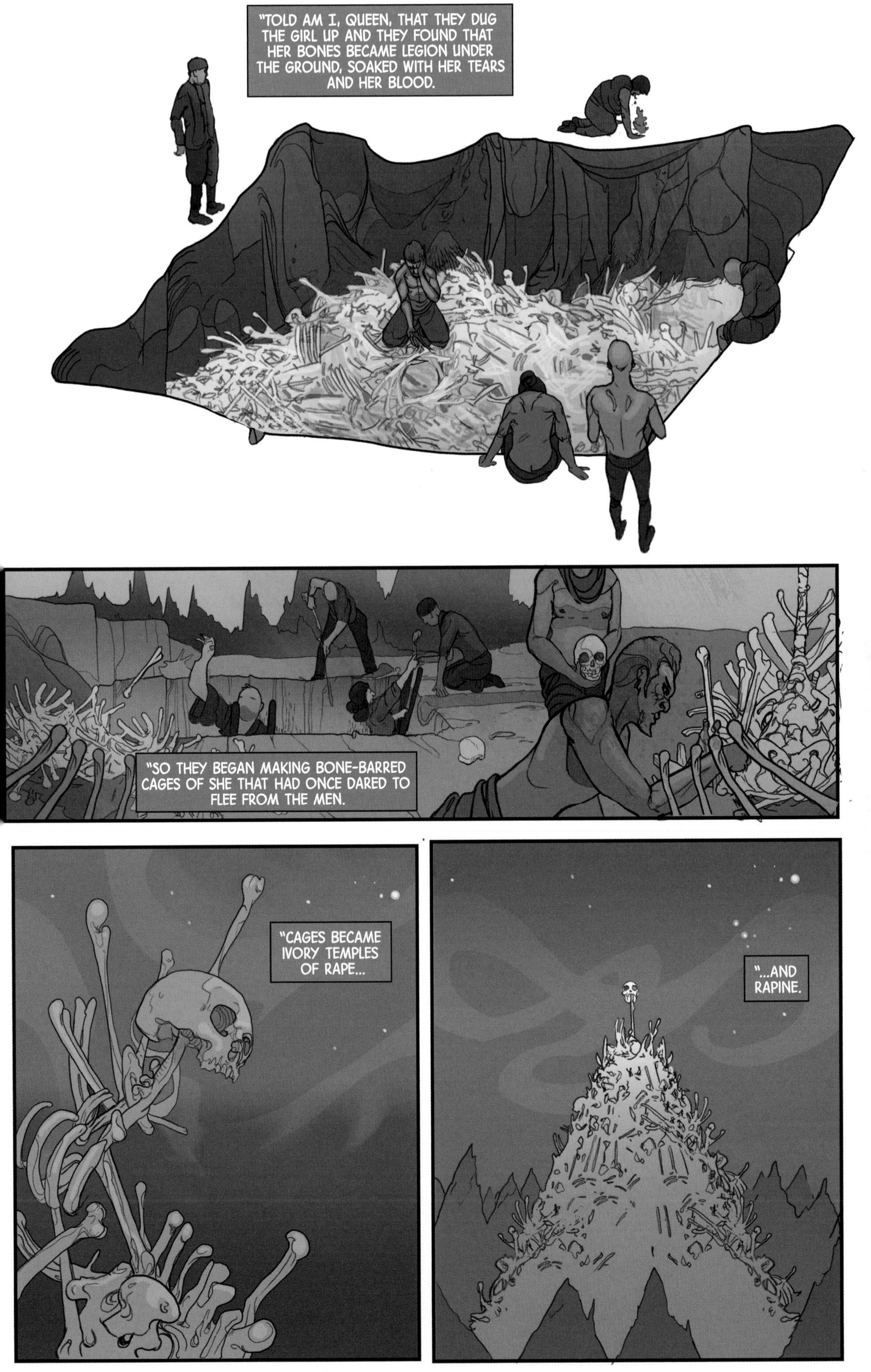
"TOLD AM I, QUEEN, THAT THEY DUG THE GIRL UP AND THEY FOUND THAT HER BONES BECAME LEGION UNDER THE GROUND, SOAKED WITH HER TEARS AND HER BLOOD.
"SO THEY BEGAN MAKING BONE-BARRED CAGES OF SHE THAT HAD ONCE DARED TO FLEE FROM THE MEN.
"CAGES BECAME IVORY TEMPLES OF RAPE...
"...AND RAPINE.

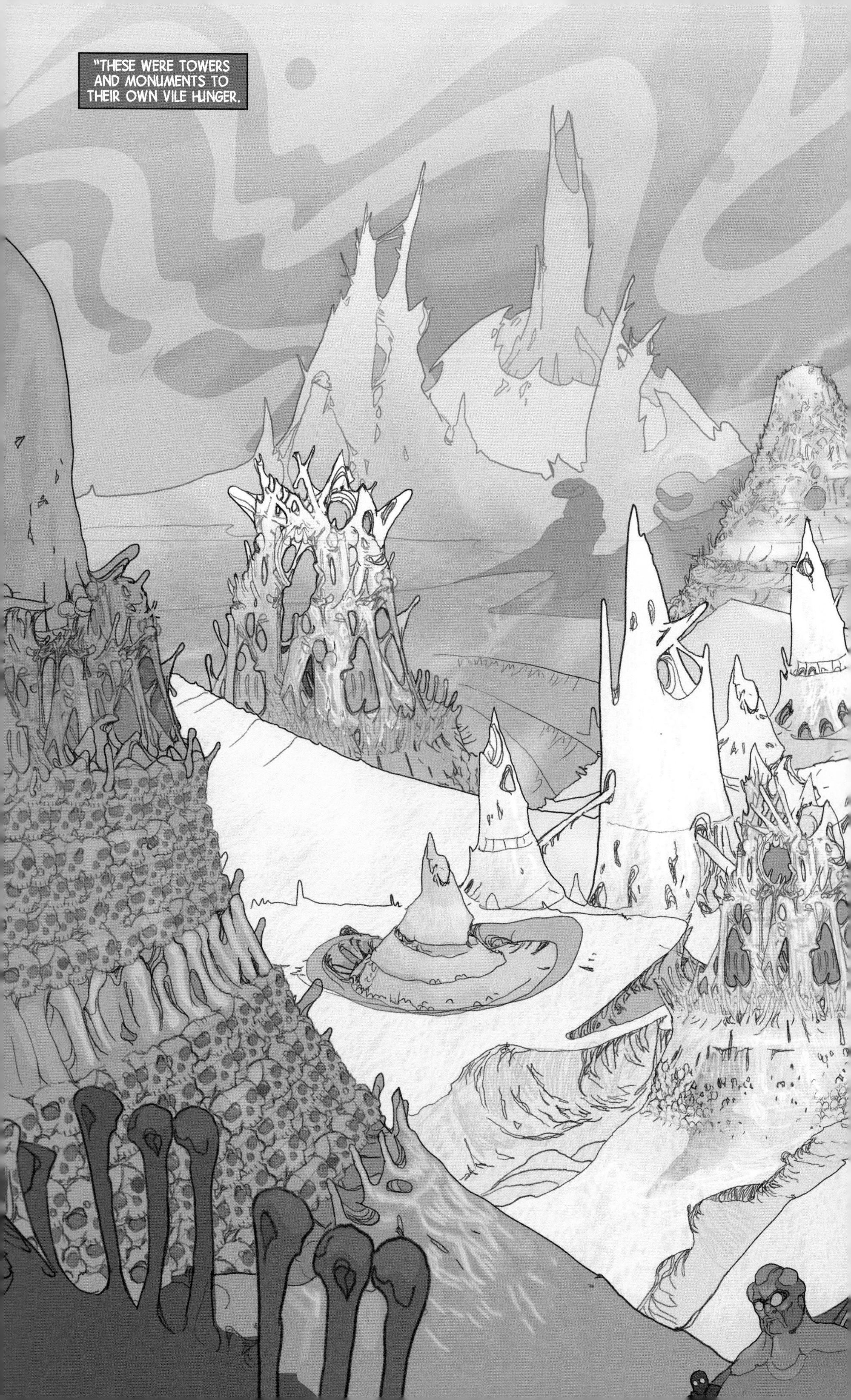
"THESE WERE TOWERS AND MONUMENTS TO THEIR OWN VILE HUNGER.

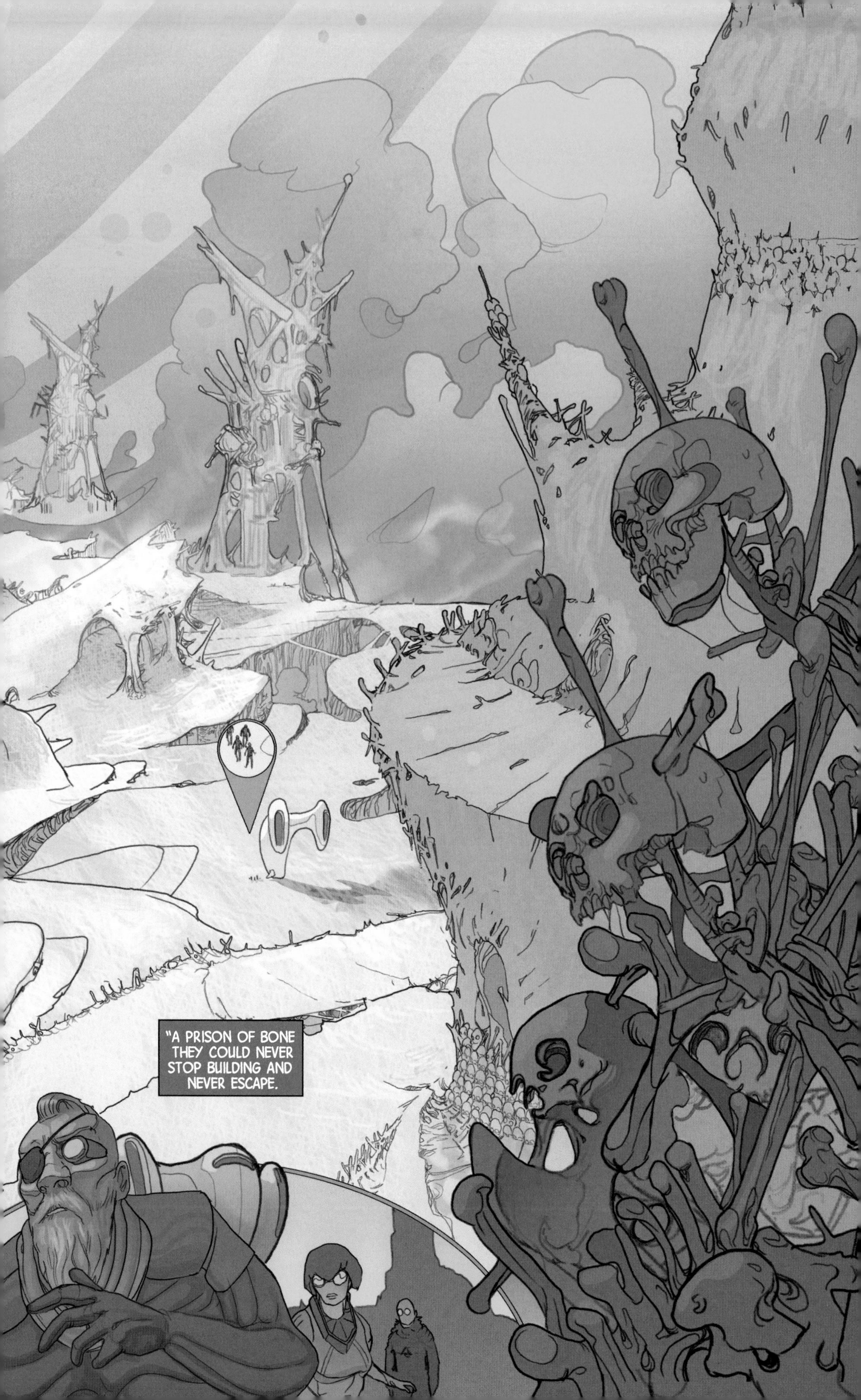
"A PRISON OF BONE THEY COULD NEVER STOP BUILDING AND NEVER ESCAPE.

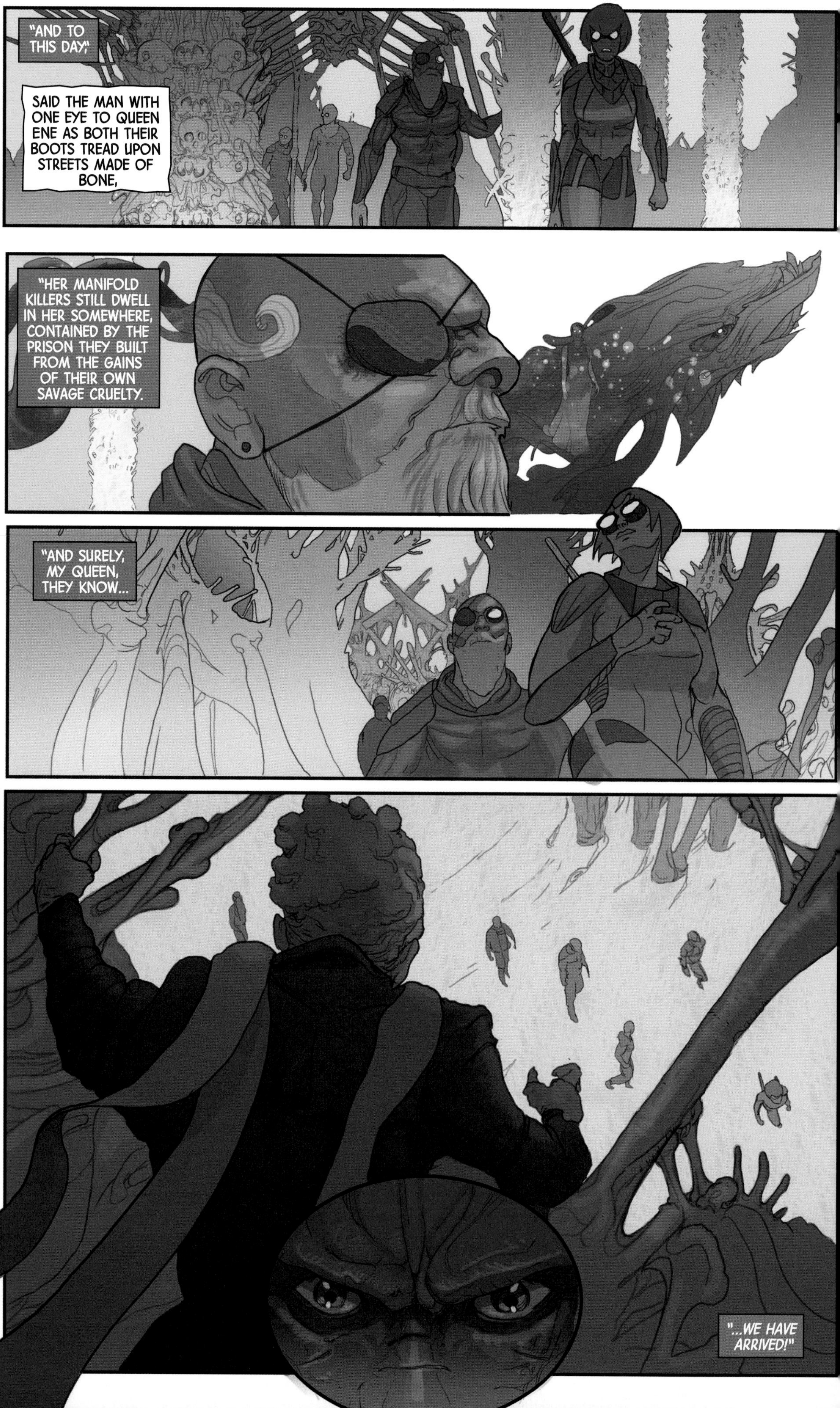
"AND TO THIS DAY,"
SAID THE MAN WITH ONE EYE TO QUEEN ENE AS BOTH THEIR BOOTS TREAD UPON STREETS MADE OF BONE,
"HER MANIFOLD KILLERS STILL DWELL IN HER SOMEWHERE, CONTAINED BY THE PRISON THEY BUILT FROM THE GAINS OF THEIR OWN SAVAGE CRUELTY.
"AND SURELY, MY QUEEN, THEY KNOW...
"...WE HAVE ARRIVED!"

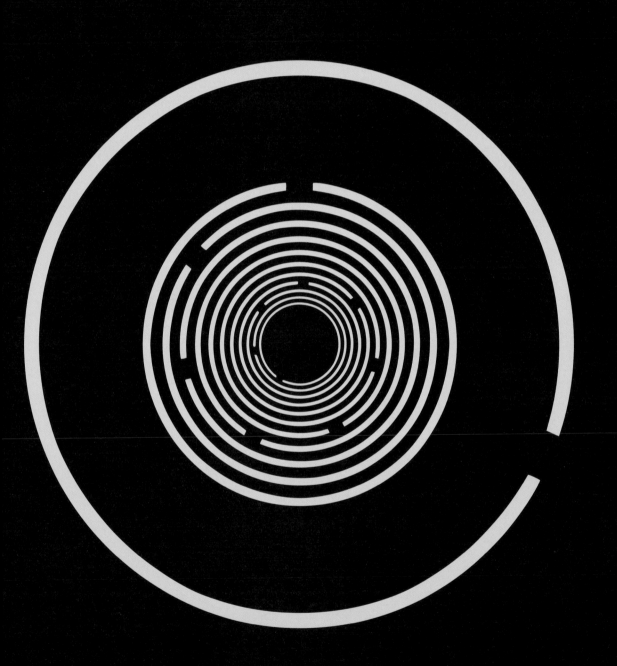

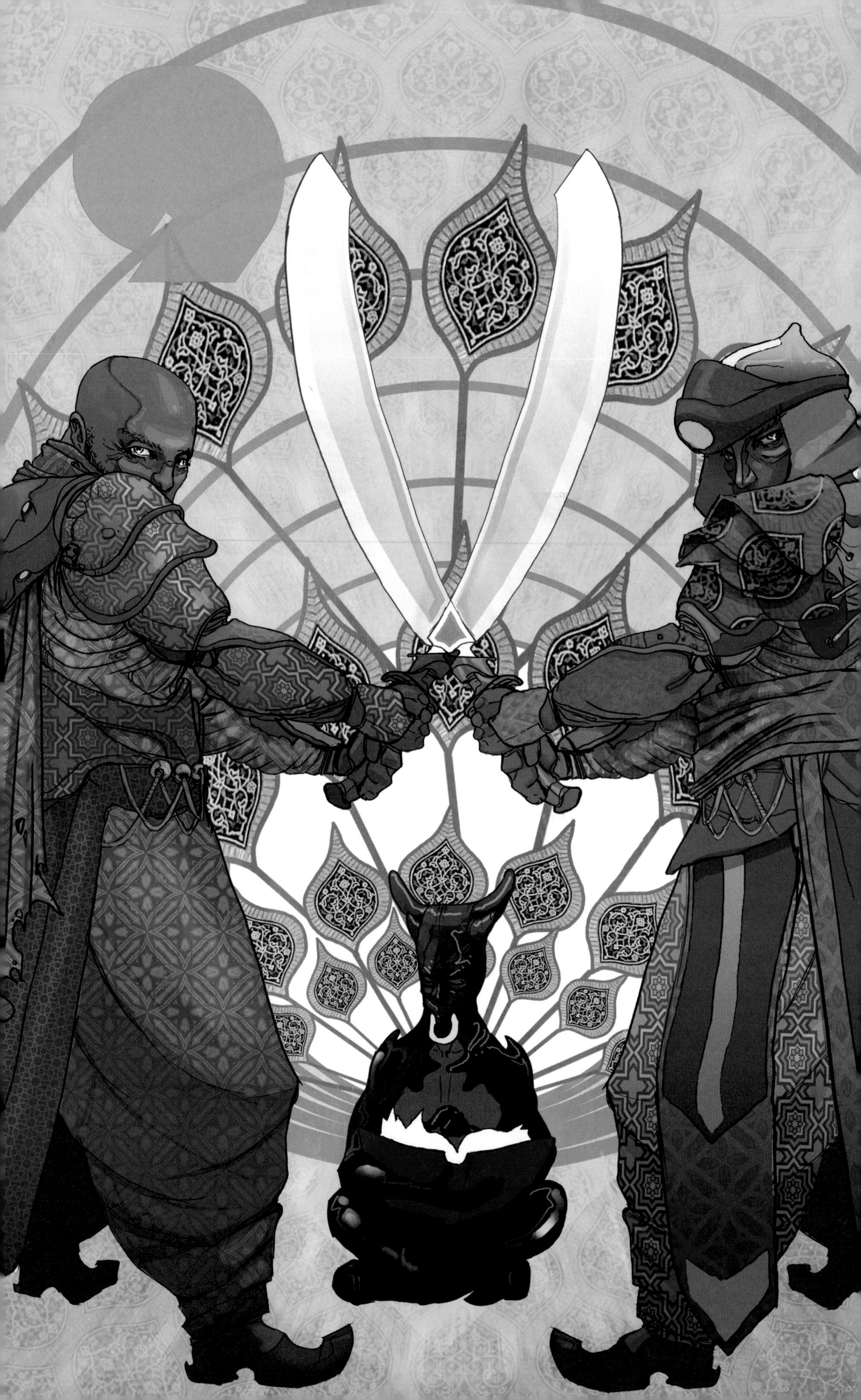

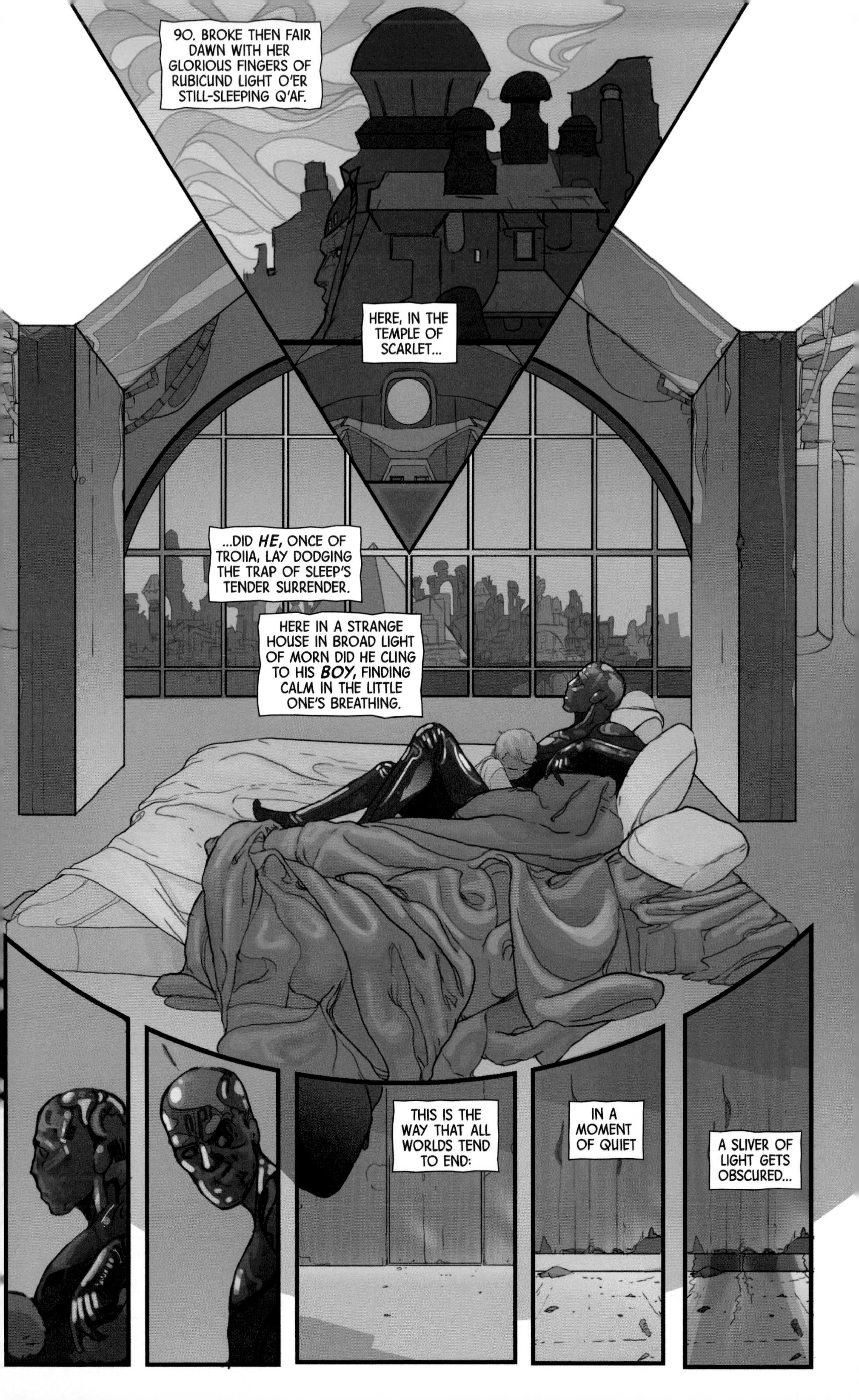
90. BROKE THEN FAIR DAWN WITH HER GLORIOUS FINGERS OF RUBICUND LIGHT O'ER STILL-SLEEPING Q'AF.
HERE, IN THE TEMPLE OF SCARLET...
...DID HE, ONCE OF TROIIA, LAY DODGING THE TRAP OF SLEEP'S TENDER SURRENDER.
HERE IN A STRANGE HOUSE IN BROAD LIGHT OF MORN DID HE CLING TO HIS BOY, FINDING CALM IN THE LITTLE ONE'S BREATHING.
THIS IS THE WAY THAT ALL WORLDS TEND TO END:
IN A MOMENT OF QUIET
A SLIVER OF LIGHT GETS OBSCURED...

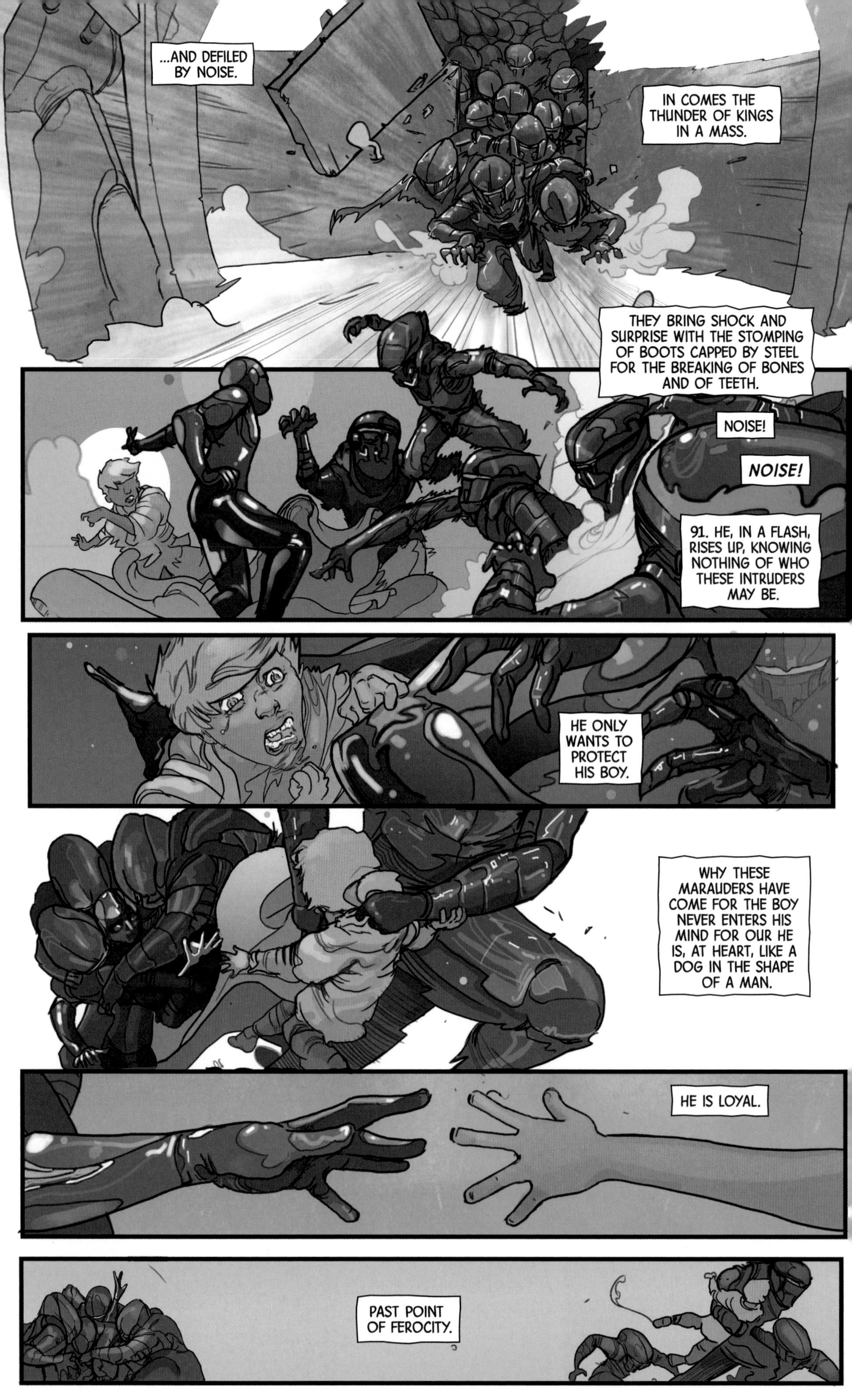
...AND DEFILED BY NOISE.
IN COMES THE THUNDER OF KINGS IN A MASS.
THEY BRING SHOCK AND SURPRISE WITH THE STOMPING OF BOOTS CAPPED BY STEEL FOR THE BREAKING OF BONES AND OF TEETH.
NOISE!
NOISE!
91. HE, IN A FLASH, RISES UP, KNOWING NOTHING OF WHO THESE INTRUDERS MAY BE.
HE ONLY WANTS TO PROTECT HIS BOY.
WHY THESE MARAUDERS HAVE COME FOR THE BOY NEVER ENTERS HIS MIND FOR OUR HE IS, AT HEART, LIKE A DOG IN THE SHAPE OF A MAN.
HE IS LOYAL.
PAST POINT OF FEROCITY.

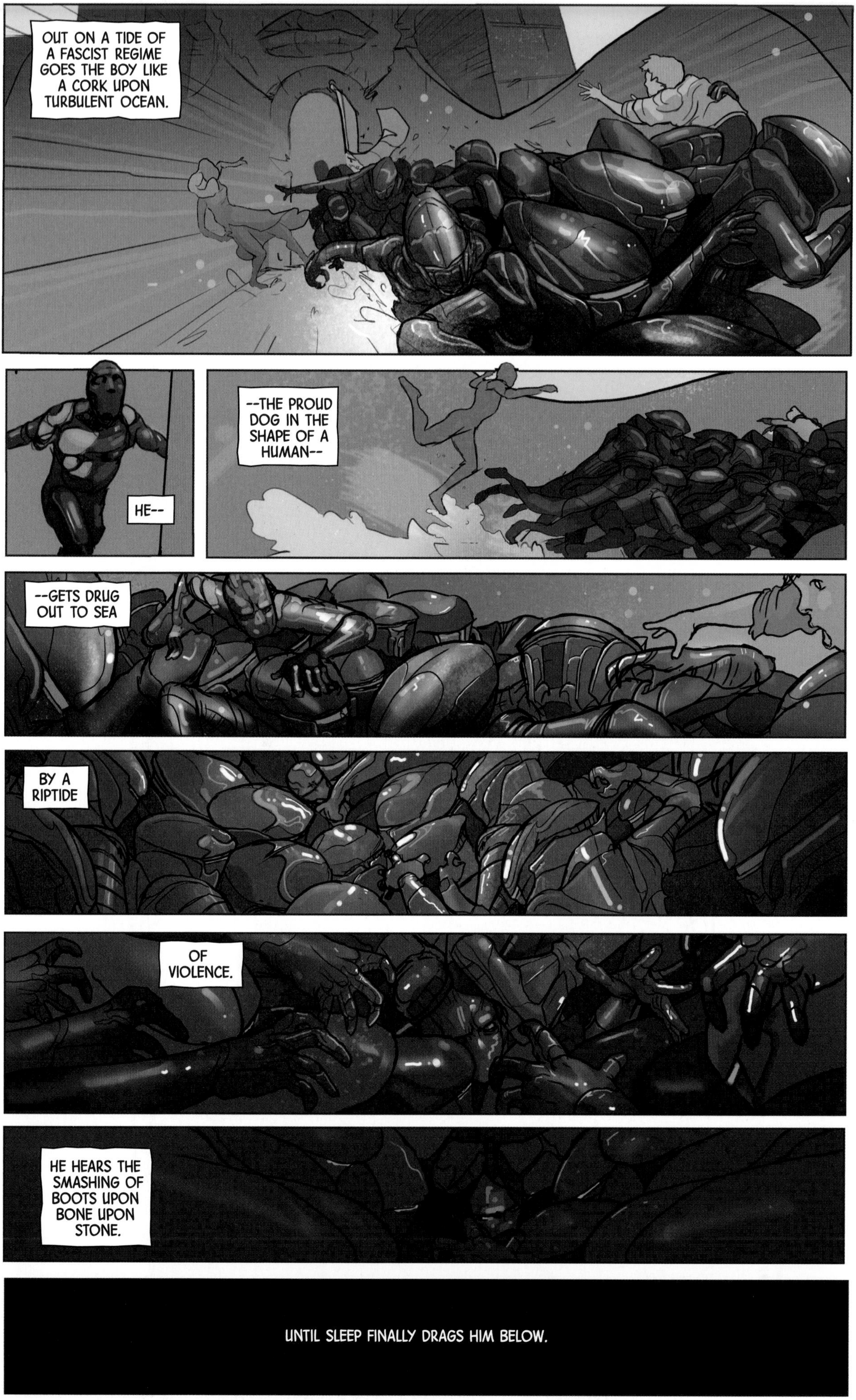
OUT ON A TIDE OF A FASCIST REGIME GOES THE BOY LIKE A CORK UPON TURBULENT OCEAN.
HE--
--THE PROUD DOG IN THE SHAPE OF A HUMAN--
--GETS DRUG OUT TO SEA
BY A RIPTIDE
OF VIOLENCE.
HE HEARS THE SMASHING OF BOOTS UPON BONE UPON STONE.
UNTIL SLEEP FINALLY DRAGS HIM BELOW.

92. CUT TO: THE *PALAIS ROYALE*

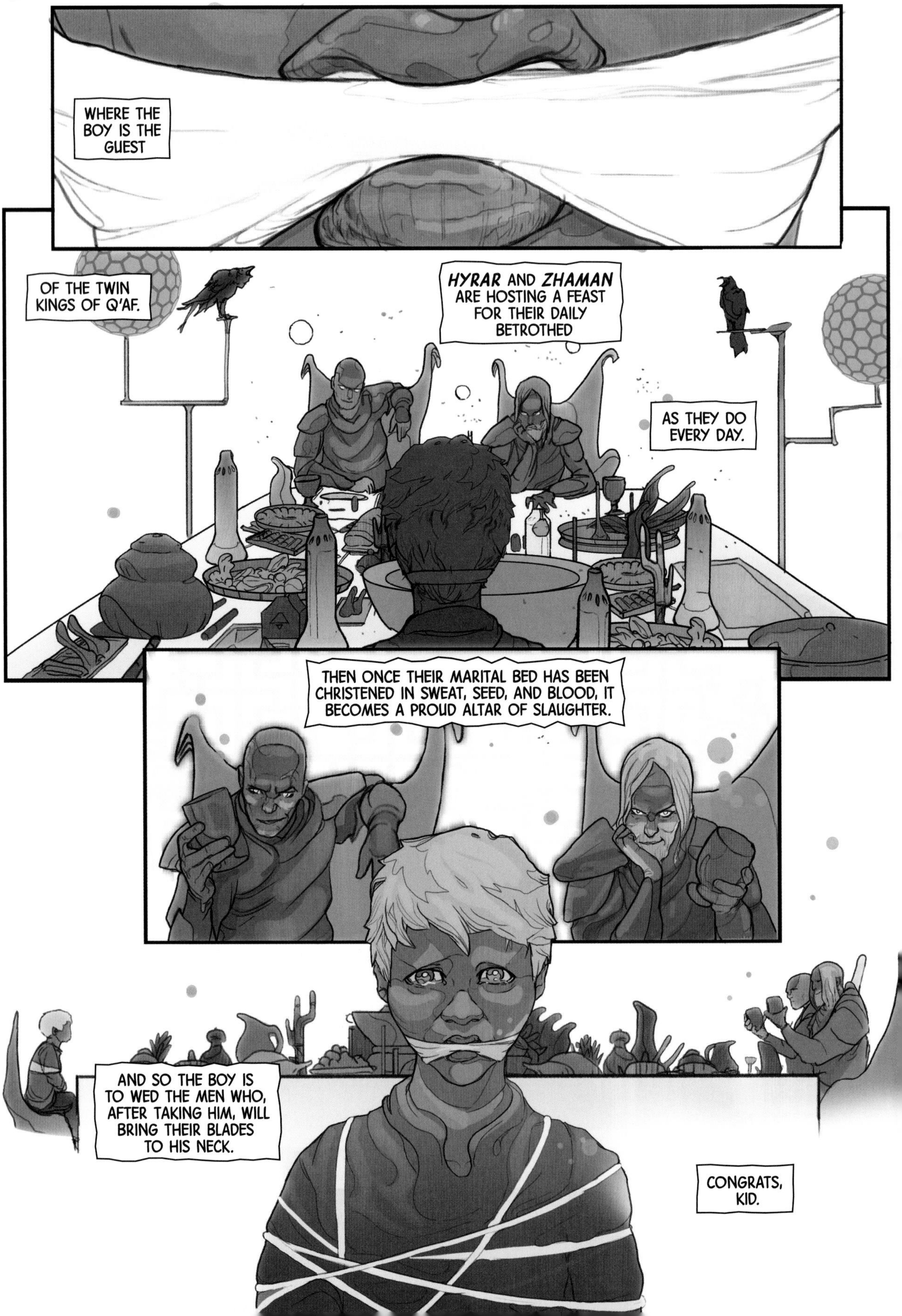

WHERE THE BOY IS THE GUEST
OF THE TWIN KINGS OF Q'AF.
HYRAR AND *ZHAMAN* ARE HOSTING A FEAST FOR THEIR DAILY BETROTHED
AS THEY DO EVERY DAY.
THEN ONCE THEIR MARITAL BED HAS BEEN CHRISTENED IN SWEAT, SEED, AND BLOOD, IT BECOMES A PROUD ALTAR OF SLAUGHTER.
AND SO THE BOY IS TO WED THE MEN WHO, AFTER TAKING HIM, WILL BRING THEIR BLADES TO HIS NECK.
CONGRATS, KID.

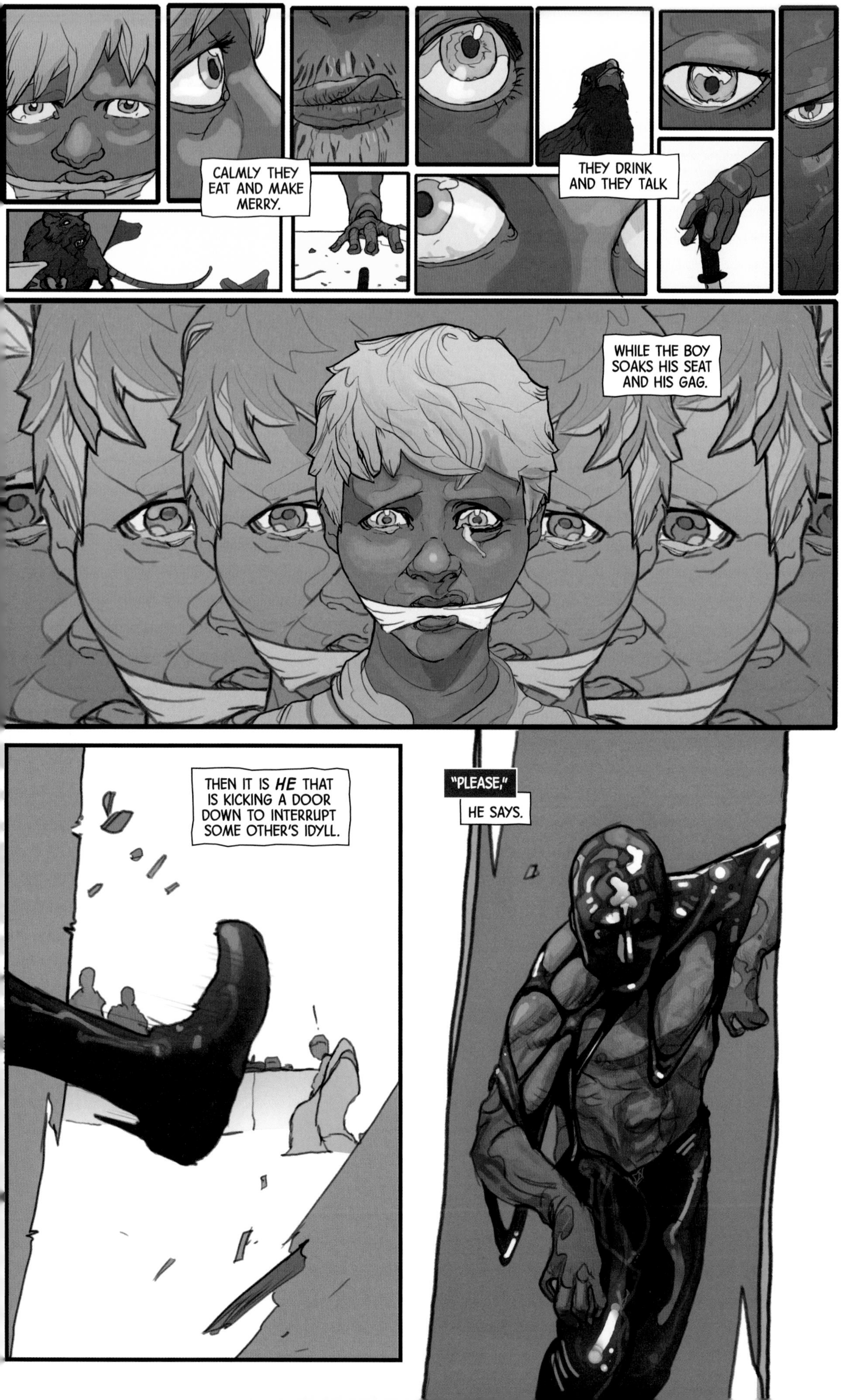
CALMLY THEY EAT AND MAKE MERRY.
THEY DRINK AND THEY TALK
WHILE THE BOY SOAKS HIS SEAT AND HIS GAG.
THEN IT IS HE THAT IS KICKING A DOOR DOWN TO INTERRUPT SOME OTHER'S IDYLL.
"PLEASE,"
HE SAYS.

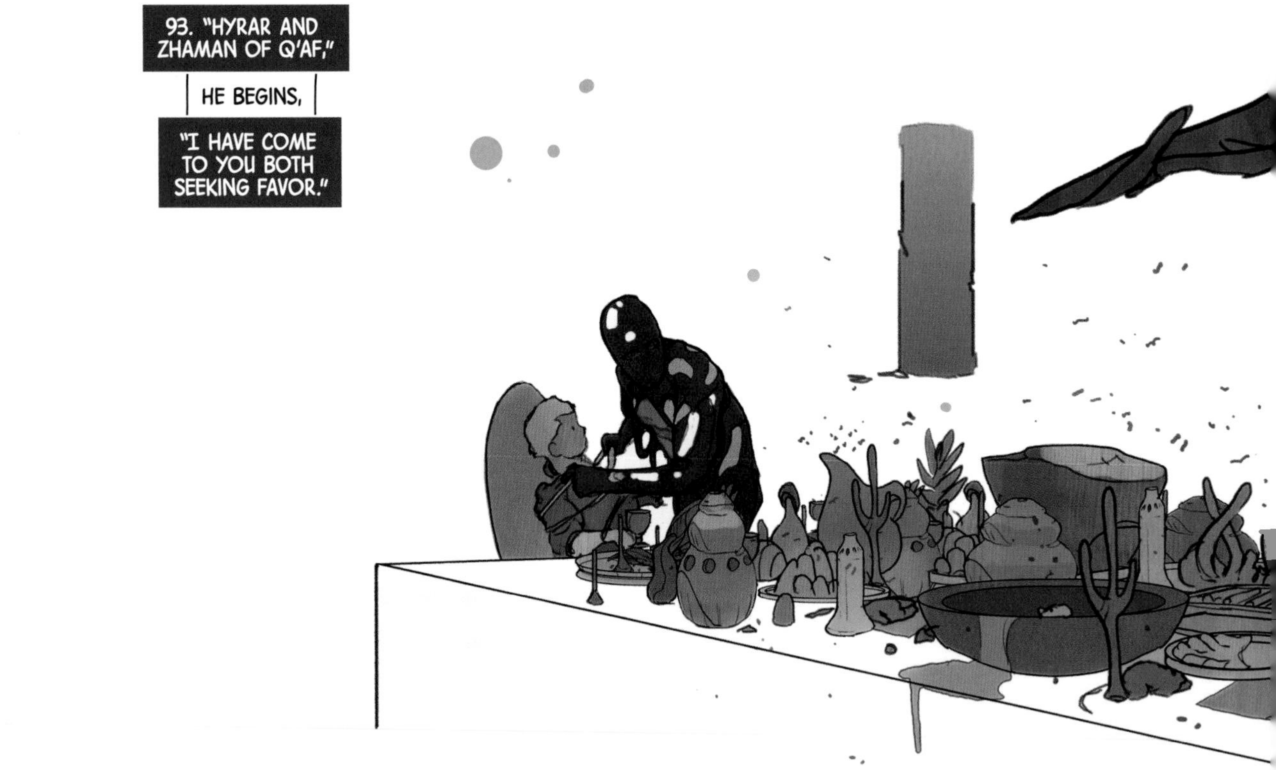
93. "HYRAR AND ZHAMAN OF Q'AF,"
HE BEGINS,
"I HAVE COME TO YOU BOTH SEEKING FAVOR."

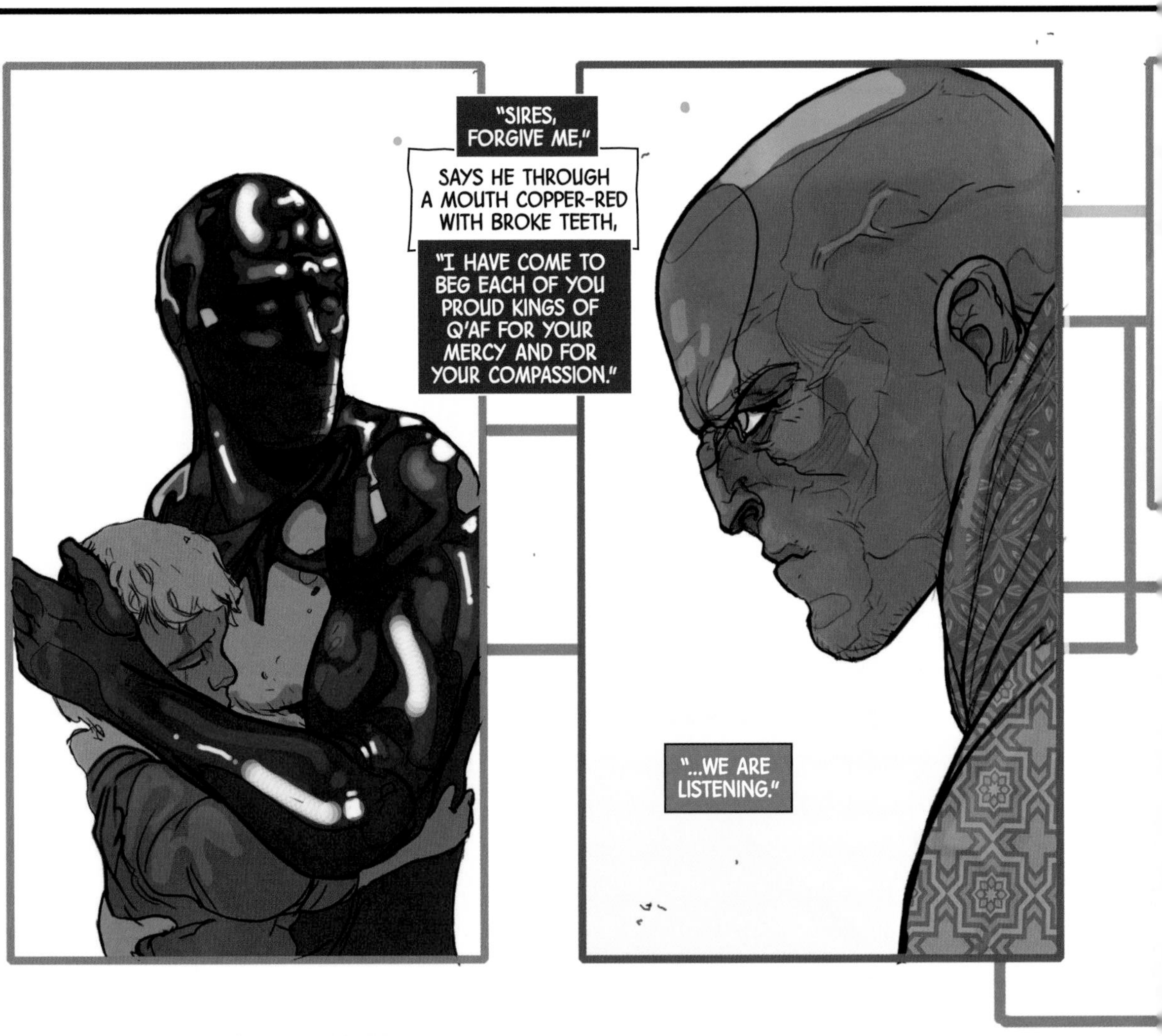
"SIRES, FORGIVE ME,"
SAYS HE THROUGH A MOUTH COPPER-RED WITH BROKE TEETH,
"I HAVE COME TO BEG EACH OF YOU PROUD KINGS OF Q'AF FOR YOUR MERCY AND FOR YOUR COMPASSION."
"...WE ARE LISTENING."

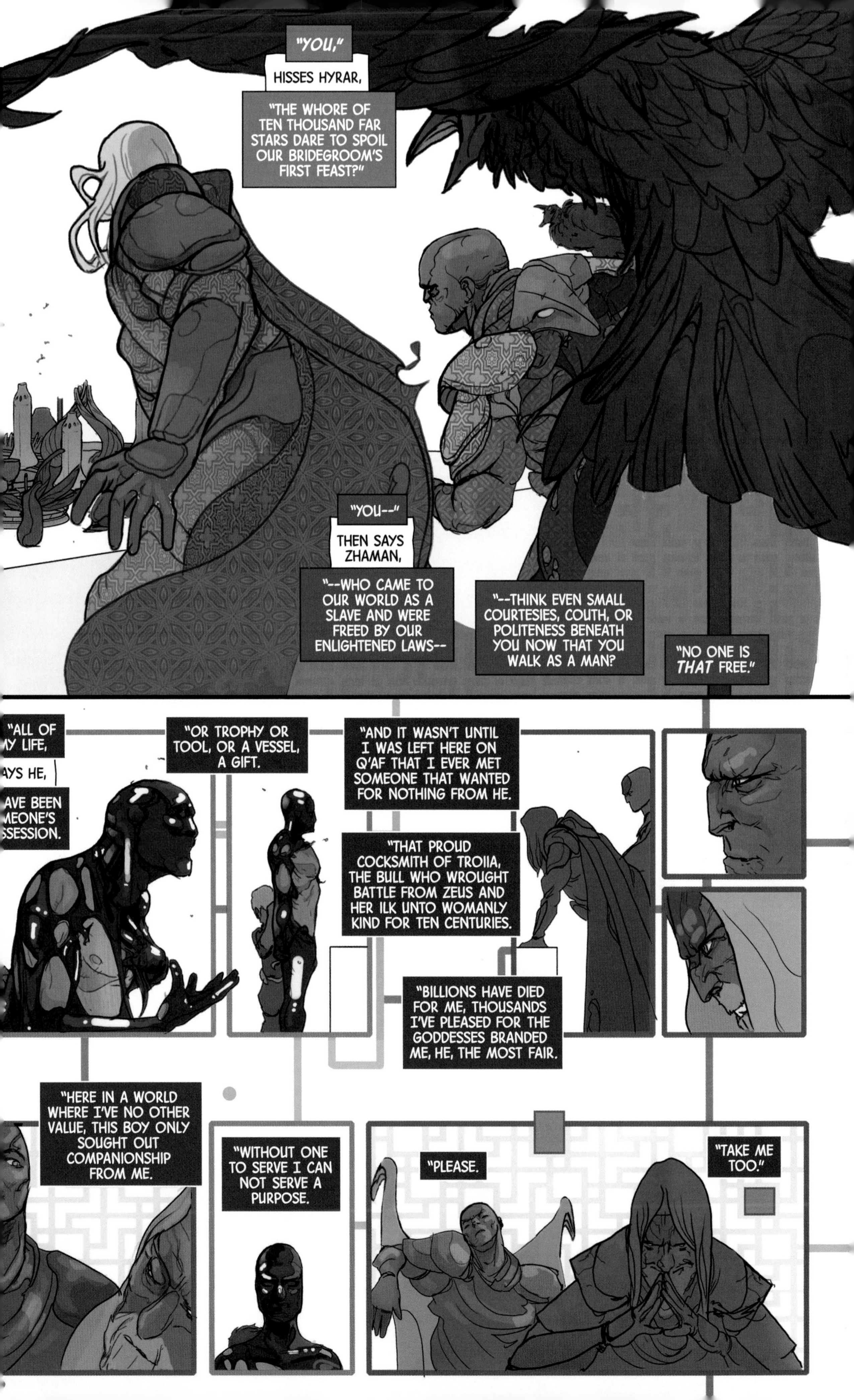
"YOU,"
HISSES HYRAR,
"THE WHORE OF TEN THOUSAND FAR STARS DARE TO SPOIL OUR BRIDEGROOM'S FIRST FEAST?"
"YOU--"
THEN SAYS ZHAMAN,
"--WHO CAME TO OUR WORLD AS A SLAVE AND WERE FREED BY OUR ENLIGHTENED LAWS--
"--THINK EVEN SMALL COURTESIES, COUTH, OR POLITENESS BENEATH YOU NOW THAT YOU WALK AS A MAN?
"NO ONE IS THAT FREE."
"ALL OF
Y LIFE,
AYS HE,
AVE BEEN
MEONE'S
SSESSION.
"OR TROPHY OR TOOL, OR A VESSEL, A GIFT.
"AND IT WASN'T UNTIL I WAS LEFT HERE ON Q'AF THAT I EVER MET SOMEONE THAT WANTED FOR NOTHING FROM HE.
"THAT PROUD COCKSMITH OF TROIIA, THE BULL WHO WROUGHT BATTLE FROM ZEUS AND HER ILK UNTO WOMANLY KIND FOR TEN CENTURIES.
"BILLIONS HAVE DIED FOR ME, THOUSANDS I'VE PLEASED FOR THE GODDESSES BRANDED ME, HE, THE MOST FAIR.
"HERE IN A WORLD WHERE I'VE NO OTHER VALUE, THIS BOY ONLY SOUGHT OUT COMPANIONSHIP FROM ME.
"WITHOUT ONE TO SERVE I CAN NOT SERVE A PURPOSE.
"PLEASE.
"TAKE ME TOO."

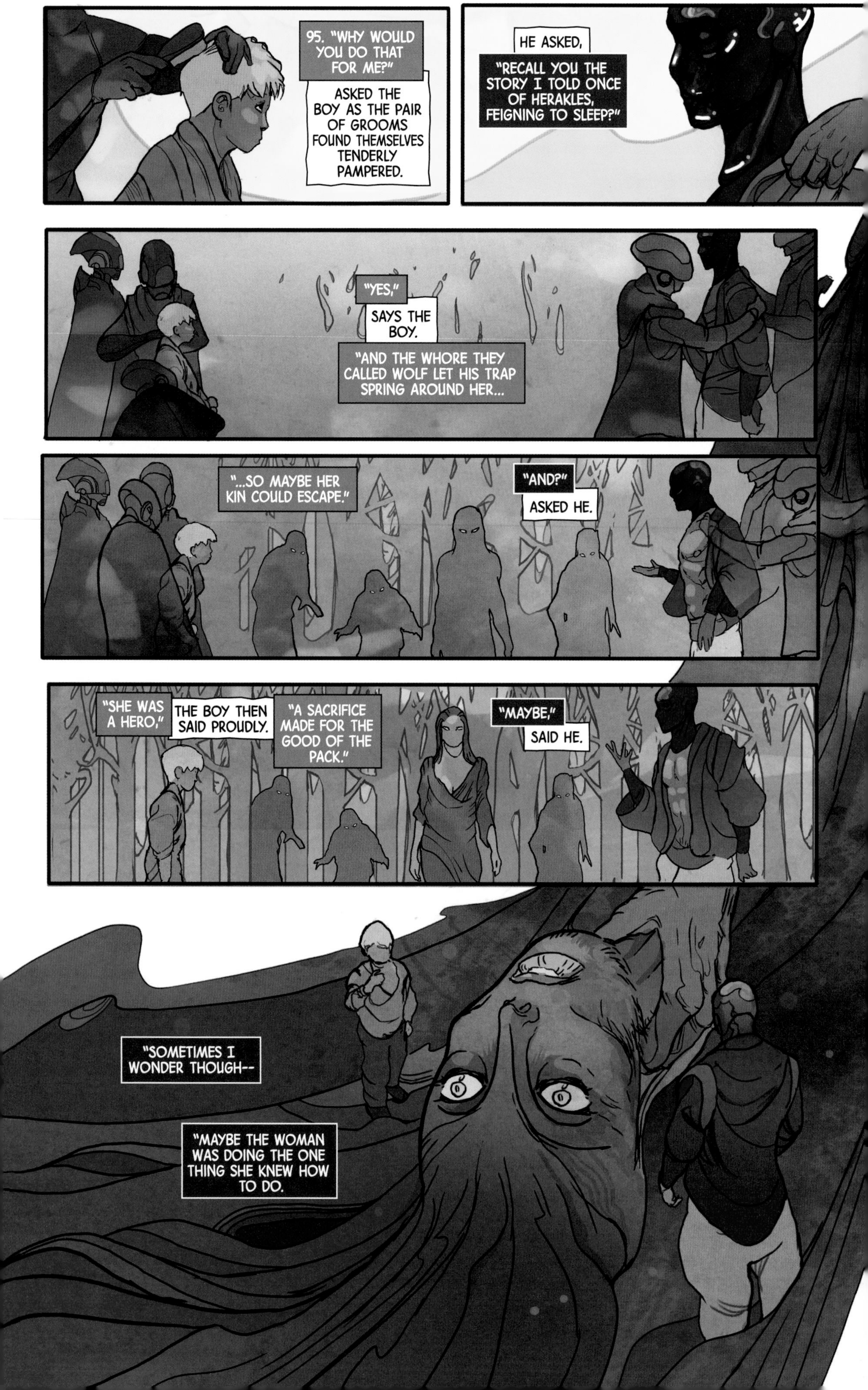

95. "WHY WOULD YOU DO THAT FOR ME?"
ASKED THE BOY AS THE PAIR OF GROOMS FOUND THEMSELVES TENDERLY PAMPERED.
HE ASKED,
"RECALL YOU THE STORY I TOLD ONCE OF HERAKLES, FEIGNING TO SLEEP?"
"YES,"
SAYS THE BOY.
"AND THE WHORE THEY CALLED WOLF LET HIS TRAP SPRING AROUND HER...
"...SO MAYBE HER KIN COULD ESCAPE."
"AND?"
ASKED HE.
"SHE WAS A HERO,"
THE BOY THEN SAID PROUDLY.
"A SACRIFICE MADE FOR THE GOOD OF THE PACK."
"MAYBE,"
SAID HE.
"SOMETIMES I WONDER THOUGH--
"MAYBE THE WOMAN WAS DOING THE ONE THING SHE KNEW HOW TO DO.

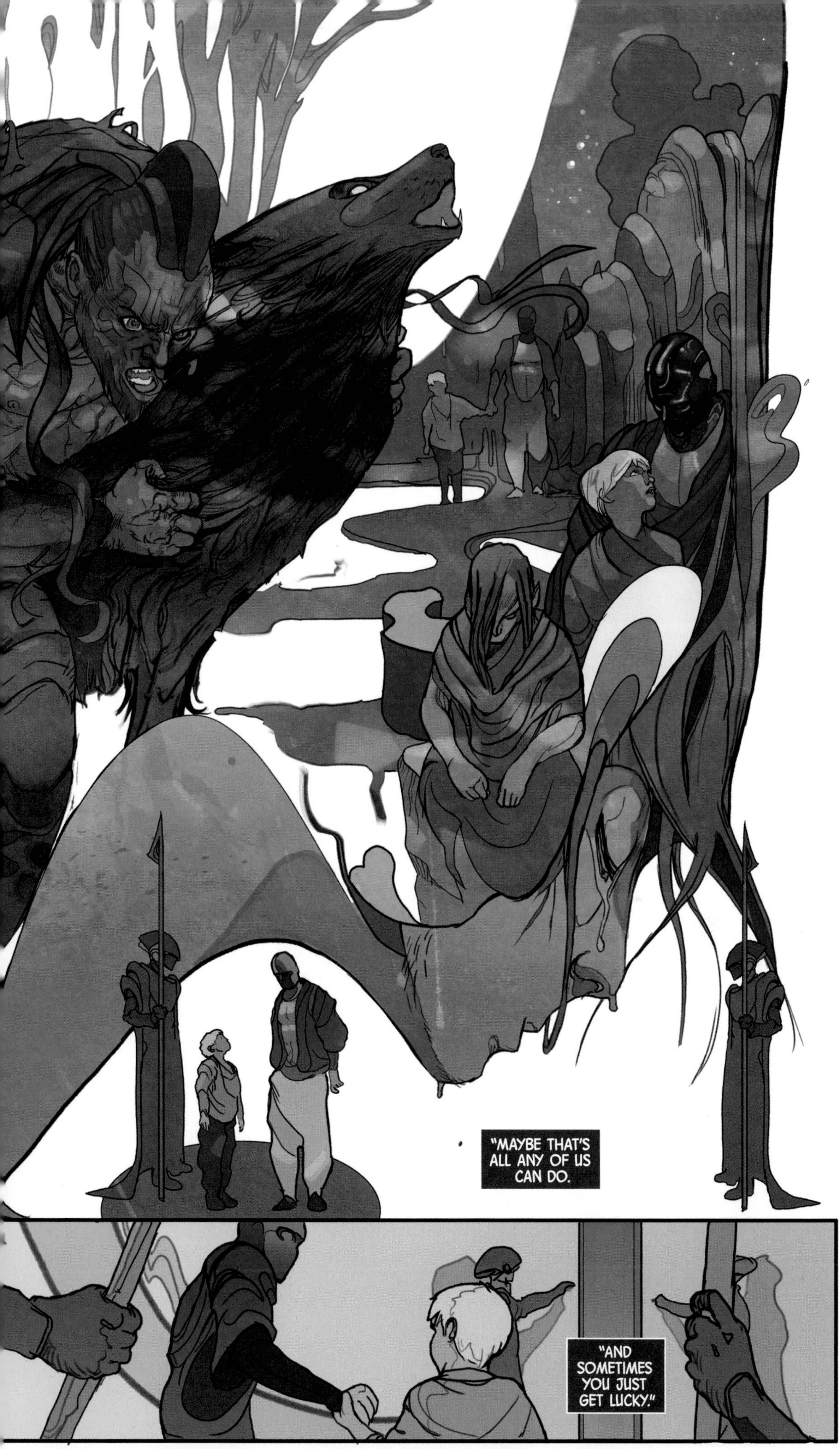
"MAYBE THAT'S ALL ANY OF US CAN DO.
"AND SOMETIMES YOU JUST GET LUCKY."

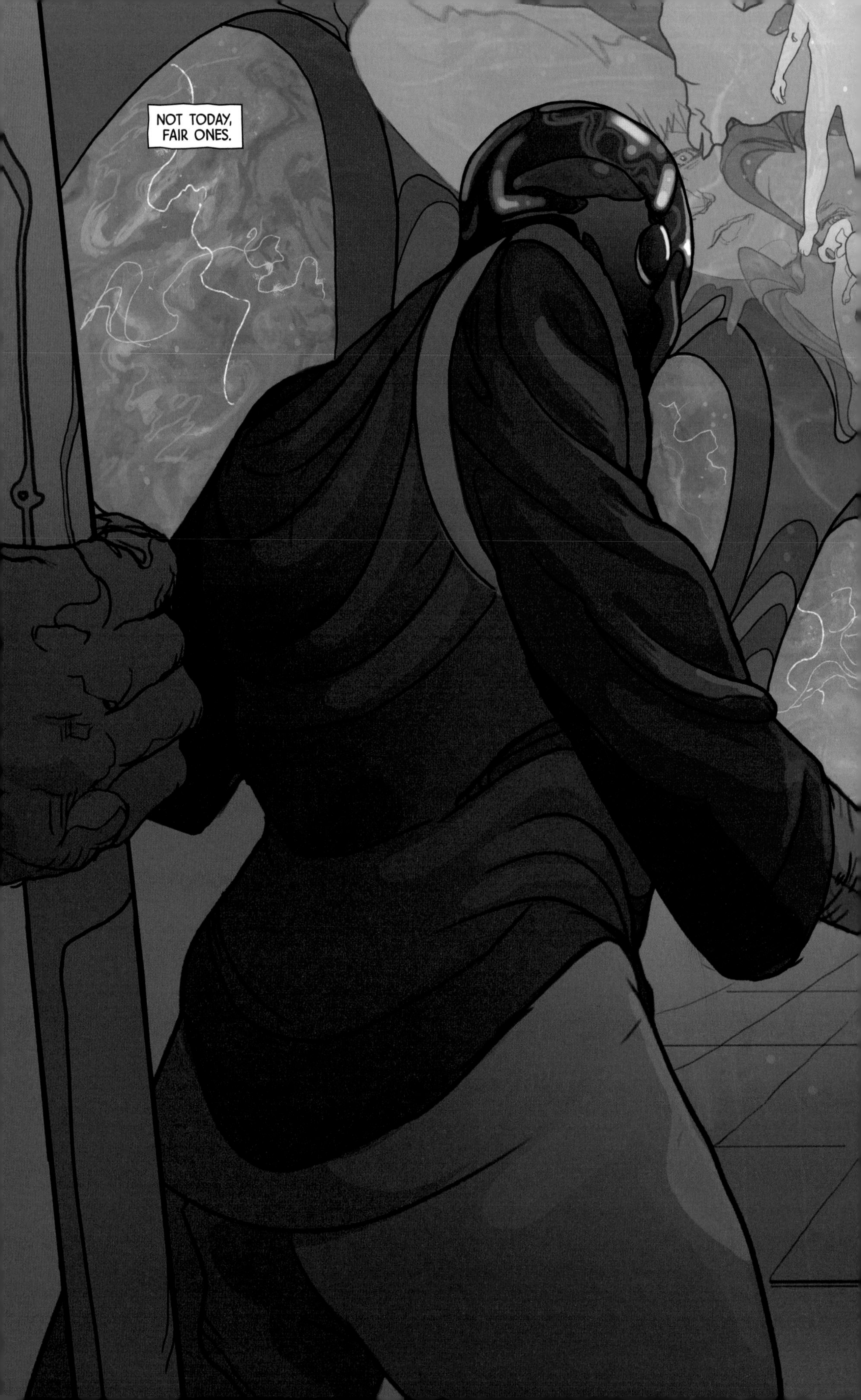
NOT TODAY,
FAIR ONES.

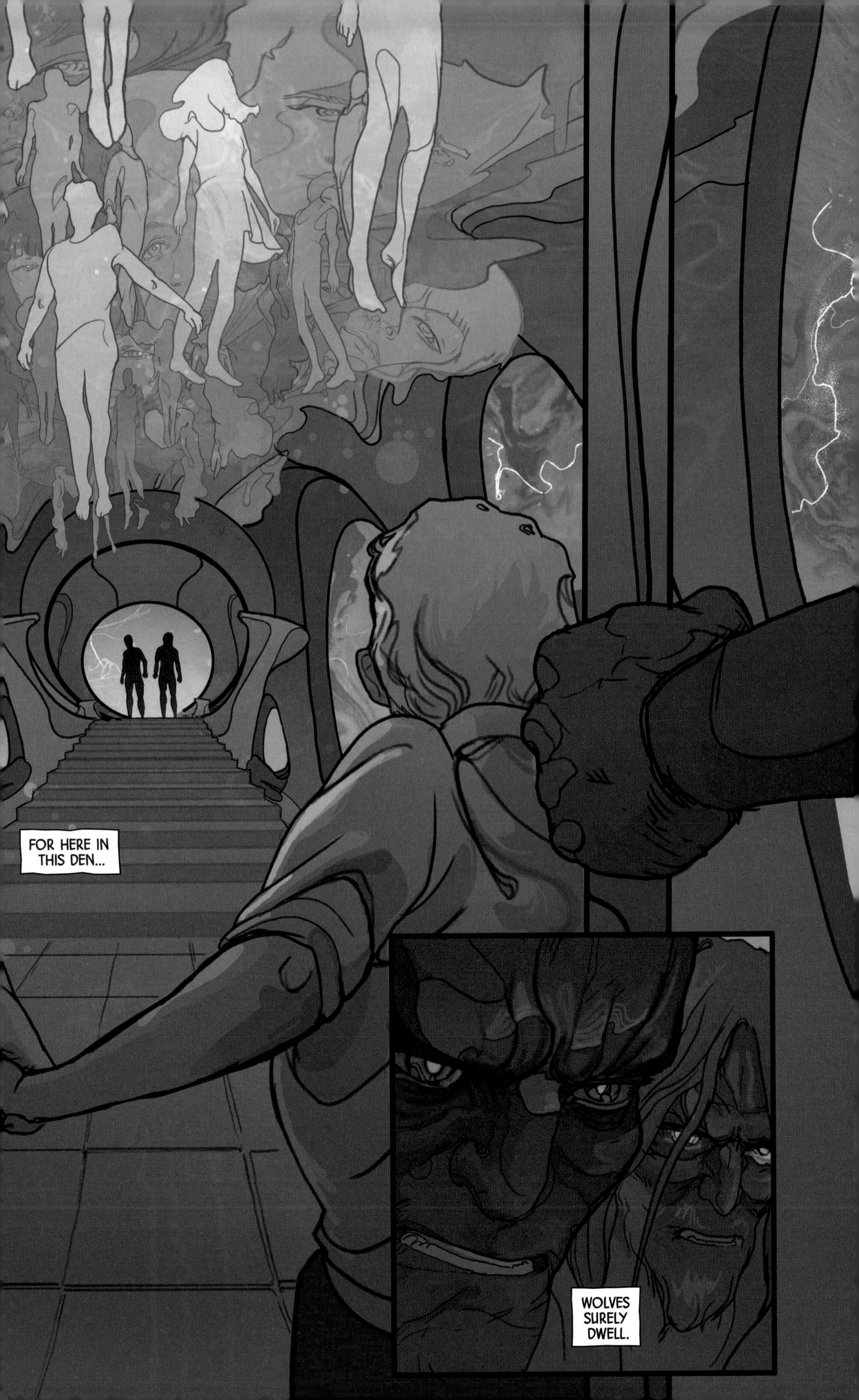
FOR HERE IN THIS DEN...
WOLVES SURELY DWELL.

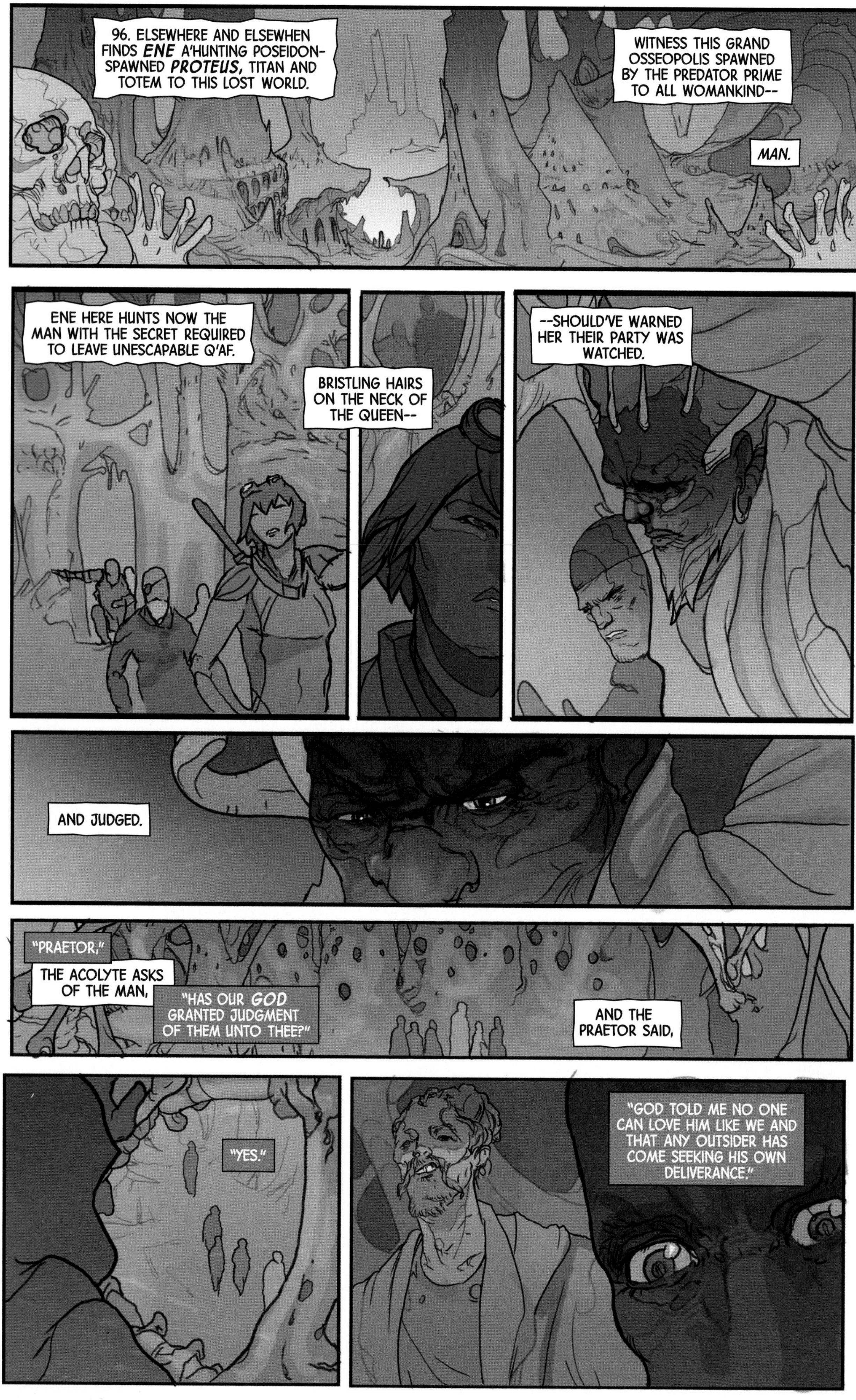
96. ELSEWHERE AND ELSEWHEN FINDS ENE A'HUNTING POSEIDON-SPAWNED PROTEUS, TITAN AND TOTEM TO THIS LOST WORLD.
WITNESS THIS GRAND OSSEOPOLIS SPAWNED BY THE PREDATOR PRIME TO ALL WOMANKIND--
MAN.
ENE HERE HUNTS NOW THE MAN WITH THE SECRET REQUIRED TO LEAVE UNESCAPABLE Q'AF.
BRISTLING HAIRS ON THE NECK OF THE QUEEN--
--SHOULD'VE WARNED HER THEIR PARTY WAS WATCHED.
AND JUDGED.
"PRAETOR,"
THE ACOLYTE ASKS OF THE MAN,
"HAS OUR GOD GRANTED JUDGMENT OF THEM UNTO THEE?"
AND THE PRAETOR SAID,
"YES."
"GOD TOLD ME NO ONE CAN LOVE HIM LIKE WE AND THAT ANY OUTSIDER HAS COME SEEKING HIS OWN DELIVERANCE."

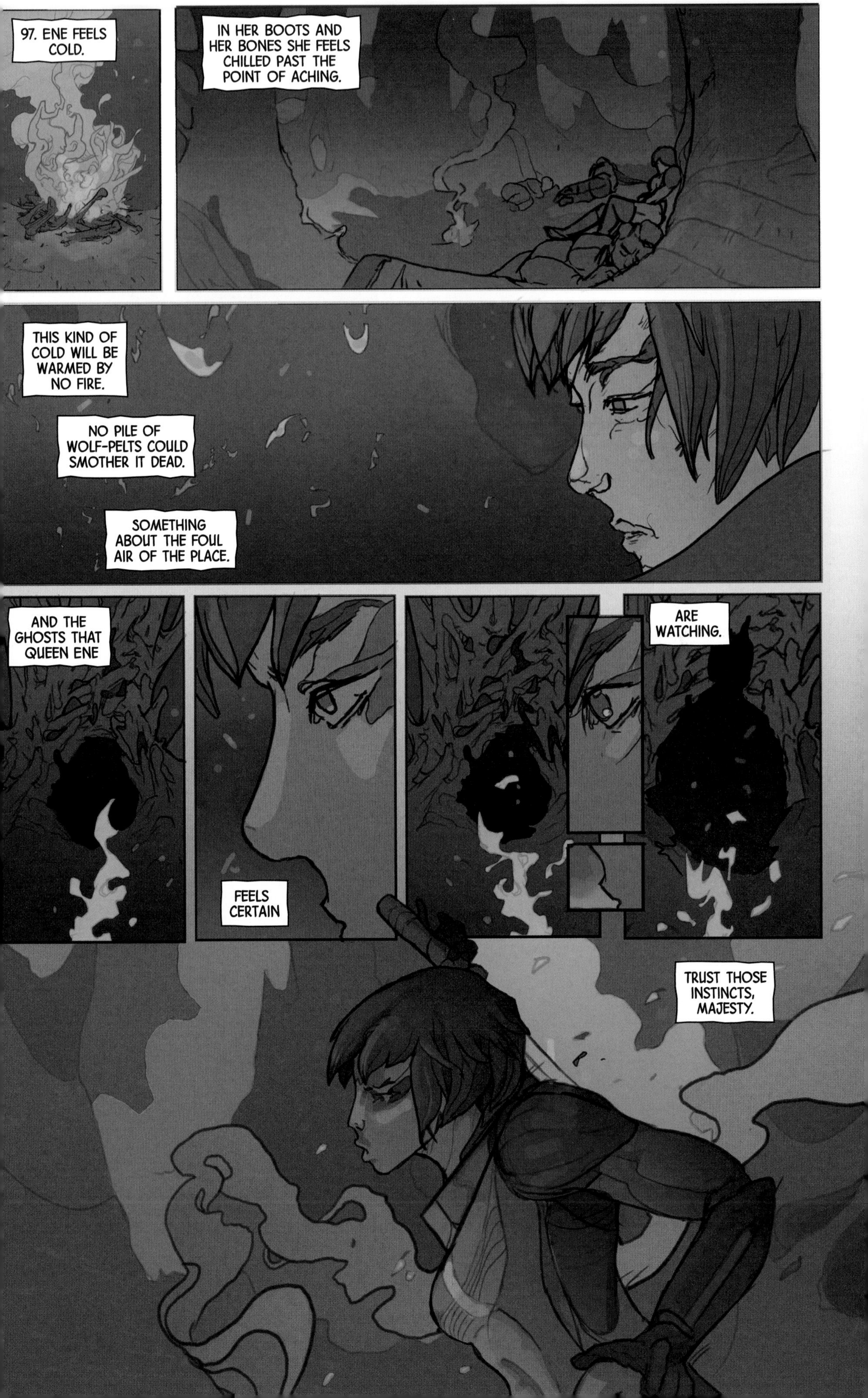
97. ENE FEELS COLD.
IN HER BOOTS AND HER BONES SHE FEELS CHILLED PAST THE POINT OF ACHING.
THIS KIND OF COLD WILL BE WARMED BY NO FIRE.
NO PILE OF WOLF-PELTS COULD SMOTHER IT DEAD.
SOMETHING ABOUT THE FOUL AIR OF THE PLACE.
AND THE GHOSTS THAT QUEEN ENE
FEELS CERTAIN
ARE WATCHING.
TRUST THOSE INSTINCTS, MAJESTY.

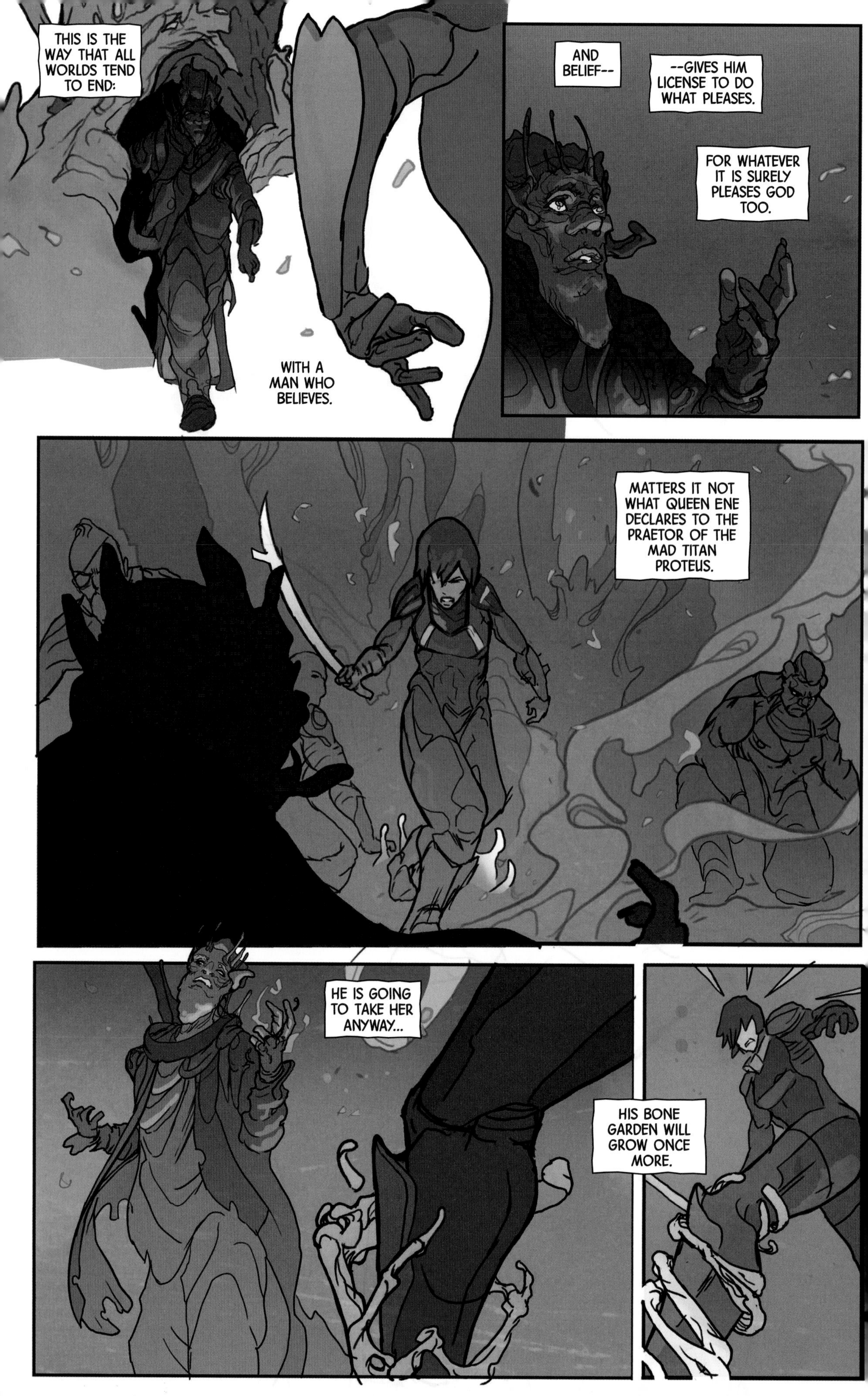
THIS IS THE WAY THAT ALL WORLDS TEND TO END:
WITH A MAN WHO BELIEVES.
AND BELIEF--
--GIVES HIM LICENSE TO DO WHAT PLEASES.
FOR WHATEVER IT IS SURELY PLEASES GOD TOO.
MATTERS IT NOT WHAT QUEEN ENE DECLARES TO THE PRAETOR OF THE MAD TITAN PROTEUS.
HE IS GOING TO TAKE HER ANYWAY...
HIS BONE GARDEN WILL GROW ONCE MORE.

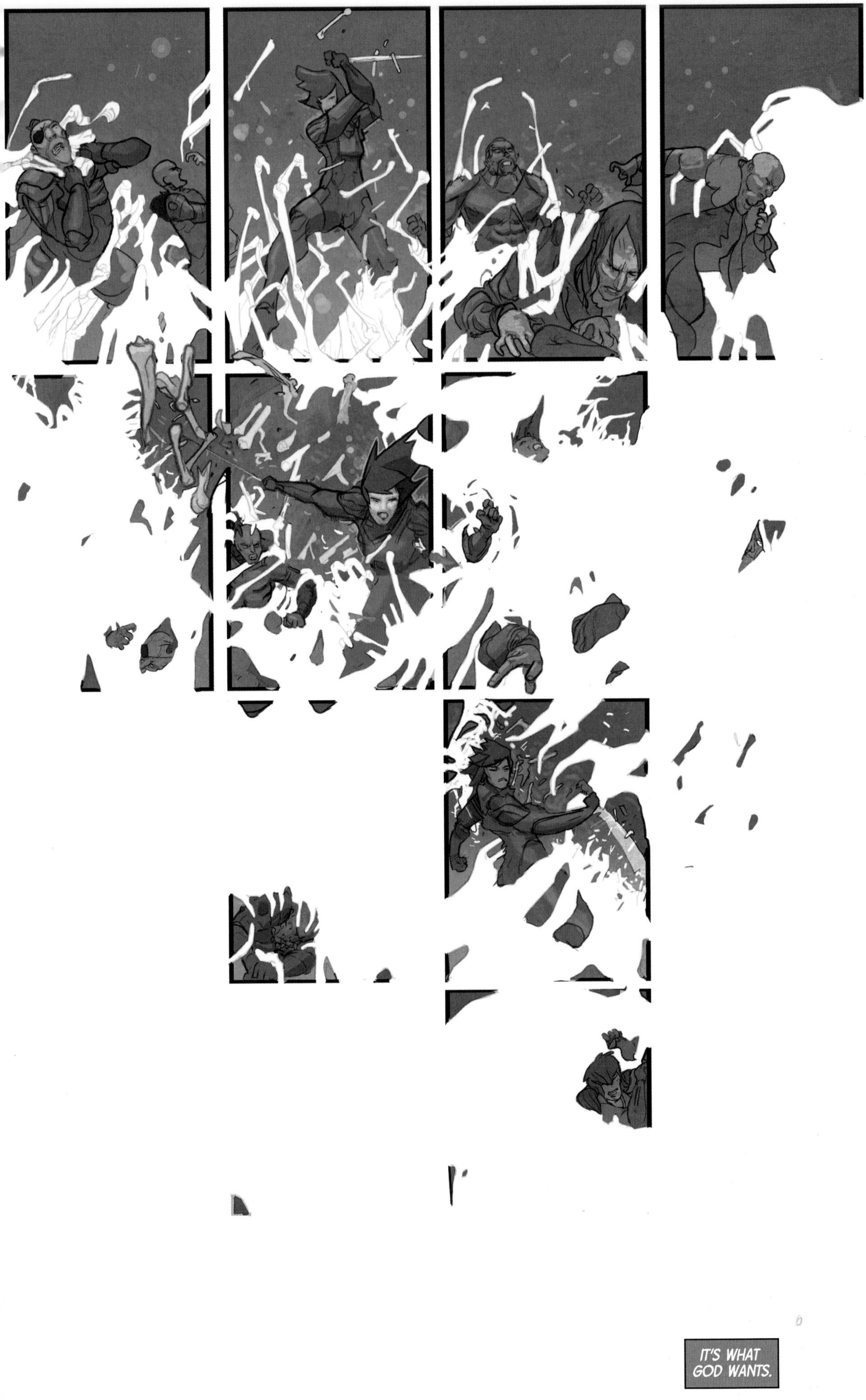
IT'S WHAT
GOD WANTS.

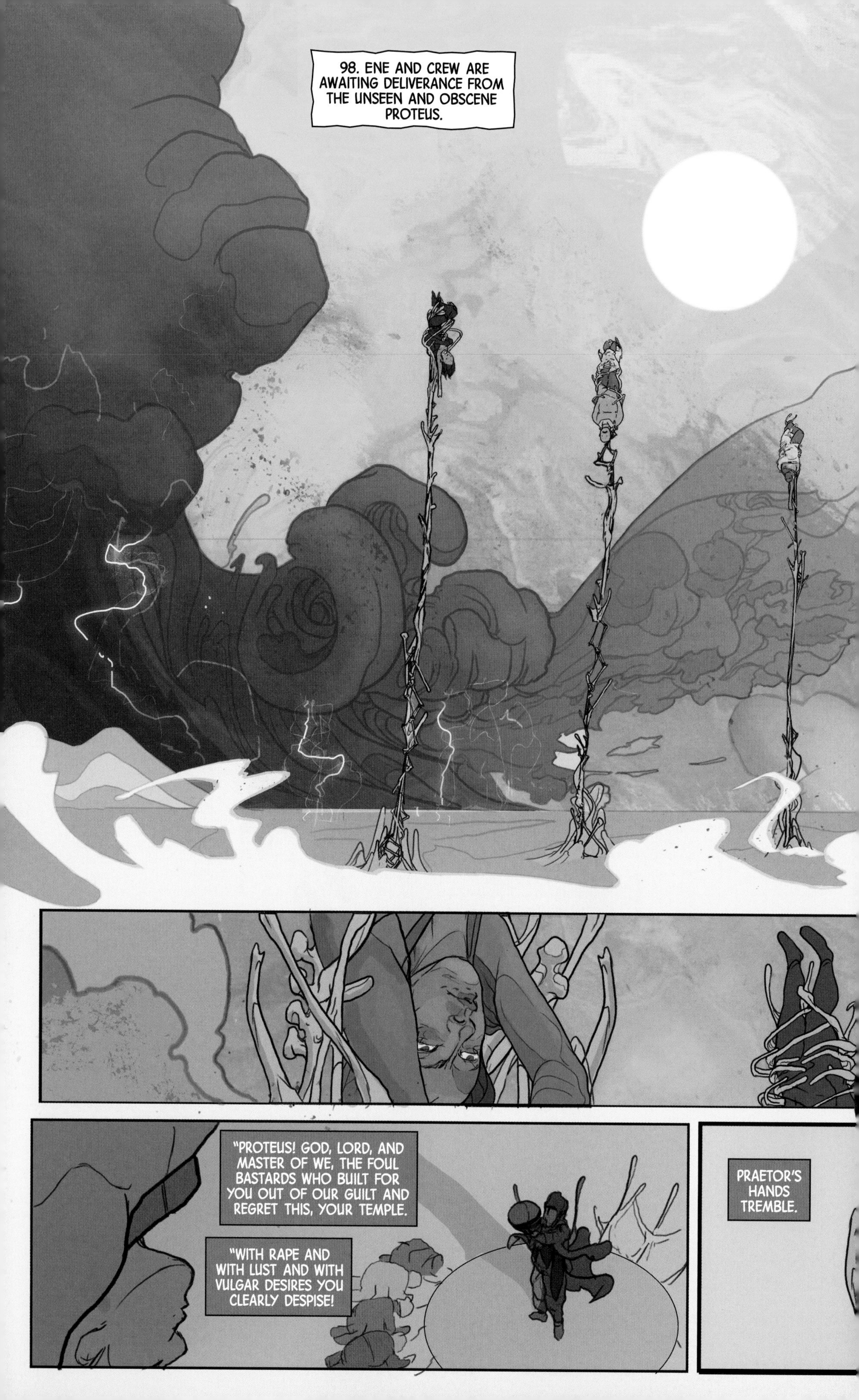
98. ENE AND CREW ARE AWAITING DELIVERANCE FROM THE UNSEEN AND OBSCENE PROTEUS.
"PROTEUS! GOD, LORD, AND MASTER OF WE, THE FOUL BASTARDS WHO BUILT FOR YOU OUT OF OUR GUILT AND REGRET THIS, YOUR TEMPLE.
"WITH RAPE AND WITH LUST AND WITH VULGAR DESIRES YOU CLEARLY DESPISE!
PRAETOR'S HANDS TREMBLE.

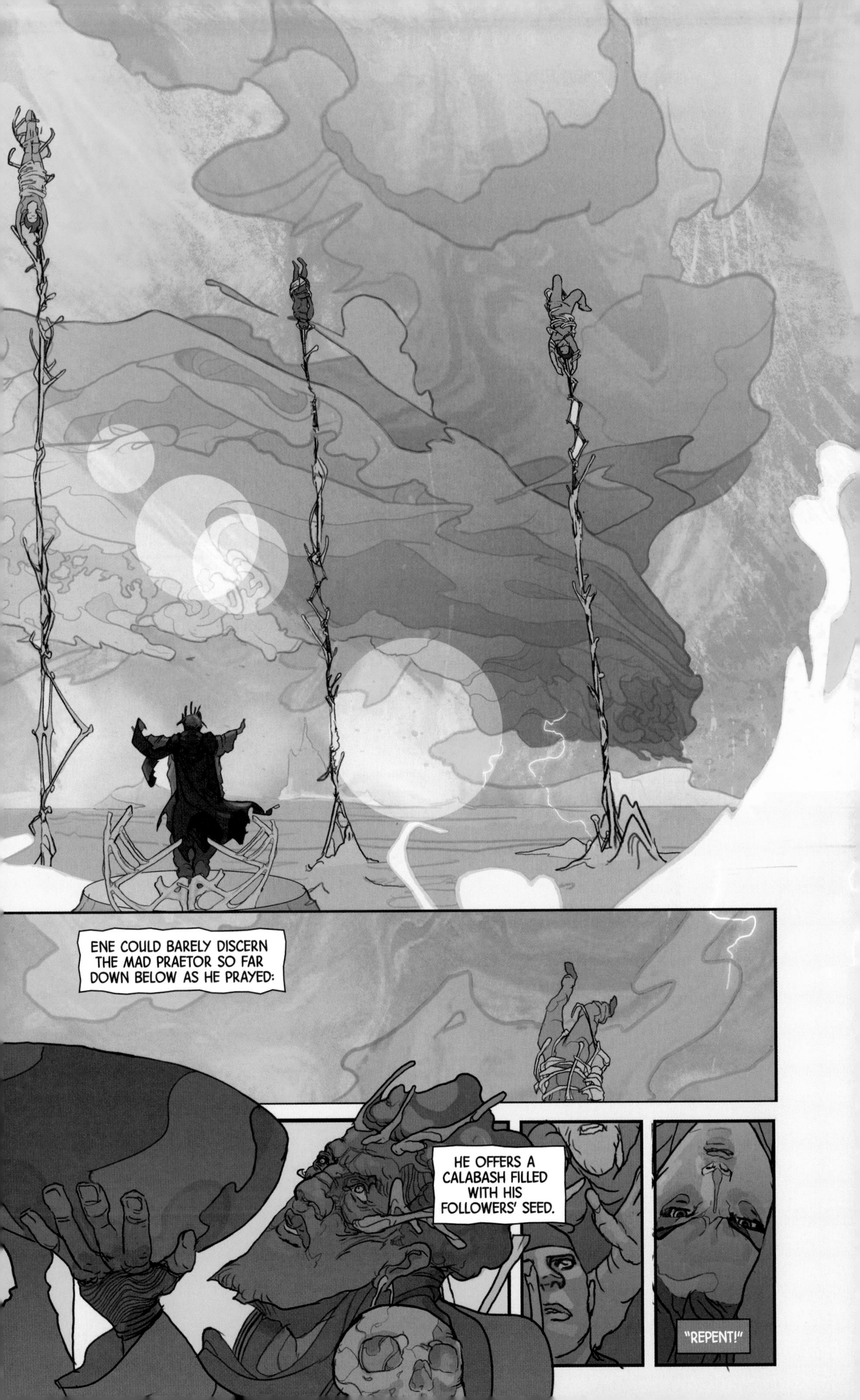
ENE COULD BARELY DISCERN THE MAD PRAETOR SO FAR DOWN BELOW AS HE PRAYED:
HE OFFERS A CALABASH FILLED WITH HIS FOLLOWERS' SEED.
"REPENT!"

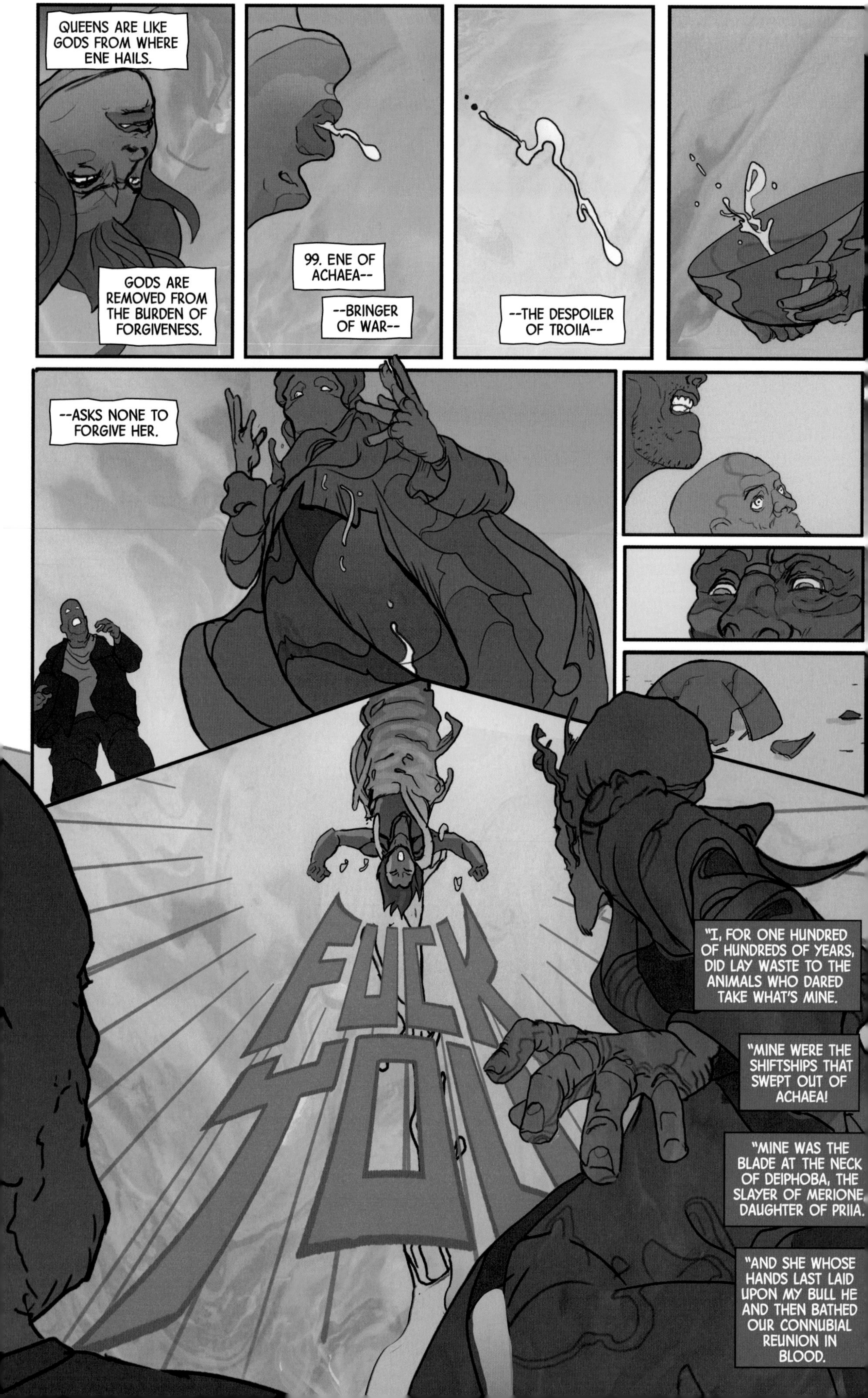
QUEENS ARE LIKE GODS FROM WHERE ENE HAILS.
GODS ARE REMOVED FROM THE BURDEN OF FORGIVENESS.
99. ENE OF ACHAEA--
--BRINGER OF WAR--
--THE DESPOILER OF TROIIA--
--ASKS NONE TO FORGIVE HER.
FUCK YOU
"I, FOR ONE HUNDRED OF HUNDREDS OF YEARS, DID LAY WASTE TO THE ANIMALS WHO DARED TAKE WHAT'S MINE.
"MINE WERE THE SHIFTSHIPS THAT SWEPT OUT OF ACHAEA!
"MINE WAS THE BLADE AT THE NECK OF DEIPHOBA, THE SLAYER OF MERIONE DAUGHTER OF PRIIA.
"AND SHE WHOSE HANDS LAST LAID UPON MY BULL HE AND THEN BATHED OUR CONNUBIAL REUNION IN BLOOD.

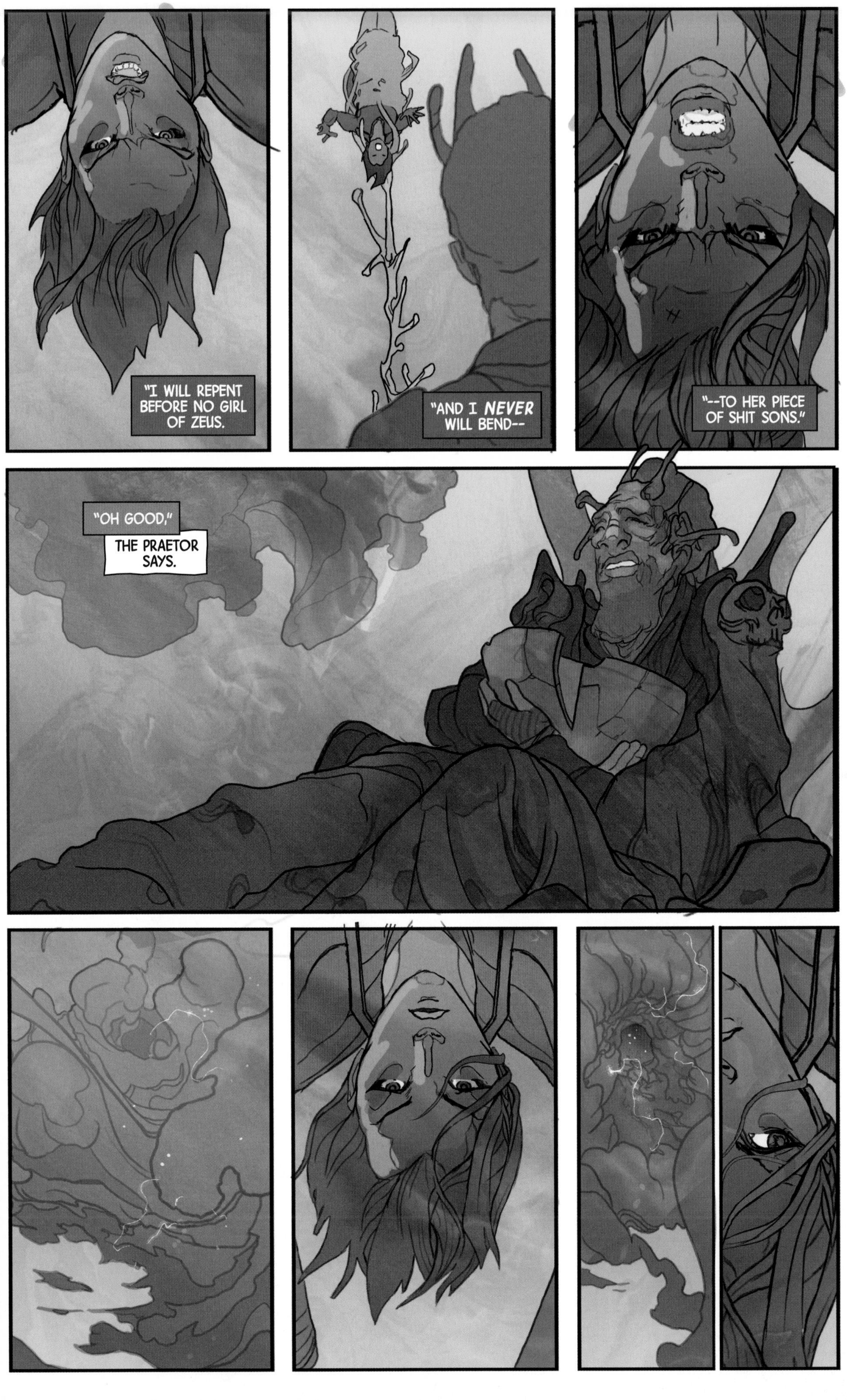
"I WILL REPENT BEFORE NO GIRL OF ZEUS.
"AND I ***NEVER*** WILL BEND--
"--TO HER PIECE OF SHIT SONS."
"OH GOOD,"
THE PRAETOR SAYS.

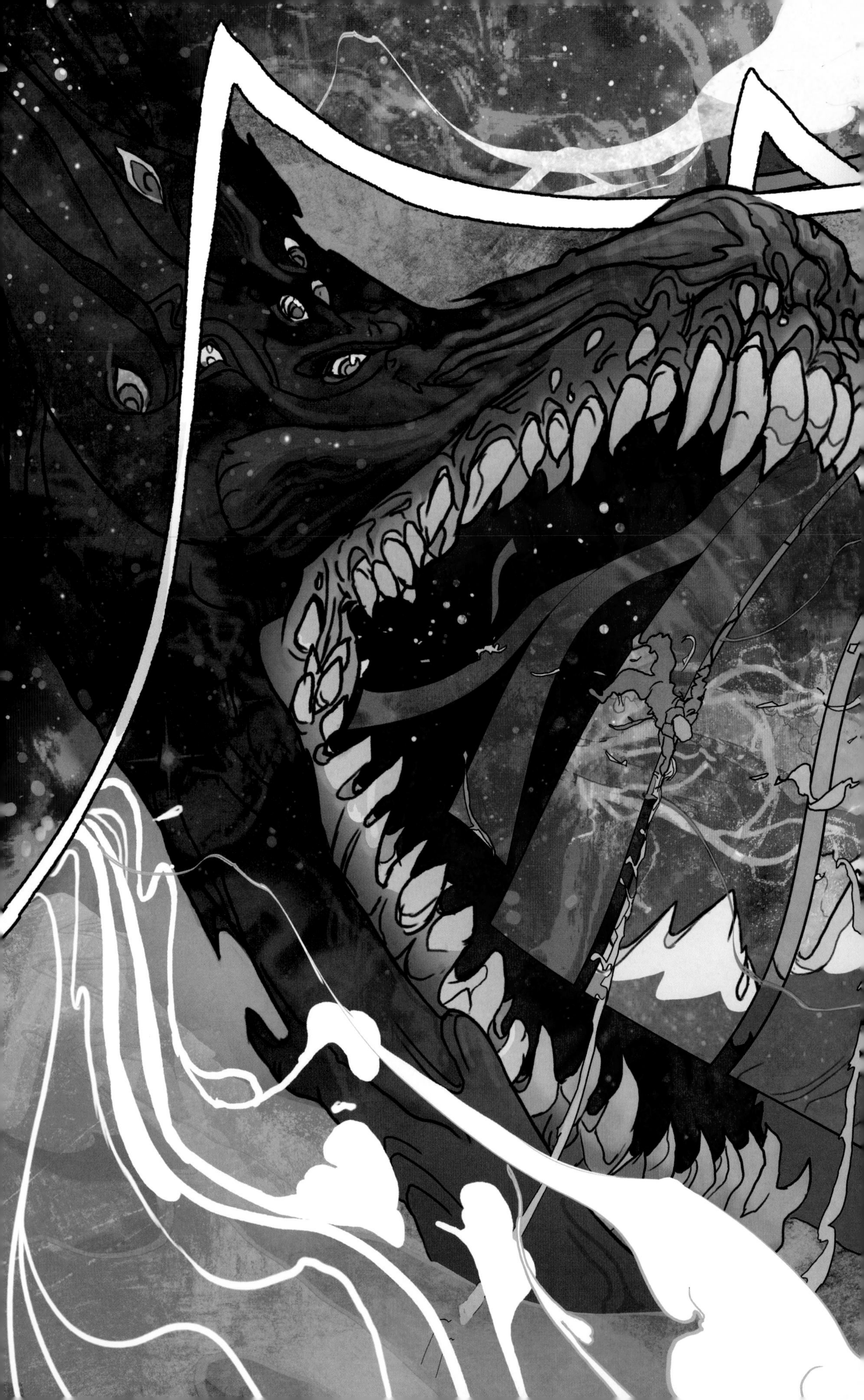

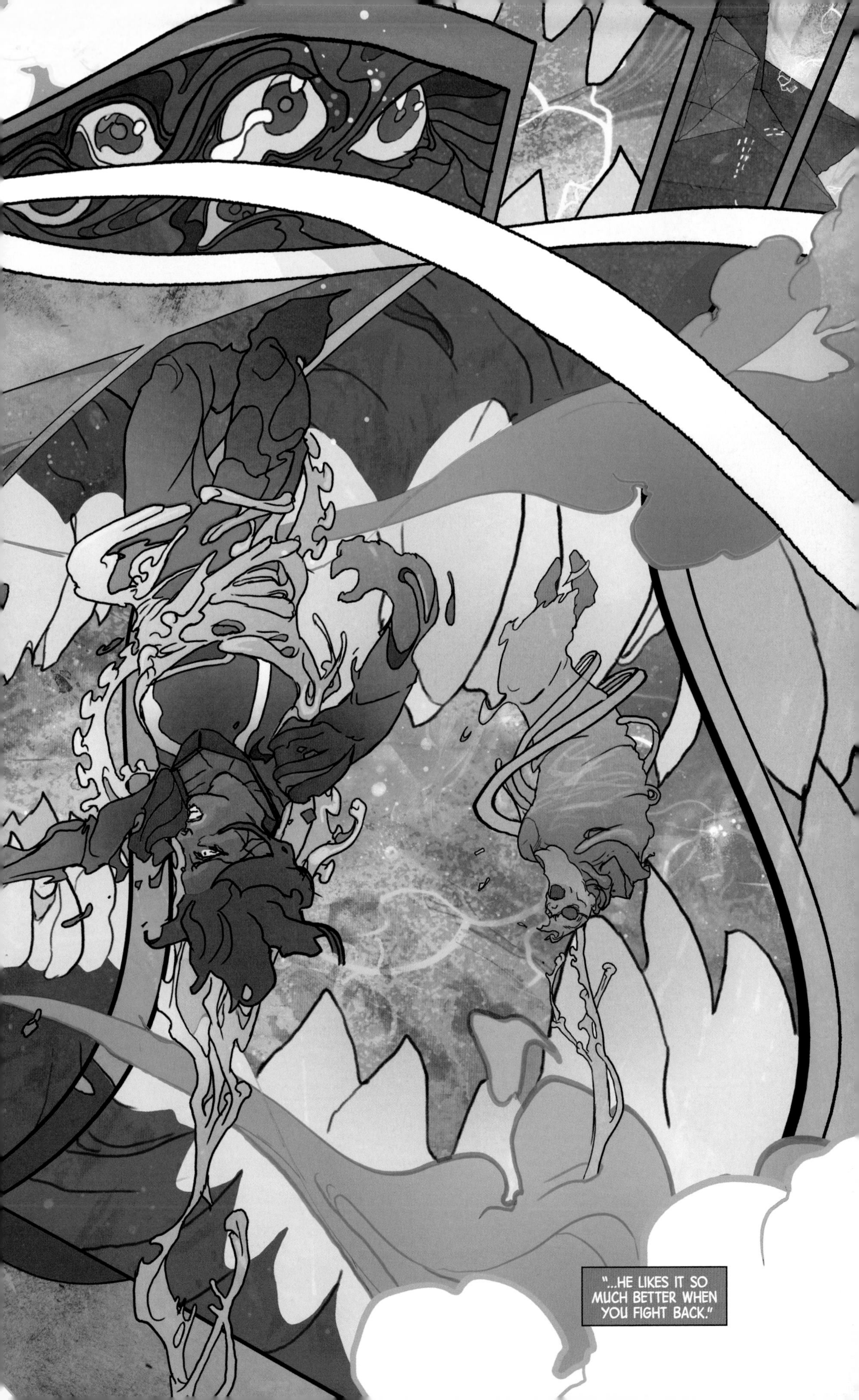
"...HE LIKES IT SO MUCH BETTER WHEN YOU FIGHT BACK."

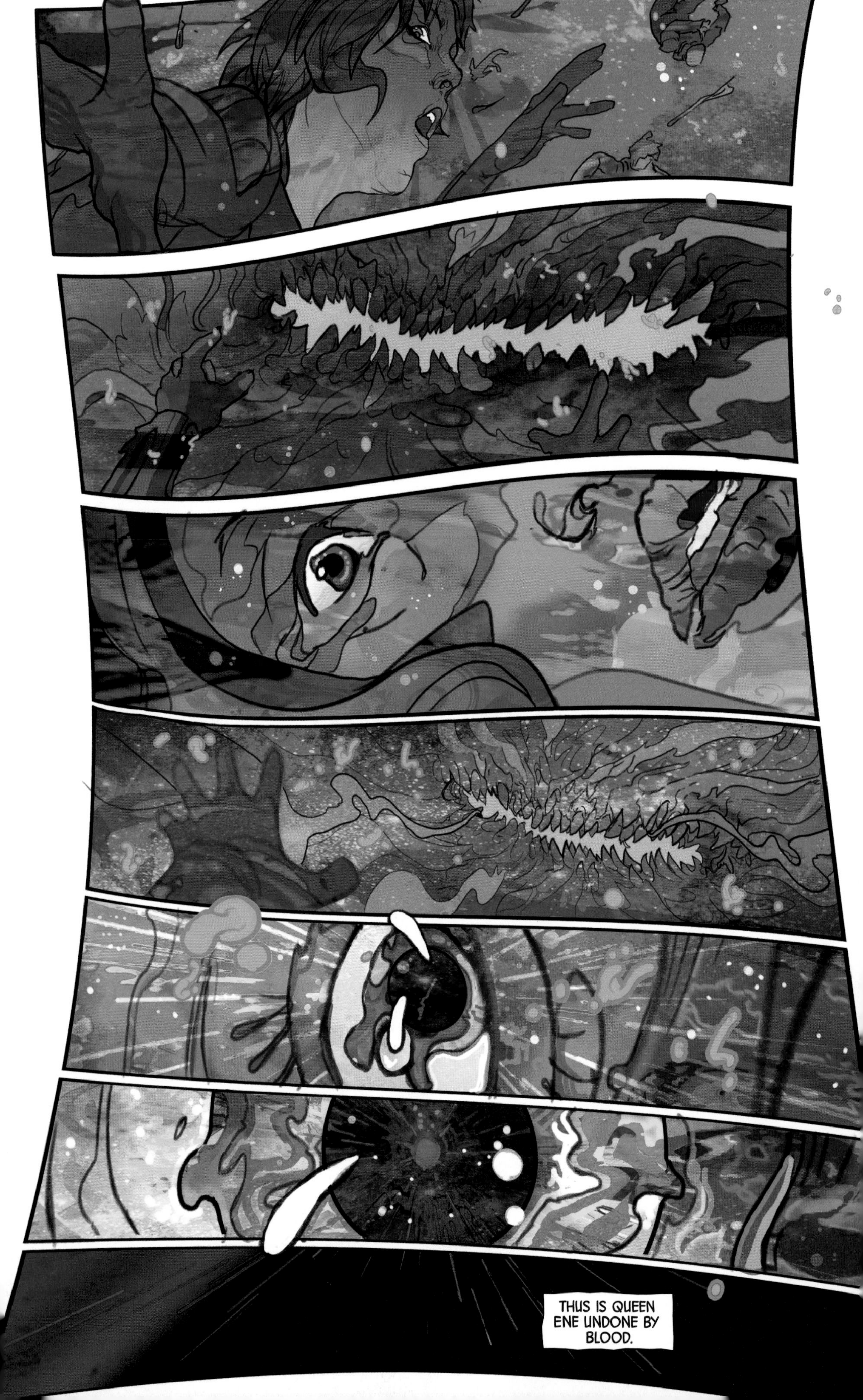
THUS IS QUEEN ENE UNDONE BY BLOOD.

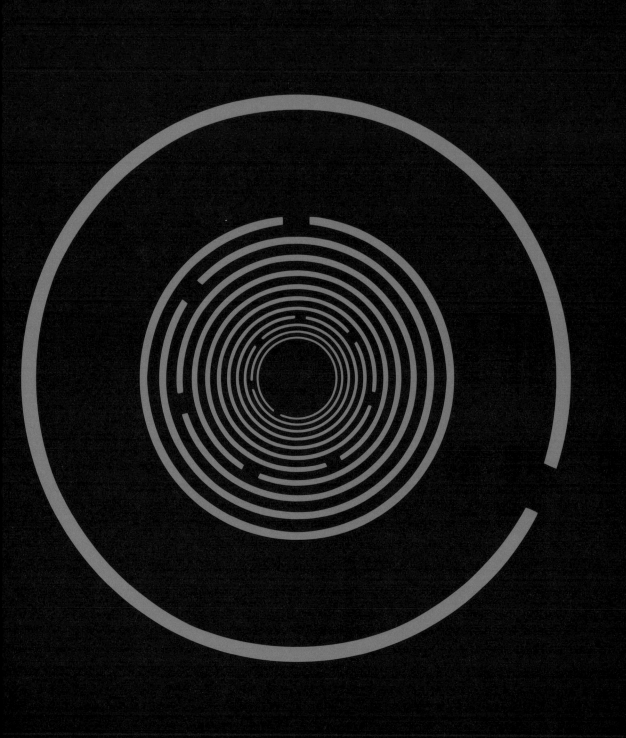

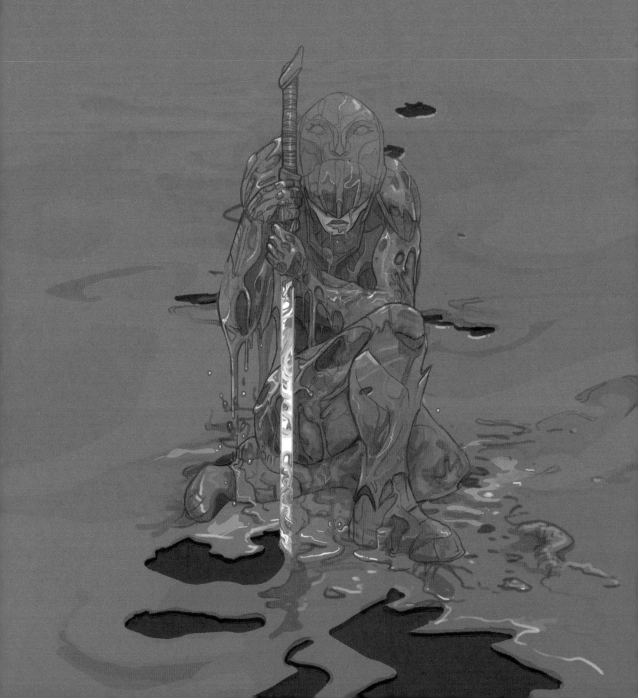

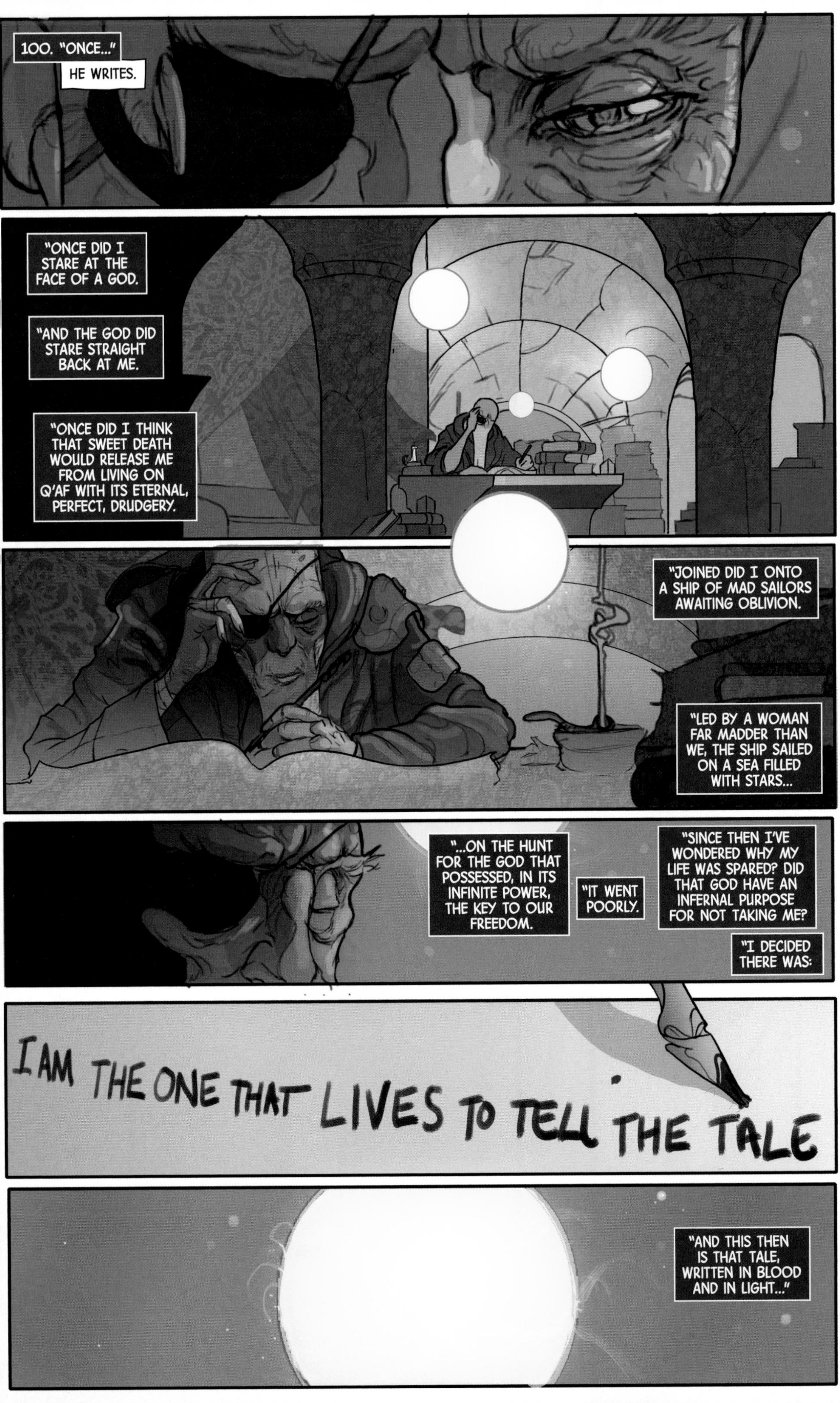
100. "ONCE..."
HE WRITES.
"ONCE DID I STARE AT THE FACE OF A GOD.
"AND THE GOD DID STARE STRAIGHT BACK AT ME.
"ONCE DID I THINK THAT SWEET DEATH WOULD RELEASE ME FROM LIVING ON Q'AF WITH ITS ETERNAL, PERFECT, DRUDGERY.
"JOINED DID I ONTO A SHIP OF MAD SAILORS AWAITING OBLIVION.
"LED BY A WOMAN FAR MADDER THAN WE, THE SHIP SAILED ON A SEA FILLED WITH STARS...
"...ON THE HUNT FOR THE GOD THAT POSSESSED, IN ITS INFINITE POWER, THE KEY TO OUR FREEDOM.
"IT WENT POORLY.
"SINCE THEN I'VE WONDERED WHY MY LIFE WAS SPARED? DID THAT GOD HAVE AN INFERNAL PURPOSE FOR NOT TAKING ME?
"I DECIDED THERE WAS:
I AM THE ONE THAT LIVES TO TELL THE TALE
"AND THIS THEN IS THAT TALE, WRITTEN IN BLOOD AND IN LIGHT..."

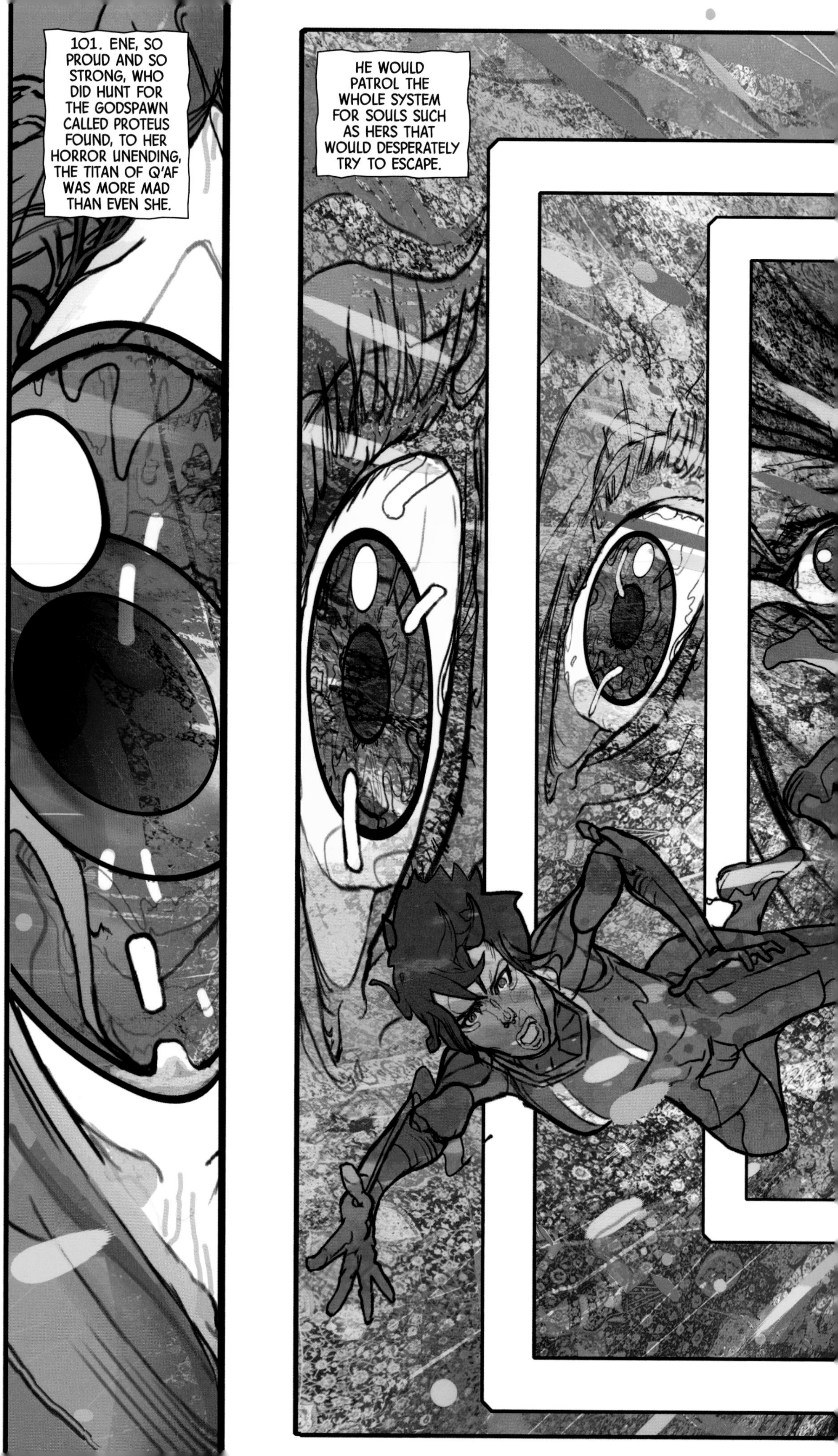
101. ENE, SO PROUD AND SO STRONG, WHO DID HUNT FOR THE GODSPAWN CALLED PROTEUS FOUND, TO HER HORROR UNENDING, THE TITAN OF Q'AF WAS MORE MAD THAN EVEN SHE.
HE WOULD PATROL THE WHOLE SYSTEM FOR SOULS SUCH AS HERS THAT WOULD DESPERATELY TRY TO ESCAPE.

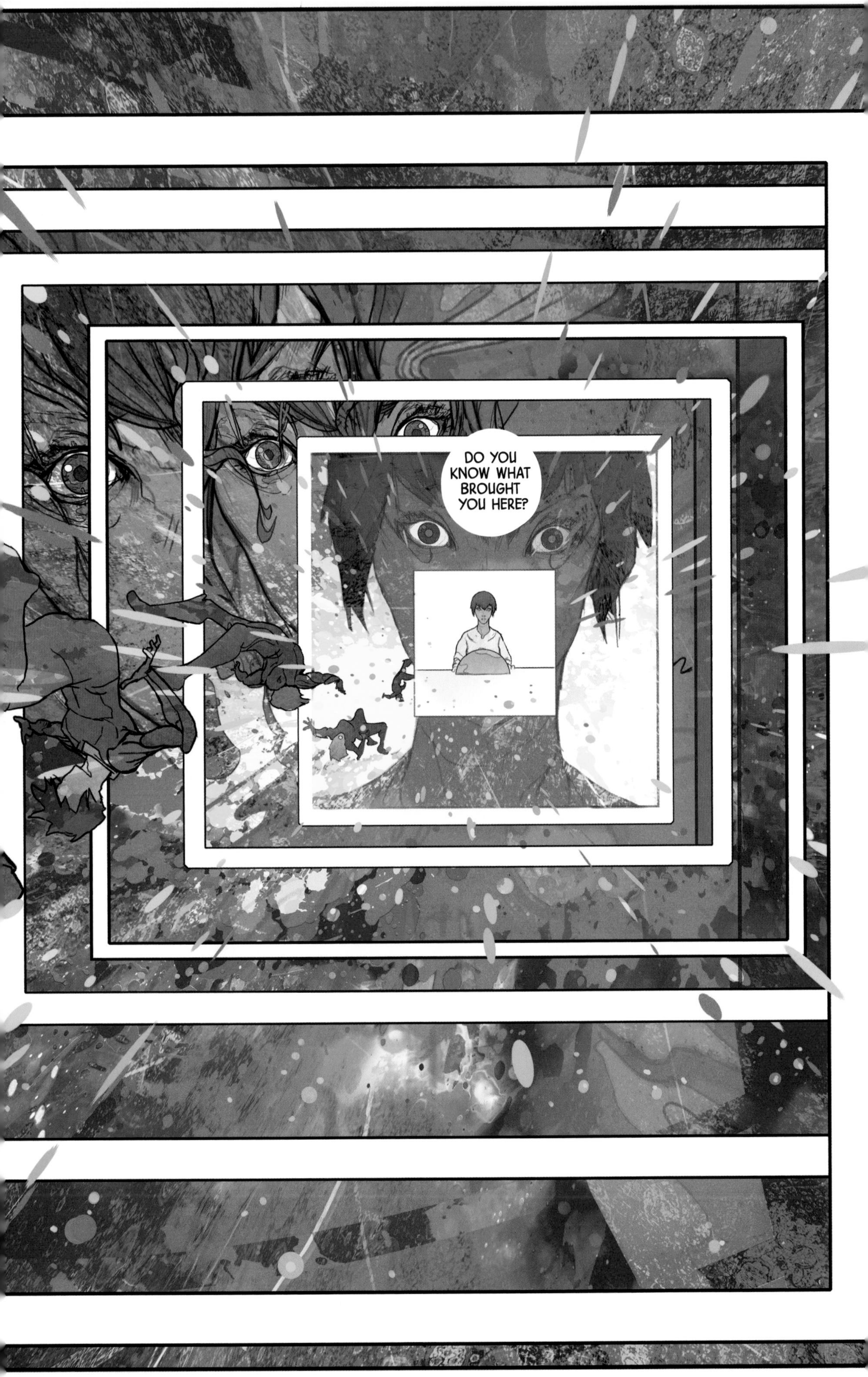
DO YOU KNOW WHAT BROUGHT YOU HERE?

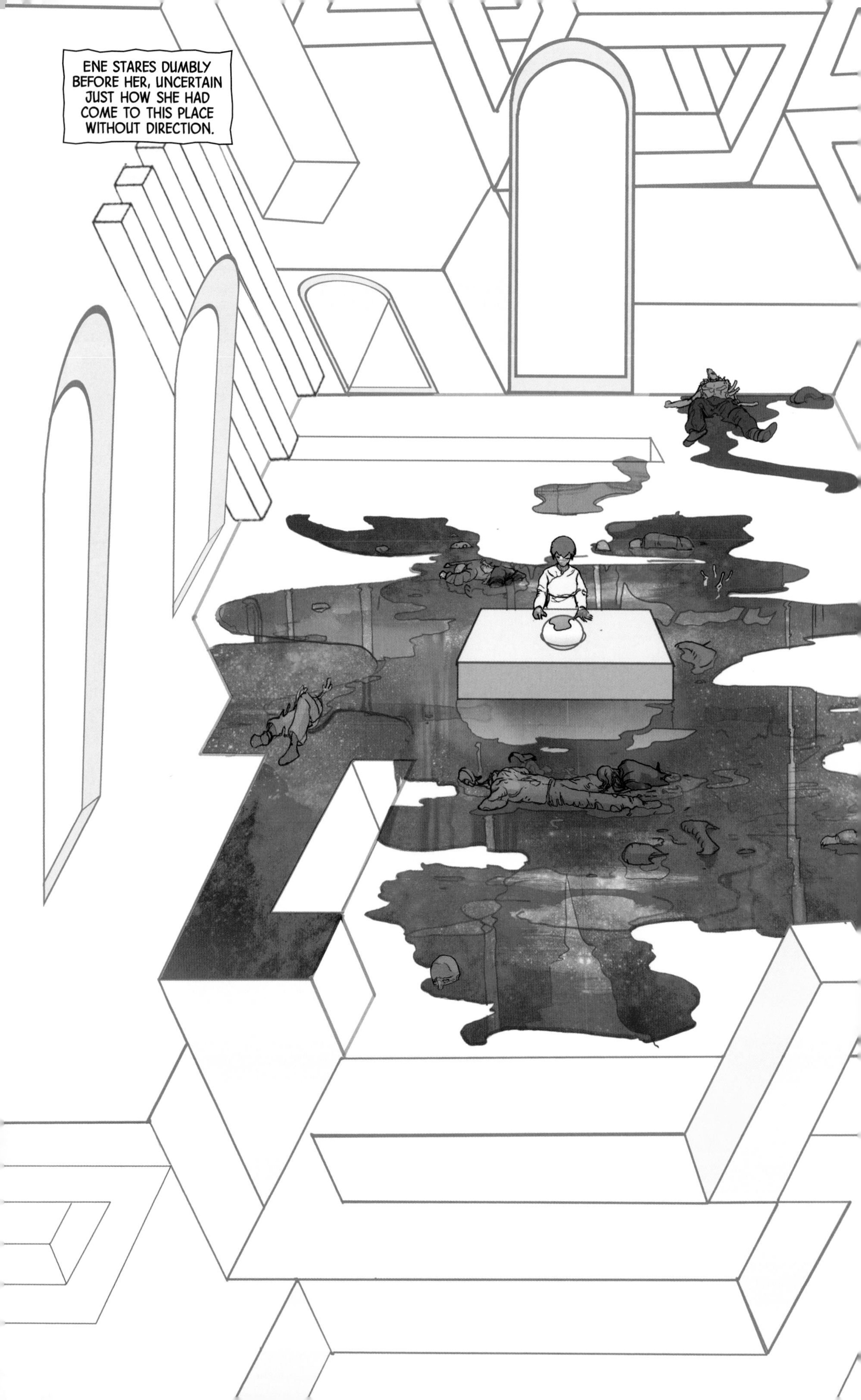
ENE STARES DUMBLY BEFORE HER, UNCERTAIN JUST HOW SHE HAD COME TO THIS PLACE WITHOUT DIRECTION.

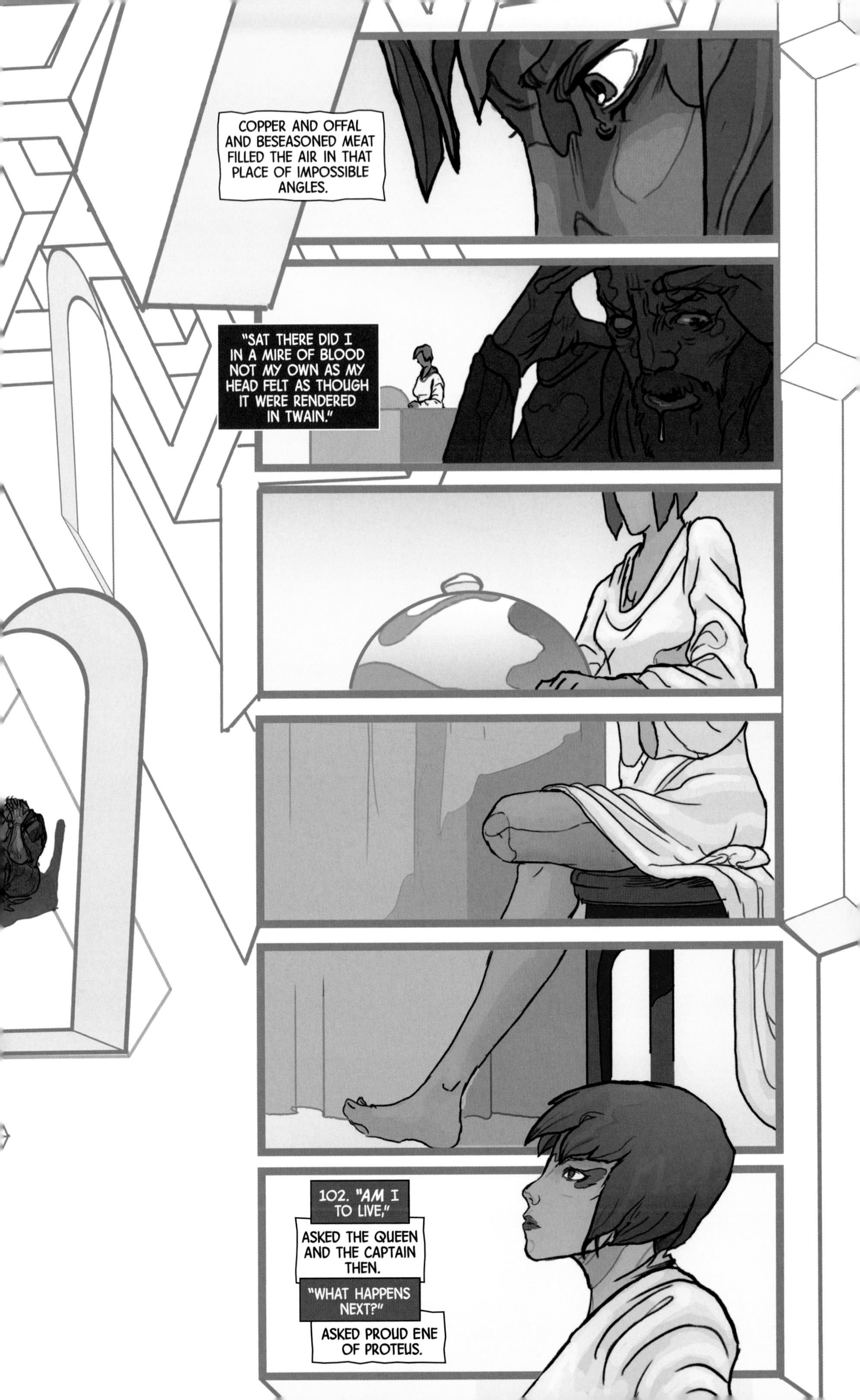
COPPER AND OFFAL AND BESEASONED MEAT FILLED THE AIR IN THAT PLACE OF IMPOSSIBLE ANGLES.
"SAT THERE DID I IN A MIRE OF BLOOD NOT MY OWN AS MY HEAD FELT AS THOUGH IT WERE RENDERED IN TWAIN."
102. "AM I TO LIVE,"
ASKED THE QUEEN AND THE CAPTAIN THEN.
"WHAT HAPPENS NEXT?"
ASKED PROUD ENE OF PROTEUS.

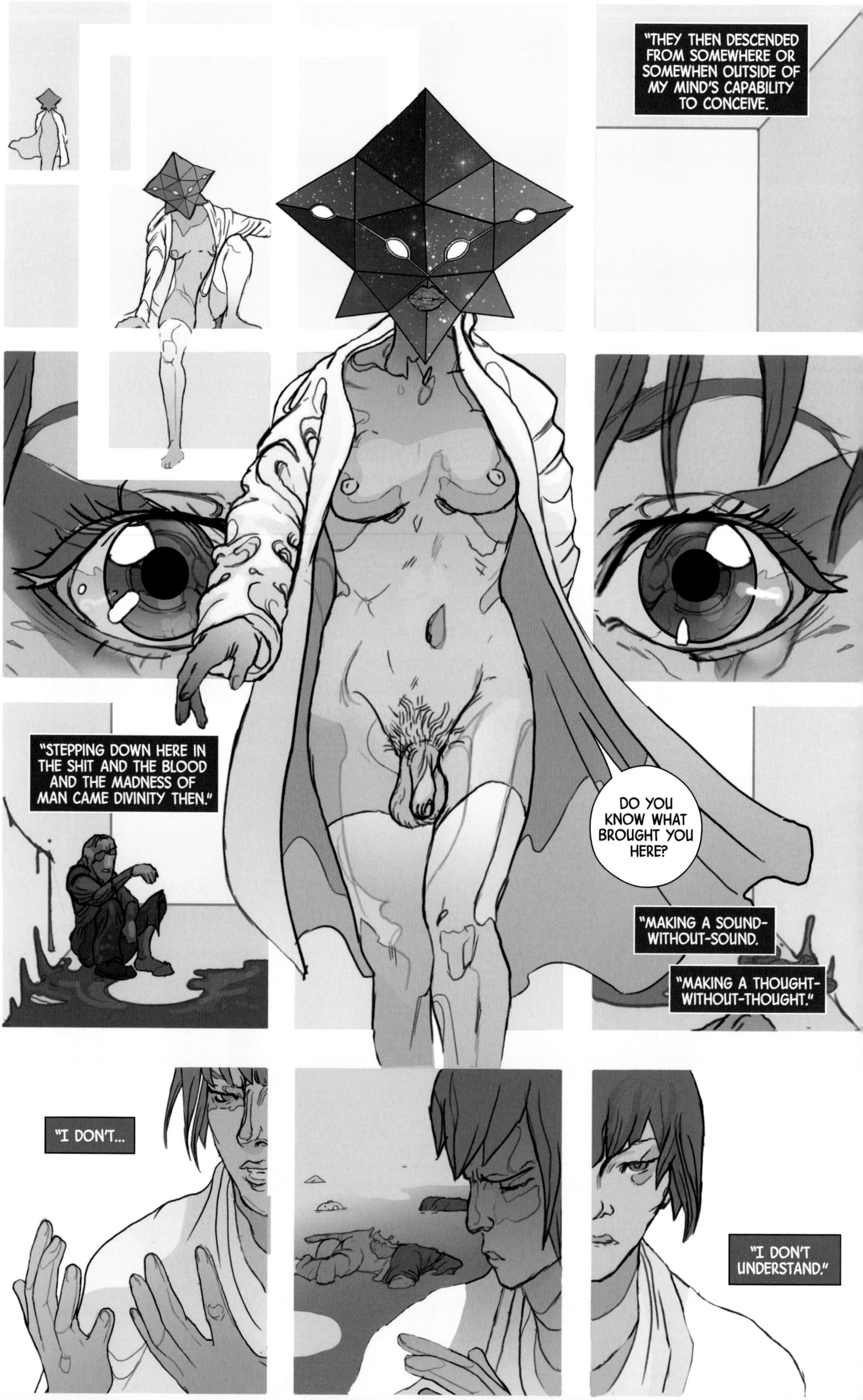
"THEY THEN DESCENDED FROM SOMEWHERE OR SOMEWHEN OUTSIDE OF MY MIND'S CAPABILITY TO CONCEIVE.
"STEPPING DOWN HERE IN THE SHIT AND THE BLOOD AND THE MADNESS OF MAN CAME DIVINITY THEN."
DO YOU KNOW WHAT BROUGHT YOU HERE?
"MAKING A SOUND-WITHOUT-SOUND.
"MAKING A THOUGHT-WITHOUT-THOUGHT."
"I DON'T...
"I DON'T UNDERSTAND."

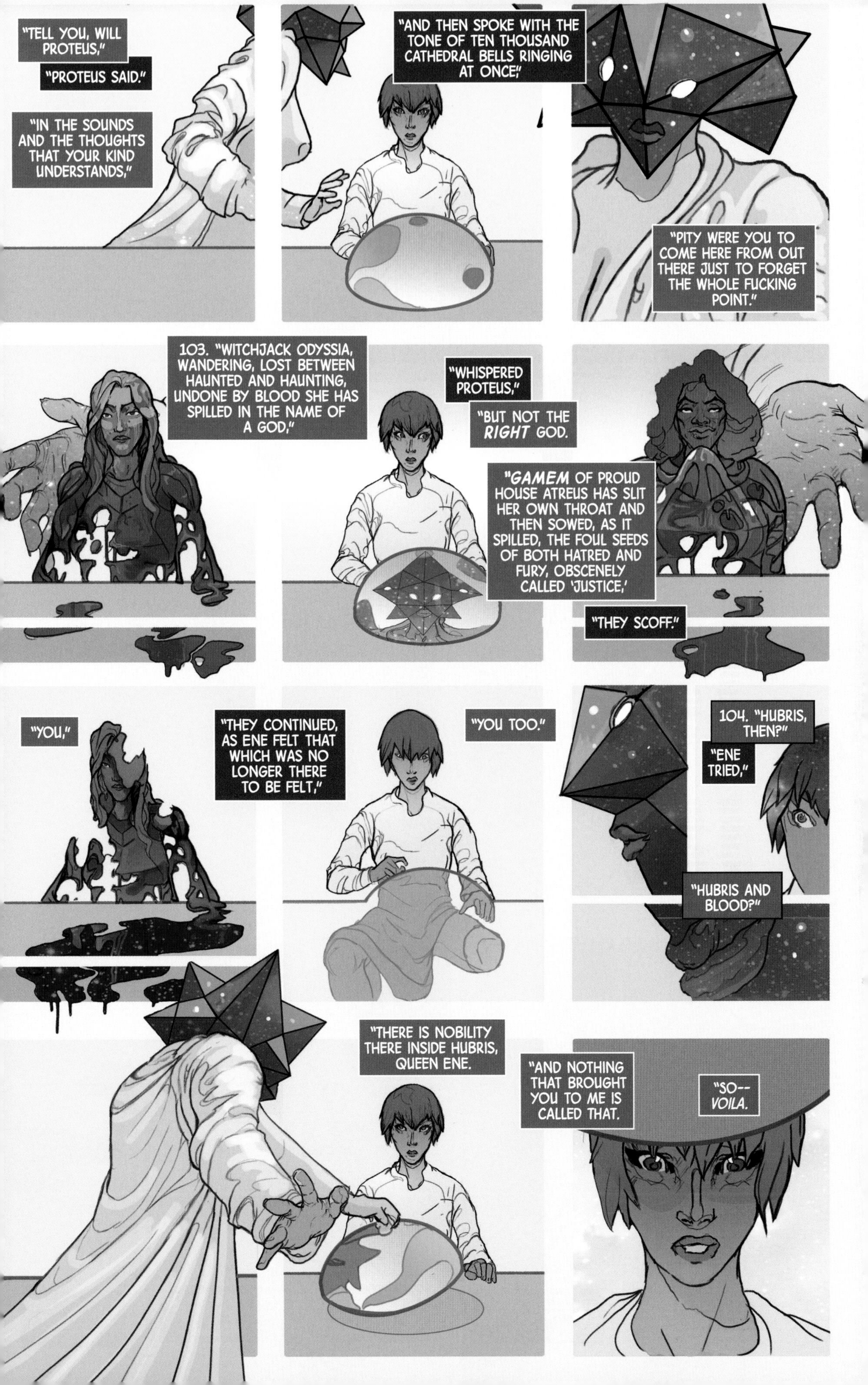
"TELL YOU, WILL PROTEUS,"
"PROTEUS SAID."
"IN THE SOUNDS AND THE THOUGHTS THAT YOUR KIND UNDERSTANDS,"
"AND THEN SPOKE WITH THE TONE OF TEN THOUSAND CATHEDRAL BELLS RINGING AT ONCE,"
"PITY WERE YOU TO COME HERE FROM OUT THERE JUST TO FORGET THE WHOLE FUCKING POINT."
103. "WITCHJACK ODYSSIA, WANDERING, LOST BETWEEN HAUNTED AND HAUNTING, UNDONE BY BLOOD SHE HAS SPILLED IN THE NAME OF A GOD,"
"WHISPERED PROTEUS,"
"BUT NOT THE *RIGHT* GOD.
"*GAMEM* OF PROUD HOUSE ATREUS HAS SLIT HER OWN THROAT AND THEN SOWED, AS IT SPILLED, THE FOUL SEEDS OF BOTH HATRED AND FURY, OBSCENELY CALLED 'JUSTICE,'
"THEY SCOFF."
"YOU,"
"THEY CONTINUED, AS ENE FELT THAT WHICH WAS NO LONGER THERE TO BE FELT,"
"YOU TOO."
104. "HUBRIS, THEN?"
"ENE TRIED,"
"HUBRIS AND BLOOD?"
"THERE IS NOBILITY THERE INSIDE HUBRIS, QUEEN ENE.
"AND NOTHING THAT BROUGHT YOU TO ME IS CALLED THAT.
"SO-- *VOILA*.

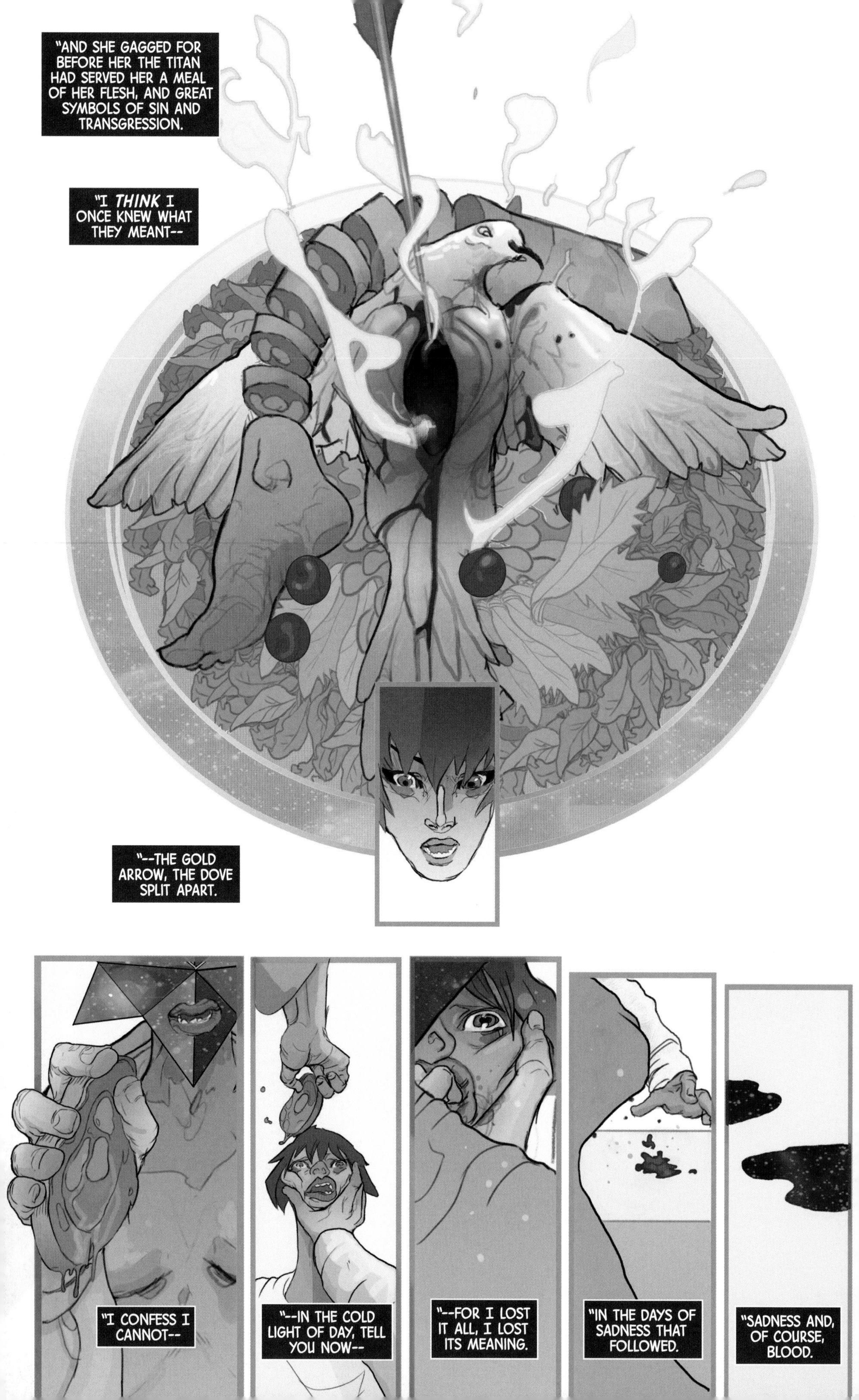
"AND SHE GAGGED FOR BEFORE HER THE TITAN HAD SERVED HER A MEAL OF HER FLESH, AND GREAT SYMBOLS OF SIN AND TRANSGRESSION.
"I *THINK* I ONCE KNEW WHAT THEY MEANT--
"--THE GOLD ARROW, THE DOVE SPLIT APART.
"I CONFESS I CANNOT--
"--IN THE COLD LIGHT OF DAY, TELL YOU NOW--
"--FOR I LOST IT ALL, I LOST ITS MEANING.
"IN THE DAYS OF SADNESS THAT FOLLOWED.
"SADNESS AND, OF COURSE, BLOOD.

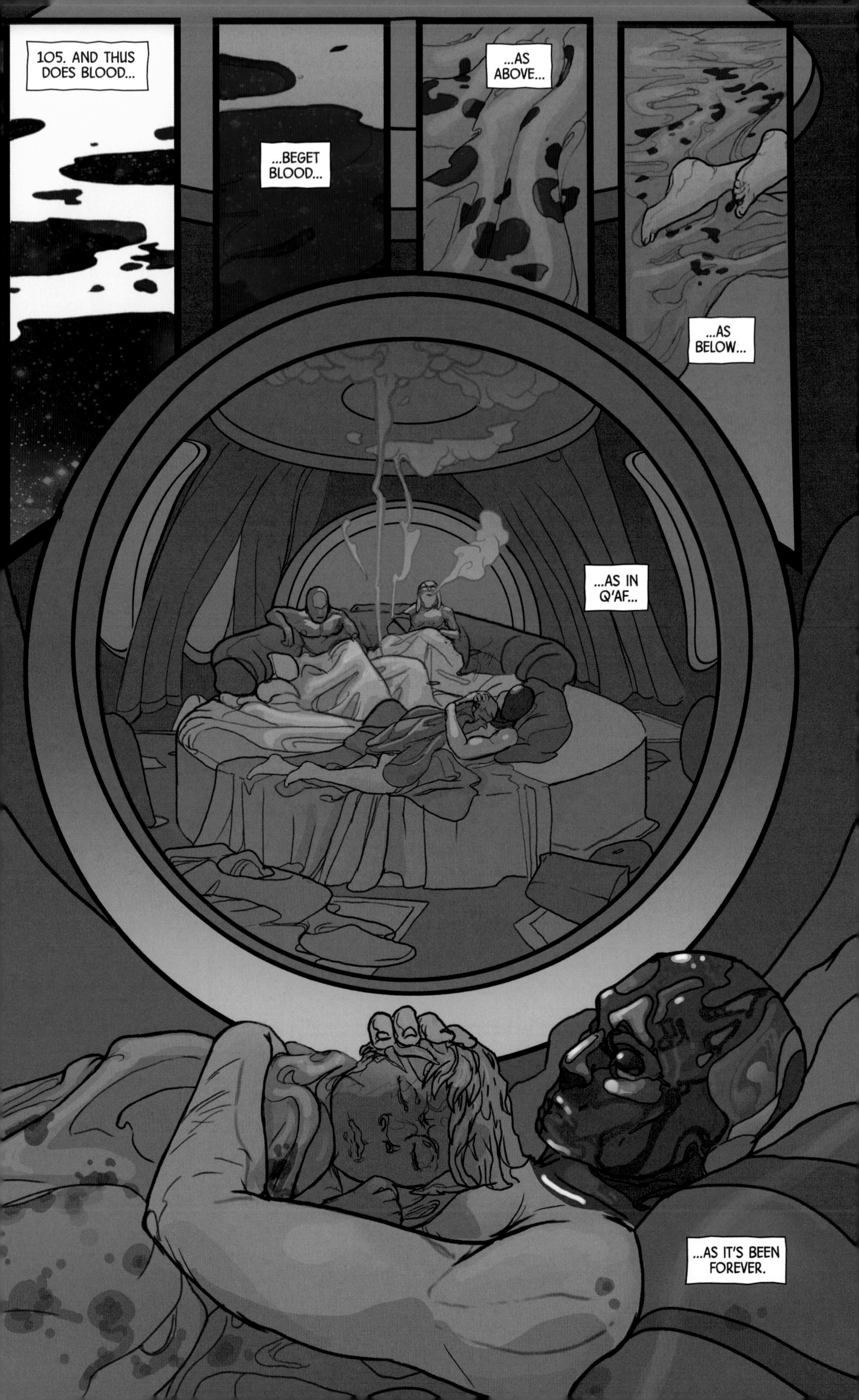
105. AND THUS DOES BLOOD...
...BEGET BLOOD...
...AS ABOVE...
...AS BELOW...
...AS IN Q'AF...
...AS IT'S BEEN FOREVER.

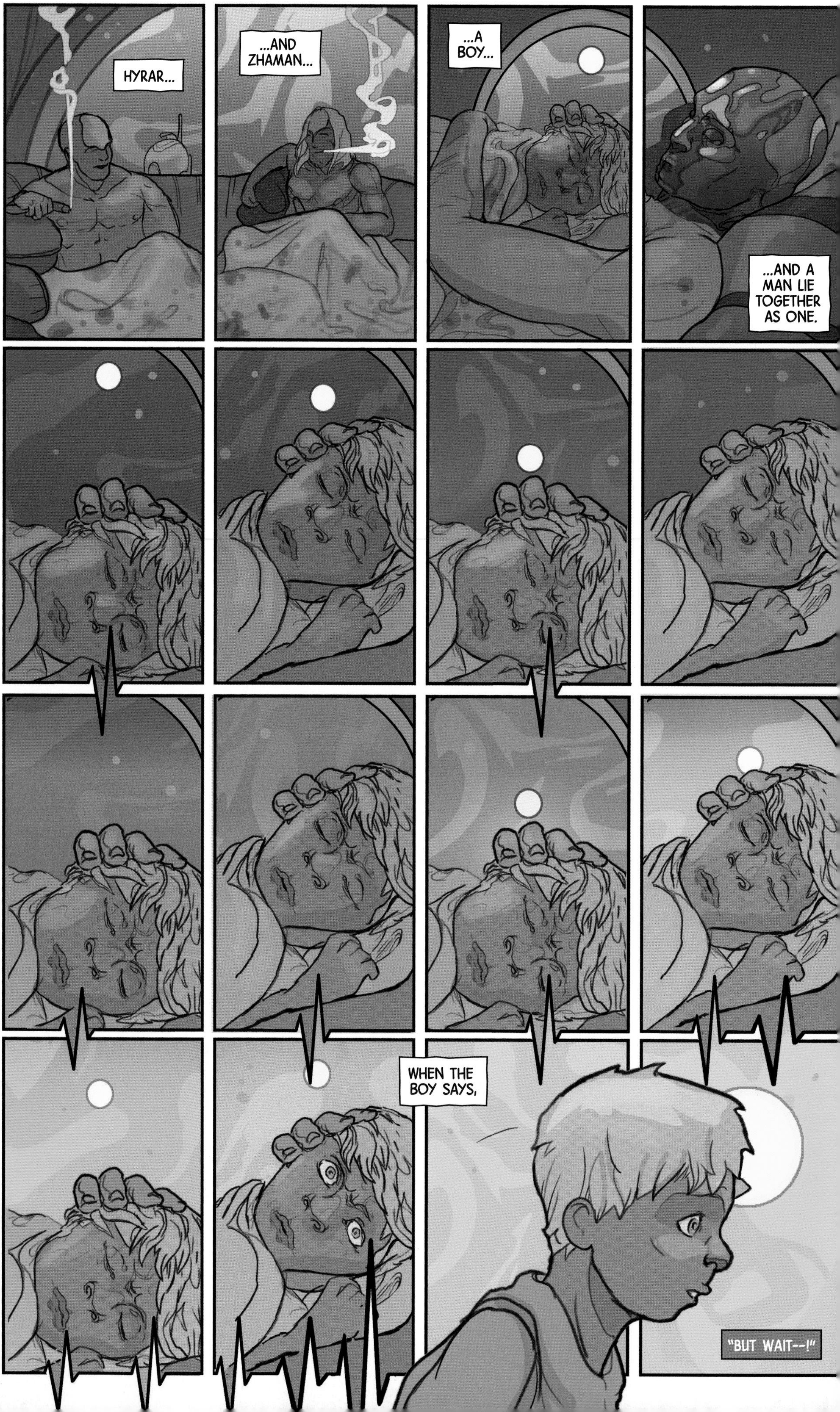
HYRAR...
...AND ZHAMAN...
...A BOY...
...AND A MAN LIE TOGETHER AS ONE.
WHEN THE BOY SAYS,
"BUT WAIT--!"

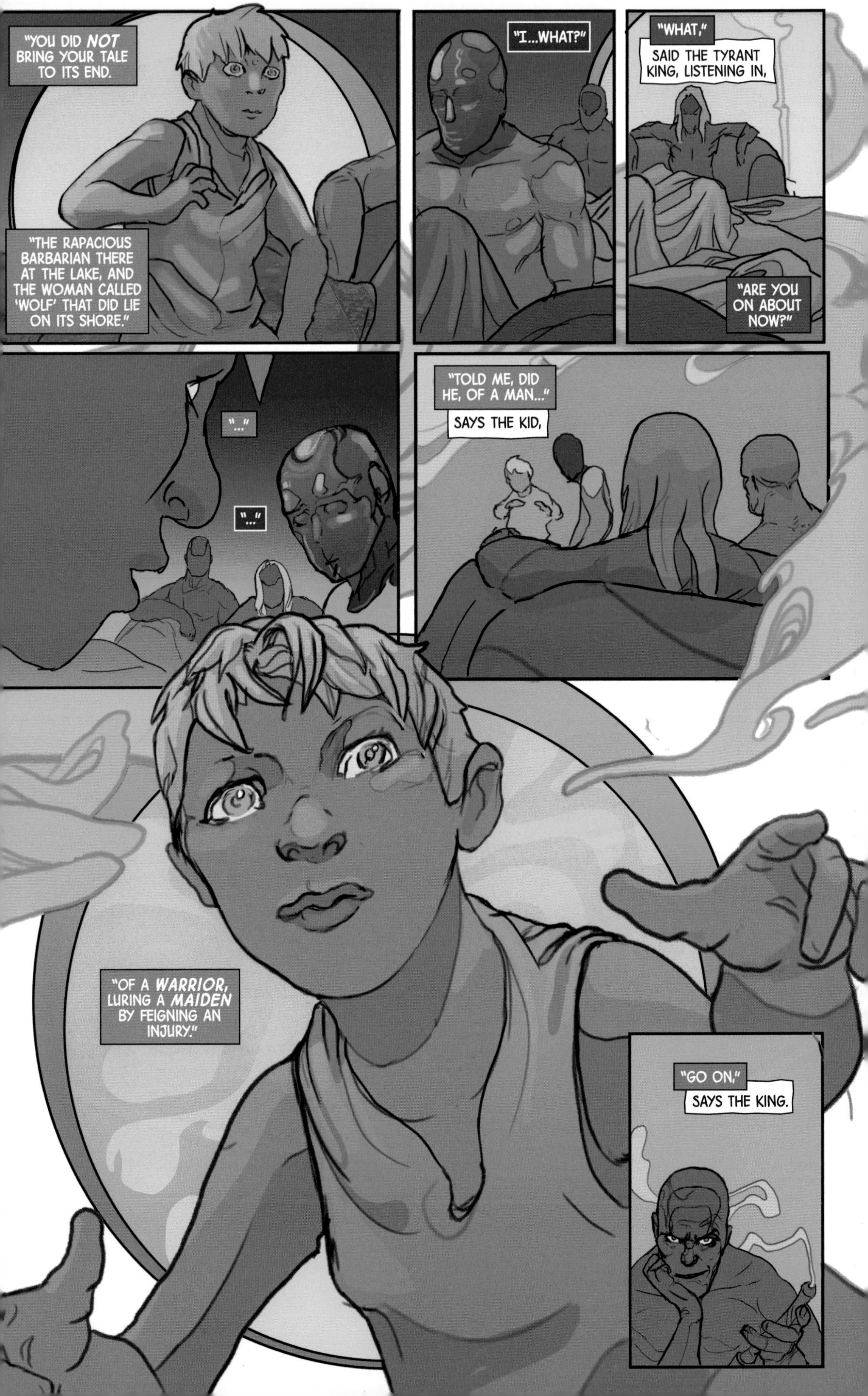
"YOU DID NOT BRING YOUR TALE TO ITS END.
"THE RAPACIOUS BARBARIAN THERE AT THE LAKE, AND THE WOMAN CALLED 'WOLF' THAT DID LIE ON ITS SHORE."
"I...WHAT?"
"WHAT,"
SAID THE TYRANT KING, LISTENING IN,
"ARE YOU ON ABOUT NOW?"
"..."
"..."
"TOLD ME, DID HE, OF A MAN..."
SAYS THE KID,
"OF A WARRIOR, LURING A MAIDEN BY FEIGNING AN INJURY."
"GO ON,"
SAYS THE KING.

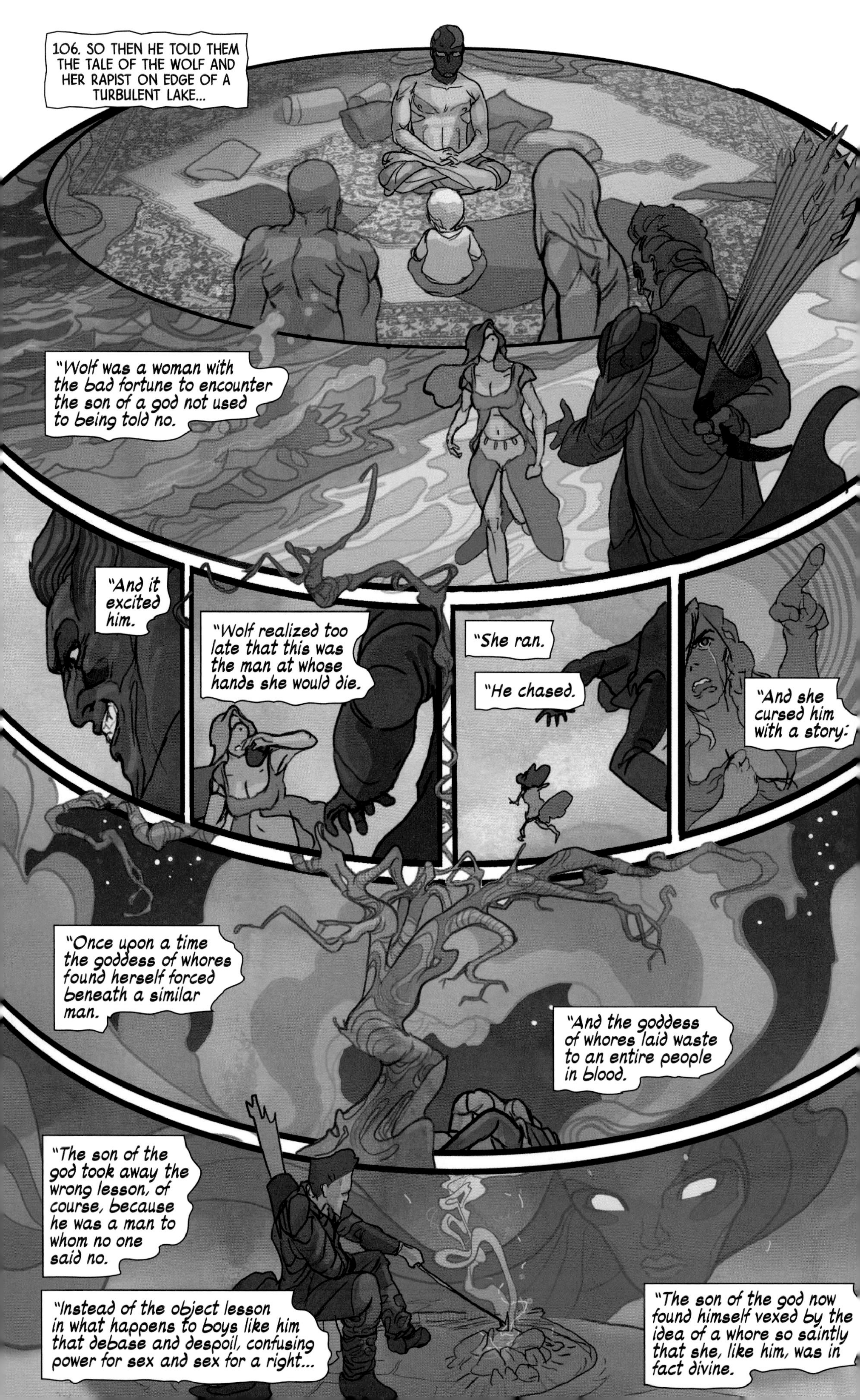
106. SO THEN HE TOLD THEM THE TALE OF THE WOLF AND HER RAPIST ON EDGE OF A TURBULENT LAKE...
"Wolf was a woman with the bad fortune to encounter the son of a god not used to being told no.
"And it excited him.
"Wolf realized too late that this was the man at whose hands she would die.
"She ran.
"He chased.
"And she cursed him with a story:
"Once upon a time the goddess of whores found herself forced beneath a similar man.
"And the goddess of whores laid waste to an entire people in blood.
"The son of the god took away the wrong lesson, of course, because he was a man to whom no one said no.
"Instead of the object lesson in what happens to boys like him that debase and despoil, confusing power for sex and sex for a right...
"The son of the god now found himself vexed by the idea of a whore so saintly that she, like him, was in fact divine.

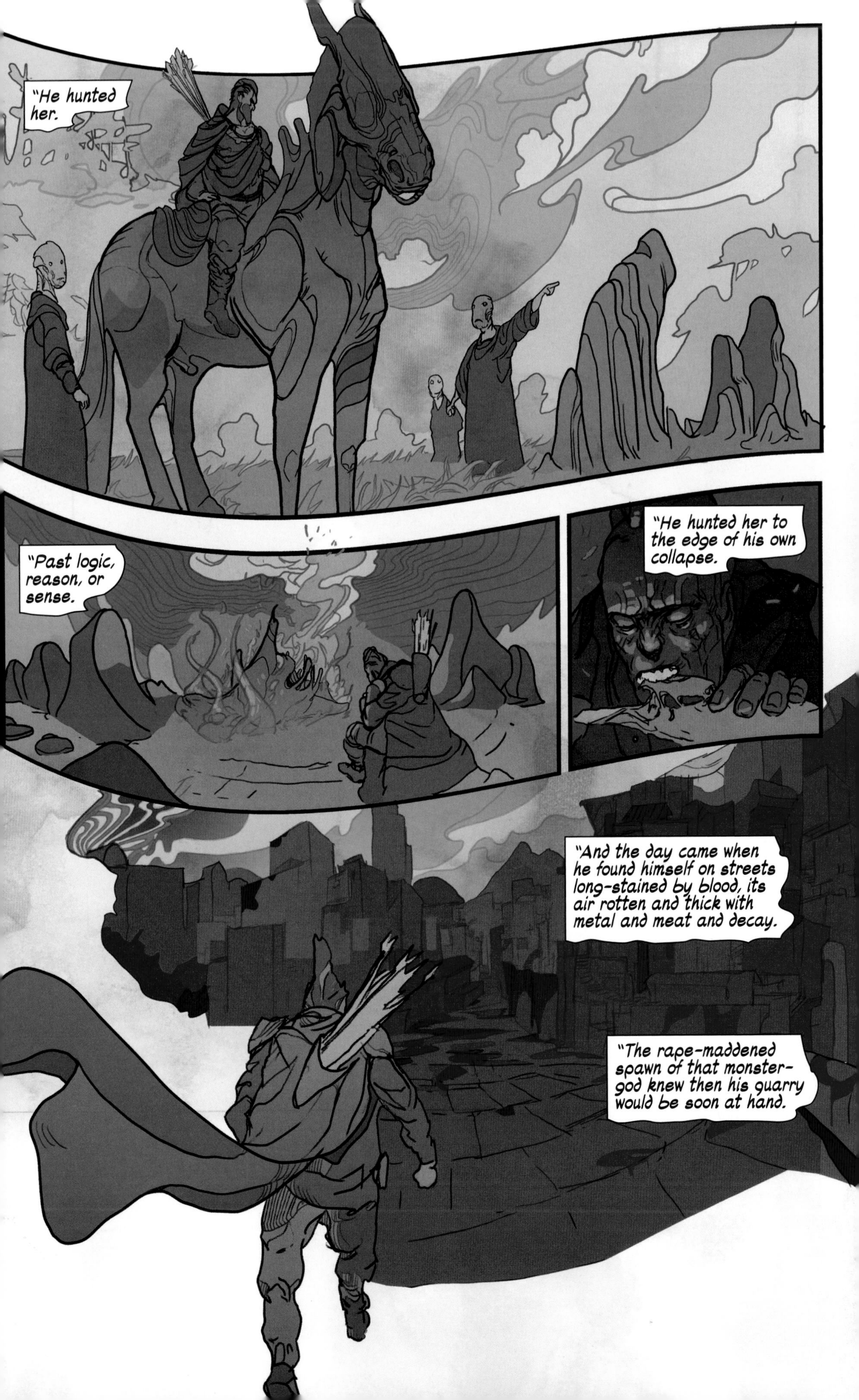
"He hunted her.
"Past logic, reason, or sense.
"He hunted her to the edge of his own collapse.
"And the day came when he found himself on streets long-stained by blood, its air rotten and thick with metal and meat and decay.
"The rape-maddened spawn of that monster-god knew then his quarry would be soon at hand.

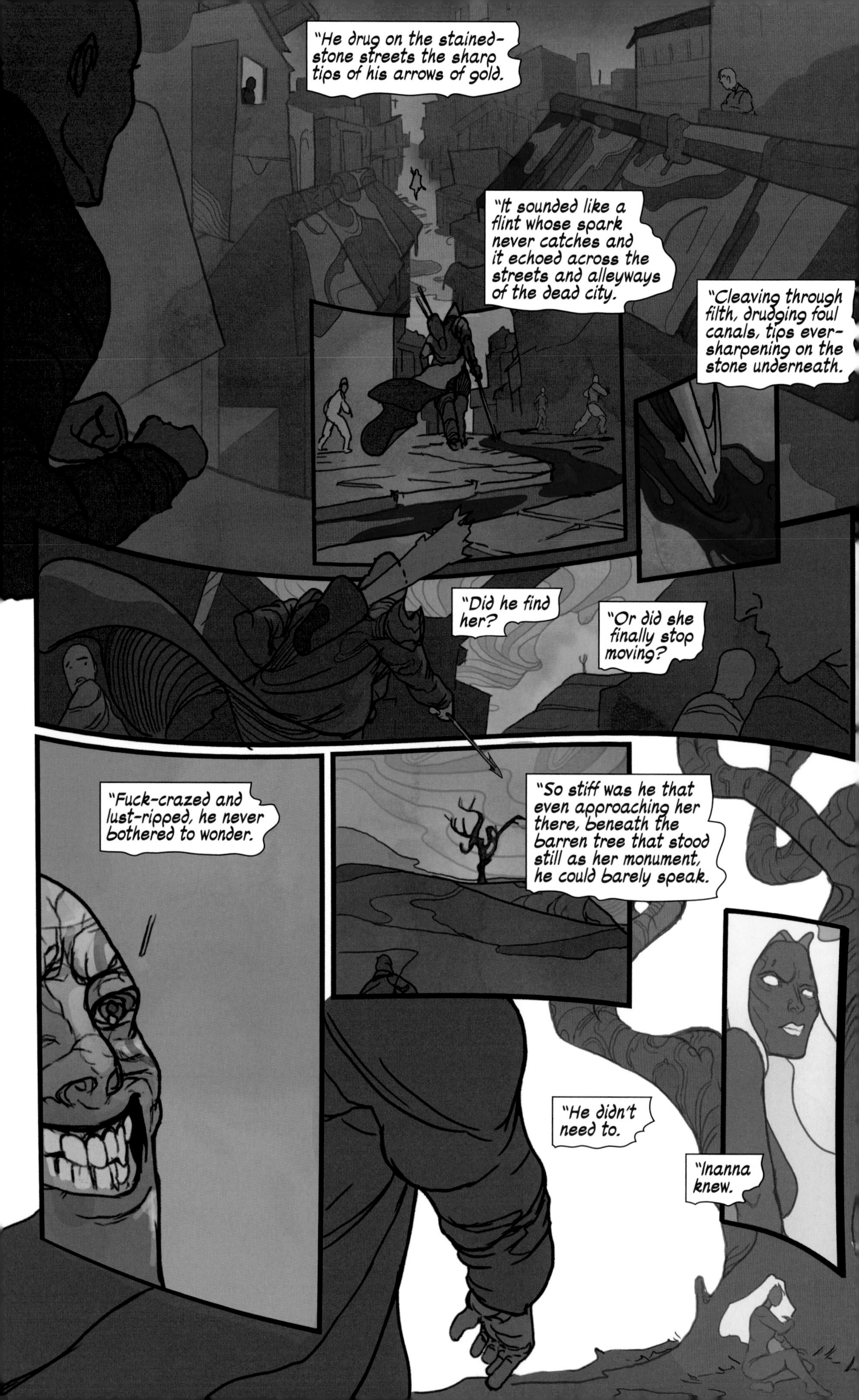
"He drug on the stained-stone streets the sharp tips of his arrows of gold.
"It sounded like a flint whose spark never catches and it echoed across the streets and alleyways of the dead city.
"Cleaving through filth, drudging foul canals, tips ever-sharpening on the stone underneath.
"Did he find her?
"Or did she finally stop moving?
"Fuck-crazed and lust-ripped, he never bothered to wonder.
"So stiff was he that even approaching her there, beneath the barren tree that stood still as her monument, he could barely speak.
"He didn't need to.
"Inanna knew.

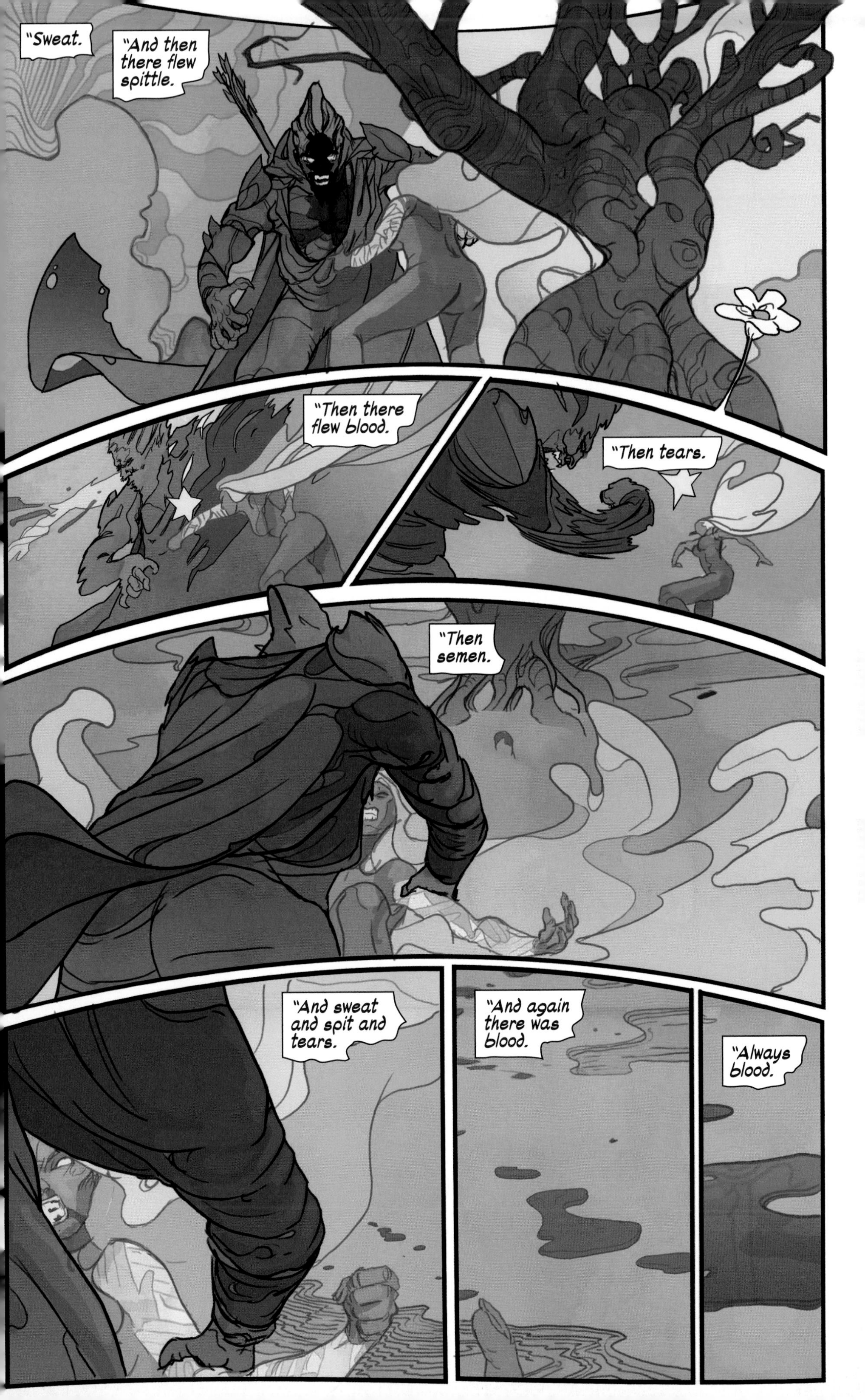
"Sweat.
"And then there flew spittle.
"Then there flew blood.
"Then tears.
"Then semen.
"And sweat and spit and tears.
"And again there was blood.
"Always blood.

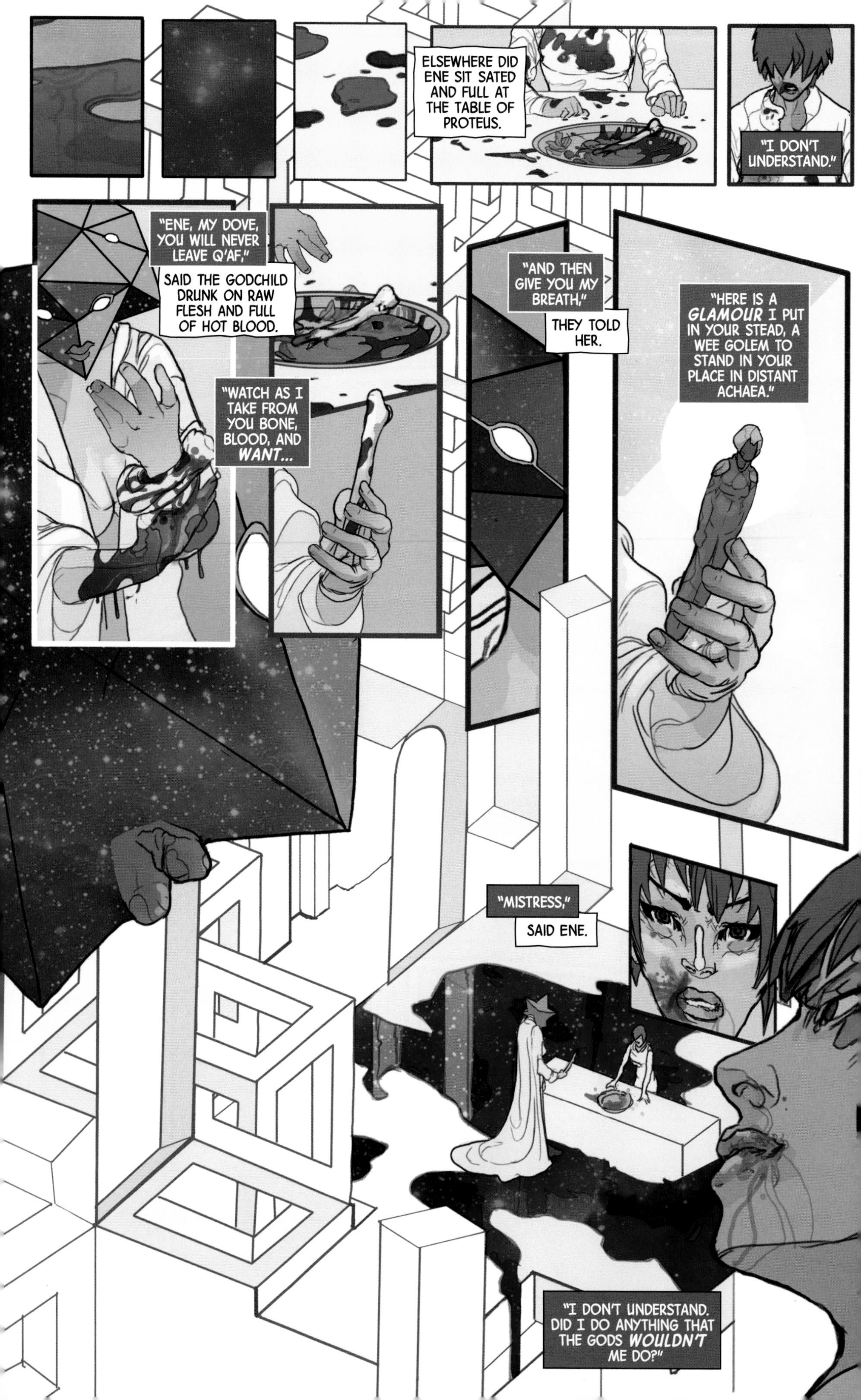
ELSEWHERE DID ENE SIT SATED AND FULL AT THE TABLE OF PROTEUS.
"I DON'T UNDERSTAND."
"ENE, MY DOVE, YOU WILL NEVER LEAVE Q'AF,"
SAID THE GODCHILD DRUNK ON RAW FLESH AND FULL OF HOT BLOOD.
"WATCH AS I TAKE FROM YOU BONE, BLOOD, AND WANT...
"AND THEN GIVE YOU MY BREATH,"
THEY TOLD HER.
"HERE IS A GLAMOUR I PUT IN YOUR STEAD, A WEE GOLEM TO STAND IN YOUR PLACE IN DISTANT ACHAEA."
"MISTRESS,"
SAID ENE.
"I DON'T UNDERSTAND. DID I DO ANYTHING THAT THE GODS WOULDN'T ME DO?"

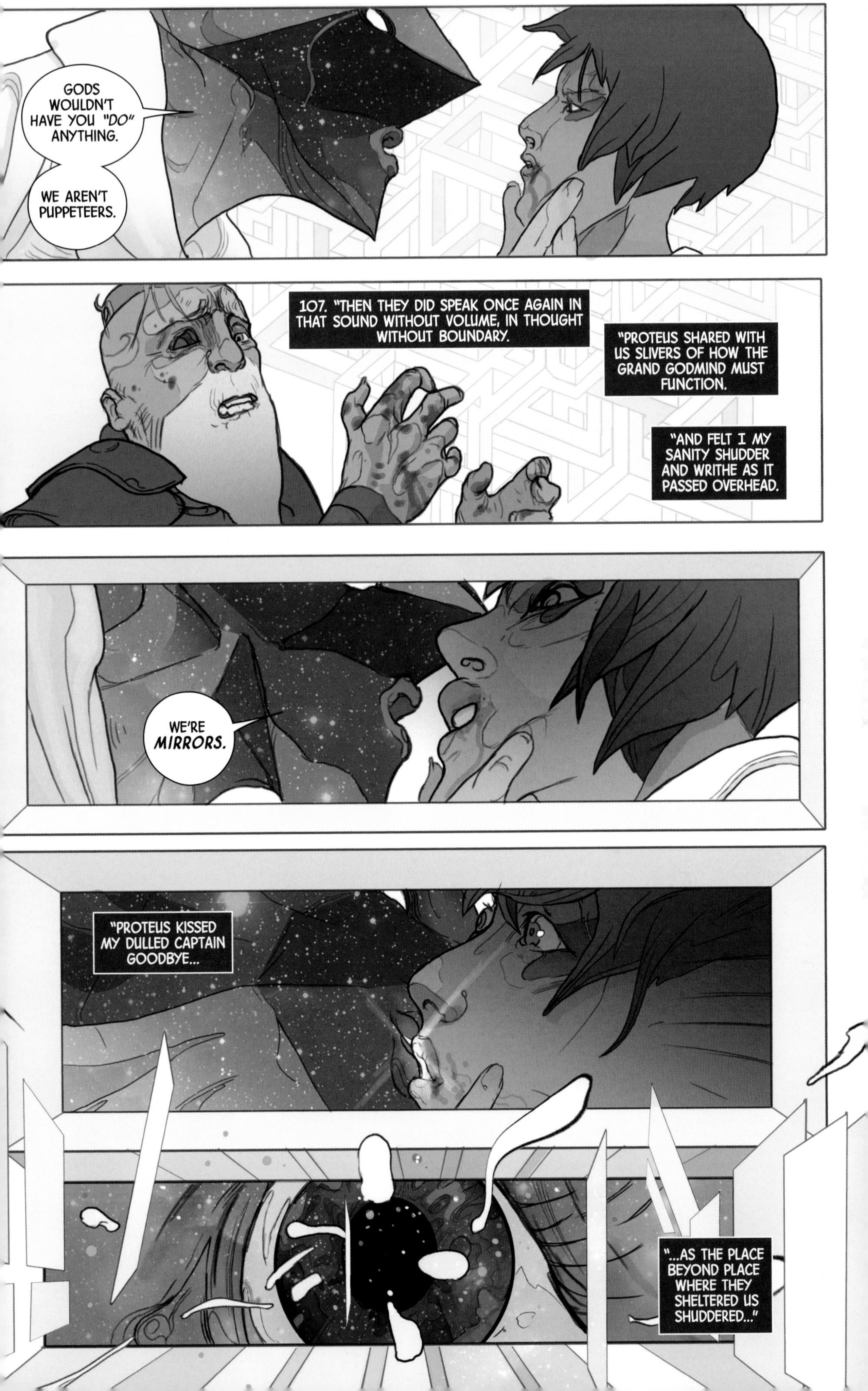
GODS WOULDN'T HAVE YOU "DO" ANYTHING.
WE AREN'T PUPPETEERS.
107. "THEN THEY DID SPEAK ONCE AGAIN IN THAT SOUND WITHOUT VOLUME, IN THOUGHT WITHOUT BOUNDARY.
"PROTEUS SHARED WITH US SLIVERS OF HOW THE GRAND GODMIND MUST FUNCTION.
"AND FELT I MY SANITY SHUDDER AND WRITHE AS IT PASSED OVERHEAD.
WE'RE MIRRORS.
"PROTEUS KISSED MY DULLED CAPTAIN GOODBYE...
"...AS THE PLACE BEYOND PLACE WHERE THEY SHELTERED US SHUDDERED..."

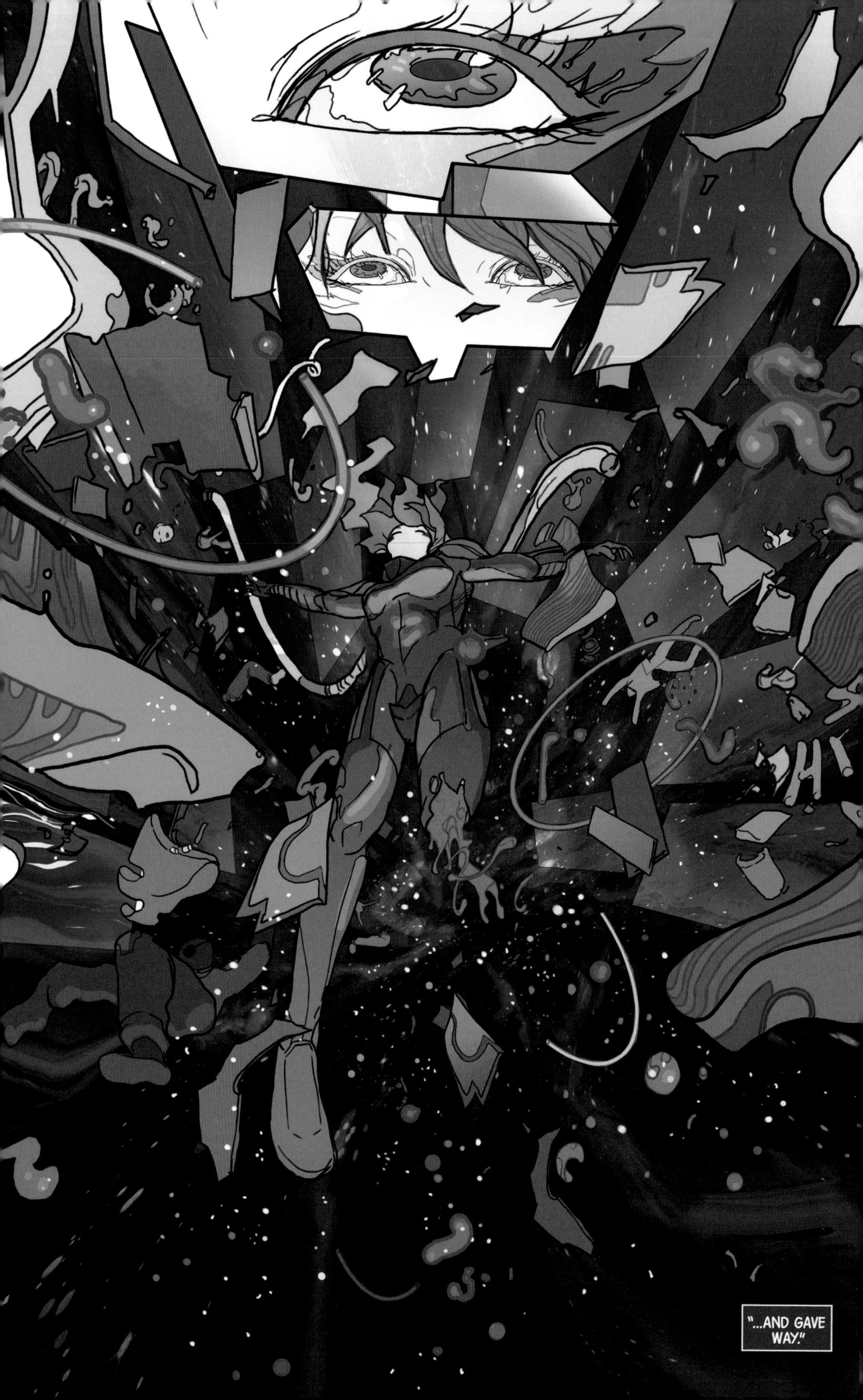
"...AND GAVE WAY."

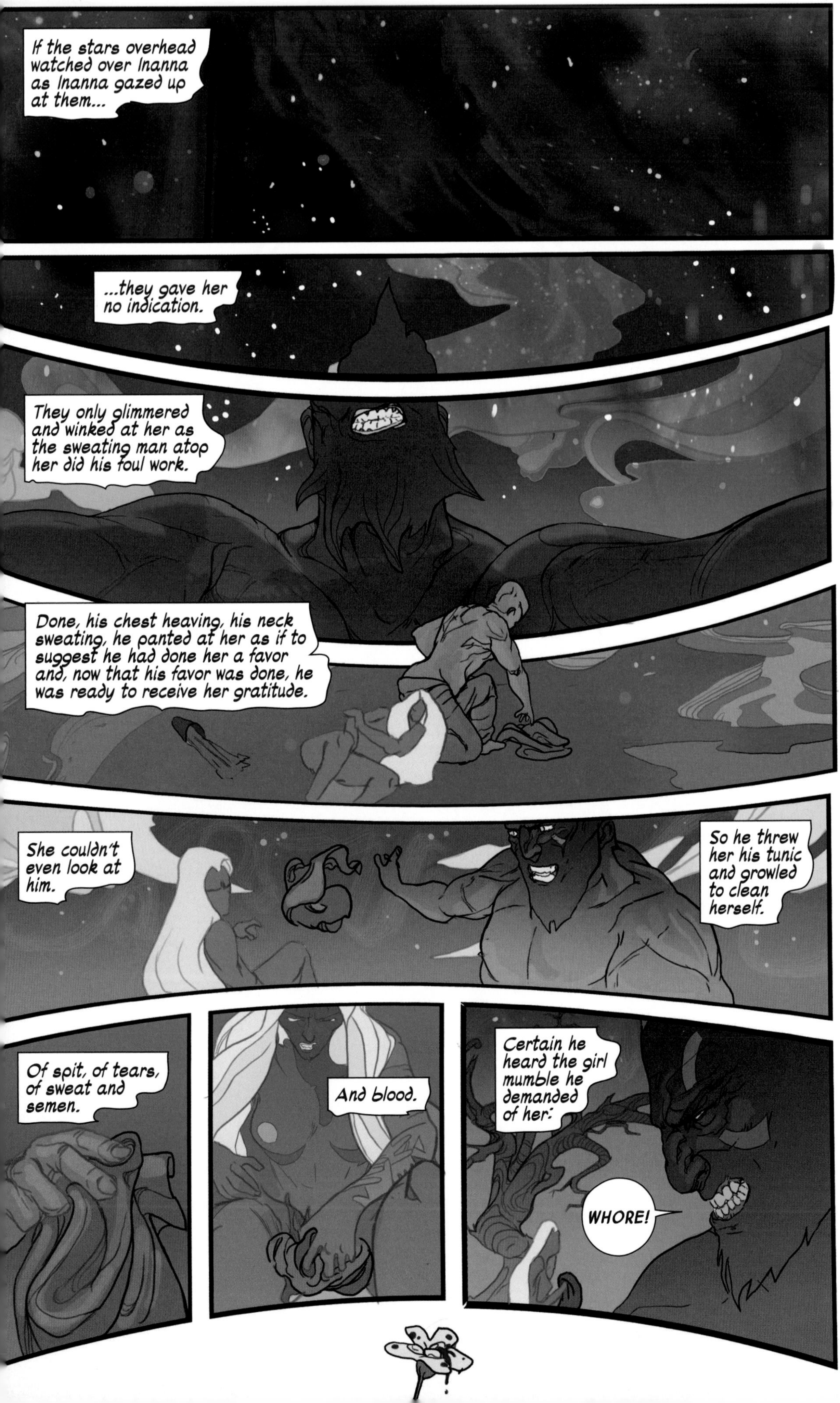
If the stars overhead watched over Inanna as Inanna gazed up at them...
...they gave her no indication.
They only glimmered and winked at her as the sweating man atop her did his foul work.
Done, his chest heaving, his neck sweating, he panted at her as if to suggest he had done her a favor and, now that his favor was done, he was ready to receive her gratitude.
She couldn't even look at him.
So he threw her his tunic and growled to clean herself.
Of spit, of tears, of sweat and semen.
And blood.
Certain he heard the girl mumble he demanded of her:
WHORE!

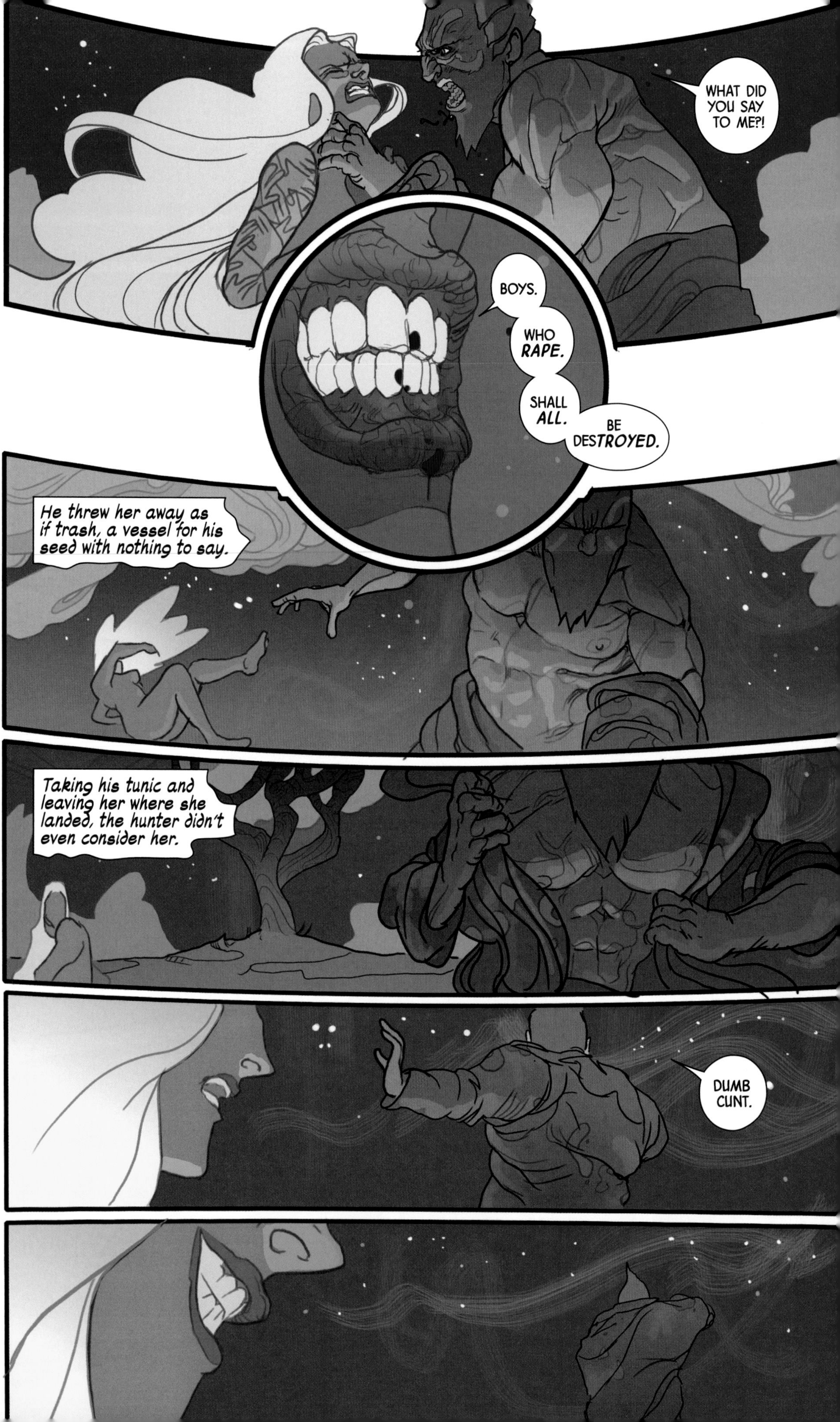
WHAT DID YOU SAY TO ME?!
BOYS.
WHO RAPE.
SHALL ALL.
BE DESTROYED.
He threw her away as if trash, a vessel for his seed with nothing to say.
Taking his tunic and leaving her where she landed, the hunter didn't even consider her.
DUMB CUNT.

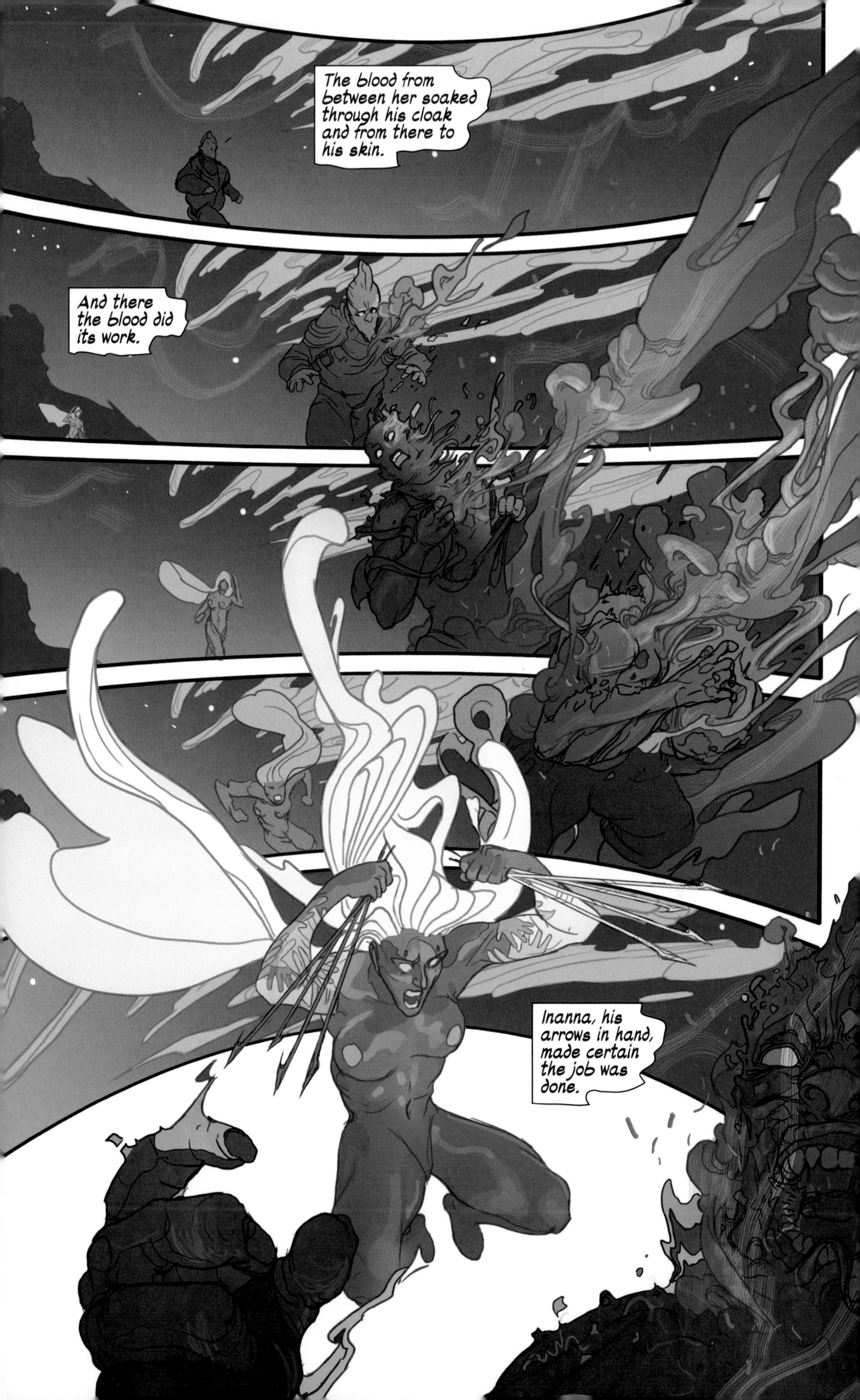
The blood from between her soaked through his cloak and from there to his skin.
And there the blood did its work.
Inanna, his arrows in hand, made certain the job was done.

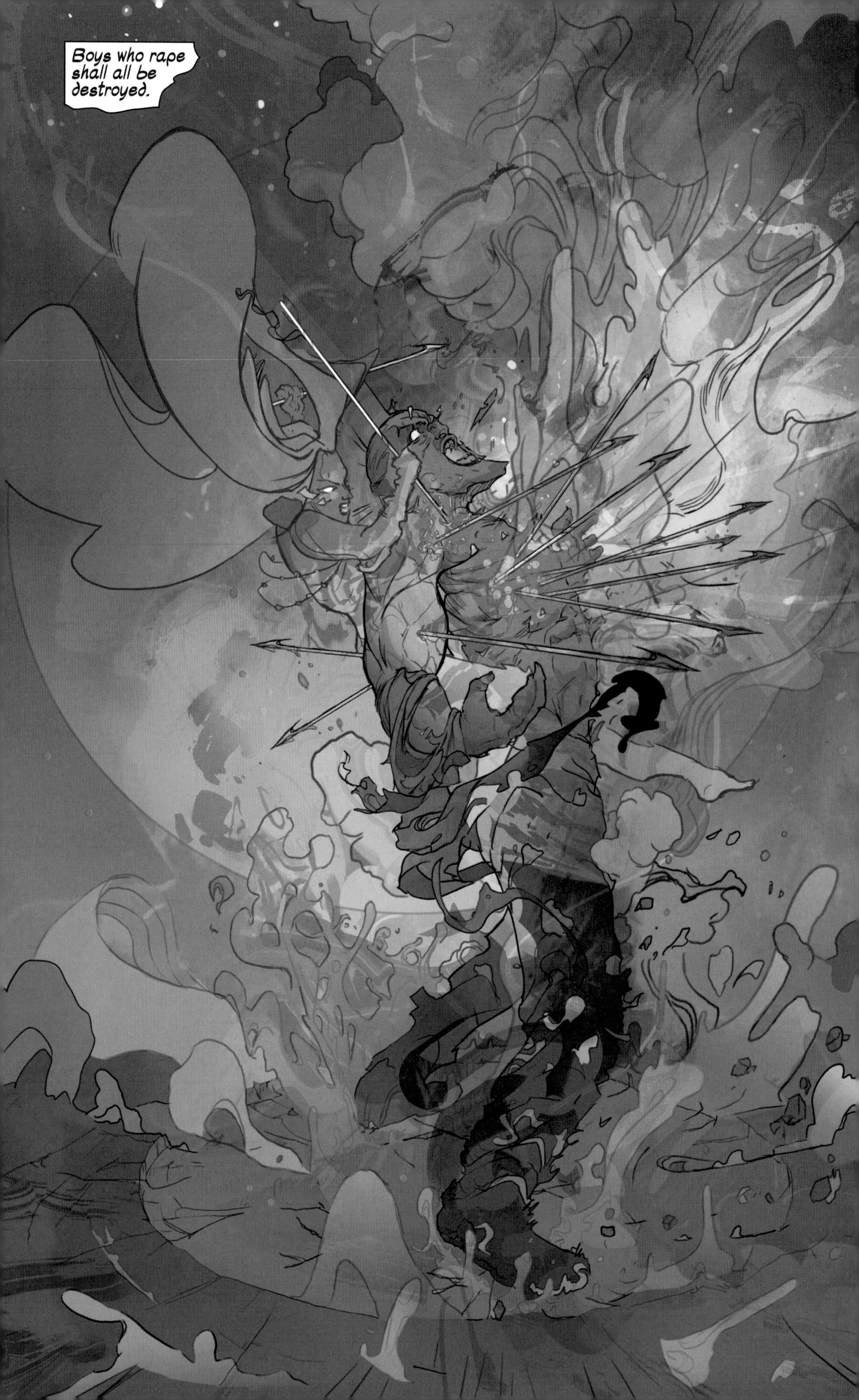
Boys who rape shall all be destroyed.

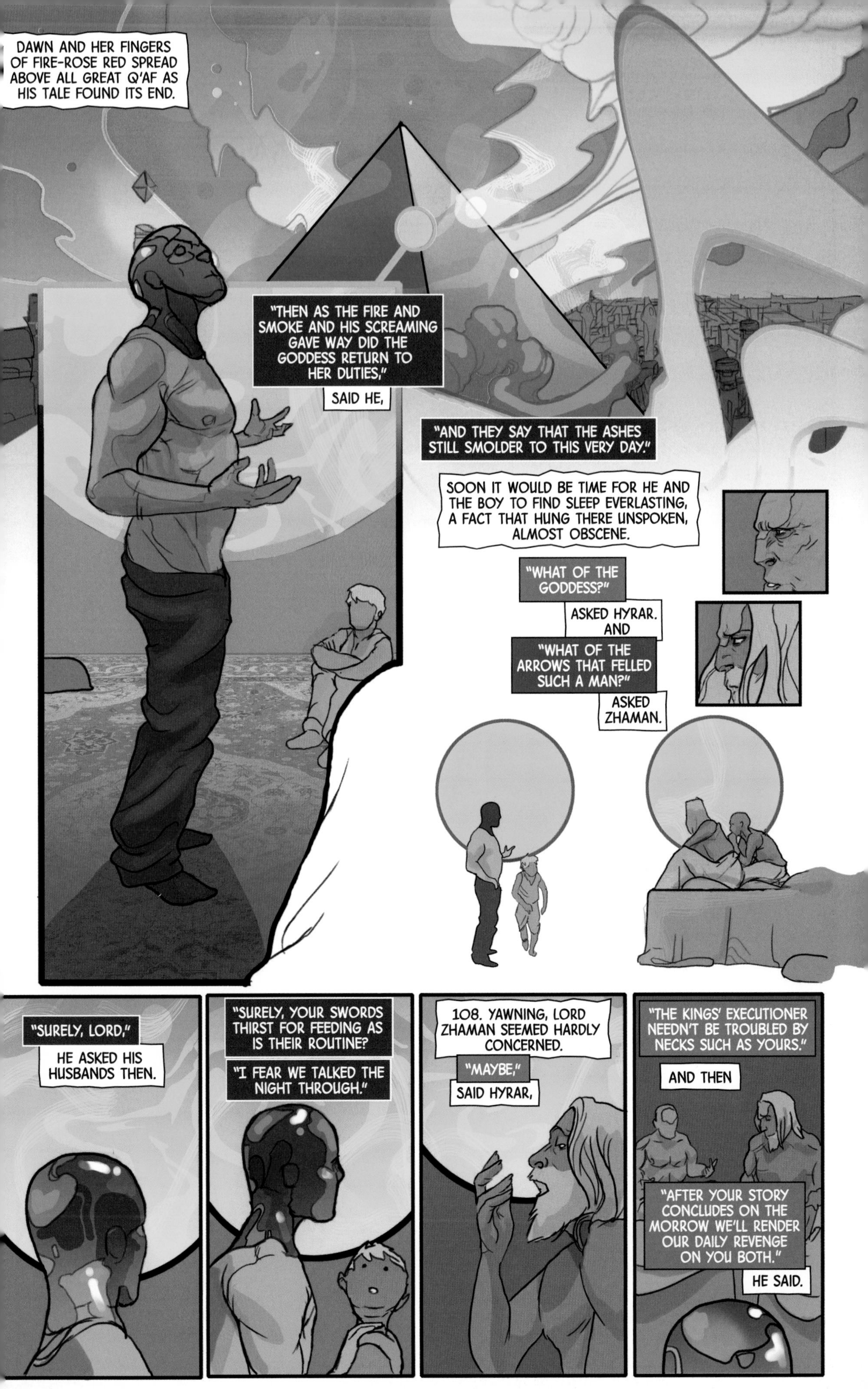
DAWN AND HER FINGERS OF FIRE-ROSE RED SPREAD ABOVE ALL GREAT Q'AF AS HIS TALE FOUND ITS END.
"THEN AS THE FIRE AND SMOKE AND HIS SCREAMING GAVE WAY DID THE GODDESS RETURN TO HER DUTIES,"
SAID HE,
"AND THEY SAY THAT THE ASHES STILL SMOLDER TO THIS VERY DAY."
SOON IT WOULD BE TIME FOR HE AND THE BOY TO FIND SLEEP EVERLASTING, A FACT THAT HUNG THERE UNSPOKEN, ALMOST OBSCENE.
"WHAT OF THE GODDESS?"
ASKED HYRAR. AND
"WHAT OF THE ARROWS THAT FELLED SUCH A MAN?"
ASKED ZHAMAN.
"SURELY, LORD,"
HE ASKED HIS HUSBANDS THEN.
"SURELY, YOUR SWORDS THIRST FOR FEEDING AS IS THEIR ROUTINE?
"I FEAR WE TALKED THE NIGHT THROUGH."
108. YAWNING, LORD ZHAMAN SEEMED HARDLY CONCERNED.
"MAYBE,"
SAID HYRAR,
"THE KINGS' EXECUTIONER NEEDN'T BE TROUBLED BY NECKS SUCH AS YOURS."
AND THEN
"AFTER YOUR STORY CONCLUDES ON THE MORROW WE'LL RENDER OUR DAILY REVENGE ON YOU BOTH."
HE SAID.

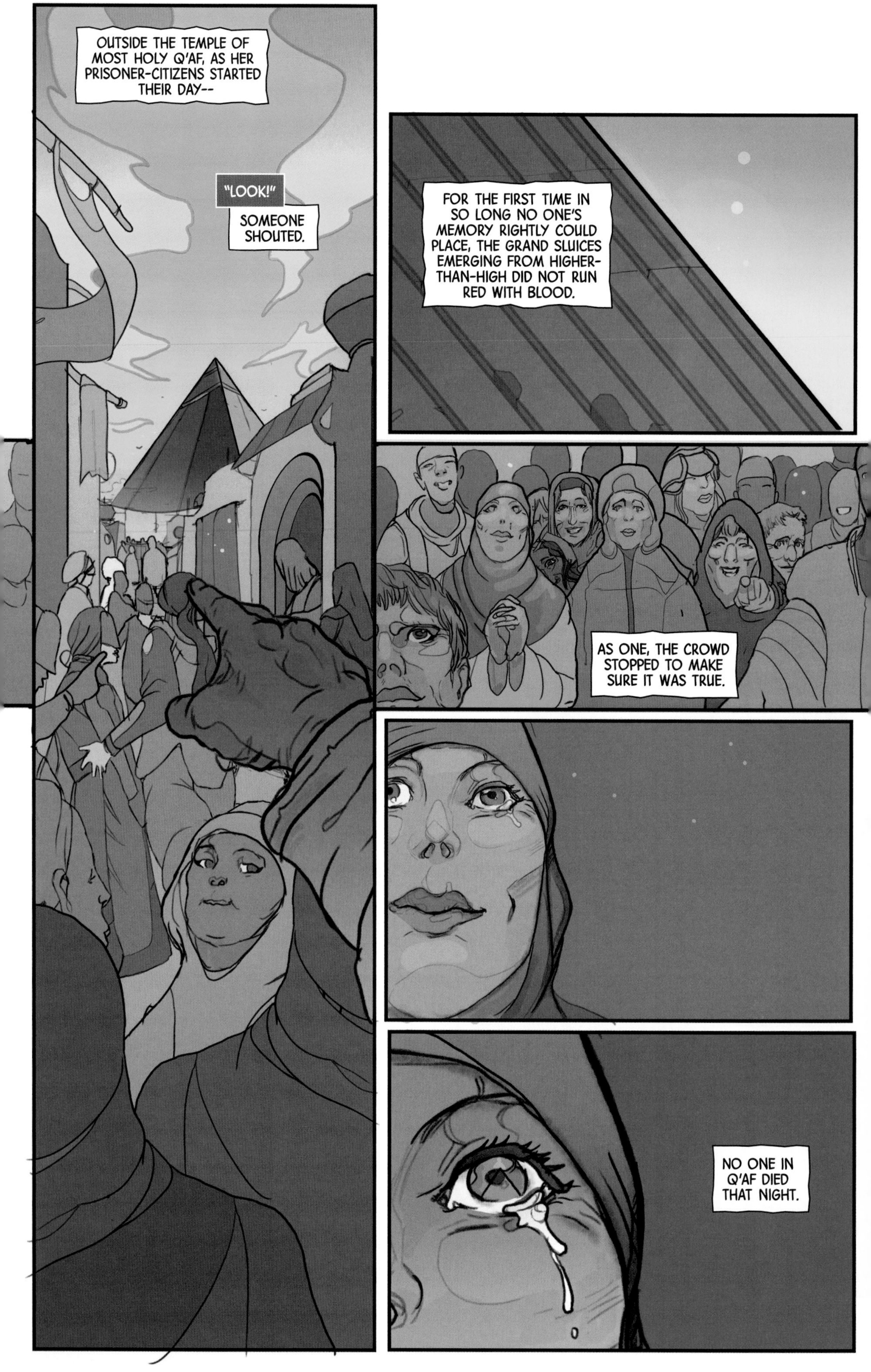
OUTSIDE THE TEMPLE OF MOST HOLY Q'AF, AS HER PRISONER-CITIZENS STARTED THEIR DAY--
"LOOK!"
SOMEONE SHOUTED.
FOR THE FIRST TIME IN SO LONG NO ONE'S MEMORY RIGHTLY COULD PLACE, THE GRAND SLUICES EMERGING FROM HIGHER-THAN-HIGH DID NOT RUN RED WITH BLOOD.
AS ONE, THE CROWD STOPPED TO MAKE SURE IT WAS TRUE.
NO ONE IN Q'AF DIED THAT NIGHT.

109. "ENE NOR I, YOUR MOST HUMBLE NARRATOR, DID DIE AFTER PROTEUS EXPELLED US FROM HEAVEN.

"THOUGH IN THE CENTURIES SINCE THEN I'VE WISHED IT WEREN'T SO.

"SO I'VE SPENT ALMOST ALL OF THE YEARS SINCE THAT DAY TELLING ANYONE ANYWHERE WHO MIGHT LISTEN MY TALE.

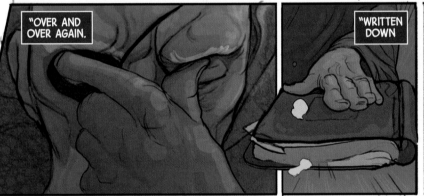

"OVER AND OVER AGAIN.

"WRITTEN DOWN

"OR SUNG OUT

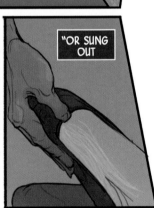

"OR WITH PICTURES AND WORDS."

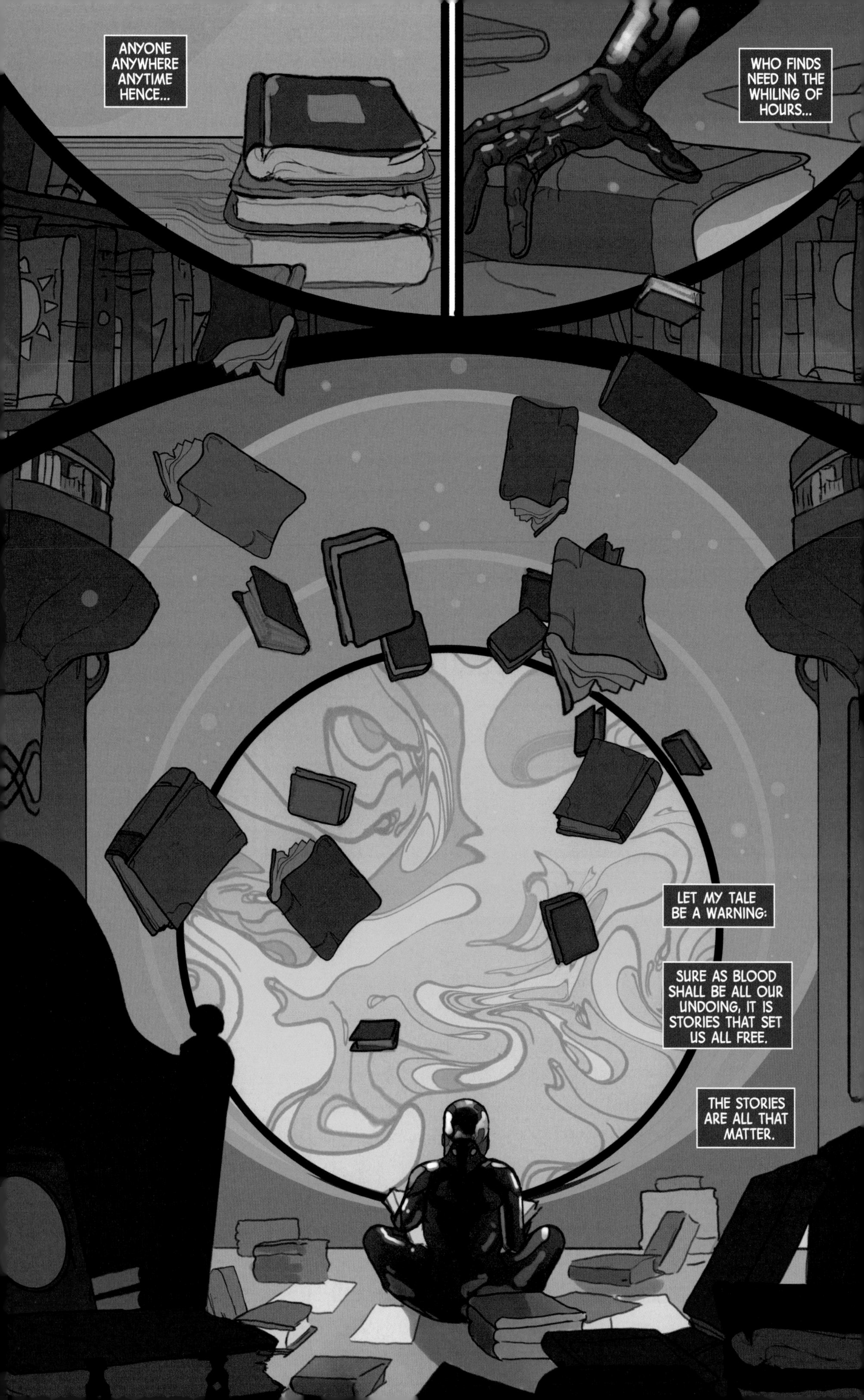
ANYONE ANYWHERE ANYTIME HENCE...
WHO FINDS NEED IN THE WHILING OF HOURS...
LET MY TALE BE A WARNING:
SURE AS BLOOD SHALL BE ALL OUR UNDOING, IT IS STORIES THAT SET US ALL FREE.
THE STORIES ARE ALL THAT MATTER.

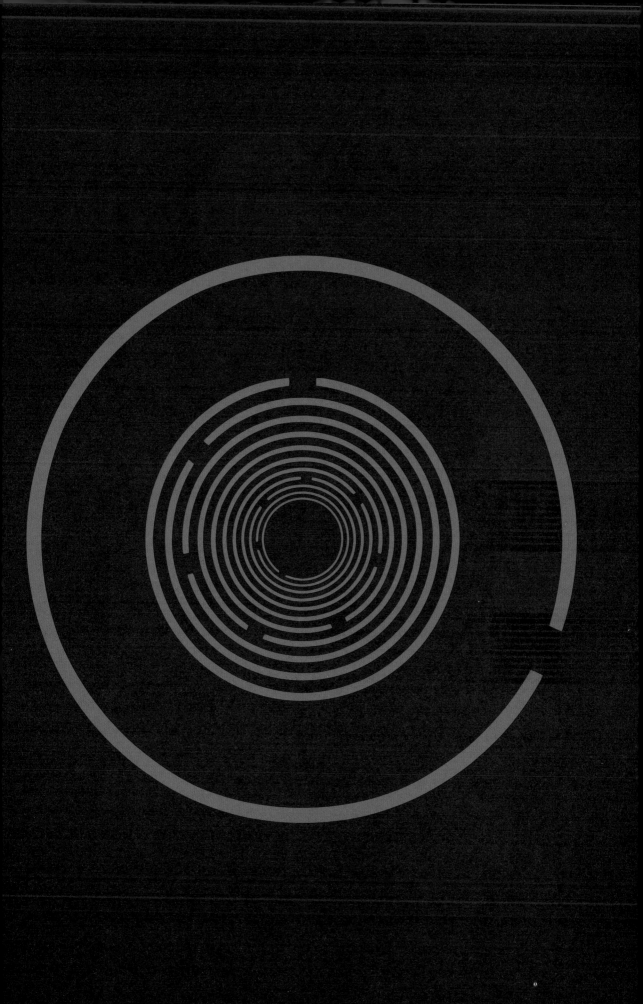

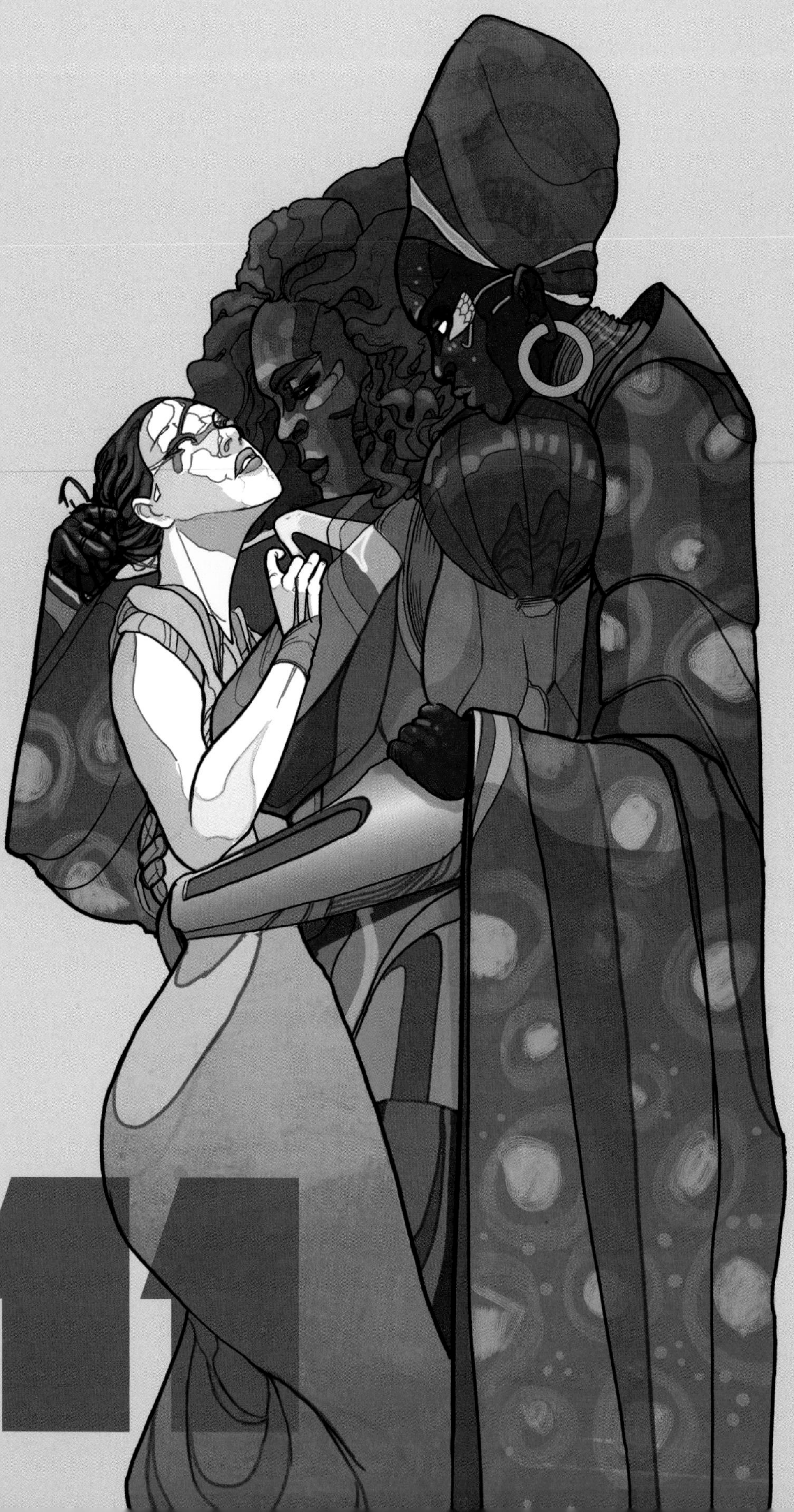

11

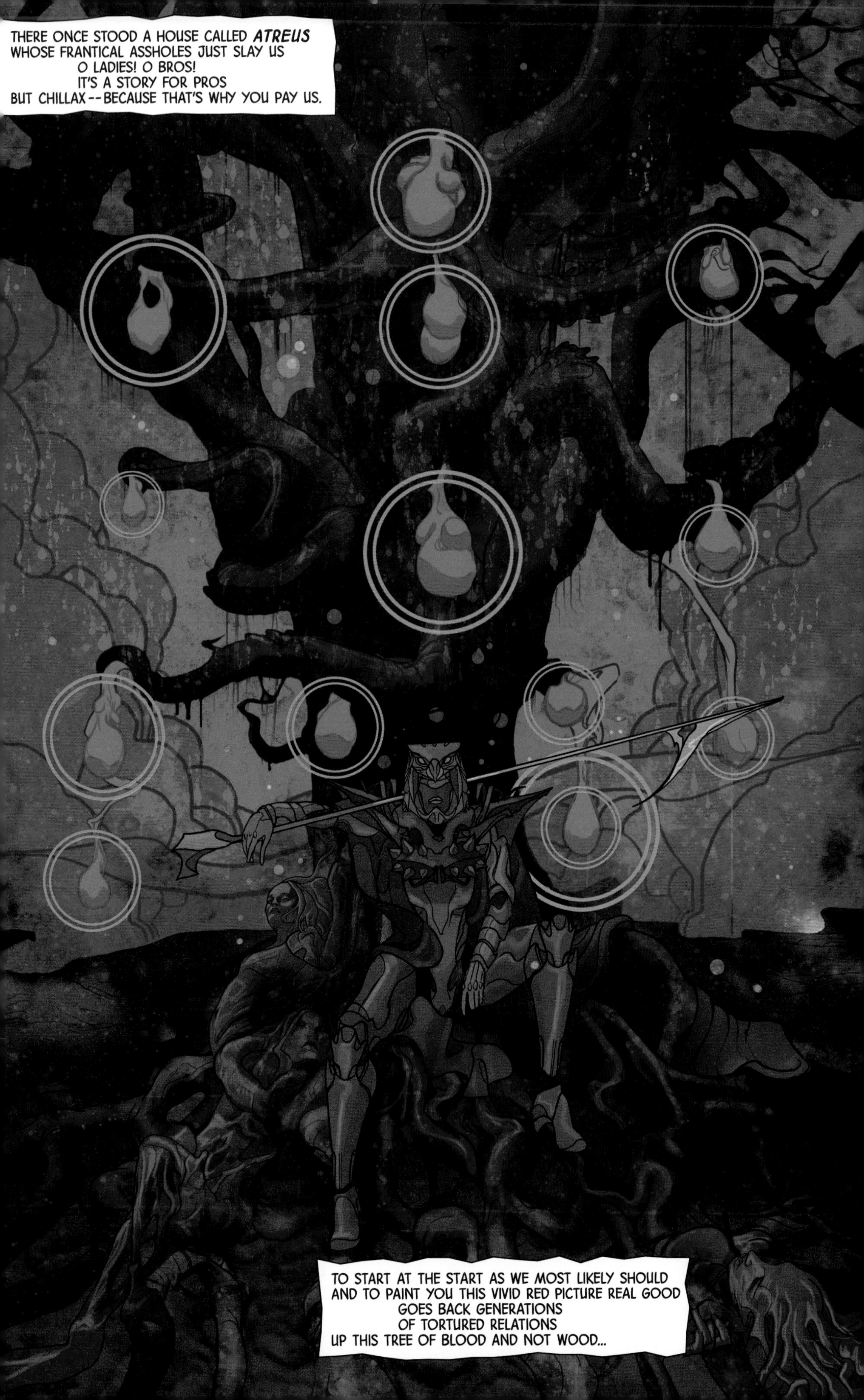
THERE ONCE STOOD A HOUSE CALLED ATREUS
WHOSE FRANTICAL ASSHOLES JUST SLAY US
O LADIES! O BROS!
IT'S A STORY FOR PROS
BUT CHILLAX--BECAUSE THAT'S WHY YOU PAY US.
TO START AT THE START AS WE MOST LIKELY SHOULD
AND TO PAINT YOU THIS VIVID RED PICTURE REAL GOOD
GOES BACK GENERATIONS
OF TORTURED RELATIONS
UP THIS TREE OF BLOOD AND NOT WOOD...

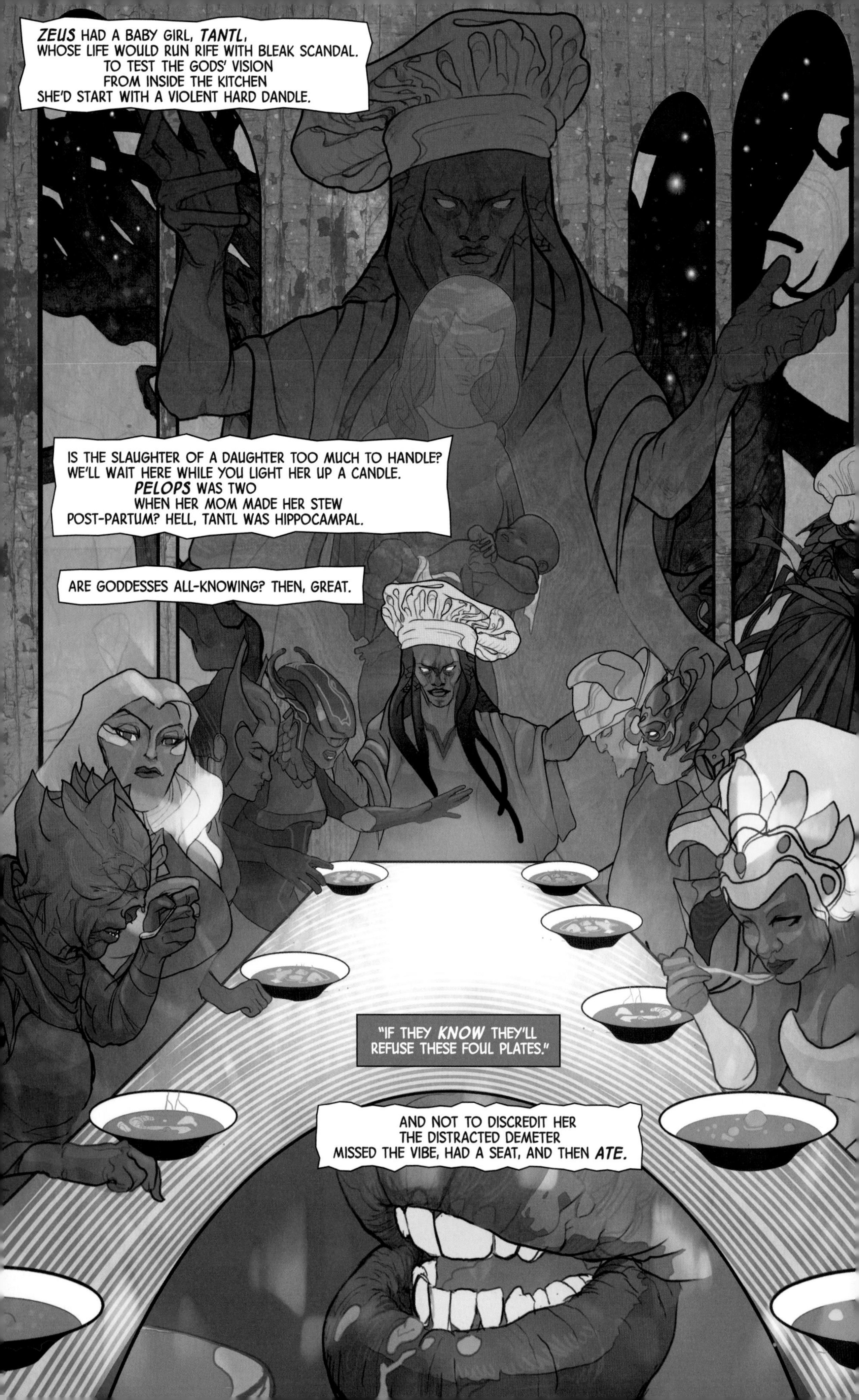
ZEUS HAD A BABY GIRL, TANTL,
WHOSE LIFE WOULD RUN RIFE WITH BLEAK SCANDAL.
TO TEST THE GODS' VISION
FROM INSIDE THE KITCHEN
SHE'D START WITH A VIOLENT HARD DANDLE.
IS THE SLAUGHTER OF A DAUGHTER TOO MUCH TO HANDLE?
WE'LL WAIT HERE WHILE YOU LIGHT HER UP A CANDLE.
PELOPS WAS TWO
WHEN HER MOM MADE HER STEW
POST-PARTUM? HELL, TANTL WAS HIPPOCAMPAL.
ARE GODDESSES ALL-KNOWING? THEN, GREAT.
"IF THEY KNOW THEY'LL REFUSE THESE FOUL PLATES."
AND NOT TO DISCREDIT HER
THE DISTRACTED DEMETER
MISSED THE VIBE, HAD A SEAT, AND THEN ATE.

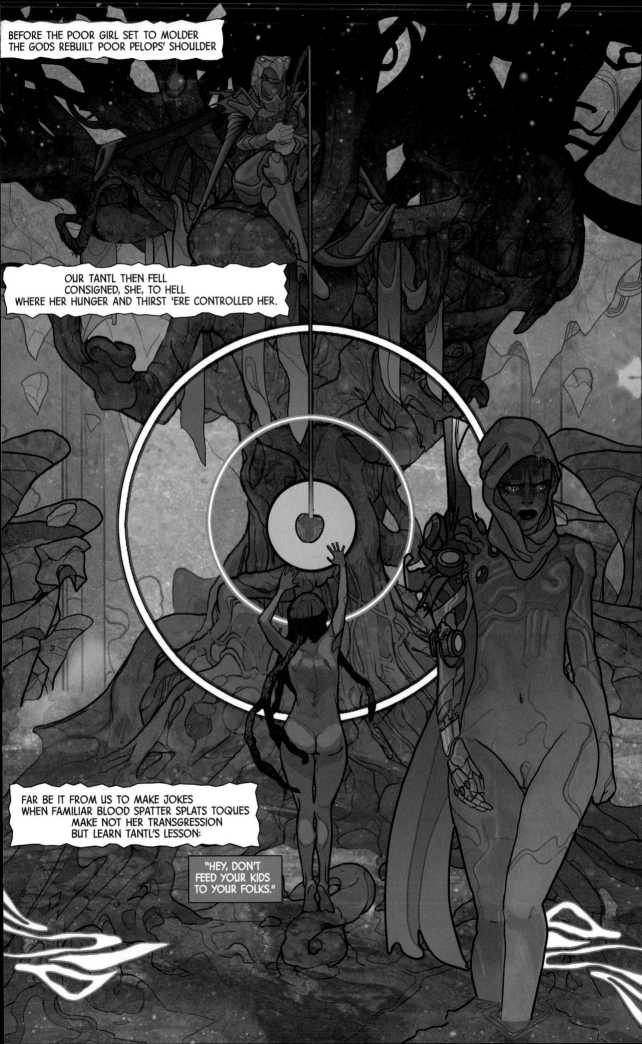

BEFORE THE POOR GIRL SET TO MOLDER
THE GODS REBUILT POOR PELOPS' SHOULDER

OUR TANTL THEN FELL
CONSIGNED, SHE, TO HELL
WHERE HER HUNGER AND THIRST 'ERE CONTROLLED HER.

FAR BE IT FROM US TO MAKE JOKES
WHEN FAMILIAR BLOOD SPATTER SPLATS TOQUES
MAKE NOT HER TRANSGRESSION
BUT LEARN TANTL'S LESSON:

"HEY, DON'T
FEED YOUR KIDS
TO YOUR FOLKS."

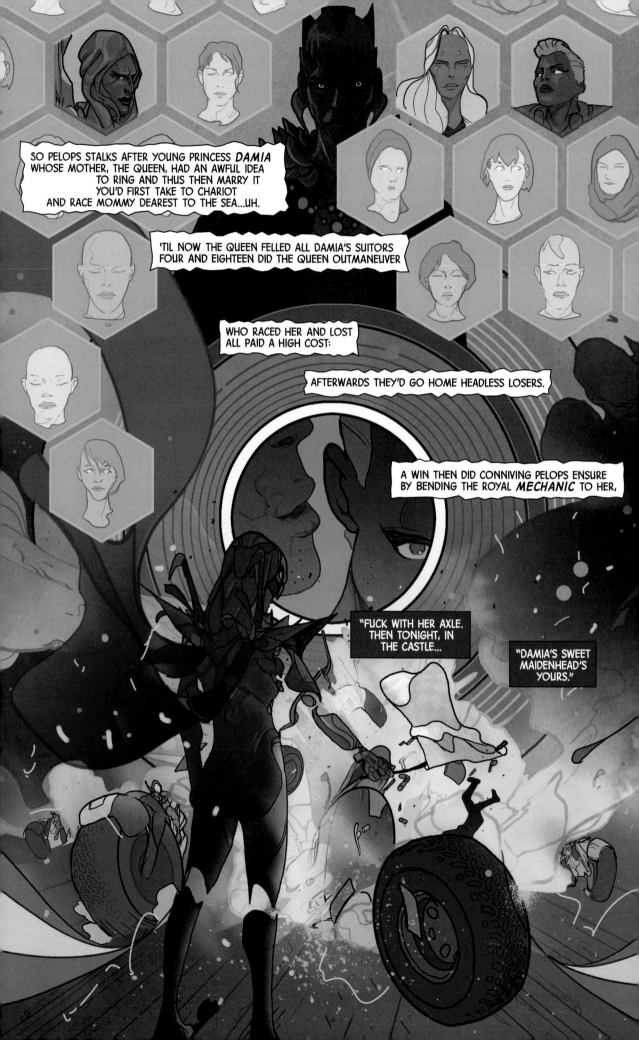

SO PELOPS STALKS AFTER YOUNG PRINCESS *DAMIA* WHOSE MOTHER, THE QUEEN, HAD AN AWFUL IDEA TO RING AND THUS THEN MARRY IT YOU'D FIRST TAKE TO CHARIOT AND RACE MOMMY DEAREST TO THE SEA...UH.

'TIL NOW THE QUEEN FELLED ALL DAMIA'S SUITORS FOUR AND EIGHTEEN DID THE QUEEN OUTMANEUVER

WHO RACED HER AND LOST ALL PAID A HIGH COST:

AFTERWARDS THEY'D GO HOME HEADLESS LOSERS.

A WIN THEN DID CONNIVING PELOPS ENSURE BY BENDING THE ROYAL *MECHANIC* TO HER,

"FUCK WITH HER AXLE. THEN TONIGHT, IN THE CASTLE...

"DAMIA'S SWEET MAIDENHEAD'S YOURS."

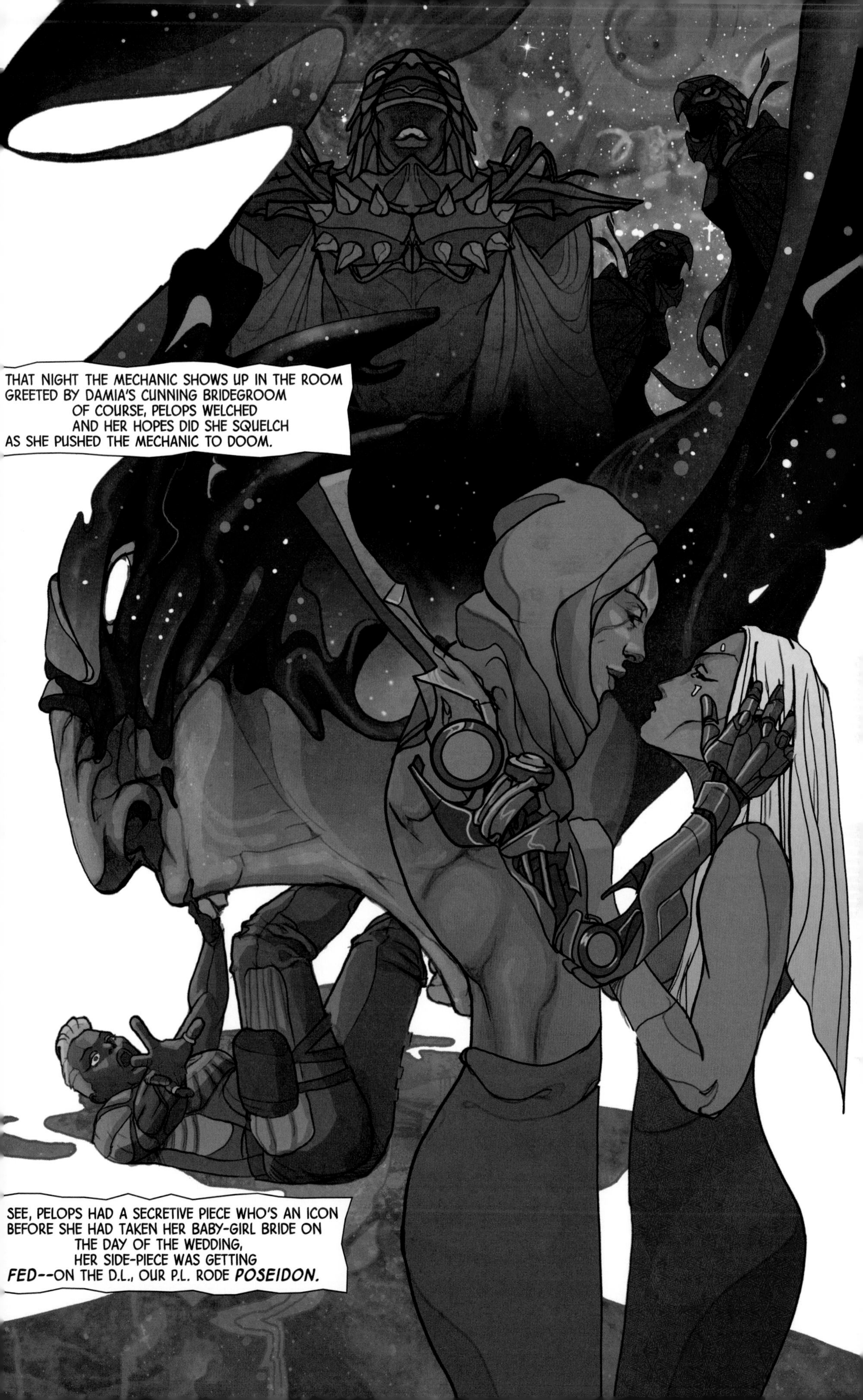
THAT NIGHT THE MECHANIC SHOWS UP IN THE ROOM
GREETED BY DAMIA'S CUNNING BRIDEGROOM
OF COURSE, PELOPS WELCHED
AND HER HOPES DID SHE SQUELCH
AS SHE PUSHED THE MECHANIC TO DOOM.
SEE, PELOPS HAD A SECRETIVE PIECE WHO'S AN ICON
BEFORE SHE HAD TAKEN HER BABY-GIRL BRIDE ON
THE DAY OF THE WEDDING,
HER SIDE-PIECE WAS GETTING
FED--ON THE D.L., OUR P.L. RODE POSEIDON.

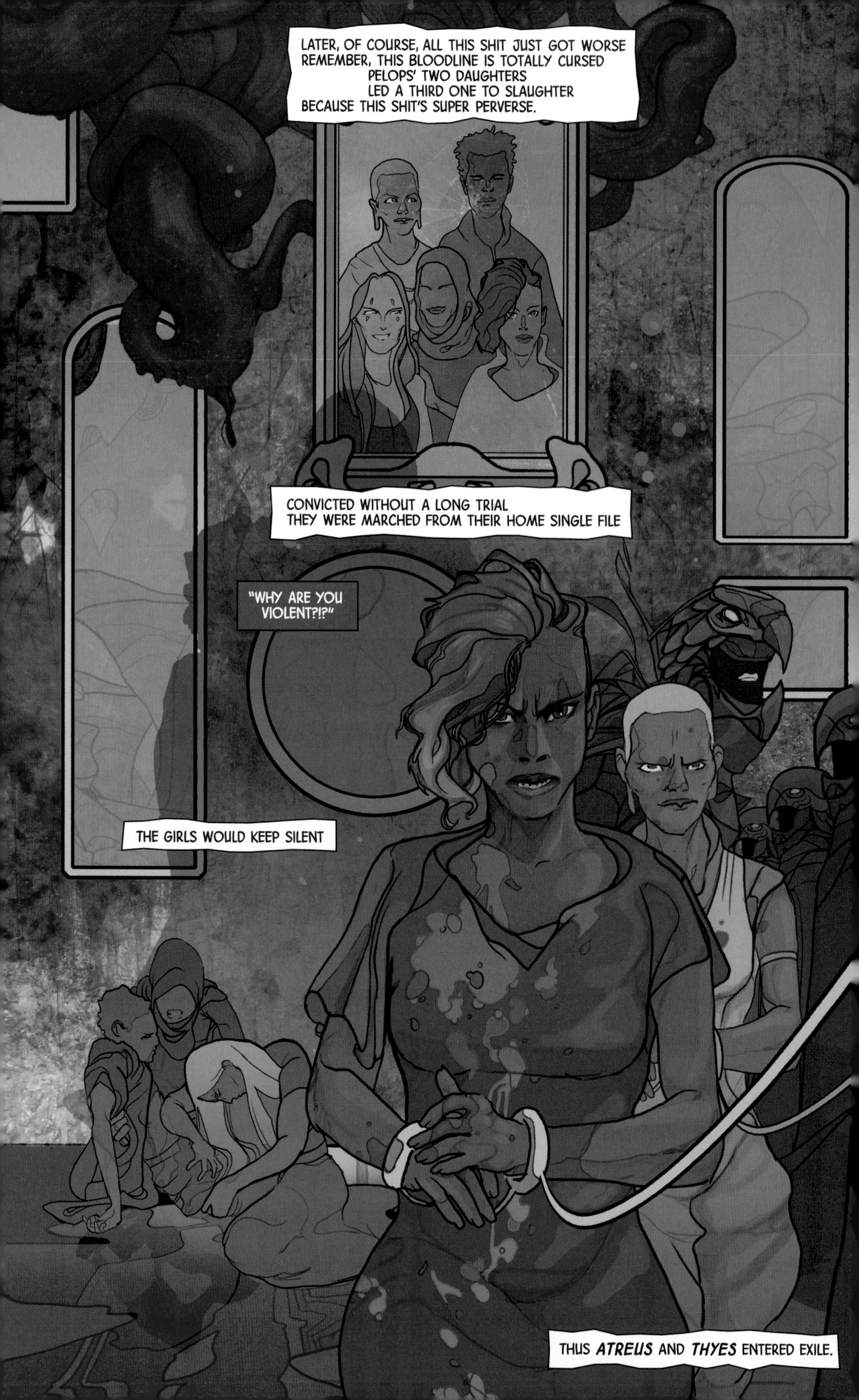
LATER, OF COURSE, ALL THIS SHIT JUST GOT WORSE
REMEMBER, THIS BLOODLINE IS TOTALLY CURSED
PELOPS' TWO DAUGHTERS
LED A THIRD ONE TO SLAUGHTER
BECAUSE THIS SHIT'S SUPER PERVERSE.
CONVICTED WITHOUT A LONG TRIAL
THEY WERE MARCHED FROM THEIR HOME SINGLE FILE
"WHY ARE YOU VIOLENT?!?"
THE GIRLS WOULD KEEP SILENT
THUS *ATREUS* AND *THYES* ENTERED EXILE.

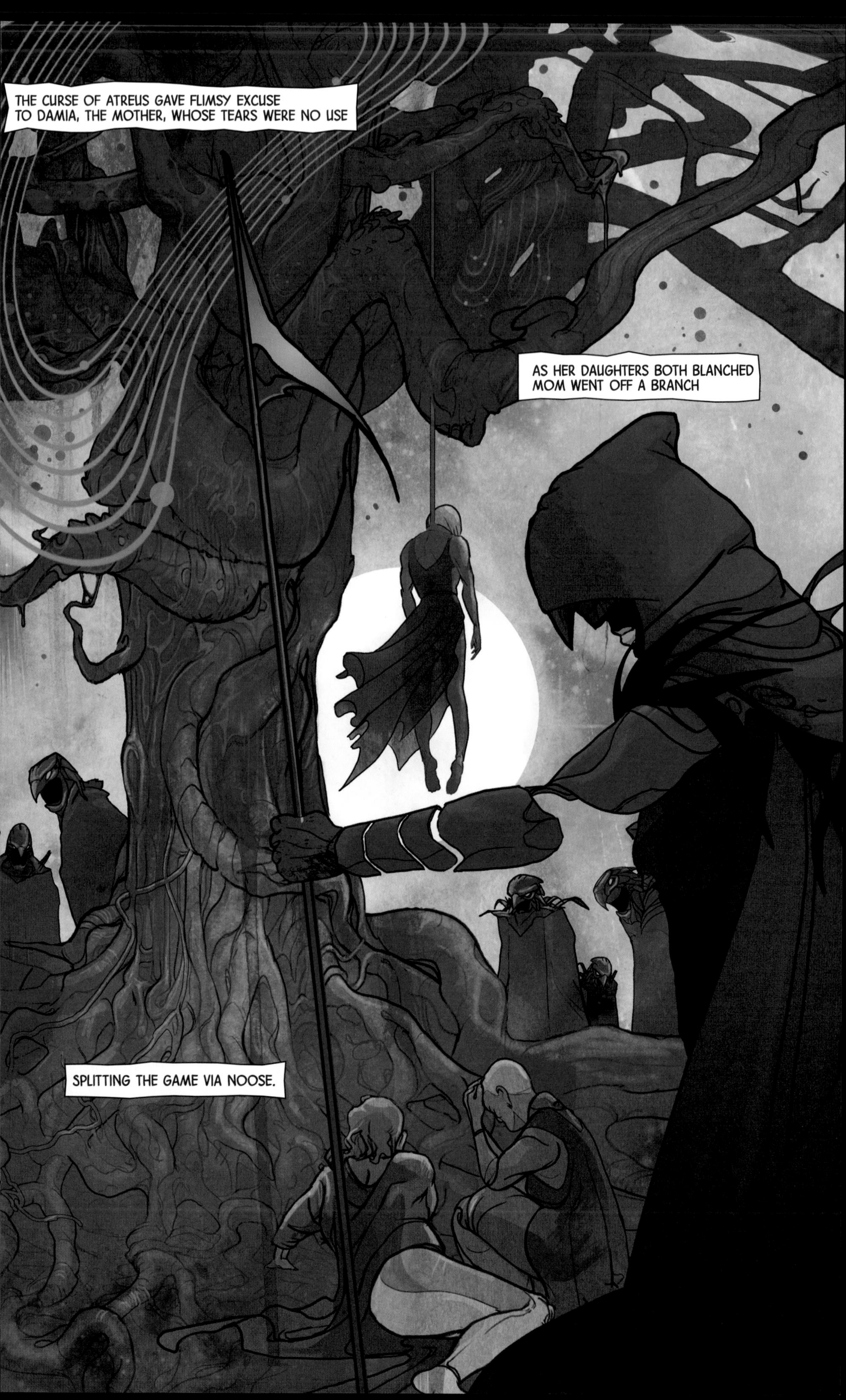
THE CURSE OF ATREUS GAVE FLIMSY EXCUSE
TO DAMIA, THE MOTHER, WHOSE TEARS WERE NO USE
AS HER DAUGHTERS BOTH BLANCHED
MOM WENT OFF A BRANCH
SPLITTING THE GAME VIA NOOSE.

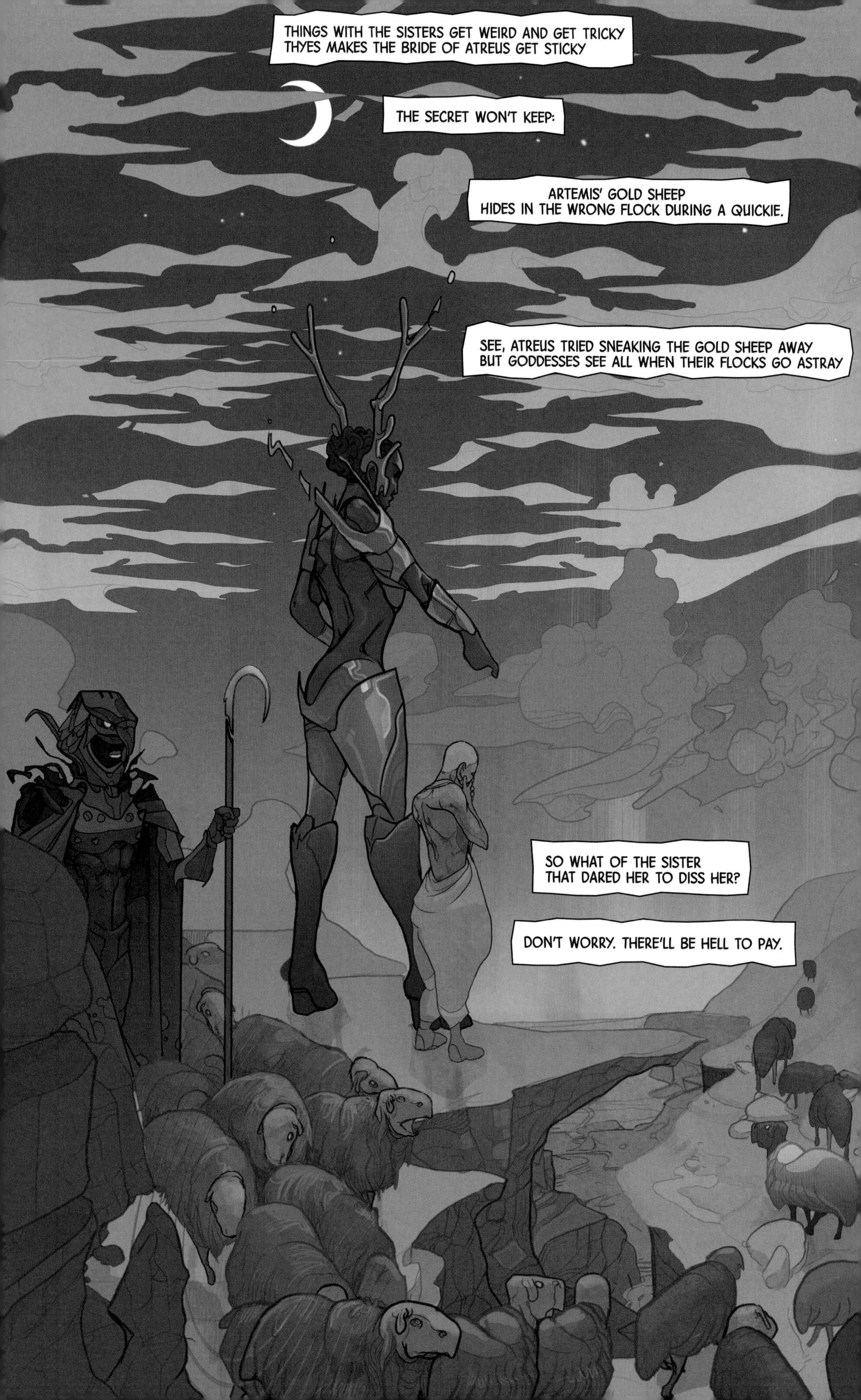
THINGS WITH THE SISTERS GET WEIRD AND GET TRICKY
THYES MAKES THE BRIDE OF ATREUS GET STICKY
THE SECRET WON'T KEEP:
ARTEMIS' GOLD SHEEP
HIDES IN THE WRONG FLOCK DURING A QUICKIE.
SEE, ATREUS TRIED SNEAKING THE GOLD SHEEP AWAY
BUT GODDESSES SEE ALL WHEN THEIR FLOCKS GO ASTRAY
SO WHAT OF THE SISTER
THAT DARED HER TO DISS HER?
DON'T WORRY. THERE'LL BE HELL TO PAY.

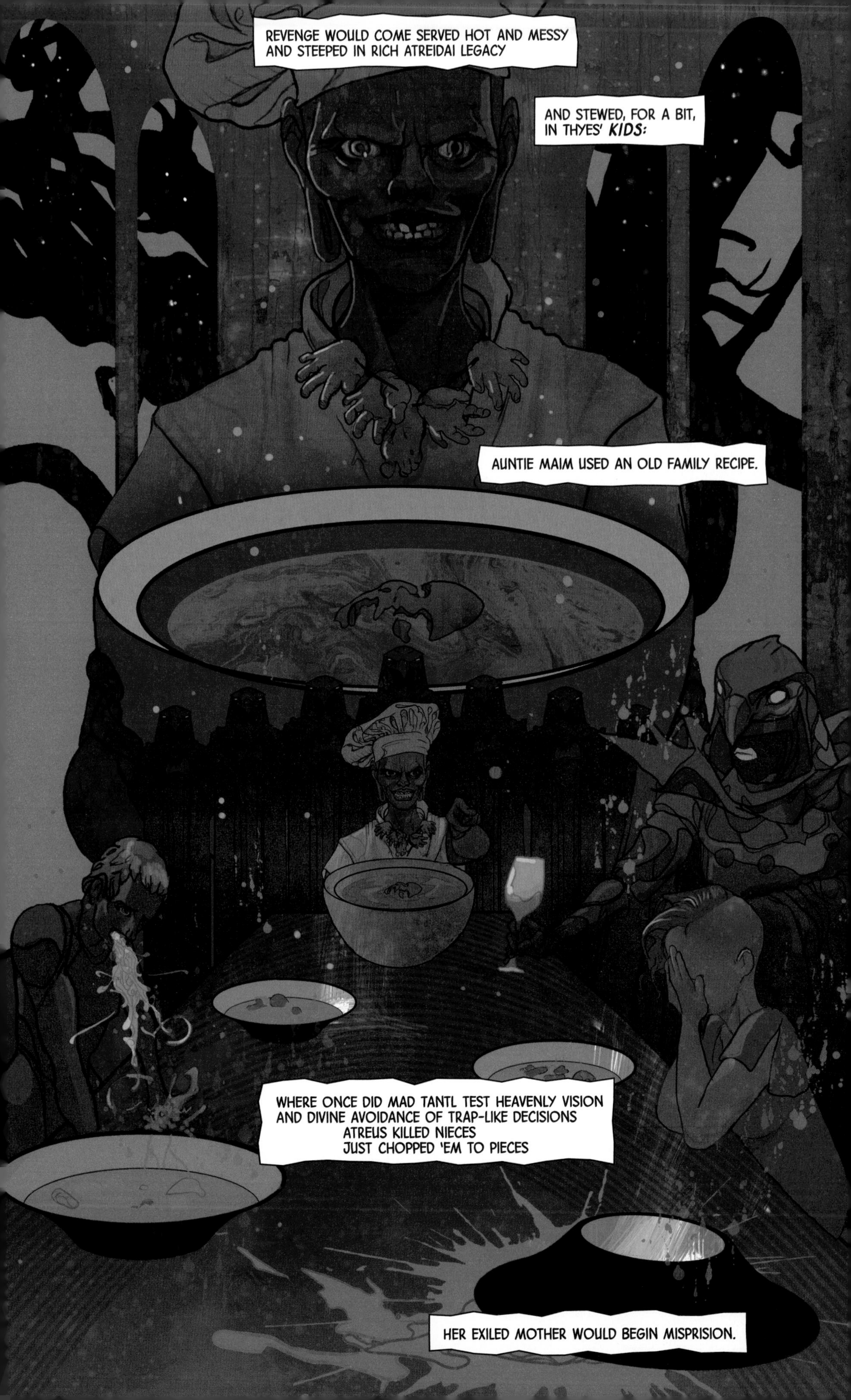
REVENGE WOULD COME SERVED HOT AND MESSY
AND STEEPED IN RICH ATREIDAI LEGACY
AND STEWED, FOR A BIT,
IN THYES' ***KIDS:***
AUNTIE MAIM USED AN OLD FAMILY RECIPE.
WHERE ONCE DID MAD TANTL TEST HEAVENLY VISION
AND DIVINE AVOIDANCE OF TRAP-LIKE DECISIONS
ATREUS KILLED NIECES
JUST CHOPPED 'EM TO PIECES
HER EXILED MOTHER WOULD BEGIN MISPRISION.

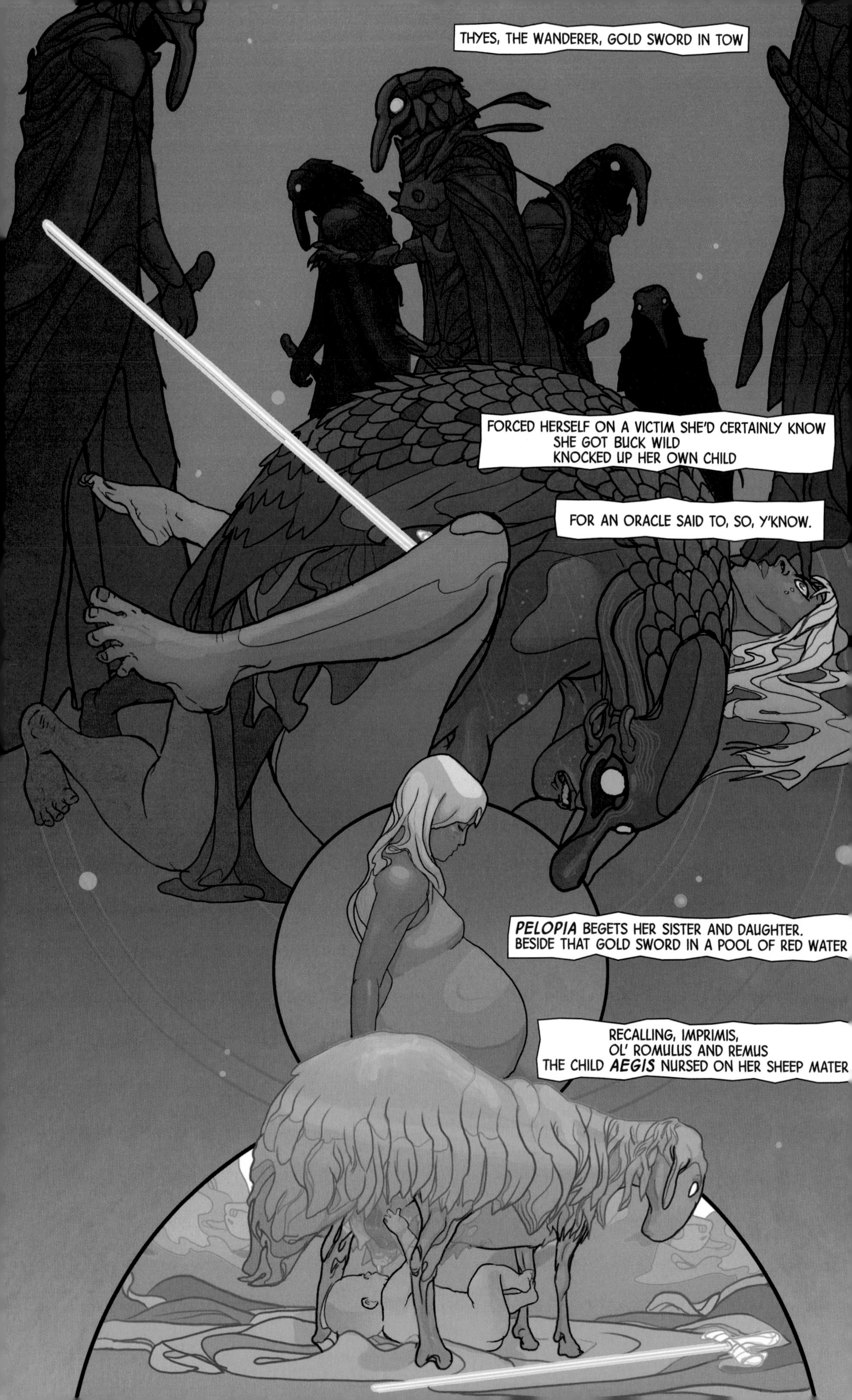
THYES, THE WANDERER, GOLD SWORD IN TOW
FORCED HERSELF ON A VICTIM SHE'D CERTAINLY KNOW
SHE GOT BUCK WILD
KNOCKED UP HER OWN CHILD
FOR AN ORACLE SAID TO, SO, Y'KNOW.
PELOPIA BEGETS HER SISTER AND DAUGHTER.
BESIDE THAT GOLD SWORD IN A POOL OF RED WATER
RECALLING, IMPRIMIS,
OL' ROMULUS AND REMUS
THE CHILD AEGIS NURSED ON HER SHEEP MATER

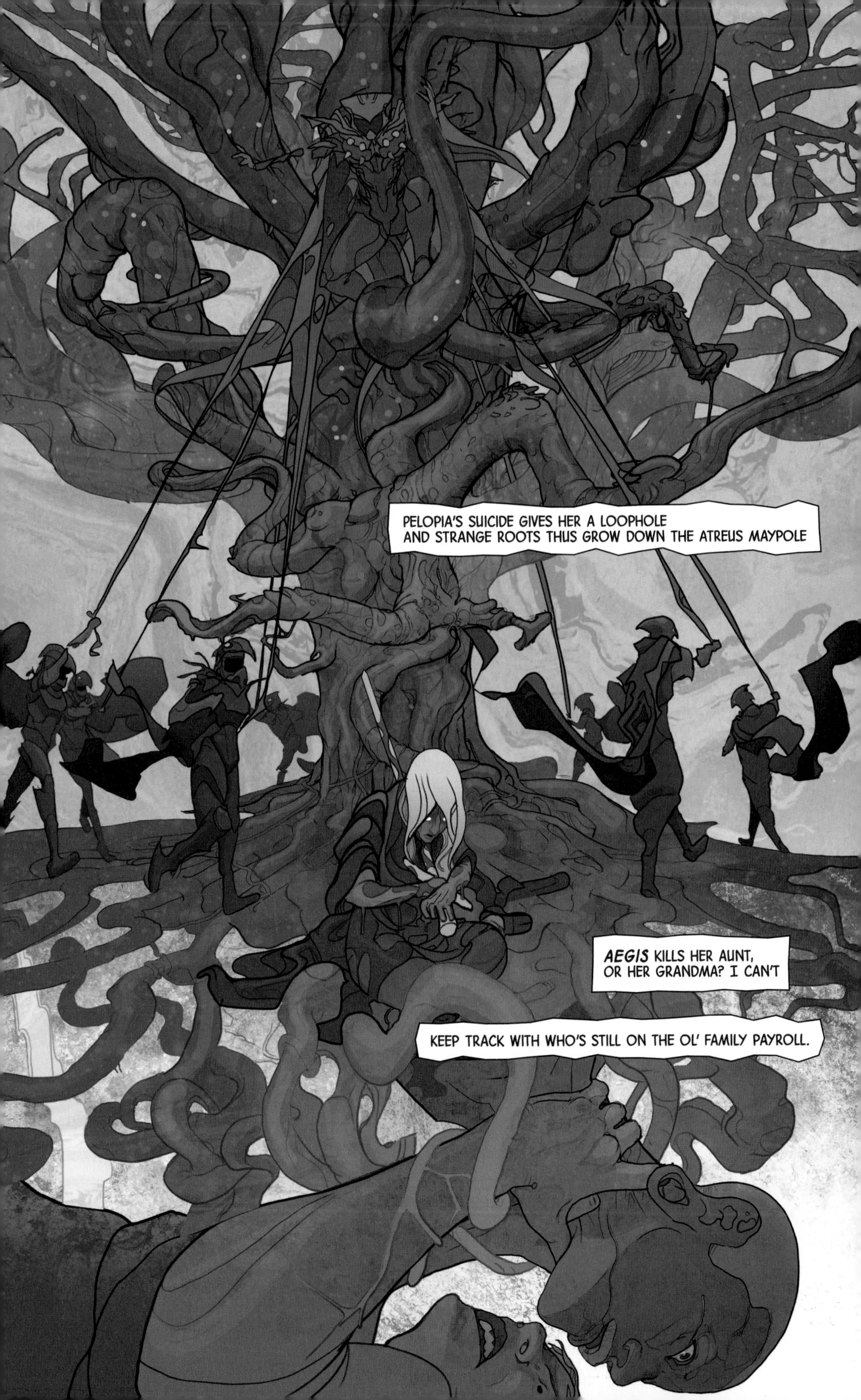
PELOPIA'S SUICIDE GIVES HER A LOOPHOLE
AND STRANGE ROOTS THUS GROW DOWN THE ATREUS MAYPOLE
AEGIS KILLS HER AUNT, OR HER GRANDMA? I CAN'T
KEEP TRACK WITH WHO'S STILL ON THE OL' FAMILY PAYROLL.

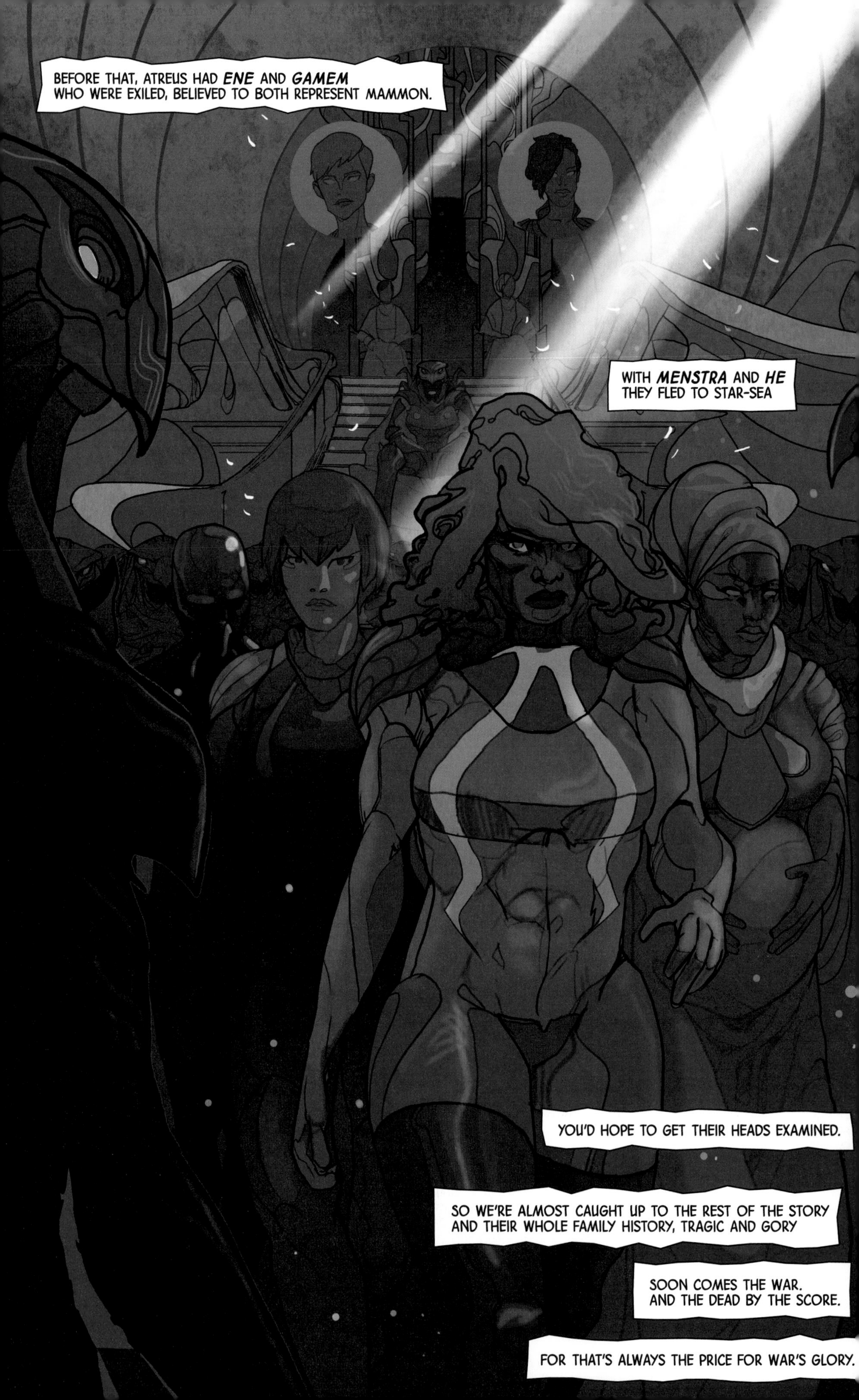
BEFORE THAT, ATREUS HAD ENE AND GAMEM
WHO WERE EXILED, BELIEVED TO BOTH REPRESENT MAMMON.
WITH MENSTRA AND HE
THEY FLED TO STAR-SEA
YOU'D HOPE TO GET THEIR HEADS EXAMINED.
SO WE'RE ALMOST CAUGHT UP TO THE REST OF THE STORY
AND THEIR WHOLE FAMILY HISTORY, TRAGIC AND GORY
SOON COMES THE WAR.
AND THE DEAD BY THE SCORE.
FOR THAT'S ALWAYS THE PRICE FOR WAR'S GLORY.

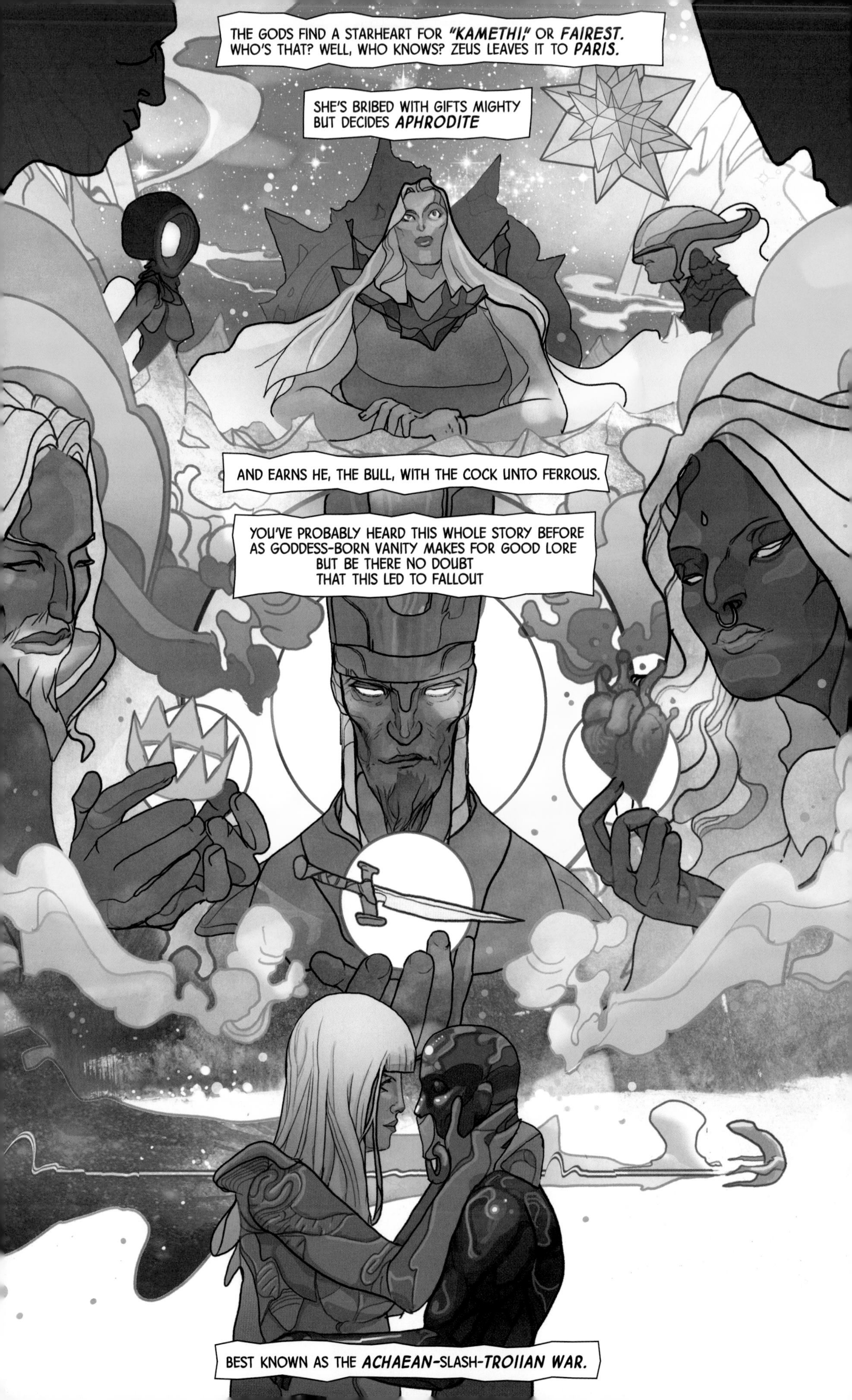
THE GODS FIND A STARHEART FOR "KAMETHI," OR FAIREST. WHO'S THAT? WELL, WHO KNOWS? ZEUS LEAVES IT TO PARIS.
SHE'S BRIBED WITH GIFTS MIGHTY BUT DECIDES APHRODITE
AND EARNS HE, THE BULL, WITH THE COCK UNTO FERROUS.
YOU'VE PROBABLY HEARD THIS WHOLE STORY BEFORE AS GODDESS-BORN VANITY MAKES FOR GOOD LORE BUT BE THERE NO DOUBT THAT THIS LED TO FALLOUT
BEST KNOWN AS THE ACHAEAN-SLASH-TROIIAN WAR.

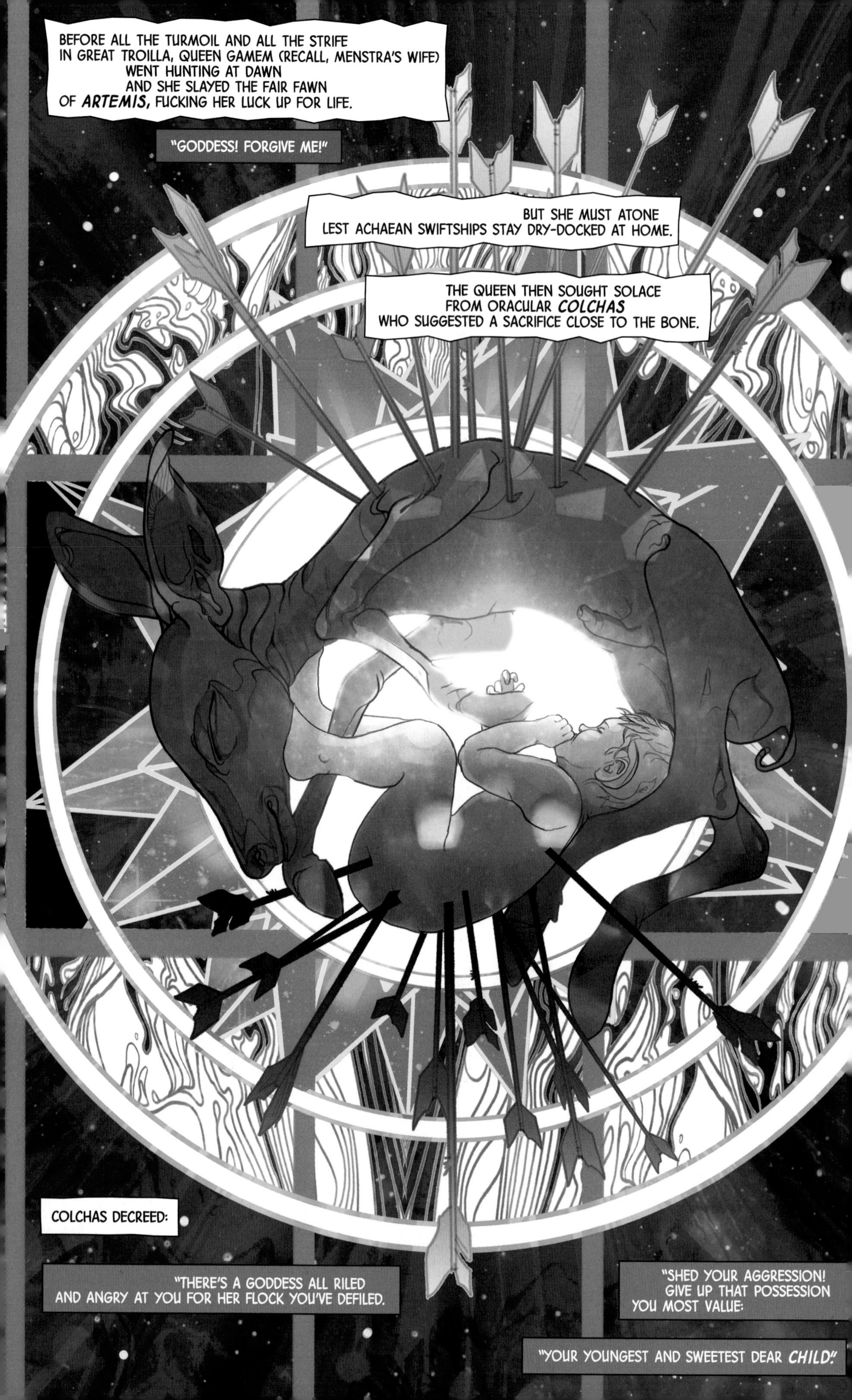
BEFORE ALL THE TURMOIL AND ALL THE STRIFE
IN GREAT TROILLA, QUEEN GAMEM (RECALL, MENSTRA'S WIFE)
WENT HUNTING AT DAWN
AND SHE SLAYED THE FAIR FAWN
OF ARTEMIS, FUCKING HER LUCK UP FOR LIFE.
"GODDESS! FORGIVE ME!"
BUT SHE MUST ATONE
LEST ACHAEAN SWIFTSHIPS STAY DRY-DOCKED AT HOME.
THE QUEEN THEN SOUGHT SOLACE
FROM ORACULAR COLCHAS
WHO SUGGESTED A SACRIFICE CLOSE TO THE BONE.
COLCHAS DECREED:
"THERE'S A GODDESS ALL RILED
AND ANGRY AT YOU FOR HER FLOCK YOU'VE DEFILED.
"SHED YOUR AGGRESSION!
GIVE UP THAT POSSESSION
YOU MOST VALUE:
"YOUR YOUNGEST AND SWEETEST DEAR CHILD."

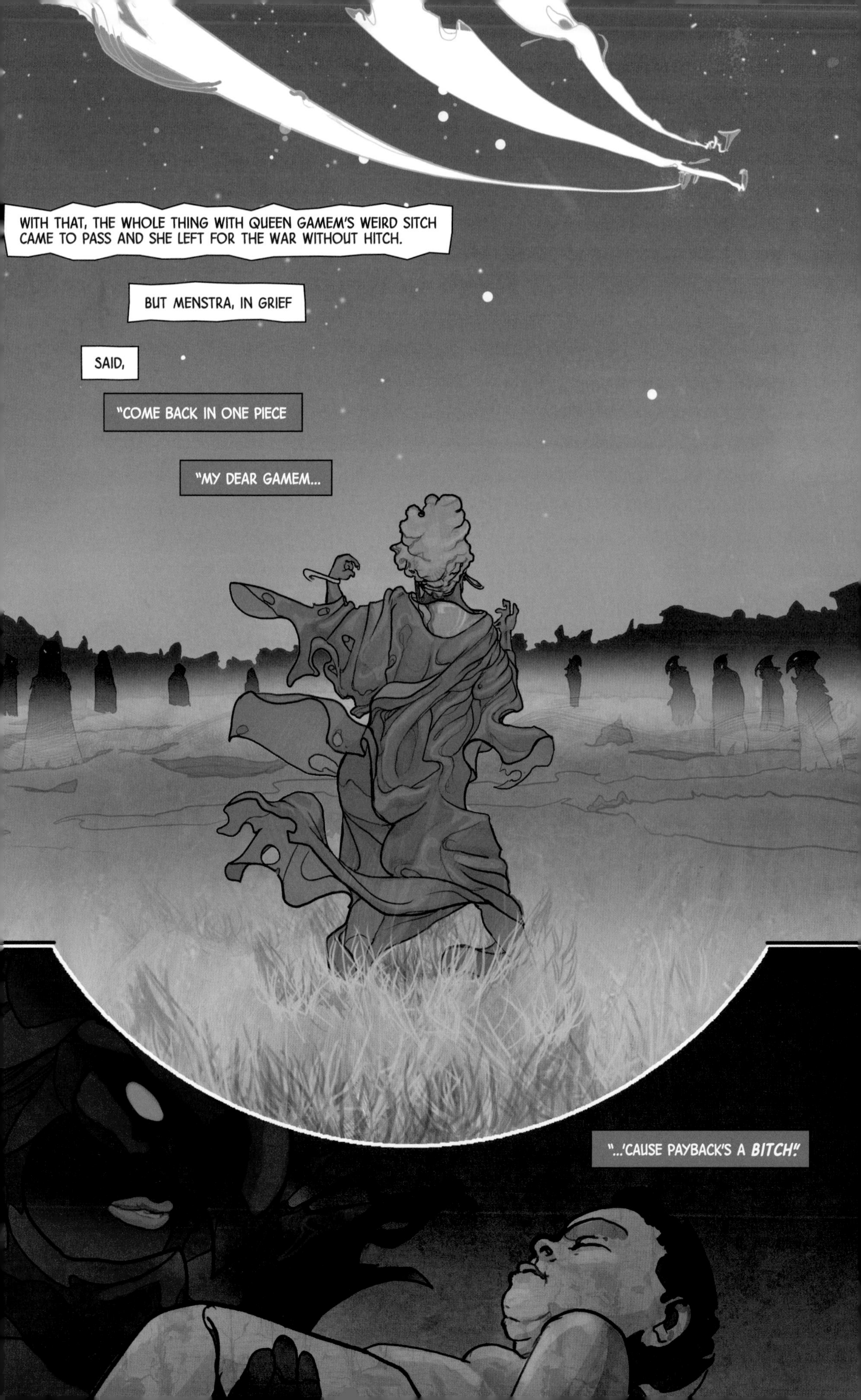
WITH THAT, THE WHOLE THING WITH QUEEN GAMEM'S WEIRD SITCH CAME TO PASS AND SHE LEFT FOR THE WAR WITHOUT HITCH.
BUT MENSTRA, IN GRIEF
SAID,
"COME BACK IN ONE PIECE
"MY DEAR GAMEM...
"...'CAUSE PAYBACK'S A *BITCH*!"

THE FALL OF

THE HOUSE

OF ATREUS

. GAMEM PART ONE, OR, TRAGEDY TOMORROW

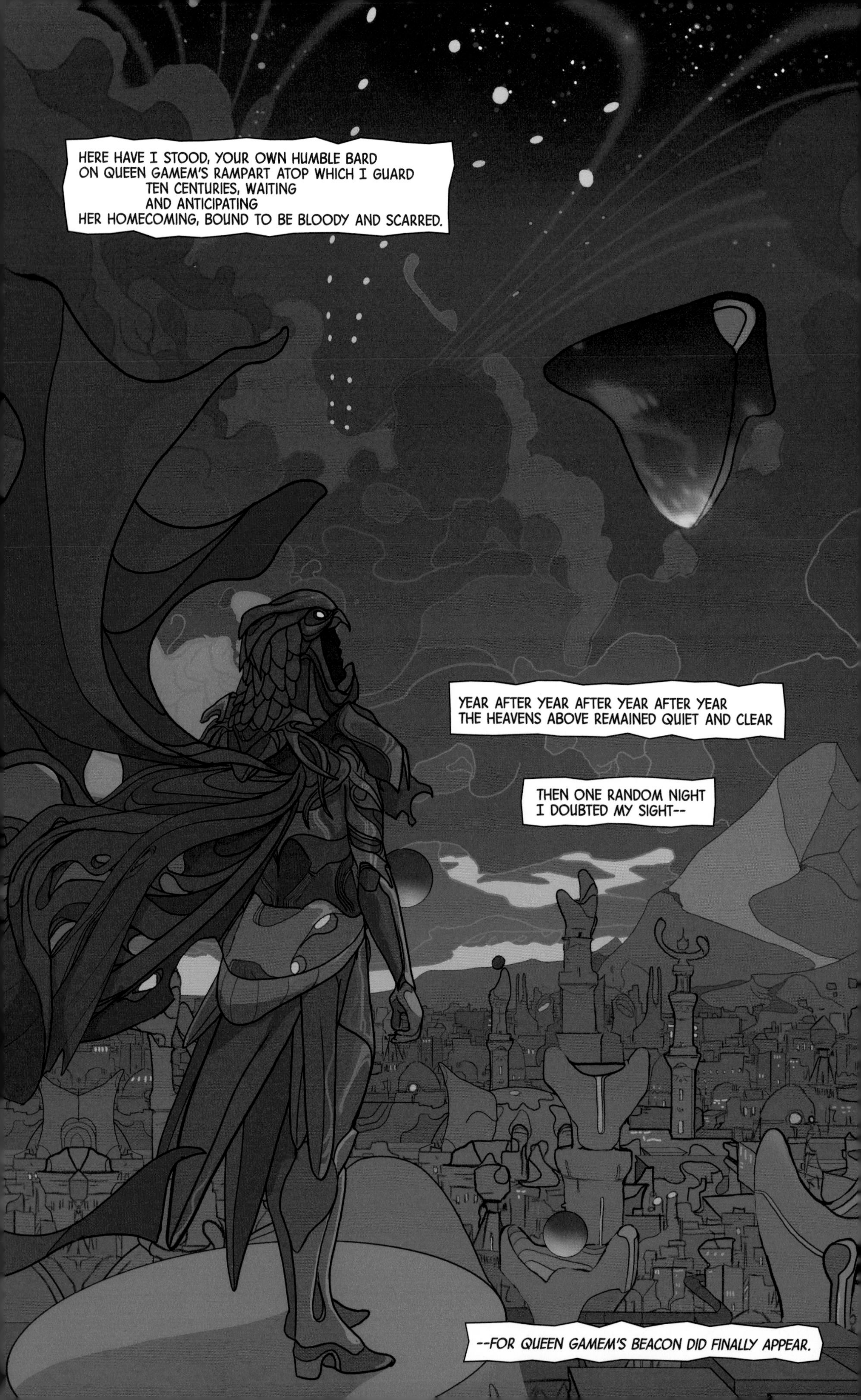
HERE HAVE I STOOD, YOUR OWN HUMBLE BARD
ON QUEEN GAMEM'S RAMPART ATOP WHICH I GUARD
TEN CENTURIES, WAITING
AND ANTICIPATING
HER HOMECOMING, BOUND TO BE BLOODY AND SCARRED.
YEAR AFTER YEAR AFTER YEAR AFTER YEAR
THE HEAVENS ABOVE REMAINED QUIET AND CLEAR
THEN ONE RANDOM NIGHT
I DOUBTED MY SIGHT--
--FOR QUEEN GAMEM'S BEACON DID FINALLY APPEAR.

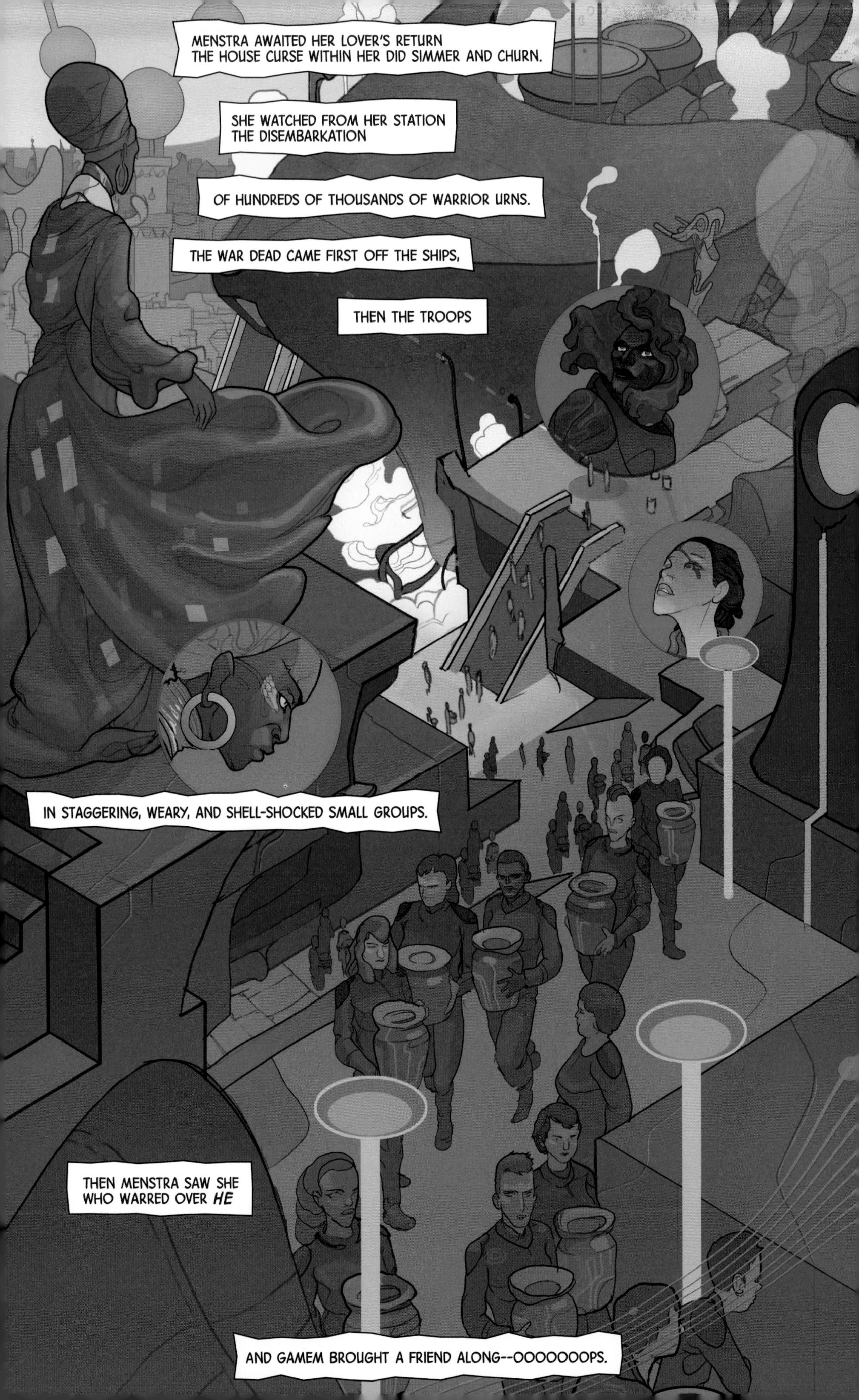
MENSTRA AWAITED HER LOVER'S RETURN
THE HOUSE CURSE WITHIN HER DID SIMMER AND CHURN.
SHE WATCHED FROM HER STATION
THE DISEMBARKATION
OF HUNDREDS OF THOUSANDS OF WARRIOR URNS.
THE WAR DEAD CAME FIRST OFF THE SHIPS,
THEN THE TROOPS
IN STAGGERING, WEARY, AND SHELL-SHOCKED SMALL GROUPS.
THEN MENSTRA SAW SHE
WHO WARRED OVER *HE*
AND GAMEM BROUGHT A FRIEND ALONG--OOOOOOOPS.

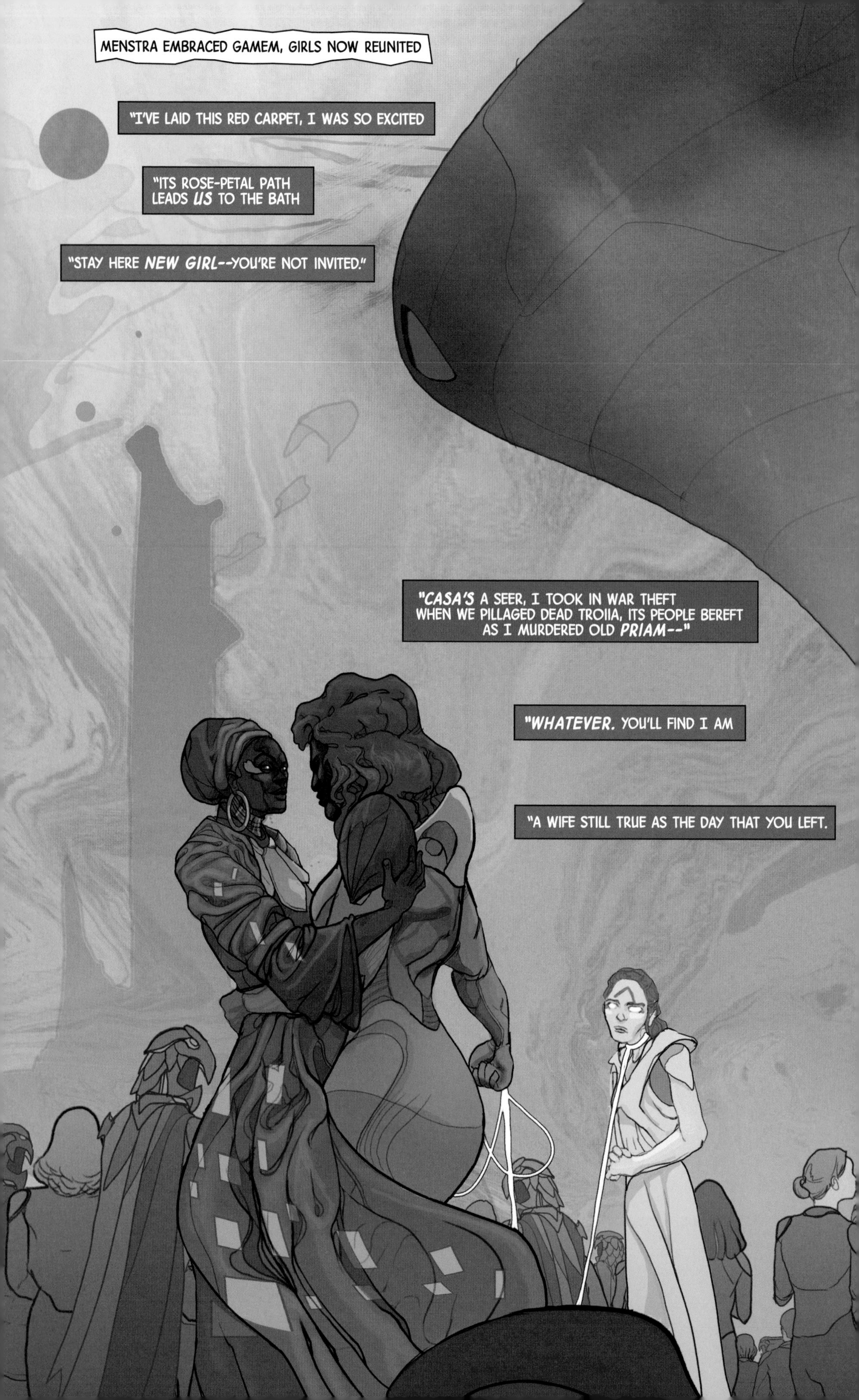
MENSTRA EMBRACED GAMEM, GIRLS NOW REUNITED
"I'VE LAID THIS RED CARPET, I WAS SO EXCITED
"ITS ROSE-PETAL PATH LEADS US TO THE BATH
"STAY HERE NEW GIRL--YOU'RE NOT INVITED."
"CASA'S A SEER, I TOOK IN WAR THEFT WHEN WE PILLAGED DEAD TROIIA, ITS PEOPLE BEREFT AS I MURDERED OLD PRIAM--"
"WHATEVER. YOU'LL FIND I AM
"A WIFE STILL TRUE AS THE DAY THAT YOU LEFT.

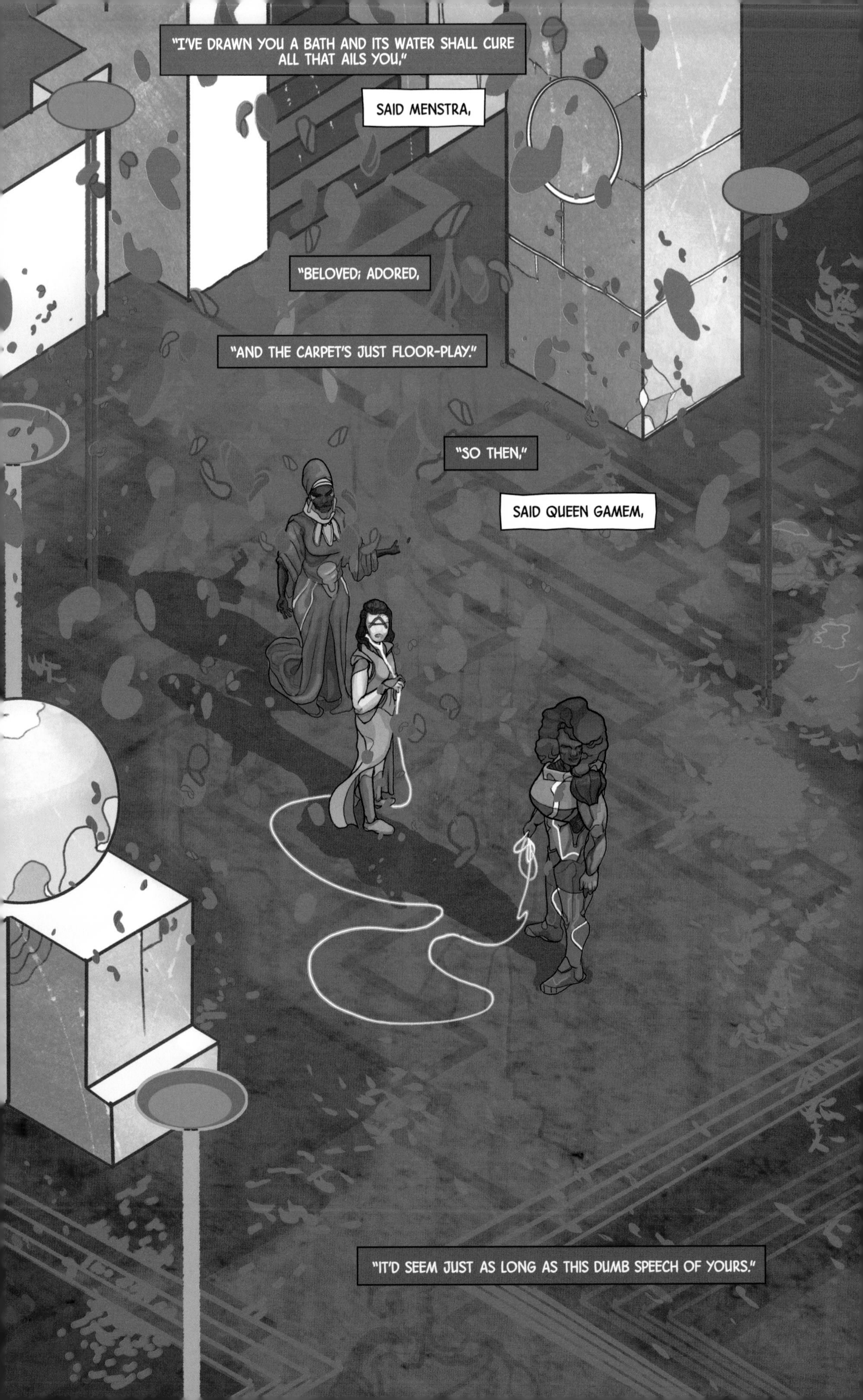
"I'VE DRAWN YOU A BATH AND ITS WATER SHALL CURE ALL THAT AILS YOU,"
SAID MENSTRA,
"BELOVED; ADORED,
"AND THE CARPET'S JUST FLOOR-PLAY."
"SO THEN,"
SAID QUEEN GAMEM,
"IT'D SEEM JUST AS LONG AS THIS DUMB SPEECH OF YOURS."

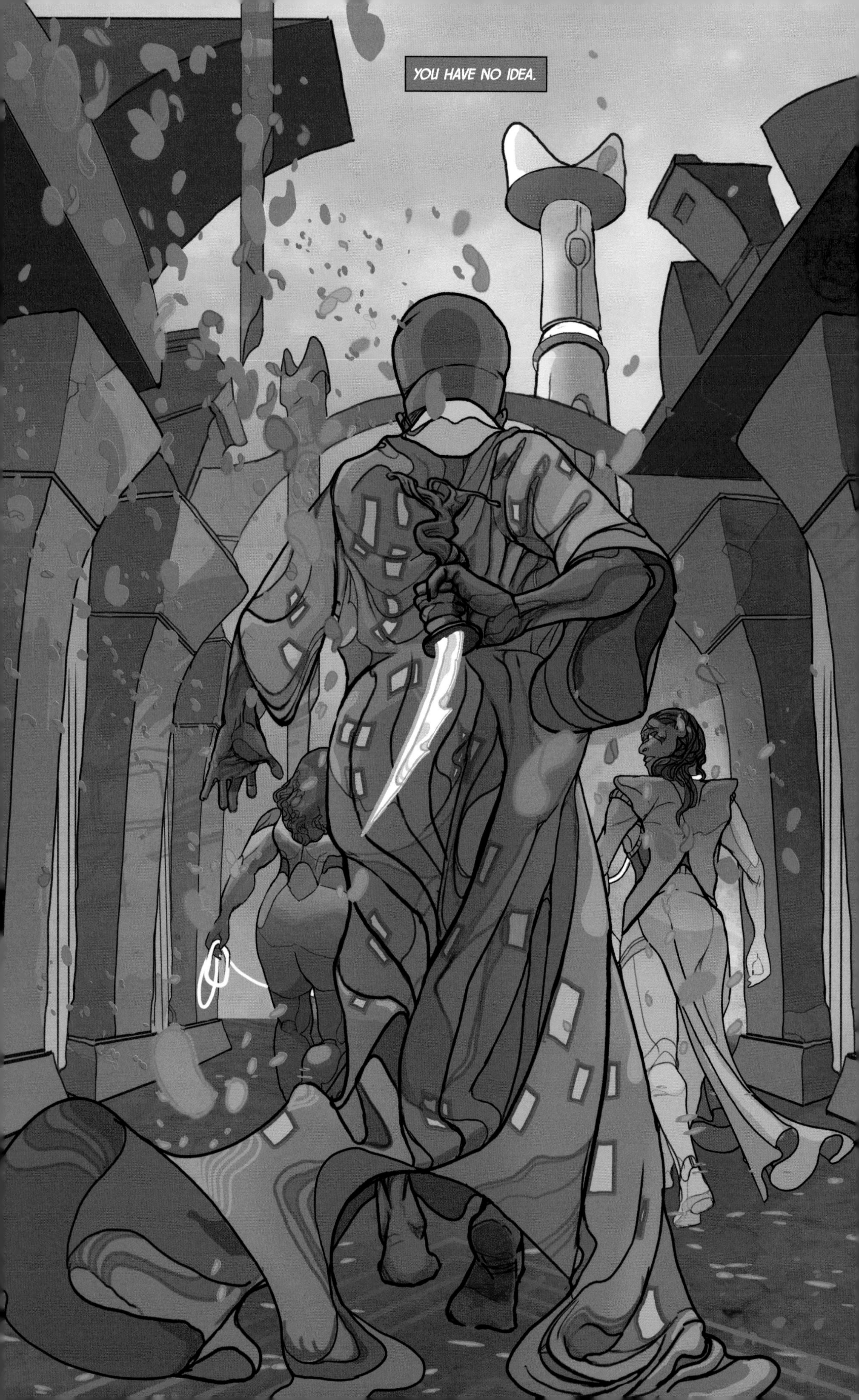
YOU HAVE NO IDEA.

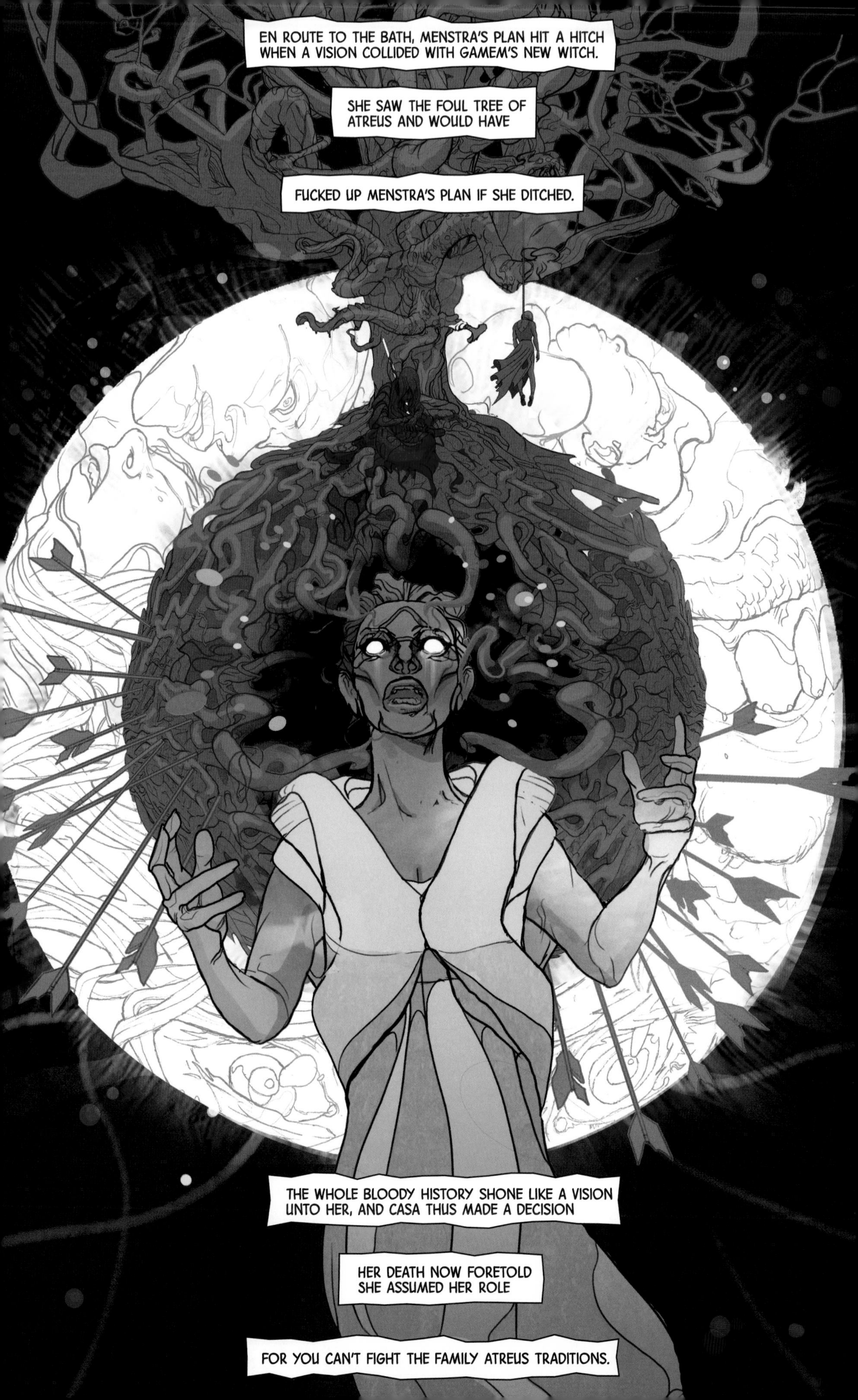
EN ROUTE TO THE BATH, MENSTRA'S PLAN HIT A HITCH
WHEN A VISION COLLIDED WITH GAMEM'S NEW WITCH.
SHE SAW THE FOUL TREE OF
ATREUS AND WOULD HAVE
FUCKED UP MENSTRA'S PLAN IF SHE DITCHED.
THE WHOLE BLOODY HISTORY SHONE LIKE A VISION
UNTO HER, AND CASA THUS MADE A DECISION
HER DEATH NOW FORETOLD
SHE ASSUMED HER ROLE
FOR YOU CAN'T FIGHT THE FAMILY ATREUS TRADITIONS.

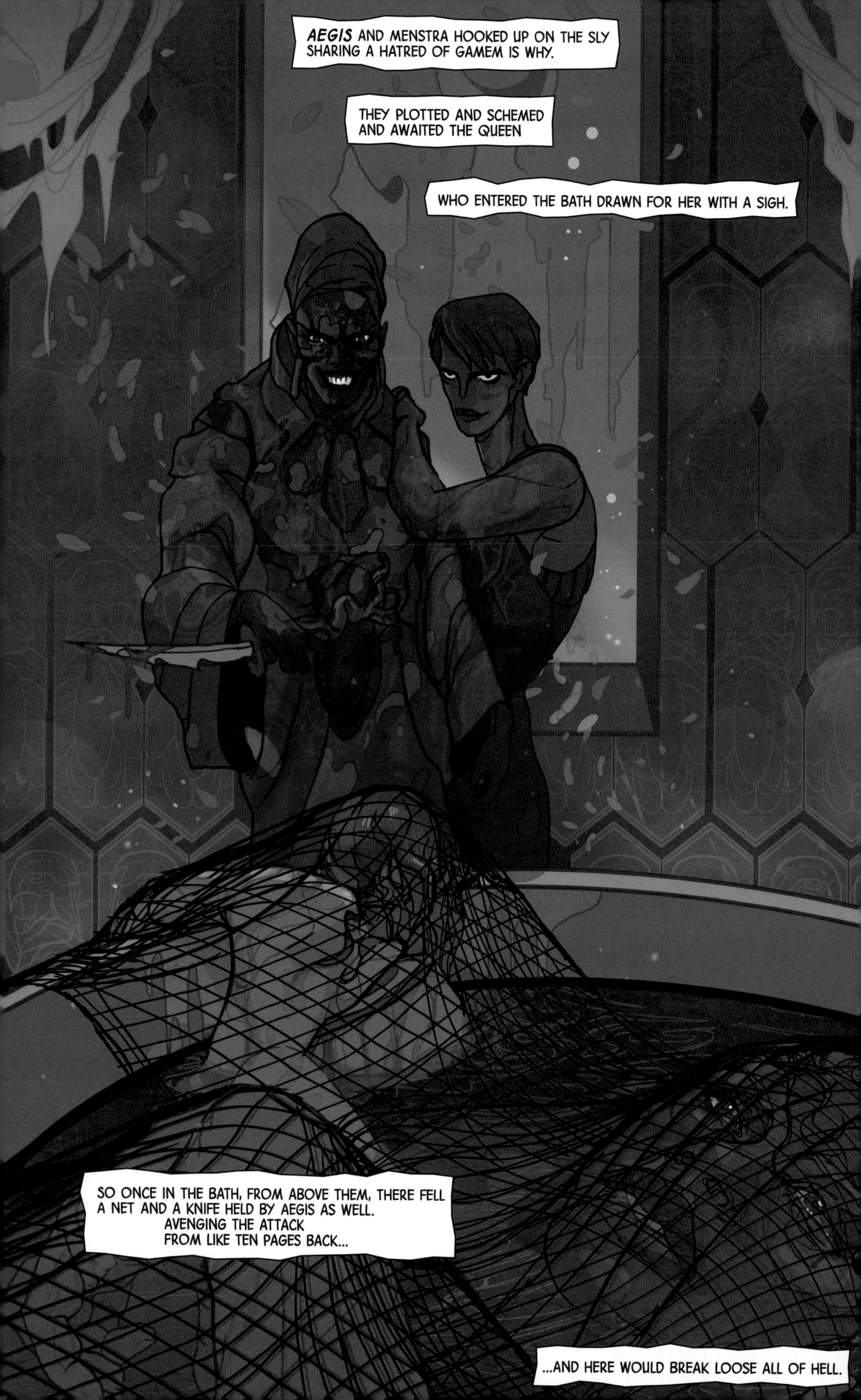
AEGIS AND MENSTRA HOOKED UP ON THE SLY
SHARING A HATRED OF GAMEM IS WHY.
THEY PLOTTED AND SCHEMED
AND AWAITED THE QUEEN
WHO ENTERED THE BATH DRAWN FOR HER WITH A SIGH.
SO ONCE IN THE BATH, FROM ABOVE THEM, THERE FELL
A NET AND A KNIFE HELD BY AEGIS AS WELL.
AVENGING THE ATTACK
FROM LIKE TEN PAGES BACK...
...AND HERE WOULD BREAK LOOSE ALL OF HELL.

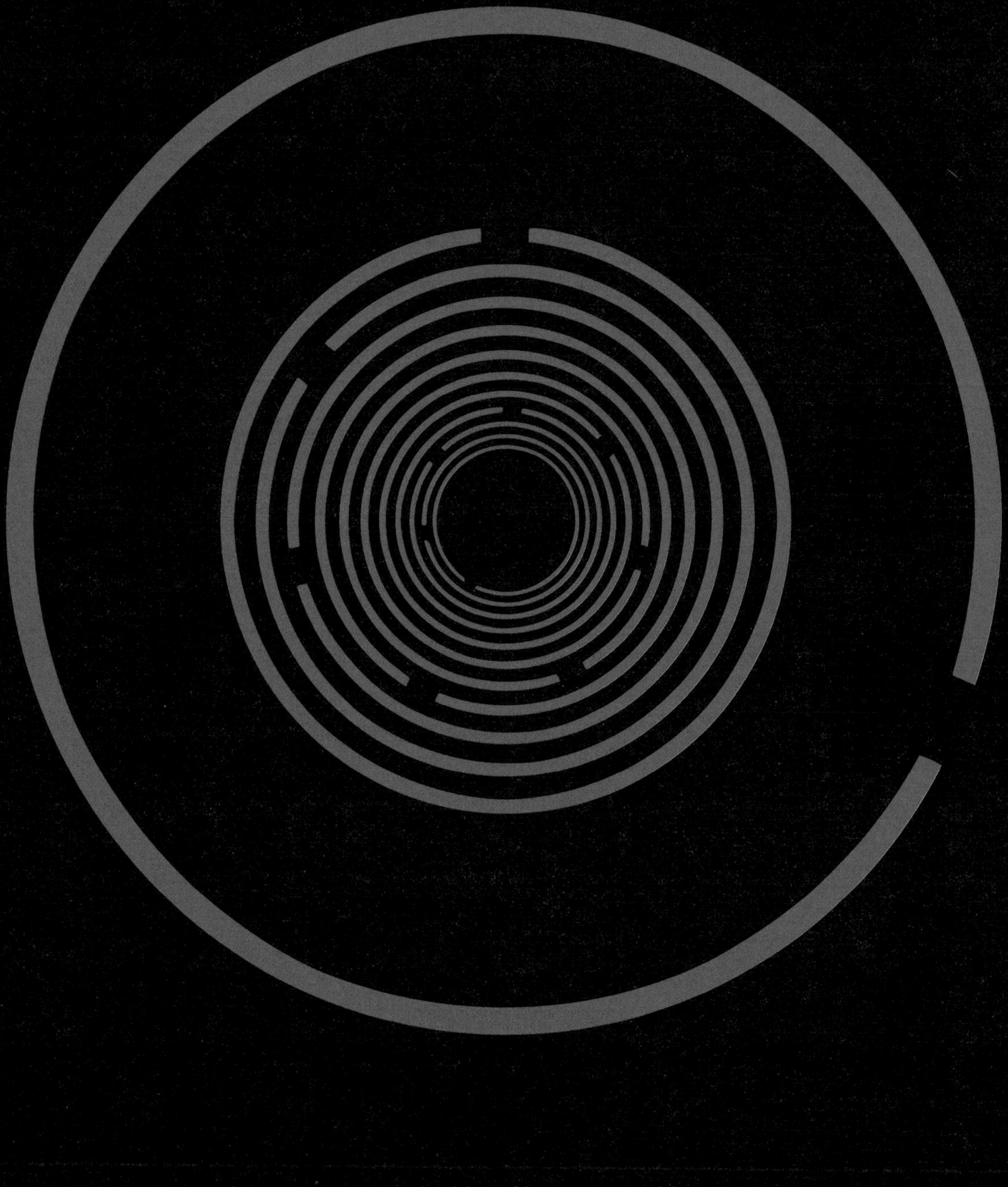

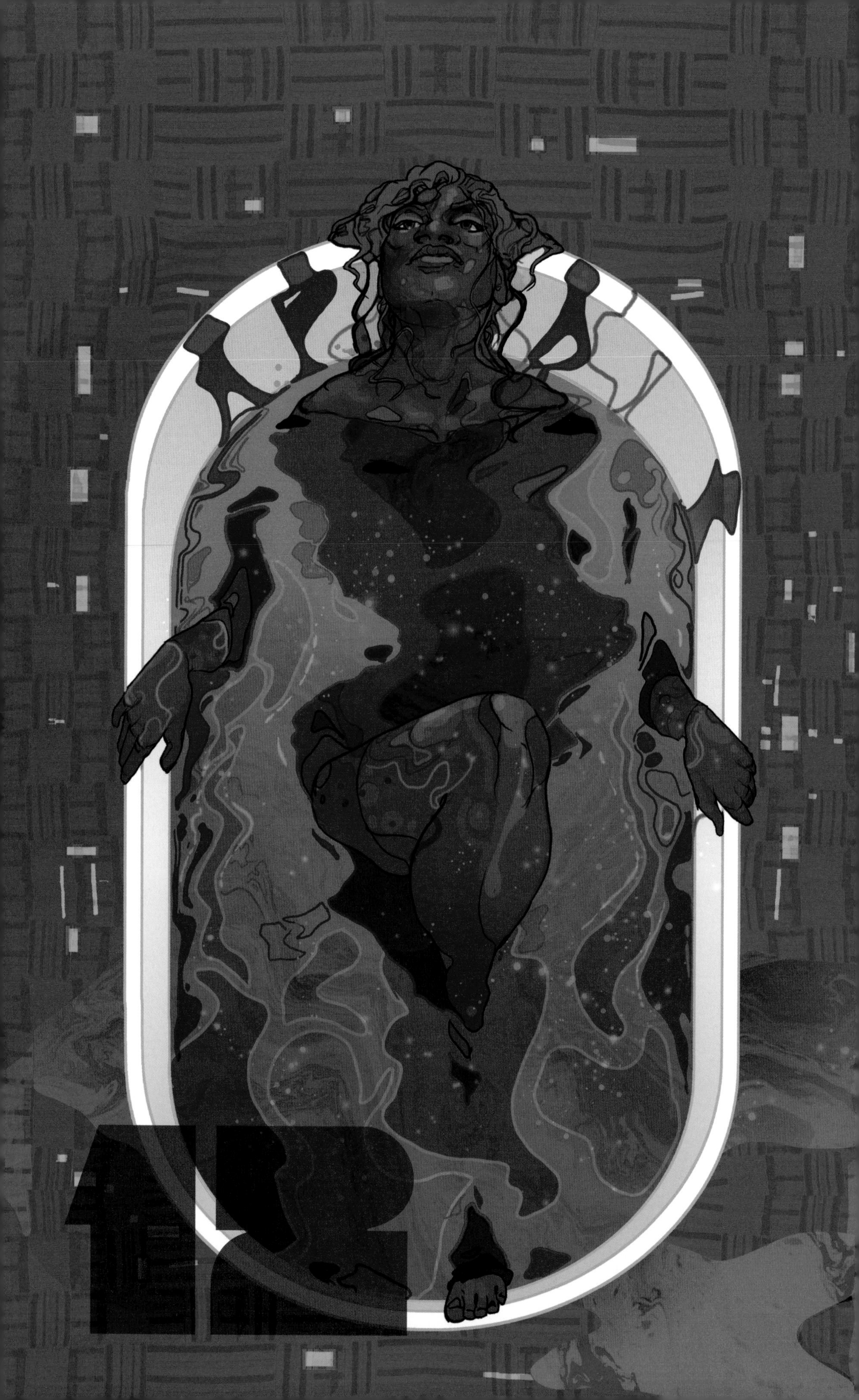
12

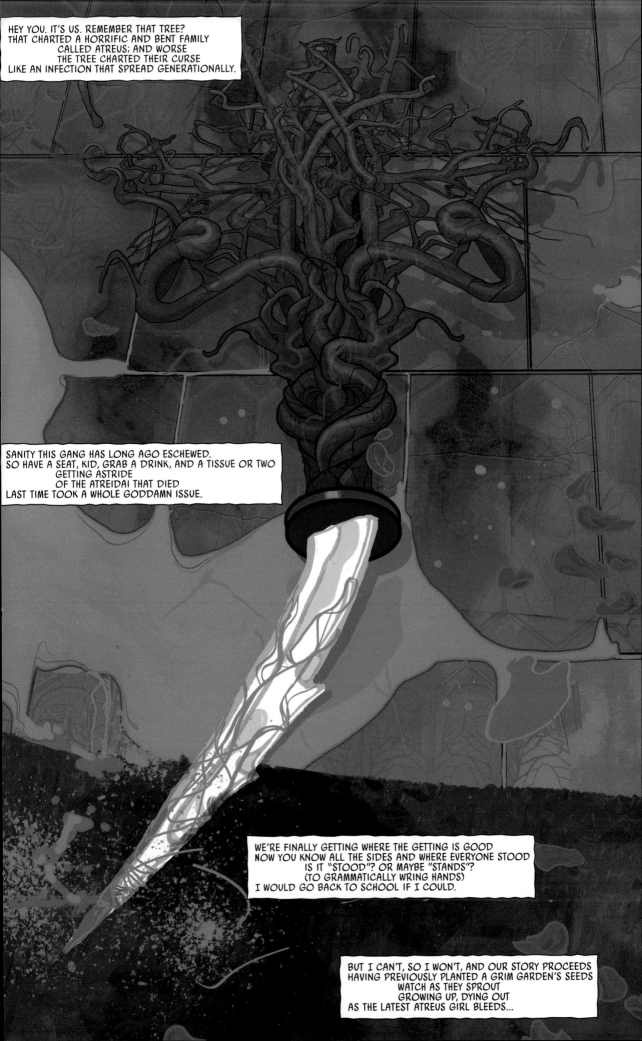

HEY YOU. IT'S US. REMEMBER THAT TREE?
THAT CHARTED A HORRIFIC AND BENT FAMILY
CALLED ATREUS; AND WORSE
THE TREE CHARTED THEIR CURSE
LIKE AN INFECTION THAT SPREAD GENERATIONALLY.

SANITY THIS GANG HAS LONG AGO ESCHEWED.
SO HAVE A SEAT, KID, GRAB A DRINK, AND A TISSUE OR TWO
GETTING ASTRIDE
OF THE ATREIDAI THAT DIED
LAST TIME TOOK A WHOLE GODDAMN ISSUE.

WE'RE FINALLY GETTING WHERE THE GETTING IS GOOD
NOW YOU KNOW ALL THE SIDES AND WHERE EVERYONE STOOD
IS IT "STOOD"? OR MAYBE "STANDS"?
(TO GRAMMATICALLY WRING HANDS)
I WOULD GO BACK TO SCHOOL IF I COULD.

BUT I CAN'T, SO I WON'T, AND OUR STORY PROCEEDS
HAVING PREVIOUSLY PLANTED A GRIM GARDEN'S SEEDS
WATCH AS THEY SPROUT
GROWING UP, DYING OUT
AS THE LATEST ATREUS GIRL BLEEDS...

THE FALL OF
THE HOUSE

OF ATREUS

. GAMEM PART TWO, OR, COMEDY TONIGHT

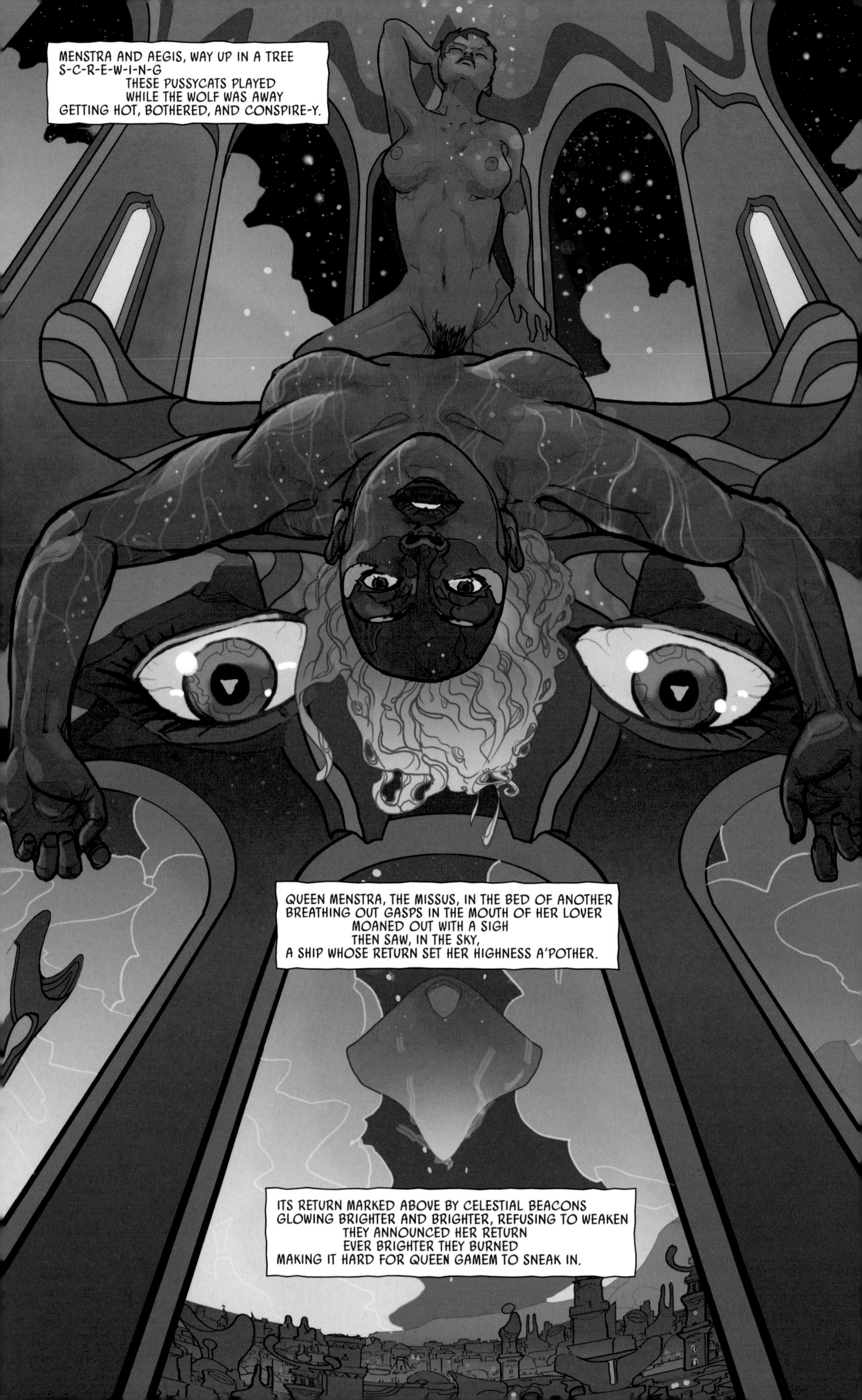
MENSTRA AND AEGIS, WAY UP IN A TREE S-C-R-E-W-I-N-G THESE PUSSYCATS PLAYED WHILE THE WOLF WAS AWAY GETTING HOT, BOTHERED, AND CONSPIRE-Y.
QUEEN MENSTRA, THE MISSUS, IN THE BED OF ANOTHER BREATHING OUT GASPS IN THE MOUTH OF HER LOVER MOANED OUT WITH A SIGH THEN SAW, IN THE SKY, A SHIP WHOSE RETURN SET HER HIGHNESS A'POTHER.
ITS RETURN MARKED ABOVE BY CELESTIAL BEACONS GLOWING BRIGHTER AND BRIGHTER, REFUSING TO WEAKEN THEY ANNOUNCED HER RETURN EVER BRIGHTER THEY BURNED MAKING IT HARD FOR QUEEN GAMEM TO SNEAK IN.

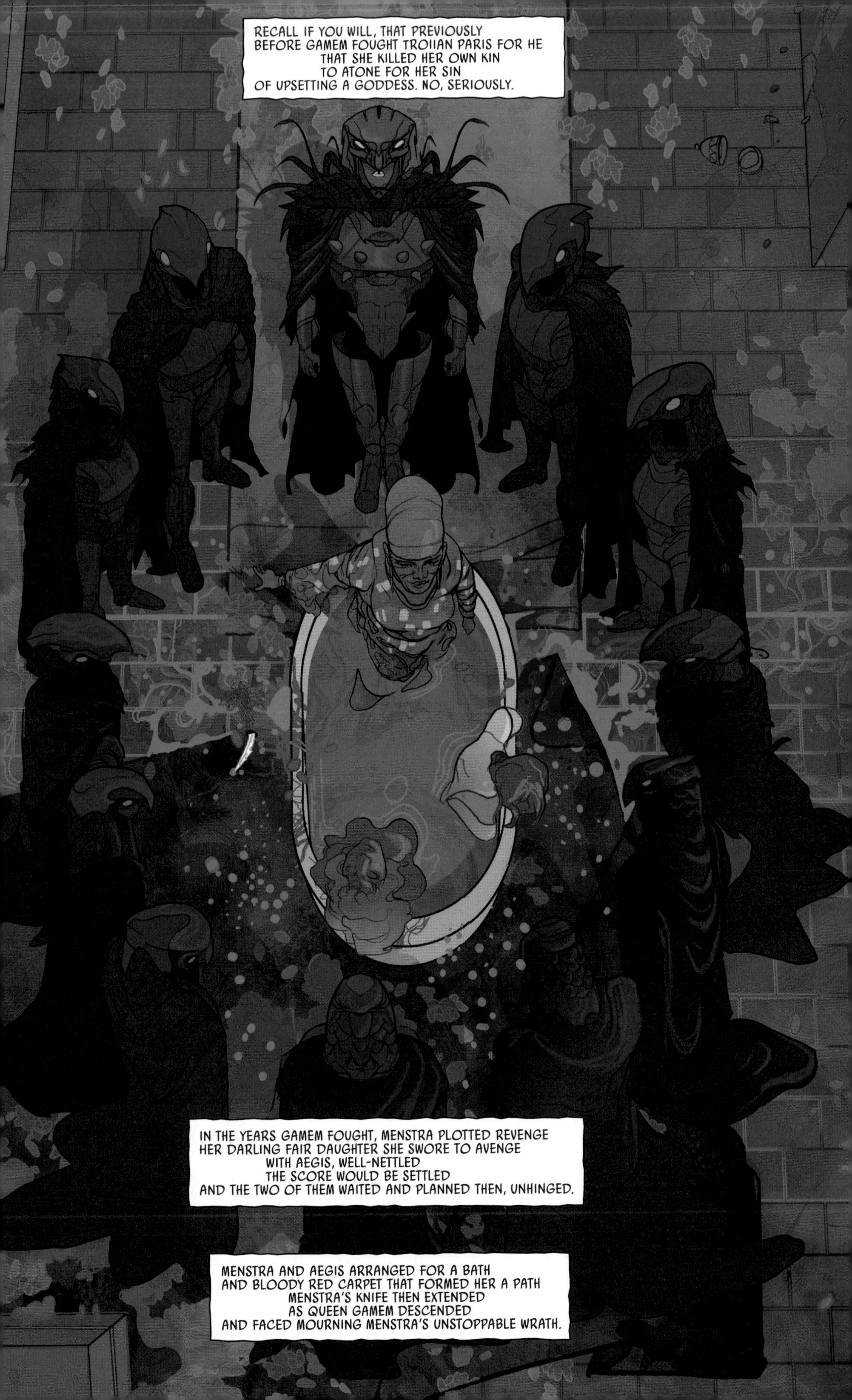

RECALL IF YOU WILL, THAT PREVIOUSLY
BEFORE GAMEM FOUGHT TROIIAN PARIS FOR HE
THAT SHE KILLED HER OWN KIN
TO ATONE FOR HER SIN
OF UPSETTING A GODDESS. NO, SERIOUSLY.
IN THE YEARS GAMEM FOUGHT, MENSTRA PLOTTED REVENGE
HER DARLING FAIR DAUGHTER SHE SWORE TO AVENGE
WITH AEGIS, WELL-NETTLED
THE SCORE WOULD BE SETTLED
AND THE TWO OF THEM WAITED AND PLANNED THEN, UNHINGED.
MENSTRA AND AEGIS ARRANGED FOR A BATH
AND BLOODY RED CARPET THAT FORMED HER A PATH
MENSTRA'S KNIFE THEN EXTENDED
AS QUEEN GAMEM DESCENDED
AND FACED MOURNING MENSTRA'S UNSTOPPABLE WRATH.

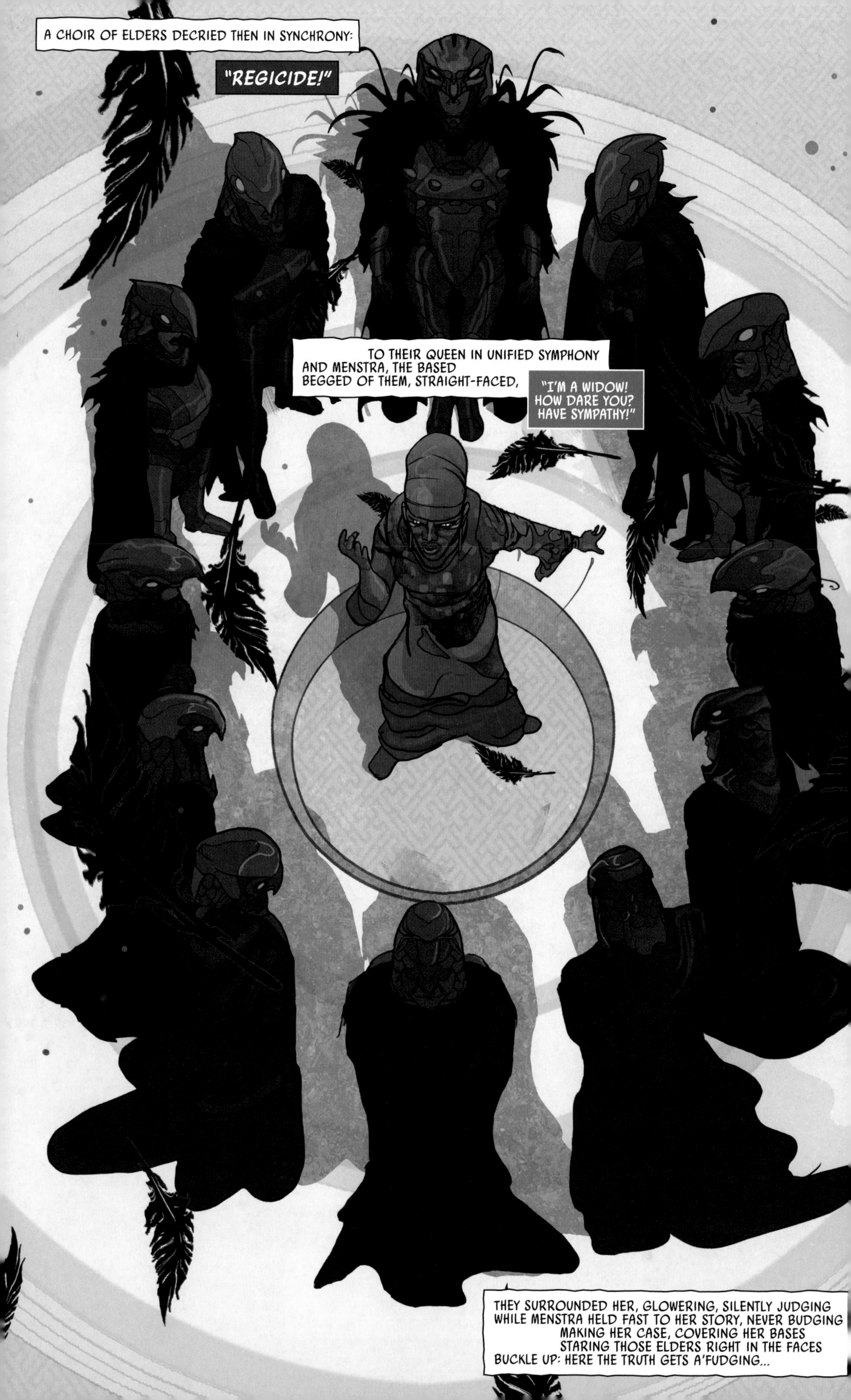
A CHOIR OF ELDERS DECRIED THEN IN SYNCHRONY:
"REGICIDE!"
TO THEIR QUEEN IN UNIFIED SYMPHONY
AND MENSTRA, THE BASED
BEGGED OF THEM, STRAIGHT-FACED,
"I'M A WIDOW! HOW DARE YOU? HAVE SYMPATHY!"
THEY SURROUNDED HER, GLOWERING, SILENTLY JUDGING
WHILE MENSTRA HELD FAST TO HER STORY, NEVER BUDGING
MAKING HER CASE, COVERING HER BASES
STARING THOSE ELDERS RIGHT IN THE FACES
BUCKLE UP: HERE THE TRUTH GETS A'FUDGING...

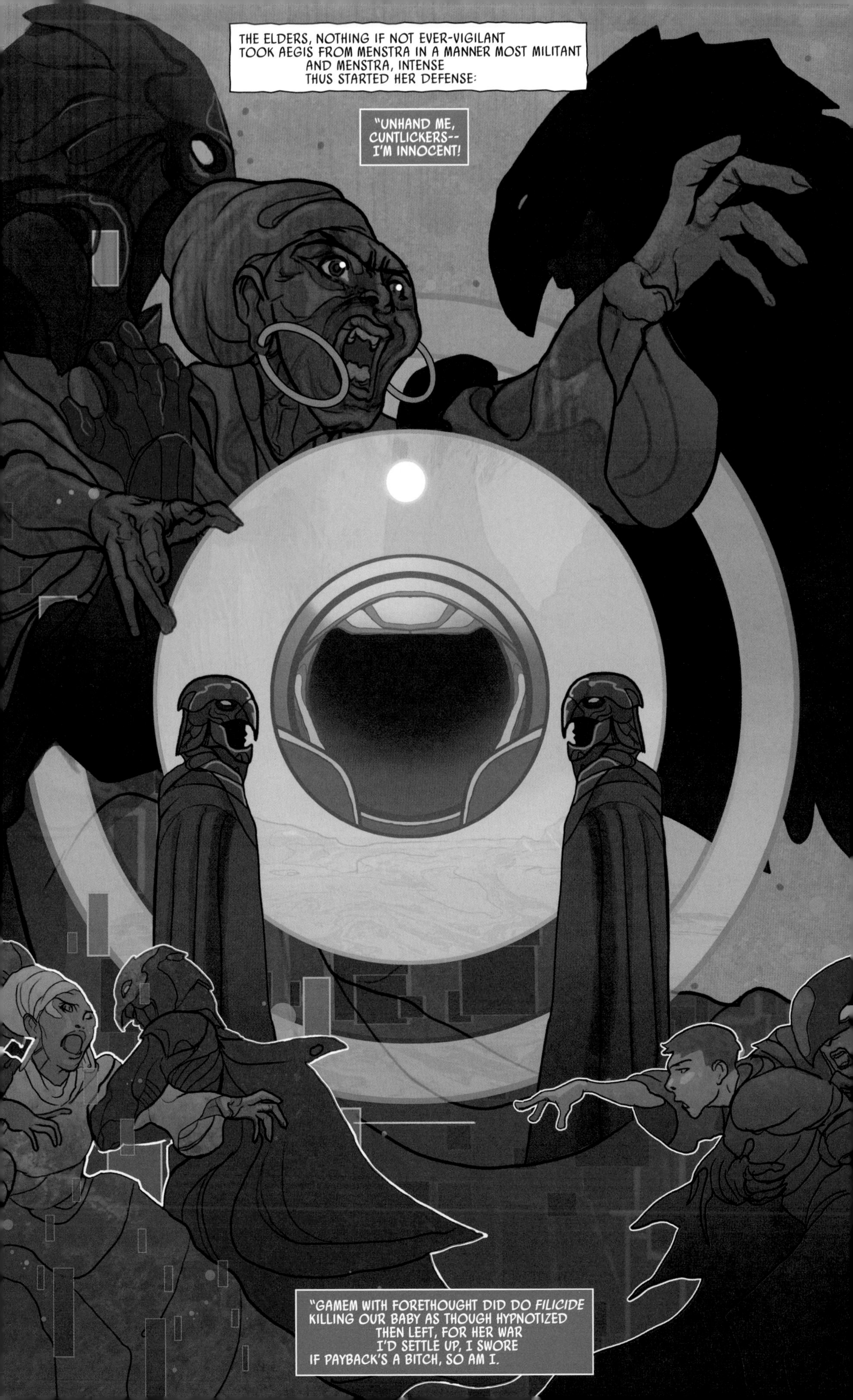
THE ELDERS, NOTHING IF NOT EVER-VIGILANT TOOK AEGIS FROM MENSTRA IN A MANNER MOST MILITANT AND MENSTRA, INTENSE THUS STARTED HER DEFENSE:
"UNHAND ME, CUNTLICKERS-- I'M INNOCENT!
"GAMEM WITH FORETHOUGHT DID DO *FILICIDE* KILLING OUR BABY AS THOUGH HYPNOTIZED THEN LEFT, FOR HER WAR I'D SETTLE UP, I SWORE IF PAYBACK'S A BITCH, SO AM I.

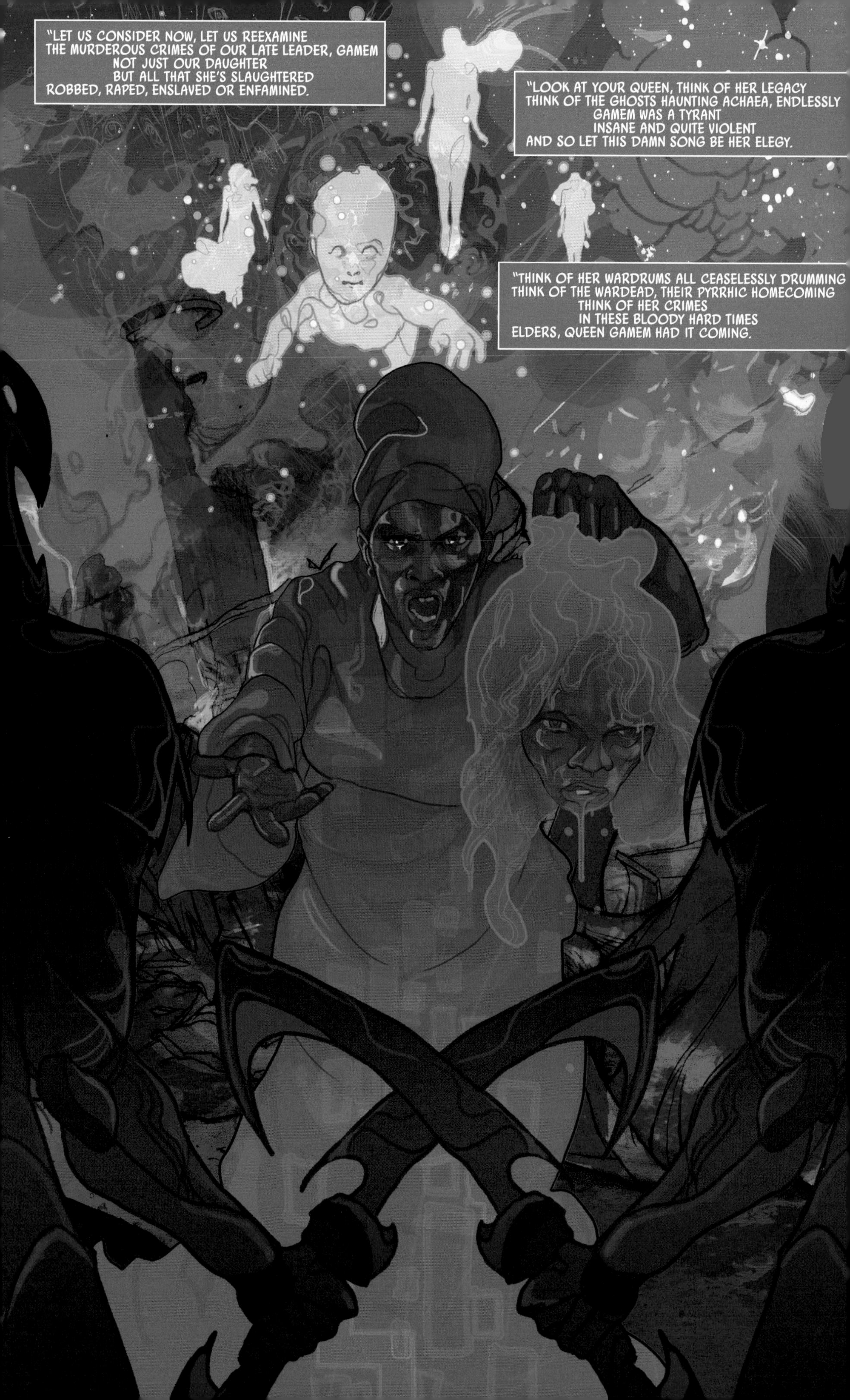
"LET US CONSIDER NOW, LET US REEXAMINE
THE MURDEROUS CRIMES OF OUR LATE LEADER, GAMEM
NOT JUST OUR DAUGHTER
BUT ALL THAT SHE'S SLAUGHTERED
ROBBED, RAPED, ENSLAVED OR ENFAMINED.
"LOOK AT YOUR QUEEN, THINK OF HER LEGACY
THINK OF THE GHOSTS HAUNTING ACHAEA, ENDLESSLY
GAMEM WAS A TYRANT
INSANE AND QUITE VIOLENT
AND SO LET THIS DAMN SONG BE HER ELEGY.
"THINK OF HER WARDRUMS ALL CEASELESSLY DRUMMING
THINK OF THE WARDEAD, THEIR PYRRHIC HOMECOMING
THINK OF HER CRIMES
IN THESE BLOODY HARD TIMES
ELDERS, QUEEN GAMEM HAD IT COMING.

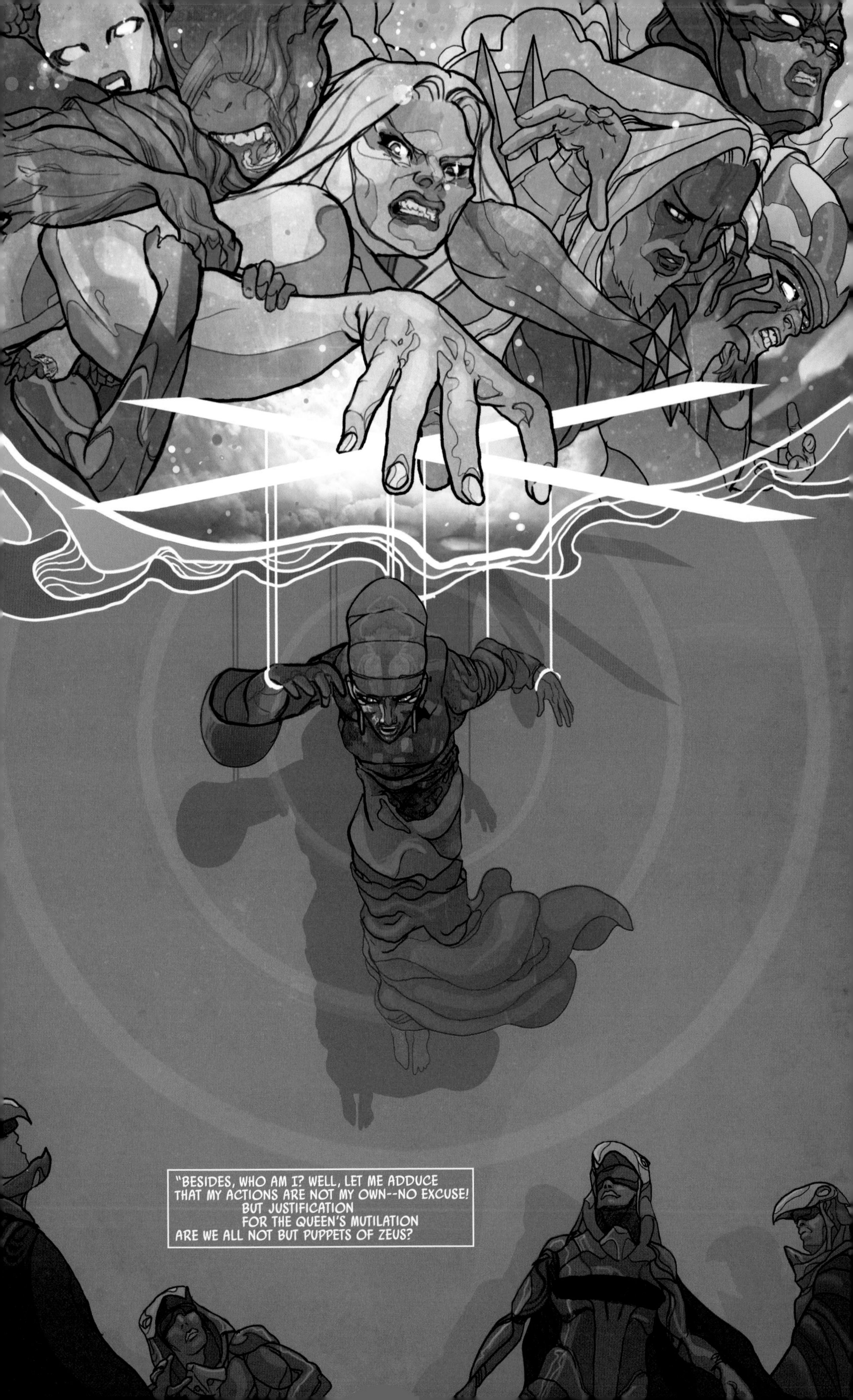
"BESIDES, WHO AM I? WELL, LET ME ADDUCE
THAT MY ACTIONS ARE NOT MY OWN--NO EXCUSE!
BUT JUSTIFICATION
FOR THE QUEEN'S MUTILATION
ARE WE ALL NOT BUT PUPPETS OF ZEUS?

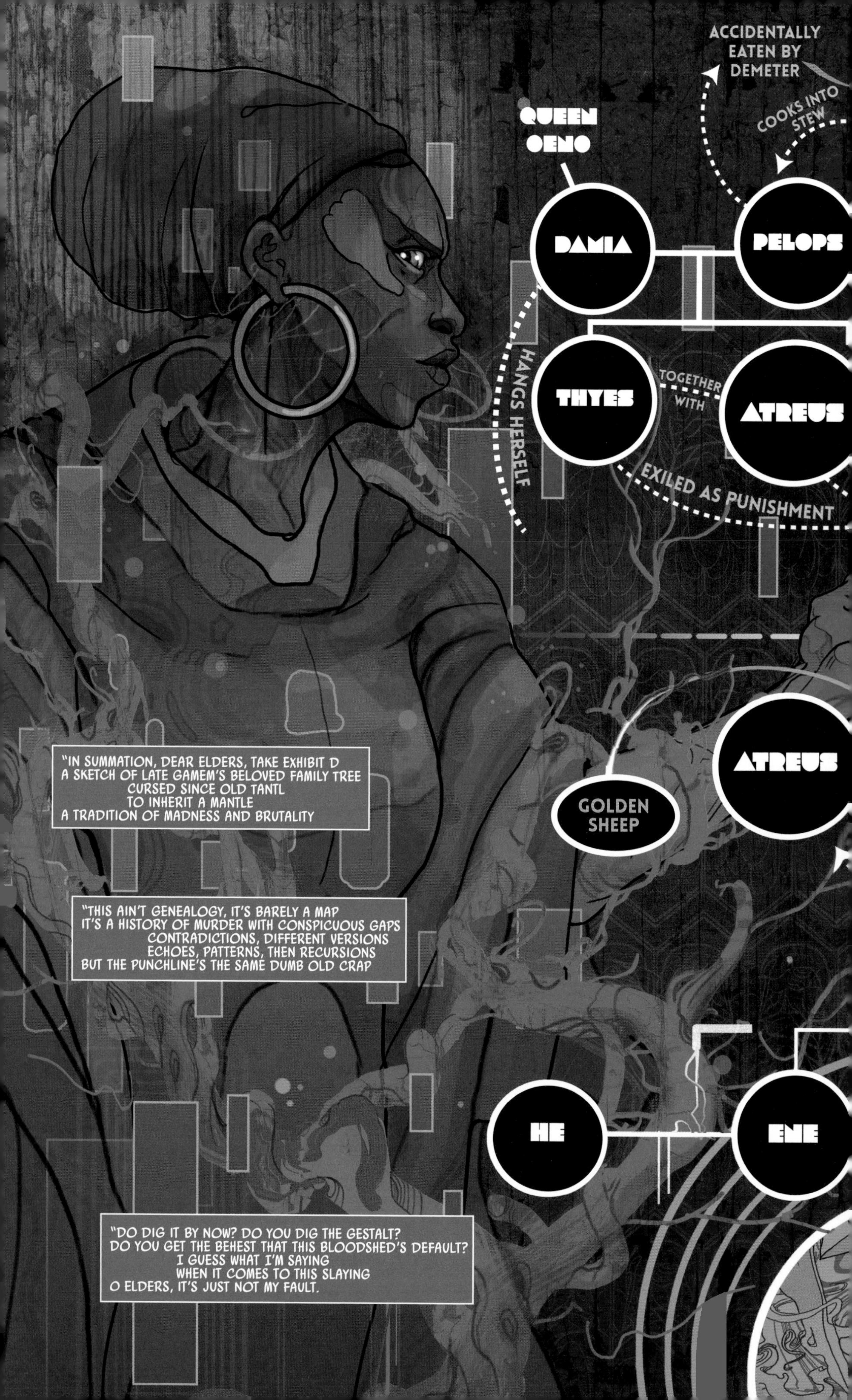

ACCIDENTALLY EATEN BY DEMETER
COOKS INTO STEW
QUEEN OENO
DAMIA
PELOPS
HANGS HERSELF
THYES
TOGETHER WITH
ATREUS
EXILED AS PUNISHMENT
"IN SUMMATION, DEAR ELDERS, TAKE EXHIBIT D
A SKETCH OF LATE GAMEM'S BELOVED FAMILY TREE
CURSED SINCE OLD TANTL
TO INHERIT A MANTLE
A TRADITION OF MADNESS AND BRUTALITY
ATREUS
GOLDEN SHEEP
"THIS AIN'T GENEALOGY, IT'S BARELY A MAP
IT'S A HISTORY OF MURDER WITH CONSPICUOUS GAPS
CONTRADICTIONS, DIFFERENT VERSIONS
ECHOES, PATTERNS, THEN RECURSIONS
BUT THE PUNCHLINE'S THE SAME DUMB OLD CRAP
HE
ENE
"DO DIG IT BY NOW? DO YOU DIG THE GESTALT?
DO YOU GET THE BEHEST THAT THIS BLOODSHED'S DEFAULT?
I GUESS WHAT I'M SAYING
WHEN IT COMES TO THIS SLAYING
O ELDERS, IT'S JUST NOT MY FAULT.

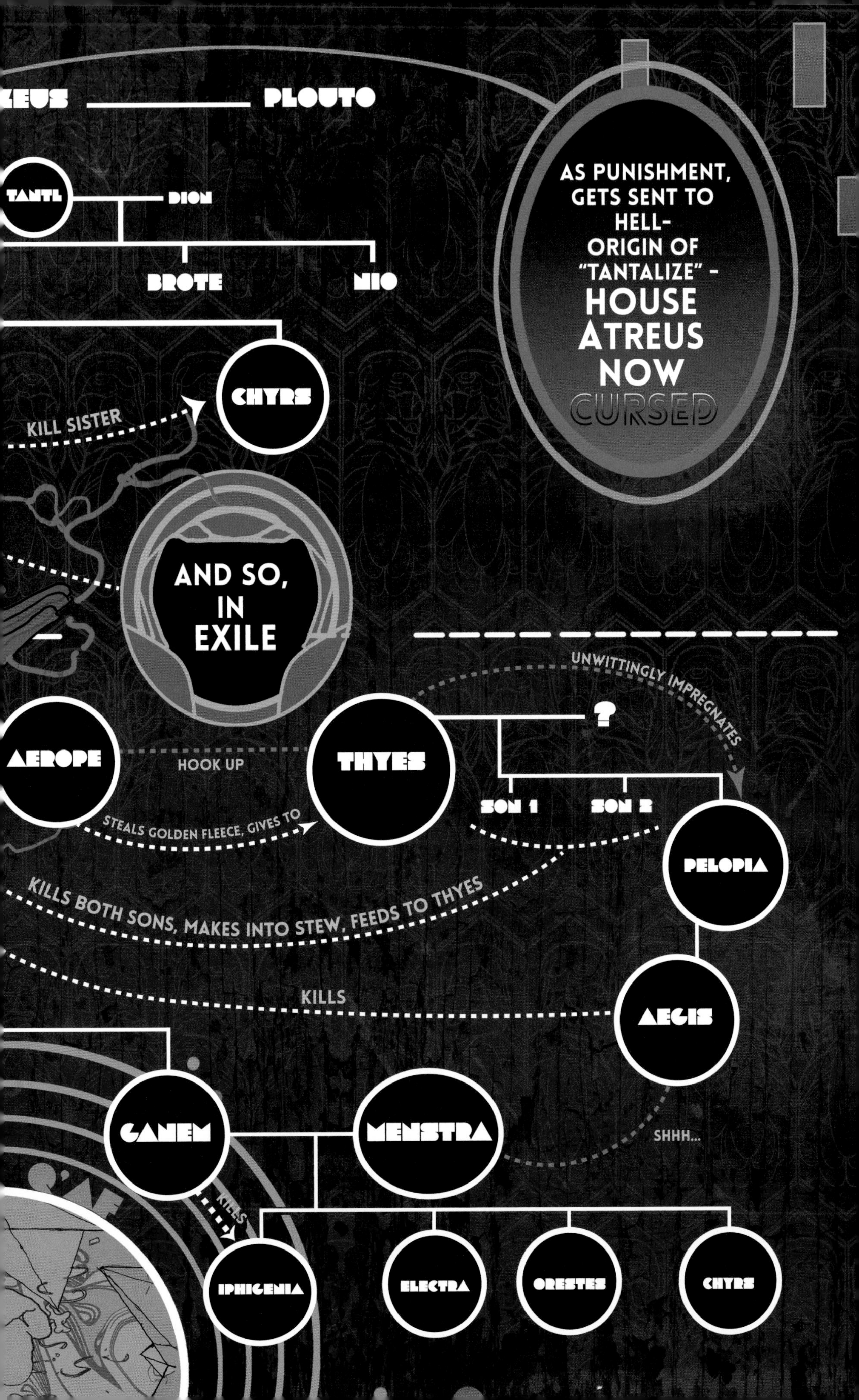

EUS
PLOUTO
TANTL
DION
BROTE
NIO
AS PUNISHMENT, GETS SENT TO HELL- ORIGIN OF "TANTALIZE" - HOUSE ATREUS NOW CURSED
CHYRS
KILL SISTER
AND SO, IN EXILE
AEROPE
HOOK UP
THYES
?
UNWITTINGLY IMPREGNATES
SON 1
SON 2
STEALS GOLDEN FLEECE, GIVES TO
PELOPIA
KILLS BOTH SONS, MAKES INTO STEW, FEEDS TO THYES
KILLS
AEGIS
GANEM
MENSTRA
SHHH...
KILLS
IPHIGENIA
ELECTRA
ORESTES
CHYRS

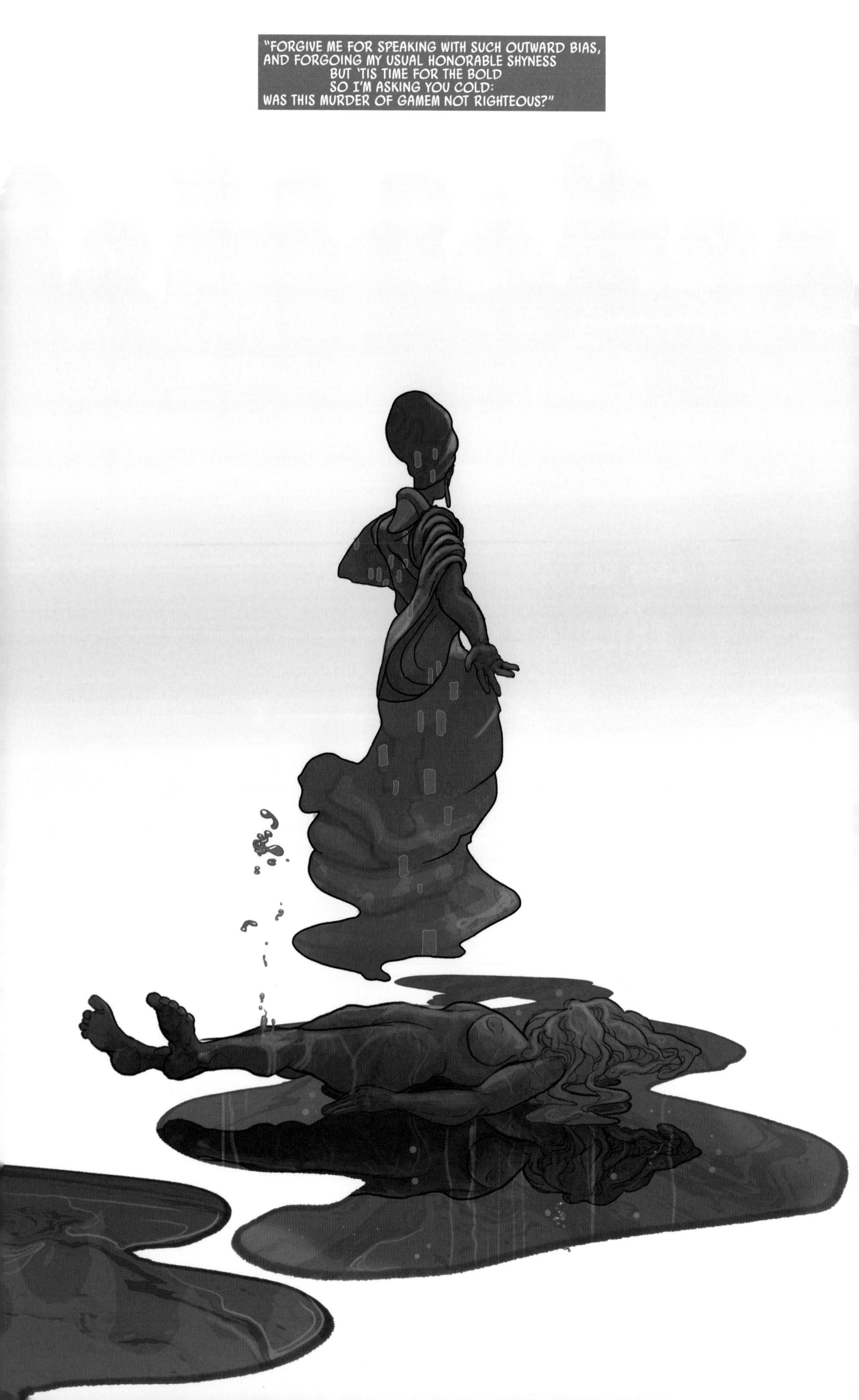
"FORGIVE ME FOR SPEAKING WITH SUCH OUTWARD BIAS,
AND FORGOING MY USUAL HONORABLE SHYNESS
BUT 'TIS TIME FOR THE BOLD
SO I'M ASKING YOU COLD:
WAS THIS MURDER OF GAMEM NOT RIGHTEOUS?"

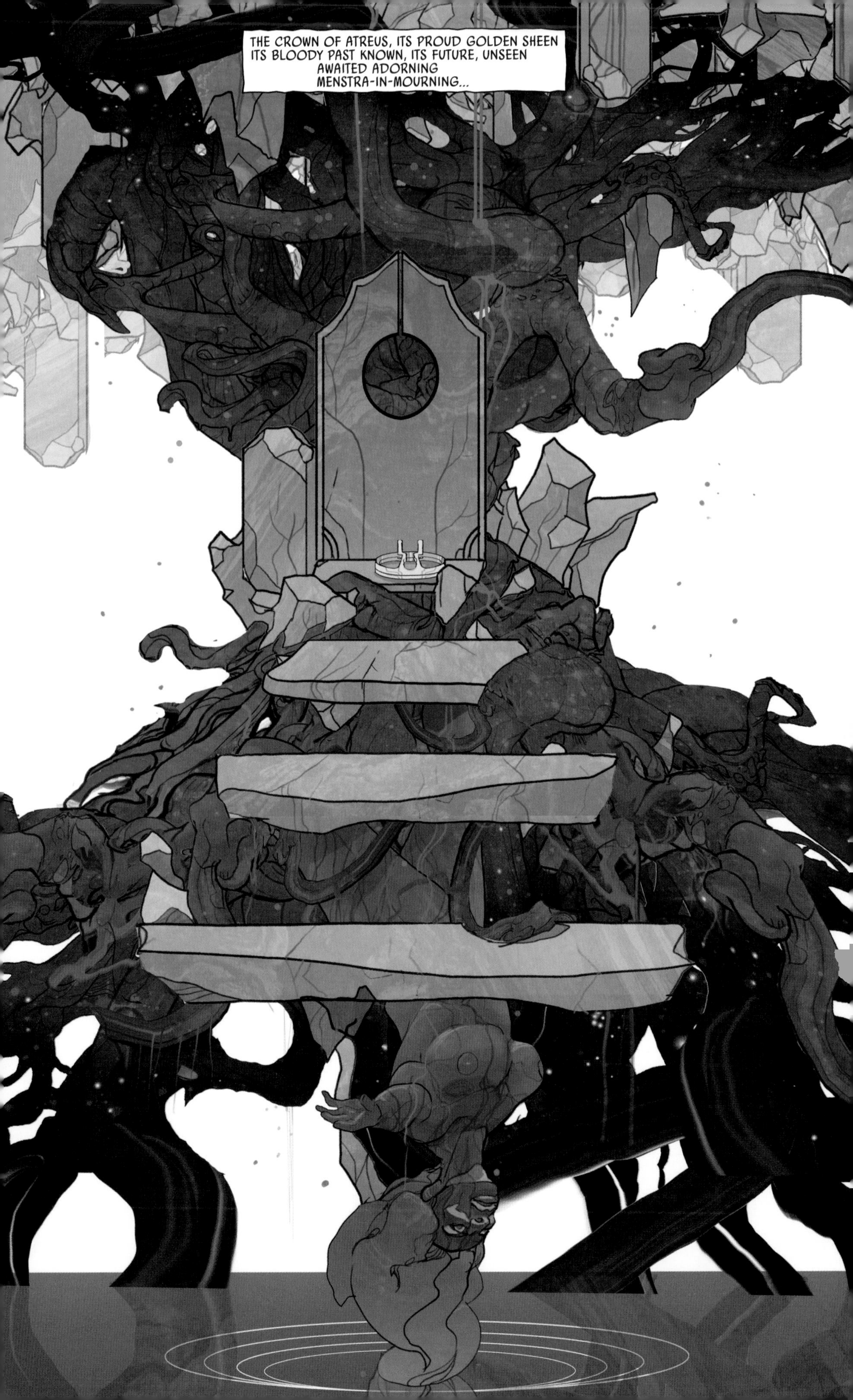
THE CROWN OF ATREUS, ITS PROUD GOLDEN SHEEN
ITS BLOODY PAST KNOWN, ITS FUTURE, UNSEEN
AWAITED ADORNING
MENSTRA-IN-MOURNING...

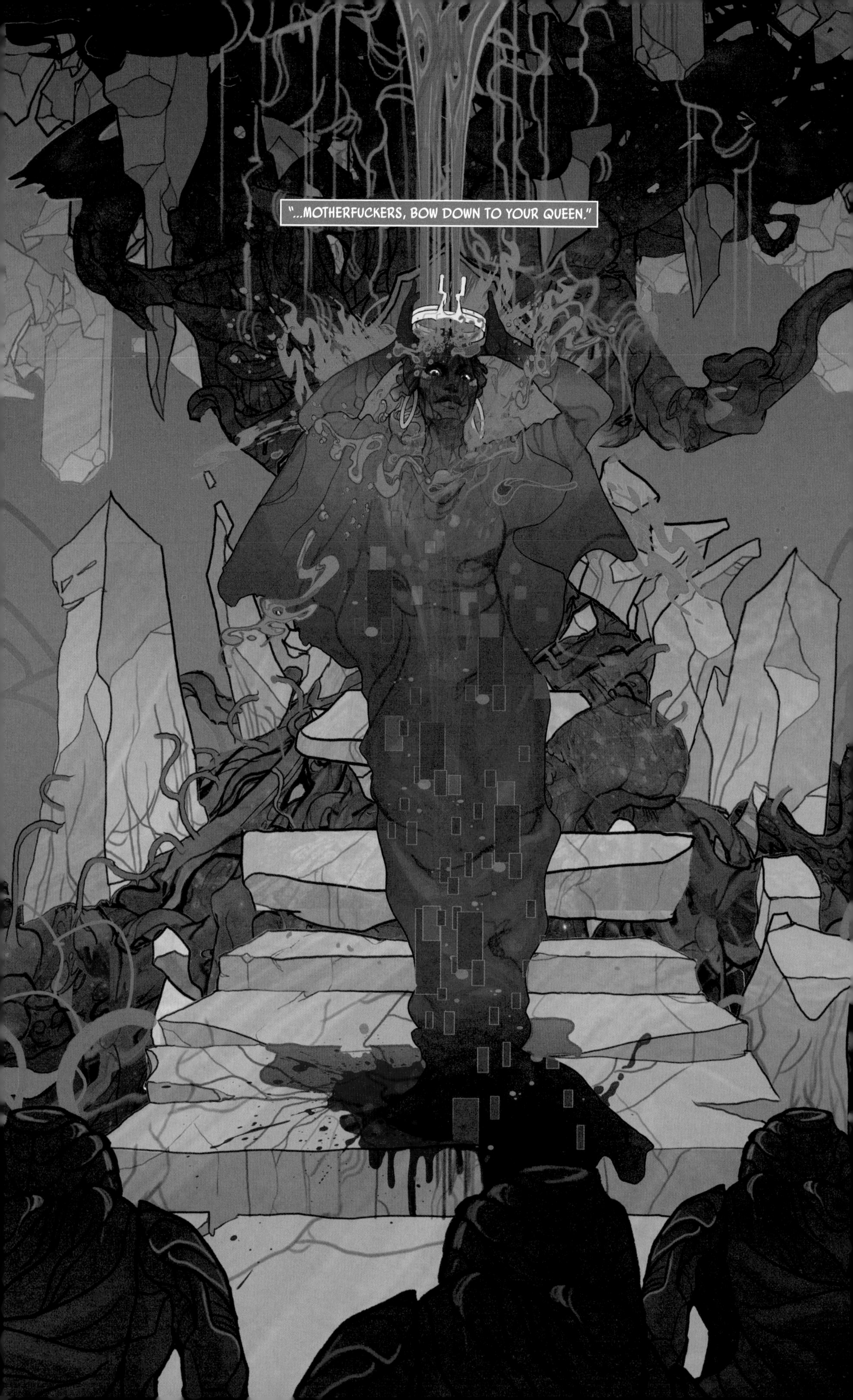
"...MOTHERFUCKERS, BOW DOWN TO YOUR QUEEN."

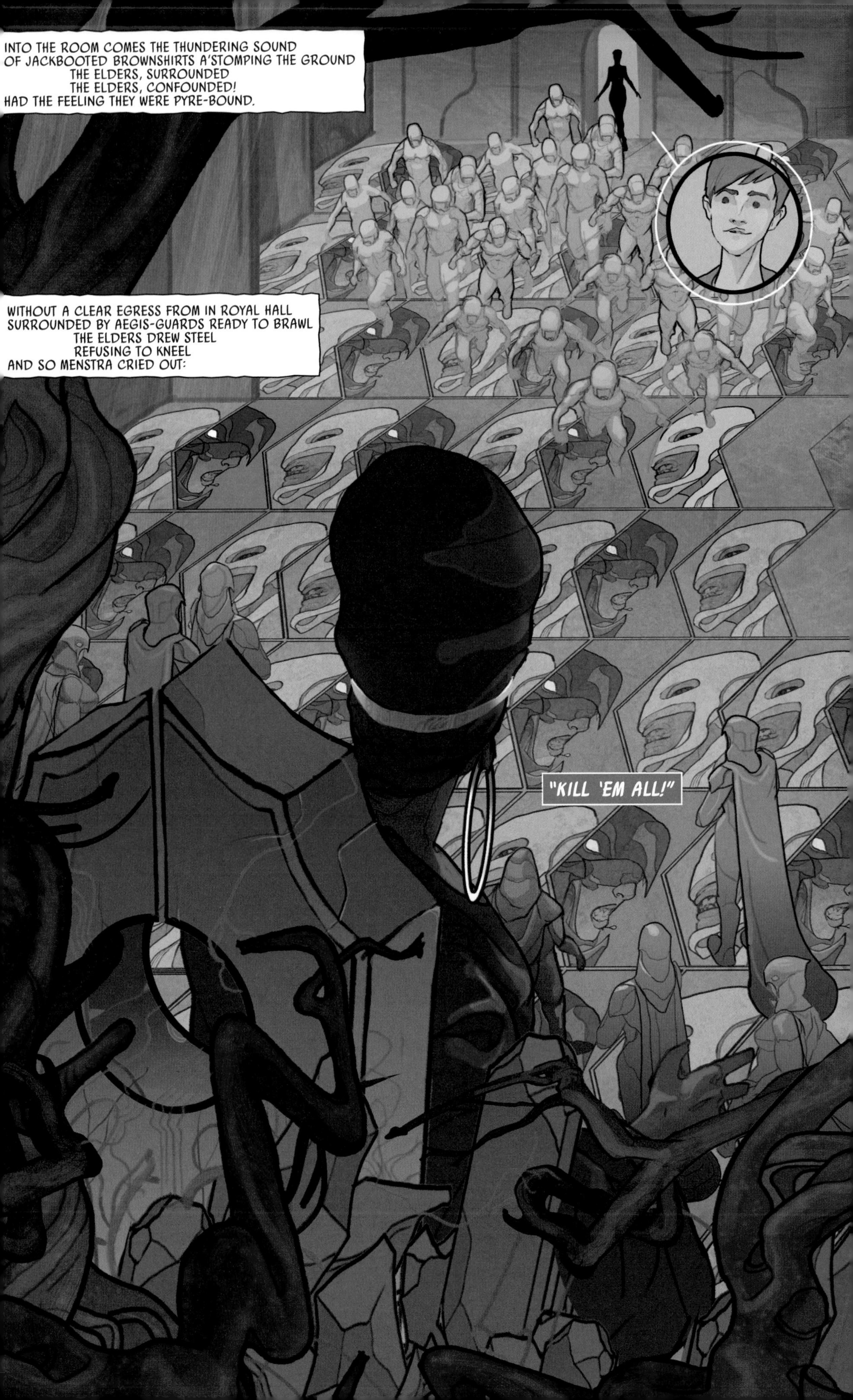
INTO THE ROOM COMES THE THUNDERING SOUND
OF JACKBOOTED BROWNSHIRTS A'STOMPING THE GROUND
THE ELDERS, SURROUNDED
THE ELDERS, CONFOUNDED!
HAD THE FEELING THEY WERE PYRE-BOUND.
WITHOUT A CLEAR EGRESS FROM IN ROYAL HALL
SURROUNDED BY AEGIS-GUARDS READY TO BRAWL
THE ELDERS DREW STEEL
REFUSING TO KNEEL
AND SO MENSTRA CRIED OUT:
"KILL 'EM ALL!"

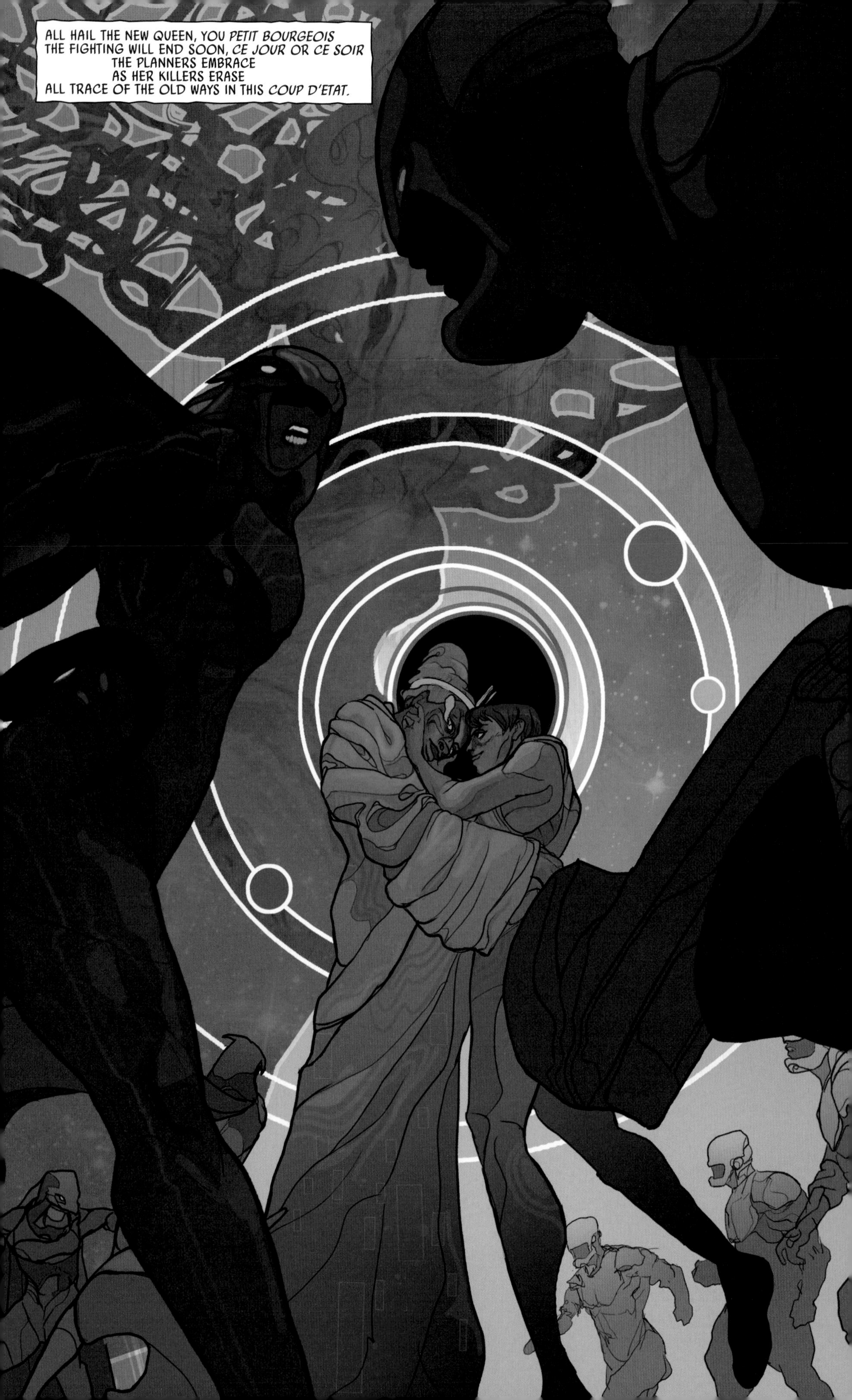
ALL HAIL THE NEW QUEEN, YOU *PETIT BOURGEOIS*
THE FIGHTING WILL END SOON, *CE JOUR OR CE SOIR*
THE PLANNERS EMBRACE
AS HER KILLERS ERASE
ALL TRACE OF THE OLD WAYS IN THIS *COUP D'ETAT.*

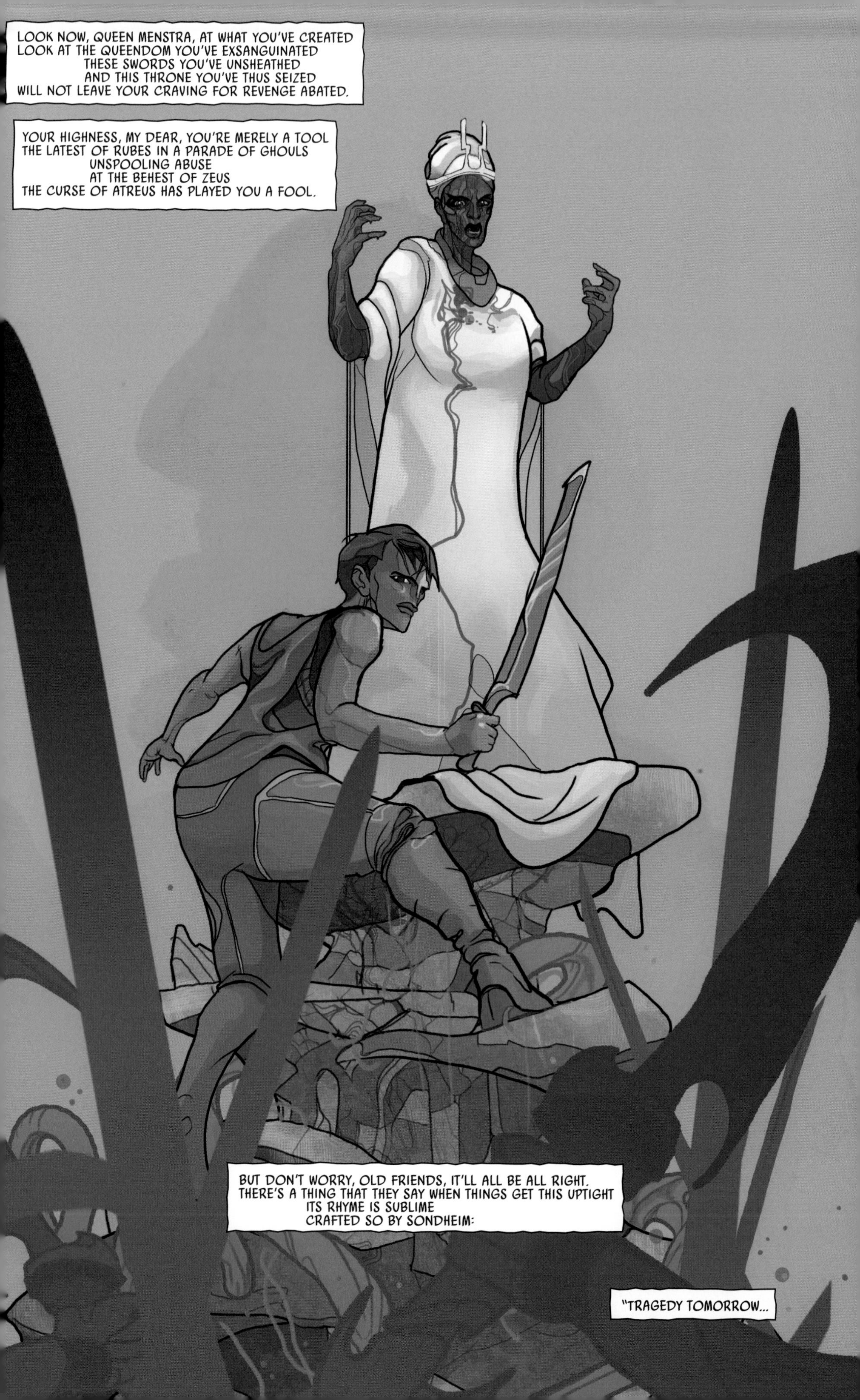
LOOK NOW, QUEEN MENSTRA, AT WHAT YOU'VE CREATED
LOOK AT THE QUEENDOM YOU'VE EXSANGUINATED
THESE SWORDS YOU'VE UNSHEATHED
AND THIS THRONE YOU'VE THUS SEIZED
WILL NOT LEAVE YOUR CRAVING FOR REVENGE ABATED.
YOUR HIGHNESS, MY DEAR, YOU'RE MERELY A TOOL
THE LATEST OF RUBES IN A PARADE OF GHOULS
UNSPOOLING ABUSE
AT THE BEHEST OF ZEUS
THE CURSE OF ATREUS HAS PLAYED YOU A FOOL.
BUT DON'T WORRY, OLD FRIENDS, IT'LL ALL BE ALL RIGHT.
THERE'S A THING THAT THEY SAY WHEN THINGS GET THIS UPTIGHT
ITS RHYME IS SUBLIME
CRAFTED SO BY SONDHEIM:
"TRAGEDY TOMORROW...

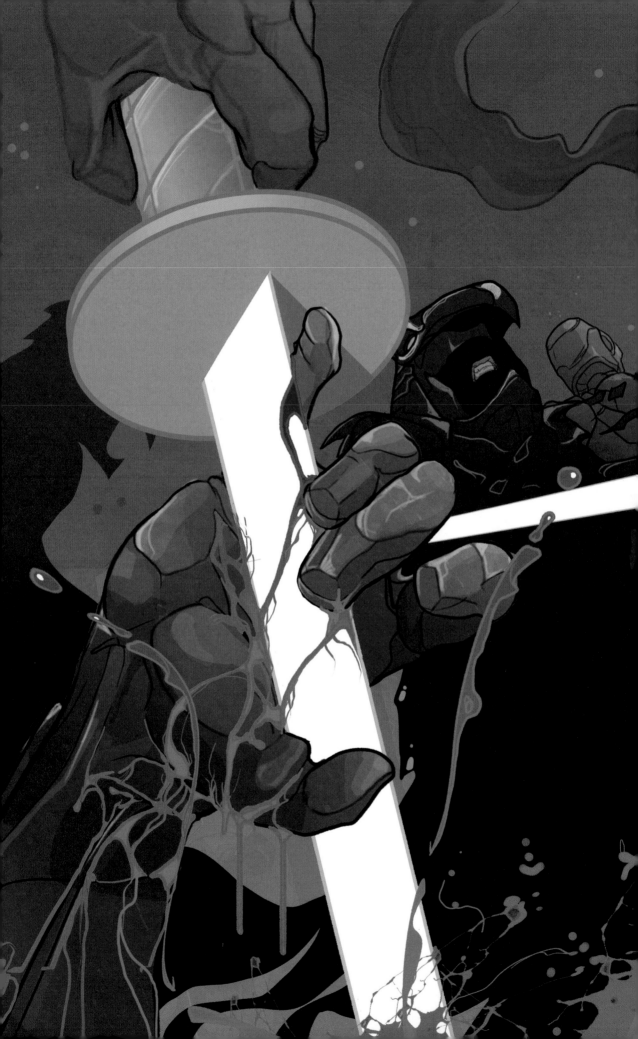

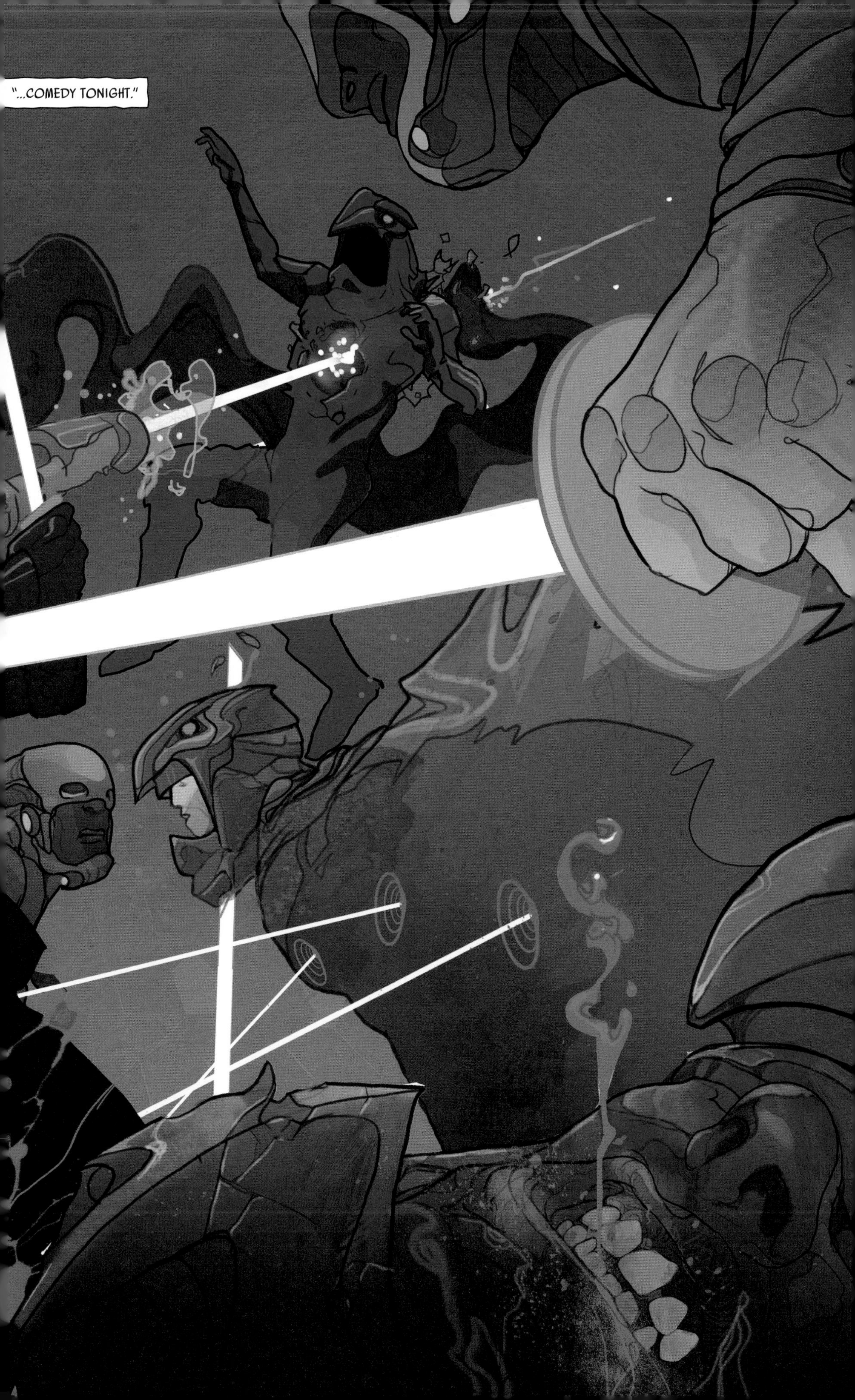
"...COMEDY TONIGHT."

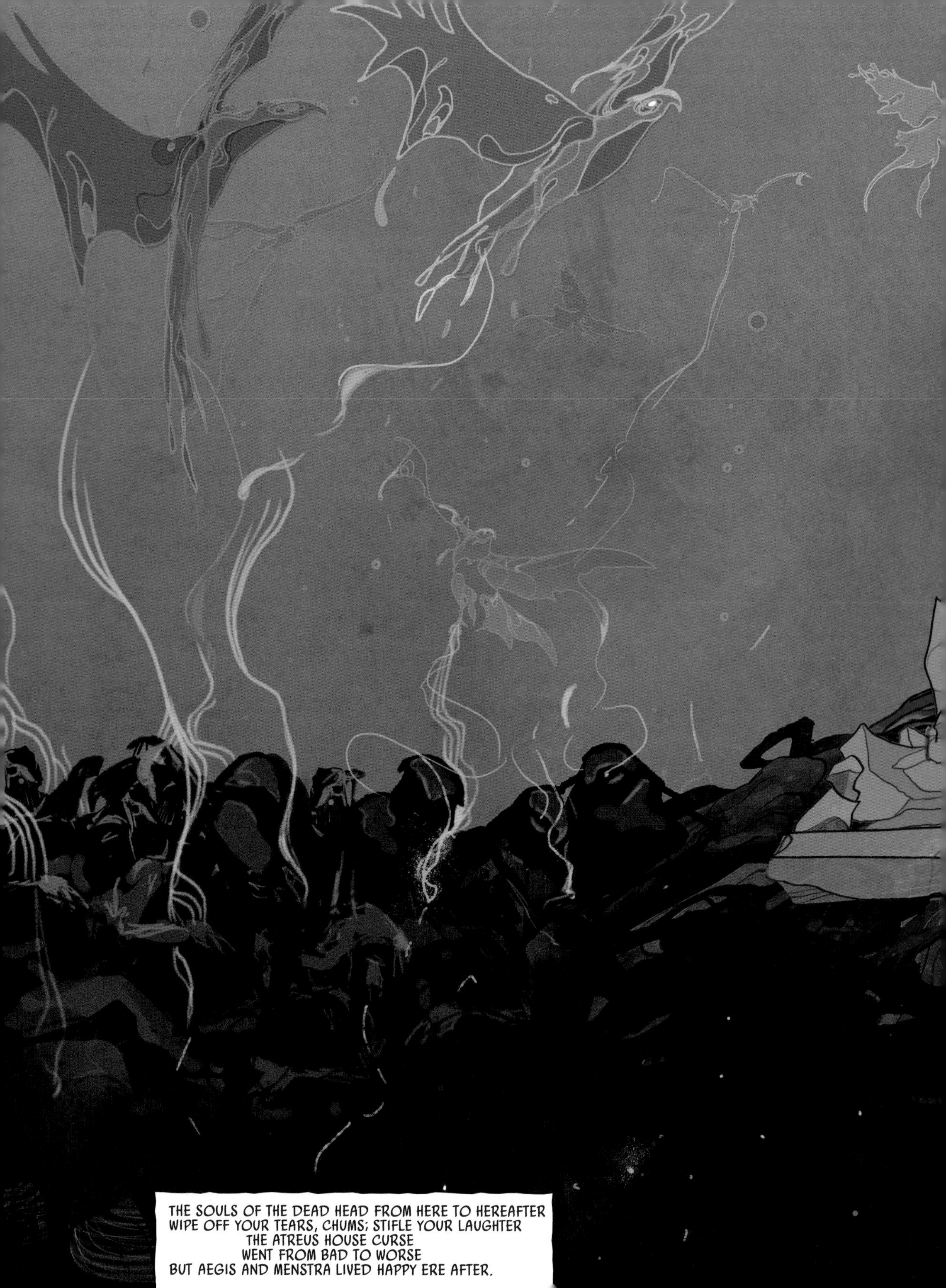
THE SOULS OF THE DEAD HEAD FROM HERE TO HEREAFTER
WIPE OFF YOUR TEARS, CHUMS; STIFLE YOUR LAUGHTER
THE ATREUS HOUSE CURSE
WENT FROM BAD TO WORSE
BUT AEGIS AND MENSTRA LIVED HAPPY ERE AFTER.

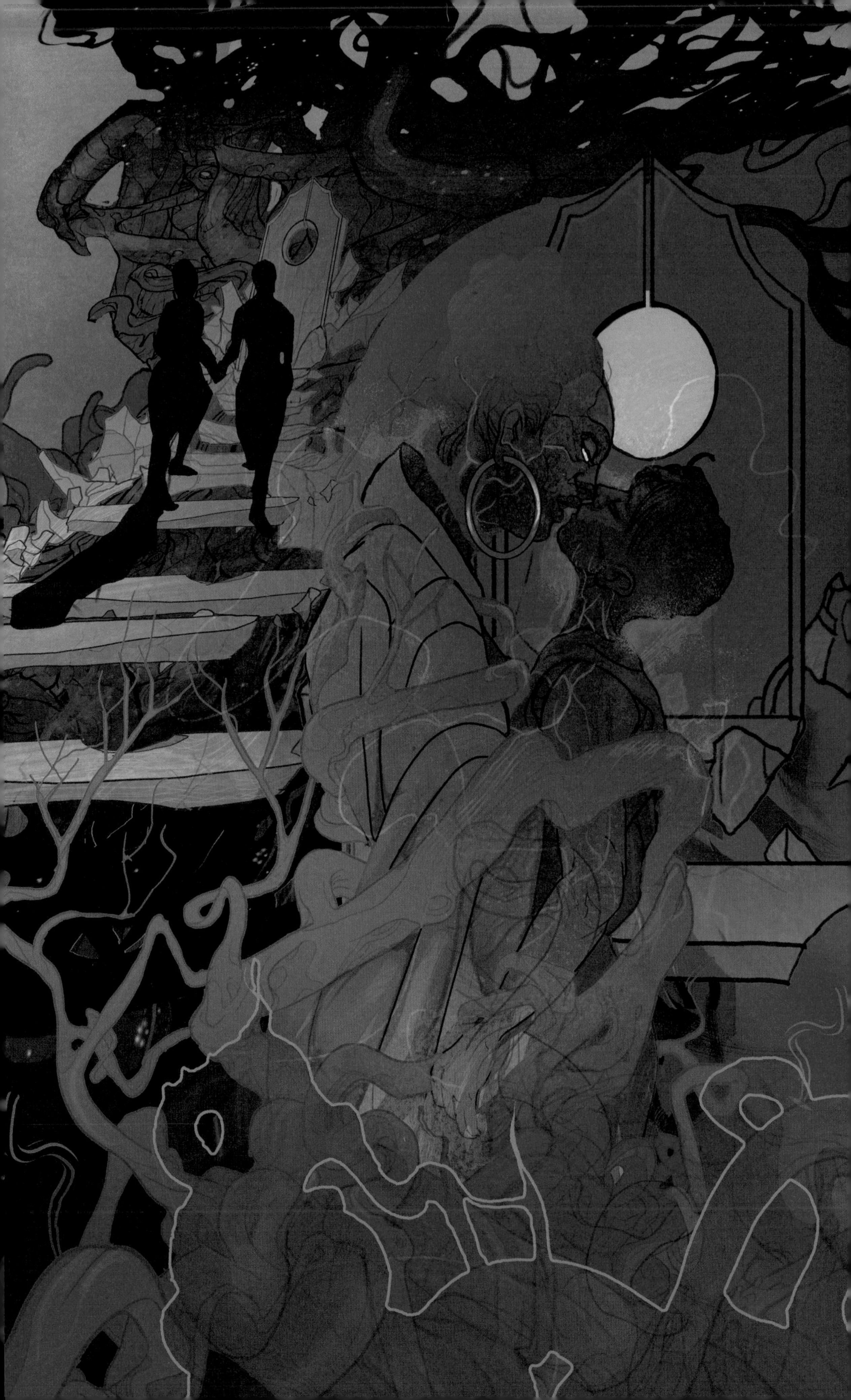

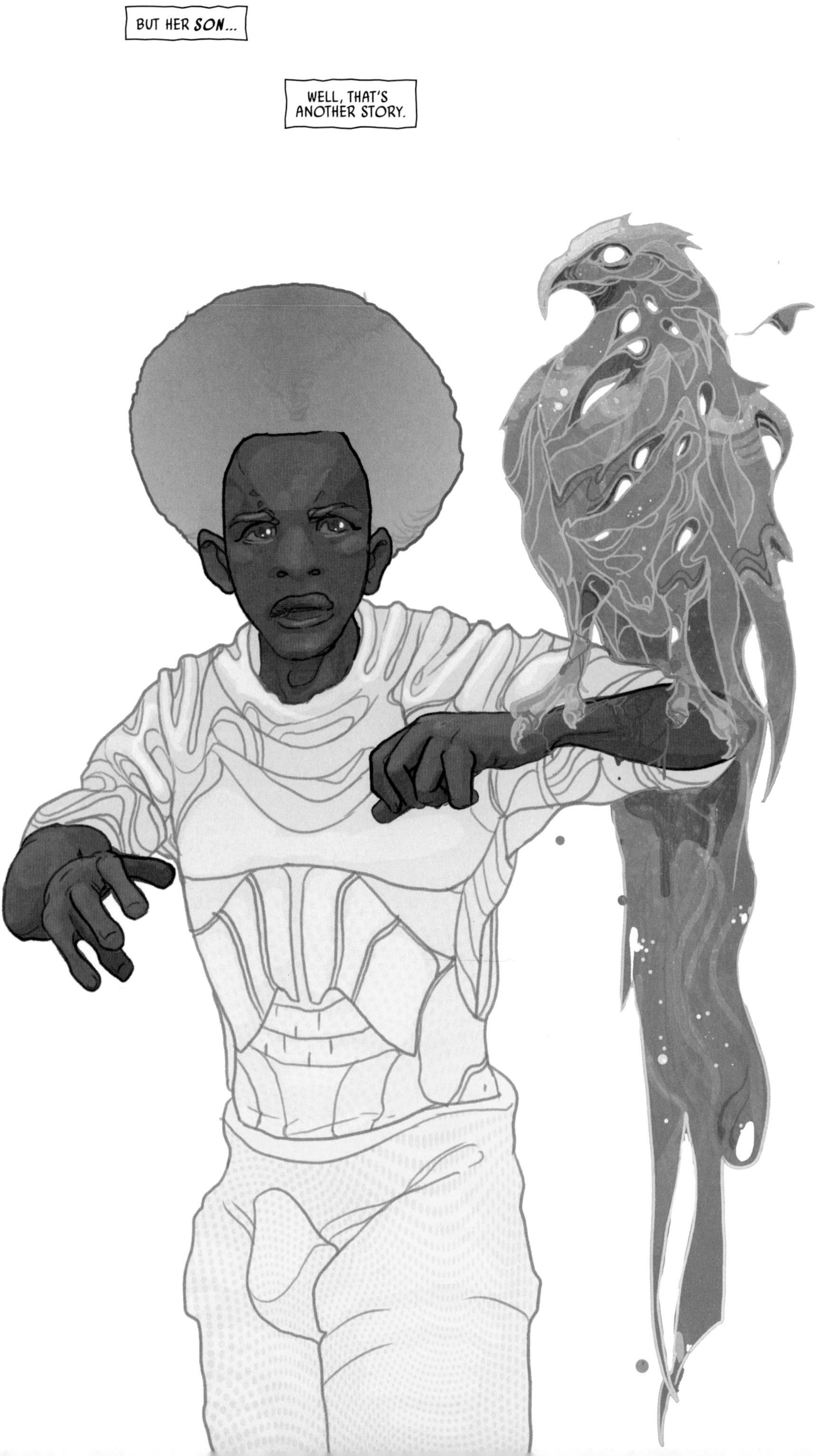
BUT HER SON...
WELL, THAT'S ANOTHER STORY.

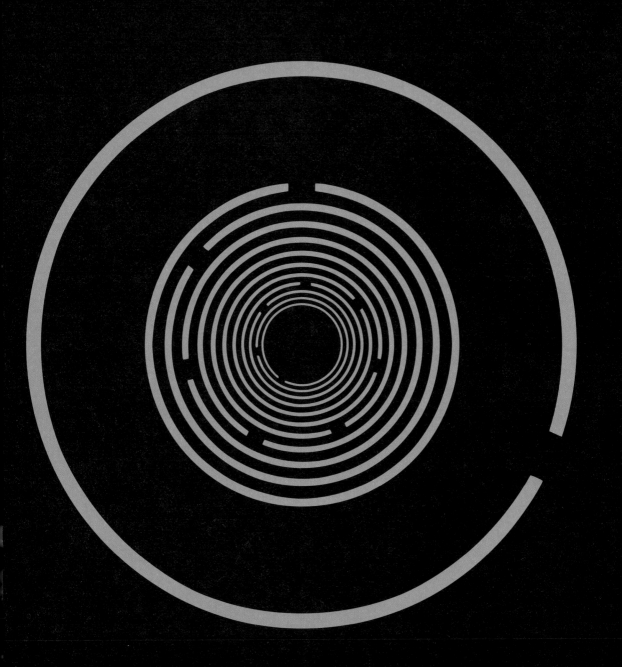

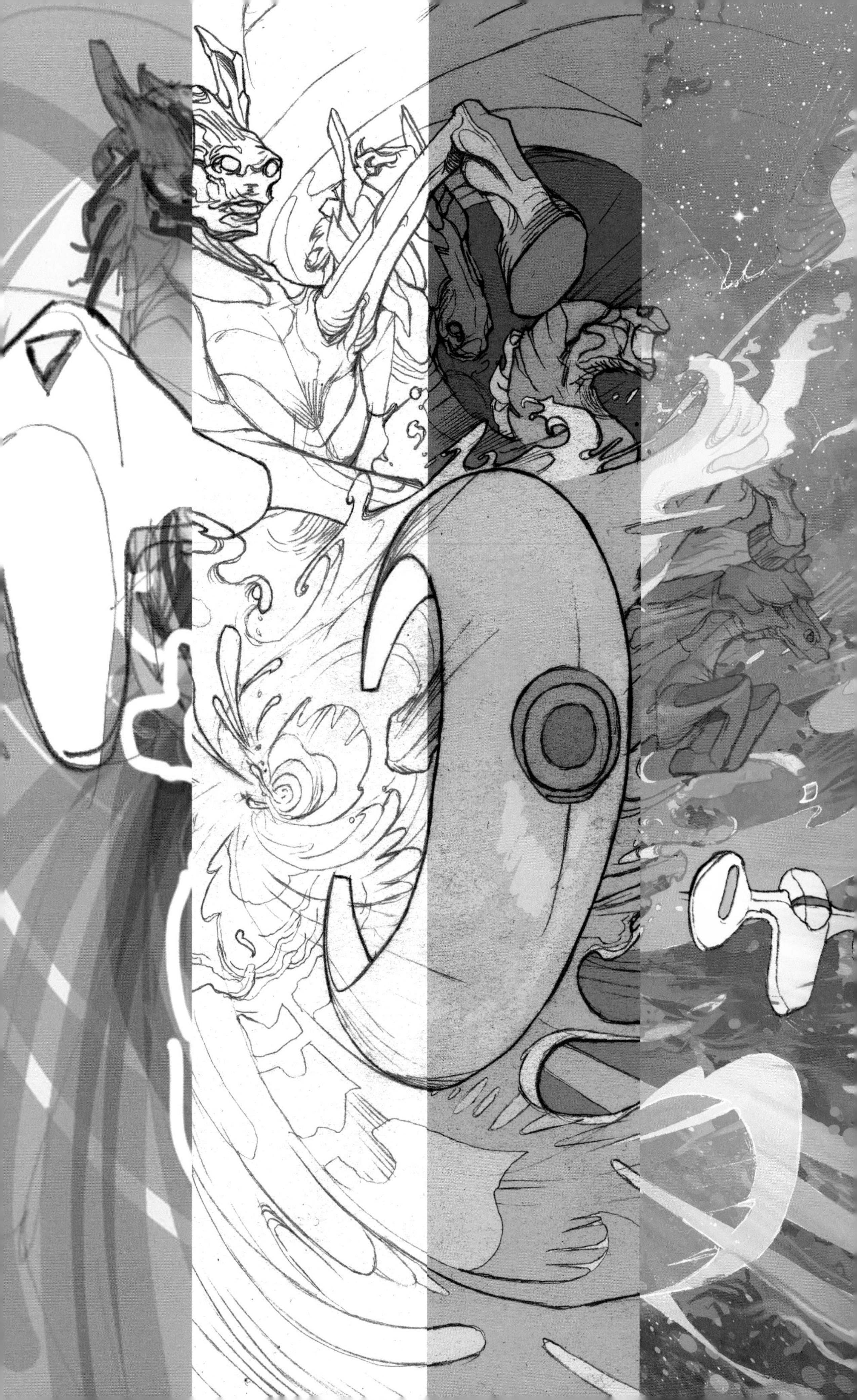

THE KYKLOS
THE MAKING OF ODY-C

A Beginner's Guide to Homeric Verse

by Dani Colman

Homer composed the *Iliad* and the *Odyssey* – the two greatest works of Greek poetry – in the eighth century BCE. The first time either poem was written down was more than three hundred years later, when an already thriving cult of Homeric scholarship in Hellenic Greece started keeping written record of their literature. For three hundred years, long after the poet himself was dead, the *Iliad* and the *Odyssey* were recited word-for-word by singers and poets, until the works were finally recorded and placed in the library at Alexandria, in the versions that scholars still study today.

Homer himself was an *aoidos*, which was an ancient minstrel poet. *Aoidoi* were the freestyle rappers of the ancient world: accompanying themselves on four-stringed lutes, they told epic, sprawling poems commemorating myths and heroes, recounting history and even commenting on current events, extemporising as they went. A good *aoidos* could recite hundreds of lines of poetry from a combination of memory and improvisation; *aoidoi* competed against each other in public events, trying to out-declaim each other for prestige, fame, and their own places in a kind of literary hero cult. Many *aoidoi*, like Homer himself, were blind, giving rise to a myth that the gods took their sight in exchange for the greater gift of poetic inspiration.

As impressive as professional *aoidoi* were, when Homer wrote the *Iliad* and the *Odyssey*, he elevated the *aoidos*

game to a whole new level. Many of the stories, including parts of the sacking of Troy, had been the subject of epic poetry before, but Homer decided to canonise it, creating a single, unified version of the siege of Troy and the homeward journey of Odysseus that would be remembered, word for word, millennia later. To do this, Homer drew on the techniques of his fellow *aoidoi* and his own prodigious poetic skill to write poetry so epic that it would give rise to a whole new generation of poet-performers: the *rhapsodes*, who, unlike their predecessors, recited pre-written epic poems from memory.

Almost all Classical – that is to say Latin and Greek – epic poetry is written in *dactylic hexameter,* which is a rhythmic structure that uses units of syllables like bars of music to create phrases of fixed length. English poetry uses rhythmic structures too: the most common is *iambic pentameter,* which was used often by Shakespeare to mimic the cadence of natural speech. Divided into five beats of unstressed and stressed syllables, iambic pentameter gives us some of the most famous lines in English literature:

> Oh *she* doth *teach* the *torch*-es *to* burn *bright.*

Or, in more mundane speech, the most English phrase in the world:

> I *think* I'm *going* to *make* a *cup* of *tea.*

English has a quirk, though: there's a natural cadence to which syllables are stressed, but it isn't set in stone. You can change the stress of any word to change the emphasis of the sentence:

> I think *I'm* going to make a cup of *tea.*

By changing the stress on particular words, you add extra meaning to the sentence: you might have made yourself a cup of coffee, but I'm going to stick to my Earl Grey, thank you very much.

Homeric Greek is very different. Rather than being divided into stressed and unstressed syllables, Greek syllables are long and short, with no interchangeability between the two. A phrase like πολυμητις Οδυσσευς – *polumetis Odysseus,* or "cunning Odysseus" – always has the same rhythm: *po-lu-***me***-tis* O-**dyss-eus**. It's a poetic Morse code, and one that *aoidoi* like Homer could use to help memorise and extemporise long passages of poetry. Every line is divided into six "feet"; each foot was either made up of a *dactyl* (a long syllable followed by two short syllables), or a *spondee* (two long syllables). Every line of epic poetry ended with a dactyl followed by a spondee, giving the end of a line the rhythm of *shave and a haircut.*

For the early *aoidoi*, dactylic hexameter was a skeleton around which they could build their improvised poems, like a jazz musician improvises over a

For Homer, though – the blind bard whose poetry was so magnificent that it influenced the way epics were told for two thousand years – the rhythms of his verse were a way to get the words of the *Iliad* and the *Odyssey* under people's skins.

blues scale. As long as he could fit four feet before the shave-and-a-haircut, an *aoidos* could piece extemporaneous poetry into the rest of the line like a rapper aiming for the final rhyme. And there were more tricks than just the cadence up a good *aoidos'* sleeve: generations of poets improvising epics on the fly built up a repository of stock descriptive phrases that could be slotted into a line of poetry as the hexameter required, like ῥοδοδάκτυλος Ἠώς (rosy-fingered dawn) or οἴνοπι πόντῳ (wine-dark sea).

When Homer started writing the *Iliad* and the *Odyssey*, dactylic hexameter and descriptive epithets were synonymous with epic poetry, and Homer used these techniques to build poetry that was both magnificent in scope, and relatively easy for him and his fellow *aoidoi* to recite verbatim. By the time Homer died, the *rhapsodos* was already beginning to replace the *aoidos*, and reciting the fifteen thousand lines of the *Iliad* and the twelve thousand lines of the *Odyssey* to a rapt audience became the first and only true measure of a *rhapsodos'* skill.

Later poets in Greek and Latin would push dactylic hexameter to its absolute limits, using combinations of dactyls and spondees to imitate the galloping of horses or the earthshaking footsteps of Titans. For Homer, though – the blind bard whose poetry was so magnificent that it influenced the way epics were told for two thousand years – the rhythms of his verse were a way to get the words of the *Iliad* and the *Odyssey* under people's skins. Unable to write his poetry down himself, and living in a time before written records were commonplace, Homer used the natural musicality of Greek to hack the language, and make himself – and his work – functionally immortal.

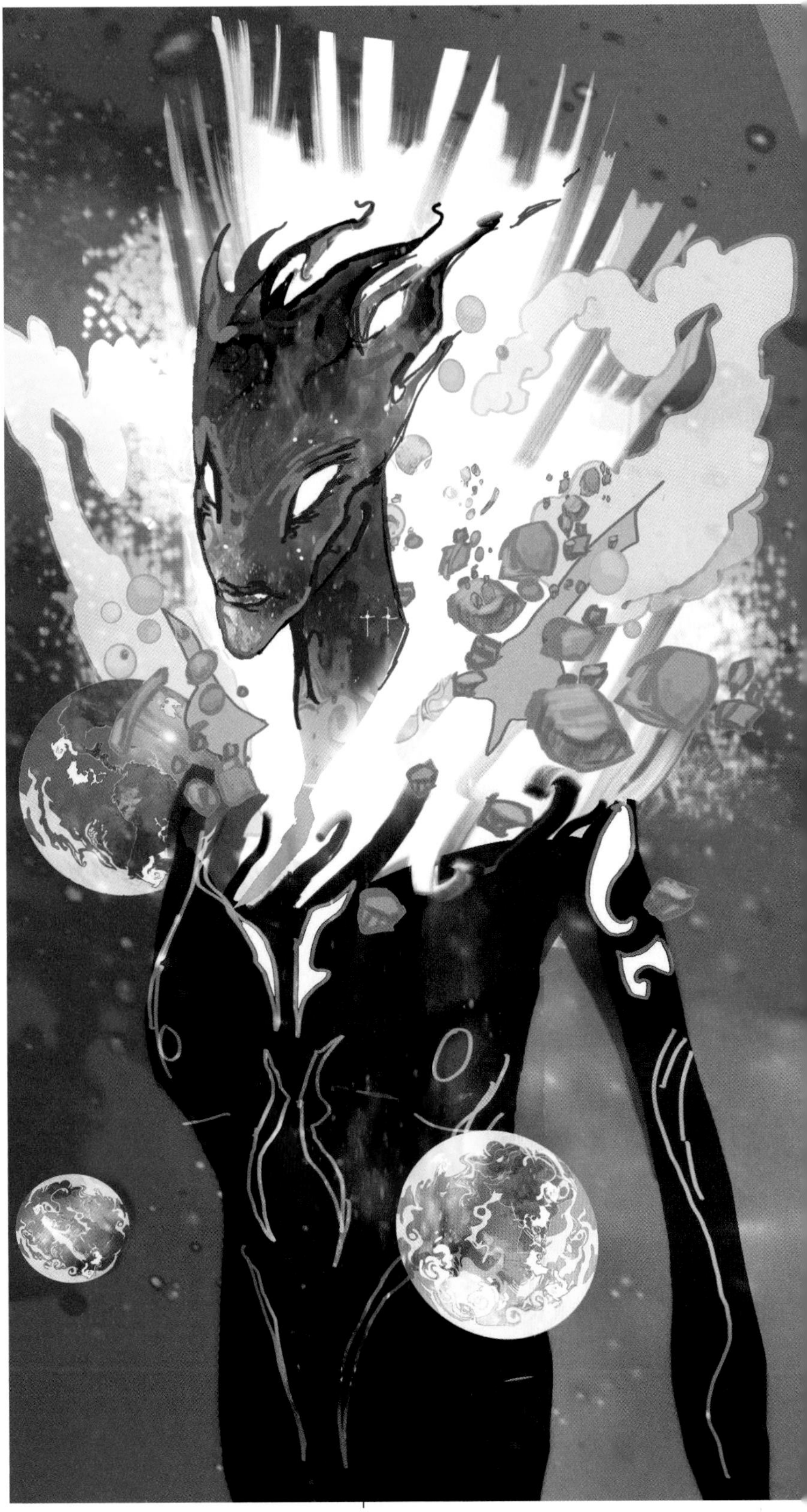

Poseidon concept by Christian Ward.

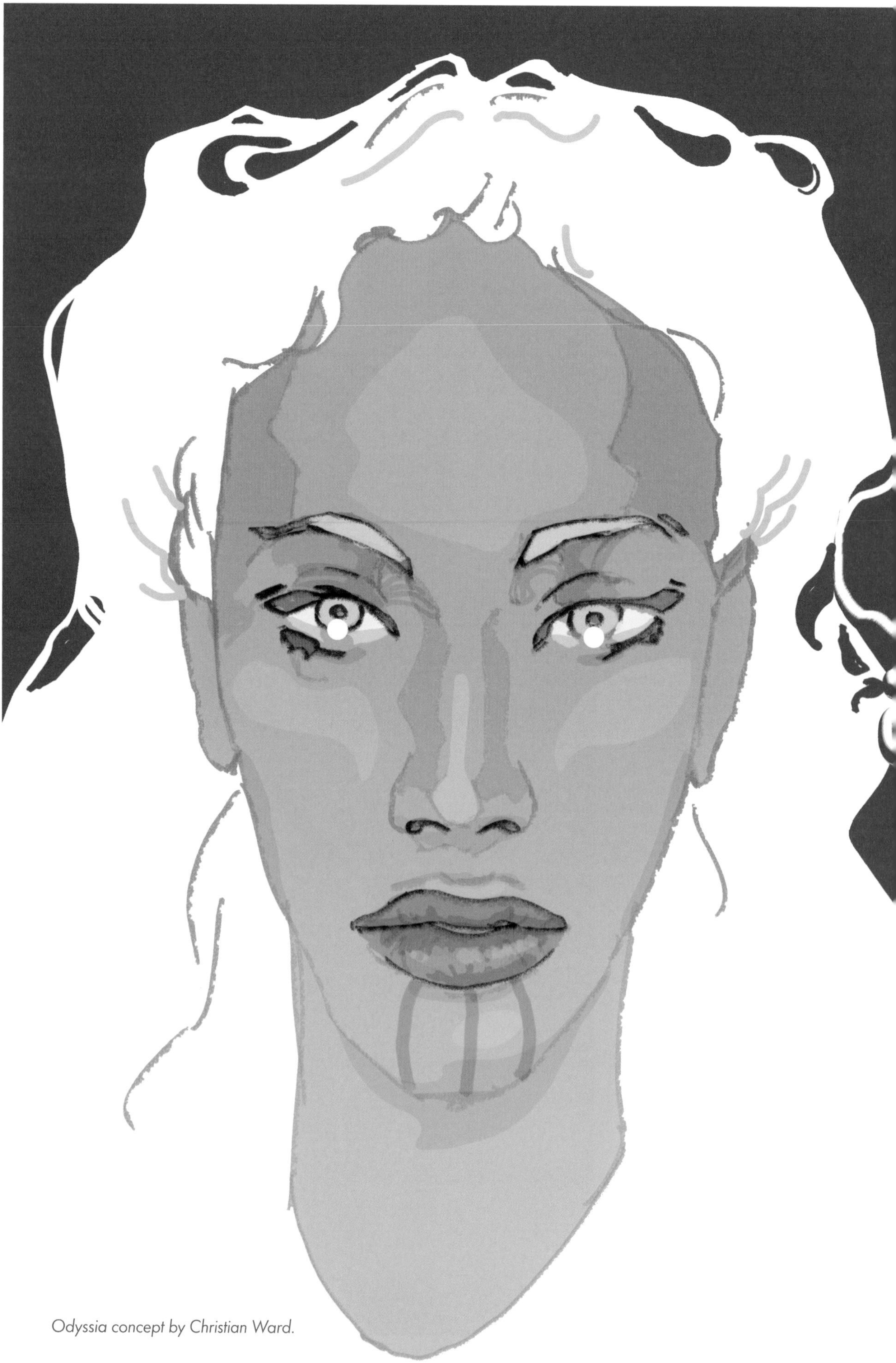

Odyssia concept by Christian Ward.

Homeric Heroes and Manly Tears

by Dani Colman

Odysseus gets a lot of epithets over the course of the *Odyssey*, but the most common is *polumetis*, which roughly translates to "of many wiles". *Metis* is what gets Odysseus out of the worst of his troubles: it's his *metis* that lets him outwit the Cyclops, just as it's *metis* that provides him the idea of the Trojan Horse. *Metis* was such an important concept to the Greeks that it got a personification: one of the titans, and Zeus' first wife. Metis passed on her gift for cunning to her daughter, Athena, who is Odysseus' champion throughout his journey. *Metis* was borne of women and passed down to women, yet heroic Odysseus literally lives or dies based on whether he follows his masculine *thumos* or his feminine *metis*.

To say epic Greek poetry was androcentric is an understatement at best. In fact, there are plenty who would say that the *Iliad* is almost entirely about masculinity: the warlike, leonine masculinity of heroes like Hector and Achilles contrasted with the feminine cowardice of Paris, or the duplicitous femininity of Helen. So it can be kind of jarring, expecting a story of red-blooded triumph in battle, to realize just how much time Homeric heroes spend crying their eyes out.

Odysseus weeps a lot over the course of his journey home to Ithaca. He weeps at the loss of his men; he weeps with homesickness; he weeps with desire and frustration and anger. Shedding tears was actually not considered unmasculine among heroes: indeed, a fundamental part of a hero's *thumos*, or spirit, was the feeling of strong passions and emotions, a surfeit of which was supposed to manifest as an outpouring of tears. Even Achilles, the manliest of Greek men, weeps openly when confronted with a grieving Priam, crying both in sympathy for Priam's loss and in shame for his part in the death and desecration of Priam's son Hector. Tears of emotion weren't just acceptable for masculine heroes of epic poetry: they were an almost exclusively masculine trait.

Greek women wept rather differently from Greek men. While women were expected to be emotional creatures, crying was considered unseemly for women of good breeding. The exception – and the one time a woman was not only allowed but encouraged to weep – was when a woman was in mourning. For a fallen husband or son, especially one lost in battle, all bets were off: women were expected to weep so ostentatiously that funeral keening was actually considered a form of music.

So Odysseus' tears aren't just admissible: by Homeric standards they're positively manly. There's one exception, though: when Odysseus is sojourning at the court of Alcinous, the blind bard Demodocus entertains the guests with the story of the sacking of Troy, and Odysseus loses it in a particularly unmanly fashion:

> "As a woman weeps, when she falls on her beloved husband…
> …and as she sees him gasping and dying, she throws her arms around him and shrilly keens…"

Odysseus' explicitly feminine tears – so unrestrained that Demodocus keeps having to stop his song – are a needle-scratch moment in what looks otherwise like a tale of unbridled manliness. After all, Odysseus doesn't just engineer the downfall of Troy; he also screws his way across most of the Mediterranean, shacking up with princesses, nymphs and witches on his way. But Homer was more subtle and less sexist than that, because if the *Iliad* is the story of masculinity causing Achilles' downfall, the *Odyssey* is all about Odysseus' femininity letting him win the day and survive the journey home.

Even Odysseus' sexual prowess has its roots in the feminine. In the same breath that Hector insults Paris' manhood, he also sneers at his reputation as a lover. Sure, a manly Greek was expected to have a wife and father children, but being guided by love and libido was something that women did. But for Odysseus, love and lust are almost as important as *metis* in leading him safely home. It's not his sword, though drawn, that allows Odysseus to save his men from the witch Circe's enchantment: it's his willingness to sleep with her. Odysseus' love for his wife Penelope persuades him to leave the island of the sea-nymph Calypso, but not before she builds him the boat that will take him home as thanks for his time as her lover.

There's never been any doubt among classicists that Odysseus is as manly a Greek hero as they come, but it's telling that by the time of the great tragedians like Aeschylus, tears of emotion had already become something that women shed, not men. Still, to this day, Odysseus surpasses almost all the heroes of tragedy as an icon of epic heroism. Perhaps it's because a poet as great as Homer had to know that, to quote classicist Helene Foley, "a man is never so much a man as when there is something of a woman in him."

Odysseus' explicitly feminine tears – so unrestrained that Demodocus keeps having to stop his song – are a needle-scratch moment in what looks otherwise like a tale of unbridled manliness.

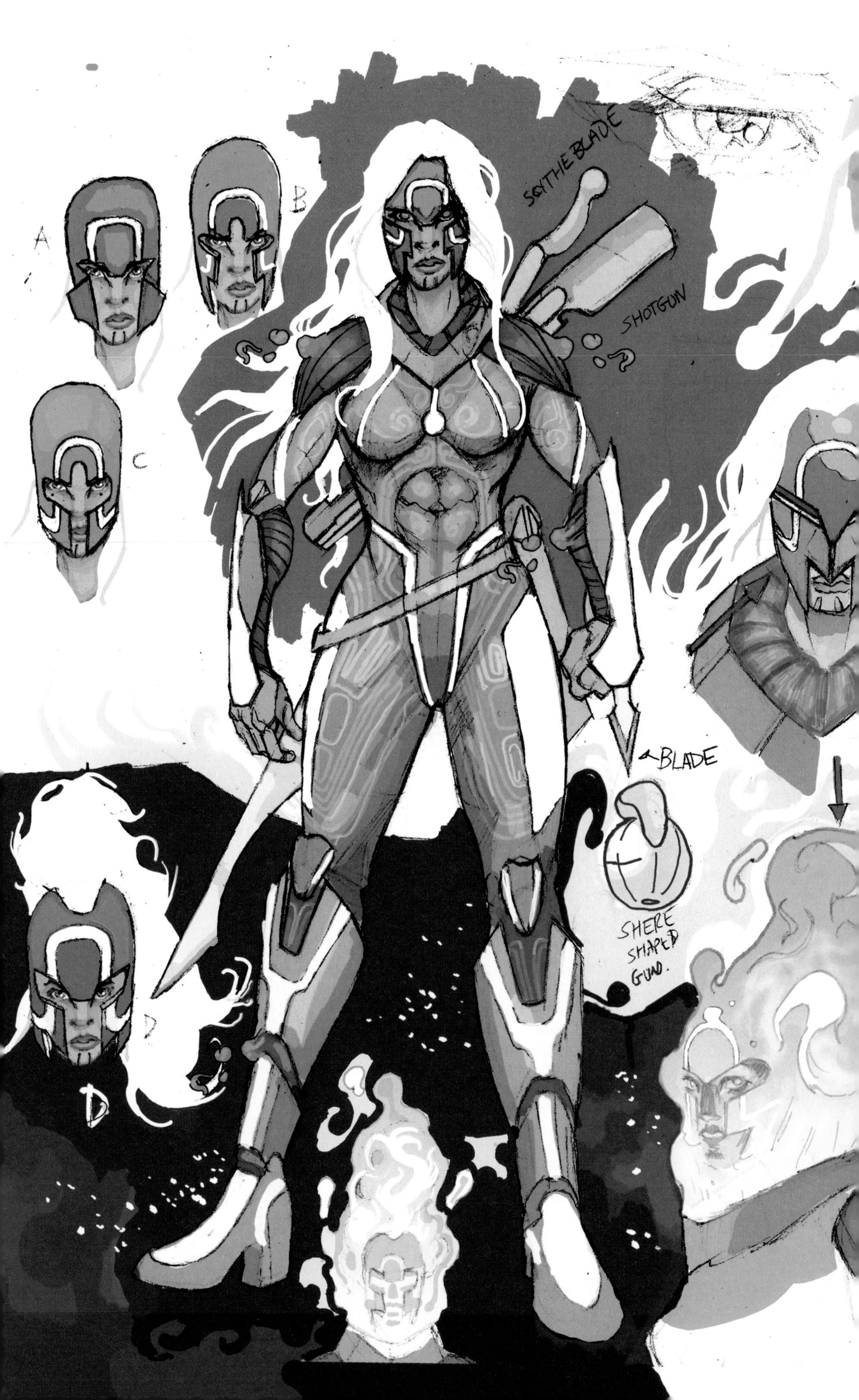
A
B
C
SCYTHE BLADE
SHOTGUN
BLADE
SHERE SHAPED GUN.
D
D

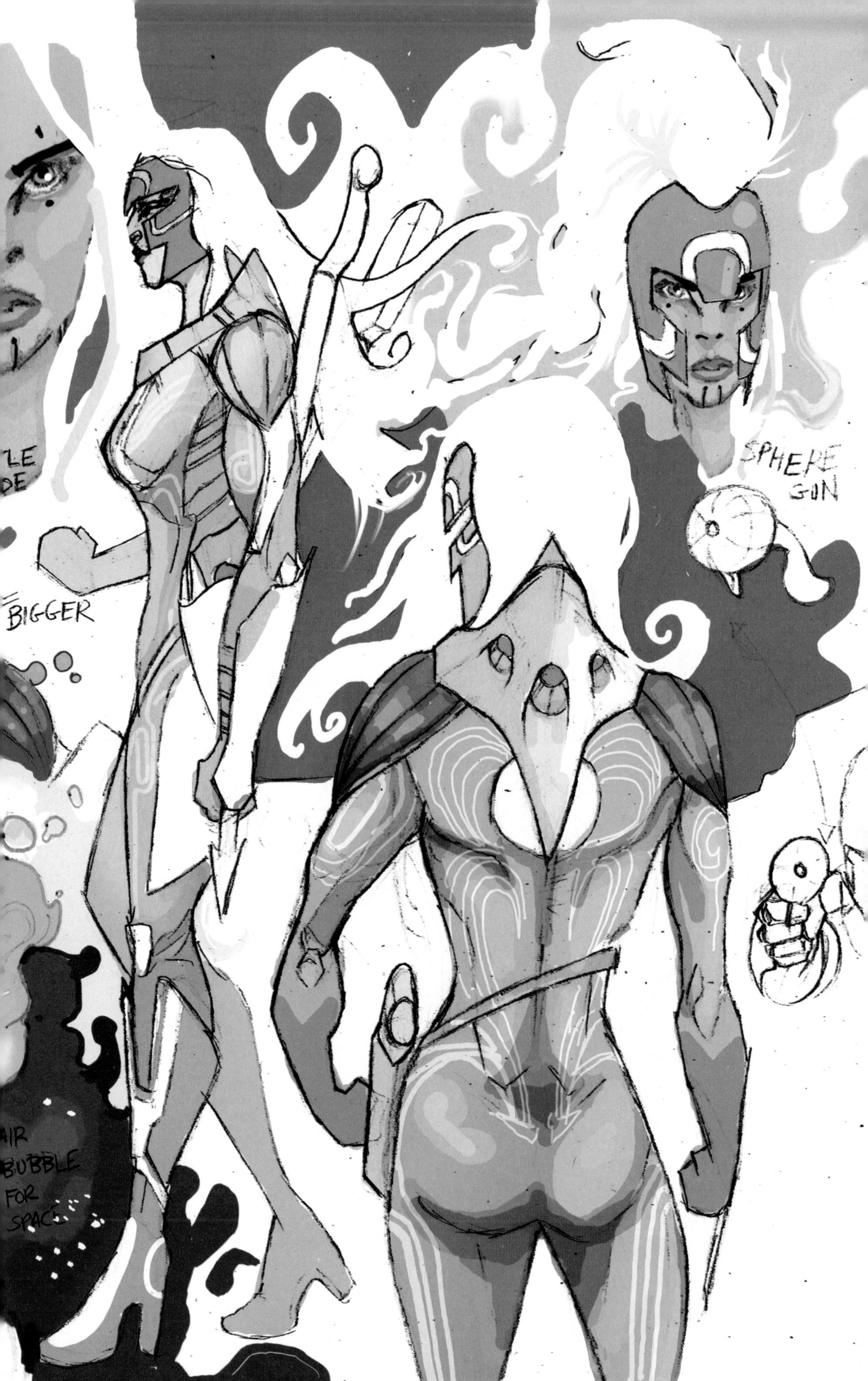
BIGGER
SPHERE GUN
AIR BUBBLE FOR SPACE

Odyssia costume concept by Christian Ward.

The Wives of Homer

by Dani Colman

Modern readings of the *Odyssey* have a lot of love for Circe and Calypso, the powerful, sexually liberated single ladies of Odysseus' journey, but they are outliers in a story that is not just about warfaring male heroes. Two wives motivate the *Illiad* and the *Odyssey*: Helen, whose beauty started the Trojan War, and Penelope, whose loyalty brought Odysseus home to Ithaca.

As queen of Sparta, Helen was privileged with unusual status. Sparta was one of very few Greek city-states that allowed women to own property; in fact, the women of Sparta enjoyed massive wealth and a great deal of influence. Sparta's militaristic culture meant that any man of status spent a great deal of time away at war, and Spartan society quickly realized that letting women actually run things while the men were off fighting was far wiser than leaving the city leaderless. From childhood, Helen would have trained with her brothers to fight, hunt, and engage in politics precisely so that she could rule Sparta if ever her husband had to fight on foreign soil.

Helen's lifestyle would not have changed much once she reached Troy: Troy was also one of the few places in the classical world where women enjoyed relative freedom and privilege. Helen wasn't much favored by Trojan society, especially once the Greeks came knocking at the walls, but by Trojan law she was allowed to own property, run a household and even take up a profession. The progressive attitudes towards women in Sparta and Troy make it a peculiar irony that the woman who should, historically, have had the most status and freedom ended up more of a bargaining chip than any other Homeric woman.

Helen is described as "the face that launched a thousand ships", but it was her political status, not her beauty, that kicked off the Trojan War. Sparta's dangerous army made it a valuable ally, so when Helen came of marriageable age, numerous suitors approached her father, Tyndareus, for her hand. Faced with a potential war if he denied any of them, Tyndareus asked wily Odysseus – himself one of the suitors – for advice, whereupon Odysseus suggested that all the suitors swear an oath to protect each other no matter who was chosen. Tyndareus seized this opportunity to choose Menelaus, the adoptive son he was already grooming to rule Sparta; more importantly, it was this Tyndarean Oath upon which Menelaus called when he set out to reclaim Helen from Paris, turning the Trojan War from a spurned husband's folly into the bloody siege of legend.

Ultimately, even Helen's "choice" to run off with Paris wasn't actually her choice at all. Helen's love was promised by Aphrodite as a bribe in an Olympic beauty pageant, making Helen perhaps the only Homeric woman to be used as a political tool by another woman. After Paris' death, the disgraced Helen was given to his brother Deiphobus as a spoil of war, until Menelaus killed him and took Helen back to Sparta. Not much is known about Helen's fate after that – some accounts have her living a quiet life of privilege with Menelaus, while others describe her being tricked to her death by the grieving wife of another king killed in the Trojan War. Still others say that she never made it to Troy at all: blown off-course on his way home, Paris landed in Egypt, where King Proteus realized that Helen was far too valuable a commodity to be taken to a city bound for war, and commanded that Helen stay in Egypt with him.

Back in Ithaca, Odysseus' wife Penelope didn't quite enjoy the freedoms of a Spartan woman, but she had something far more valuable than joint ownership of Odysseus' estate. Greek noble descent was matrilineal; a king's eldest daughter brought her father's kingdom to her marriage as a dowry, while sons were expected to claim their own kingdoms by marrying princesses from other city-states. A noblewoman without natural inheritance of her own, Penelope became the rightful queen of Ithaca when she married Odysseus, and would remain queen until her death. Had Penelope and Odysseus had a daughter then the next king of Ithaca would have been her husband, not first-born male Telemachus. So none of Penelope's many suitors were interested in her for her winning personality – and, though she is usually described as easy on the eyes, none of them cared about her looks either.

To an ambitious nobleman taking advantage of Odysseus' presumed death at sea, Penelope represented one thing: rule over Ithaca, and with it a potent alliance with the other allegiants of the Tyndarean Oath. Ithaca was a powerful island state, home to great wealth and influence. Penelope's family ties to Sparta and Mycenae only made her more valuable as a political tool, and that's all she was to her suitors. Any of Penelope's suitors' ultimate plans would have looked something like this:

1. Marry Penelope.
2. Sleep with Penelope – as soon and as often as possible.
3. Get Penelope pregnant.
4. Arrange a nice, convenient death for Telemachus to secure the line of succession.

Steps three and four were interchangeable (two of Penelope's least appealing suitors try to get Telemachus killed as their first order of business), but the aim was the same: win Penelope to win Ithaca. Penelope's legendary loyalty to her absent husband was about far more than just love or propriety. Penelope represented the ideal wife in Greek society, not just because she was faithful to her husband, but because as Odysseus' wife, she owned the keys to his kingdom, and used all her wits and skill to protect them.

The progressive attitudes towards women in Sparta and Troy make it a peculiar irony that the woman who should, historically, have had the most status and freedom ended up more of a bargaining chip than any other Homeric woman.

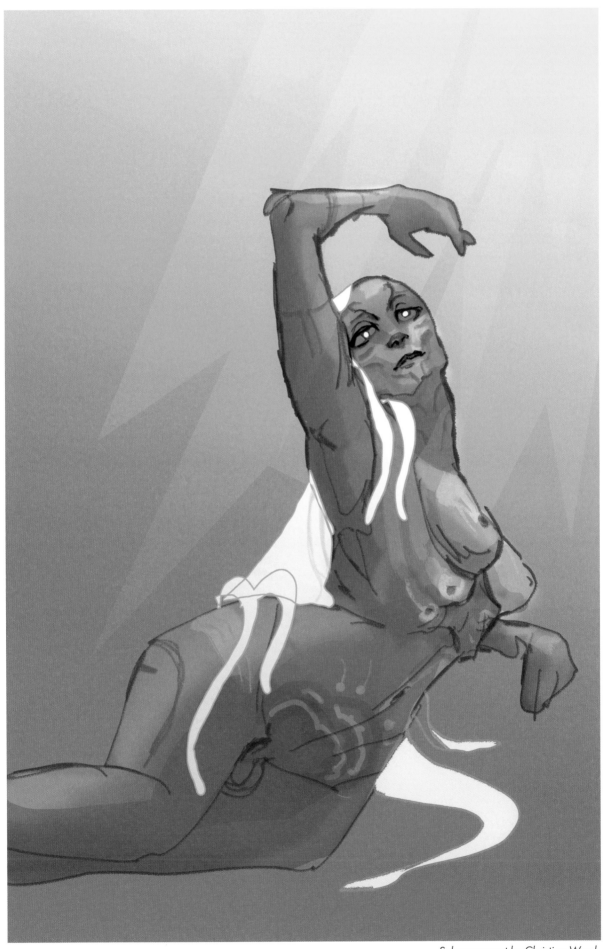

Sebex concept by Christian Ward.

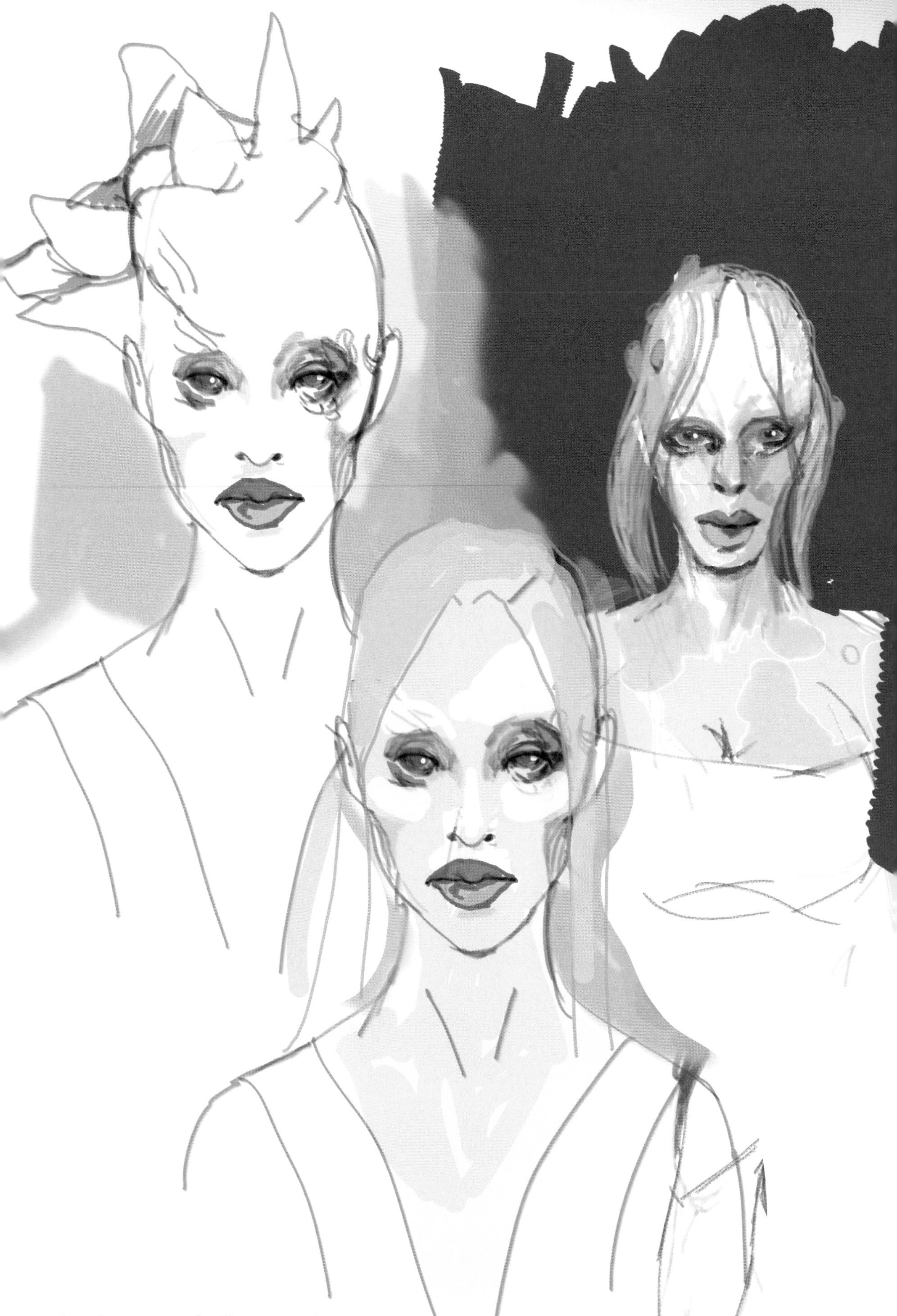

Lotus Eaters concept by Christian Ward.

Women of Mytheme

by Dani Colman

In language there is a phenomenon called the false cognate, in which two languages that cannot possibly have any connection share words with strikingly similar sounds and meanings. Though these word pairs defy explanation other than coincidence, their existence points tantalisingly towards a kind of global linguistic unity, in which contemporary English speakers and ancient Australian aborigines share the same word for "dog" because we're all just human, aren't we?

Storytelling has its own version of false cognates, embedded in what we now think of as tropes and archetypes. Even more than their cognate cousins, these mythemes weave themselves throughout mythology, painting a picture of interconnected humanity through scattered fragments of common story. Thus, in both China and France, sometime in the 17th century, a little girl meets a beast along the road who tricks her into thinking it is her grandmother; and in both Ionic Greece, and 8th-century Persia, two women use extraordinary cunning to escape the whims of cruel and capricious men.

The last essay introduced us to Odysseus' wife Penelope, who was kept busy during her husband's long absence by a string of unpleasant suitors vying for her hand and her throne. Refusing these suitors outright was politically complicated: many of them were noblemen and commanded considerable power; but to accept any one's proposal would condemn Penelope's son Telemachus to death, and Penelope herself to rape and probable assassination as soon as she bore a child.

A continent and several centuries away, newlywed Scheherazade had a marital outlook just as bleak as Penelope's. Caliph Shahryár, her new husband, held a particularly spectacular grudge: after his first wife was unfaithful, he devel-oped a hatred of women that makes GamerGate look like an ACLU parade, marrying and then beheading a new wife every day so no woman would ever have the chance to cuckold him again. Volunteering as the thousand-and-first bride, Scheherazade knew that she was on a suicide mission, with only the hours between sunrise and sunset to stop the vicious cycle for herself and every single woman in Persia.

For both these women, escape and violence were not options. Penelope bore responsibility for Ithaca and for her son, neither of which were safe without her claim to rule. Scheherazade was prisoner inside the palace and bound by a ticking clock the moment she married the Caliph. Unable to fight or flee, Penelope and Scheherazade had no choice but to delay.

Penelope was the model of a good Greek wife, and in that virtue she found her reprieve. Laertes, Odysseus' father, was in poor health and likely soon to die, and as the dutiful daughter-in-law it fell to Penelope to weave his ornate burial shroud. To appease the suitors, she promised that she would marry when the shroud was done. Every day she wove, and every night she picked apart her weaving, holding off the suitors for one more day as she claimed continuation with her unfinished work.

Scheherazade's solution was also, night by night, to delay, but instead of weaving cloth, the Persian princess wove stories. Her sister, planted as a handmaiden among her entourage, forestalled Scheherazade's appointed execution by begging her to tell a tale, and the resulting stories became the famous *One Thousand and One Nights*. The child of storytellers herself, Scheherazade was a master, using framing narratives to stretch out tales over several nights and keep the Caliph too enraptured to kill her until the story was over.

Most of Scheherazade's stories were tales of heroic men: the seafaring Sinbad even has a few mythemes in common with Odysseus. The women of the Arabian Nights were usually slaves and concubines, and, perhaps to appease the Caliph's own misogyny, they spend a lot of time being beaten, ordered about and even killed. But, degraded as they are, Scheherazade's women are rarely passive or obedient. The wives cheat; the slaves steal; scorned women exact often unreasonable revenge.

What's the point? Scheherazade could easily have told tale after tale of heroic, good and faithful women, building Shahryar a personal mythology of perfect womanhood that might have persuaded the Caliph to give up his grudge and once again to see women as beautiful and worthy. How could she know that her stories of concubines, cuckolders, connivers and cheats — even interspersed with tales of princesses and goddesses — wouldn't enrage the Caliph and hasten her own execution?

Scheherazade isn't around to ask, but if she were, her answer might have been that of any observant woman: that giving the Caliph an ideal of womanhood would only make the problem worse, in the end. Scheherazade never had any guarantee that her strategy wouldn't one day fail and end in her death, but she did know that the thousand wives before her died because they were being held up to an unattainable ideal. Scheherazade's stories paint a complex, flawed and fascinating portrait of womanhood, and they do so not to protect her own safety, but to protect all the potential wives who might come after her. A Caliph who lusted after a perfect myth of women could only ever be disappointed; a Caliph enraptured with stories of women both beautiful and flawed might one day love a woman for real.

This was how women of myth survived: they used their *metis* — the same quality of cunning that makes Odysseus such an unusual hero. More combative women — and we'll meet one next time — fared badly, brought low by patriarchal disgust of violent women. But with cunning, a woman could hope to slip her agenda past the eyes of watchful men, changing her circumstances by inches until she had shaped the world to her image.

Scheherazade's stories paint a complex, flawed and fascinating portrait of womanhood, and they do so not to protect her own safety, but to protect all the potential wives who might come after her.

Stories That Save

by Dani Colman

*It was a dark and stormy night,
And the wind was blowing a gale
When the captain said to his
shipmate,
"Shipmate, tell me a tale!"*

And this was the tale he told:

"It was a dark and stormy night..."

Unless there's something dolphins are saying to each other that we are just not getting, storytelling might be the last true barrier between humans and other animals. Neither zebras that mourn their dead nor crows that solve complex puzzles tell bedtime tales to their children, yet the telling of stories is absolutely universal throughout every single human collective across the globe and across all of time.

Why?

We don't know exactly how it started, but we do know that the human brain is literally built to respond to stories. A Princeton study imaged the brains of speakers and listeners to find out why stories resonate the way they do, and discovered something amazing. When the speaker was delivering facts alone, the listener's brain responded in a localized fashion: number-processing areas for figures, language-processing areas for words and so on. But when the speaker told a *story*, with characters, settings and narrative flow, the listen-

er's brain lit up like a Christmas tree. Neurological areas for processing smell, color, movement and emotion went into overdrive, lighting up in patterns that exactly matched the brain activity of the storyteller. The act of telling a story – especially of telling one well – turns your audience's brain into a photocopy of your own, overriding any other stimuli that the listener is experiencing independently. When a story is so good you feel like you were actually there in the middle of it, it's because, at least as far as your brain is concerned, you actually were.

The power of a story to neurologically transport someone goes a long way towards explaining why, for storytellers like Scheherazade, the stories they told were the literal tools of their salvation. It's easy to ascribe the importance of Scheherazade's storytelling gambit to her clever use of the cliffhanger and the tale-within-a-tale, by which she ensured none of her stories had a truly satisfying end until she herself was truly satisfied that ending them wouldn't end her own life. But Scheherazade's brave gambit would not have worked in the first place were it not for the primal power of storytelling itself. In the worst of situations, surrounded by the worst of people, a good story can momentarily change the question of survival from "Where do I find food?" or "How do I endure?" to "What happens *next*?"

Scheherazade lived centuries too early to understand the neuroscience behind why stories work, but she survived her marriage to Caliph Shahryár because she understood the other thing that gives stories immense power. Because we are hardwired to respond to stories, human beings tend to frame everything around them – including our own lives – in narrative terms. And, because it takes a particularly low view of oneself to play the sidekick in one's own story, we tend to cast ourselves as the heroes in our own lives, bending our experience of reality around us to fit the stories we think the world is telling on our behalf. When Scheherazade married Shahryár, she was the heroine of a story of tragic sacrifice, but that wasn't the Caliph's story. Cuckolded by his former wife and betrayed, as he saw it, by all womankind, Shahryár was the hero of a revenge story. If Scheherazade was to turn her story of sacrifice into one of triumph, she was going to have to pull a genre switch on the Caliph as well.

Night after night, for almost three years, Scheherazade used her narrative gift to hack into her husband's brain and reshape it in her own image. Story to story, her immediate goal was to build such an emotional response in her husband that the need to know what happened next became more important than his role in his own story – his heroic need to kill her to sustain his vengeful narrative. Over the long haul, Scheherazade needed to convince Shahryár that he was the hero of a different story than the one he thought he was: a love story, with Scheherazade as his leading lady. The stories of *One Thousand and One Nights* have been changed and added to over the years, but if you read carefully you can start to see exactly what kind of game Scheherazade was playing with the Caliph, and how she managed to pull off his eventual change of heart.

Scheherazade's brave gambit would not have worked in the first place were it not for the primal power of storytelling itself. In the worst of situations, surrounded by the worst of people, a good story can momentarily change the question of survival from "Where do I find food?" or "How do I endure?" to "What happens *next*?"

The story cycle begins as base entertainment, with wicked women subject to brutal revenge in stories that mirrored the one Shahryár thought he was living. But as the cycle continues, they grow in complexity: adulteresses grow personalities and demand sympathy for their lapses; criminals have reasons for their crimes; and – most importantly – the heroes begin to exercise compassion and mercy, demonstrating wisdom and temperance and taking the advice of counsellors. After three years of hearing these stories, the Caliph could no longer be the hero of a revenge story; to his changed mind, such men were no longer heroes at all. A hero acted wisely and loved deeply, and eventually that's exactly what Caliph Shahryár did.

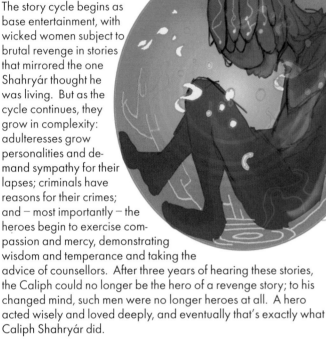

Captain's pod design by Christian Ward.

Even today, stories retain their extraordinary power to overcome difficult reality. In a San Diego Comic-Con panel[1], writer Gail Simone told the story of how she found this out in person: a fan approached her, emotional, and told her that during his struggles with suicidal impulses he had turned to her run on *Batgirl* to get by. Caught up in the story Simone was telling, he realised he couldn't kill himself without finding out what Barbara Gordon was going to get up to in the next issue. The strange neurological link between storyteller and listener let him borrow Gail Simone's brain when his own was working against him, and the question of what happens next became more powerful than the desire to end it all. Over months of chipping away at his depression while *Batgirl* gave him a reason to stay alive, he managed to change his own genre as well, turning himself from the antihero of a tragedy to the hero of a story of triumph over adversity. In pictures or prose, on stage or on screen, stories create shared experience across vast time and distance, and that shared experience is a powerful tool for good.

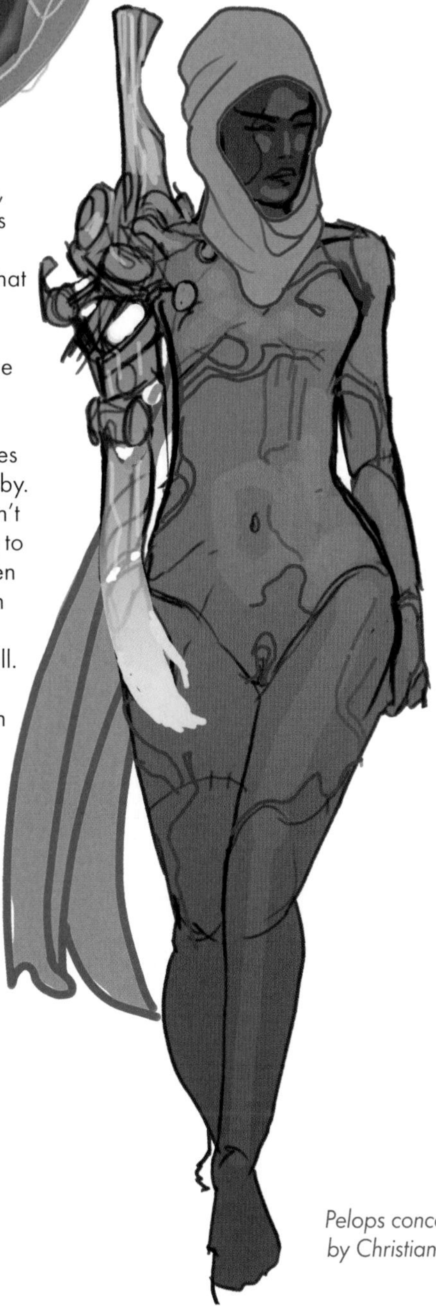

Pelops concept by Christian Ward.

1. "India Inkblot Test: Why Comics Are Good For Mental Health" (San Diego Comicon 2015), http://tiny.cc/SimonePanel

Call Me Ishmael

by Dani Colman

*"How very like a whale." –
Hamlet, by way of a Sub-Sub
Librarian, by way of Herman
Melville.*

While you have to admire his
commitment to telling us about the
misadventures of mad Captain
Ahab and his great white whale,
it's hard to argue that *Moby Dick's*
Ishmael is anything but a really
lousy narrator. He comments on
conversations he can't possibly
have heard, he disappears from the
story for chapters at a time, and,
thanks to chapter upon chapter
about the various uses of blubber
(and some far-too-serious insistence
that whales are actually fish), he
doesn't even invite his readers
onto the *Pequod* until chapter
21. Even when Ishmael stops
getting distracted by questionable
cetology, he still attacks his
narration with all the focus and
consistency of a hyper-caffeinated
literature student confusing classes
during finals, telling parts of the
story in verse, in play form, and,
at one point, in the form of a
sermon. Half of the appeal (and

frustration) of *Moby Dick* is the
frenetic inconsistency of Ishmael's
narration, and, in a book about a
mad captain's quest for a murderous
albino sperm whale, that's saying
something.

What is it about Ishmael that makes
him as memorable to a reader as
a vengeful whale, despite being
absent for a good third of the book?
Why do the fantastical stories of the
One Thousand and One Nights
need Scheherazade to hold them
together? Why does Homer hand
off parts of his epic poems to bards,
to Odysseus himself, and even to
one of Penelope's dead suitors in
the Underworld?

We've already explored the
strange neurological link between
storytellers and their listeners[1]: When
someone tells a story to someone

1. See "Stories That Save", ODY-C #8

else, even impersonally via a book
or tape, the brains of both the teller
and the listener light up in tandem[2],
temporarily becoming carbon
copies of each other. When a
storyteller adds a narrator to the
mix, that psychic chain gains a link,
and the teller gets to filter the story
through an intermediary's brain.
Readers care far less about stories
than they do about characters, and
adding a narrator allows an author
to give an entire story a character
to whom a reader can narrate, and
about whom a reader can care.

A closer look at *Moby Dick* shows
us just how aware Melville was of
the power of character to connect
a story to the reader. Even before
Ishmael gets down to the business
of telling the story, Melville pulls us
in with glossaries and epigraphs:
where most authors present
epigraphs without context as a sort
of literary figurehead to a chapter,

2. Stephens GJ, Silbert LJ, Hasson U. "Speaker-
listener neural coupling underlies successful
communication." Proc Natl Acad Sci U S A.
2010 Aug 10;107(32):14425-30.

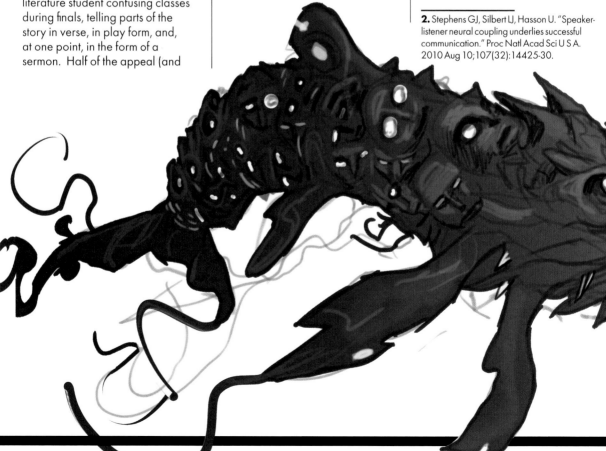

Melville goes to great lengths to ensure us that his epigraphs were in fact collated by a "mere painstaking burrower and grub-worm of a poor devil of a Sub-Sub [Librarian]", who "appears to have gone through the long Vaticans and street-stalls of the earth, picking up whatever random allusions to whales he could anyways find in any book whatsoever, sacred or profane". There is absolutely no need to tell the reader that anyone collected the series of quotes and idioms about whales that precedes the story of *Moby Dick*, yet in doing so Melville reframes them with their own mini-story, and more than a little humor.

Ishmael's job, then, is to hand-hold the reader through points of view, using the reader's personal connection to him to navigate the sometimes rocky waters of admiration for Ahab, awe of the whale, and affection for the fearsomely striking Queequeg. The story doesn't work if the reader sees through Ahab's zeal to madness too quickly; the story particularly doesn't work if the 19th century readers are guided by their 19th century prejudices against men of color like Queequeg, so Melville uses Ishmael's relatable voice to tell his readers how to think. With his very first invocation − "Call

What is it about Ishmael that makes him as memorable to a reader as a vengeful whale, despite being absent for a good third of the book? Why do the fantastical stories of the *One Thousand and One Nights* need Scheherazade to hold them together?

me Ishmael" − Ishmael makes it personal, and that colors how we experience the story.

Note, though, that the insertion of a narrator is not always to guarantee the reader's sympathies. In late verses of the *Odyssey*, when Penelope's suitor Amphimedon tells us of the slaughter at the feast, we aren't supposed to side suddenly with a man whose plan was to rape Penelope and murder Telemachus. In this case, it's our knowledge of his treachery that colors our reading of his tale, inviting us to defy the natural sympathy between storyteller and listener to call him out on his lies. In other cases, such as Nabokov's

Lolita, the trustworthiness of the narrator is far less clear, and the act of reading it becomes a choice by the reader of whether or not to trust the narrator's appeal to our sympathy. Agatha Christie even uses our built-in trust of the narrator in one of her murder mysteries to set up a devastating twist that is almost impossible to see coming.

We've already seen this interplay of narrators start to work in the pages of *ODY-C*, where our sympathies for the characters color their tellings of parts of the tale. When Wolf, via He's book, tells Herakles the story of Inanna's rape, we know the moral of the story before Wolf's biting last words. And when He retells that same story to the boy, we feel sadness that the story should end so, before the boy himself, who has already helped save He from a terrible fate, gives the story a note of hope by taking it up himself. The same story, by three narrators, means something entirely different in each context. Add in the narrators of *ODY-C* itself − Matt Fraction and Christian Ward − and the story becomes as multi-colored as one of its own pages, given a new shade by each voice that helps in the telling of it.

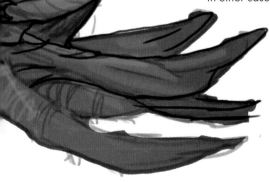

Proteus concept by Christian Ward.

The Tyndarean Triangle

by Dani Colman

When we talk of the Tyndarean Oath – the promise Odysseus brokered that the suitors of Helen would pledge allegiance to whomever she chose as husband – we think of Helen as the woman at its heart. If we dig a little deeper, we might recall that Odysseus brokered this agreement in exchange for the hand of Penelope, daughter of Icarius of Sparta and an heir to land, title and the formidable Spartan army. Helen and Penelope, however, were just two sides to a triangle of women who connected the most powerful and influential figures of the day. The third, Tyndareus' daughter Clytaemnestra, *definitely* got the raw end of the deal.

Clytaemnestra's story starts with the question of whether she was actually Tyndareus' daughter at all. According to legend, Tyndareus' wife, Leda, was one of the god Zeus' conquests: in one of his frequent bestial episodes, Zeus took a shine to Leda and assumed the form of a swan to seduce – or, more probably, rape – her, impregnating her. The same night, Leda slept with her husband Tyndareus, and nine months later she laid two eggs. Out of one, unquestionably the result of her copulation with Zeus, were born the twins Helen and Pollux; the other, believed to be from the seed of Tyndareus, bore Clytaemnestra and her brother Castor. Tyndareus wasn't known for causing the women he slept with to lay eggs; nonetheless, it was widely accepted that Clytaemnestra and Castor were his true children, while Helen and Pollux were his stepchildren.

Despite being Tyndareus' legitimate daughter – and remember, Greek descent was matrilineal, so the women were the keys to their fathers' kingdoms – Clytaemnestra played a resounding second fiddle to her half-sister Helen. Famous as the most beautiful woman alive and revered as a daughter of Zeus, Helen had immense value in a strategic marriage, and it was the fight for her hand that first almost split, then ultimately united, the Greek city-states prior to the Trojan War. Relatively little is known about Clytaemnestra's childhood and adolescence in Sparta: like Helen, she would have grown up running and fighting with her brothers; unlike Helen, she didn't lose her characteristically Spartan pugnaciousness when she grew up. Strong-willed and often abrasive, Clytaemnestra was a funhouse-mirror version of her beautiful, aristocratic sister, and she got the funhouse-mirror marriage to match.

Menelaus, who ultimately won Helen's hand, was a member of the cursed house of Atreus – a distinction he shared with his brother Agamemnon. The history of the house of Atreus is what you'd get if you ran the Lannisters and the Freys through a blender and then fed them to a direwolf: incest, murder, and an adulterer who unwittingly ate a meal of the cooked bodies of his own children. Thyestes, who did some of the murdering, most of the incest and almost all of the people-eating, vowed revenge on Atreus, who did the child-cooking, and murdered him with the help of his son, Aegisthus.

With Thyestes and Aegisthus still out for bloody revenge, Atreus' sons – Menelaus and Agamemnon – fled to Sparta, where they sought sanctuary with Tyndareus.

Once in Sparta, life got markedly better for Menelaus: he shortly thereafter became Helen's favored suitor and married her in a valuable strategic alliance. Agamemnon was not so lucky: just as one of a set of twins might inherit the lion's share of athletic prowess or musical talent, Agamemnon inherited the brunt of his family's curse. His comeuppance would come later; at the time he arrived in Sparta, Agamemnon's share of the curse manifested itself as hubris, ambition, and cruelty. According to some sources, Clytaemnestra was already married to Tantalus, King of (depending on the source) either Pisa or Lydia. Whether the marriage was a happy one is not known, but we do know that it was short: setting his sights on Clytaemnestra when it became clear Menelaus would win Helen, Agamemnon murdered Tantalus and killed Clytaemnestra's infant son, ending the Lydian line of succession and claiming Clytaemnestra as his own bride.

For Tyndareus, the situation was perfect: neither Pisa nor Lydia would have been of much value as allies, but marrying another daughter to a son of Atreus strengthened his claim to Mycenae, a valuable city-state ripe for the retaking under Aegisthus' and Thyestes' chaotic rule. Indeed, shortly after marrying Clytaemnestra, Agamemnon returned to Mycenae with the Spartan forces behind him, killing Thyestes, ousting Aegisthus and ruling Mycenae for several years with Clytaemnestra as his queen. From his seat of power in Mycenae, Agamemnon was able to spread his rule through conquest, becoming the most powerful prince in Greece and the figurehead that united the Greek forces when the Trojan War began.

> ## The history of the house of Atreus is what you'd get if you ran the Lannisters and the Freys through a blender and then fed them to a direwolf: incest, murder, and an adulterer who unwittingly ate a meal of the cooked bodies of his own children.

As for Clytaemnestra, there is nothing to suggest that she ever had any affection for Agamemnon. She bore him four children, and the legends and plays say she loved them all – not least her eldest daughter, Iphigenia. As a queen she was canny, famed for her ability to plan and scheme politically; in fact, in his famous tragedy *Agamemnon*, Aeschylus even puns with her name's etymological connection to the Greek word μήδομαι – *medomai*: to scheme or contrive. But by the time she realized her power as a queen, Clytaemnestra had already lost a husband and son to the curse of the house of Atreus, and she would be destined to lose much more. Drawn into the cycle of revenge by Agamemnon's cruelty and hubris, Clytaemnestra's fate would be to perpetuate it – not for the family she had already lost, but for the family she was yet to lose at Agamemnon's hand.

Agamemnon's years of conquest from his seat in Mycenae had not lessened his hubris, and, as he was preparing his forces at Aulis to join his brother in Troy, he managed to offend the goddess Artemis. Some sources say he killed her sacred stag; others say he claimed that he was her equal in hunting; some go for broke and insist that first he killed the stag, then he stood upon its carcass and bragged that in its slaughter, he had surpassed the goddess of the hunt herself. Either way, Artemis put her sandaled foot down and plagued the Mycenaean fleet with both poor winds and an actual plague, and Agamemnon's prophet declared that the only way to appease Artemis was with the sacrifice of his and Clytaemnestra's daughter, Iphigenia.

Iphigenia's death on the altar changed the curse of the Atreidae from one of fathers and sons to one of mothers and daughters. Clytaemnestra's indifference towards her husband became bloody vengeance, and she spent all the years of the Trojan War preparing to bring him down. Her revenge against Agamemnon was so magnificent that it inspired possibly the greatest work of Greek drama ever written – Aeschylus' *Agamemnon* – and, though Clytaemnestra would herself eventually fall victim to the cycle of revenge that plagued the house of Atreus, her own murder would be what brought the curse to its end when her son Orestes was put on trial and acquitted for matricide instead of being doomed to a vengeful death himself.

From the overlooked third side of the Tyndarean Triangle, Clytaemnestra would become the case upon which a new era of Greek justice was founded: not just another wife of some great Greek hero, but the queen who took the curse of the house of Atreus in hand and made it her own.

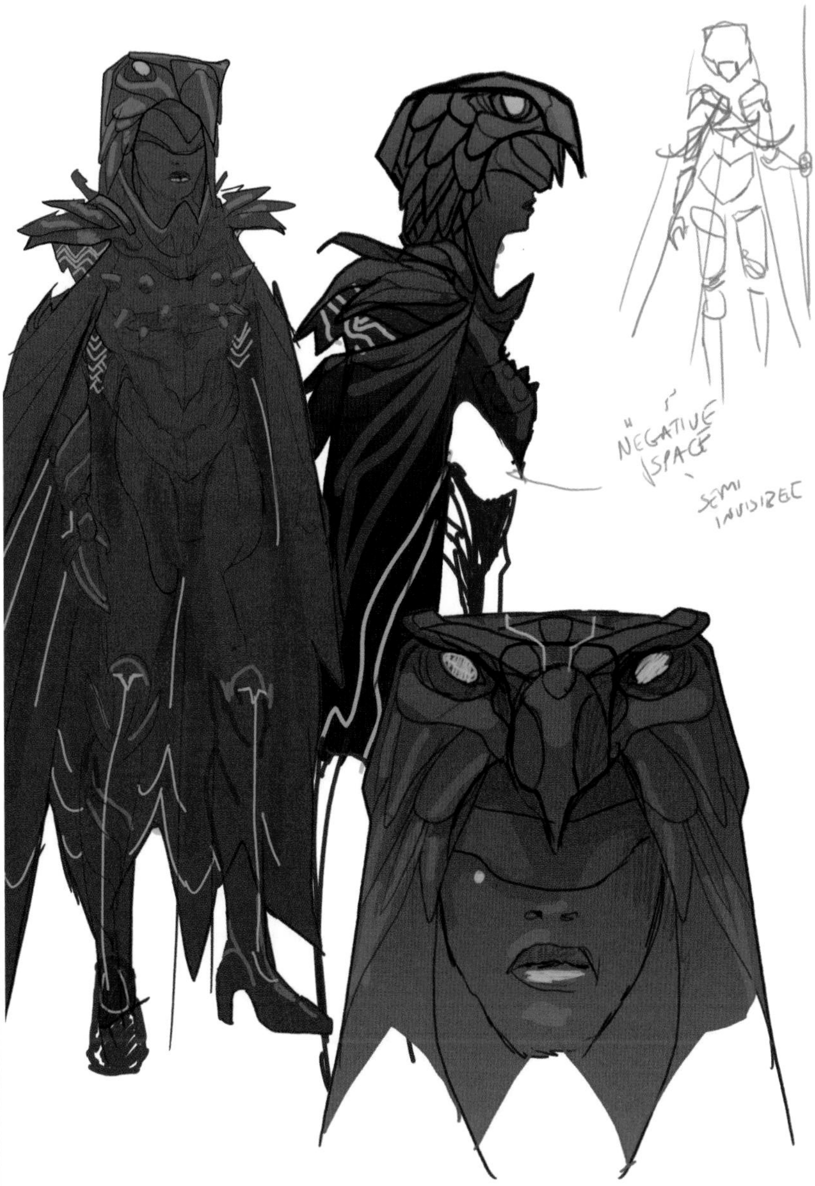
NEGATIVE SPACE
SEMI INVISIBLE

Watchhawk concept by Christian Ward.

Sex[ism] Kills

by Dani Colman

The word "feminist" is a tough one to use in the context of Greek tragedy, if for no other reason than that the concept did not exist. Plato made an argument for equality of the sexes in his *Republic*, his treatise on an ideal society, but even that was a good century after the heyday of Athenian tragedy. Different city states had different ideas about gender, but in Athens – considered to be the most educated and enlightened of the city states (particularly by those who lived there) – women were a secondary caste, expected to embody certain attributes and fulfill certain roles. There was no Greek "feminism": while women featured prominently in the earliest extant Greek tragedies, they played traditional roles, their stories revolving around marriage and family and their destinies controlled by the male characters in the stories.

Clytaemnestra belongs to the same class of dramatic leads as Hamlet and The Punisher: conflicted, determined, and so bound by her desire to avenge the wrongs done to her that she uses the line between good and evil like a jump rope. Issues of hubris and vengeance were nothing new by the time Aeschylus premiered *Agamemnon* in 458 BC, but they were the province of male protagonists, with the women of the plays often the reasons for, and victims of, the men's antics. With *Agamemnon*, Aeschylus mined the drama-rich story of the cursed house of Atreus to probe the question of what happens when the cycle of

vengeance – a pattern begun and perpetuated by men – falls to a woman to continue. In doing so, he had to tackle issues of Athenian gender politics head-on, in a way that no Athenian playwright had really done before.

Athenian culture saw women as flighty, emotional and untrustworthy, and that's the first stereotype that Clytaemnestra faces the second she steps out on stage. Announcing that she has seen the beacon that heralds Agamemnon's return from Troy, Clytaemnestra is questioned over and over again by the chorus of elderly men, all of them commenting how like a woman it would be to hear a rumor and accept it as fact because it suits her emotional narrative. Calm and haughty, Clytaemnestra sticks to her story, but it isn't until a male herald confirms it some 600 lines into the play that the chorus finally accepts that their king is returning from battle.

Clytaemnestra, however, doesn't waste her time complaining about the chorus' view of her – after all, she's had ten years of ruling Mycenae to get used to it. Instead, she leans in, exploiting the chorus' limited attitude towards a female ruler to throw them off the scent of her plan. In poetic language, she muses on what a wonder it is when a woman is reunited with her husband; because she is perfectly describing a woman's role, the chorus accepts her seeming joy at Agamemnon's return as fact, not noticing that every word

of her speech is loaded with hints that she is planning to murder him in the bathtub as soon as he gets home.

The *Agamemnon* begins and ends with violence. As was the case with all Greek tragedy, the violence happened offstage, recounted to the audience after the fact by the chorus or one of the actors. Aeschylus, a prodigiously skilled playwright, used this convention not just to tell the story but to offer insight into the narrators of the action. In the opening verses – a kind of "Previously, in the House of Atreus" – the chorus lets us in on why Clytaemnestra might have issue with her husband, describing Agamemnon's decision to sacrifice their daughter Iphigenia for fair winds to Troy. Though their recounting of the girl's preparation for sacrifice is heart-wrenching, describing the clothes torn from her body as she cries out to her father to save her, they turn away at the moment of her death, skipping over the part where Agamemnon actually kills her to lay the blame on Calchas, the prophet who suggested the sacrifice in the first place. Narrating the action secondhand, the chorus chooses to absolve their king of blame by taking the violence out of the story entirely.

Clytaemnestra, narrating her own action after she murders Agamemnon, takes absolute ownership of what she does. Where the chorus of the opening verses shied away from the moment of Iphigenia's death, handwaving the brutality of Agamemnon's act by refusing to describe it, Clytaemnestra recounts Agamemnon's death in glorious blank verse, describing her actions blow-by-blow and narrating every gout of Agamemnon's blood in terms that deserve a film treatment by Eli Roth. Even though the action happens offstage, Clytaemnestra forces the chorus to bear witness to every gory moment of it, refusing them the option to delicately turn away and pretend the gods took over.

Clytaemnestra belongs to the same class of dramatic leads as Hamlet and The Punisher: conflicted, determined, and so bound by her desire to avenge the wrongs done to her that she uses the line between good and evil like a jump rope.

Moreover, when the anguished chorus calls for Clytaemnestra's banishment, she slaps them in the face with their own hypocrisy. "Where," she asks, "were your cries for Agamemnon's banishment when he sacrificed Iphigenia?" The chorus, in their protests, promptly do exactly what they accused Clytaemnestra, as a woman, of doing in the opening: they twist the facts of Iphigenia's sacrifice to fit their own emotional narrative.

Agamemnon has an odd little coda to it. The natural dramatic ending of the story is when Clytaemnestra, having done the deed, tells the chorus that Iphigenia will meet her father in the Underworld, embracing him with love. 2500 years after the fact, it's hard to say whether that line was supposed to drip with the sarcasm that seems obvious now, but it brings the play full circle as it forces Agamemnon to face the daughter whose sacrifice doomed him. It's a powerful and emotional moment — and it is promptly swept aside for the entrance of Aegisthus, Clytaemnestra's lover and another member of the cursed House of Atreus. Aegisthus grandstands for a little while, crowing about wrongs righted and vengeance enacted, but, in their first real display of clarity in the entire play, the chorus refuses to take any of his crap.

"If you planned this, as you say," they cry, "why did the woman strike the killing blow?"

The phrasing is no accident, especially coming after Aegisthus' blustering that treachery is women's work. What makes Clytaemnestra something close to a feminist two millennia before the term existed is not that she took on the man's role in murdering Agamemnon. Clytaemnestra may have taken a very masculine action in stabbing her husband to death, but she got there by being what Athenians would describe as

feminine: scheming, calculating, and willing to lie and twist the truth. For all his claim to being the mastermind behind Agamemnon's death, Aegisthus' final screaming match with the chorus is nothing but him trying to parry their direct attacks on his masculinity, oblivious to the fact that Clytaemnestra is now both man and woman in the eyes of the chorus.

And where is Clytaemnestra, the true architect of the murders, in all

Art by Christian Ward.

this? She's over it. She always knew that killing Agamemnon would only perpetuate the curse, and she accepted that wholeheartedly. That's what she tells the chorus as they rail at Aegisthus; that's what she tells her lover as he tries to defend his shriveled machismo.

"That is what this woman has to say," she declares. "Can you accept the truth?"

A Gender-Bender Agenda

by Dani Colman

The internet calls it Rule 63; TvTropes.org calls it the "gender-flip". There's no formal term for it in literary criticism, but the recasting of male roles as female and vice-versa is something that has arguably never before been more manifest in popular culture, nor more entangled with how we view gender as a whole.

Gender-flipping is almost as old as storytelling itself: many of the best-known folk and fairy tales, including Little Red Riding Hood and Cinderella, have gender-flipped versions almost as old as the originals. In most of these cases, however, the reason for the gender-flip has little to do with any kind of commentary and everything to do with sheer statistical certainty. Cinderella has more than 500 catalogued variations[1] : tell a single story enough times, in enough languages and across enough cultures, and it's pretty much a given that at least one version turns the princess into a prince.

Deliberate gender-flipping – the reversal of genders of original characters in order to say something new with the story – is actually an incredibly recent phenomenon in storytelling. Just as it is impossible to look at a fairy tale and say for certain whether the prince version or the princess version came first, it is near-impossible to go back further than the middle of the 20th century and find an example of a writer deliberately deciding to change a character's gender in the course

of an adaptation. Why? Most likely because, for the great bulk of Western history, gender roles were so cast in stone that exploring or commenting on them via a gender-flip might literally have been outside the bounds of a writer's imagination.

Of course, to a certain degree, all of theater engaged in partial gender-flipping for most of its history. Only relatively recently in theater's millennia-long history has it been acceptable for women to be seen on stage, and for what we might consider theater's formative periods – Athenian tragedy and Elizabethan theatre, in particular – nominally female roles were played by boys and men.[2]

Only very rarely was this partial gender-bend commentative. The suspension of disbelief needed to accept a man in a woman's role would have been much less than the shock caused by a woman appearing on stage; in fact, it's doubtful whether Athenian women were even permitted to attend the theatre, much less to act in plays. Any commentary on femininity or gender roles came from the text itself, not from the gender of the actor doing the speaking.

That began to change with the Renaissance, which, with its renewed focus on the arts, ushered in a new level of literary complexity. Plays became political, commenting on the social dynamics of the day, and by the time Queen Elizabeth's historic reign was underway, gender was

an intrinsic part of that commentary. The fledgling fluidity of gender roles in Elizabethan England was not just about women taking on the offices of men; masculinity was also changing, with dandyism on display in men's high heels and powdered wigs, and younger men affecting traditionally "feminine" traits while under the patronage – economic, and often sexual – of older aristocrats. Several of Shakespeare's women donned breeches in order to buck the limitations of their gender and further the plot; in each case, the accompanying commentary on gender and sexuality was deliberate, but none more so than *The Merchant of Venice*.

First performed in 1600 – and for an audience that almost certainly had Elizabeth I in it – *The Merchant of Venice* introduces a character who would have been impossible in the real world at the time: a female lawyer. Though she has to dress as a man in order to exercise her legal prowess, Portia easily holds her own in a court of men as she defends Antonio from Shylock's knife. Portia's crossdressing was not all that notable in itself – several of Shakespeare's heroines spend more scenes in drag – but her considerable acumen in court is, as even highly educated Elizabethan noblewomen were banned from the study of medicine or law.[3] More notable still is that Portia's crossdressing puts her in a position to witness Bassanio saying outright, in front of the disguised Portia, that he values Antonio's life over his wife's love; taken alongside the attraction between Viola (disguised as a man) and Orsino in *Twelfth Night*, it becomes clear that Shakespeare used these so-called "trouser" roles as a way to comment on the strong homosocial bonds between Elizabethan men.

While the Reformation shut down British theater in the early 1600s,

---

1. http://www.ala.org/offices/resources/multicultural

2. P. E. Easterling, "Cambridge companion to Greek tragedy" (1997)

3. Joseph Papp, and Elizabeth Kirkland, "The Status of Women in Shakespeare's Time" (2003)

Deliberate gender-flipping – the reversal of genders of original characters in order to say something new with the story – is actually an incredibly recent phenomenon in storytelling.

when the Restoration revived it half a century later, the ban on female actors was lifted. Bouncing back quickly, theater companies began casting women in male roles as well as female, playing the sight of a woman in breeches for comedy. Just like the early performances of men as women, these trouser roles were rarely commentative: in fact, the draw of a woman in a man's role was not what subtlety she might bring to the character, but the fact that a man's stockings and breeches showed off the shape of her legs to an enthusiastic audience.

Around the same time that women started appearing on stage in Britain, opera – over on the continent – was doing the same thing. Thanks to a papal edict forbidding women from singing in church, music had, for a long time, assigned its soprano and mezzo-soprano roles to castrati: promising young trebles who had their testicles removed before their voices broke to preserve their high singing registers into adulthood. The earliest operas, breaking out as they did from semi-staged religious oratorios, put castrati in the lead roles, but, as the dramatic purview of opera increased, castrati began to take on female roles, donning dresses and acting as the love interests for the heroic tenors and baritones.

Despite the demand for their voices, castrati were notoriously bad actors, and known for histrionics both on and off the stage.[4] As the demands on their voices increased, composers found that trained female singers – many of whom already understudied for the fickle castrati – outclassed the castrati both musically and dramatically: no castrato of the day could have hit the notes of *The Magic Flute*'s Queen of the Night aria, but a talented soprano could soar that high and retain the gravitas needed to really sell the role. As leading ladies became

more popular than leading castrati, mezzo-sopranos started filling the vocal range for which the castrati were known, and, while some of the lower-voiced women had leading female roles written for them, many donned breeches to fill the parts of adolescent men and – ironically enough – eunuchs.

Despite the gender politics of 18th-century Europe, the opera-going audience was accustomed enough to seeing castrati in dresses that trouser roles were part of the opera's built-in suspension of disbelief, and, if the singers were good enough, the audience went willingly along. But just as Shakespeare occasionally leaned in to the boys-in-drag nature of his female roles for some metatextual gender-play, the best composers of opera found ways to make women in breeches part of the fabric of their theater. In Mozart's *The Marriage of Figaro*, the page Cherubino – one of the most famous and demanding trouser roles – is an irrepressibly horny adolescent, lusting indiscriminately over every woman in the opera. When Count Almaviva, angry at Cherubino's philandering, orders that Cherubino leave to join the military, Countess

Rosina and her chambermaid Susanna attempt to save Cherubino from his fate by dressing him up in women's clothing, all while he sings about how unhappy he will be while away from the both of them. Even early productions of the opera would stage the scene to give Cherubino maximum opportunity to paw at the two women while they are dressing him, letting the mezzo-soprano playing Cherubino indulge in all the

Athena by Christian Ward.

4. Roger Pickering, "Reflections upon theatrical expression in tragedy" (1755)

raunchy romping that would have been denied her in a traditional skirt role. In a rare self-aware twist to the breeches role in operatic comedy, Cherubino returns from the military to find happiness with Barbarina, a serving-girl who is every bit as horny as he is.

Trouser and skirt roles in theater and opera notwithstanding, gender flipping didn't really take off substantially until the advent of film. From its very earliest days, film was most commercially viable when it included some romantic tension, so sidekick roles from adapted plays and books had their genders flipped so that the hero could have a love interest. The best-known example is the two male journalists of the 1928 stage play *The Front Page* becoming a journalist and his wife in 1940's *His Girl Friday*[5] , but several lesser-known movies did the same. By the 1980s, film and television had begun not only deliberately flipping genders to change the dynamics between characters in adaptation, but even occasionally leaving the genders of characters blank, to be filled in during casting as with Ellen Ripley in 1979's *Alien*.

Serialized storytelling in the form of both comics and television leaned into the gender-bend hard, from gender-flipped roles in adaptation to entire universes of gender-flipped heroes. While some flips, like Starbuck in Syfy's reboot of *Battlestar Galactica*, are notable for hardly changing the character's role in the story at all, most modern flips use the device to provide additional commentary on the relationships between characters. In a TV adaptation of *The Jungle Book*[6], Bagheera becomes female, giving Mowgli a mother figure; in Netflix's *Jessica Jones*, attorney Jeryn Hogarth becomes the female Jeri, injecting an LGBT+ character by flipping only one side of the romantic pairing between Jeri and her girlfriend Pam.

Between bearded-lady gods, gender-flipped heroines, gender-uncertain sebex and the odd character who keeps the same

5. http://www.tcm.com/tcmdb/title/206/His-Girl-Friday/articles.html
6. "Adventures of Mowgli", 1967-1971, Soviet Union (released in the US in 1973 under Films by Jove)

gender as their source, ODY-C is less a gender-bent *Odyssey* than it is an *Odyssey*-flavored gender pretzel. Rather, ODY-C is an early next step into what comes after the gender flip: the unfurling of the gender spectrum both to comment on and to dismiss outright what we understand as gender roles and norms in classic literature. On writing ODY-C in the first place, co-creator Matt Fraction recounts: "...[I] thought, what if it was about a mother trying to come home instead of a father. That was the start of it: I wanted to write a heroic warrior-mother for my daughter."

In changing heroic husband Odysseus to heroic mother Odyssia, ODY-C does exactly what any good gender-flip does, both actively and passively commenting on the part a character's gender plays in their story. Women in fiction often play the role of mother lion, motivated by their children more than by their love interests, and, while a male Odysseus certainly thinks of his son Telemachus as he dreams of home, the face he sees when he closes his eyes is that of his wife Penelope. With female Odyssia, though the motivation of her waiting child is part of the story being told, it's also part of her new role as woman – a role that we, as readers, unconsciously give her. Ero, Odyssia's third-gendered and female-pronouned lover, wants not just children but a life spent raising them rather than waiting for her warrior-bride to stop fighting; the fiercely maternal, fiercely clever, and fiercely afraid-of-domesticity Odyssia does not. Hryar and Zhaman, fraternal kings of Q'af, marry, fuck and decapitate men and women indiscriminately; though their story has its roots in the misogynistic rapes of Inanna and Wolf, the violence of sex has no gender in their own lives, becoming instead an instrument of war declared on anyone capable of doing them harm. Above it all, the bearded, breasted and often phallused gods do their best to pull the strings, but the world of ODY-C is more complicated than even they can control. After all, when Zeus in her fury rids the world of men, it doesn't simplify the world by reducing it to a single gender. It leads to the sebex, and explodes the customary binary out into a spectrum, created once more by unruly children refusing to do as they're told.

ODY-C is on the front lines of this kind of gender twist, but it is increasingly not unique. In *Mr. Robot*, Whiterose occupies the traditionally masculine roles of businessman and hacker, but slips fluidly between genders from scene to scene; in *Rat Queens*, the adventuring ladies wear the armour, weapons and even beards of their roles, not their nominal genders. The more stories play with casting men, women, and trans, intersex, genderqueer and agender people outside the roles that society has traditionally assigned them, the more these stories get to play with the traditional trappings of those roles, and the more diverse and dimensional these characters become.

Fiction tends to imitate life, before life turns around and imitates fiction right back. Even before there were trouser roles in plays and operas, Hua Mulan and Joan of Arc disguised themselves as men to participate in battle, and queens, stateswomen, artists and scientists assumed nominally masculine roles without trading their dresses for breeches. Just as Shakespeare's often formidable women were written to earn the favor of Queen Elizabeth I, storytellers throughout history have drawn inspiration from the trailblazers of their day. It is the stories, however, that normalize what once was strange and aberrant behavior, by inviting readers and audiences to step into a fictional world and experience it as truth for a while. To put it another way: little girls have known they could bust ghosts since Bill Murray first rode in the Ecto-1, but now *everyone* knows it. As fiction continues to move towards a gender spectrum instead of a binary, life in turn will imitate that fiction, giving those in every shade of that spectrum more freedom, more visibility and more acceptance.

Dani's writing can be found online at medium.com/@DirectorDaniC and at toovia.com/user/dani-colman. Follow her on Twitter: @DirectorDaniC.

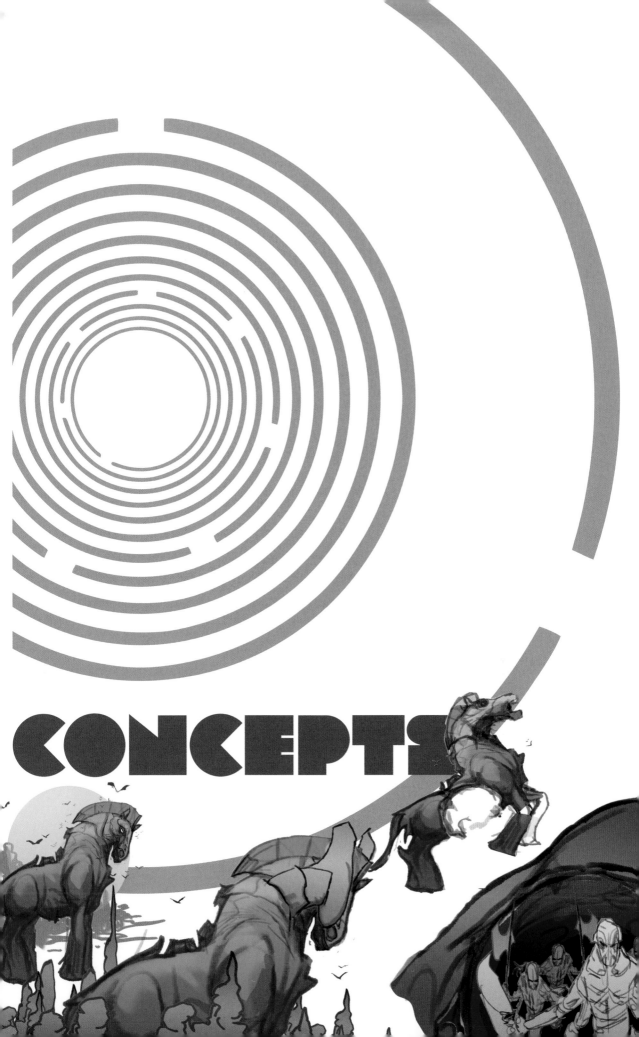

CONCEPTS

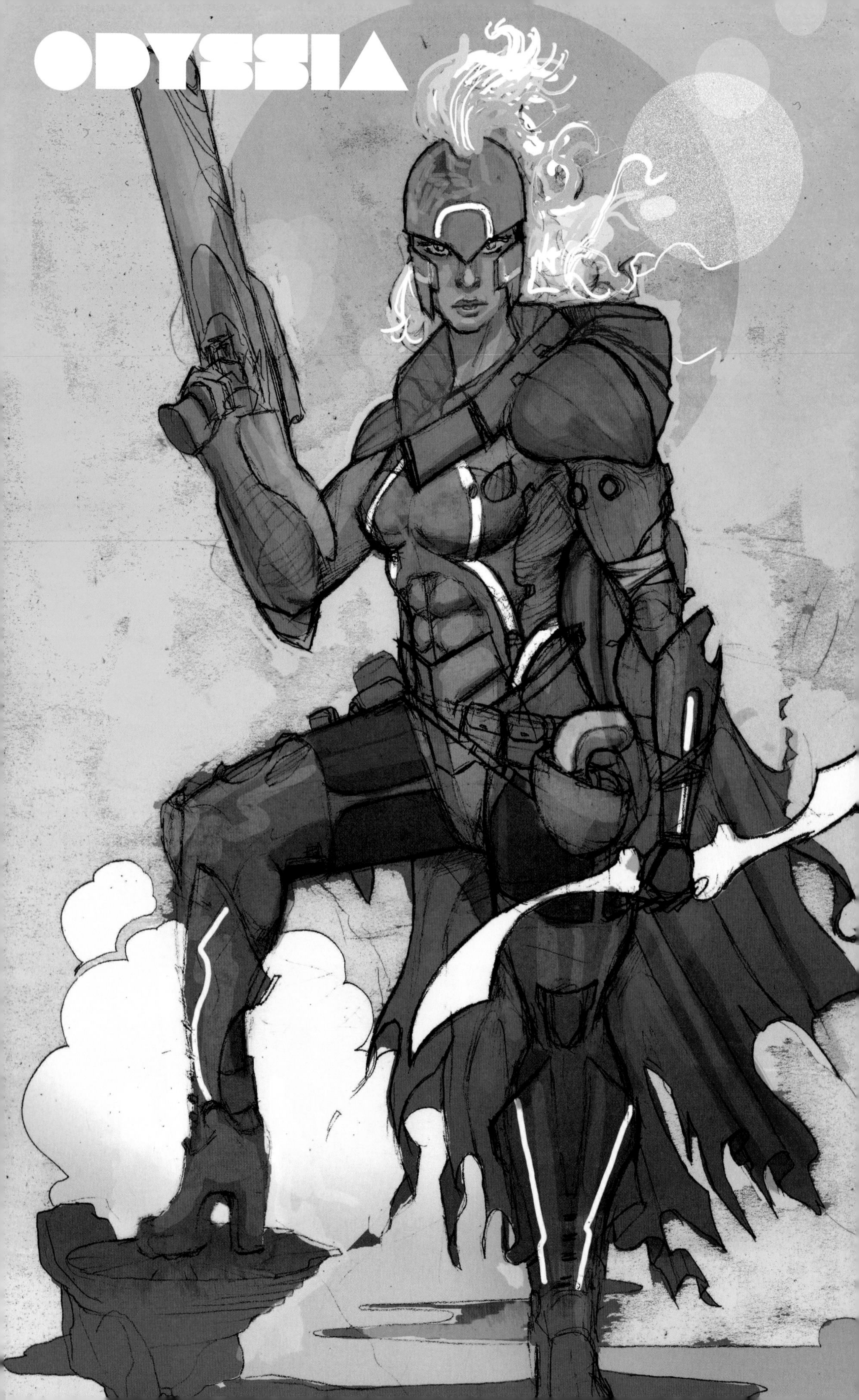
ODYSSIA

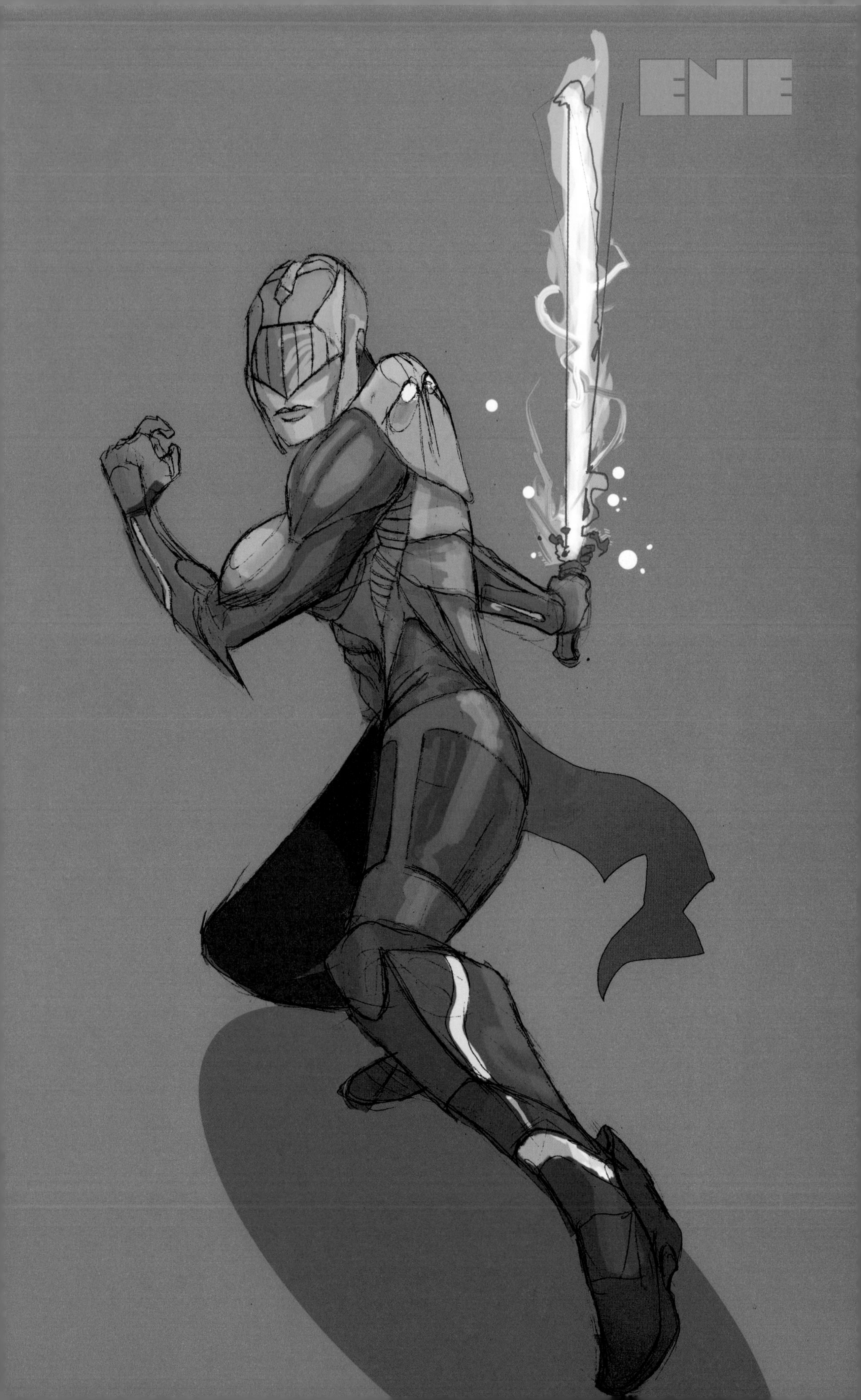
ENE

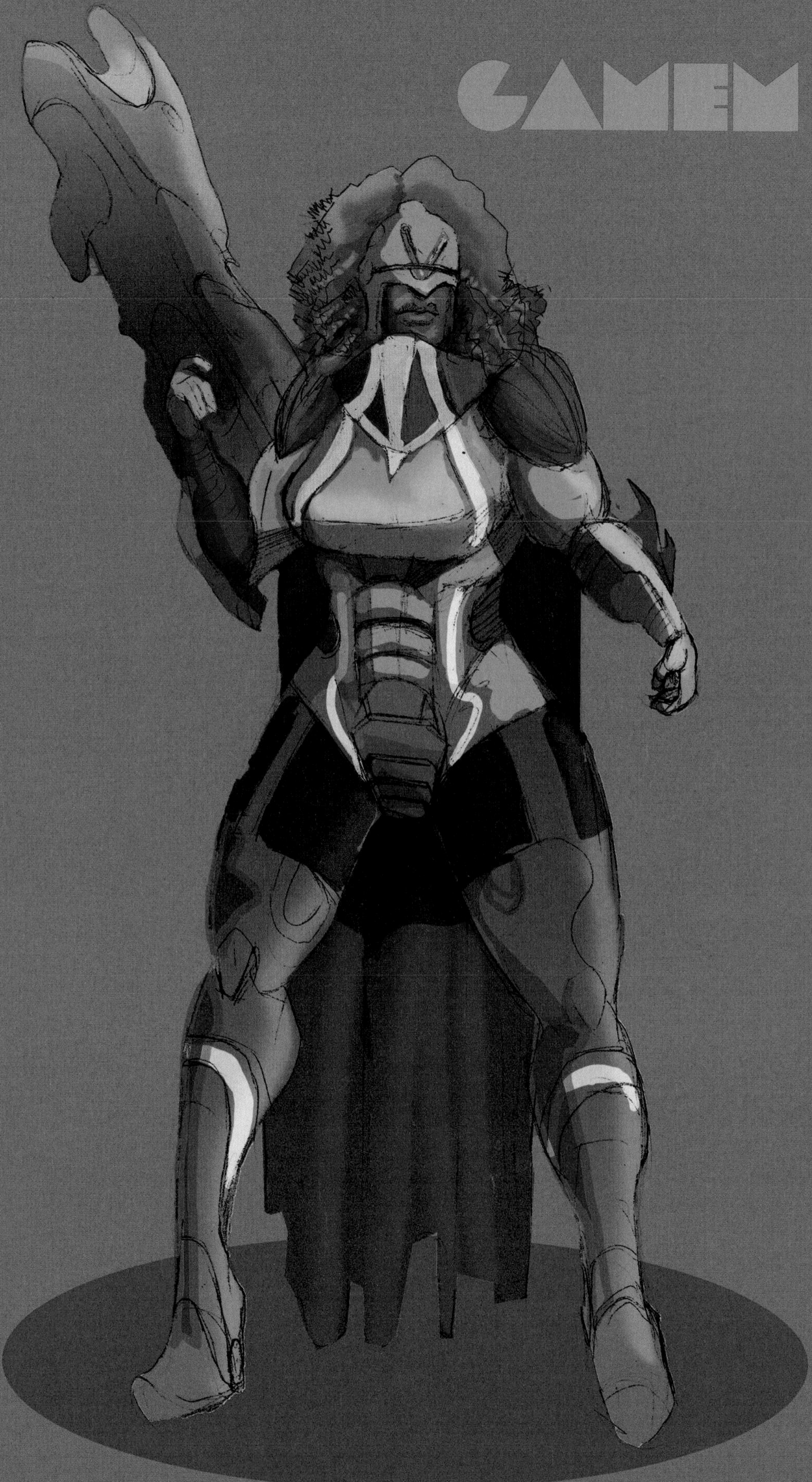
GAMEM

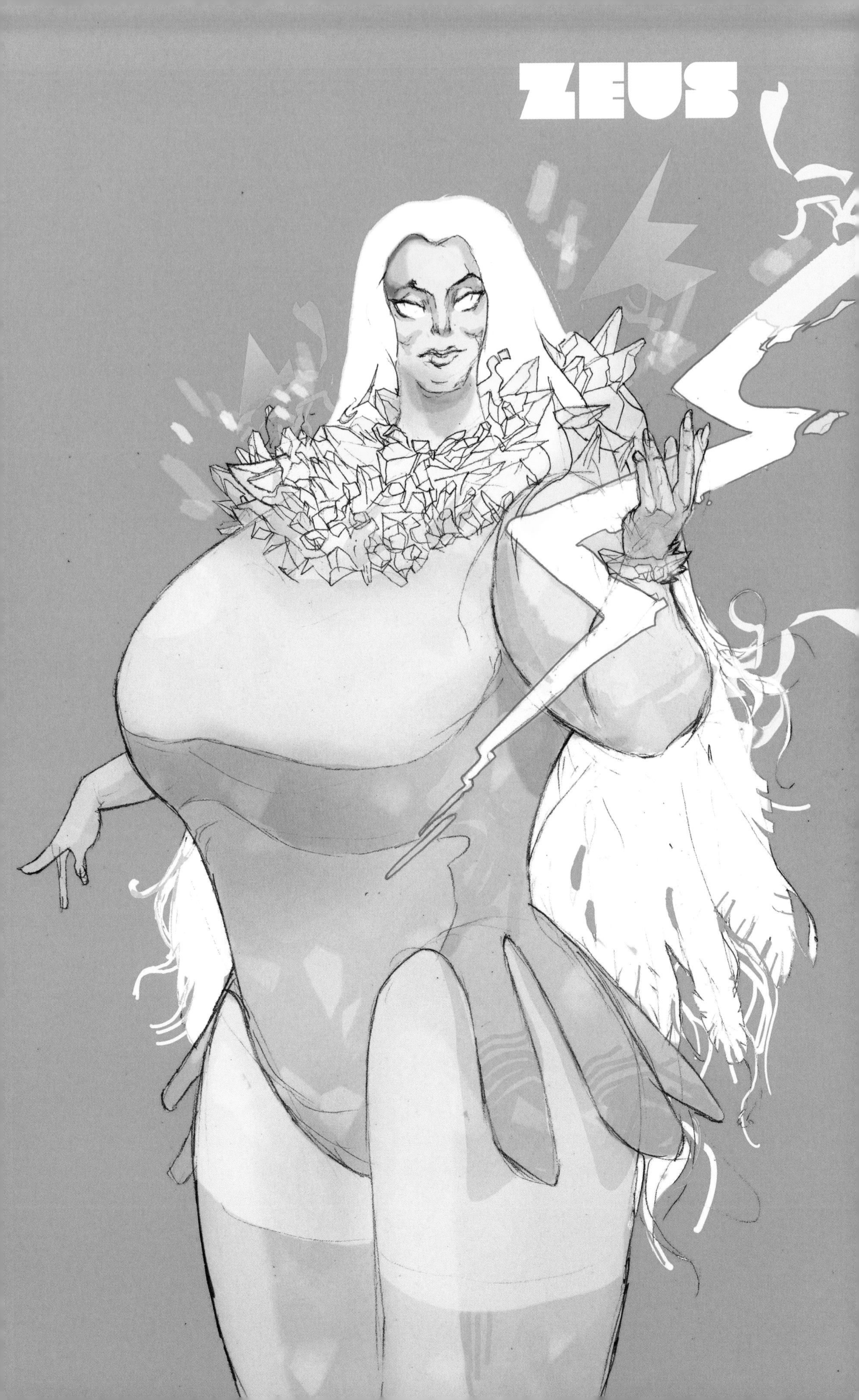
ZEUS

POSEIDON (CONCEPT)

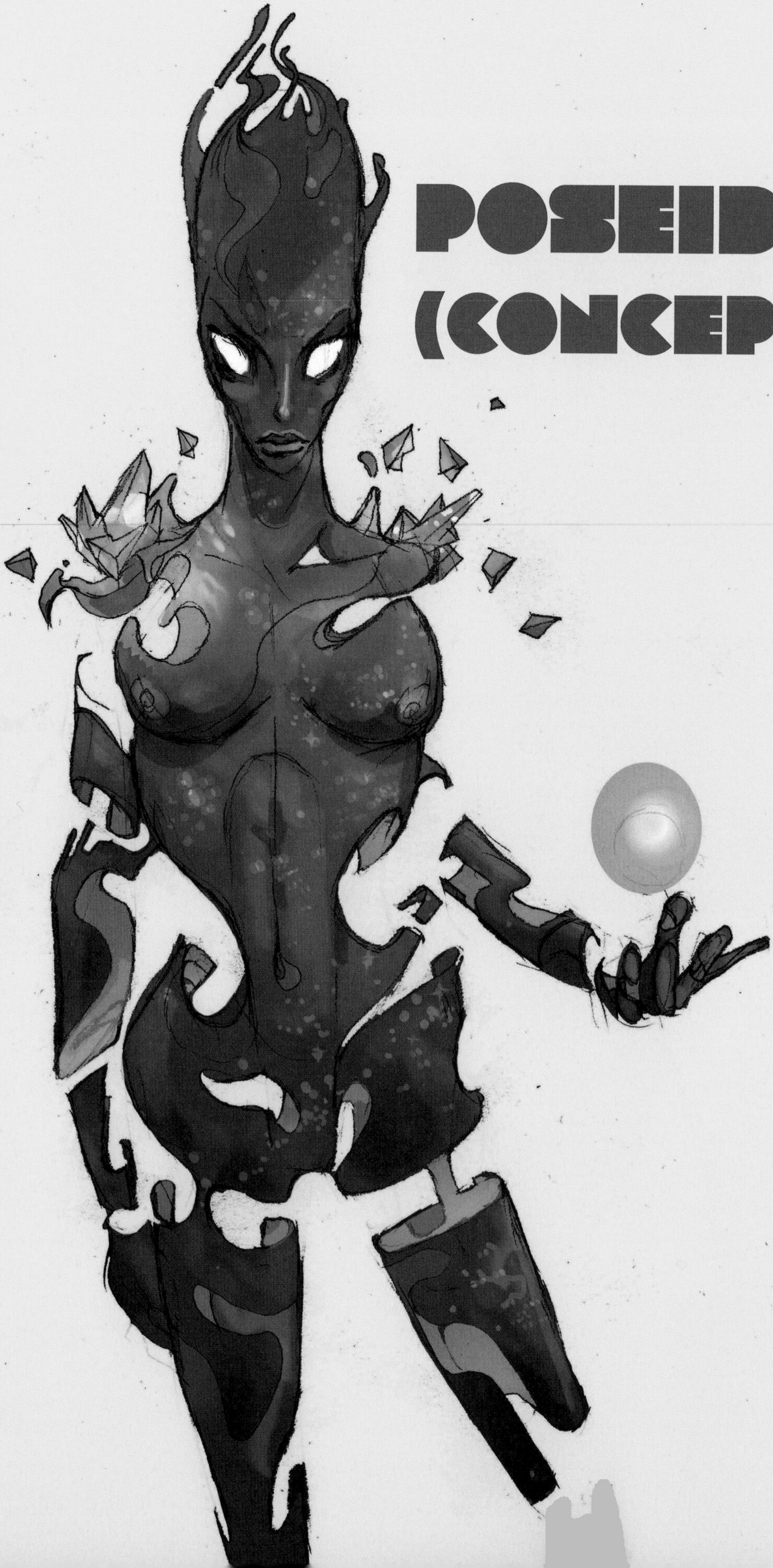

POSEIDON (FINAL)

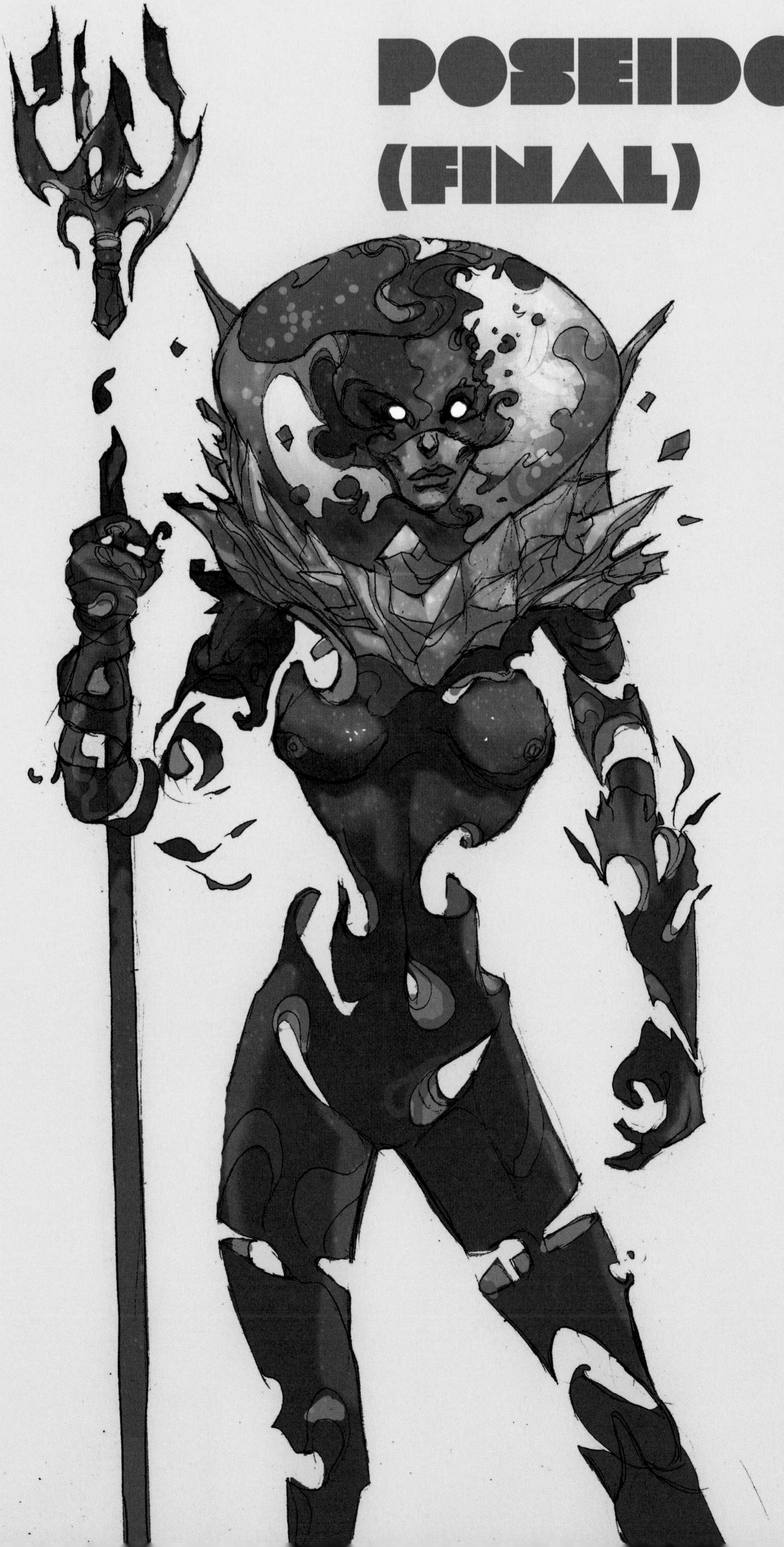

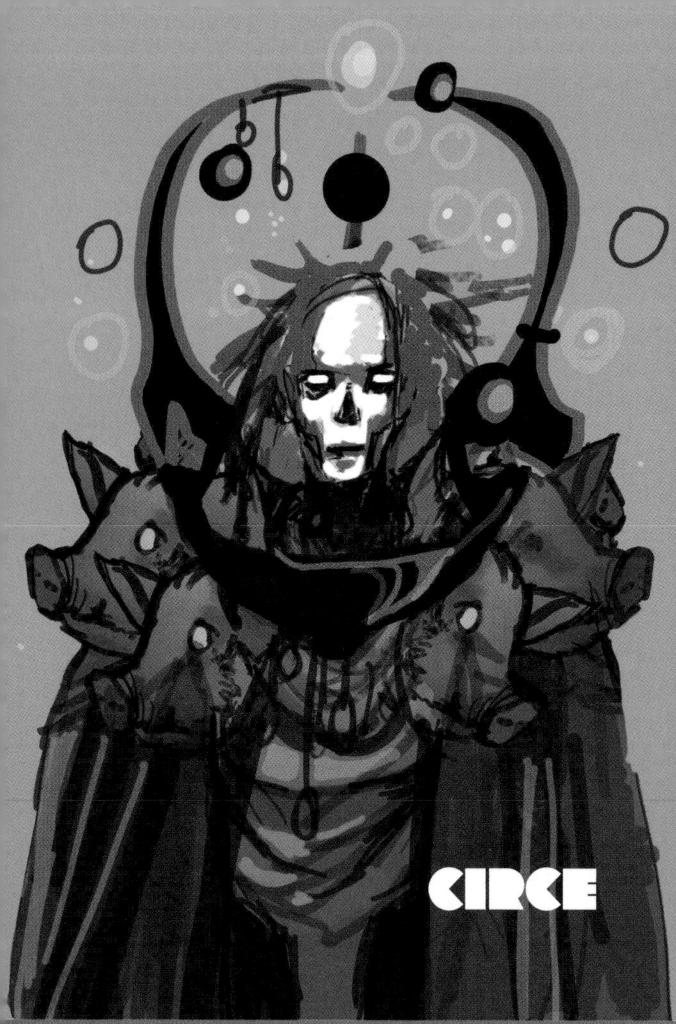
CIRCE

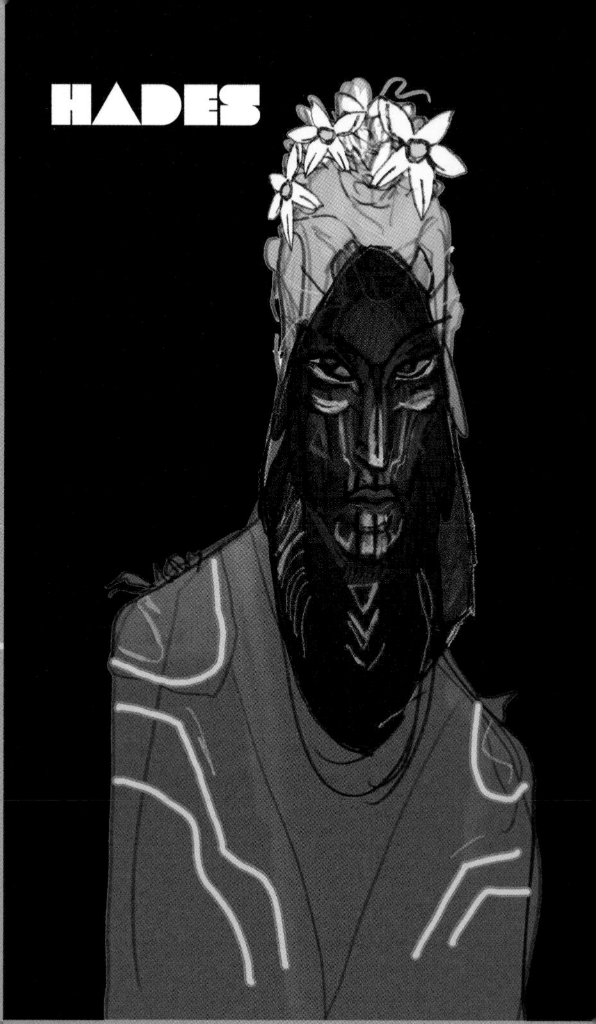
HADES

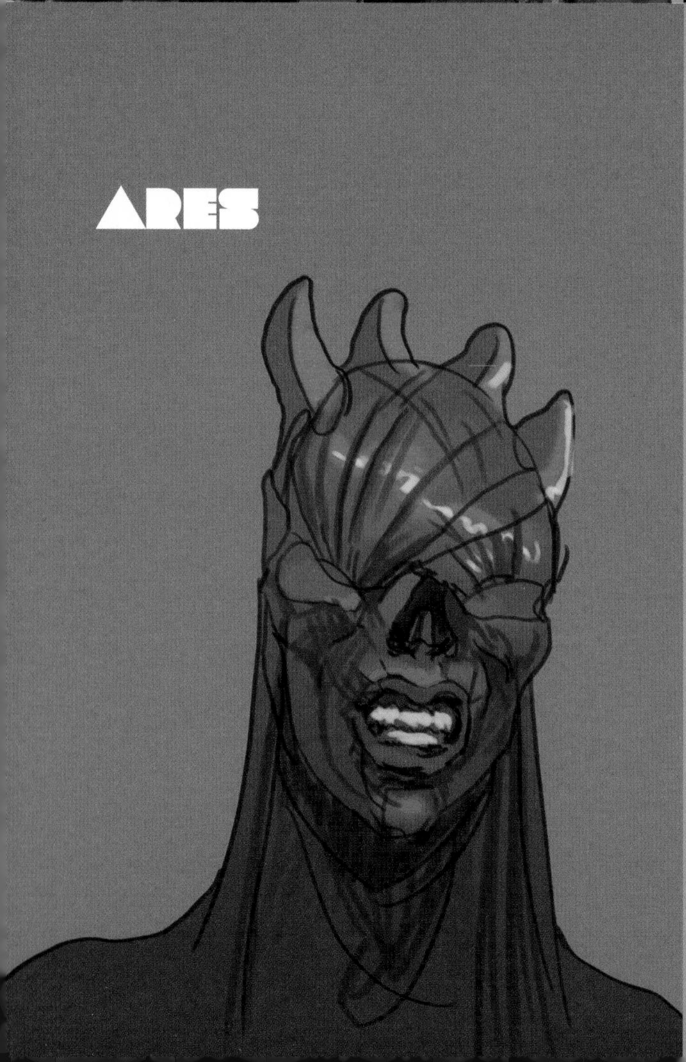
ARES

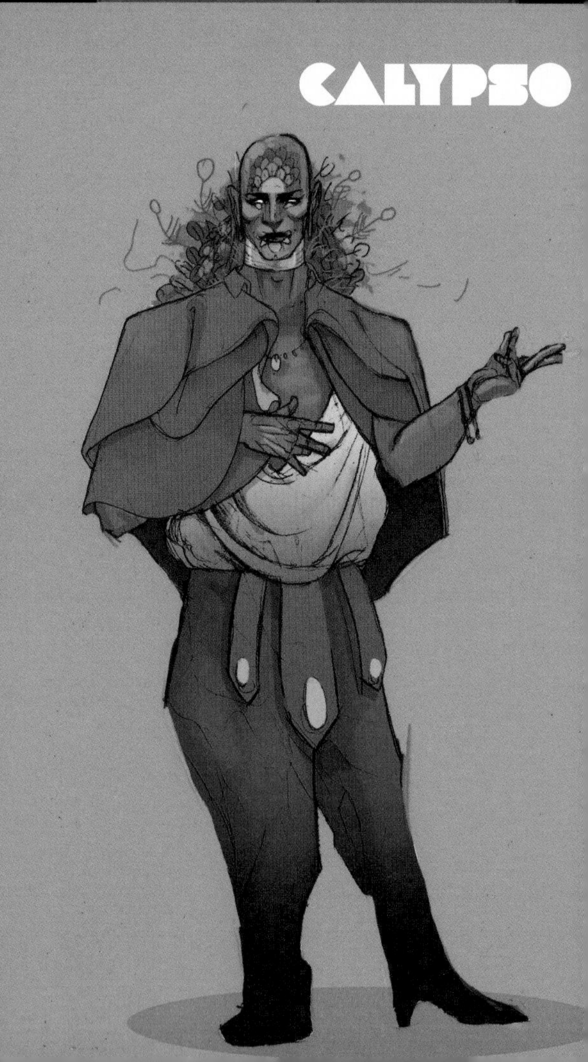
CALYPSO

CYCLOPS

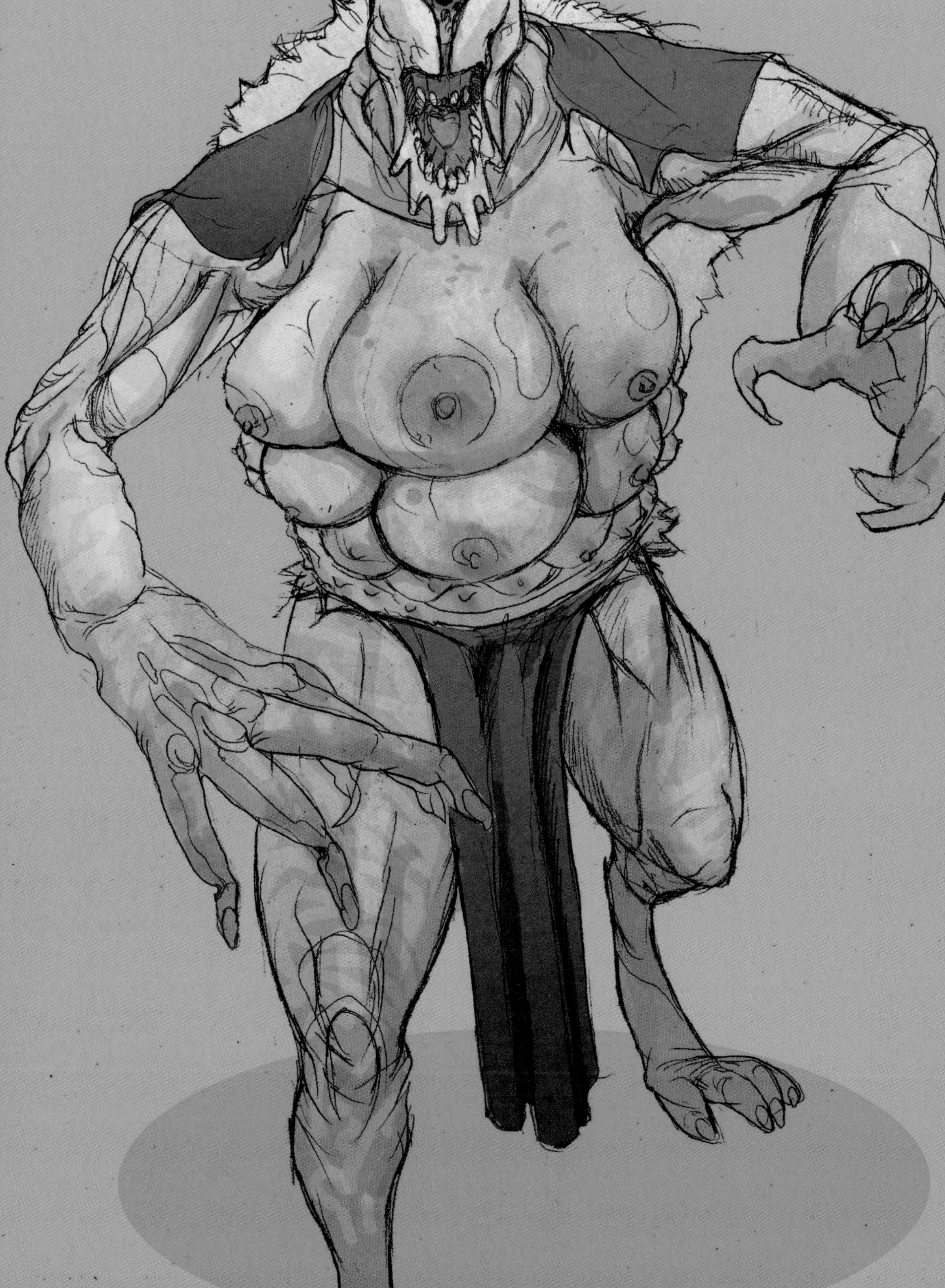

THE PRIMORDIAL GODS

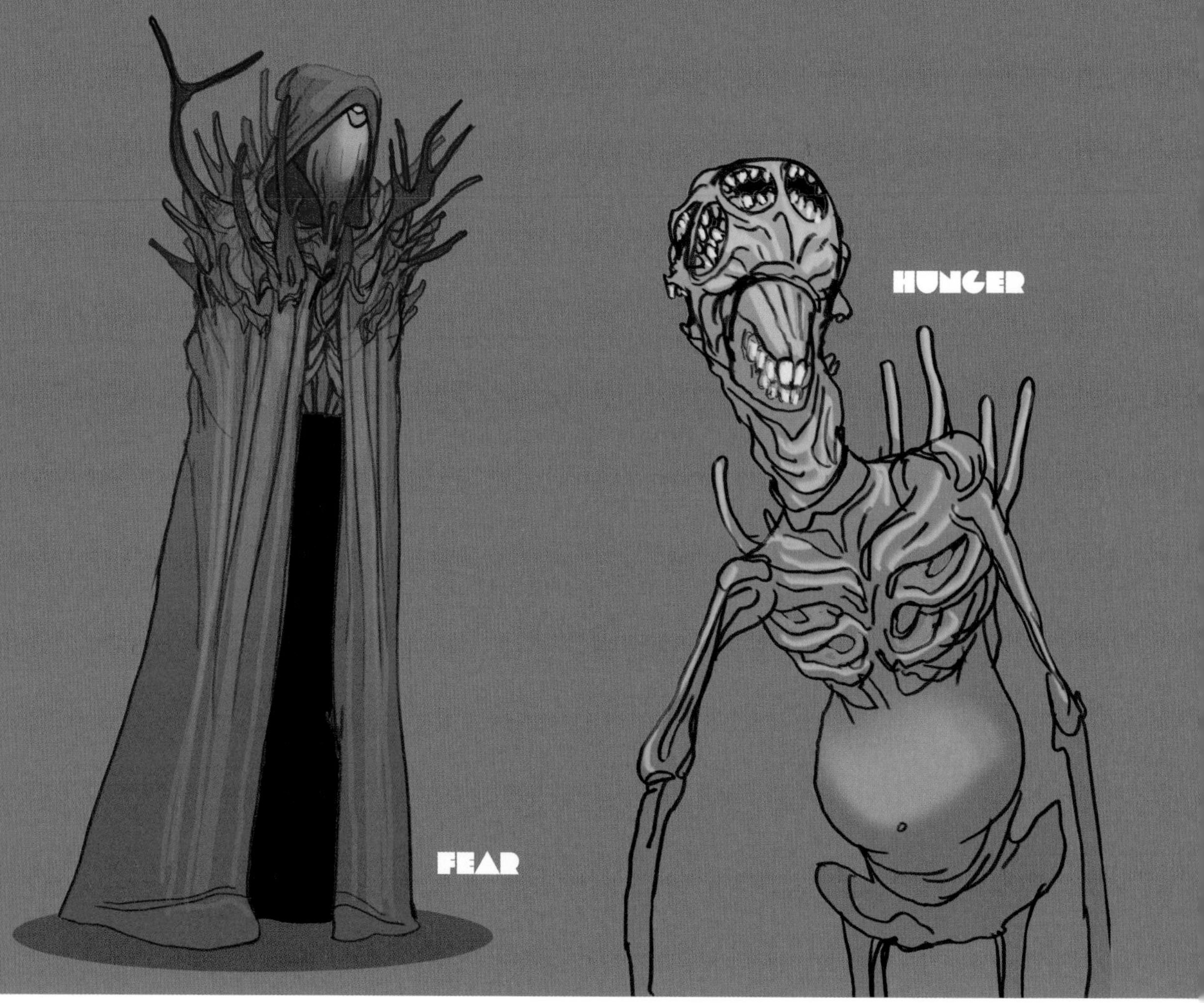
HUNGER
FEAR

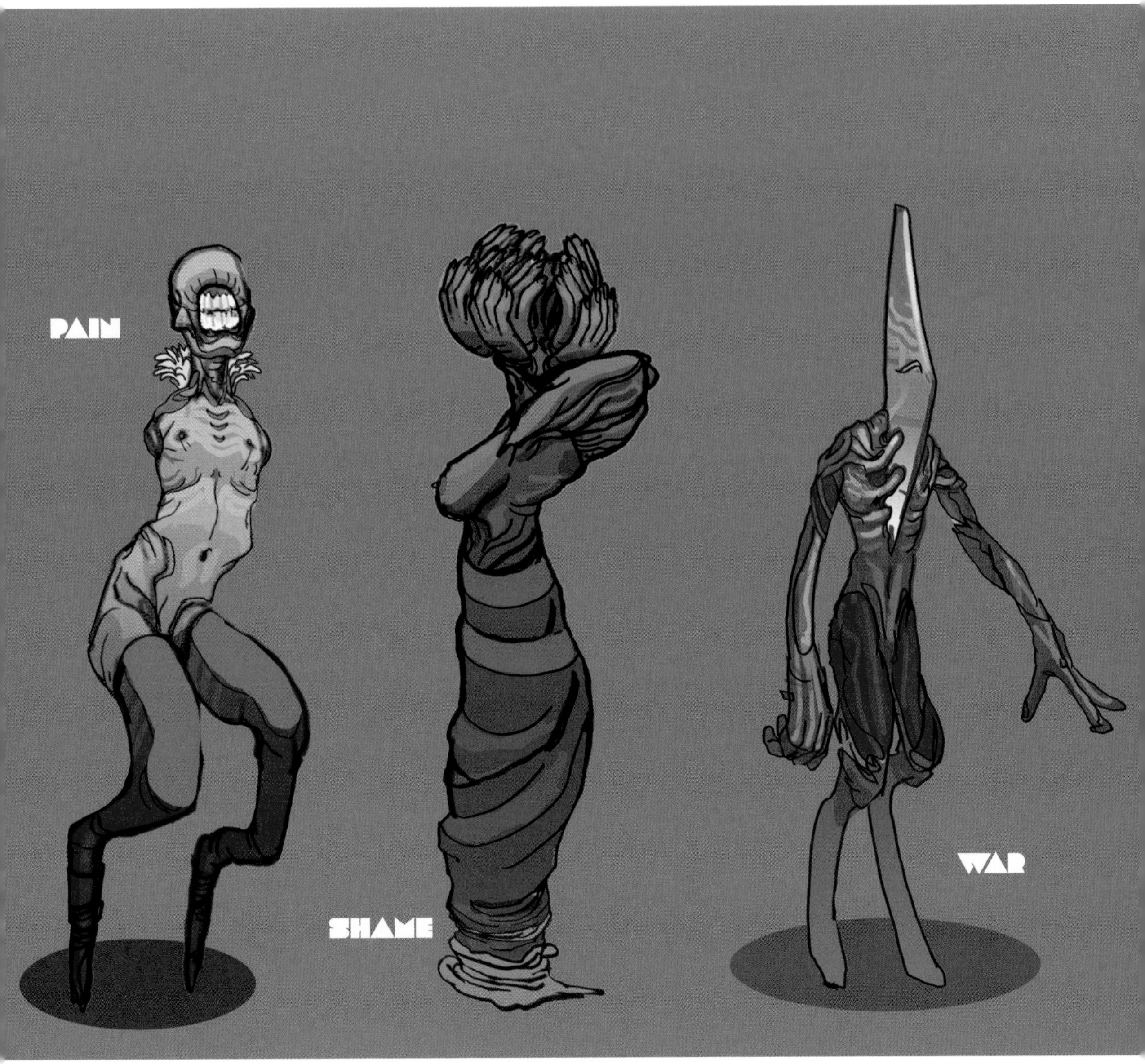
PAIN
SHAME
WAR

COVER PROCESS

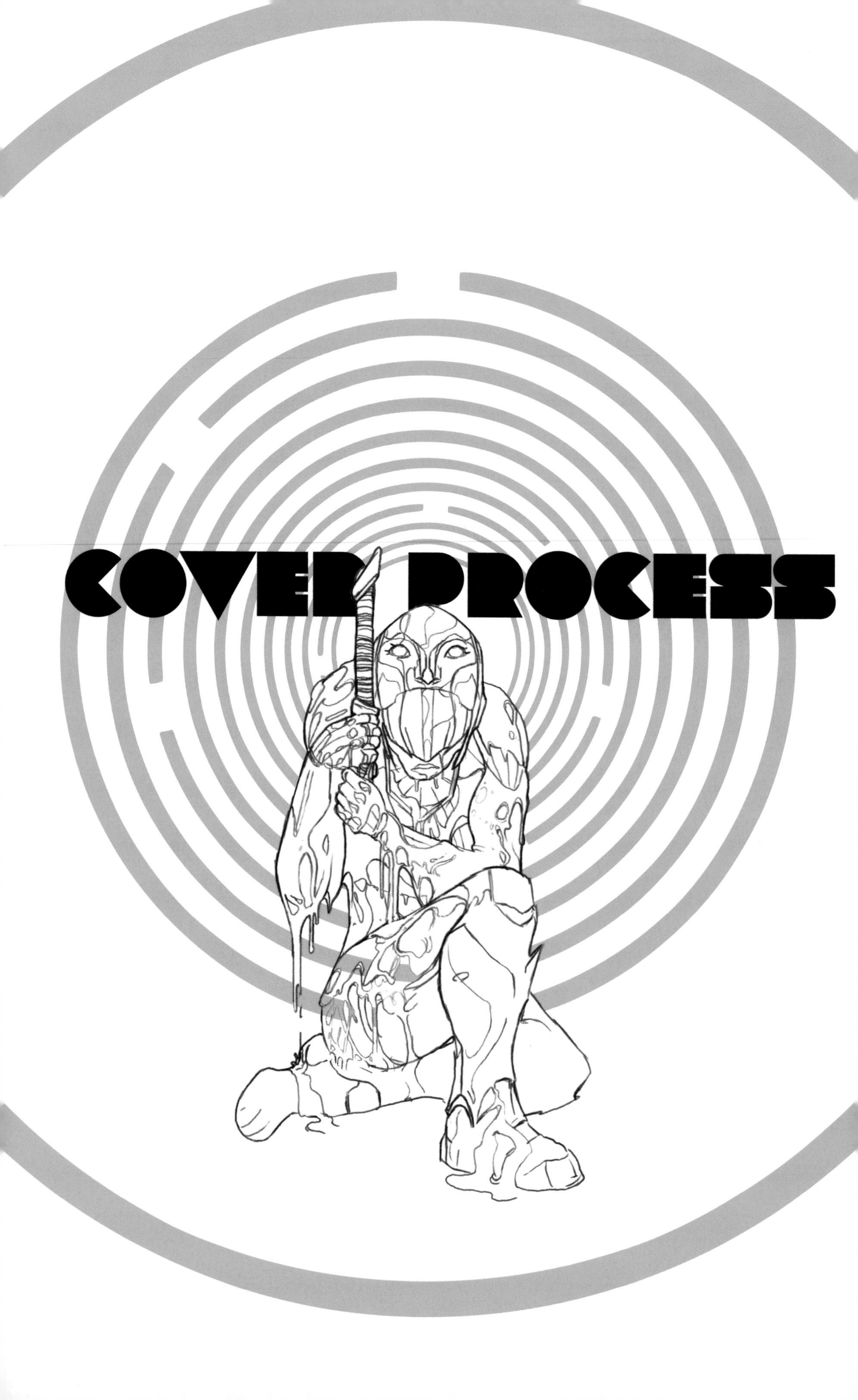

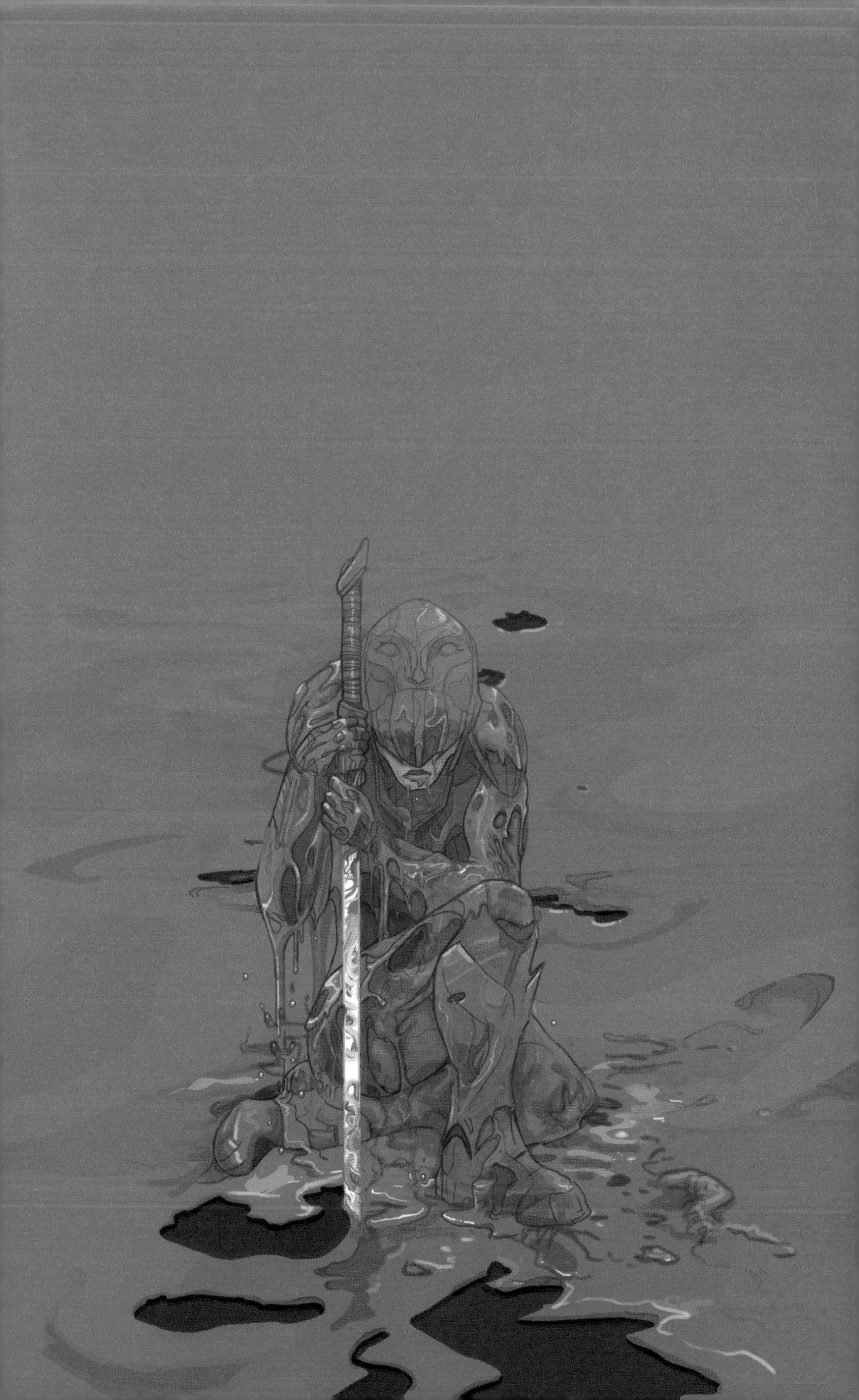

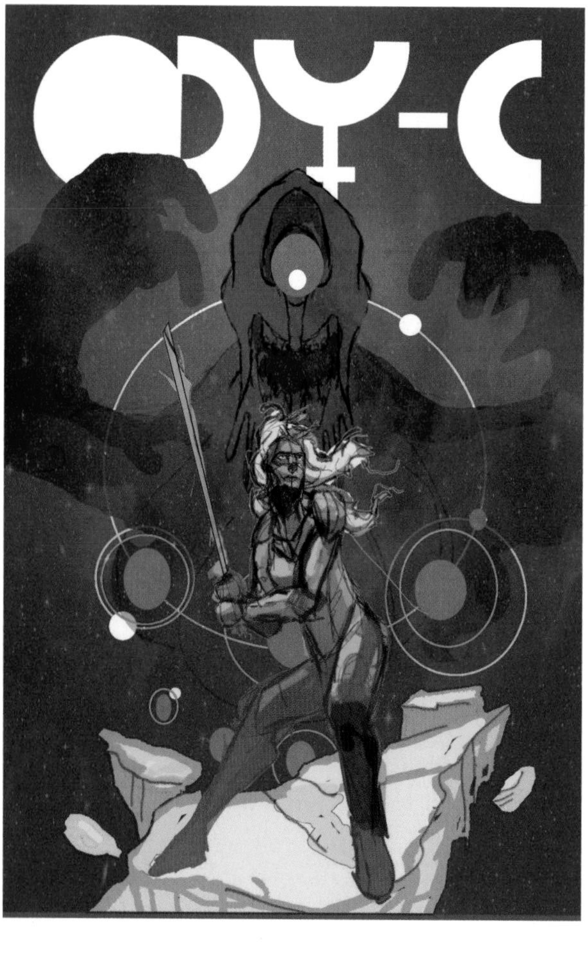
ODY-C

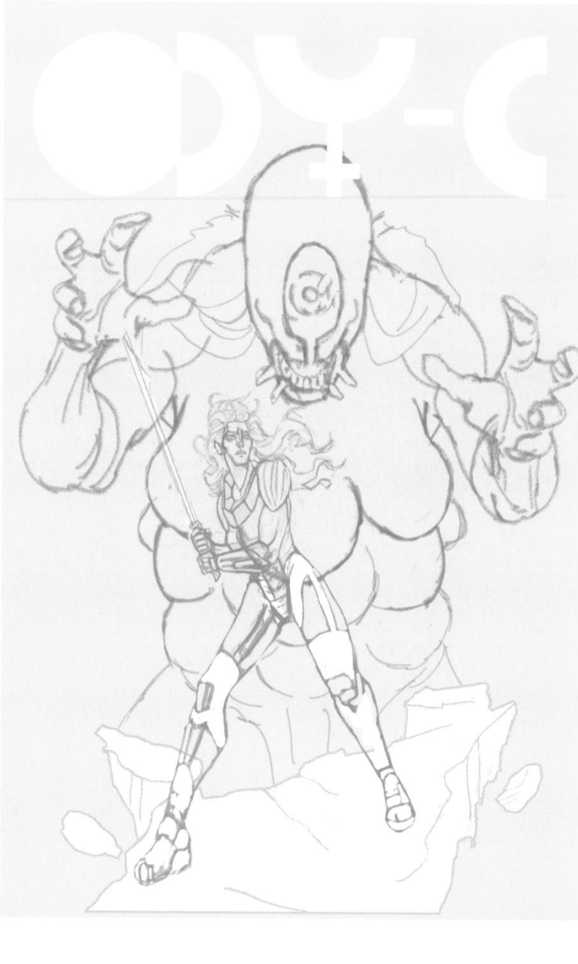
ODY-C

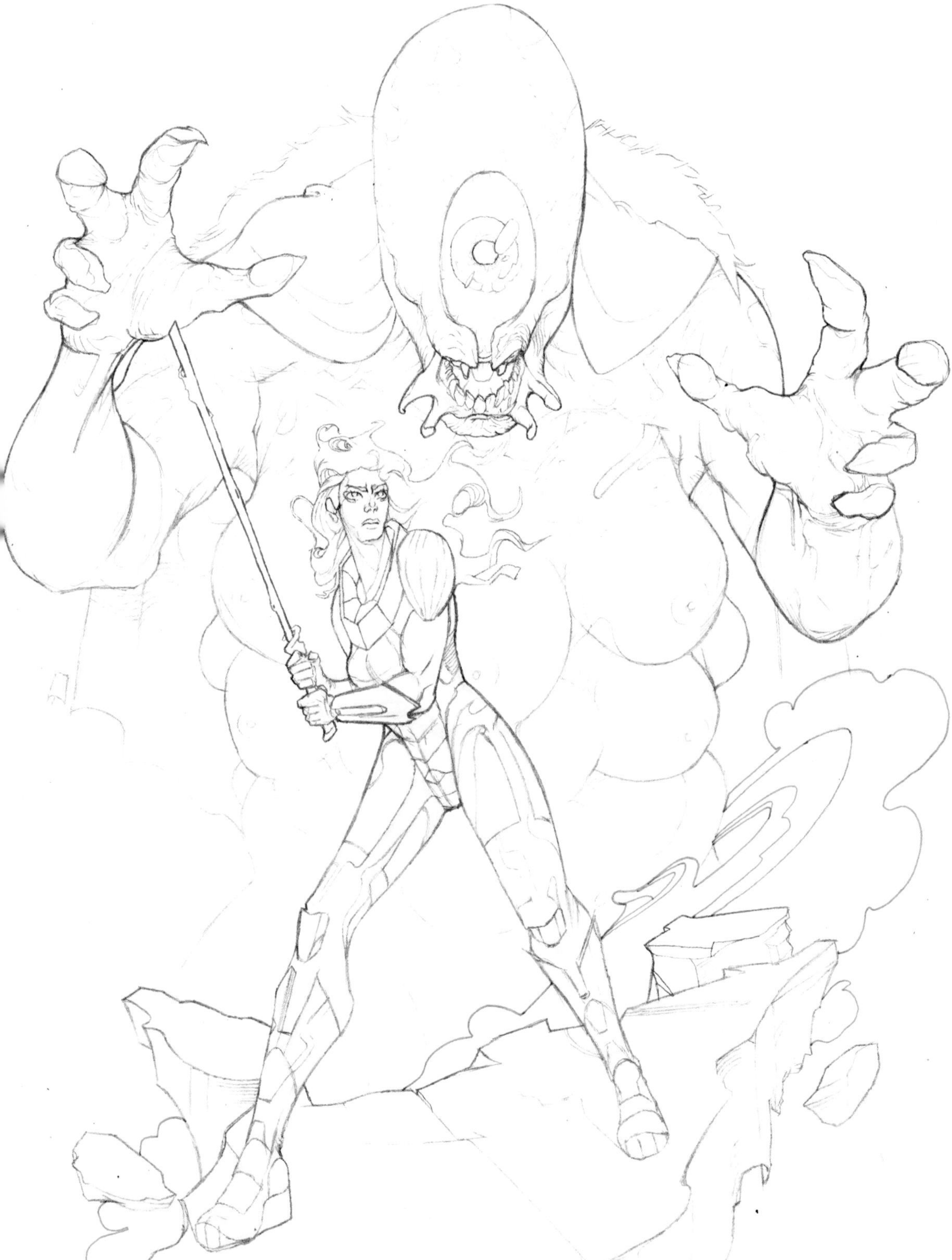

TRADITIONAL PENCILS

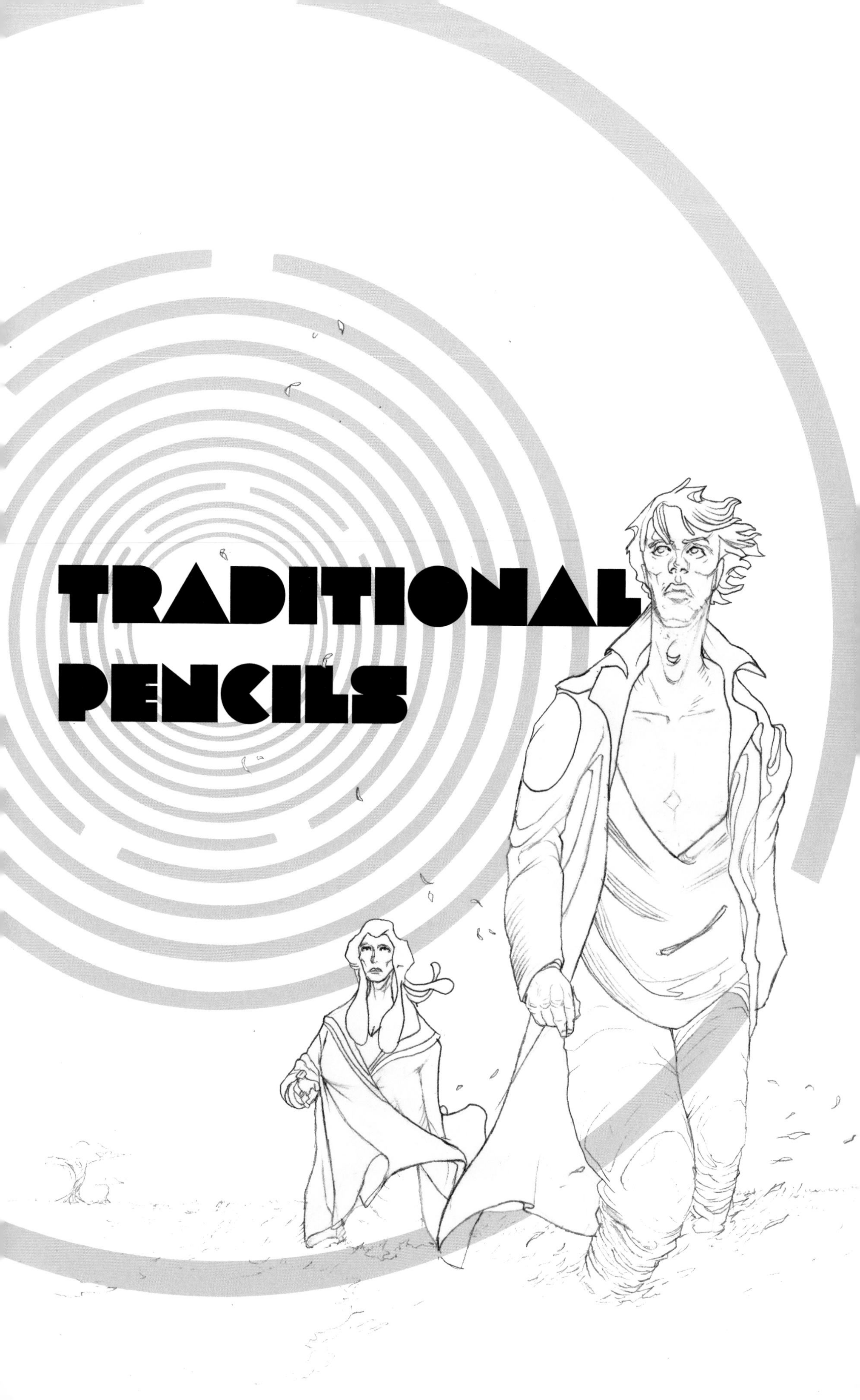

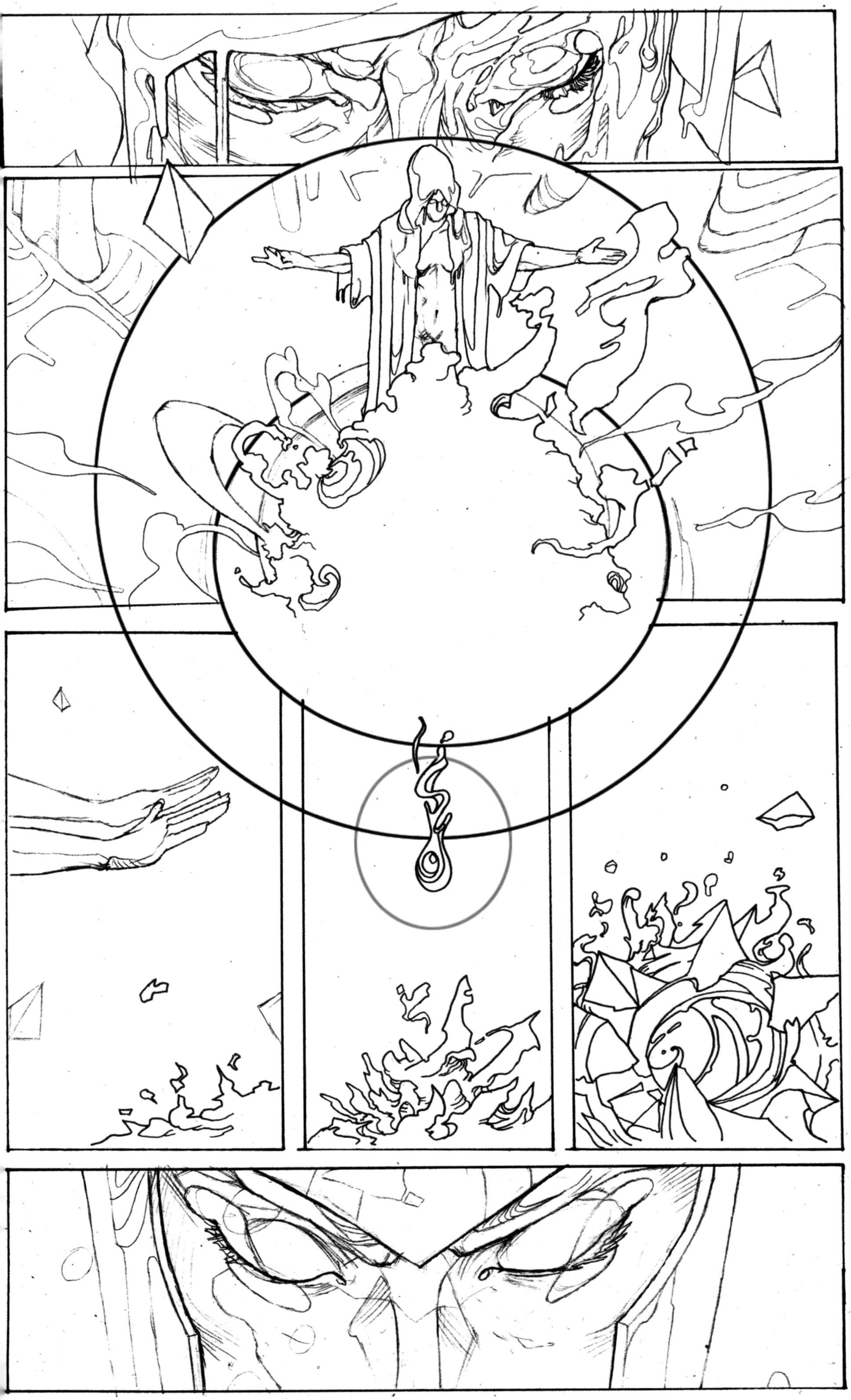

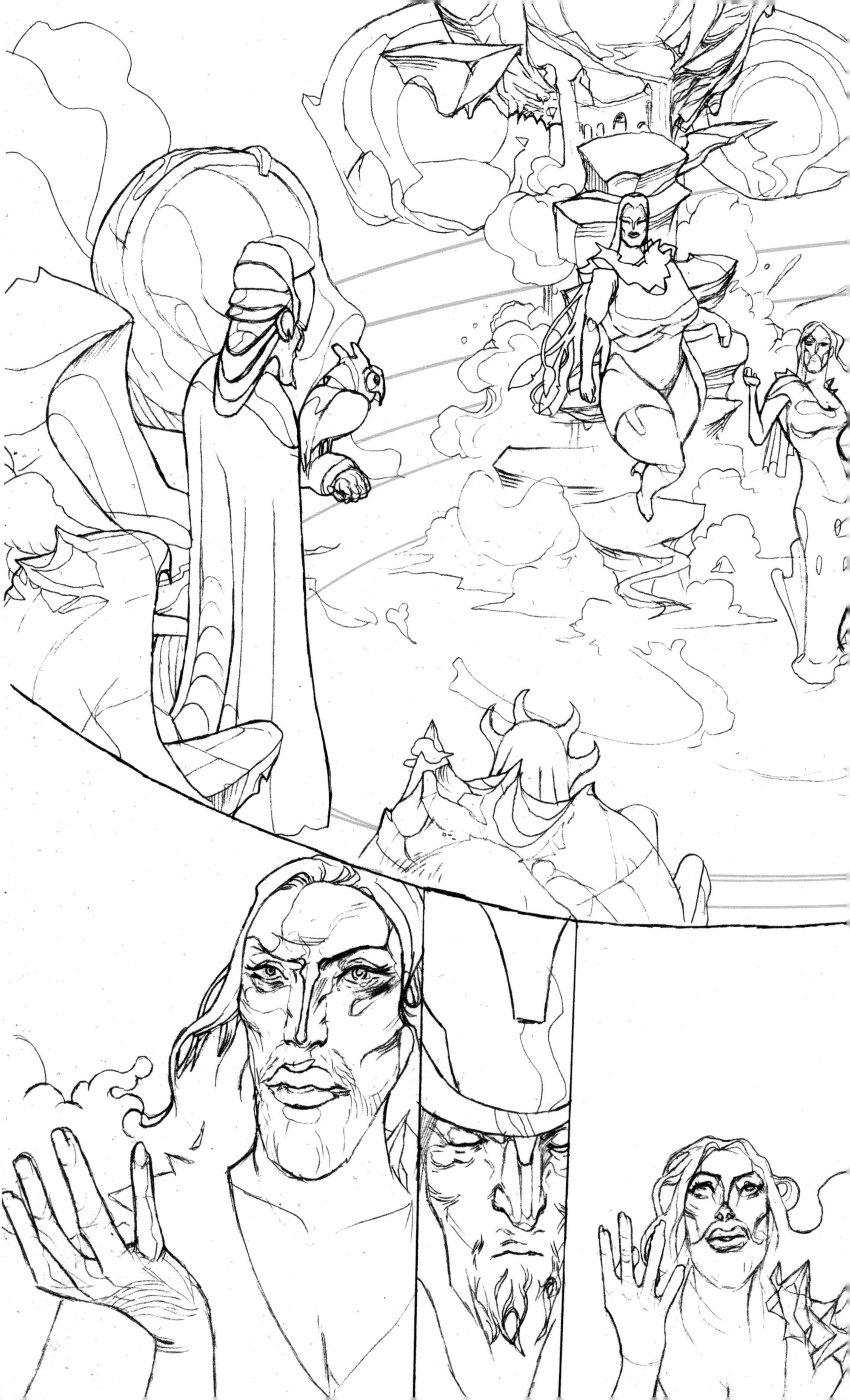

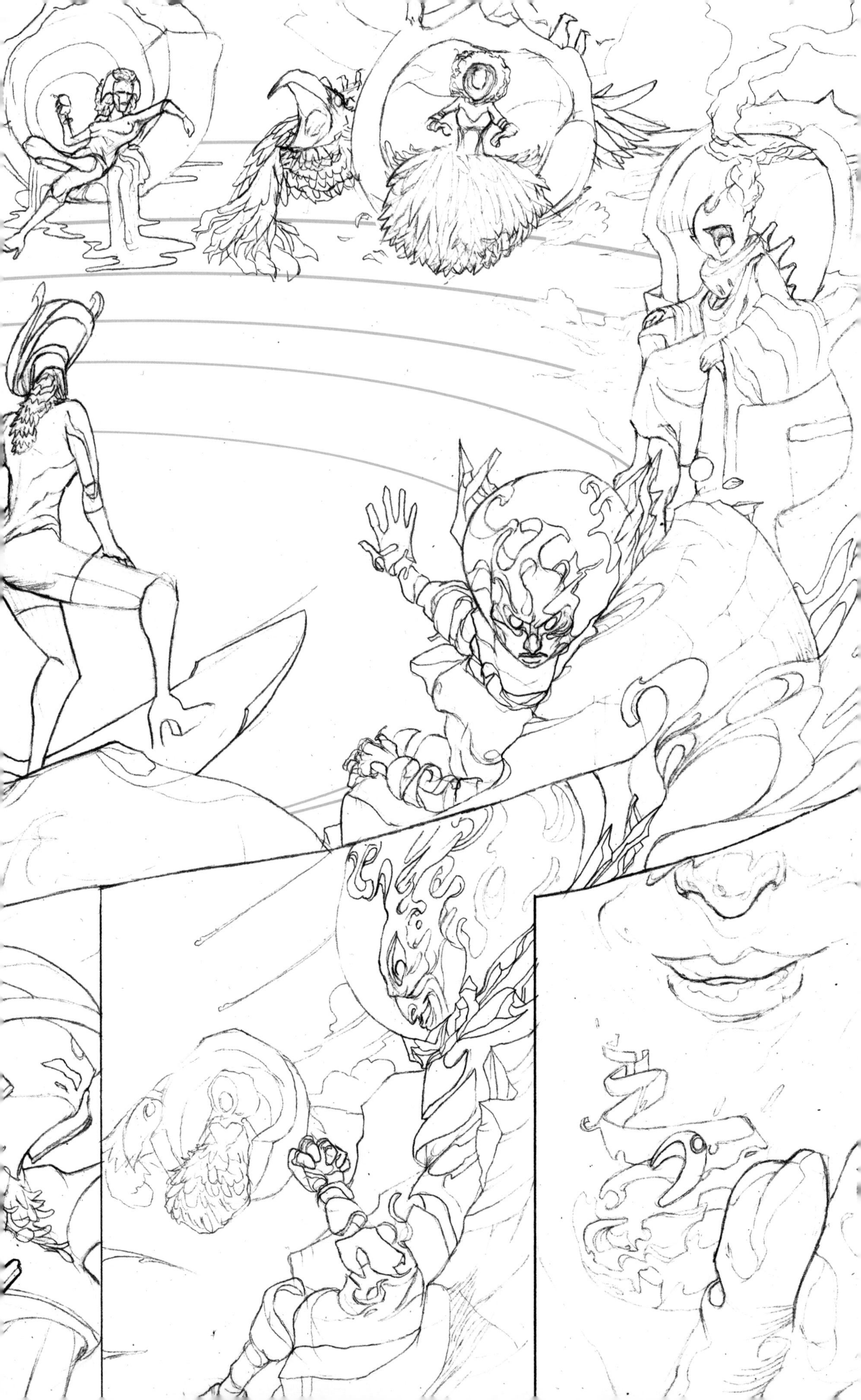

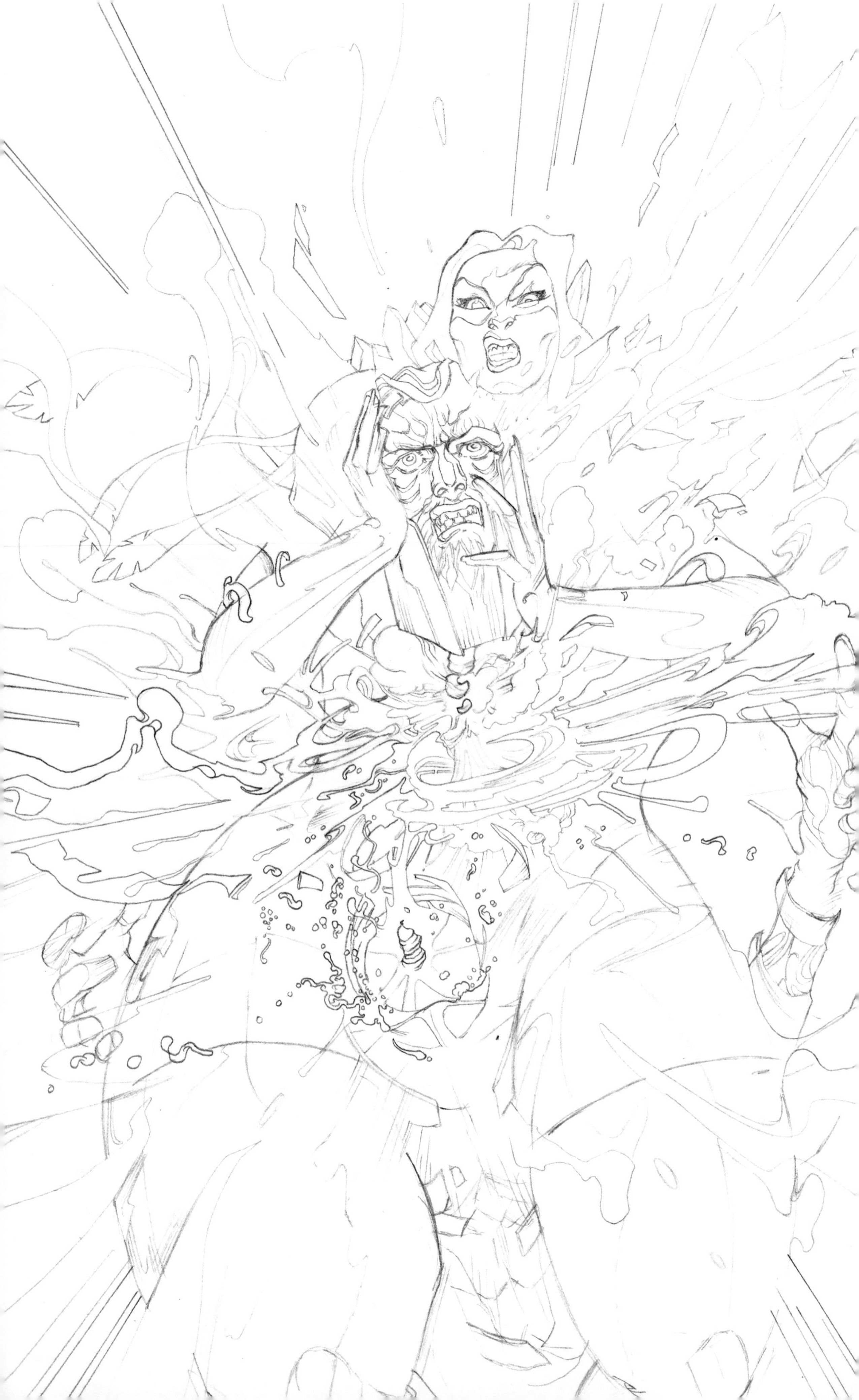

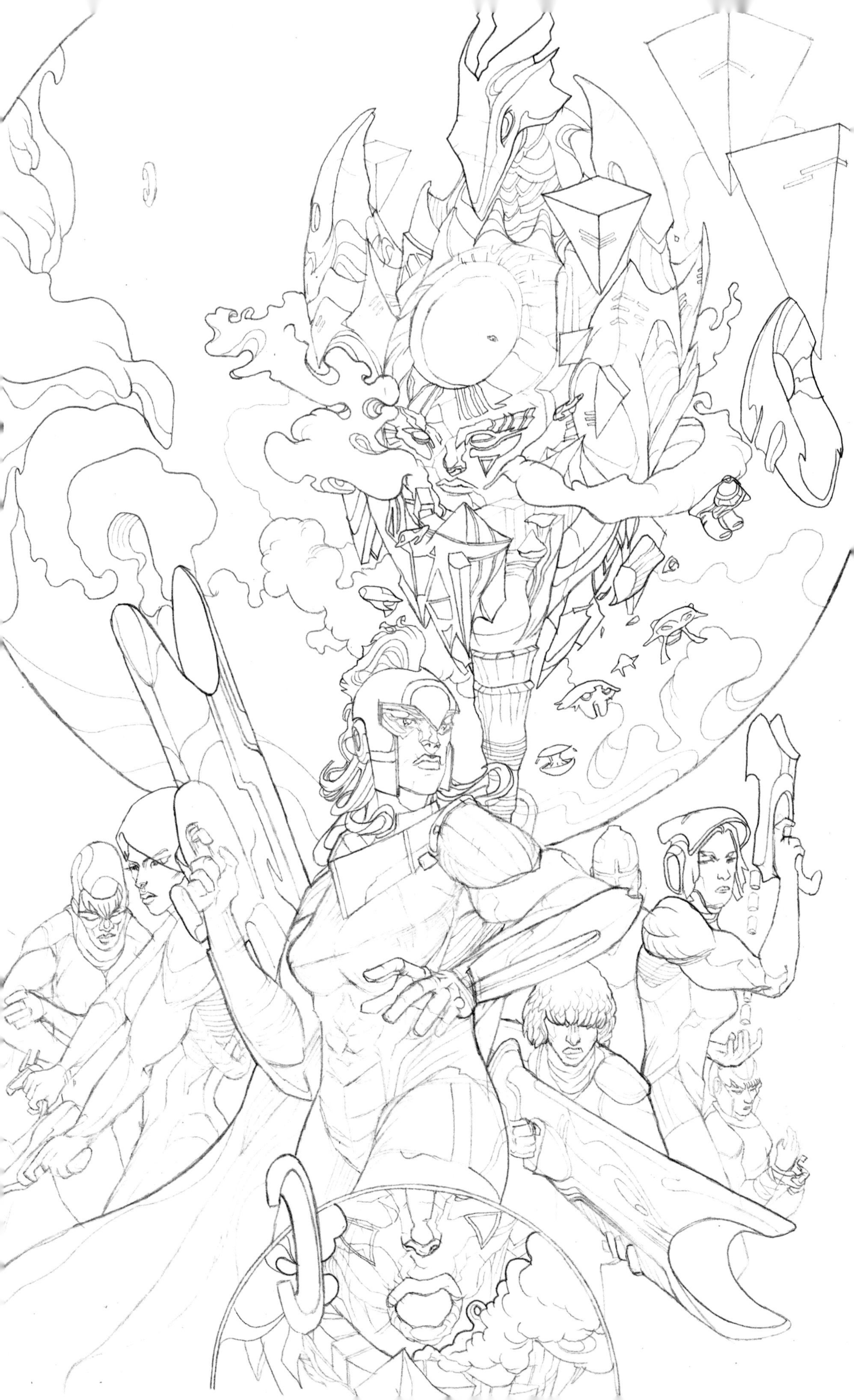

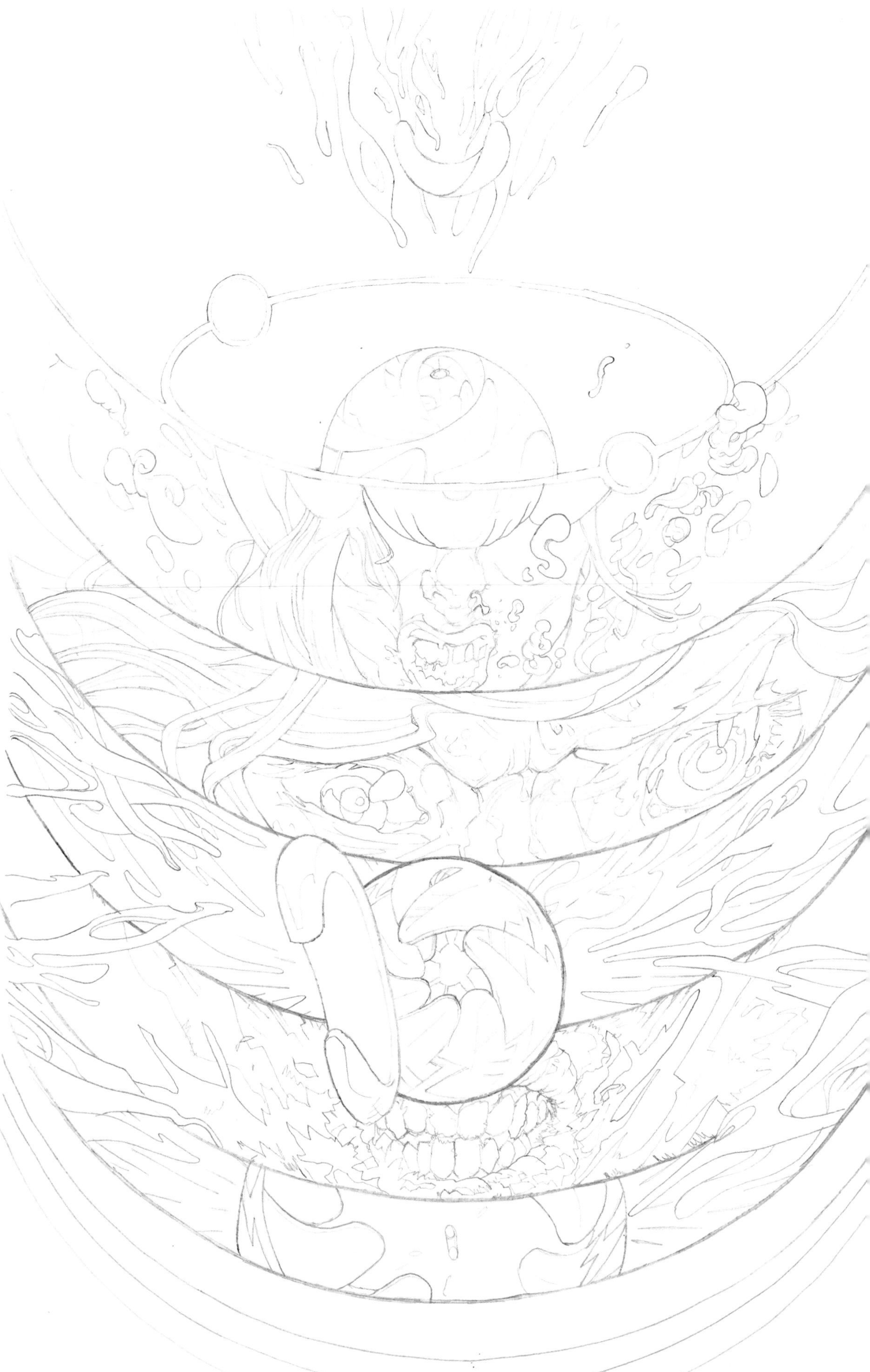

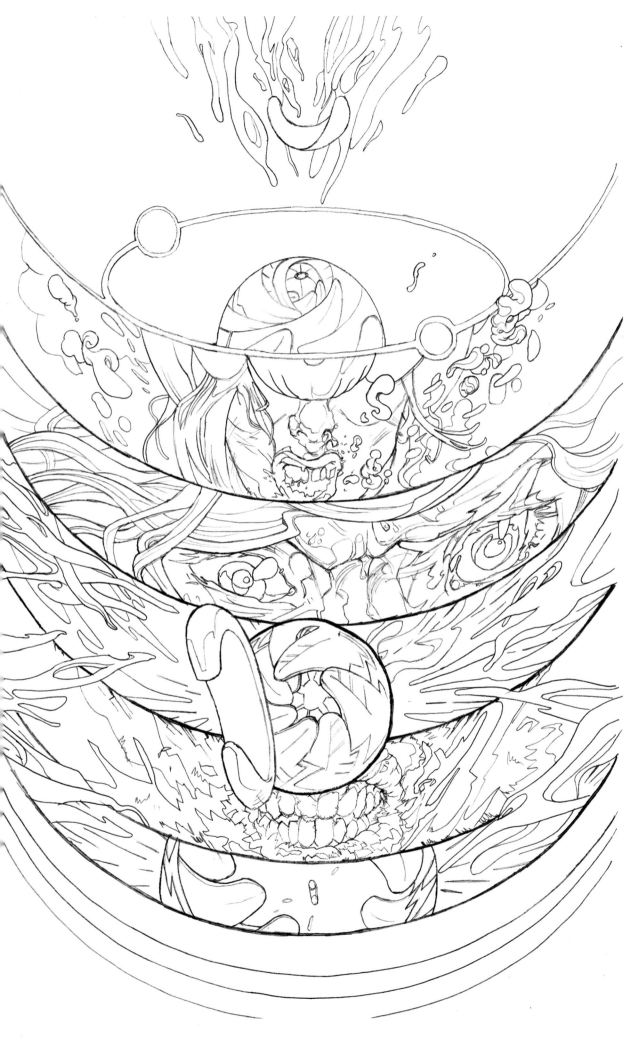

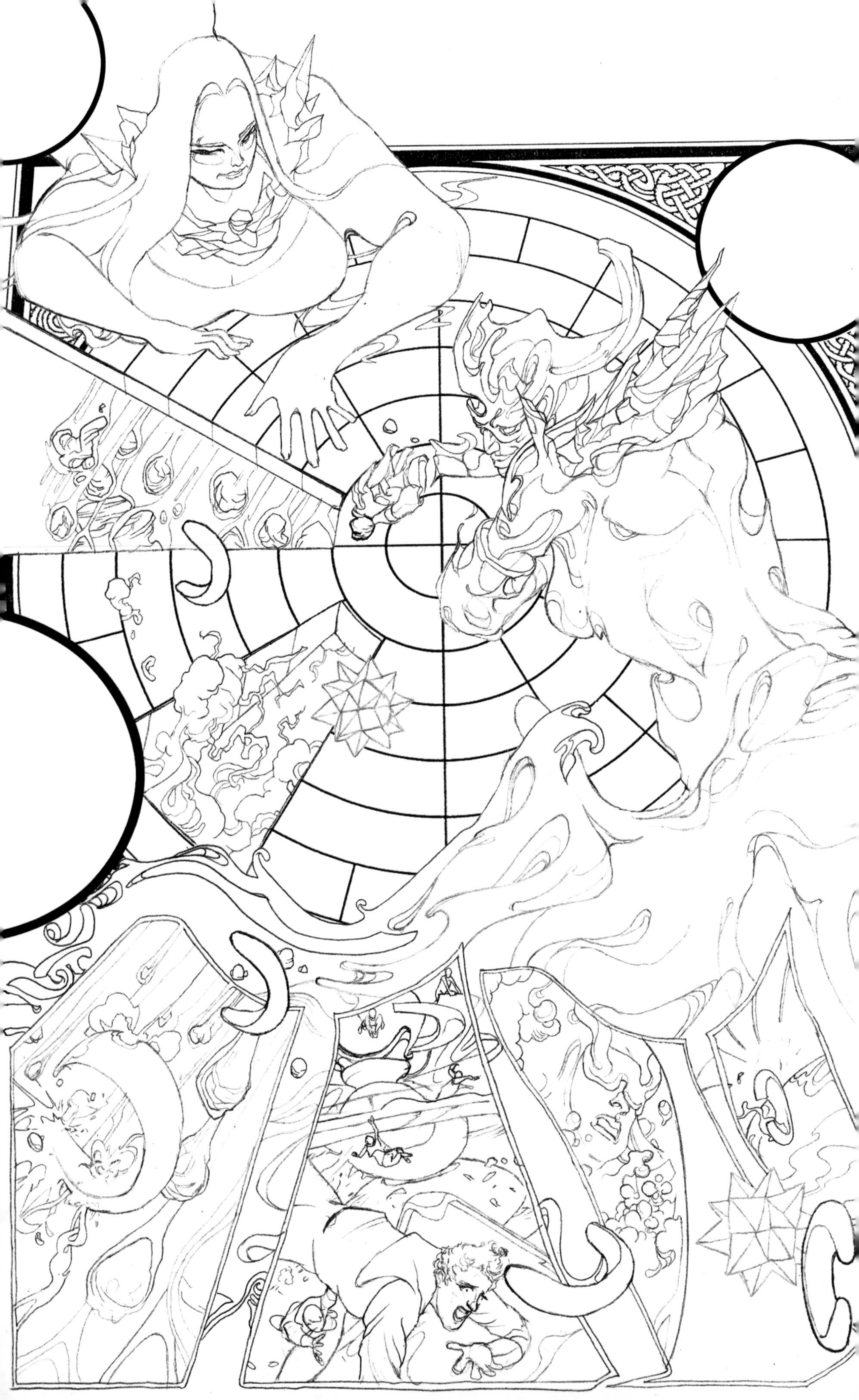

DIGITAL PENCILS

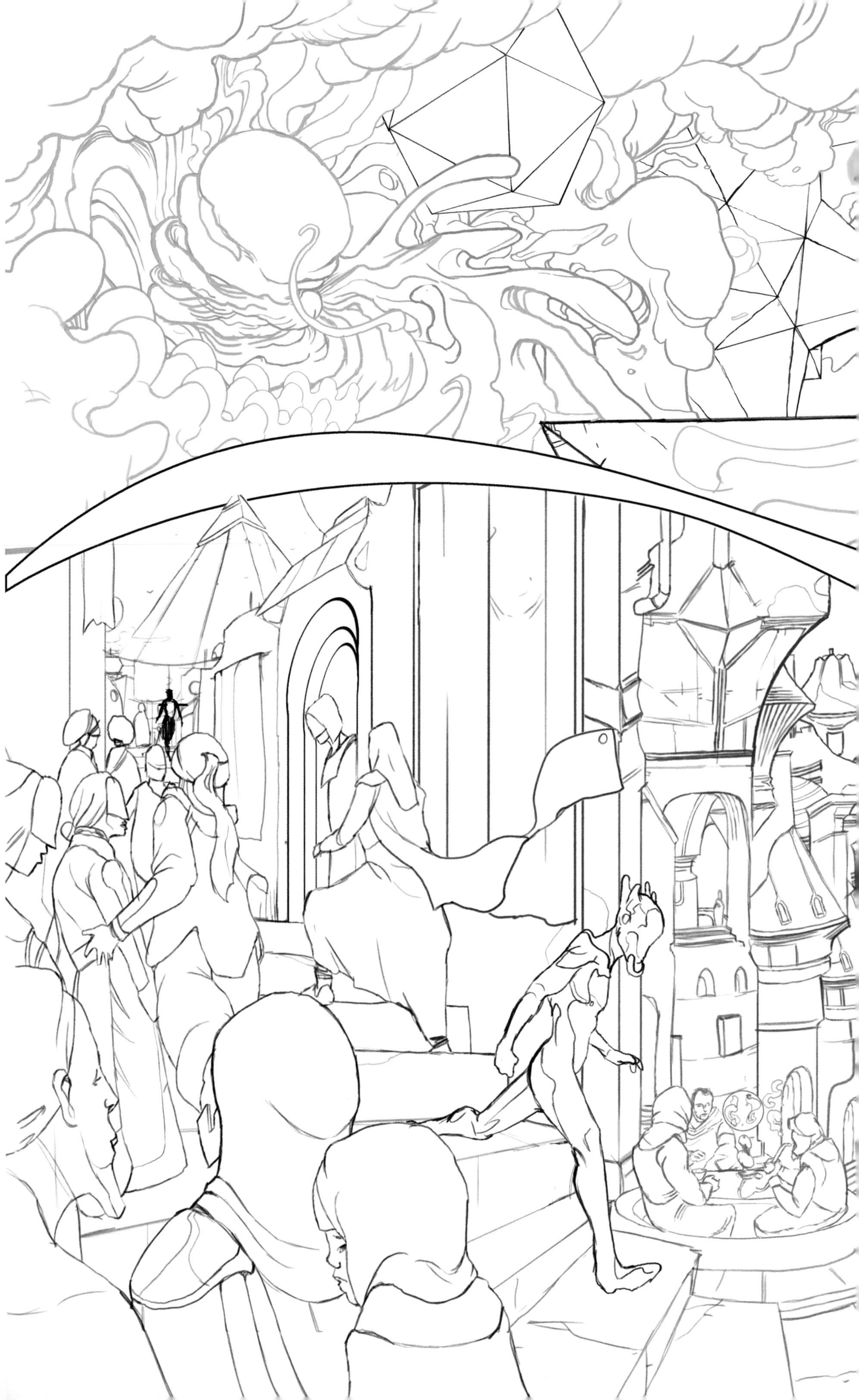

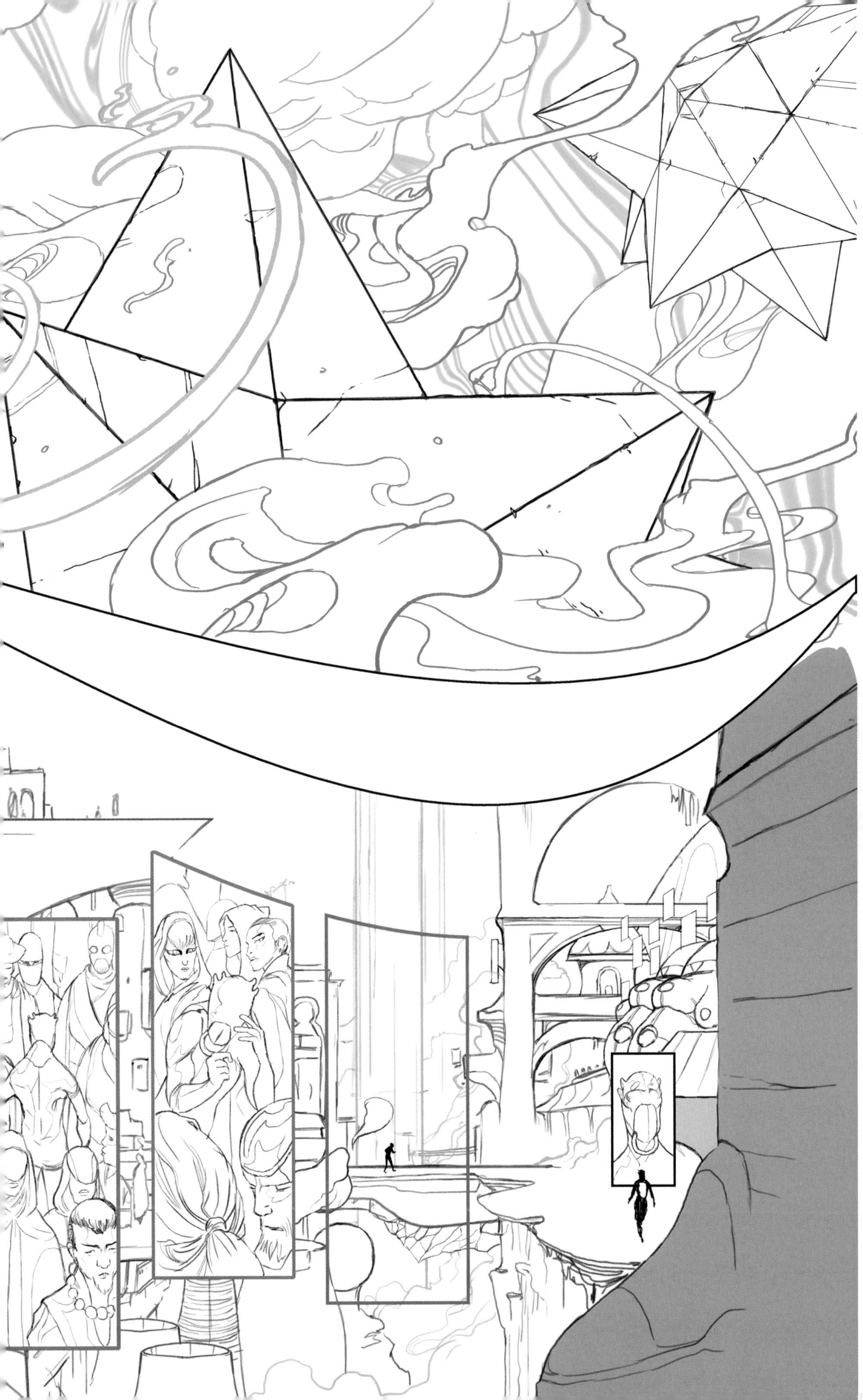

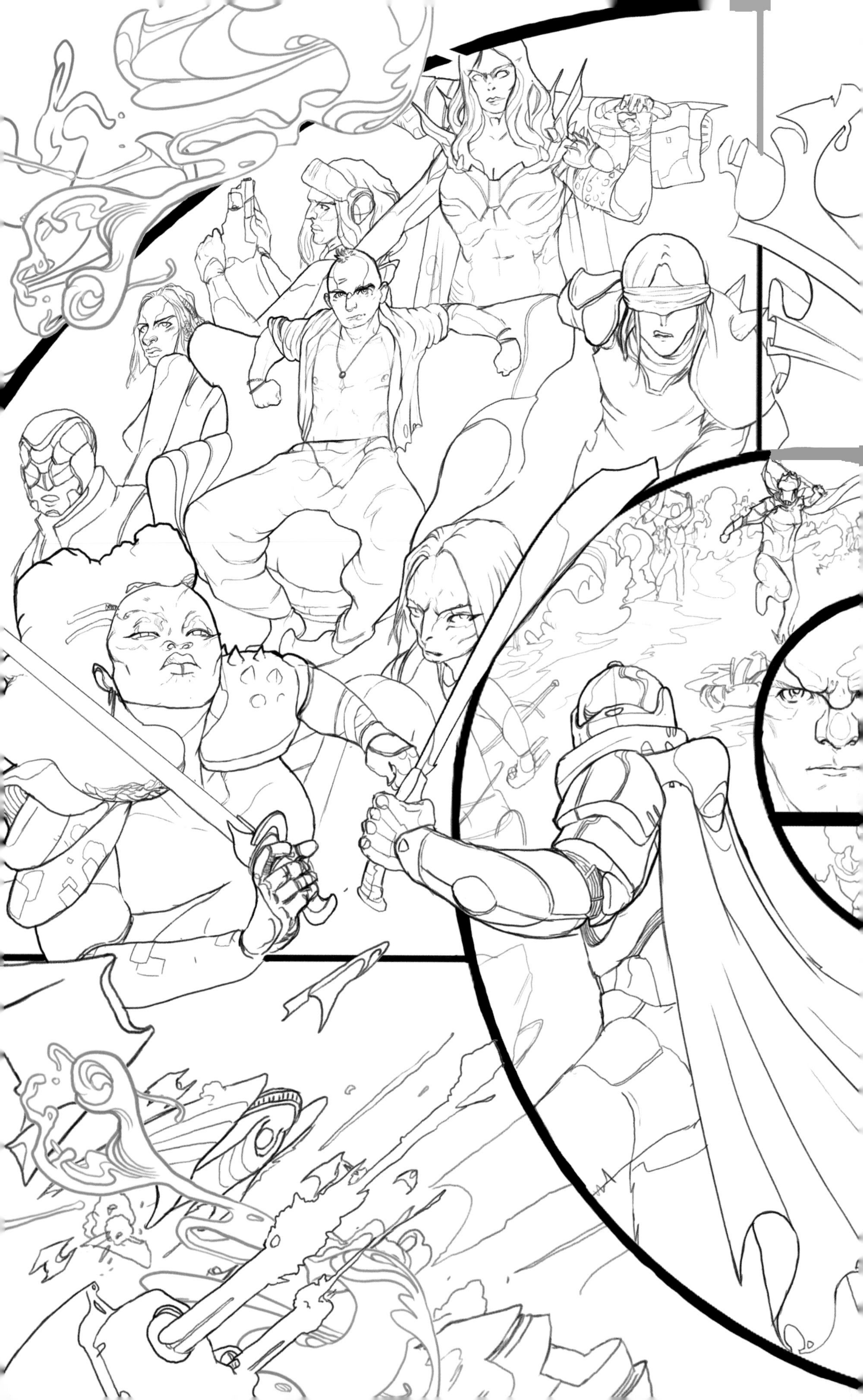

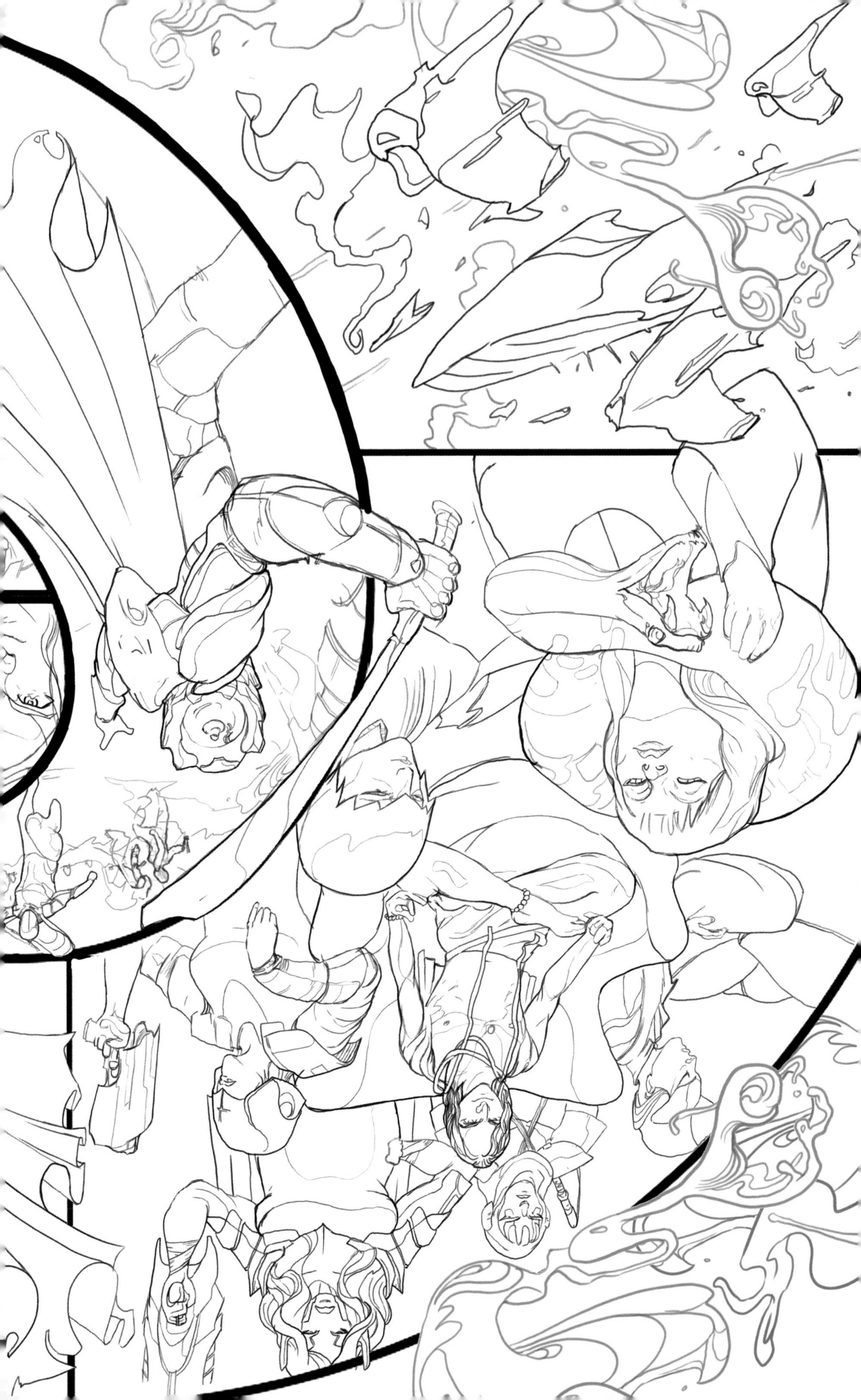

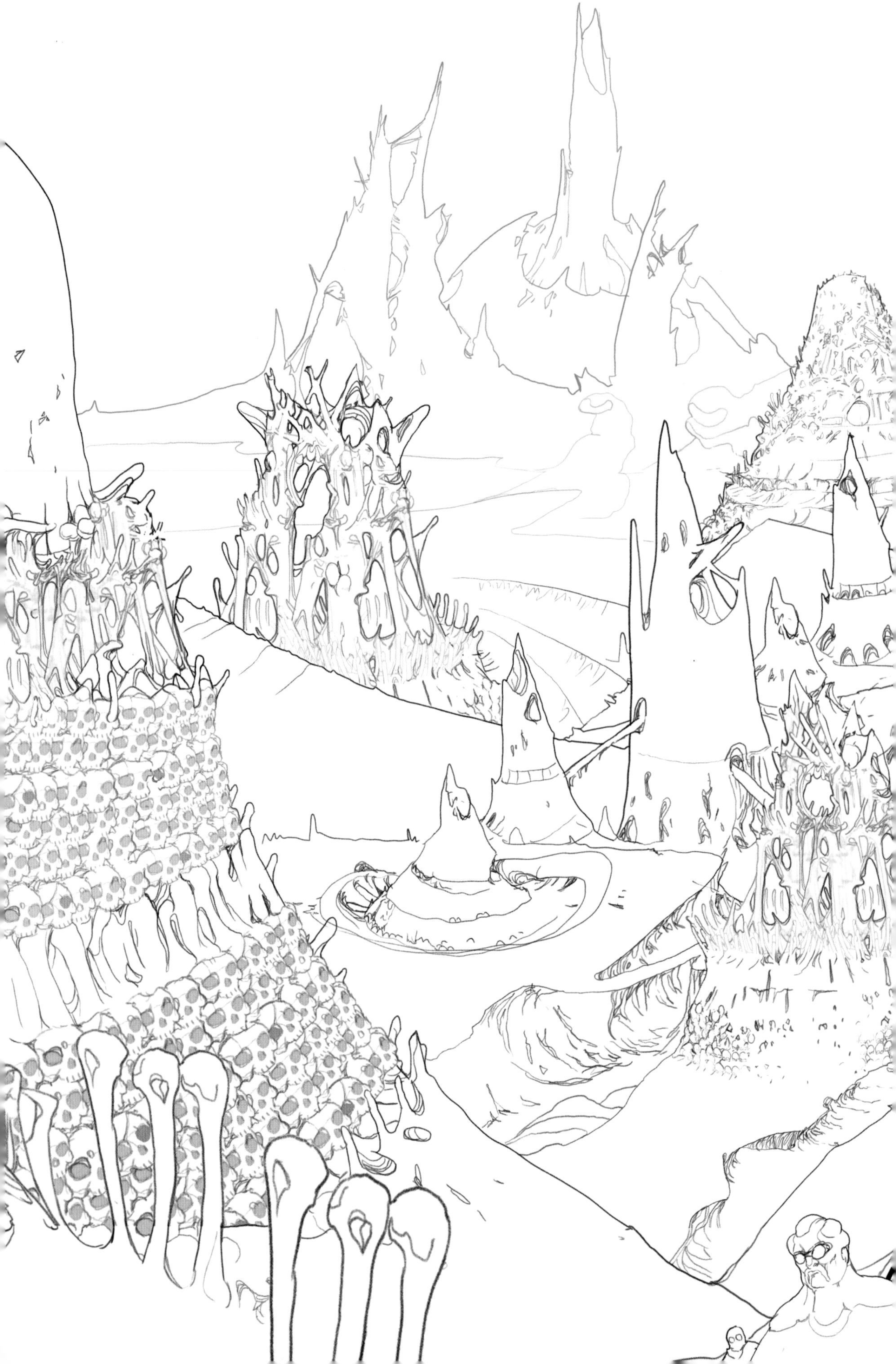

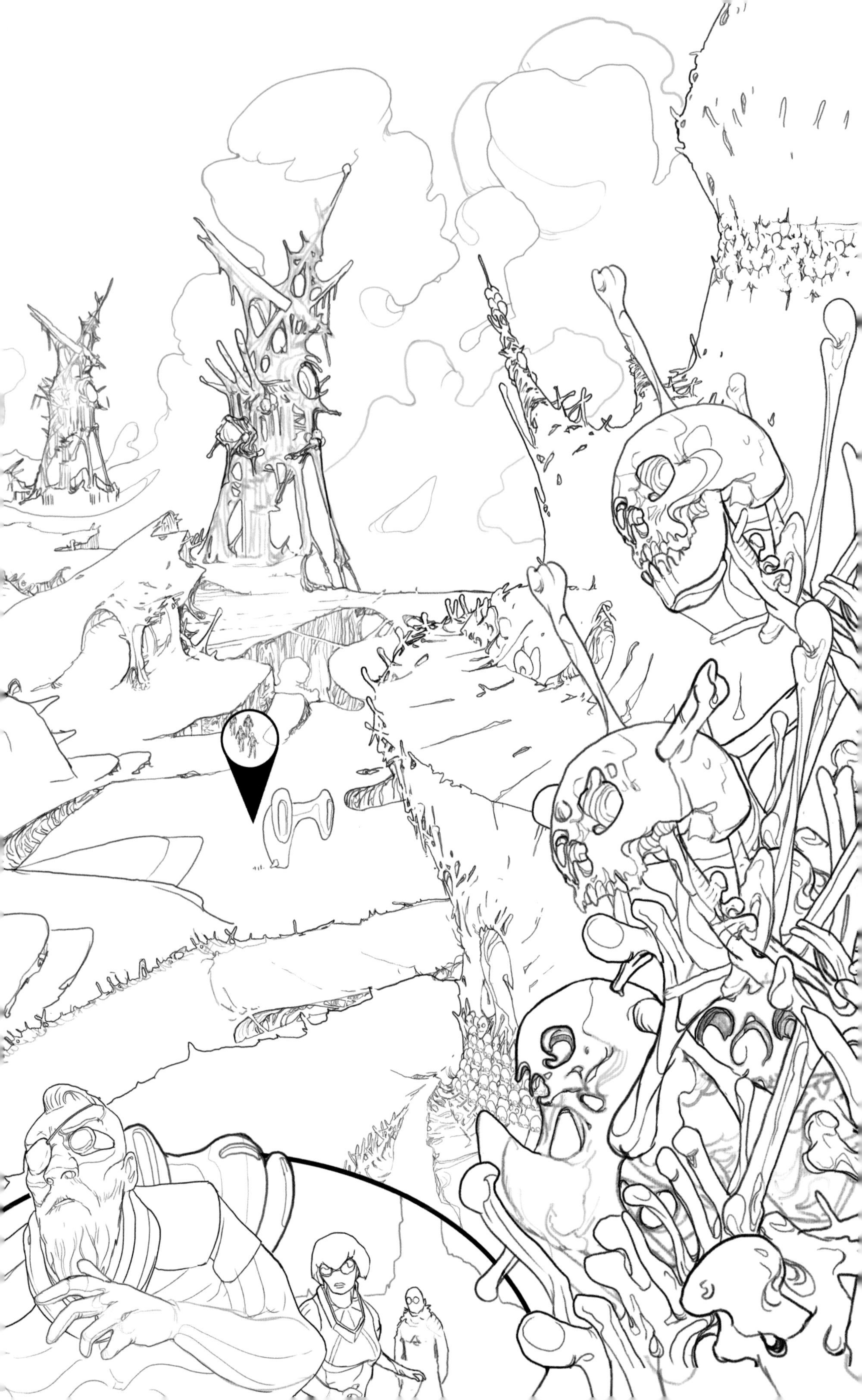

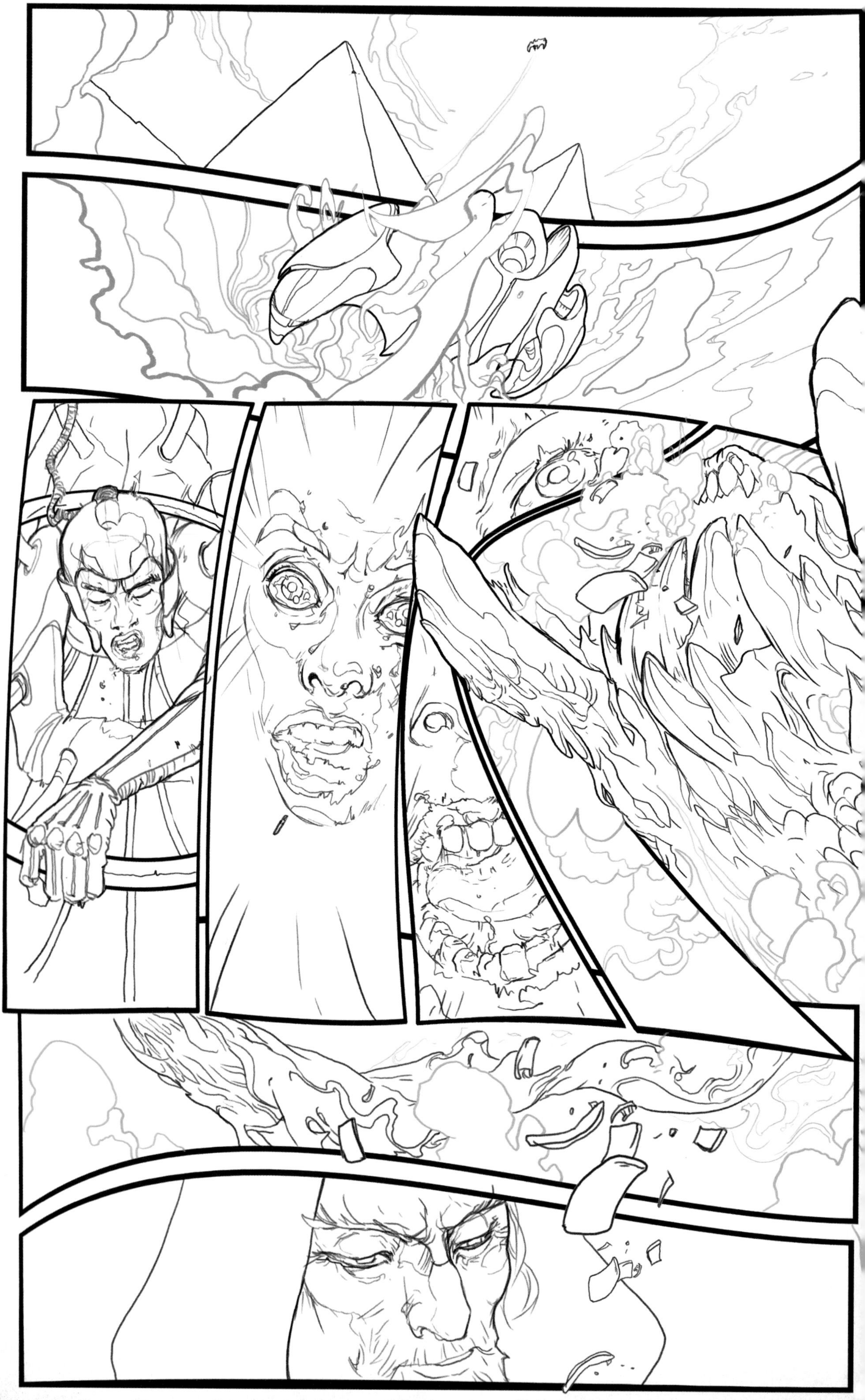

PAGE PROCESS

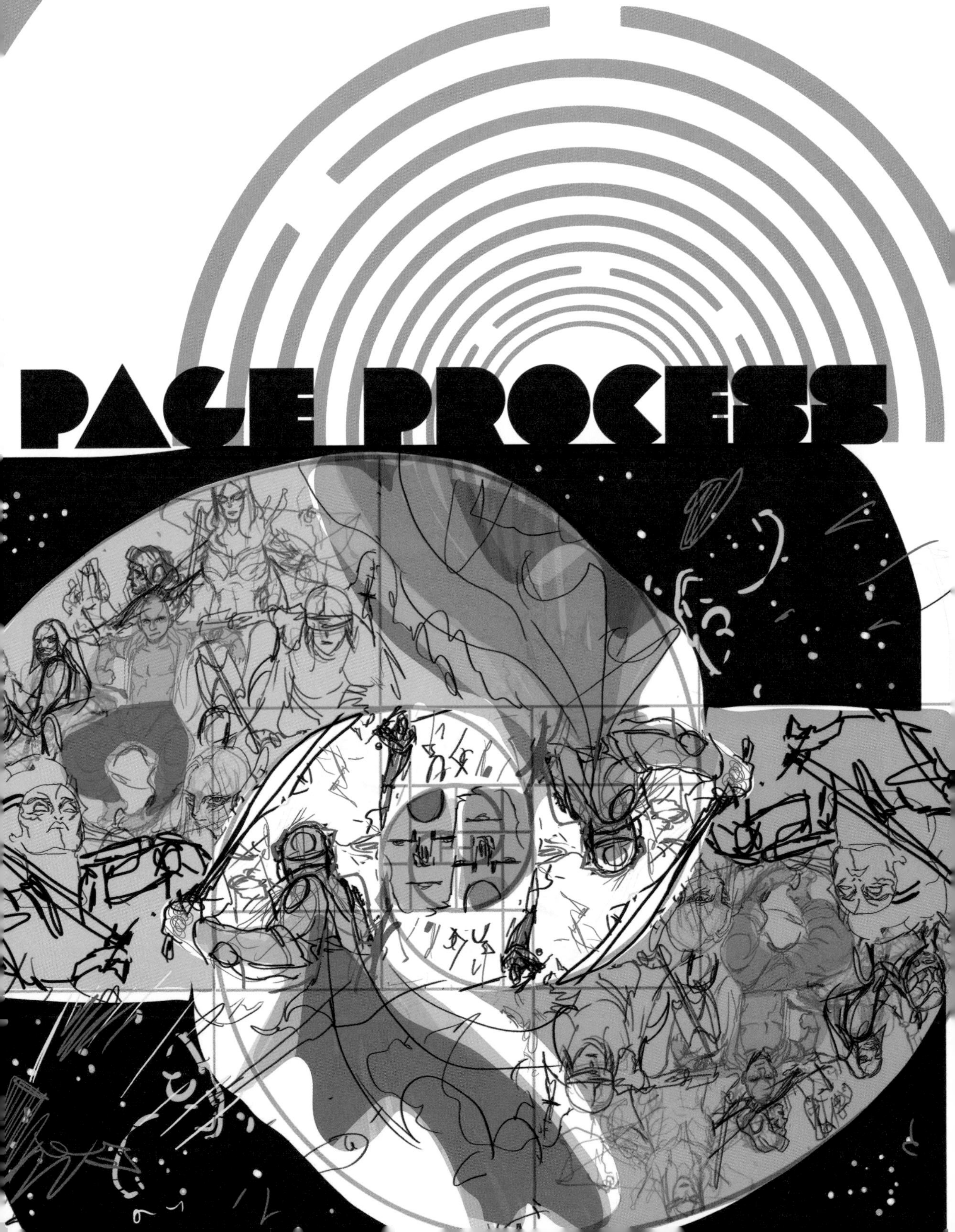

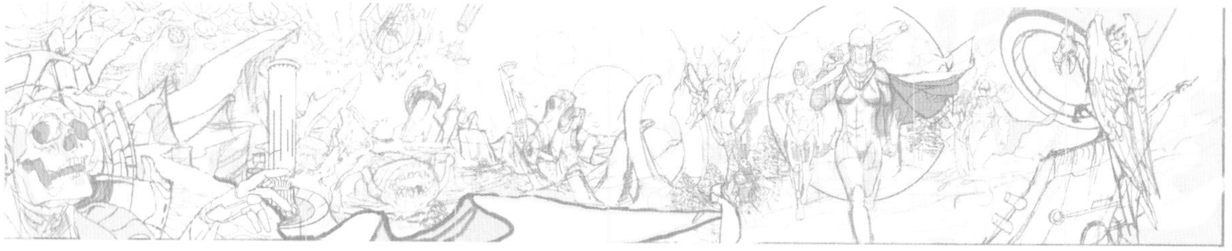
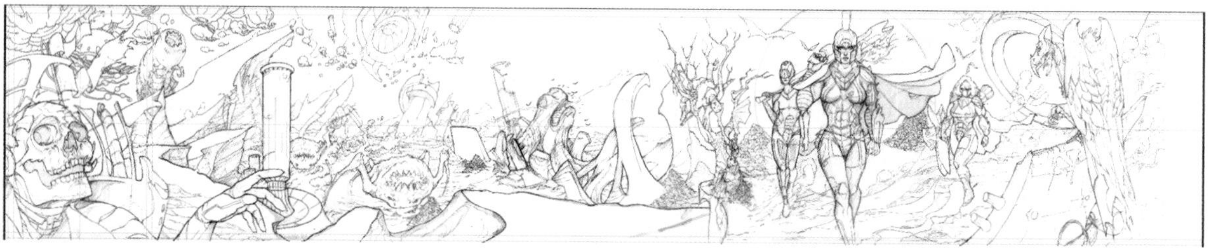
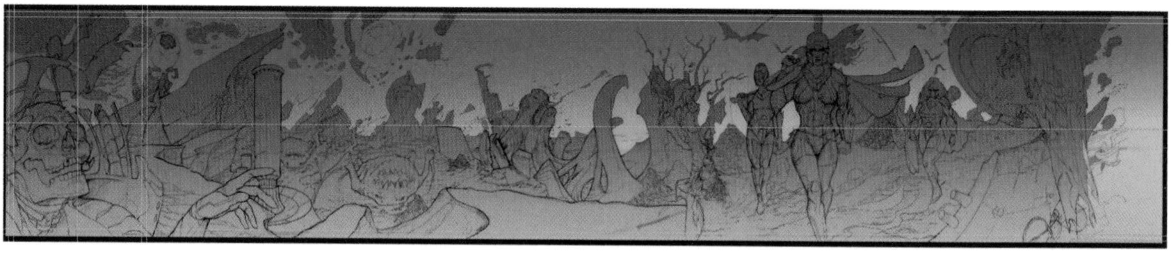
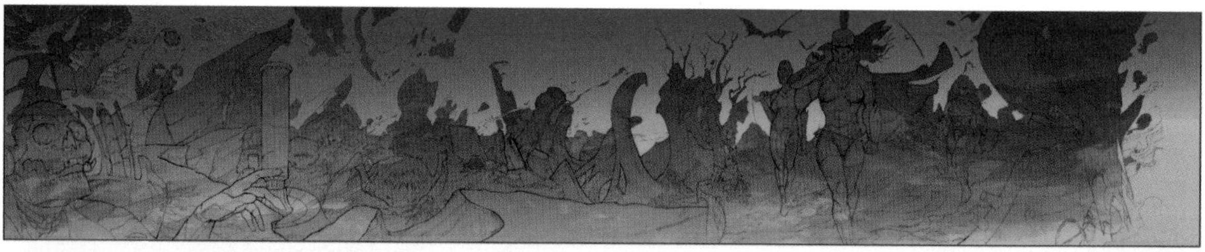
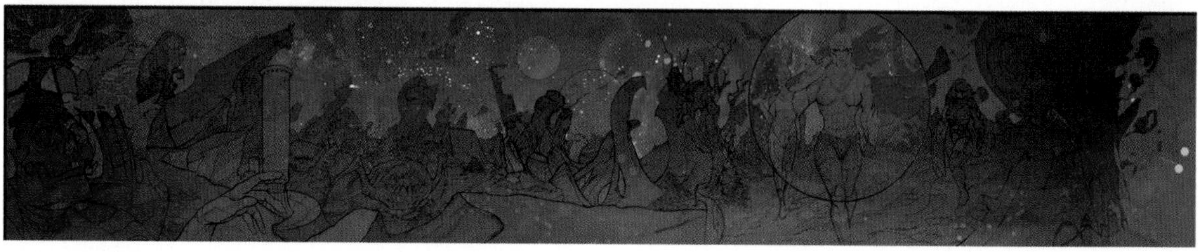
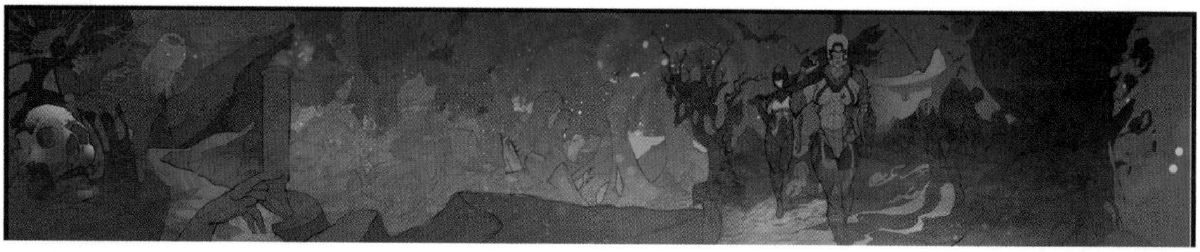
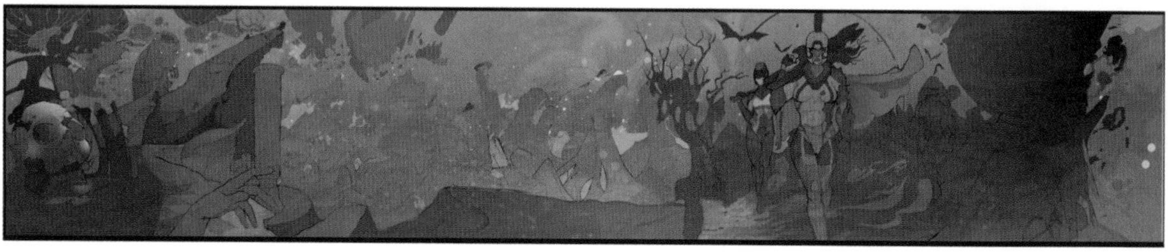

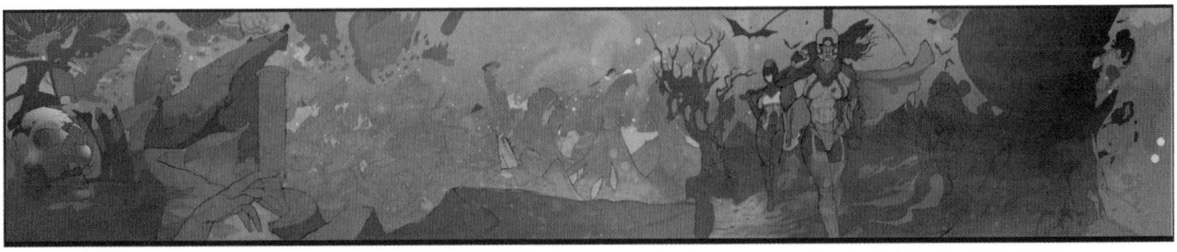

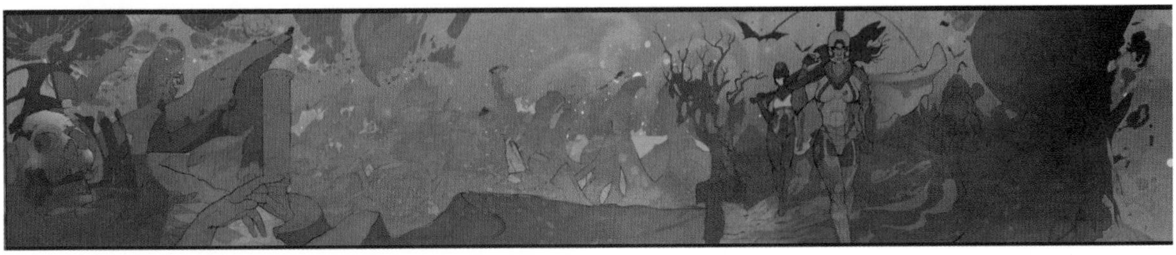

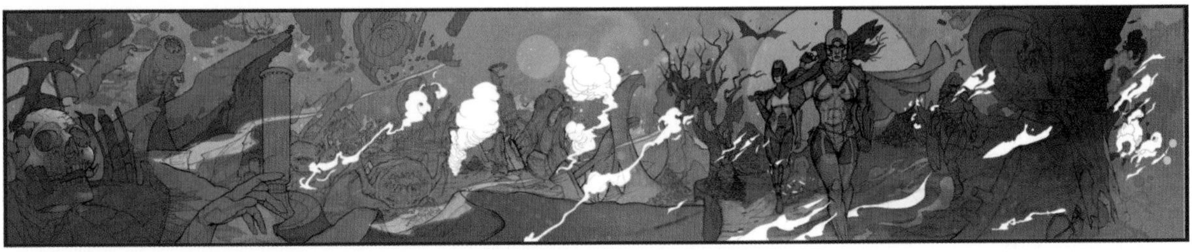

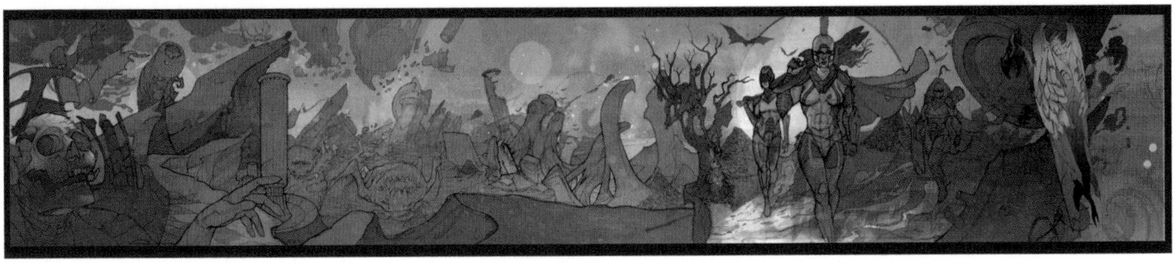

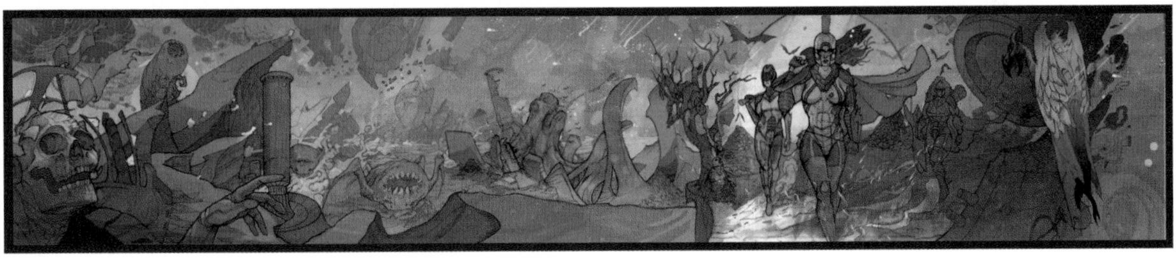

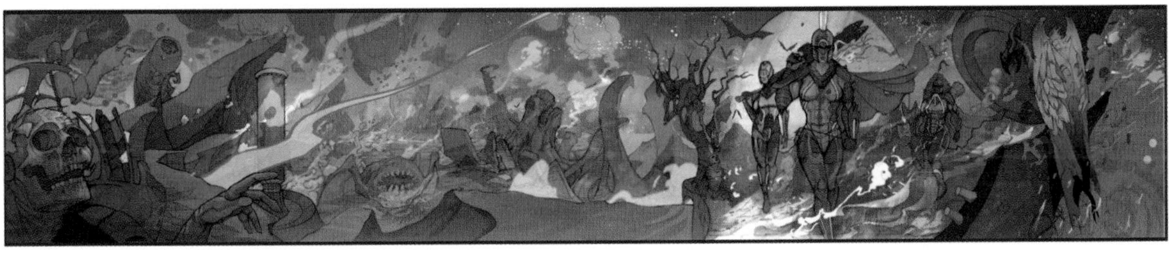

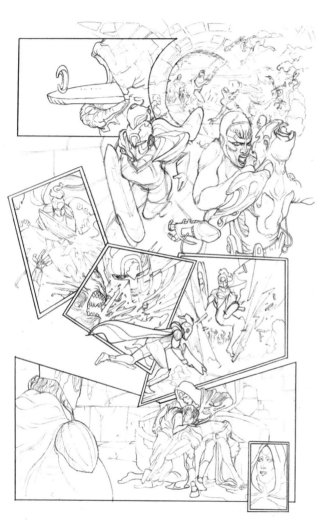

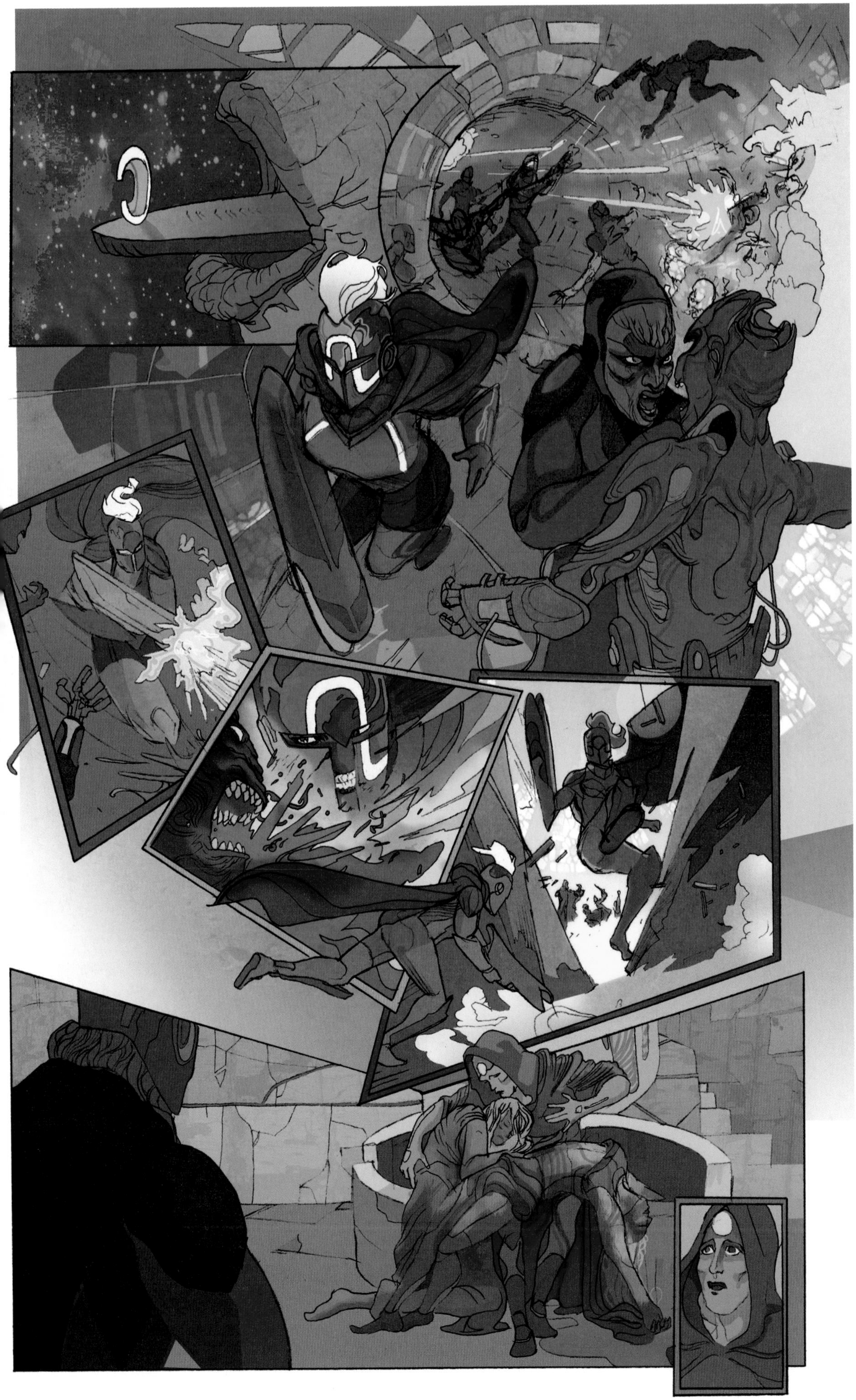

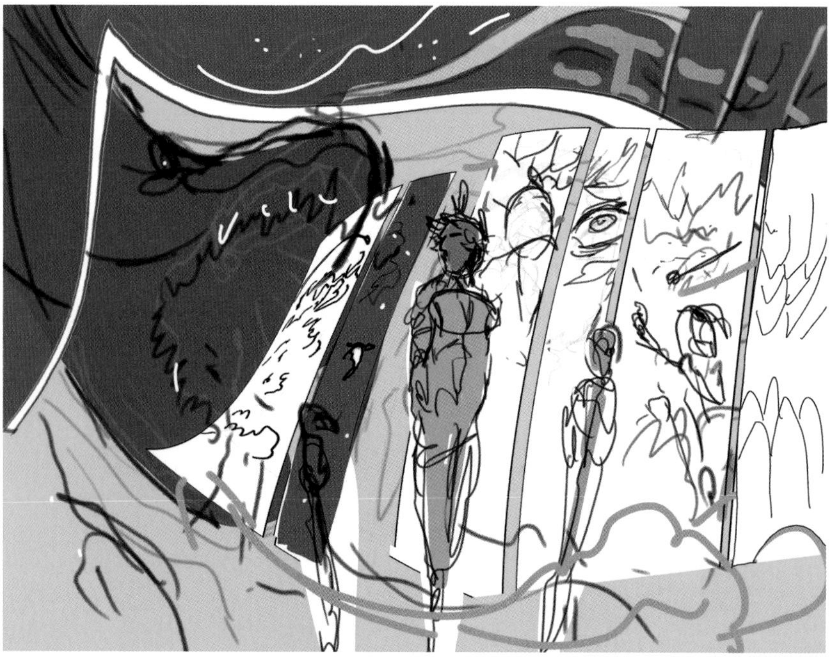
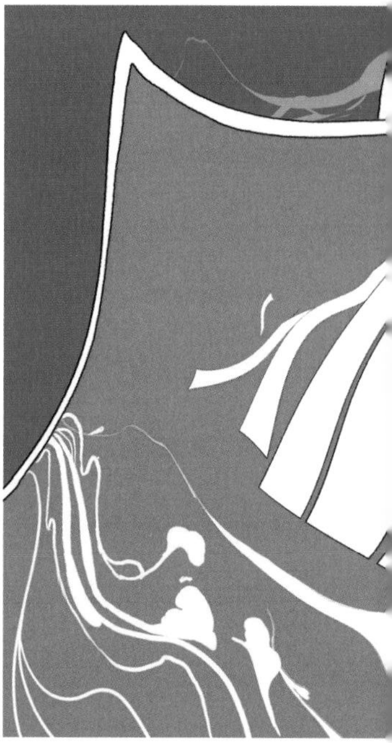
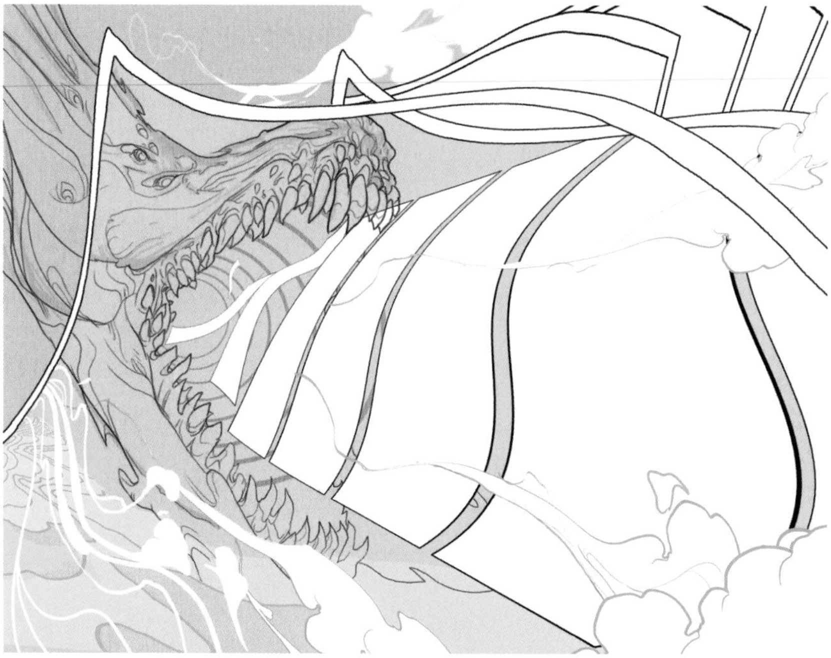
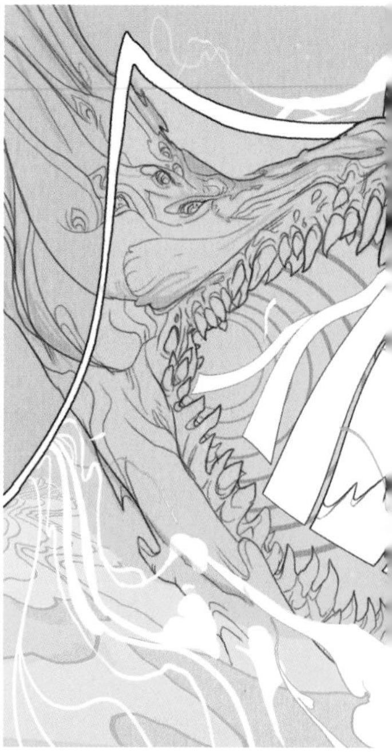
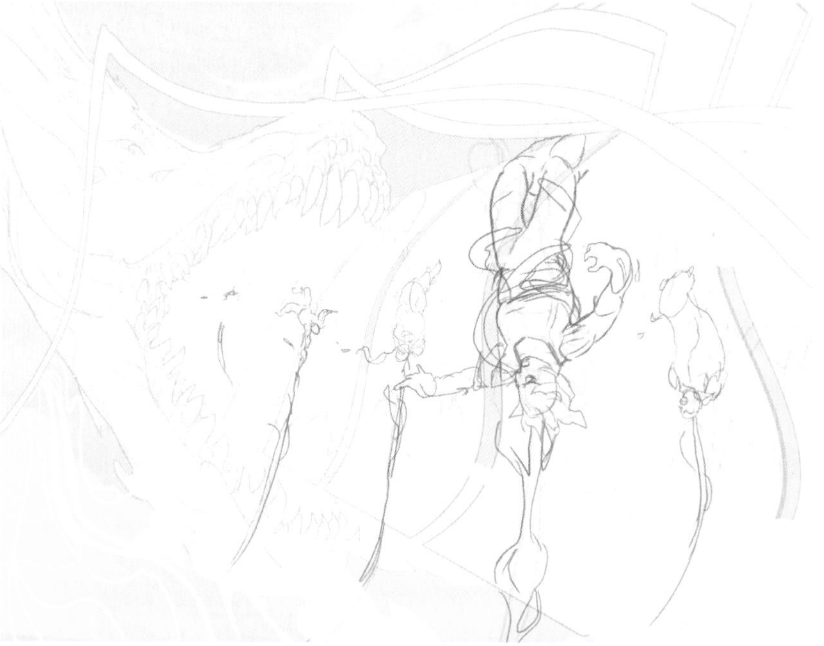
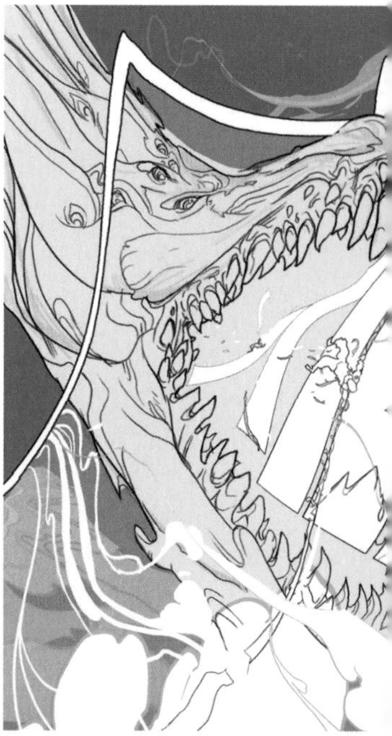

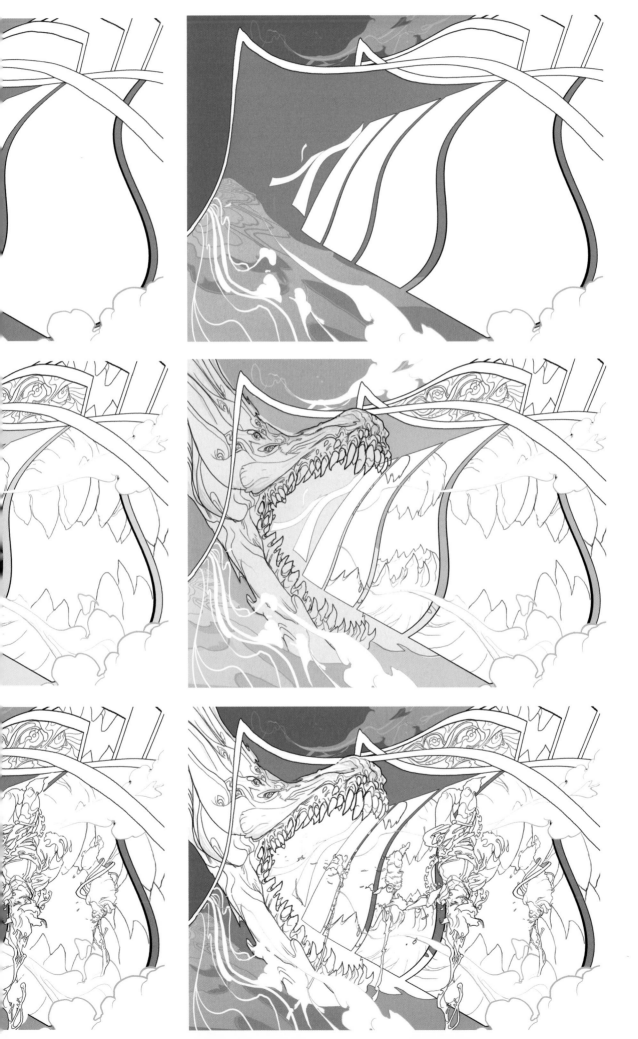

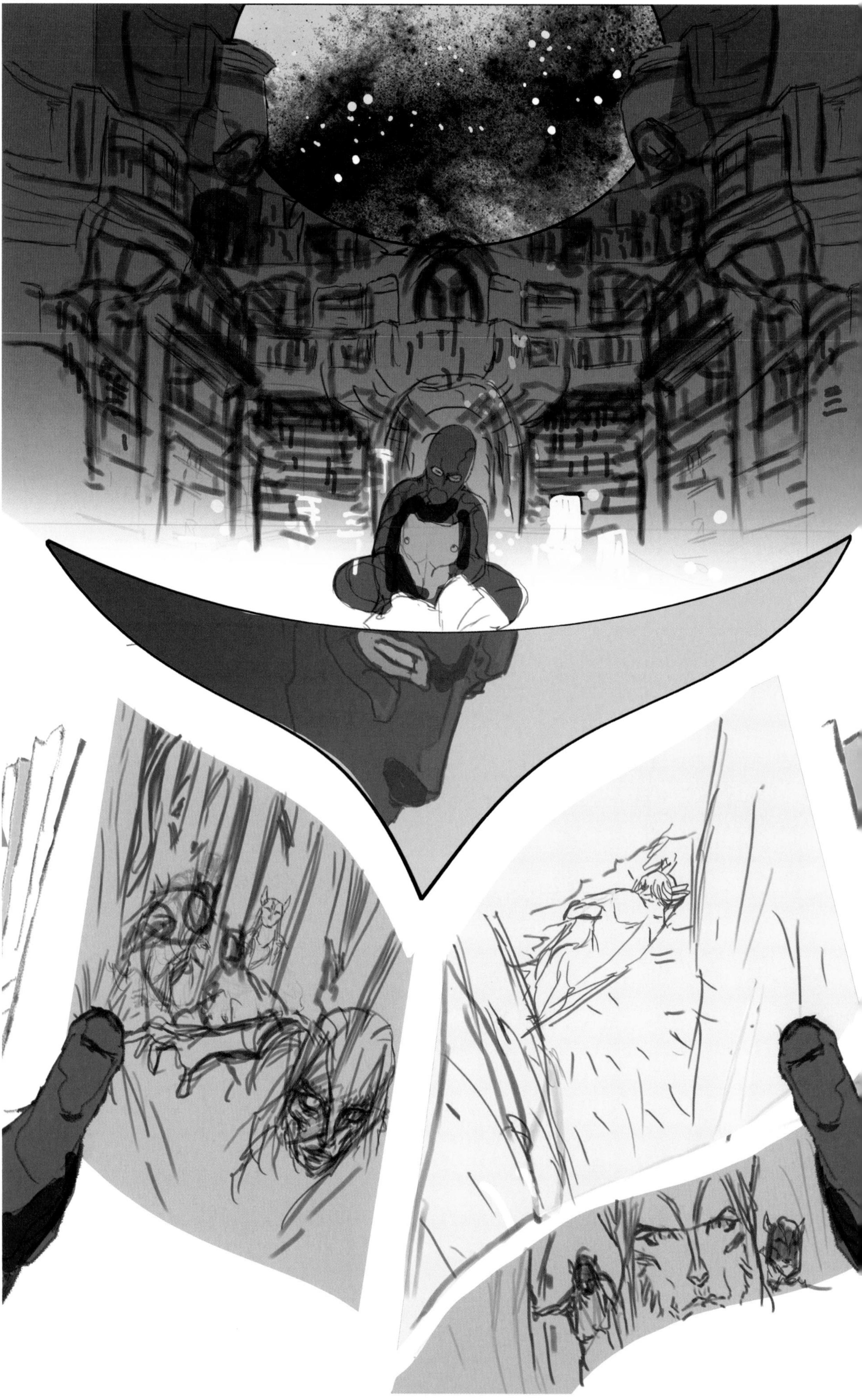

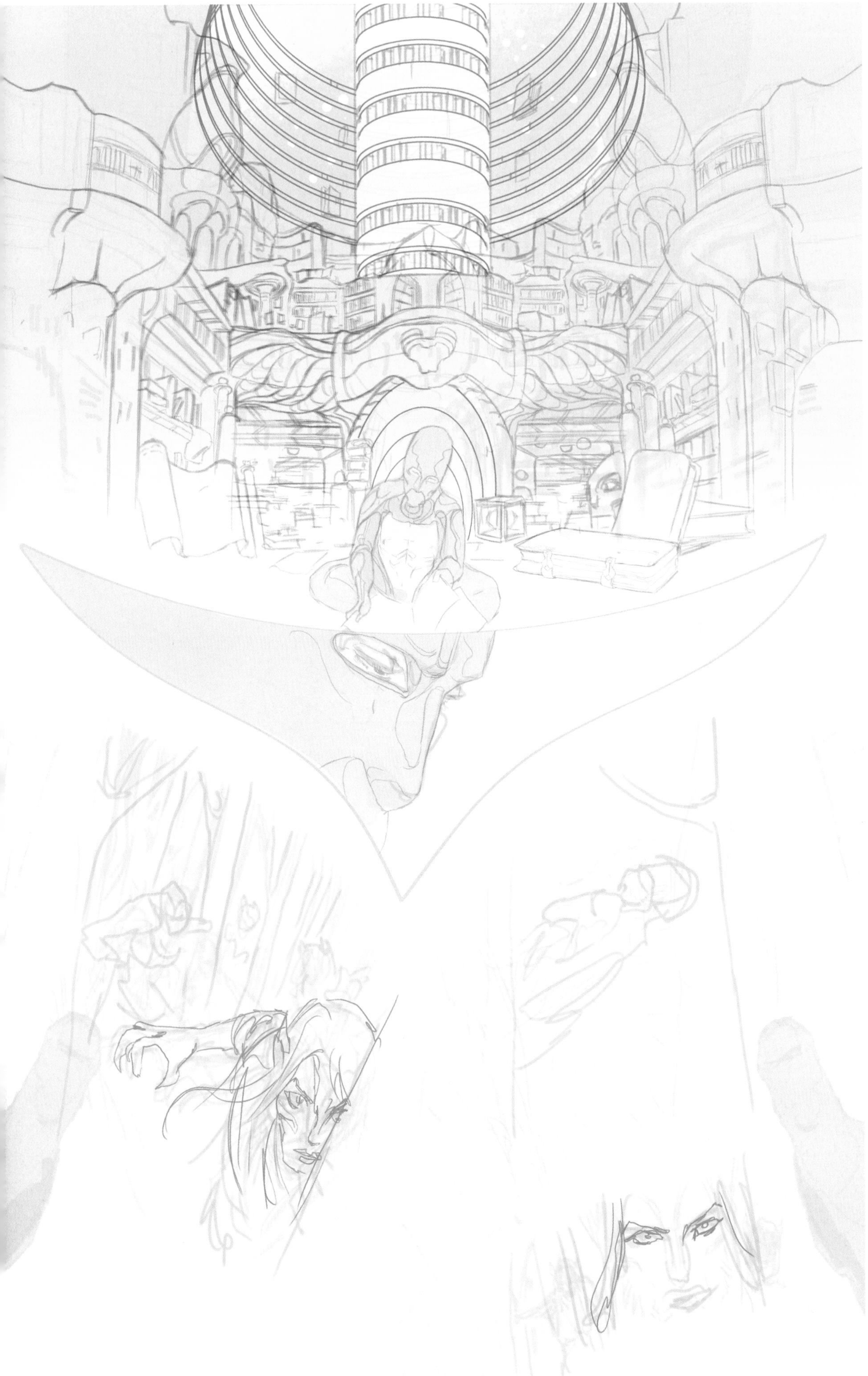

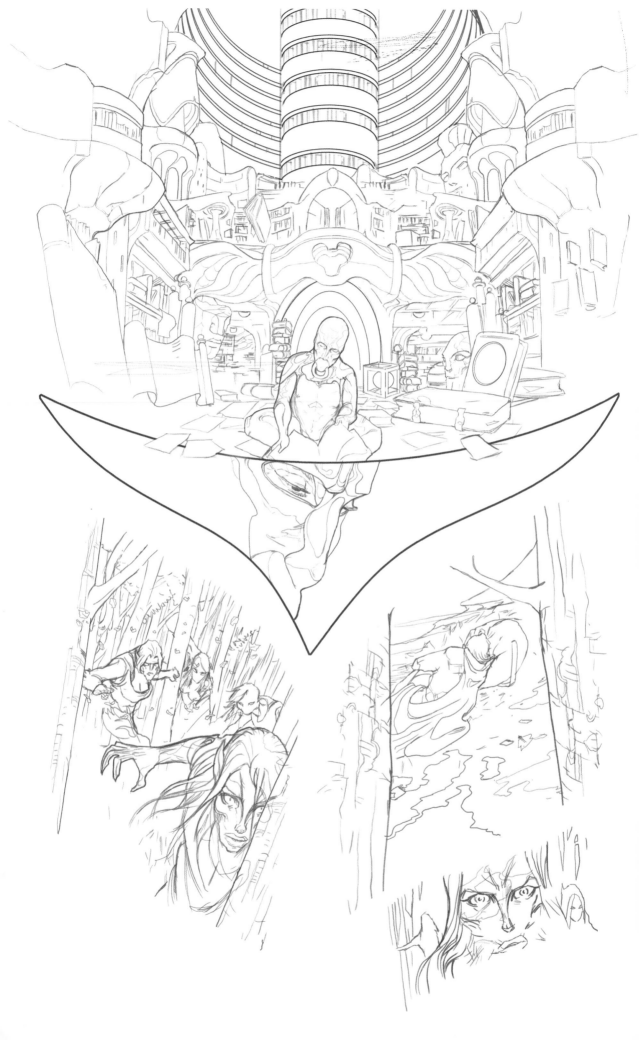

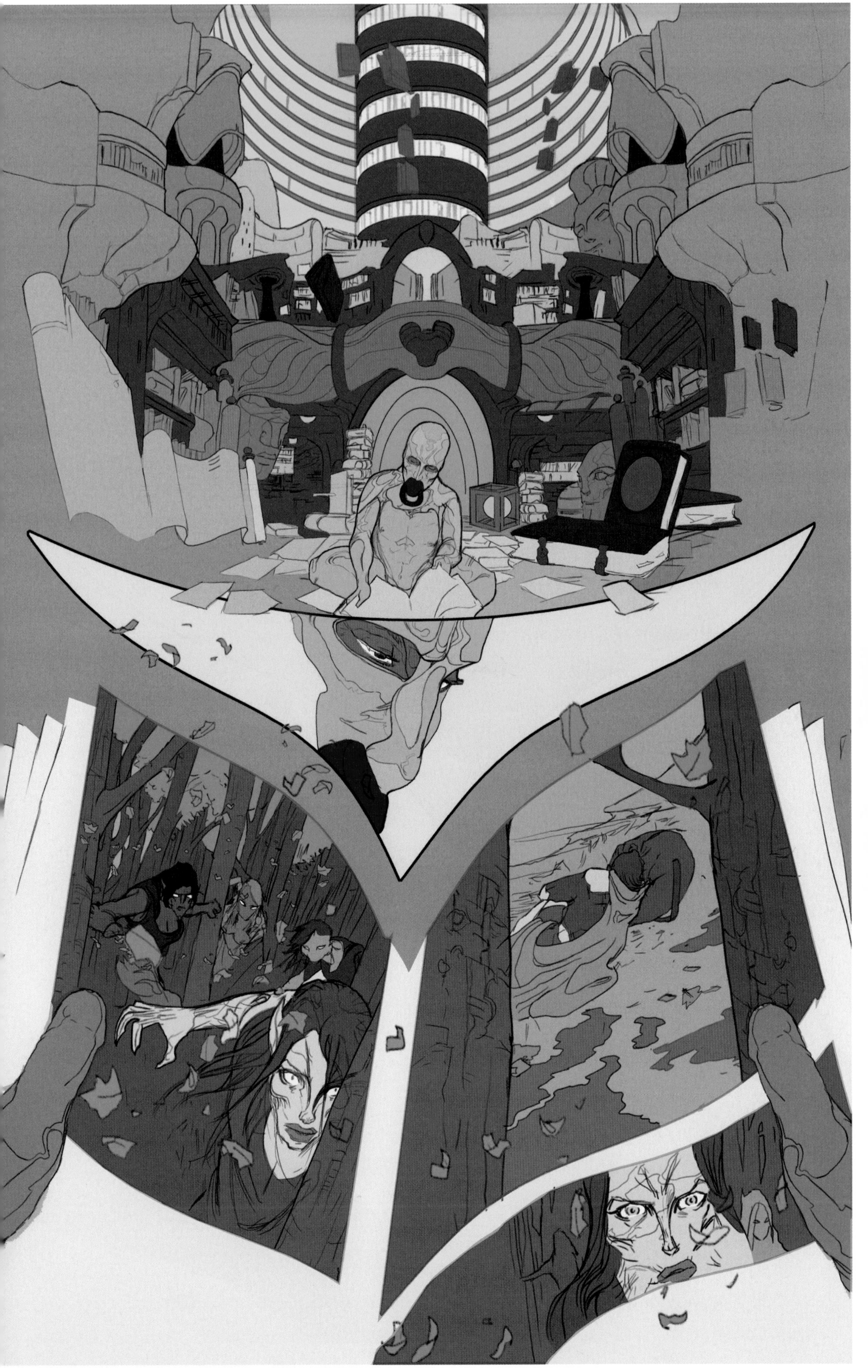

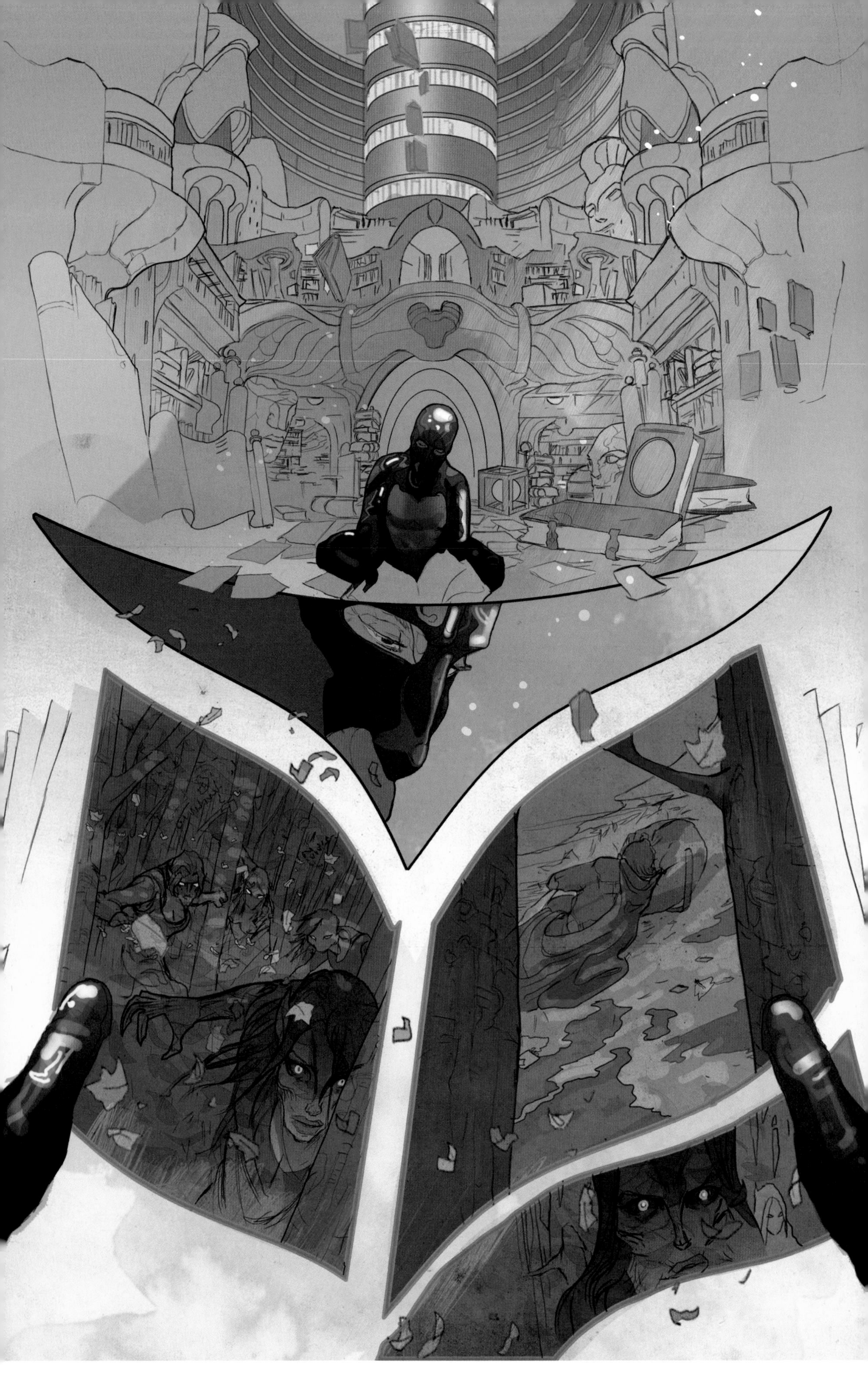

VARIANT COVERS

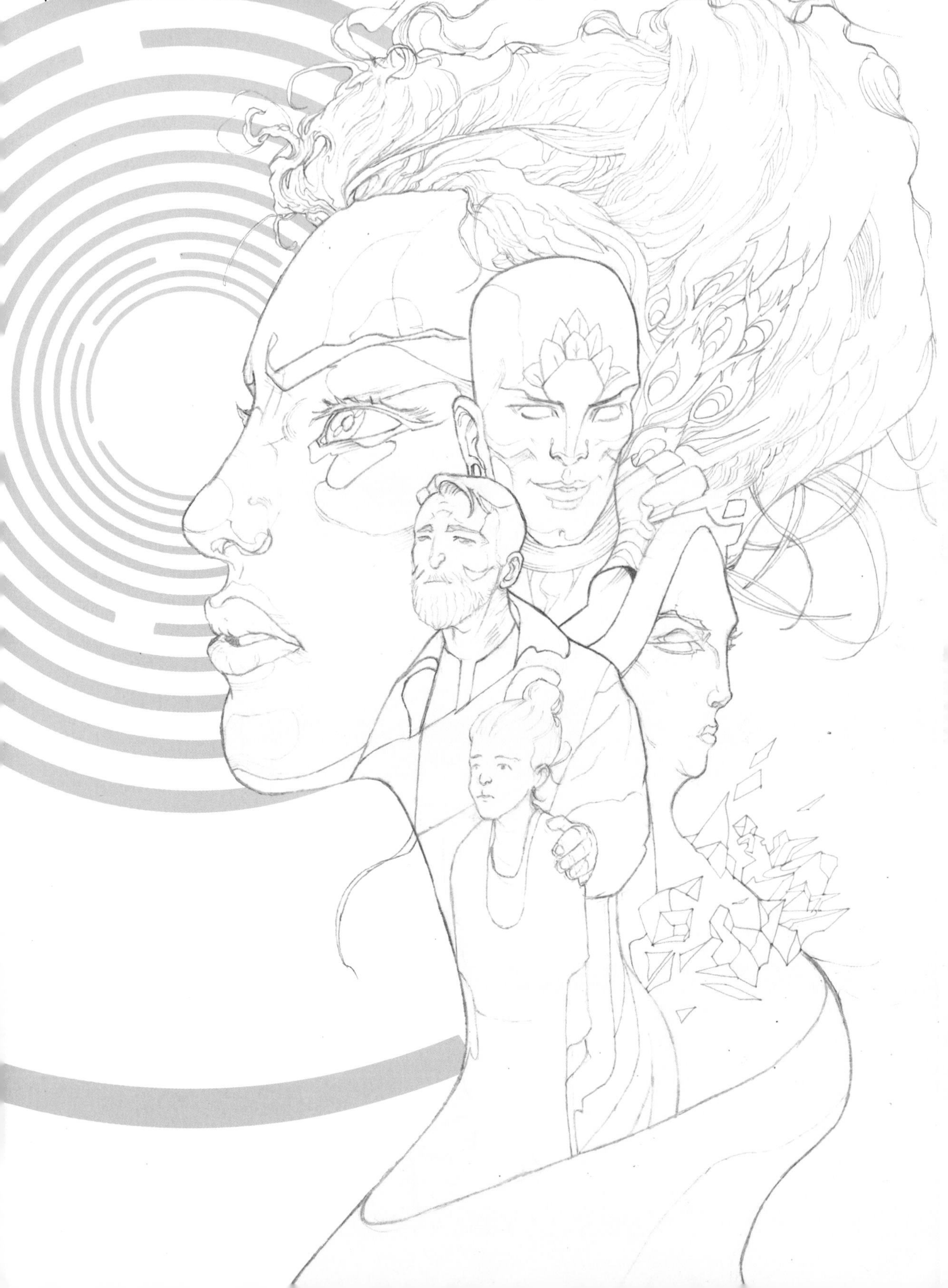

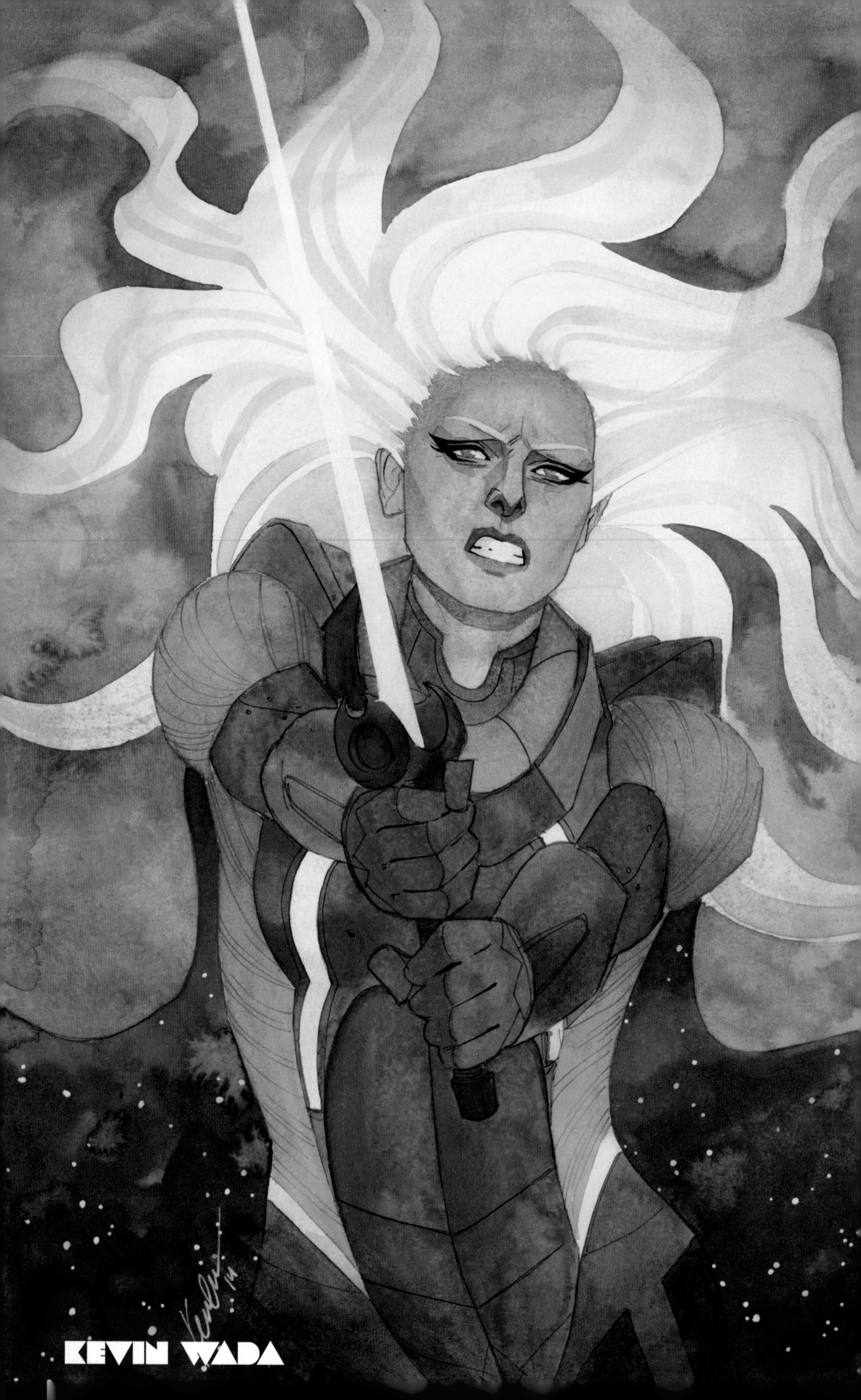
KEVIN WADA

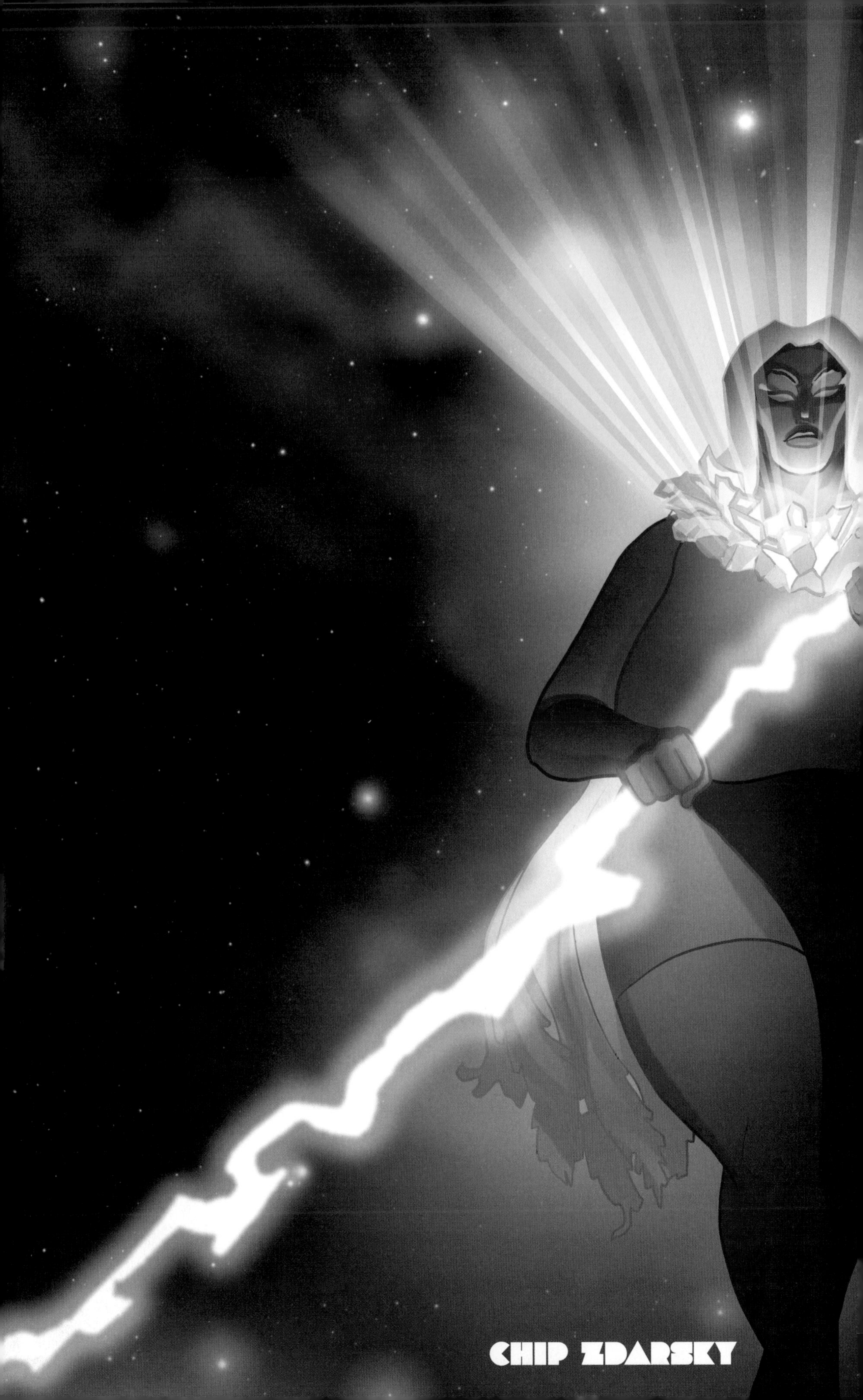
CHIP ZDARSKY

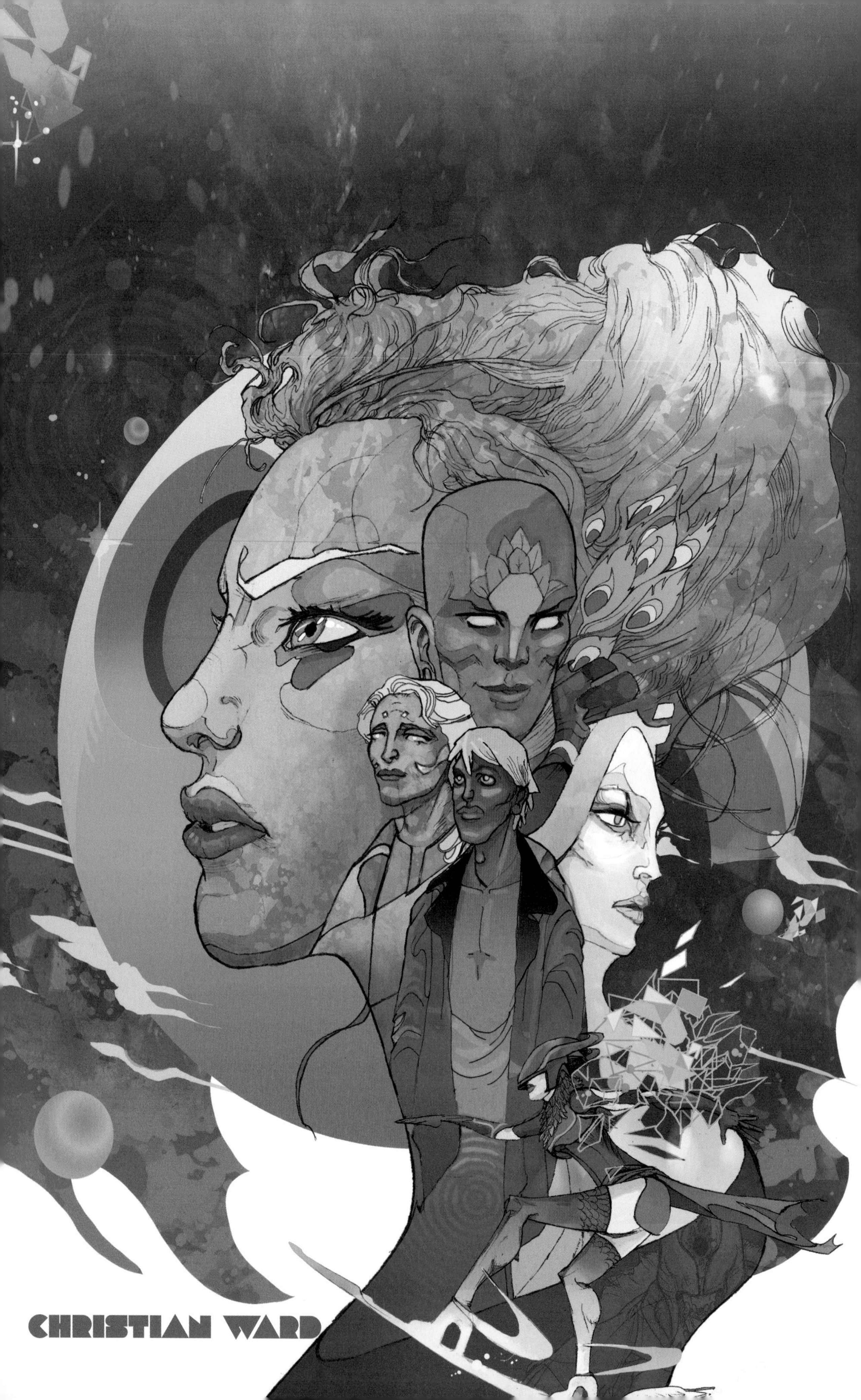
CHRISTIAN WARD

EXTRAS

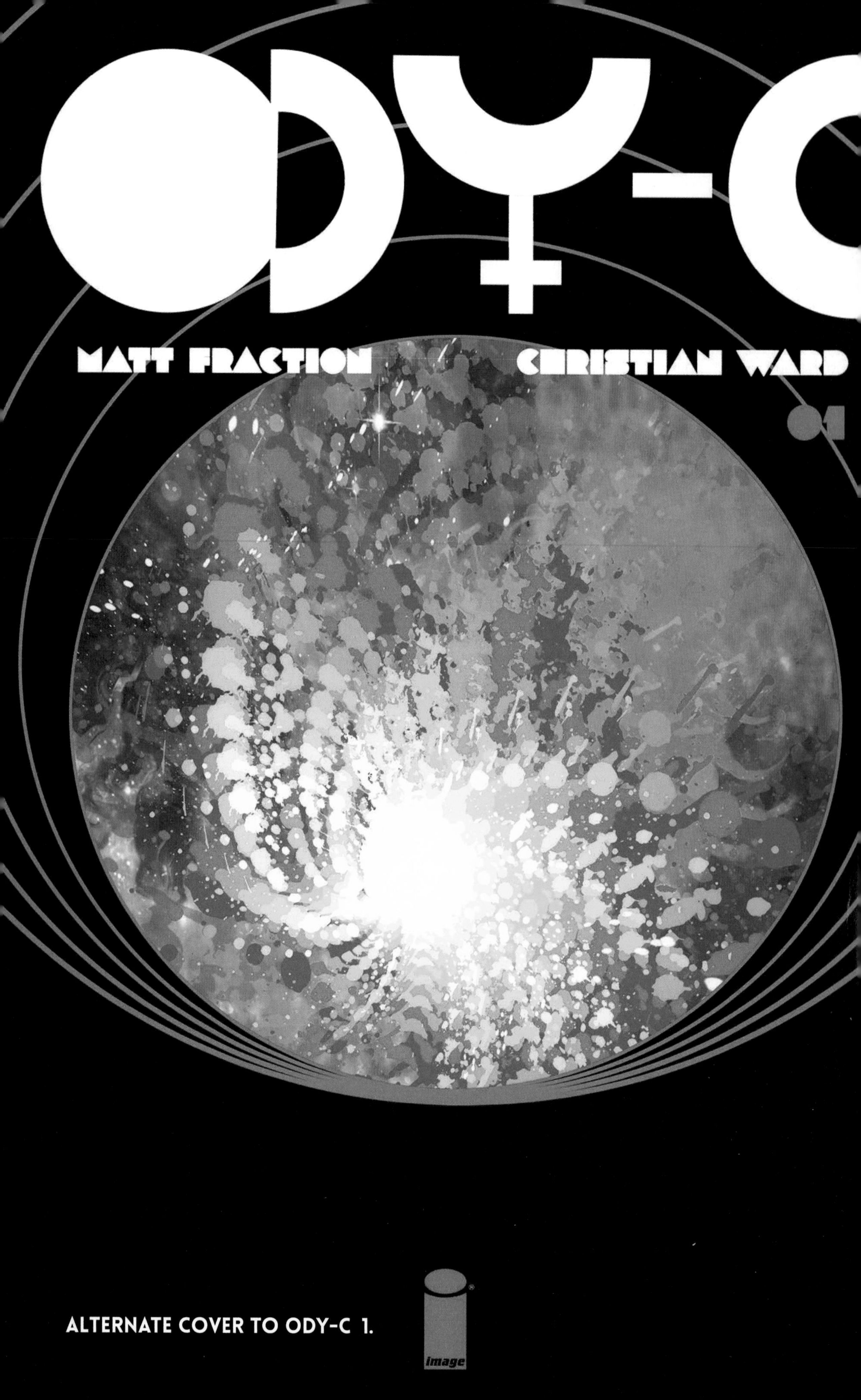
ODY-C
MATT FRACTION
CHRISTIAN WARD
01

ALTERNATE COVER TO ODY-C 1.

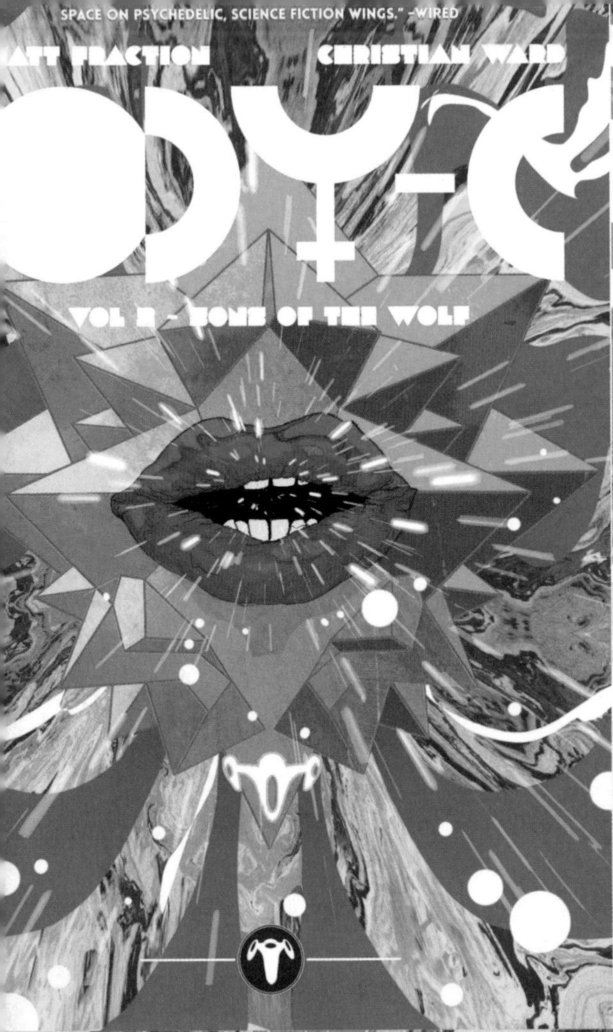
SPACE ON PSYCHEDELIC, SCIENCE FICTION WINGS." -WIRED
CHRISTIAN WARD
VOL 2 - SONS OF THE WOLF

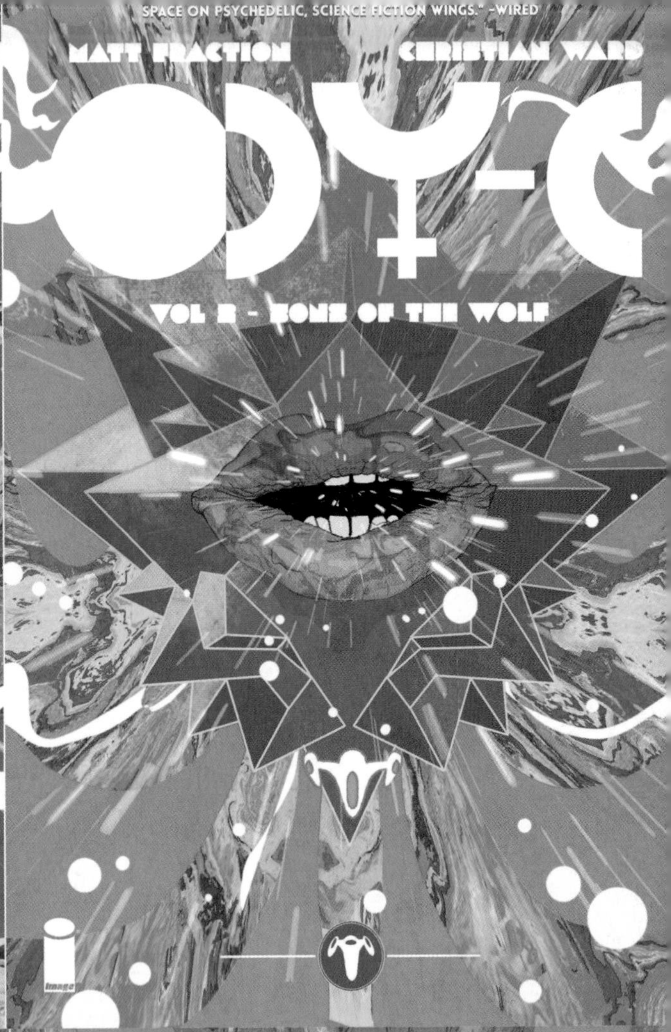
SPACE ON PSYCHEDELIC, SCIENCE FICTION WINGS." -WIRED
MATT FRACTION
CHRISTIAN WARD
VOL 2 - SONS OF THE WOLF

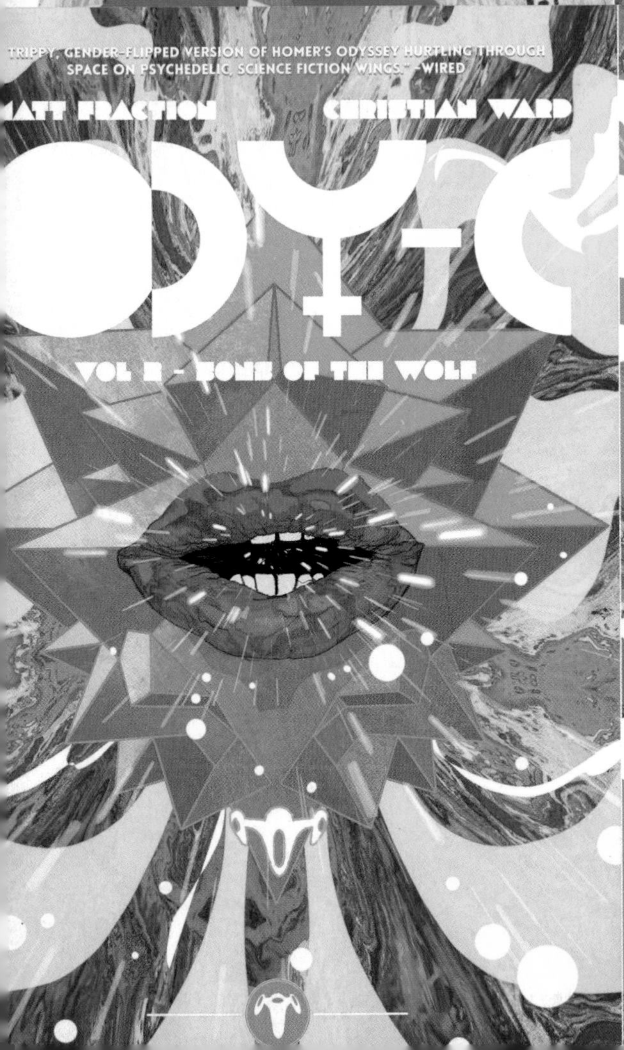
SPACE ON PSYCHEDELIC, SCIENCE FICTION WINGS." -WIRED
CHRISTIAN WARD
VOL 2 - SONS OF THE WOLF

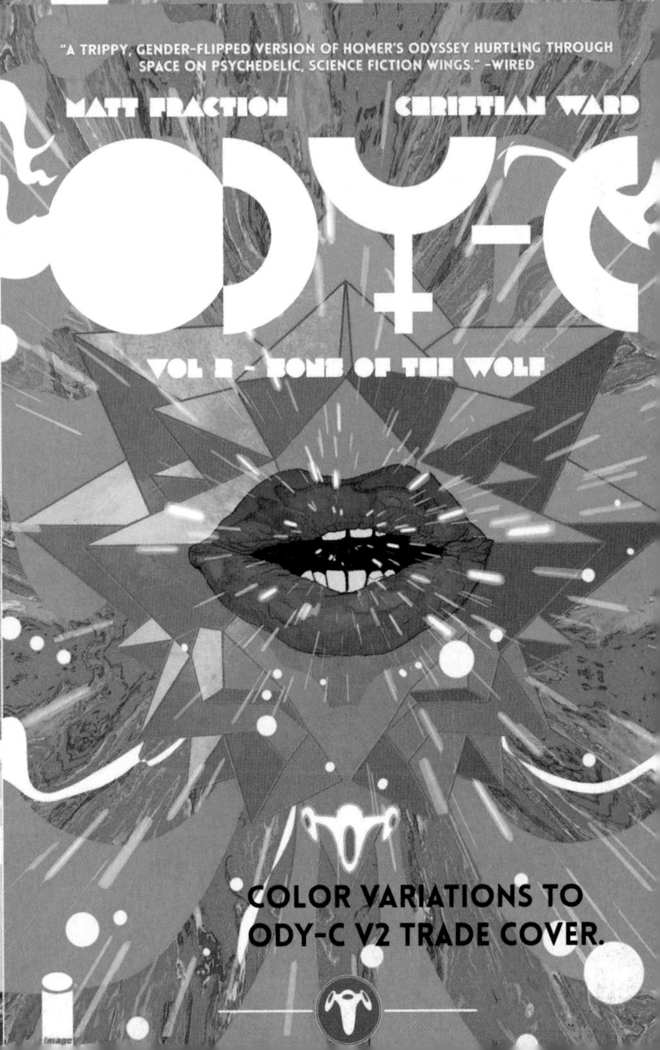
"A TRIPPY, GENDER-FLIPPED VERSION OF HOMER'S ODYSSEY HURTLING THROUGH SPACE ON PSYCHEDELIC, SCIENCE FICTION WINGS." -WIRED
MATT FRACTION
CHRISTIAN WARD
VOL 2 - SONS OF THE WOLF

COLOR VARIATIONS TO ODY-C V2 TRADE COVER.

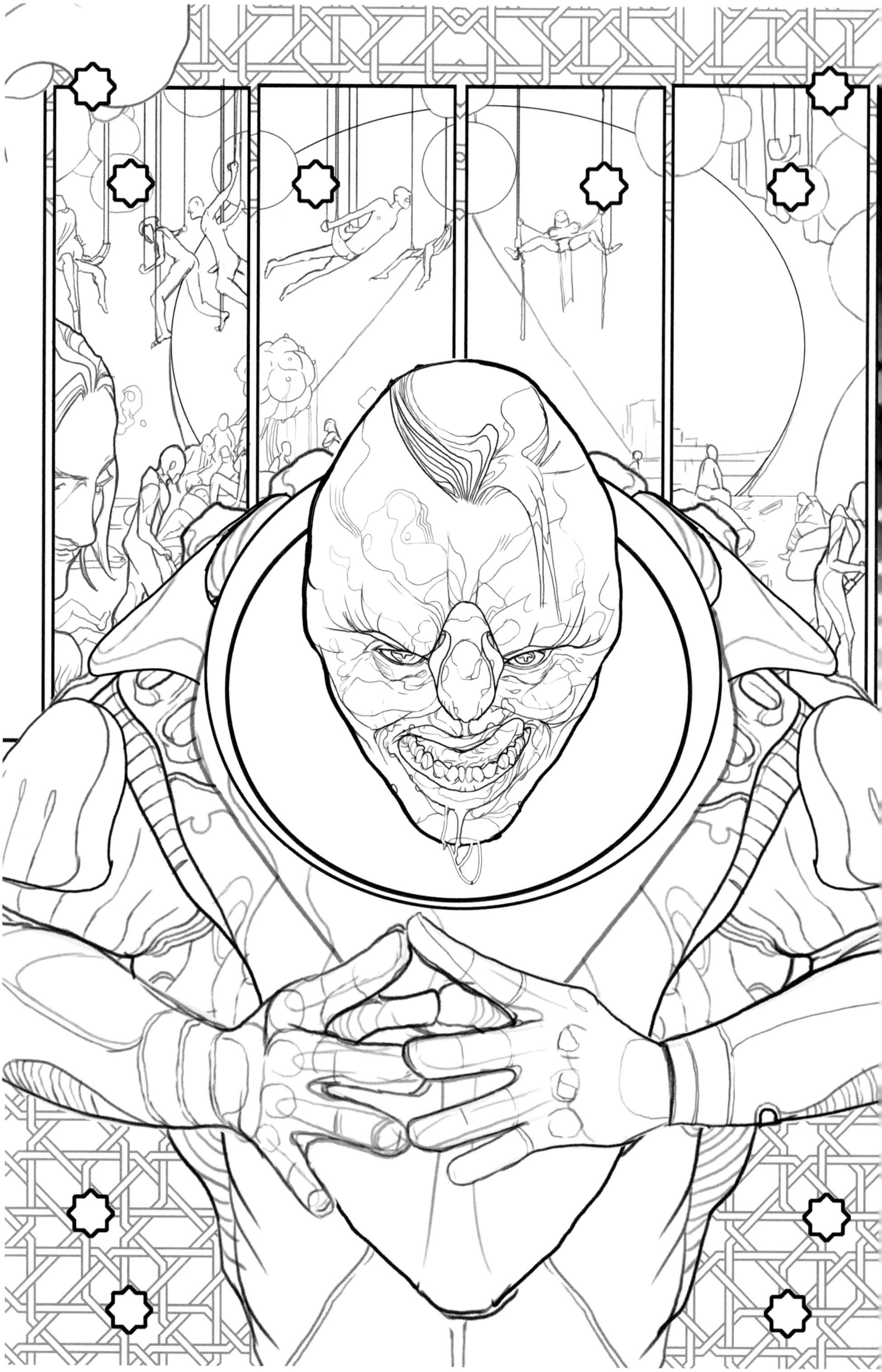

UNUSED COLORING BOOK PAGE OF THE SPECIALIST.

BIBLIOGRAPHY

NOVELS

Atwood, Margaret. *The Penelopiad*. Edinburgh: Canongate, 2005.
al-Shaykh, Hanan. *One Thousand and One Nights: A Retelling*. New York: First Anchor Books, 2014.
Byatt, A.S. *The Djinn in the Nightingale's Eye*. New York: Random House, Inc., 1994.
Jelloun, Tahar Ben. *The Sand Child*. Translated by Alan Sheridan. Baltimore: Johns Hopkins University Press, 2000.
Jelloun, Tahar Ben. *The Sacred Night*. Translated by Alan Sheridan. Baltimore: Johns Hopkins University Press, 2000.
Jelloun, Tahar Ben. *This Blinding Absence of Light*. Translated by Linda Coverdale. New York: Penguin Group, LLC, 2006.
Lightman, Alan. *Einstein's Dreams*. New York: Random House, Inc., 1993.
Mason, Zachary. *The Lost Books of the Odyssey*. New York: Farrar, Straus, and Giroux, 2010.
Rakoff, David. *Love, Dishonor, Marry, Die, Cherish, Perish*. New York: Random House, Inc., 2013.
Shay, Jonathan. M.D., Ph.D. *Achilles in Vietnam: Combat Trauma and the Undoing of Character*. New York: Scribner, 2003.
Shay, Jonathan. M.D., Ph.D. *Odysseus in America: Combat Trauma and the Trials of Homecoming*. New York: Scribner, 2002.

COMICS

Duggan, Gerry & Phil Noto. *The Infinite Horizon*. Berkeley: Image Comics, 2012.
Goodwin, Archie & Walter Simonson. *Alien: The Illustrated Story*. London: Titan Books, 2012.
Toppi, Sergio. *Sharaz-De: Tales from the Arabian Nights*. Los Angeles: Archaia, 2013.

CLASSICAL LITERATURE

Aeschylus. *The Oresteia*. Translated by Robert Fagles. New York: Penguin Group, LLC, 1979.
Haddawy, Husain, trans. *Sinbad and Other Stories from the Arabian Nights*. London: W.W. Norton & Company Inc. 1996.
Herodotus. *The Histories*. Translated by Tom Holland. New York: Penguin Group, LLC, 2014.
Homer. *The Iliad*. Translated by Robert Fagles. New York: Penguin Group, LLC, 1991.
Homer. *The Iliad of Homer*. Translated by Alexander Pope. Indiana: Ex Fontibus Co., 2012.
Homer. *The Odyssey*. Translated by Robert Fagles. New York: Penguin Group, LLC, 1991.
Homer. *The Odyssey*. Translated by Robert Fitzgerald. New York: Random House, Inc., 1990.
Homer. *The Odyssey*. Translated by Alexander Pope. Indiana: Ex Fontibus Co., 2012.
Lyons, Malcolm C. & Ursula Lyons, trans. *The Arabian Nights: Tales of 1001 Nights Vol.1*. New York: Penguin Group, LLC, 2010.
Lyons, Malcolm C. & Ursula Lyons, trans. *The Arabian Nights: Tales of 1001 Nights Vol.2*. New York: Penguin Group, LLC, 2010.
Lyons, Malcolm C. & Ursula Lyons, trans. *The Arabian Nights: Tales of 1001 Nights Vol.3*. New York: Penguin Group, LLC, 2010.
Mahdi, Muhsin. *The Arabian Nights*. Translated by Husain Haddawy. London: W.W. Norton & Company Inc. 1995.
Melville, Herman. *Moby-Dick*. London: W.W. Norton & Company Inc., 2002.
Petronius. *The Satyricon*. Translated by P.G. Walsh. Oxford: Oxford University Press, 2009.
Pullman, Philip, edit. *Fairy Tales from the Brothers Grimm*. New York: Penguin Group, LLC, 2013.
R. Scott Smith and Stephen M. Trzaskoma. *Apollodorus' Library and Hyginus' Fabulae*. Indianapolis: Hackett, 2007.
Seneca. *Six Tragedies*. Translated by Emily Wilson. Oxford: Oxford University Press, 2010.
Shakespeare, William. *Macbeth*. New York: Simon & Schuster, Inc., 2013.

REFERENCE

Campbell, Joseph. *The Hero with a Thousand Faces*. Princeton: Princeton University Press, 1972.
Campbell, Joseph. *The Power of Myth*. New York: Bantam Doubleday Dell Publishing Group, Inc., 1988.
Chetwynd, Tom. *Dictionary of Symbols*. London: Harper Collins Publishers, 1993.
Cirlot, J.E. *A Dictionary of Symbols*. New York: Dover Publications, Inc. 2002.
Cooper, J.C. *An Illustrated Encyclopedia of Traditional Symbols*. New York: Thames and Hudson, 1979.
Cotterell, Arthur & Rachel Storm. *The Ultimate Encyclopedia of Mythology*. London: Anness Publishing Ltd, 2009.
Frazer, Sir James. *The Golden Bough*. Hertfordshire: Wordsworth Editions Limited, 1993.
Hamilton, Edith. *Mythology*. New York: Hachette Book Group, 1998.
Holland, Tom. *Rubicon: The Last Years of the Roman Republic*. New York: Random House, Inc., 2004
Hyde, Lewis. *Trickster Makes this World: Mischief, Myth, and Art*. New York: Farrar, Straus, and Giroux.
Guirand, Felix, edit. *Larousse Encyclopedia of Mythology*. Paris: Librairie Larousse, 1959.
Manguel, Alberto & Gianni Guadalupi. *The Dictionary of Imaginary Places*. Orlando: Harcourt Inc., 1974.
Metzner, Ralph. *The Well of Remembrance*. Boston: Shambhala Publications, Inc., 1994.
Paradiz, Valerie. *Clever Maids: The Secret History of the Grimm Fairy Tales*. New York: Perseus Books Group, 2005.
Rockwood, Camilla, edit. *Brewer's Dictionary of Phrase & Fable*. London: Chambers Harrap Publishing, Ltd., 2009.
Ruck, Carl A.P. & Danny Staples. *The World of Classical Myth: Gods and Goddesses, Heroines and Heroes*. Durham: Carolina, Academic Press, 1994.
SparkNotes. *SparkNotes: Moby-Dick*. New York: Spark Publishing, 2014.
Staples, Blaise Daniel, et al., *The Hidden World: Survival of Pagan Shamanic Themes in European Fairytales*. Durham: Carolina Academic Press, 2007.
Tresidder, Jack, edit. *The Complete Dictionary of Symbols*. San Francisco: Chronicle Books LLC, 2004.
Warner, Marina. *Stranger Magic: Charmed States and the Arabian Nights*. Cambridge: Harvard University Press, 2013.

MATT FRACTION WRITES COMIC BOOKS OUT IN THE WOODS AND LIVES WITH HIS WIFE, THE WRITER KELLY SUE DECONNICK, HIS TWO CHILDREN, TWO DOGS, A CAT, A BEARDED DRAGON, AND A YARD FULL OF COYOTES, STAGS, AND CROWS. SURELY THERE IS A METAPHOR THERE. HE'S A NEW YORK TIMES BESTSELLING DONKUS OF COMICS LIKE SEX CRIMINALS (WINNER OF THE 2014 WILL EISNER AWARD FOR BEST NEW SERIES, THE 2014 HARVEY AWARD FOR BEST NEW SERIES, AND NAMED TIME MAGAZINE'S BEST COMIC OF 2013), SATELLITE SAM, ODY-C, AND HAWKEYE (WINNER OF THE 2014 WILL EISNER AWARD FOR BEST SINGLE ISSUE). UNDER THEIR COMPANY MILKFED CRIMINAL MASTERMINDS, INC., FRACTION AND DECONNICK ARE CURRENTLY DEVELOPING TELEVISION FOR NBCUNIVERSAL.

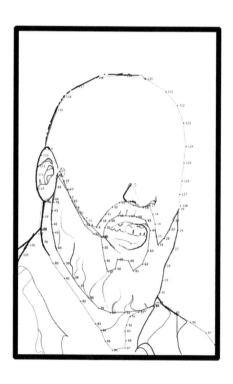

AFTER 10 YEARS OF ENCOURAGING LONDON TEENAGERS TO DRAW ANYTHING OTHER THAN COMICS, CHRISTIAN WARD IS NOW A FULL-TIME COMIC BOOK ARTIST, ILLUSTRATOR AND WRITER. ALONGSIDE BEING AN ARTIST AT MARVEL (IRON MAN, NEW AVENGERS, THE ULTIMATES, AGENTS OF S.H.I.E.L.D.), HE IS ALSO THE CO-CREATOR OF ODY-C WITH MATT FRACTION FOR IMAGE COMICS. HE'S ALSO COLLABORATED WITH WRITERS SUCH AS NICK SPENCER, KIERON GILLEN AND MARGARET ATWOOD. CHRISTIAN CURRENTLY LIVES IN THE UK WITH HIS WIFE CATHERINE AND A PUG NAMED THOR.